MW01069828

ONCE THERE WERE HEROES

A TIME OF DRAGONS: BOOK ONE

PHILIP C. QUAINTRELL

First edition published 2023.

Cover Illustration by Chris McGrath
Book design by BodiDog Design
Edited by David Bradley

ISBN: 978-1-916610-33-0 (hardback)
ASIN: B0CG6J12M5 (ebook)

Published by Quaintrell Publishings

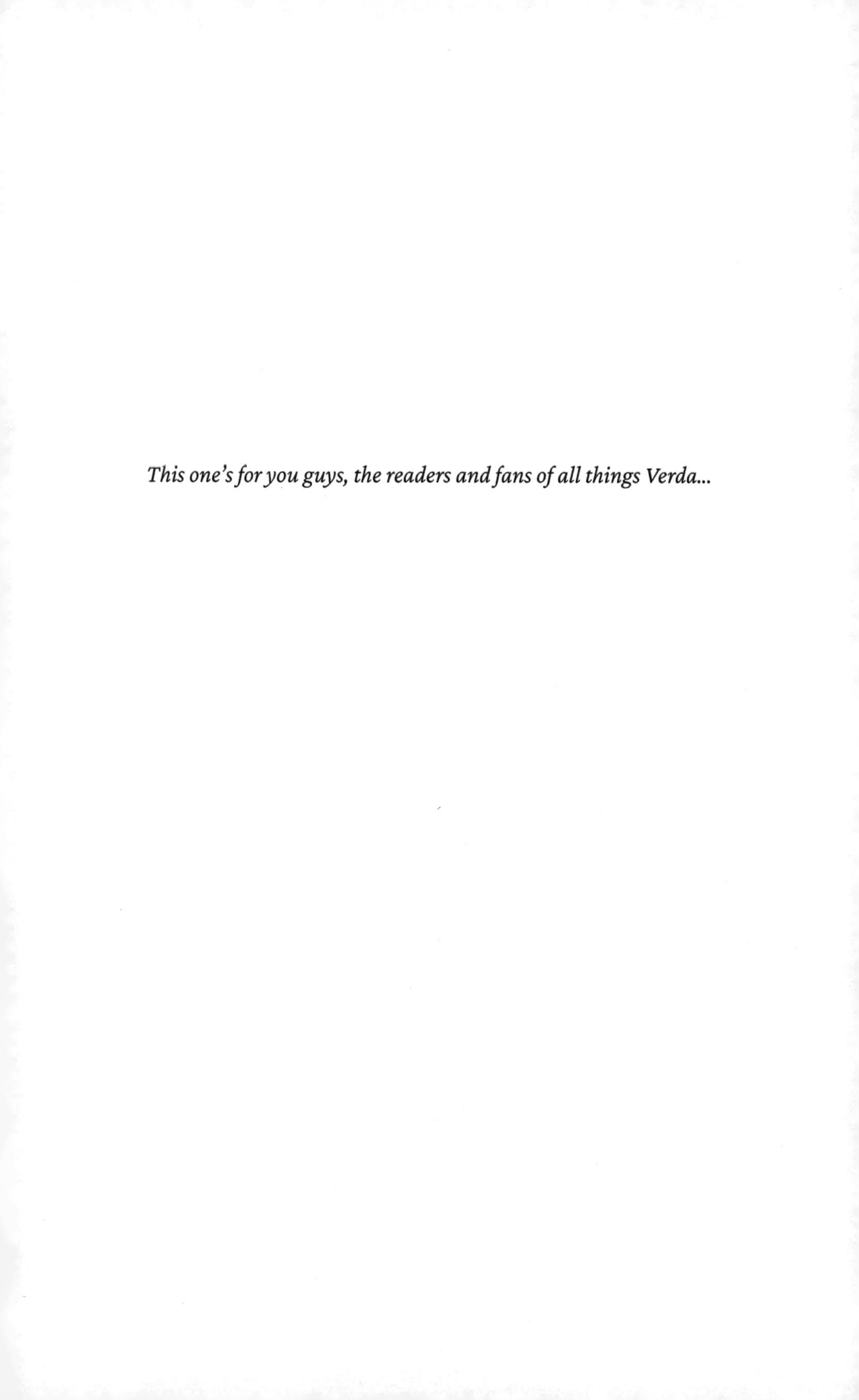

This one's for you guys, the readers and fans of all things Verda...

ALSO BY PHILIP C. QUAINTRELL

THE ECHOES SAGA: (9 Book Series).

1. Rise of the Ranger
2. Empire of Dirt
3. Relic of the Gods
4. The Fall of Neverdark
5. Kingdom of Bones
6. Age of the King
7. The Knights of Erador
8. Last of the Dragorn
9. A Clash of Fates

THE RANGER ARCHIVES: (3 Book Series).

1. Court of Assassins
2. Blood and Coin
3. A Dance of Fang and Claw

A TIME OF DRAGONS:

1. Once There Were Heroes

THE TERRAN CYCLE: (4 Book Series).

1. Intrinsic
2. Tempest
3. Heretic
4. Legacy

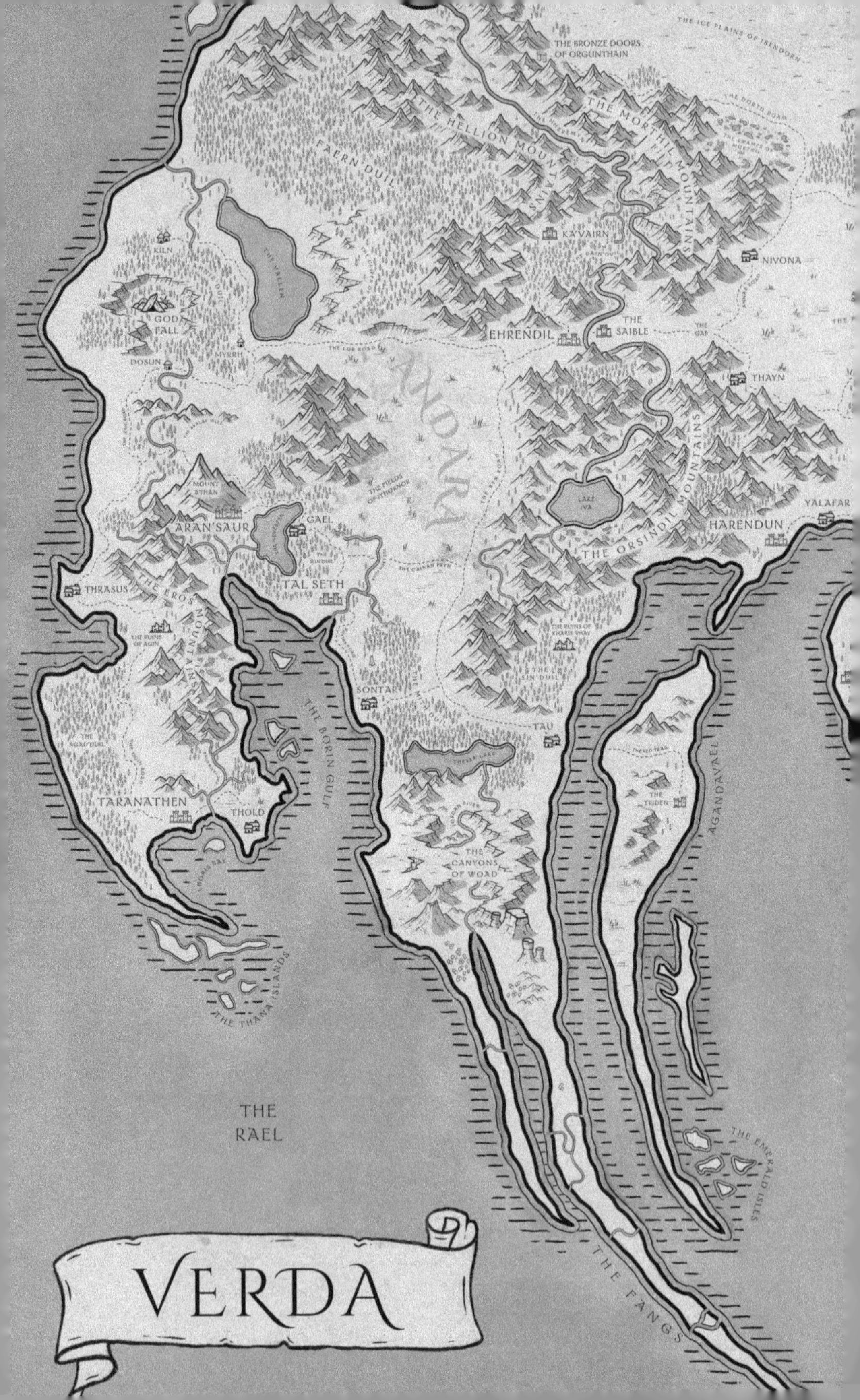

THE ICE PLAINS OF ISENDORN
THE BRONZE DOORS OF ORGUNTHAIN
THE MORTHIL MOUNTAINS
THE HELLION MOUNTAINS
FAERN DUIL
KA'VAIRN
NIVONA
KILN
GOD FALL
DOSUN
MYRRH
EHRENDIL
THE SAIBLE
THE GAP
THAYN
ANDARA
MOUNT ATHAN
ARAN SAUR
GAEL
TAL SETH
LAKE IVA
THE ORSINDIL MOUNTAINS
HARENDUN
YALAFAR
THRASUS
THE EROS MOUNTAINS
SONTAR
THE BORIN GULF
TAU
TARANATHEN
THOLD
THE CANYONS OF WOAD
THE TRIDEN
AGANDAVAEL
THE THANA ISLANDS
THE RÄEL
THE EMERALD ISLES
THE FANGS
VERDA

THE NIGHT SEA
THE DREAD WOOD
STORM'S REACH
THE BROKEN MOUNTAINS
THE WATCHTOWER OF ARGUNSUUN
WHITE TOWER
DRAKANAN
THE DRAGON PATH
THE FOREST OF RUIN
DRAYSHON
THE RED FIELDS OF DUNMAR
SUNHOLD
THE SEA TRAIL
FREYGARD
THE NORTH ROAD
THE DEEP
THE SILVER TREES OF ARMAR
MOUNT KALIBAN
ERADOR
RIVERWATCH
VALGALA
THE TOWER OF JAIN
THE RED HOLD
HEMON
ELDERHALL
FARNFOSS
THEDARIA
TORINN
WARTH
THE MORN'S WOOD
LAKE TALON
THE DAWNING ISLES
CARTHAM
HARAN'S TOWN
ALLISANDER
BROADCASTLE
QALANOATH
THE GOLD RISE
OLD DRIFT

DRAMATIS PERSONAE

Abel Set-Sedaas
Weaver

Androma
Ex Dragon Rider

Cob
ranger

Gallien Drakalis
Smuggler

Grarfath
Dwarven Smith

Handuin
First Vahlken

Ilithranda
Vahlken

DRAMATIS PERSONAE

Joran
Half Andaren/half human

Kitrana Voden
Nimean

Kovun
Vahlken

Melios
Weaver

Naelin
Vahlken

Aphrandhor
Wizard

Slait
Vahlken

Soveana
Weaver

Soyra
Vahlken

The Valtorak
Master if Ka'vairn

Yamnomora
Dwarf

Yendi
Vahlken

PROLOGUE

He was bleeding again.

Looking down at his hands, Talo watched fresh blood follow the contours of his wrists and drip onto the polished floor. It seemed absurdly red against the lustrous gold of the imperial sigil, the sunburst of House Lhoris, printed upon the stark white marble. He tried to adjust his manacles, his constant companions of late, but only succeeded in disturbing older scabs that would go on to crust the irons in more blood.

Hopelessly, Talo tried to wipe the blood away with a bare foot. There was no fighting the inherent need to protect the sigil. He had proudly worn that sunburst and its broken circle on his breastplate for decades, centuries in fact. Just the thought of it moved a hand to his chest, but the pain he found there was far worse than that of his wrists. A *deserter*, they had branded him, quite literally. It had been weeks now since the glowing iron had seared his skin, but Talo knew he would carry that pain for the rest of his life.

Lifting his head, a near-blinding light arrested his attention, bringing that same hand up to his face. Eyes narrowed, Talo soon adjusted to the light of the setting sun as it dipped below the great arches and cut through the palace. 'Twas not the sun, however, that had pained his sight but its reflection in the gilded doors that now bathed in the early evening light.

They loomed before him, arching into the high ceiling as if they were the gates to paradise itself. The gold faces upon them were brought to life all the more by the golden light from the west. So serene were their expressions, there at the feet of the emperor, whose image became whole when the entrance was sealed.

Talo had been approaching the doors for hours, shuffling along the pristine hall as so many others had. One by one, he had watched those in front step closer to the gleaming doors. It was the honour of a lifetime to approach them, to be so close to the Empyreal Throne.

To be so close to *him*.

Again and again, one golden slab would open and another from the line would disappear, lost to the other side. So close now, Talo was offered an inkling of what lay beyond the doors, an impression of light and resplendence. He had even sighted one of the six fabled pillars that supported the throne room's exalted roof.

It was all so brief, that glimpse of another world. When the doors inevitably closed again, Talo was left to the grand hall and those who shared the honour of standing in it. There were fewer than ten in front of him, after so many hundreds. The only constants were the minor clerics who wandered up and down, speaking the word of the Arkalon from scrolls or the book itself. They, and the guards, of course.

The palace guard had been doubled, the halls flooded with Andara's finest warriors, all stationed to ensure the line kept moving. Their armour glimmered in the sunlight, a shade of bronze that accentuated their ivory skin and the chalk-white hair that flowed down their backs. So too did the light catch the swords resting on their hips.

There was no going back, only forwards with the seemingly endless line of his kin who had been offered the same glory as himself.

When he finally arrived at those towering doors, he considered the choices he had made, the decisions that had put him inside the imperial palace, on that immaculate floor.

When he closed his eyes, Talo could still see the human horde as they smashed into their front line, their primitive language reduced to a primal roar. He could see his kinsmen, their centuries of life rent from existence in an instance of violence and blood.

The sights of war were almost as haunting as the sounds. Bones breaking under pressure. Flesh splitting to the edge of a blade. Boots splashing through puddles of blood. Men suffocating in the mud.

The cries for mercy, for family, at least, were something they had in common with the vile humans. It had been Talo's need of his family that had seen him turn and flee the battle.

He was again dragged back to the brand that had blackened his skin, making a ruin of his chest.

The imperial tribunal had been swift. He was to be publicly beheaded, his family shamed for eternity. He had envisioned that inevitable moment so many times before the tribunal: the shriek of horror from his family, a wail that would carve through the quietude of the onlookers. Then would come the far more horrifying sound to those who remained—the stillness of death.

There had been an alternative, however, the same alternative every poor soul in the line had chosen. It offered hope where there had only been the promise of darkness. Hope for his family's lasting honour. That was a price worth paying.

Talo gripped his left wrist until his knuckles were as white as his hair. The need to relieve himself had been pressing upon him for hours, urging him now to go right there on the palace floor. He certainly wouldn't have been the first, unable to abandon his place in the line.

One of the doors opened, the width just enough to allow him entry.

His feet hesitated, delaying his destiny. Movement in the corner of his eye—one of the guards—was enough to see Talo take a step. No sooner had he passed over the threshold than the entrance closed behind him, shut by a nameless servant who remained hidden in the shadow of their hood.

The servant could only hold Talo's attention for a moment, his cobalt eyes drawn ever upward, as the throne room's architect had intended. As the stories professed, six pillars—each covered in relief carvings that depicted the six epochs of their people—gave the chamber its impressive height. The vaulted ceiling was concealed by hanging foliage and snaking vines, a stark contrast to the golden pillars and ashen walls—a softening touch.

It did little, though, to soften the harshness created by the dulled bones of a dead dragon, its skeleton suspended between the pillars by twinkling chains. So high was it that the hanging foliage had grown to brush its smooth ridges, promising to one day conceal it altogether. Talo was sure he had heard the name of the beast in some tale, the name its human masters had branded it with, but, awed and overwhelmed as he was, the Andaren failed to conjure it.

His gaze was torn from the heavens and the nameless dragon, his path blocked by a grand cleric. Talo naturally bowed his head in submission to the keeper of the word, as he would to any positioned so highly in their divine order. Stripped of their name and identity, face hidden behind a sloping mask of polished bronze, the cleric used a key to free him of his manacles. Talo would have enjoyed the moment of relief had the cleric not tossed the manacles onto a vast pile of identical chains.

When the grand cleric turned on their heel and walked away, the deserter could but follow in their wake. He trailed the flowing red robes as they crossed a small arching bridge of stone, over the moat of black-red water that snaked around the pillars.

It was there, in that open circular space, the very heart of the Andaren Empire, that the deserter laid eyes on His Radiance.

Emperor Qeledred Isari Arad, the forty-first of his name, of House Lhoris.

Overwhelmed, Talo instantly fell prostrate, his forehead pressed firmly to the pristine marble. It had only been a glimpse, yet the image of the emperor was etched into his mind as firmly as the details etched into the pillars. Seated on the august throne of his forebears, he emanated authority and dignity, his sovereignty unquestionable. A thick mane of hair, so white it could be snow, cascaded over plum robes that complemented his violet eyes. Much like the humble circlet of silver that served as his crown, so too did his attire shimmer with aspects of glistening minerals.

"Rise," came the voice of the cleric. So deep was it that the words seemed rooted somewhere in their chest.

Talo rose on unsteady feet, a tremor running through his hands. He knew he shouldn't look upon the emperor again, just as he shouldn't look up at the sun, yet the majesty of His Radiance was undeniable, dragging his eyes up the steps to that lofty throne that stood above all.

He had expected those violet eyes to be upon him if not looking through him, but the emperor's gaze was distant, lost to the vastness of that great chamber. Unlike Talo's ivory skin, which had begun to grey through malnourishment, the emperor's pale face shone with vitality. Pale too were the fingers that gripped the arms of his throne, so many of which were adorned with rings of precious stones.

To the emperor's left, though not so elevated, sat his three wives, each a beauty to behold, their white hair braided down to within an inch of the floor. Behind them sat a gallery of children, the imperial princes and princesses of varying ages. Unlike their mothers and father, the emperor's offspring watched Talo intently, almost eagerly.

Unable to stand their gaze, let alone meet it, Talo's eyes shifted to take note of those standing to the right of the throne. Soldiers all, though most held the rank of paragon or thereabout—the generals and warmasters. Unlike the obsidian cloaks of the common soldier—as Talo had once worn—their bronze armour was draped in cloaks so white as to blend with their hair. Their scrutiny was not so eager as the children's but determined, as if their expressions had been chiselled onto their faces.

Of them all, two figures caught and held his attention, the pair lingering on the end of the line. They were taller than all in that chamber and seemingly wider with their sloping leather pauldrons keeping their fur cloaks at their backs. Talo knew them to be Vahlkens, Andara's most lethal, if not rarest, of warriors.

They weren't the only warriors present, however, who were accredited with lethal proficiency. Dotted about the throne and dais were the legendary Praetorian Guard. It had taken a little longer for Talo's eyes to find them but, now that he had, he couldn't help but stare. Clad in white armour from head to toe, their faces concealed behind masks that had been shaped to their angular features, they appeared no more than lifeless statues. Indeed, they had all adopted some form of heroic stance that might be seen in a statue, be they standing with one foot on a step or even sitting on the dais with their jaw resting on one hand. It was said their presence always lent the emperor an added aura of regality, as if, wherever he went, he was always in some imperial garden. Talo agreed.

Two more grand clerics stepped into Talo's view, redirecting his attention to the circular pool that sat not far from the base of the throne. Like the moat that joined it either side, the pool was so intensely red as to be black. If there was any doubt as to what had given the pool this colour, there was a thick smear of red marring the marble, a snaking line that led away from the imperial family and through a side door.

Blood.

Even on the battlefields he had never seen so much blood in one place. It was enough to put ice in his bones and a cold dread in his gut.

Again, Talo's bare feet hesitated. While the cleric who had led him thus far remained at his back, the other two of their order framed the short steps that led down into the bloody pool.

"No one can be forced," said the cleric at his back. "But your honour can only be reclaimed in there."

With trembling hands, Talo's slender frame slipped between the clerics and down the steps. The pool was warm and heavy, his body lost to sight from the waist down.

The rustle of parchment interrupted Talo's contemplation,

turning him to a fourth grand cleric seated beside the nearest pillar. In front of him was a small desk and a scroll of parchment that draped over the edge, down to his feet, and unravelled across the floor for more than ten feet. The keeper of the word was sat ready, a quill pinched between fingers and thumb.

A presence behind him directed Talo to a lowly servant entering the pool, their bare feet previously unheard on the marble. But for a simple loincloth, the young man was naked and already coated in blood from the waist down. This wasn't his first time in the pool. The servant's presence fell away when the deserter noticed that which he held in his hands.

Talo was instantly enraptured.

Clasped between a pair of armoured gauntlets—preventing the holy relic from being stained by the servant's lowly hands—was the helm of a *god*.

Talo liked to think that he would have laid his head low were it not for the bloody water. In truth, however, the helm gripped him, holding him fast. In that moment, everything melted away, even the opulence of the throne room and the splendour of the imperial family.

Before him, within reach, was an object that had been crafted by godly hands and worn by a being of creation itself. Talo had only seen drawings and paintings of it, though he had read of the helm many times in the scriptures of the Arkalon.

The Helm of Ahnir, the god who had seen *The End*.

It stole Talo's breath away and brought tears to his eyes. The metal could have been mistaken as common steel were it not for the multitude of colours that danced across its sleek surface where it caught the light. Its design was mystifyingly simple for that of a god, with naught but an overlaying pattern of the same metal. Perhaps its most notable feature was the red gem fixed into the helm, above and centred between the eyes. It was no bigger than a single noht—a mere coin—though surely worth more than all the nohts in the empire. Situated at the gem's heart lay a black stone, a prisoner inside a gilded cage.

Quite naturally, Talo's attention shifted to the charred gash where the helm had been gouged above the right eye. The blow that had killed the immutable Ahnir.

The servant holding the helm straightened his arms all the more and bowed his head to his chest, desperate, possibly, to be free of the pool.

"Take it," one of the clerics commanded.

Talo's brow of pale slate pinched into a frown and he swallowed once. An order from a grand cleric carried the weight of the emperor himself, their words never to be denied. But surely they could not have been serious? None but those of imperial blood were permitted to touch the helm and rightly so. He was not worthy.

"It is not too late to face the block," another cleric voiced.

Talo tore his eyes from the helm but could not guess as to which of them had spoken to him.

"Take it."

Licking his dry lips, his hands came up, his undeserving fingers outstretched as he grasped the helm. So deeply profound was the moment that he nearly dropped it into the bloody soup.

It was cool to the touch, as any steel might be. Turning it over, he peered inside. It was there that the helm revealed a portion of its celestial nature and drew Talo in all the more. Flecks of obsidian crystal, like the stone within the ruby, decorated the interior. Each shard was pressed flat to the steel, giving no impression to his fingers.

The Andaren had no idea what was to happen next and so he returned his questioning gaze to the three grand clerics.

"Put it on," came the order.

Talo stood frozen in the warm pool. *Put it on.* The words seemed hollow to him, each without meaning. He had known this was coming for he had chosen this path rather than face the block and the disgrace that came with it. But now, holding the Helm of Ahnir... It was so vanquishing as to rob him of sense. Surely he was tainting such a holy relic.

Under the scrupulous gaze of the clerics, and to a vast chamber of anticipation, Talo slowly raised the helm and lowered it onto his head. It covered all but his mouth, the cheek guards curving down just past his jaw line. It wasn't nearly as oppressive as a god's helm should have been and, he was certain, he felt the helm alter its size to better fit him.

Turning to face his emperor, he could only wait—even if he couldn't fathom what he was waiting *for*. The servant retreated from the pool and disappeared behind the wall of clerics that now looked down on Talo, their expectant expressions felt even through their masks.

Something passed over the surface of the pool, a reflection that had no source. It drew Talo's scrutiny until his entire vision was filled by the bloody water. The Andaren frowned at the scene playing out in the reflection, for there was nothing but the ceiling and hanging foliage above. And yet, with his own eyes, he witnessed a savage battle being waged in the blood.

Talo looked up at those around him, wondering if they too could see what the blood was showing him. Their collective attention, however, was on him alone. Unable to bear it, he turned back to the surface of the pool.

He might as well have plunged beneath the surface, for he was there, on that very battlefield. Gone was the throne room and the palace with it. He now stood under black clouds that rained blood upon the armies of Erador and Andara. The hideous rain stopped abruptly when the source of the blood fell from the sky and thundered into the ground with a mighty crash, killing humans and Andarens alike.

A dragon.

A *dead* dragon.

Its body had been torn asunder by thick and unrelenting talons capable of tearing away dragon scales. Talo was driven back, his hair swept out by the fanned wings of an Aegre. He had seen them in battle before but never so close as this. The humans called them horned eagles, a crude name for the creatures, though quite typical from the dulled imagination of man. The Aegre swooped low over its victim, its impressive feathered wings stretched almost to equal those of a dragon.

Four bird-like legs descended on the corpse, talons sinking easily into dragon meat before its armour-plated beak pierced the monster's neck.

Upon its back sat one of the Vahlken, who had, long ago, tamed the deadly Aegres. Like the birds they flew, Talo had never seen one so close before. He decided they were just as terrifying as their mutated mounts.

Talo had only to turn on the spot to see an opposing scene, as a dragon brought down an Aegre in the distance. The great bird was pinned to a cliff face, helpless to prevent the dragon from unleashing its fiery breath. How quickly the fire spread across its feathers, enveloping it in flames.

The familiar cries of war surrounded Talo, redirecting him to the frenzied battles between his people and the humans. They each fell in droves, their shared blood soaked up by the dirt.

A bolt of pain racked Talo's mind, dropping him to his knees. He shut his eyes tight yet it did nothing to block out the sight of war. Of death. The environment had changed with the pain that burdened him, revealing that he was now in the middle of an open field under a clear blue sky. The fighting, however, remained exactly the same.

Dragons and Aegres collided with talons and claws.

Humans and Andarens slaughtered each other with abandon.

Machines of war spat their bolts and burning missiles across the battlefield.

The pain intensified and the environment changed once more, shredding Talo's mind into ruins as he watched human ships invade Andara's eastern coast. Human soldiers poured out of those ships like fire from the maws of their dragons.

Again and again, the surroundings changed and the war lived on, a never-ending cycle of death and destruction. Countless battles over countless years, creating a civilisation of corpses.

How many had died in the war and found naught but the Black Abyss, the chasm that awaited them all in the absence of the gods?

There was no more room for thought. Fire began to fill Talo's veins, eliciting a sharp wail that drowned out the constant warring. An eternity passed before the burning pain subsided and the Andaren was able to make sense of the vision thrust upon him.

The world had split like a shattered mirror, each side of the battlefield a perfect reflection of the other with Talo on the dividing line. Catching his breath, he required another moment to see the truth of the scene before him. It wasn't a *perfect* reflection. The environment was an exact copy and the opposing armies stood to mimicking attention, but he saw clearly now that one side was human and the other Andaren.

There stood a single figure, however, a lone man who walked towards him, along that dividing line. Talo narrowed his eyes to focus on the approaching stranger, but his image shifted like sand caught in the wind. The constant change lent him the pink flesh of man and the white hair and pointed ears of an Andaren all at once, as if he were a creature of both worlds. He came to a stop but ten feet away, one foot coming to rest upon a rock. There he stood, illustrious, powerful even, his eyes as violet as the emperor's.

A cape billowed in his wake, caught by ethereal winds. One moment, it appeared light as air and tanned in the style of the Dragon Riders, the next it became the heavy furs of a Vahlken cloak.

So too did the stranger's attire slip between two distinct designs. Seconds would go by while he wore the dark and well-fitted armour of the dreaded Dragon Riders. But there was no mistaking the thick leathers of the Vahlken, a slaiken blade planted in the ground beside him, the weapon tall and slightly curved. The banners of both orders danced about the chameleon, flapping in the same wind that caught his cloak.

Who was this man? *What* was this man? The answers that came with those questions flooded Talo's mind with terrible revelation. Naught but the gods should have to witness so much death. It brought tears to his eyes before hollowing him out.

With that, the Helm of Ahnir had spent all that Talo had to offer—all that his mind could withstand. His moment of divinity was over, returning what remained of himself to the present.

No sooner was the helm removed from his smoking head than

he vomited blood. His breathing came in shallow but rapid breaths. Blood trickled from his eyes, ears, and nose, streaking red down his pale face, adding more of the viscous fluid to the pool.

Talo had no memory of ever speaking, yet, to his left, the cleric was busy scribing, their quill scratching incessantly against the parchment. Quite naturally, his eyes soon found the base of the Empyreal Throne, taken there by the steps that led to the emperor's feet. Where before His Radiance had sat as a pillar of regality, he now sat upon his throne as the father, a young child perched upon his lap while his fingers combed through her immaculate hair.

Those violet eyes had finally found him.

Talo's ability to form coherent thoughts was diminishing by the second, a degeneration that was hastened under the emperor's hard stare. Before his mind could truly flee, his legs gave out, plunging him beneath the vile black water. The rough hands of servants grasped at him and dragged him back into the light and onto the smear of blood that stained the marble, where so many others had been laid.

One of the faceless clerics stepped forward. "At last, Your Radiance—*progress*. The abomination has a name."

While Talo lay, his body spasming, Emperor Qeledred's attention wandered over him, to the grand clerics. "*Pendain*," he announced impassively, his voice slicing through the air as a blade would cleave through flesh.

"A human name, Your Radiance," the cleric went on. "A pity. That will make finding him all the harder."

The name sounded familiar to Talo, the shape of it feeling right on his lips, yet he had no memory of voicing it.

The sound of vomiting filled the grand chamber, turning all eyes back to Talo. Blood gushed from his mouth and splashed across the white floor, pooling about his wrists and knees.

"He must be found," the emperor declared, moving on from the gruesome scene. "This *Pendain* cannot be allowed to bring about such a vision. The destiny of Andara and its people cannot be steered by an abomination," he added, flexing the fingers of his free hand.

"Of course, Your Radiance," the same cleric agreed. "We will..." The masked priest trailed off, his gaze drawn down to Talo.

The Andaren deserter blinked hard, gathering droplets of blood about his lashes. When his vision cleared he saw the image he had painted onto the floor with his own blood. His mind was sluggish, his thoughts and memories slowed by the Helm of Ahnir. Still, he recognised the symbol he had scrawled, the bloody image the size of his chest.

The grand cleric shoved him aside and his weak body gave no protest. The priest studied the symbol, his red robes hanging about him. "Your Radiance," he began, his voice no more than a whisper. "The *Eikor*."

The word was enough to send a ripple of discord through the imperial family and soldiers alike. Lying on his side, Talo registered the word as well, just as he had the symbol itself. Every Andaren knew that word, had seen its symbol in the last volume of the holy Arkalon. It had but one meaning.

The servant closest to Talo retreated from the symbol. "The Dark Ones," he muttered, garnering the attention of the grand clerics.

Like a coiled snake, the most vocal of the grand clerics advanced on the servant. Talo hadn't seen the curved dagger before it was in the cleric's grip and, even then, he barely saw the steel before it was plunged into the servant's throat. Without any signal, the other clerics in the chamber cornered every servant in attendance to the royal family and unceremoniously slaughtered them.

The clerics weren't the only ones to have exploded into action. The Praetorian Guard went from statues to wraiths. Of the dozen, some wielded spears while others brought scimitars to bear, and all accompanied by a rounded shield. Impassive were the expressions etched into their masks but aggressive was their stance; knees bent and weapons pointed out from the emperor.

As quickly as it had begun, the bloodshed came to an end. The first grand cleric to have incited violence rose from the servant, now dead at their feet. The curved dagger was cleaned with a kerchief and carefully replaced within the red robes. "Prudence, Your Radiance," he said by way of explanation. "It would be best if the abomination's name and any mention of the Eikor remain with a trusted few."

"Agreed," the emperor decided, his response and even tone enough to stand down the Praetorian Guard. "I would know more from the helm," he said, as the bodyguards resumed their previous positions.

The grand cleric hesitated. "We have exhausted near on two thousand to learn this much, Your Radiance."

The emperor continued to brush his hand through his daughter's hair. "Then imagine what we will learn after another two thousand."

The cleric bowed their head before turning to the golden doors, beyond the moat. "Bring forth the next!"

"But father," the child began, curiosity in her melodic tone, "why hasn't his head gone *pop*?" She whined with a dramatic pout, "All the others did! That's my favourite part."

Talo's unravelling mind could hardly comprehend the words she used, but something innate within him knew her question was a horror unto itself, a question he didn't want answering.

But the answer came all the same.

The latent pressure that had been quietly building crested the limits of any Andaren skull, spelling the end of Talo the deserter. There came no wail from kin as he had once imagined of his doom. Instead, it was his violent death that carved through the quietude of the onlookers. Then, as he had predicted, came the far more horrifying sound.

The stillness of death.

That yawning abyss.

PART ONE

1

MOVING SHADOWS

"YOU NEED TO *PUSH*, ILITHRANDA." ANDROMA'S WORDS WERE A FIRM directive. "Push *now*."

Leaning on the end of the bed, Androma could feel the sheets crease as they were clenched within Ilithranda's knotted fists. She could smell the sweat that lingered on the air, long having overpowered the lavender water prepared days earlier—a calming scent that had achieved little in the end. The Andaren warrior exhaled, letting loose a long moan, replacing all else in Androma's sensitive ears. The latter was a blessing given the sounds that invaded from beyond the walls.

What madness there was out there. What death.

"Push," she repeated, her hands moving up the bed and between Ilithranda's legs.

"I can't," the Andaren cried, her arduous labour taking its toll.

Indeed, Androma had recorded three sunrises since Ilithranda's first contraction. Warrior or not, the Andaren was exhausted.

"You must," Androma insisted. "The time is now. The babe is ready. You must *push*."

"I can't," Ilithranda said again, her head falling back onto the mounded pillows. "I'm... I'm too tired."

Androma cocked her head, though it did nothing to help her see past the ragged strip of cloth that concealed her eyes. "Tired? I'm blind, not deaf. There is yet strength in your voice. Where's that Vahlken mettle? You were bred to never stop."

Ilithranda groaned. "We were bred to never stop... killing!" she countered. "This is quite the... opposite." The next surge was upon her.

The walls shook around them and the timber beams creaked, threatening to lose their place in the ceiling. Somewhere, not too far away, another building was brought down in a shower of stone and rubble. So too were the fires rising, their reaching flames burning anything and everything. Androma could smell them. As always, amidst the chaos of war, there were the constant sounds of ringing steel and pained screams.

It was a battle that would have to wait.

"*Push*, Ilithranda."

The Andaren's head rolled forwards, her jaw clenched by the sound being forced between her teeth. It might have been years since she had seen the effect with working eyes, but Androma knew that the Andaren's silvery skin would be flushing a dull grey under such strain. Digging into reserves not idly found in most, sweat coating every inch of her skin, Ilithranda turned onto all fours, breathing and pushing with the rhythms of her body.

"That's it," Androma encouraged. "Feel it. Push."

Despite Ilithranda's efforts and the invariable frenzy of violence outside, Androma's aural abilities still detected the distinct flap of wings that batted the air beyond the roof. There came a squawk too, though it was quickly drowned out by an ear-splitting roar and another set of mighty wings.

"It's Tovun," Ilithranda declared, the name forced from her lips.

"Yes," Androma agreed. "He battles Herragax this day," she added ominously.

"You know the dragon by sound?" Ilithranda questioned.

"I know all their voices," Androma admitted, "few though they are."

"Vander is here," Ilithranda concluded with dismay.

"Yes," Androma answered, her tone relaying more than an ounce of derision for Herragax's Rider.

"Where is Daijen?" Ilithranda asked, her voice laced with concern.

"You ask a blind woman?" Androma quipped.

"He said he would be here," came the Andaren's groaning response.

"Daijen Saeth will be wherever he is needed to be—such is his way." Androma waved the topic away. "Neither Daijen nor Tovun are of any consequence," she instructed. "I need you focused..." Her attention snapped away, taken by the sound of the door being slammed open downstairs. "What now?" she growled.

The clamour of armour and imperial boots pounding up the spiral staircase soon followed, bringing out a sigh from Androma. Aware that Ilithranda was on the cusp of giving birth, she slipped off the bottom of the bed. She knew there were five steps between the edge of the bed and the northern wall, where she had left her staff resting against the stone.

Her arm outstretched, fingers flexing for the familiar touch, she found and grasped the staff of maple wood as the door was opened. Multiple boots entered, ruffling the strip of weathered rug that ran out from the threshold.

Four was Androma's count. But she had been wrong before.

"*What in the Black Abyss is going on here?*" one of them demanded in his native tongue.

"*GET OUT!*" Ilithranda roared without even looking at them.

Androma's Andarneese slipped from her tongue as if it was her first language. "*Can I help you, gentlemen?*"

By the sound of their scraping helms, the group had turned from the unlikely scene of an Andaren woman giving birth in the middle of a battle to the blind woman pointing her staff in their direction. Androma held it deliberately high, irritatingly so for the Andaren soldier who considered it to be in his face.

"*She's human!*" declared one from the back of the group.

"*Human?*" another questioned incredulously.

The first to speak, his voice deeper and richer than the others, uttered, "*What in the emperor's name...*"

"*Don't you have a war to be fighting?*" Androma interjected, jabbing her staff at the air.

The Andaren soldier gripped the flat end of the staff. "*Get that out of my face!*" he barked, shoving it aside. It gave away his exact position and informed Androma which hand wielded his sword.

The wicked smirk that curled but one of her cheeks would not have been hard to miss for the sighted.

That length of maple wood jabbed forwards with enough force to break the soldier's nose and push him back into the Andaren behind. What followed was a blur, the staff arcing round to slam one in the side of the helm before breaking the knee of another and, finally, being thrust up into the groin of a third. Androma's next, but considerably more powerful, attack whipped the staff up into the jaw of the third, flipping him up and over until he landed on the back of his neck.

"Androma!" Ilithranda screamed.

The soldier who had received the blow to the helm recovered first and leapt from the floor, barrelling into Androma with a strong arm around her waist. Her response to Ilithranda was taken from her lips, along with the air in her lungs as she greeted the wall with force. Two successive fists rammed into her gut before a swift right hook caught her in the face and dropped her to one knee.

But the soldier wasn't done with her yet.

As he tried to pull her up for another beating, Androma pushed him back and he dragged the rags over her head in the process. Staggering back with naught but clothing for his efforts, the Andaren looked back at the blind woman, perhaps expecting to see her naked.

He was wrong.

"*That armour,*" he muttered in his rich baritone, obviously staring at the close-fitted panels of firm but well-worn leather the rags had been concealing. "*You're a...*"

"*She's a Dragon Rider!*" another exclaimed, though the sound of his voice suggested he had a broken nose.

What a surprise that must have been, to have tackled a blind woman, and of age by her weathered skin, pallor, and cropped greying hair, only to behold a *Dragon Rider*. Their nerves were immediately frayed by the reputation that accompanied such a title.

Whether that was the whole truth of the matter or not, Androma used the moment of revelation and thrust a boot out, hammering the soldier holding her ragged tunic in the chest. The broken nose stepped in, for while the broken leg naturally failed to stand, the other was unconscious, if not already dead from a broken neck.

Arms held out and absent her staff, Androma stepped away, giving herself time and space. She heard the sound of a sword being raised and swiftly so by the way it cut through the air. Her left heel knocked against her staff, causing it to move a few inches. She stepped over it and rolled the wood onto her toes before kicking it up into her waiting hands.

Head down and tilted slightly to one side, she listened and waited. To the blind, the world was moving shadows, black on black. It was a life of quietude and chaos entwined, a life that had taken Androma years to master after several lifetimes of enjoying sight.

But mastered it she had.

Weaving left then right, she evaded the two swings that would have taken her head, and deflected a third swing with her right vambrace, the steel glancing off the small blue dragon scales that plated the armour. Having now taken the necessary steps to position not just herself but her opponent too, Androma jabbed the soldier in the throat, her staff robbing him of breath. A quick twist of the maple wood brought the staff up behind the Andaren and launched him through the shutters and window.

The sound of war was exaggerated for a moment, the violence

and mayhem spilling into the room. Moving away from the noise, Androma detected movement at the end of the bed. The soldier who had snatched her tunic was rising. Closer to the door, the fool with the broken leg, who had yet to have his say in the fight, was crawling back to the stairs.

"Androma," Ilithranda moaned again, pulling at her attention.

On his feet, the soldier dropped the tunic and drew a dagger from his belt, the steel ringing short and sharp as it tasted the air. He spat on the floor. "*Now you die, witch,*" he promised.

Equally short and sharp was the breath that escaped Androma's nose as she resigned herself to the final obstacle. He jabbed first, coming for her face, before rounding back to slice her neck. She felt the sting of it and knew it wasn't a mortal blow. Rather than dwell on the near-miss, she brought her staff into the melee, forcing the soldier to rely on his footwork to stay in the fight. He took three strikes to the chest and one to the top of his arm, all of which were armoured and saved him from broken bones.

"*Maybe you're not a Dragon Rider after all!*" the Andaren sneered. He countered with a backhand that bloodied Androma's lip, before the edge of his dagger carved across her ribs, staggering her.

Androma didn't need eyes to know the Andaren was smiling. She cared little for his revels, or his words for that matter. Her hand moved over her compact armour and found the damage her foe had wrought. Her fingers traced the torn leather and felt the hard scales that formed the hidden underlayer of her armour.

Scales. *His* scales.

Don't think about him, she commanded of herself.

Though he didn't know it, the soldier was coming at her now with a dulled blade. He might yet have wielded it to victory, but victory was not his to claim that day, nor any that might follow.

Androma lashed out and stunned him with a single blow to his jaw. Before he knew what was happening, she was repositioning not only herself but the staff until she was behind him and the maple wood rested in front of his neck. Then she twisted.

The body dropped, leaving Androma with the sound of her

own blood pumping like thunder in her ears. Chest heaving, she could but listen to the world as it came back to her. The soldier with the broken knee was gone. The remaining two didn't move. Battle raged as it had for days and quickly returned to no more than a background noise.

It was then that she heard it. The cry of a baby. At last, on the sparrow day, in the year 3117 of the sixth epoch, and in the middle of a fierce invasion, a baby of two worlds had been born.

"Ilithranda?" she breathed.

"*Come,*" the Vahlken replied, her words slurring. "*Feel him.*"

Androma could hear her smile. "*Him?*"

Using her staff, she found the edge of the bed and worked her way around to the head. She sat beside Ilithranda and let the Andaren guide her hands to the child. He was draped in the blanket previously laid out and already rooting for his mother's breast.

"*This is... Joran.*" Though she said his name with pride, Ilithranda's voice was growing distant.

"*A good name,*" Androma replied, though her concern was growing. Ilithranda's exhaustion was considerable, her three days of labour having taken its toll. Voicing such concern to her—or any Vahlken—would only fall on deaf ears. Instead, she explored Joran's hands, counting ten digits in total, before running her fingers up his arm and neck until she could stroke his head.

"*He has a lot of hair for a babe,*" she remarked, a rare smile of genuine warmth on her face.

"*It's white,*" Ilithranda informed her softly.

Androma nodded along. "*And his skin?*"

"*He has... the pink of man,*" the Vahlken replied. "*The skin of his father,*" she added quietly.

Androma lowered her hand and traced the edges of the boy's left ear. It was pointed, shaped like his mother's. "*And his eyes?*" she enquired.

"*He has mine,*" Ilithranda uttered.

"*Violet then,*" Androma said, recalling the warrior's face from distant memory.

"*He's... beautiful,*" the new mother observed.

"*He's complicated,*" Androma opined.

"*He's... minutes old, Androma.*" Despite the obvious fatigue that was upon her, Ilithranda managed to insert an edge of defensive venom into her tone.

"*I had only hoped he would adopt one side or the other. At least then we would know where to hide him, where he would be safe. As he is, he will be hunted in both realms.*"

"*No one,*" Ilithranda stated with as much verve as she could muster in her deteriorating condition, "*is touching... my son!*"

It was hard to make that emotional connection without her eyes to find Ilithranda's, as she had once done as no more than a reflex. Instead, she searched for the Andaren's hand and squeezed it, her features softening for the moment.

"*That too,*" Androma whispered, "*is* my *vow.*" She felt Ilithranda squeeze her hand in return. "*Now,*" she began, her mind returning to more immediate tasks, "*has the sack come with the babe?*" Her hands were already searching for the baby's cord.

"*Yes,*" Ilithranda uttered.

"*Very good,*" Androma said, impressed with the speed and efficiency of Vahlken anatomy.

"*You're sure... you know what you're... doing?*"

"*Quite sure,*" Androma answered confidently, even if that wasn't entirely the case. "*As a child, I witnessed my mother assist in bringing dozens of children into the world.*"

"*How long ago... was that?*"

Androma licked her lips. "*Some years, I suppose,*" she said offhandedly, aware that it was closer to six centuries now.

After tying the cord close to Joran, with a length of string, she sliced through it and separated him from the sack. She would have left them attached for much longer, but Harendun was not a city in which they could afford to linger.

"*Androma,*" Ilithranda murmured, her voice distant despite their close proximity. "*I...*"

A terrible sinking feeling took hold of Androma. With one hand she investigated the sheets between Ilithranda's legs. Blood. Far too much blood. It was a great volume, the likes of which no human or Andaren could survive without. She couldn't say why—an instinctual memory perhaps—but she began to rub Ilithranda's stomach in the hope of staunching it.

"It's alright," she lied, her words slipping back into man's tongue. "Everything's going to be alright."

There came no response from Ilithranda.

Then the baby began to cry.

Androma stopped rubbing and moved further up the bed. "Ilithranda?" Still nothing. "Ilithranda?" She found Joran, loosely held in his mother's slack grip, and took him in her own. "There, there," she cooed, her tone betraying a lack of knowledge where mothering was concerned.

"Ilithranda?" she tried again, this time reaching out to find her face. Like all of her pale race, her features were sharp and beautiful. She had no response to Androma's probing fingers.

While it wasn't common knowledge to most of the realm, Androma's highly-regarded training included much about the body. She pressed two fingers against the Vahlken's throat and waited for the feel of a pulse, a telltale sign that her heart was still pumping blood around her body.

She felt nothing.

Androma's shoulders sagged as a quick and sudden depression took hold of her. She cradled Joran all the more. He had only been in the world mere minutes and already he had beheld so much death. And what a loss it was for the world, that it should know another day without the light of Ilithranda in it. Of course, there was no greater tragedy than Joran growing up in a world without his mother to guide him. And what a guide she would have been.

Joran cried again, cutting through her mounting grief. There would be time to mourn her, time to cry until there were no more tears to be had. But, right now, there was only one thing on Androma's ever pragmatic mind.

Milk.

2
THE STRINGS OF FATE

80 Years Ago...

Harendun burned, as it had so many times before over the last two hundred years. At least half of it did. The flaming ruins belonged to Erador now, taken with steel and blood. From the rooftop gardens of the ancient Rune Tower, the icy blue eyes of Daijen Saeth spied their ships through the smoke, brought to Andara's shores on red sails.

Though the ruination of Harendun hazed the afternoon sky, the Andaren warrior could still see the exchanging fireballs and lancing ballista bolts that streaked through the blue. Each brought destruction down upon the city or sank an Eradoran warship, sending its soldiers to the depths.

So much death.

From such a lofty vantage, he couldn't hear the fighting taking place in the streets or the screams of the dying. Steel would be clashing and blood would be spilling onto the stone but, as always, Daijen was only to observe the battlefield, never to enter it.

A skirmish broke out on one of the connecting bridges below, redirecting the Andaren's attention. Two of his kin had burst through the door before the pursuing humans followed in their wake. The two warriors were forced to turn and fight, and fight well they did. In less than a minute, they succeeded in throwing four humans over the rail as they cut their way through the group of seven.

Exhausted, the two Andarens clasped forearms in celebration of their victory. Daijen couldn't imagine what that felt like, to have fought such odds and survived by skill and grit alone. He considered his armour, its shade of bronze undisturbed by combat or blood. Even his dark cloak remained pristine save for the dirt that collected about the hem.

His sword was more decoration than weapon.

The same could also be said of Ondris, beside him. Both had been assigned their duty years earlier, to guard the messengers sent forth from The Saible in The Gap. While some had argued that Ondris had landed such a risk-free position on account of his father—who served those on the emperor's war council—most had determined that Daijen simply wasn't fit to fight the human horde. Those same people had also informed him as much on numerous occasions.

Daijen didn't know what to believe, but watching the two warriors below succumb to the works of a catapult, their bridge obliterated in an explosion of fire and debris, he was thankful for his position all the same.

"They're gaining ground," Ondris observed, a hint of fear in his voice.

Daijen disagreed but he didn't say as much. Ondris's house was of higher standing, a fact that formed the foundation of his personality and, ultimately, made him something of a prig. Rather than give his opposing opinion, and suffer Ondris's biting retort, Daijen continued to watch from the edge of the gardens, where the defenders below pushed the enemy back, street by street. Still, it only took one barricade to fail and the human invaders would find their way to The Rune Tower.

Daijen turned to the bushes that marked the corner of the

garden path. There, he saw Ailen Torth, the messenger they had set out from The Saible with. He was vomiting. A lithe creature of no more than thirty years, this was not only Ailen's first time delivering the war council's word but also his first time east of The Gap.

"Sir," Daijen began, intending to usher the messenger along.

Ailen shot up a finger to silence him, as he would have to the servants of his house, superior even to Ondris's. He retched one more time before straightening up and smoothing his robes down. He glanced at the two guards, suspiciously so, and cleared his throat.

"All those blasted steps," he complained, as if it hadn't been the sight of the red sails that had upset his nerves.

"We're running out of time, Sir," Ondris reported, his open stance leading the messenger to the vista of ruin.

Ailen Torth raised a hand to stop him from saying another word, a lump forming in his throat. He couldn't even bring himself to look beyond the balcony.

"Announce me," he instructed sharply, gesturing to the double doors on the other side of the gardens.

Abandoning the cityscape, Daijen led the way at a quick pace, his obsidian cloak moving lightly in the air. They were met by two more guards in identical armour, one of whom opened the doors for them. Daijen opened his mouth, prepared to voice his superior's name and title, but chaos reigned therein.

He didn't know where to look or whom to address. Soldiers were storming about the chamber as they coordinated their counterattack. Missives were scribed, bound, and put into the hands of numerous runners. Castellans and imperators pored over the large map that blanketed the central table, which was overlaid with smaller, more detailed maps of the streets and alleyways. At the head of the table stood a paragon, his white mane bound into a tight braid that fell over his cuirass. He was the quietest of them all, a man of ancient focus befitting his station.

A glancing elbow from Ondris reminded Daijen of his duty. "Council..." Daijen cleared his throat and tried again. "Council

Messenger, Ailen, of House Torth, with word from The Saible!" he declared.

The buzz faded to utter silence and all eyes fell on Daijen Saeth. Since the ground didn't swallow him whole as he would have liked, the young Andaren moved aside so his superior might be seen.

"Paragon Sorn," the messenger began, overcoming his recent fear to enunciate clearly. "I have come with—"

"Words aren't going to save this city," Sorn interjected with his barking voice, "be they from The Saible or the emperor himself. So unless you've come with ten thousand soldiers at your back, you can stand over there and keep quiet."

As quickly as it had faded, the chamber's busy activities resumed as if it had suffered no interruption at all. Runners pushed their way past Ailen, no mind given to the fact that he hailed from one of the highest houses in all of Andara.

Ailen himself was left with naught but a lump in his throat, his ivory skin somewhat flushed to blue. As commanded, however, he slowly slunk away and stood by the north wall, as if he were no more than a part of the furniture. Embarrassed as he was, the highborn spared Daijen and Ondris a scolding look that brought them to his side.

The hubbub experienced another pause, if briefly, when a tremor ran through the tower. Dust rained down from the vaulted ceiling and decanters were toppled, spilling water across the floor. Daijen maintained his stoical facade to hide the concern growing in his bones. He had been close to the battlefield before, but never had he been ordered to stand around and wait to die. And what would he be dying for? Failing to deliver a message from the war council, and that a message he hadn't even been trusted with. Worse still, he would die because the war simply demanded it. It might help, of course, if he knew exactly *why* they were at war, for the reasons he had been given made little sense to him. Not that they needed to when a foreign people were literally bombarding the shore.

"Paragon."

The voice that had bitten off the title belonged to a woman on the far side of the table. She appeared to be one of a group, though the other two remained immobile, slightly back from the central table, where she pressed her hands onto the edges of the map. Her white hair flowed over marred pauldrons, framing her angular face and sharp lips. It might have been brief, but her violet eyes met Daijen's across the table before shifting to Paragon Sorn.

Fierce was the word that came to Daijen's mind, be it the look in those violet eyes or in the clipped way she addressed the highest ranking Andaren in all of Harendun.

"Give me the men and I'll drive through to the Sea Gate," she claimed. "From there we can—"

"All die," Sorn cut in. "We're pushing them back, but the latest report has the southern square compromised. The defences there have fallen through. You would be set upon from both sides as well as by those you aim to push back to the beach."

"It can be done," the fierce Andaren protested, her tone absent any respect.

"Perhaps, but not by you," the Paragon stated firmly. "Word has already been sent. Ka'vairn is expecting three of you and three of you I intend to deliver." Sorn turned immediately to the soldier on his right. "Why isn't their escort ready?" he demanded.

"We're here, Paragon!" the female Andaren pointed out. "Use us now! Let us fight!"

"You *have* fought!" Sorn retorted, his patience run dry. "And bravely so," he added, his voice shaking. "Why else would I have picked you three of all the thousands? Look out there!" he snapped, one hand thrown out to the gaping window. "Do you see any Aegre in the sky? We *need* Vahlken," he intoned. "So no, you cannot fight, Ilithranda. You must survive today and survive the trials and fight *another* day. Trust me, the war will still be here when you claim your slaiken blade."

Daijen looked upon Ilithranda and her two companions with new eyes. He had never seen a Vahlken in person or even those chosen to take the trials, as these three had. So few were considered worthy to be handpicked from the battlefield, for it was said that only the bravest and most skilled could withstand the trials of Ka'vairn. Daijen gazed at them as a child might, they who would one day soar through the clouds like gods.

Put in her place, the one called Ilithranda could do naught but step back from the table and join her comrades in their small line. Her sullen features were soon concealed when her place at the table was taken by one of the prime chiefs.

Several minutes went by, precious minutes in which the Eradorans searched for a way past the defences. Distant impacts sent new tremors up The Rune Tower, but it was clear their accuracy was improving.

Inevitably, Daijen's fears became manifest.

The first missile struck the tower at its foundations, knocking most from their feet, but the second was hurled slightly higher. Without warning, the wall behind Ilithranda exploded into the room. The sound alone blasted the occupants with an ear-piercing shockwave, though it wasn't nearly as devastating as the flaming missile itself.

The great stone and a wave of debris rammed through everything, taking no prisoners as it demolished the table, flattening commanders and soldiers alike, before continuing through the opposite wall.

The ramifications were so much worse than two holes in the tower and a dozen dead, for the arched roof was immediately compromised. Two thick beams, damaged by flying debris, lost their place and fell into the chamber, killing more of their elite planners. Adding to the turmoil, the flames from the missile had reached out and spread patches of fire across the room, masking the air with smoke.

Over the sounds of pained calls for help, Daijen heard the roof creaking and wood splintering. It was coming down and fast.

"We need to get out of here!" he yelled, picking himself up and turning to Ondris.

Ondris wasn't there. Nor was Ailen Torth.

Where they had been standing was now a jagged hole through which the afternoon sun poured in, unaware that it was shining down on such a dark day. Daijen peered out of the hole and discovered no more than a handful of ruined buildings and marred rooftops. He swallowed the sharp cut of revelation he felt, his instinct to survive pushing him past the shock of it all.

Turning back to the chamber, the paragon was being dragged towards the double doors by a pair of commanders. They made it no further than the end of the table before another beam snapped and swung down on one side. The common soldier to Sorn's left was killed instantly, his skull hammered by the unrelenting wood. The jolt of it knocked the other soldier aside and the paragon fell face down.

While Daijen's instincts told him to flee the tower at once, his duty to protect spoke the loudest, urging him to the paragon's side. A slave to the tenets drilled into him, the young Andaren began dragging him by the wrists.

The double doors were already open, the exterior guards having entered after the attack. Daijen felt the sun on his pale skin as he heaved his superior to safety, if there was such a place in Harendun. A short sharp scream turned Daijen back to the smoking chamber. He hadn't seen her cry out, but he knew it had been Ilithranda.

Again, his survival instincts reminded him that he had escaped the Black Abyss, so why put that in jeopardy?

As more staggered into the daylight, bleeding and dazed, Ilithranda called out again, her voice strained from exertion. Daijen squeezed the hilt of his virgin sword, a tactile source of strength for any warrior. Before that small voice in the back of his mind could tell him he was anything but a warrior, Daijen of House Saeth marched back into the burning chamber.

He coughed with almost every breath while one hand waved the smoke from his vision. More than one of his kin bumped into him as they escaped the unstable roof. Still, he pressed on, determination in his steps. That determination faltered when another beam broke and thundered into the floor beside him.

On his hands and knees now, he felt the cool air where the catapult had shattered the first wall. In that moment of clarity, he saw her, trapped beneath a beam and the body of one of her chosen companions. Scrambling, Daijen navigated two of the dead and crouched beside Ilithranda.

Using both hands, he dragged the body off her legs before moving on to the beam. Damned if it wasn't the heaviest thing he had ever lifted. Urged on by impending doom, however, Daijen found the strength to raise it just enough for Ilithranda to crawl out.

"It's coming down!" he warned her, his gaze flitting to the roof.

"Wait!" she commanded. "Help me with Elivar!"

Daijen was directed to another body a few feet away—one of the chosen three. Elivar sported a nasty gash to the side of his head but his hands were slowly exploring the area about him. Together, they hooked his arms around their shoulders and carried him towards the door.

A loud splintering of wood came from above, informing Daijen that they were out of time. "Jump!" he shouted, one hand gripping Elivar by the waist.

As one, they leapt for safety, passing over the threshold as The Rune Tower lost its roof altogether. A plume of smoke and dust washed over them and spread into the gardens. The burst of activity had put some life back into Elivar's bones, who was now resting on his elbows.

"Can you stand?" Ilithranda asked him.

"Yes," Elivar managed, his throat dry.

"Order a full advance."

The words caught the attention of the three survivors and turned them all to Paragon Sorn, who was returned to his feet, his white cloak marred and stained to match his features. He was looking out over the city, as Daijen had with Ondris.

"Split our force in two," the Paragon went on. "We will sweep round from the east and the west to let the humans slip through the heart and believe they have gained ground. Then we will attack from their rear. From there we will..." Sorn trailed off as he caught sight of Ilithranda and Elivar. "You live," he remarked, a touch of relief about him. He then regarded Daijen beside them, a stranger to his amber eyes. "You," he said with some recognition now. "You saved my life." The paragon glanced at the chosen pair, who had only survived because of Daijen's efforts. "Where is Rondir?"

Ilithranda half turned to face the imploded chamber. "He did not survive," she said quickly. "Paragon, let us join your force—"

"No," Sorn bit back. "You fought well for three hard weeks. You kept Harendun alive; you bought its people time. But I promised Ka'vairn three initiates. I shall see they receive three," he vowed, amber eyes falling on Daijen.

It seemed then to Daijen Saeth that the Black Abyss had manifested inside his stomach, a tangible thing that pulled his organs down to a cold, cold place.

"Him?" Ilithranda spat. "He's a messenger guard!"

"*He's* the reason we draw breath," the paragon corrected. "Besides, it's not for me to determine whether he, or any of you, become a Vahlken or not. I can but send you. And so I shall. What's your name, boy?"

Daijen's lips, dry as old bones, caught in his response, slowing him just enough for another to speak over his name.

"Red cloaks!" The call came from the railing, where other survivors were watching the streets and bridges below.

Paragon Sorn straightened his back, a flex that pinched his brow in pain, and drew his sword. "We must close the breach!" he commanded.

Ilithranda's sword cleaved through the air as it tasted freedom. Daijen didn't miss the dried blood that clung to the blade. Elivar succeeded in separating sword from scabbard but his arm failed to keep the weapon aloft, the edge falling to meet the garden path.

"Stay behind me," Ilithranda told him.

"I can still fight," he insisted.

"And you will," Ilithranda replied sternly. "But if you want to make it to Ka'vairn you will stay behind me."

Elivar nodded dourly.

Ilithranda looked at Daijen, her gaze darting from his sword—

still on his hip—to his face. In response, he pulled the sabre free, the steel embarrassingly clean.

"Die here or die in Ka'vairn," Ilithranda stated. "It makes no difference to me." With that, she moved on and with Elivar close on her heels.

As one, the survivors of The Rune Tower descended its many steps and rushed out into the streets, swords bristling. Indeed, the human invaders had breached one of the defensive lines and found their way through to the tower. In armour that would have gleamed silver were it not for the blood and grime that coated it, they charged with red cloaks flowing behind them.

Daijen wished he could have said he rushed to meet them, sword raised. But that was not what happened. He hesitated before the mob of killers, just enough that their assault was met by others in a collision of violence and death.

Paragon Sorn counted himself among those on the front line, his centuries of fighting plain to see. Equally talented in the art of delivering death, Ilithranda danced between her foes, sabre lancing and slashing with deadly efficiency. Humans piled up around her, they who had been fated to taste the bite of her steel. Even Elivar, wounded as he was, showed his quality, ducking and weaving between attacks before bringing his good arm to bear.

Among the throng of humans, a lone red cloak broke through, his blade backhanding one of the tower survivors, sending them to the Black Abyss. With a primal cry and a face of rage, the Eradoran came for Daijen's life.

Naturally, the young Andaren backed off a step, giving himself —if not his honed reactions—time to respond. In a two-handed grip, his sabre came up and blocked the incoming sword not once but twice before he shoved a boot into the Eradoran's cuirass. Thinking only to survive, Daijen then swept his sword into his enemy's neck.

He hadn't the strength to decapitate the man, and so his blade remained lodged between the bones. The blow was still enough to send the soldier to his knees, his expression claimed by shock. A strong tug freed the weapon as well as the man's blood, which poured out with abandon before he fell face down.

Panting for breath, Daijen looked down on his work. He had seen thirty-five winters since being born into a war that had raged for somewhat over two-hundred years. He was naught but lucky, if not blessed, to have come this far without taking a life.

The civilised part of his mind demanded that he stop and take stock of the profound moment. But it had been so simple. More so, it had left him feeling strong, perhaps even hungry for more. The violence bubbled up within him, turning him to another red cloak that had fought his way through the Andaren line.

Ilithranda beat him to it, her sabre slashing low then high, bringing the man to one knee before slicing his head from jaw to brow.

Then it was done. Over.

Only the laboured breathing of a dozen Andarens filled the street. Daijen could still feel the fire coursing through his veins. He wanted to taste it again.

Victory.

It was all the sweeter when standing on the edge of the Black Abyss, knowing that his very life had been in the balance. The rush of it had turned him into a raw nerve, making him hyper-aware of everyone around him.

"Your first?" Elivar asked him, his silvery skin streaked with the blood of his foes.

Daijen needed an extra second to process the question, though Elivar, it seemed, had gleaned the truth of it.

"You're never going to survive Ka'vairn," the wounded Andaren remarked with a smirk.

"He won't even survive the journey," Ilithranda sniped on her way past.

"You two!" Paragon Sorn called, beckoning two of his soldiers. "Escort them to the eastern gate and see they have horses."

"Paragon!" Ilithranda retorted, her protests mounting.

"Enough!" Sorn snapped, whirling on her. "I would have thought *you* desired this."

Ilithranda's argument died on her lips. She looked sheepishly from face to face before landing on her superior's again. "I only desire to fight for my people," she stated firmly, if quietly.

"Complete the trials," the paragon replied, "and you *will* fight for your people. More importantly," he added, "you will win victories for your people. Now go. That's an order."

Daijen didn't feel as if he belonged beside Ilithranda and Elivar, even with a bloody sword in hand, and so he stood apart while they watched the others peel away to reclaim the city.

Ilithranda growled and kicked one of the corpses over. "Black Abyss!" she cursed.

Elivar and Daijen followed her lead when she stormed off towards the eastern gate. There were few, if any, citizens left in Harendun. As with the previous invasions, the people knew to evacuate at the first sign of trouble, taking The Sael Road north to Yalafar to await reinforcements from The Saible. Daijen still caught sight of stragglers darting between buildings, fools who thought they could outlast the human occupation.

At the edge of the city, they found war horses, and already saddled. He looked back at Harendun and its crown of smoke, thinking of the man he had just sent to the Black Abyss. He thought then of the battle taking place in the streets and how close he had been to it... to *war*. Shrinking his world, Daijen reached up with one hand and massaged the ram-like horns protruding from his horse's brow.

How strange it was to be leaving without Ondris. They had ridden out from The Saible together more times than he could count. Daijen knew he wouldn't miss his arrogant disposition or the pretentious way in which he conducted himself, both always to remind him that House Saeth was the lesser. That didn't mean he wouldn't miss the familiar company. Ilithranda and Elivar possessed an intimidating edge that left him unsettled in their presence.

"We resupply in Yalafar," Ilithranda stated, deftly taking to her new mount. "We make for The Saible from there." The fierce Andaren guided her horse to block Daijen's path. "If you wish to get... *lost* along the way, you may return to The Saible in your own time and resume your duties without report from us."

It might have been a cruel assessment of his abilities, but her offer was generous. The path he had been set upon was a knife's edge. "I have been *ordered* to Ka'vairn," he pointed out, having known little else.

"Paragon Sorn won't remember your face by day's end," Ilithranda told him. "Nor did he know your name. You have a chance to get lost in the ranks again."

"*Messenger guard* does have a ring to it," Elivar mocked.

Daijen didn't know what to say, stuck between the urge to survive and his desire to prove himself.

"Think on it," Ilithranda said in his silence, her horse now turned to the road.

Daijen watched her slowly ride away. He hardly knew Ilithranda, but what he had gleaned in their short but eventful time together was how directly she spoke. Her words were wielded as any weapon might be and she didn't apologise for it. Yet, her proposal to him—to disregard his orders—had been voiced indirectly.

"She's trying to save your life," Elivar told him, having noticed, perhaps, the lingering and inquisitive gaze that kept Daijen tethered to Ilithranda.

"Save my life?" Daijen questioned, his vision still occupied by Ilithranda's departure.

"You saved her life," Elivar reminded him, his injured arm slowing his ascent to the saddle. "This is her returning the favour. If you're smart," he went on, eventually settling into the foreign saddle, "you'll forget Sorn's orders. Ka'vairn has enough of our kin buried in its grounds." With that, the wounded warrior put his horse to the road. "Oh," Elivar called back. "I'm assuming you have a name besides *messenger guard*."

"Daijen Saeth," was his reply, though he could have said it with more pride.

"Very good. Should you decide to accompany us all the way to Ka'vairn, you would know my name. Elivar T'saren," the warrior announced, his voice growing distant. "Remember it well, Daijen of House Saeth! For one day, you will boast that you knew the greatest Vahlken who ever lived!"

Daijen watched the pair a while longer. For the first time in his life, the path before him was his to choose. In truth, he had no idea what he was going to do. He would start, however, by putting Harendun behind him.

3
THE UNDYING CITY

PRESENT DAY...

Harendun was set to flames, its great fires banishing the night as if the city wore a halo of light. Swathes of its buildings and spires had been brought down by the unrelenting warships of Erador, the city's stone no match for the mounted ballista and catapult barges.

The docks were in disarray, crowded with too many ships and boats, some of which had simply rammed through the jetties to get soldiers as close to the city as possible. Further south, more ships had run themselves onto the beach and unloaded their hold of soldiers onto Andaren sand.

So many had the king of Erador commanded into battle that his navy could not carry their numbers. Every privateer, merchant, and all those in between had been offered thousands of marks to ferry the brave and the bold who bore the sigil of the royal house Etragon—the plunging sword of dragon scales.

From the port side of The Raven, the fiery scene was reflected in the glassy eyes of Gallien Drakalis. "This isn't even the first time I've watched it burn," he remarked, taking a large bite out of his ruby red apple. "We've sacked this city... what? Nine times? Ten? We knock it down, they rebuild it." The smuggler shook his head and sighed. "War..."

"Let them sack it," came the response, turning Gallien to his companion, her face awash in the moonlight. "Makes our job easier."

Gallien regarded his roguish companion—Kitrana Voden; *Kit* to him. Her callous attitude towards war didn't surprise him. "*The wars of men mean little to me,*" she would often remark. Of course, he had seen her weep in quiet moments when their work had spilled into places where the war had made itself known, where it had ruined lives. For all her bravado when on the hunt, Kit could be a woman of unbridled emotion and exhibit an irritating sense of justice that was guaranteed to strike at the wrong moment. Damn if he didn't love that about her.

"You're doing it again," she commented, no more than a hint of a smile behind her stern expression.

"Doing what?" Gallien asked innocently enough, her observation breaking his thoughts.

"*Staring.*"

"Apologies," he offered, and half-heartedly so. After all, Nimeans had no idea how beautiful they were in the eyes of humans. It was as if the ocean had sculpted them from the dreams of men, lending them a form and physique so symmetrical as to be uncomfortably attractive.

"You're still doing it," Kit reminded him, any hint of amusement wiped away.

Gallien shrugged off the distraction and turned to the dark waves beyond The Raven. "You know," he began wistfully, "we never did talk about what happened in Valgala."

"That was the luckiest night of your life," Kitrana was quick to respond. "That kind of luck doesn't strike twice," she added at no more than a whisper.

Rebuffed and keen to move things along, Gallien flicked his head towards the city. "I honestly didn't think there'd be another invasion in my lifetime. I wouldn't have said it could be done without a dragon at our backs." He gave a mirthless laugh. "Now you don't even see Aegres in the sky, never mind dragons."

Kit moved closer to him, though her sight was set firmly on the city beyond. "I wouldn't be so sure this was done without a dragon..." Her voice trailed off, leading Gallien to narrow his eyes on Harendun.

The city's dark and jagged shape of broken buildings and toppled towers began to move, as if Harendun itself was trying to rise. It became all the clearer when two bat-like wings arched over the city and a snaking neck brought the dragon's head into the light of the fires. The smuggler's lips parted as he saw it, his eyes not daring to blink. The beast roared, almost, it seemed, in defiance of Gallien's assumption.

Those terrifying wings flapped but once and the dragon left its perch. Gallien could have watched it soar and glide all night, every facet of it so magnificent and mysterious, but the creature disappeared within the ruins and pluming smoke.

"I saw one in battle once," he uttered, his voice caught by memory. "A Rider, that is. I've never seen anything like it. They are to us as dragons are to sheep," he opined.

"Hm," was Kit's sharp and disinterested response. "I've seen things under the water that could swallow a dragon whole."

It was comments like that—comments he had heard many times before—that would keep Gallien Drakalis from dipping a single toe in the ocean for the rest of his life.

"Over here," he said, moving to starboard. He led the way across the deck, navigating the crew who had brought The Raven and its cargo of soldiers from Caster Hold. The smuggler narrowed his eyes at the cliff face that rose up from the sea in the north. "It should be... There!"

Kit followed his pointing finger to the crack that tore up through the cliff face, narrowing the higher it rose in the shape of an arrowhead. The waves crashed against the rock, posing danger to any who might attempt to enter the crevice.

"You're sure?" Kit probed, doubt in her voice.

"Of course I'm sure," Gallien defended. "When am I ever

wrong?" He regretted asking that particular question as soon as the words left his mouth.

"How about that time in Cartham?" Kit was quick to point out. "Or Haran's Town? We nearly didn't make it out of there. Hell, we would have been dead and buried in Freygard if it wasn't for me. You're lucky the city is surrounded by water."

Gallien nodded his way through every point. "But was I right?" he asked her, his broad grin spreading his thick blond beard. "Hmm? Didn't we walk away from every one of those places a little richer?"

"We nearly didn't walk away at all," Kit replied dryly, never one to agree with him.

"It doesn't matter," Drakalis said, moving from one side of his companion to the other. "This was *Corben's* plan." Gallien swallowed and pushed on as if his brother's name hadn't put a lump in his throat. "He read every word my father ever wrote about the ancient world and then some. Corben had a way of seeing things, a way even the old man couldn't." Again, Gallien pointed at the narrow crevice. "He was sure—*certain*—that—"

"Whenever you say you're *certain*," Kit interrupted, "I always end up running for my life."

"I said *Corben* was certain," Gallien corrected.

"Your brother," Kit pointed out, her voice still laden with scepticism. "A *Drakalis* boy, aye?"

"Don't go painting us all with the same brush," the smuggler told her, well aware that he alone was the bad apple, though there might have been some who said that about his father. "Corben didn't even want to make any coin from our findings. He just wanted people to know... how things used to be," he finished with a shrug.

Kit's expression suggested she was weighing the brothers up. "Sounds like I would have got on better with him than you."

"You're not wrong," Gallien muttered, though he again recalled their night in Valgala where they got on *very* well. He failed to hold on to the pleasant memory, his attention drawn back to the city of flames, where another building succumbed to the recent bombardment.

"In all the years I've had the misfortune of knowing you," Kit said, watching the plume of smoke and ash rise over Harendun, "I could count on one hand the number of times you've mentioned your brother." She looked at him intently, her face framed by the locks of her raven hair. "Is this where it happened?"

There was that lump again. He swallowed it down and cast his eyes out across the black waters. "A *lot* of men have died in those walls," he deflected. "And many more yet to be born," he wagered. Gallien sucked in a breath and straightened his back, as if he might physically rise above his emotions. "Let's focus on the treasures inside that cave, shall we?"

Kit's emerald eyes narrowed for but a moment before they relaxed and drifted out to the crevice. "I seek only one," she breathed, content to move on.

Gallien couldn't help but look down at the sword on her belt, the blade shattered a little under halfway down. "Aye," he said slowly. "Perhaps this is the site you've been looking for, eh?"

There came no immediate reply from her, those sharp eyes desperately trying to pierce the cliff face. "Are you sure you're up to this?" she asked suddenly, her tone having developed a hard edge.

Gallien expressed an exaggeration of hurt, his skin too thick to be pierced by mere words. "Of course. Corben and I raided more of these sites than I've had hot meals. Besides," he added with his easy mischievous grin, "I'm a Drakalis boy, remember. This is what we do."

Kit looked far from convinced. "What you *do* changes like the wind, Gallien. A week ago you were a smuggler—worse, you were a smuggler for the Padoshi of Thedaria. Before *that*," she conceded, "you were no more than a rogue seeking lost treasures. Or were you a soldier before that?" The Nimean shrugged. "Your dedication to any one course is... temporary."

Gallien licked his lips and took a breath. Perhaps his skin wasn't that thick after all. "I'm a smuggler and a damned good one," he protested, a thumb in his chest.

"The Padoshi of Thedaria doesn't seem to think so," Kit quipped.

"That's just a... *misunderstanding*," Gallien articulated.

"A misunderstanding that's forced you back into *this* life," Voden pointed out. "How big a treasure do you need to find in order to buy your way back into the Padoshi's good graces?"

"Let me worry about the details," Drakalis replied, ending any talk about his previous employer. "I've drifted here and there, I'll admit," he went on, "but I'm always dedicated to whatever I'm doing." His own words sat with him for a moment, each feeling as hollow as the next.

"Then I hope you're feeling dedicated," Kit said, flicking her chin at the crevice. "If this *is* what your brother believed it to be, it's likely not known visitors for millennia. It will be dangerous."

"Don't be fretting about me," Gallien assured. "You do your part and I'll do mine. Come sunrise, we'll both be richer for it."

"Back at Caster Hold," Kit went on, her head nodding back the way they had come, as if they could still see the fort and harbour from which The Raven had set sail, "you said there were *two* entrances. Yours is in there?" The Nimean's nod turned Gallien back to the burning city.

"Well I won't be getting in *that way*," he replied bemusedly, eyeing the partially submerged crevice.

"And you know where it is?" Kitrana asked, a subtle edge of concern in her tone. "It's likely to be a little... *fraught* in there."

Gallien licked his lips, the distant flames dancing in his eyes again. "I've been there before," he uttered.

Whether she sensed his unease or merely decided not to delve into his reply, Kit gestured at the cliff face in the north. "He could be right; your brother. The sea was not always so high. Ancient Andarens could have once entered on foot."

Drakalis blinked at the remark. "Not always so high?" he echoed, the notion absurd.

There was that knowing smile Kit was so fond of. "There is so much about the world you do not know, humble smuggler," she said patronisingly. "Not that you could understand it all if you tried," she added, lightly tapping the side of his head.

"I don't need *all* the knowledge, Kit," he replied, patting the rolled up scroll poking out of the inside pocket of his longcoat. "Just enough."

The clamour of armour tugged at Gallien's attention, turning him back to the main deck. Three soldiers had ventured topside, there to see the battlefield that awaited them.

"Come on!" one of them bellowed, hyping himself up.

"Andaren scum!" another sneered at the flaming vista.

"This is what all that training was for, boys," the last of the trio voiced, knocking his gauntlet against his chest plate.

"This ain't war, fellas!" came the call from the command deck, turning all to Captain Addison, a broad-shouldered man with a barrel for a gut and a face full of greying beard that he liked to collect in a knot about his chest. "It *was* war... about *six* days ago!" he laughed. "You're a little late to the party me thinks! You're just here to sit on the place and make sure it stays under your king's pretty banner!"

"Take a care of your words, *pirate*!" one of the soldiers spat back. "*Our* king is *your* king!"

Captain Addison leaned slightly over the railing, his bloodshot eyes fixed on the man. "It be you who best be taking a care, lad. On The Raven, there ain't no king but me. So take me word as law when I tell you to take your sorry selves below deck and get ready to hit sand!"

Gallien didn't even try to hide his amusement as he watched the trio skulk off, his focus quickly turned to Addison's crew and their preparations to make shore. "Well said, Captain!" he called up.

"You can shut it and all, Drakalis!" came the biting retort. Addison tugged at the waist of his breeches before taking to the steps that led to Gallien and Kit. His thunderous approach came to a stop directly in front of them. "I don't know what you're up to, Gallien, but I know it weren't the king's coin that put *you* on me ship. Come to think of it," he went on, if dramatically so, "I don't recall nearly enough coins crossing me palms for your weight upon me ship. At war time no less."

"We've been at war for three centuries," Gallien remarked dryly.

"That," the captain spat, one finger pointed at Harendun's fiery doom, "raises me prices. You promised me more coin from your ventures here, enough to pay for both crossings."

Kit's head swivelled on Gallien. "You said you paid."

Drakalis gave her no more than a glance. "And I will fulfil that promise," he assured the pirate.

"Good," Addison intoned. "Because if you can't, I might have to remember the big fat bounty on your head."

Gallien tried to look surprised. "A bounty?" he repeated, noting Kit beside him. Damned if she wasn't wearing that blasted smile again.

"We go back a long way, Drakalis. That's why I'm choosing—*at this time*—to ignore such sweet temptations. And that," Captain Addison continued, "leads me to what you're doing here exactly. I know for a fact that you put the war behind you. Hell, you wouldn't have half the tricks up your sleeve if it weren't for meeting me when you did. So what on Kaliban's humble earth would Gallien Drakalis be doing in Harendun while it's on fire? And how might that make *me* a richer man?"

"We *are* old friends," Gallien said, doubling down. "Ours was a friendship made in how many places just like this?" he questioned, gesturing to the scorched Harendun. "We both know there's fortunes to be made in places like this. You just have to know where to look, eh?" Drakalis tapped the scroll again. "I happen to be in possession of some information thought to be long lost, information that will lead us to a great—"

"If you say *treasure*," Addison cut in sharply, "I'll be returning you to Thedaria myself."

Gallien stumbled over his next words and, ultimately, swallowed them. "Artefacts," he eventually settled on. "Ancient ones. *Extremely* valuable to the right people."

Gallien caught that smile drop from Kit's face. "You're

complicating things again," she told the smuggler plainly, if quietly.

"Hmm," Addison voiced sceptically. "And I suppose you just happen to know the right people."

Drakalis held up a hand to hold off any further complaints from Kit. "Would I be here if I didn't?" It was only after expressing his most charming of smiles that Gallien remembered such things didn't work on old Captain Addison.

Bringing his oversized head even closer to the smuggler, The Raven's captain delivered his ultimatum. "If you don't return with said artefacts, Gallien, I'm going to forget our personal history and trade you for coin."

There was no mistaking the threat of violence in his tone. "Sounds fair," Drakalis replied, a lying smile keeping his lips tightly sealed.

Addison grunted and resumed his normal height. "The soldiers will unload first. Best not get in their way, eh? They're desperate to get their swords wet. Fools." With that, Addison turned around and began barking orders at his crew for the beach was fast approaching.

"Pirates," Kitrana Voden muttered with audible disdain. "I do not trust them."

"Good," Gallien replied. "The basis of any relationship with a pirate should always start with mistrust. You can't go wrong."

Taking to his easy smile about as much as Captain Addison, Kit turned back to the sea and the burning city. "This is where I leave you then."

Gallien was reaching for the scroll inside his pocket. "Do you need to see the drawings again?" He unravelled the parchment and leaned against the railing as he examined his brother's sketch work.

"I've seen them," Kit reminded, though she gave the scroll a second glance. "I never did ask—what are the runes around the edges?"

Gallien let his eyes roam over the familiar symbols. "Corben's notes," he answered.

"I don't recognise the language."

The smuggler gave a wry smirk. "You wouldn't. We made it up. Well, my father made it up and taught us to use it." He gave half a laugh at the surfacing memories. "My mother hated it."

"Perhaps you should have imparted it to someone else," Kitrana suggested. "Before you die out there," she added with amusement, her gaze searching for the city.

Gallien gave a mirthless laugh. "You're sure you don't want to go through it again?"

"I know the plan. If this is what your brother believes, I will be where I am supposed to be. You just make sure *you* are where *you're* supposed to be."

"Of course," he replied casually, seeing that his companion was looking past him, to the tragedy of Harendun.

"You're sure?" Kit pressed. "I could come with you. Double back when you're in position."

Drakalis made a face. "There you go fretting about me again," he quipped. "I'll be fine. They've been at it for six days already. If there's any fighting left to be had it'll be on the northern outskirts by now; pushing the Andarens up the road. This is just history repeating itself."

Kit scrutinised him a moment longer than was necessary, perhaps seeing through some of his bravado, as she often did. Still, she gave him no more than a nod and adjusted her teal cloak to sit further back on her shoulders. She glanced about, checking there were no prying eyes on them as she placed one hand on the rail.

Gallien never tired of watching Kitrana Voden in the water.

So smooth and graceful was her hop over the side of The Raven that it seemed the ship moved around *her*, with naught but an outstretched arm and a hand connecting her to its hull. Then she was gone, overboard and into a dive that saw her pierce the dark waters, her skin immune to its cold embrace. Gallien's blue eyes were sharper than most, but even he struggled to track Kit as she streaked through the water, just beneath the surface. It would only be seconds before she crossed the gap and entered the underwater cave, a swim that would take any man several minutes.

Any *human* that is.

"Dawn's breaking, lads!" Addison yelled from the main deck. "I want to hit that beach before the sun hits The Raven!"

"Aye, Captain!" came the unified response.

As advised, Gallien waited for the company of Eradoran soldiers to storm a beach that had long been seized. Credit to them, and after three days at sea, they still charged towards the city's Sea Gate with considerable zeal. In all their armour, however, Gallien imagined he would soon overtake them at no more than a walking pace, once he reached Harendun's streets.

"Drakalis!" Captain Addison's booming voice brought the smuggler to a halt a mere two steps onto the damp sand. "Where's your companion? I liked the look of her!"

"Gone on ahead!" he replied, not wishing to get into it.

"Make sure you don't come back empty-handed, eh?" the captain added. "Ain't no one else going to take your sorry self home!"

Gallien smiled cheerily enough, before tugging on the collar of his longcoat and striding away. "Pirates..." he muttered.

4
INTO GLORY

80 Years Ago...

The Saible stood proud upon Andara's dark soil, a grim fortress so vast it had become a city in its own right. The original walls and earliest of structures always caught Daijen's eye upon his return, their stonework scarred and partially melted by dragon fire.

Those battles had been long before Daijen's time, when the war was young and the humans had advanced into The Gap. He had grown up on stories of those bloody battles, tales of the wicked dragons and their dreaded riders.

Seeing the damage they had once wrought, Daijen thanked the gods he had never seen one of the flying monsters.

"Can you imagine it?" Elivar asked, his gaze drawn to the same structures. "Fire so hot it can sunder the stone."

Daijen slowed his horse down just enough to fall in beside his companion. "Have you ever..." He let his words trail off, as if the mere mention of the beast might conjure it.

"Seen a dragon?" Elivar finished, one hand massaging his injured shoulder. "Several times," he boasted.

"Twice," Ilithranda corrected from her saddle, ahead of the pair.

Elivar let loose a bemused smile. "Twice," he agreed. "That's two more times than I would have liked," the warrior added.

"Where were you?" Daijen asked.

"I was stationed at Argunsuun some fifty years ago," Elivar told him. "Have you ever been to the watchtower?" he enquired.

"Of course he hasn't," Ilithranda interjected. "I'd bet this was his first time east of The Gap."

Daijen considered lying just to silence her, but he couldn't even describe The Watchtower of Argunsuun, a place he had only ever heard about. "I have not," he said instead, taking some ownership over his inexperience.

"On a clear day," Elivar continued, "you can actually see White Tower."

Daijen could but imagine the two opposing towers, for he had only seen them on the map of Verda. "And you saw a dragon?" he pressed.

"That's all you do at Argunsuun," Ilithranda announced dryly. "You just *watch*."

"You guard the line," Elivar told Daijen passionately. "The soldiers at Argunsuun make sure the humans stay on their side of the line. That's no easy thing when there's dragons about." With his good arm, Elivar pointed at the sky as if he was standing atop the great watchtower. "There it was," he began. "It was all fangs and claws and carried on bat-like wings," he described dramatically. "Its scales glistened in the afternoon sun, a brilliant gold! And massive it was! I'd say it could have swallowed a Giant whole."

"It was at least a mile out and no bigger than your thumbnail," Ilithranda specified.

Elivar made a face and waved her words away. "You couldn't tell a good story if the book was in your hands," he remarked.

When Ilithranda continued to ride on, Daijen turned back to his more talkative companion. "And the second?" he asked.

"Ah..." Elivar looked wistfully into the distance. "The Battle of The Triden," he said, voicing one of those old tales Daijen had heard as a boy.

"You were there?"

"I was," Elivar replied proudly.

Daijen waited for Ilithranda to offer a nugget of truth that reduced Elivar's claim, but it never came. "My uncle told me of it. He was there too." It then occurred to Daijen that Elivar was far older than him, for The Triden—a fortress almost equal in size to The Saible—had been besieged in the first decade of the war, over two hundred years past.

"I was only there at the end—no more than seven days. That was enough. I was with the reinforcements, and the *Vahlken*," he added with emphasis. "We pushed Erador back, but I saw the last dragon to assault the keep."

"You saw it fly away," Ilithranda noted.

"I saw the Vahlken and their great eagles battle the beast," Elivar argued. "It rained blood that day. And that dragon *was* massive. For all the threat it posed," he opined, and quietly enough so that only Daijen could hear him, "its scales were the most beautiful shade of blue I've ever seen. It was like the clear waters in the south, between The Fangs."

"If we pass the trials," Ilithranda said looking back at them over one shoulder, "we'll all see our fair share of dragons."

Daijen soon realised that she was only looking at him. He could only withstand the scrutiny of those violet eyes for so long before he regarded the barracks that lined the valley. They stretched for miles out from The Saible, reaching into the east where they might one day grow so far as to touch The Plains of Palanor. Everywhere he looked, Andaren soldiers were going about their day, running through training drills, moving equipment and supplies or simply sitting around in conversation. War horses patrolled up and down, their riders searching for any who would cause trouble in the ranks. Those same riders were also overseeing the humans.

There were hundreds of them.

Men of Erador, prisoners of war, worked the stone and stirred mortar to construct new buildings. The fettered souls toiled every hour under the sun, crafting new buildings alongside the clerics, who laced the walls with their magic. None would ever see home again, their short lives sparking in the valley, before the Black Abyss. Daijen paid them little heed, a familiar sight after so many years of training on the land.

When finally in the shadow of The Saible itself, they rode beneath banners, as vast as sails that rippled in the wind, anchored to the fortress's dark stone. The sigil of House Lhoris, a black circle that never completed set inside yellow sunburst, was, perhaps, the most familiar sight of all, an image that accompanied every soldier upon their cuirass and even etched into the hilts of their swords. It was a symbol of hope and strength to all, a promise, almost, that one day they would see the world through to the last words of the Arkalon. That they would see the gods reborn.

Daijen could practically hear his uncle's voice from years gone by, reciting the scripture. He might have dwelled on it all the more, and the fact that it had been years since he had picked up his own Arkalon, had Ilithranda not brought her horse to a stop.

"This is your last chance," she stated, tearing his gaze from the towering battlements and flying banners. "You were doing your duty," she posed, offering him a plausible lie. "You escorted us back. That's all you have to say."

Daijen licked his lips and took a breath so he might speak his thoughts on the matter, a matter he had given considerable thought to over the last three weeks. Still, it was his breath alone that spoiled the frigid air.

In the absence of words, he glanced at Elivar. He dared not call him friend yet, but he had at least spoken to Daijen over the course of their journey, whereas Ilithranda had voiced no more than sharp statements. It had become clear, however, that Ilithranda cast a long shadow that Elivar could not—or would not—escape. And so the warrior averted his eyes, leaving Daijen to converse with their de facto leader alone.

"Elivar and I have fought in countless campaigns," Ilithranda informed him evenly. "We've been in the war since it began. We've *survived* the war," she added pointedly. "We were chosen for the path of Handuin because there's a chance we might survive the trials. A *chance*, Daijen Saeth. After all we've accomplished, the Black Abyss we've trodden, the humans we've slain, and, still, there is naught but a *chance* we might survive as Handuin once did."

Elivar cleared his throat. "It would not be cowardly to resume your duties, Daijen. Every soldier in the empire serves a purpose."

"Move on or begone!" came a bellowing call from The Saible's main entrance.

The trio turned to see a caravan passing under the arched gateway, a trail of horses and carts bringing fresh supplies to the city of barracks. Their discussion interrupted, the three companions guided their mounts out of the way and slipped through the gap to move beyond the fortress walls, of which there were three, each with a street between and all lined with ballista bolts, weapons, and equipment for managing the various catapults built into the thick walls.

Despite being obviously Andaren, with their ashen skin and snow-white hair, they were still stopped by an imperator who had more than a dozen soldiers to call upon should he require assistance. Even now, spiked barriers were being put back into place in the wake of the supply caravan. Archers looked down on them from a multitude of guard towers along the main road.

"You three look like you've come straight from The Black Abyss," the imperator commented, as he gestured for them to dismount.

"Harendun," Ilithranda reported on her way down.

"So I was right then," the imperator concluded. "Doesn't explain why you're here though, absent your commander or general. No one goes *west* without orders."

"We might be absent out superiors, Imperator, but we aren't absent their word." Ilithranda produced a small scroll from her belt and handed it over. "Nor is our heading *west*."

The imperator read what few lines there were, though he

spared the trio a glance before reading it again. "I see." The imperator licked his lips and cleared his throat. "I will not delay you any longer. Report to the Justiciar's office and they will see you have a bed for the night and are resupplied for the journey north. Gods be with you."

Ilithranda reclaimed Sorn's missive. "Thank you, Imperator."

Guiding their horses on foot, the three companions navigated the barriers and made for the central tower and the sprawl of buildings at its base. Daijen turned back only once to see the imperator staring at them, watching as a crowd might watch prisoners marching to the block. It sent a chill up the young Andaren's spine.

The sands of time finally ran out for Daijen, as the trio soon found themselves at a junction inside the main keep. To carry on and up would take them to the Justiciar's office and those of his staff. To their left, was the passage that led to Daijen's previous superiors, who oversaw the messages sent forth from The Saible and those that would guard them.

"Do as you will," Ilithranda said impatiently. "I for one need a good drink and a warm bed." She gave no second look, her departure sure and swift.

Elivar looked to be on the verge of some witty, if not sarcastic, comment, when he closed his mouth and reconsidered. "There's nothing wrong in wanting to live," he said earnestly. "Isn't that why we all fight?" He flashed Daijen his easy smile and patted him once on the shoulder before following in Ilithranda's footsteps.

Daijen remained in the junction, watching them walk away. He wanted to accompany them. He wanted to be a Vahlken and join the fabled heroes of Andara. Yet his feet refused to follow them. Pain and death were a certainty should he find himself in Ka'vairn. Better to guard the messengers and maybe even see the war through.

Only after Ilithranda and Elivar had vanished from sight did Daijen stable his mount and move on. He navigated the labyrinth of cold halls and spiralling stairwells, passing numerous humans as he did so. Unlike those pressed into hard labour outside, the humans inside The Saible were servants, men *and* women, who had been bred from generations of prisoners since the earliest years of the war. Daijen recalled his uncle telling him that the Eradoran soldiers had foolishly brought women to their shores—to Harendun and The Triden—to celebrate their victory with them. But the humans could never hold the city for long.

A young human female flattened herself to the wall to get out of Daijen's path. He spared her no more than a glance. The human servants were distinguished from their exterior counterparts in many ways, including their clean, if plain, attire and their razored scalps. None had ever seen Erador. They knew nothing of its culture or their kin. They were bred in camps to serve Andara and nothing more. Even the lowliest Andaren was master to them.

Continuing with his route, Daijen eventually found himself at Lornak's desk, his direct commander. With a hundred years under his belt, Lornak looked up at Daijen with his youthful face and a top knot of white hair. His sharp amber eyes looked him up and down before noting the empty spaces either side.

"Saeth," he began abruptly. "Where is Ailen Torth? Or Ondris for that matter?"

Daijen swallowed, recalling their sudden deaths. "They were killed in Harendun, Sir," he reported, doing his best to keep his voice even.

Lornak's lips parted and sucked in a breath before responding. "Dead? Both of them?"

"Yes, Sir."

The commander shot up to his feet. "It's your job to keep the messengers alive!" he spat. "*Ondris* can die. *You* can die. But not the messenger!" Lornak's eyes shifted side to side in frantic thought. "Ailen's mother is cousin to the Justiciar," he muttered. "Black Abyss," he cursed, a new revelation coming to him. "Ondris's father serves the Warmasters! What am I supposed to tell them? They died but *Daijen Saeth* yet lives! You were supposed to keep him alive!"

Something snapped in Daijen where before it would have remained dormant—integrity perhaps. "They were struck by a catapult," he argued. "It's hard to defend anyone against a flaming rock the size of a horse."

"Silence!" the commander barked. "You will not speak of this. *I* will report it and you will accept whatever comes your way. Understood?"

Daijen said nothing, his jaw locked and cobalt eyes fixed on his superior's chest.

"Is that understood?" Lornak growled.

"Yes, Sir."

"Then get out of my sight."

Daijen left without another word, his obsidian cloak fanning out behind him. It wasn't the first time he had received such verbal punishment from his superiors, but instead of feeling hollowed out, as he usually did, his blood was on fire. He had done nothing wrong. In fact, his heroic actions had seen him chosen to follow the path of Handuin. The latter didn't feel the whole truth to Daijen but he clung to it all the same and let it fuel his righteous anger.

Without meaning to, he found himself returned to that same junction, where he might enter the offices of the Justiciar. All he had to do was walk down the hall and report in with Ilithranda and Elivar. When next he returned to The Saible—and Commander Lornak—it would be on eagleback.

If he didn't die in the meantime.

That thought alone saw him turn and slowly make for the nearest barracks. He wanted to live, and there was nothing wrong with that. Daijen told himself that over and over again for the rest of the day and well into the night, until he lay on his bed. He stopped saying it then. Instead, he lay in a long line of sleeping soldiers and stared out of the adjacent window. He watched the stars move across the sky and the clouds come and go, some illuminated by the moon. There was to be no repose. Only tumultuous thoughts.

When the new day was born, Daijen simply rose with it, absent a good night's sleep. His silvery skin was dulled by the lack of rest, but he still found the energy to report for duty.

He was handed a mop and bucket.

"This is a human job," he protested.

"Now it's your job," the soldier replied simply.

He wasn't permitted to wear his sabre or even his cloak and armour. None were required to clean The Saible's floors. The orders hadn't even come from Lornak, the mop and bucket given to him by one of the soldiers who guarded the offices. It seemed he hadn't been on the lowest rung after all.

Rather sullen and wholly embarrassed, Daijen did the only thing he could: he mopped. In the halls of The Saible, he was either invisible or a hindrance to those around him. The honour of House Saeth had dwindled to its last.

Without direct oversight, and utterly depressed, Daijen granted himself a short reprieve as he came across the grand balcony that curved around the back of The Saible. It offered a western vista so bewitching it deserved to be preserved in a painting. Basking in the rising sun, The Nheremyn River glistened like a diamond-studded snake that slithered across The Gap and connected the mountains of north and south. Further still was Ehrendil, a city of spires and domes that had once sprawled across the valley floor. War had brought about the need for high walls, concealing much of its splendour. Still, it was a mark of beauty on the land.

Daijen took it all in wistfully. He hadn't been west of The Saible since his twentieth birthday. He could scarcely recall the majesty that lay beyond Ehrendil. He only knew that it was to be protected at all costs.

Movement, however distant, caught Daijen's eyes and shifted his attention across the expanse, to his right. Two riders had departed The Saible and turned north at The Nheremyn. More significantly, they had ignored the stone bridge that would take any traveller on to Ehrendil. They were heading up river, making for the cut in the northern mountains where The Nheremyn had spent millennia carving its way through. Daijen took in the mountains, if not the north itself, and knew exactly where such a path would lead.

It could only be Ilithranda and Elivar.

Pressed against the rail, Daijen watched them ride away at no more than a walk. In that moment, he didn't see two people riding to their deaths. He saw two people riding into glory. Theirs was to be a destiny of greatness. They would ride through the sky and deliver carnage to the enemy. Daijen thought on the human he had slain in Harendun. The rush of it. How pleasing it had been to see his years of training pay off, to know that he could fight *and* win. He would never feel such a thing again; not while he was forced to wield a mop.

He regarded the tools of his new trade, sitting idly beside him. Was he really going to choose cleaning floors over flying through the clouds? Before Harendun, before his *victory*, he would have picked up the mop and gone about his duty; any thoughts of becoming a Vahlken regarded as the dreams of a fool.

Daijen left the mop and bucket where they were and dashed from the balcony.

What followed was a hurried blur. He collected what he could—what he thought he would need—and made for the stables, where he saddled a horse. His armour and sword were cumbersome to attach but he didn't have to don them. He spared only the time required to clip on his cloak and drape some furs over his shoulders.

Spurring the war horse on, Daijen guided the animal to the north, putting the river on their left. He must have ridden hard for nearly three miles, putting the alchemical magic in the mount's veins to good use, before he caught sight of the pair. The sound of his horse's six thundering hooves turned both riders on the trail.

Elivar laughed at the sight of him. "You're lucky Sorn sent word ahead to Ka'vairn!" he called out on Daijen's approach. "It's a long way to go only to be turned around."

Daijen slowed the horse to come up beside Elivar. Now that he had caught up with them he didn't know what to say. His act of spontaneity had faded, leaving him with a sense of dread.

"He's not lucky," Ilithranda said, already directing her horse back to the north. "He's just doomed himself."

Elivar waited until she was a little further ahead before returning his attention to Daijen. “Feel like proving her wrong?” he asked cheerily.

A moment passed before Daijen met his companion’s expectant gaze. “I feel like proving them all wrong.”

5
THE NIMEAN

WATER IS LIFE. IT IS A WORLD WHERE HUMANS CAN BUT TASTE THE freedom of flight, and always at the cost of their breath, their precious air. They must inevitably return to their realm, where they can breathe but never fly. Kitrana Voden, however, was born to the water. To her, like all Nimeans, the ocean was *home.*

The moment her body touched the water it remembered where it had come from. Her lungs expelled every unit of pressure before sealing shut—the organs no longer required. Without thought, cutaneous respiration took control of her need for oxygen, a form of breathing that was aided all the more by the respiratory lining inside her mouth.

At the same time, the skin between her fingers secreted an oil that quickly congealed, creating a natural webbing. The same was happening between her toes, though the effect was useless when wearing her boots—one of the more irritating practices she employed to blend in with the surface dwellers.

It was all such a relief, her bodily functions returning to their preferred forms. It was like tasting life itself. Kit had always likened the experience to humans coming up for air.

As The Raven continued its gliding journey above, Kit's eyes laid bare the ocean and its secrets below, banishing the shadows of the deep and replacing them with vibrant colours. It was also a graveyard. Human bodies littered the sandy floor, dragged down by the weight of their armour. Even so close to the surface she could see the arrows that had taken them from their ships. Between them all, fish weaved and crabs investigated the new food source, their claws snipping at pallid flesh.

Movement soon caught her attention and she realised the fish and crabs weren't the only ones feasting on the cold corpses. To a human, they would have been concealed by the depths, their nightmarish features hidden within the folds of the dark sea. To Kit, there was no missing them, their snaking tails weaving endlessly through the water as their shark-like teeth and razored claws sliced through leather and flesh. The water about them was murky with blood and debris but, having the body of a sea snake from the waist down, a fact that made them three times the length of an average man, there was little that could conceal their muscled torso and arms. Dreads of hair, that looked more like seaweed than Kit's raven locks, danced hypnotically about their heads.

Like the surface-dwellers, the ocean's inhabitants put names to the monsters that stalked their world. These particular beasts had but one name, shared by all the races of the deep.

The Vorge.

Their presence came as no surprise to Kit. Where there was death and blood in the water, there were the Vorge. More so, they were known to prey upon surface dwellers. It wouldn't be long before there was nothing but hollow suits of armour and gnawed bones to find. Still, Kitrana chastised herself for not anticipating them in the wake of a bloody naval invasion. Her rich Nimean blood demanded that she sully the water with their wretched innards, but she didn't have her blade maidens at her back and she was absent any armour and even her trident, her weapon of choice. The broken sword on her hip would open them up just fine but the risk of being overrun was too great.

Turning away from them, her movements slow and smooth,

she beheld the ocean beyond the shore. Like all creatures, her sight could only perceive the world to a limit, and thereafter the sea resumed its mystique, hidden behind a veil of deepening blue.

Every fibre of her being desired that great expanse, to push back the misted curtain and take to the ocean as she was born to do. She dared not respond to that instinctual call. The deep was her true home, her ancestors' home. But her presence would not go unnoticed. Even now, in the shallows and so close to land, she was tempting fate. After all, there were far worse things out there than a few Vorge.

But life without the water was no life at all. And so, turning to the cave, Kit's mind returned to the task at hand. Hope was kindled in her at the thought of what she might find in the ruins of old Harendun. The very treasure she needed to see home again—the treasure she had spent years scouring the surface world for—could finally be within her reach. How many times had she entertained that exact same thought?

Hope was a cruel thing.

Like a dolphin taking after its prey, Kitrana speared through the water at enviable speed. Her body rippled in the manner of an arrow given flight, her bones—more cartilage than calcium—bending just enough to advance her propulsion.

Within seconds she was passing between the walls of the deep crevice and penetrating the cliff. It soon narrowed, forcing her down. She weaved with its curves, pushing further into the cave until she was beneath Harendun.

Kit paused, her legs drifting down until her boots brushed the bottom. The cave—as it had appeared to be—was roughly the width of two men abreast and just tall enough for her pass through had she been walking. In times past it had most certainly been taller, all of which raised the strong possibility that she was in a tunnel system that had been made by ancient Andarens.

She was beginning to think Gallien's brother was right.

Swimming further into the cliff, her suspicions were confirmed—she was, without a doubt, in old Harendun. The rough and jagged rock gave way to styled relief that was traced along the walls, with depictions of Andaren history, or perhaps it was no more than an expression of art. Kit couldn't say. But when the tunnel opened up, the old city took shape about her.

Shattered towers, fallen spires, and streets upon streets of hollowed buildings—shells of their former glory—dominated the enormous cavern. All manner of sea creatures swam in and out of the ruins, oblivious to the truth of their environment. It was beautiful, in its own way. It was a rare sight even for a Nimean, whose eyes had seen handcrafted kingdoms that stretched across the ocean floor for miles.

Taking to the ghost city as the fish and the eels did, Kitrana angled herself up and swam, her body rippling from head to toe. There was no fish that could compete with her speed and so their schools burst apart as she invaded their space. Recalling Corben's map, the Nimean aimed for a particular part of the city, where rock now buried a large portion of it.

She hesitated there, where the damage wrought by time and all else had ravaged the city to the extent that it no longer resembled Corben's map. She was to search for the largest tower, but there were no towers, not anymore. All that remained were broken bases and partial towers and spires that rose up into the rock itself.

Exploring what she could of the ruins, Kit moved in and out of every space that she could fit through. She dragged herself through narrow passages and twisted her limbs and torso to navigate through awkward gaps. She needed to go up, lest she never find her way back to Gallien. Thoughts of him waiting for her in the middle of a war-torn city began to gnaw at the Nimean.

Tower after broken tower she explored, her eyes and hands roaming over history itself. Having entered one of the towers that fed up into the cavern rock, Kitrana brought herself to a floating stop and closed her eyes, arms outstretched. She waited, letting her skin get a better reading on the water about her.

Giving herself a quiet moment, she began to feel a light fizz against her left hand and up her arm. Turning in that direction, she discovered a crevice in the rock itself, a narrow and jagged passage that appeared to run up through the ancient stone. Pressing herself against the crevice, her face experienced the same bubbling touch of water that possessed a higher concentration of oxygen. Kit deduced that the passage would lead to the surface and, most likely, somewhere close to Harendun's foundations.

Kitrana soon realised, however, that fitting her body into the gap would be no easy feat. Pushing any thoughts away of getting stuck halfway through, she adjusted her belt and the broken sword upon it. In her haste, she mishandled the blade and the steel sliced a portion of her palm open. Kit winced and naturally gripped the wrist of her wounded hand as blood met water. Flexing her hand into a fist, she tested the limits of her dexterity and pain. Damned if it didn't hurt. Tearing a strip from her cloak, Kitrana made a crude bandage. There were balms, secrets of the sea, that could heal such an injury in a couple of days, but the ingredients were nowhere near this part of the world.

Doing her best to shrug it off, Kit faced the tight passage. So tight was it that she could not swim, her hands and feet reduced to the steady climb a human might adopt on a cliff face. All the while traces of blood found their way past her bandage and mixed with the water.

Then she heard them.

A nightmarish choir of screeches and shrieks that pierced the sea and found her in the crevice. Kit noted the blood floating past her face. So close, she could smell the acrid iron. The Vorge, however, possessed olfactory senses beyond those of Nimeans, beyond even sharks. And now they had found her.

Powered by their mighty tails, the Vorge rushed through the ruins of Harendun in search of the wounded prey. Kitrana groaned and continued her arduous climb, though her improved speed encouraged further injury. She soon had scrapes on her head and cheeks and her knees and elbows took one knock after another. No injury could be compared to what the Vorge would do to her. The sea, like the surface world, was an unforgiving food chain where everything ate something else. Intelligent and cruel as they were, the Vorge would enjoy eating her slowly and while she lived to feel their bite.

There came another terrible shriek, and so close now that Kit felt the vibrations. Through the small and awkward gap beneath her, she spied one of the creatures of fang and claw. So too did it spy her. Large black eyes pierced the distance she had covered and looked upon her as no more than food. It was soon shoved out of the way as another of its ilk forced its way into the gap. Jaws of razored teeth spread in glee and hunger before it entered the crevice.

Kitrana doubled her efforts and ignored entirely the wounds that plagued her. Steadily, if painfully, she dragged herself up through the angled passage, daring to spare only a second now and then to check on her pursuers. One after the other they had forced their bulk into the crevice. There was no space for their tails to propel them, but their long claws and strong arms had no trouble pulling them through.

Despite the limited space, the first to come after the Nimean was closing the gap, its clawed hands dragging it through. Kitrana could feel those claws through the rock, and its scaly body slipping over the uneven stone. Pausing to look back was a mistake. One monstrous hand reached out and gripped her boot. There was no room to kick out and barely enough room to wiggle her foot. With animalistic strength, the beast pulled her down, towards its open maw. With no way to progress and no way to kick her aggressor, Kit did the only thing left to her.

She let go.

The Vorge yanked her down, fighting against a resistance that was no longer there. The result was a hard boot to the face. The creature recoiled, momentarily stunned. With what little space she now had, Kitrana used its head to push off and continue her angled ascent, her heel injuring one of the Vorge's large soulless eyes as she did so.

Free, the Nimean wasted no time in making for the other end of the passage. She squeezed through a particularly narrow gap and rounded one sharp corner before the fissure finally opened up into another tower, its heights previously inaccessible from the base. Removing herself from the crevice, she looked back to see the same wounded Vorge, stuck where its bulk couldn't fit through the gap. One clawed hand reached out helplessly for her but it was no use.

In the silent language of her people, Kitrana signed a curse at the Vorge.

The water was definitely more oxygenated now, directing the Nimean up and round where there had once been an intact spiral staircase. Swimming over the ruined steps brought her to an oval chamber and, at last, returned her to sea level. Her face broke the surface first, pushing her hair back and down her neck. The ancient dark that had swallowed that place eons ago did nothing to prevent Kitrana from seeing every inch of it.

Standing up, the water rested at her waist. Lips parting, she inhaled a breath of stale air, forcing her lungs open, while her skin ceased operating as her breathing apparatus. Wading through, she moved for the opening that had long lost its doors. Passing over the threshold, her feet discovered short steps that took her above the water and into a dank hallway. She was already missing the water, though she happily left its monsters behind.

Three steps.

Three steps was all that Kitrana made before she detected the subtle sound of water being parted behind her. She didn't want to, but she looked back over her shoulder anyway. Rising like a snake, its long arms and clawed fingers dancing hypnotically by its side, was the Vorge.

Nothing felt slower to a Nimean than running, but it was all she could do to get away from the wretch and those that followed it. Up and up she went, ascending stairwells and climbing where they had fallen into ruin. The Vorge were always right behind her, their snake-like bodies and humanoid arms keeping them in pursuit. The sound of breaking stone and tumbling rocks caught her attention, though she never stopped moving. Instead, she continued to listen, hearing the distinct sound of Vorge in pain. Their size and weight had put too much pressure on the ancient structure, bringing down a portion of the stonework and blocking their path up the tower.

Kitrana could only hope a few had been flattened at the same time.

When there was no more up, Kit sprinted along a passage that cut through the surrounding rock. Dark as it was, something overhead, hanging below the arch at the end of the passage, caught Kit's eye and brought her to a rapid stop. She recognised it immediately as a portcullis, its pointed iron tips waiting to slot into the grooves at her feet. She was alone in the ruins, but good sense told her to drop the old gate anyway. *A smart Nimean always guards her back*, her mother would tell her.

The sound of rattling chains was hideously loud in the hollow space, and made all the louder when the chain snapped and the gate fell into place. Feeling marginally safer than she had a moment earlier, Kitrana stretched her back and caught her breath. Inhaling air was far more strenuous than the process her skin used in the water, and she hated how dry it always made her mouth and throat feel.

Slowly but surely, her eyes roamed about the dark that engulfed her. The Nimean blinked in confusion, fearing, for just a moment, that she had struck her head inside the crevice. Pivoting slightly on one heel, the phenomenon she had detected wasn't just all around her but continued down the passage on the other side of the portcullis. Even in such desperate haste, she couldn't believe she had missed it.

Moved by curiosity, Kit reached out and touched one of the water droplets that hung, suspended, in the air. It broke against her finger, adding to the water that already clung to her. The droplets were everywhere, as if the water from the walls and floor had been delicately picked away and left to float endlessly. For all the years she had spent on the surface world, Kitrana could confidently say she had never seen anything like it.

Her investigation of the chamber led her to discover a set of steps carved into the wall on her left. Following them up, there was a square grill through which she could see the ladders continuing up to a circular slab of iron. She frowned, recalling the drawing Gallien had showed her at Caster Hold—a rounded chamber at the top of the tower, with two sets of ladders and a square grill between.

Kit smiled with relief.

If she was correct, Gallien was on the other side of the circular slab at the very top. The Nimean moved to reunite with her companion, one hand rising to grip the first rung, when she faltered. If this truly was the place Gallien had told her of, the place he and his brother had tried to find years earlier, then the treasures they sought should be within sight.

Turning to face the whole chamber, the ladders forgotten, Kit let her attention settle on the vast tarpaulin of leather that had been draped over a large mound that rose up to the ceiling. It had initially seemed so inconsequential compared to the floating droplets. Walking away from the ladder, the Nimean came to a stop at the base of the tarpaulin, her mind busy trying to guess what might lie hidden beneath.

One hand gripped the hilt of the broken sword, her hope rising into her throat. Could it be? Was it under there? After all this time, was she finally to see it with her own eyes? It wasn't the first time she had felt this close and the memories of those disappointments tried to dash her hope.

Taking a resolute breath, Kitrana shrugged off her feelings on the matter. It was either here, or it wasn't, and there was only one way to find out.

With both hands, she gripped the edge of the tarpaulin and began to retreat, dragging it down and away from that which it concealed. Almost immediately, her sharp eyes made sense of the *treasure* that was taking shape. Her lips parted and her jaw dropped.

6

THE PATH OF HANDUIN

80 Years Ago...

Having parted ways with the flow of The Nheremyn, Daijen had followed his two companions for days. They appeared to be on a marked trail, but the lack of a path suggested it was one that few had ever taken. Indeed, the snows had claimed most of it, though Ilithranda never struggled to keep them on their north-westerly heading. Their route took them through the fringes of The Dain'duil, a vast forest that lay nestled between the mountains.

With only one more day of travelling ahead of them, the trio made their final camp for the night. The sun, however, was slow to set, casting the world in a fiery light, lending the mountains around them a tone of gold. While something remained of the day, Daijen peeled away from the others and made for the rise they had passed only minutes before making camp. He was forced to climb certain areas of the tall outcropping, and the icy ledges provided numerous obstacles, yet still he climbed.

When finally he stood on the snow-covered top, the sun was cresting the mountains behind him, casting half of the valley in shadow. The sky was steadily fading in the east, offering glimpses of twinkling stars. The view was made all the more majestic by the sprawling forest below and the distant river that hugged the mountains. Besides being the furthest north Daijen had ever been, the young Andaren had never expected to see The Dain'duil, a forest of deep legend.

"It's good that you're not afraid of heights," Elivar voiced, his head appearing over the edge of the ascent. The older warrior pulled himself up onto the flat ground, his wounded shoulder a thing of the past.

Daijen peered over the side, wondering if Ilithranda was just behind him. She wasn't. "We should reach Ka'vairn by tomorrow?" he checked, by way of conversation.

"Around this time," Elivar confirmed, his head nodding to the north-west. "It's in shadow now, otherwise you would be able to see it."

"I've seen a painting of it," Daijen told him.

Elivar smiled, as he so liked to. "I don't think a painting is going to do it justice," he opined. "Do you know what mountains they are?" he asked, pointing to the rocky fangs that dominated the eastern horizon, beyond the weaving Nheremyn.

Daijen gave something of a hollow laugh, feeling that Elivar had taken him under his wing as a ward. "I haven't seen much of the world but I know my way around a map. Those are The Morthil Mountains," he answered. "And these are The Hellion Mountains," he added, gesturing to the mountains at their back, determined to prove himself. "The Nheremyn separates them from north to south," he continued, as if he were in a lesson and trying to impress his teacher.

Elivar waved a hand across the vista. "Many a scholar has argued that all of this should be The Hellion Mountains; that a river should not divide them."

"But it does," Daijen said, stating the fact.

"Indeed. Do you know why we acknowledge the divide?"

All but an infant knew the answer, but Daijen sensed that Elivar was building to a moment, and so he let him have it.

The warrior's eyes flashed. "Dwarves!" he exclaimed excitedly. "Have you ever met one of the old stone-bones?"

Daijen shook his head.

Elivar laughed quietly to himself and patted him on the back. "Don't worry, neither have I. Ilithranda's told me a few stories though. You recall the small bridge we used to cross The Nheremyn?"

"Of course," Daijen replied.

"It is said," Elivar continued, his voice adopting a dramatic, if ominous, tone, "that if any Andaren ignores the bridge and follows The Nheremyn along its eastern banks—for no more than fifty feet," he stressed, "the Morthil dwarves will drag you into the mountains and add you to the foundation."

A hint of amusement curled Daijen's lips. "Then it is a good thing we crossed the bridge."

It brought out a laugh in Elivar, who patted him on the shoulder this time. "I knew there was a sense of humour in there somewhere. Keep hold of it, I say," the warrior added, nodding at the shadows where Ka'vairn was perched. "The years to come will be hard."

Daijen was suddenly dazed by the timescale Elivar had used. By the time he had processed it, and with questions to follow, his companion was already beginning his descent. "Years?" he pressed.

Elivar paused with only his head and shoulders to see. A broad grin stretched his silvery cheeks and he continued his climb down.

A pit of dread began to open within Daijen, reminding him that his pursuit of glory had put him in over his head.

Concerned that the feeling would only grow and root him to the icy peak, he began his own climb down in search of a fire and his bed roll.

Having continued their journey just before the dawn, and made good ground for the day, the three companions arrived at the north-western edge of The Dain'duil while the sun still touched the face of The Hellion Mountains. Daijen turned his head up.

Ka'vairn.

The ancient fortress gripped the stone, its massive buttresses clearly defined by shadow. It protruded proud and strong from the face of The Hellions, its towers, ramparts, and great walls a monument to Andaren masons. Leading out from the fortress, snaking down and across the rocky face, was a track that would permit nothing larger than a cart.

"The Path of Handuin," Daijen muttered, his gaze tracing the path up to Ka'vairn.

Elivar was quietly laughing to himself. "We've been on the path for days, Daijen," he eventually informed. "We have been in the footsteps of Handuin since we crossed the river."

Daijen looked back the way they had come, at the humble trail framed by The Dain'duil's trees. It had been a cold hard trail, but he looked at it now with reverence. To think, he had already walked in the footsteps of the fabled Handuin.

A shadow swept over the trio.

All three turned their eyes to the sky, though they found naught but encroaching clouds. The air was buffeted in the south and the trees rustled in response.

"What is it?" Daijen whispered.

"Quiet," Ilithranda commanded as she dismounted, her sight never straying from the sky.

Something cut through the air, above the trees and to the west this time. It sent a ripple of disquiet through the forest that spilled out beyond the line and disturbed even the horses. Daijen and Elivar were quick to climb down, lest the unsettled war horses launched them from their saddles. To the sound of hooves repeatedly stomping the ground, they waited at the base of the rising path.

Elivar's right hand slowly pulled on the hilt of his sabre, revealing a sliver of steel.

"Stop," Ilithranda warned, her sharp tone enough to see the blade replaced.

A deep and uneasy silence took hold of the environment. From that quietude, there came a thunderous sound of beating wings. The tops of the trees bent away from the creature that filled the sky, as if The Dain'duil itself cowered.

In the shadow of those fanned wings, Daijen staggered back and tripped over a rock hidden beneath the snow. As he fell back and struck the ground, so too did the enormous eagle, landing in the clearing beyond the treeline. Four feathered legs crouched to take its considerable weight as it met the earth, and its sixteen talons sank deep into the hard mud.

Propped up on his elbows, Daijen could but stare at the Aegre.

Pale yellow eyes looked back at him from behind a hooked beak plated in armour. Feathers of chestnut brown surrounded a crown of chipped horns that arched back over the Aegre's head. Following the reins and sheets of chainmail draped over the creature's neck, Daijen's gaze was brought to its rider. The Vahlken was seated in his saddle, back straight as an arrow and head bowed to take in the trio.

"Get up," Elivar uttered without taking his eyes off the Aegre. "Slowly," he added, caution in his voice.

Daijen did exactly as he was instructed, leaving much of the snow to remain clinging to him. It was only then he realised the horses had assumed attack positions, fanning out with antlers dipped to precede their charge. Daijen wanted to calm his mount, but the horse was nothing if not a slave to the magic that had birthed it.

"Control your mounts," the Vahlken ordered from his saddle, his tone as unbending as steel. When the three companions didn't respond quickly enough the Vahlken spoke again. "Control them or Strix will feast."

The Aegre's name returned Daijen's attention to the mutated eagle and its predatory gaze. Its features formed a natural frown, lending the creature a menacing look, as if it saw naught but enemies. Still, the young Andaren found enough of his wits to approach his horse and take it by the reins. Some strength was required to draw the mount away but, ultimately, it was his familiar voice that calmed the animal.

Only when all three war horses were under their riders' control did the Vahlken climb from his elaborate saddle. While it was fastened to the Aegre with lengthy straps that hooked around the wing joints, it possessed a flap of leather that spread out from behind the saddle seat. It was there that Daijen glimpsed so much steel and weaponry. Try as he might, the Aegre was too tall to spot the legendary slaiken blade he had heard tales of.

The Vahlken dropped down with a *thud*, his boots displacing the snow. His white hair hung heavy on his shoulders, blending in with the thick cloak of pearl-white fur. While it covered his pauldrons, the sandy cuirass of leather was revealed, there to display a tapestry of scars that interrupted the intricate patterns carved into the leather. On his hip was a straight-edged sabre that boasted a subtle curve at its tip. Unlike those of the common soldiers, a Vahlken's sabre had no guard across the top of the hilt, making it a far more agile weapon.

When Daijen tore his eyes from the sabre, the Vahlken was already looking directly at him with a detached gaze not dissimilar to the Aegre's. "Not idly do any wander The Dain'duil," he declared, his voice as soft as snow now. "Why are you here?"

Ilithranda straightened. "We have come from battle," she answered boldly. "From Harendun. Paragon Sorn chose us for the Path of Handuin. We come with the blessing of the Justiciar."

The Vahlken's eyes, a similar shade of cobalt to Daijen's, moved from one companion to the other until, finally, lingering on Daijen himself. Was that doubt in his expression?

"I have the papers," Ilithranda offered when the Vahlken said nothing.

It was a brief exchange, the bound scroll passing from pale hand to pale hand. The Vahlken, however, didn't unravel the parchment and read Paragon Sorn's words. Instead, he held the scroll up and subtly waved it as he glanced up at Ka'vairn. Daijen craned his neck and looked at the fortress, wondering who the

Vahlken was signalling to. He saw naught but the stonework, the distance too far to discern anything else.

An awkward silence befell the clearing then, the Vahlken content to stand and say nothing.

"What now?" Elivar asked.

"Now you wait."

Elivar nodded along. "For what exactly?"

The Vahlken's cool eyes levelled on the warrior. "*This*," he replied, indicating the scroll in his hand, "does not grant passage into Ka'vairn. Only one can grant permission."

Daijen frowned where the others expressed revelation.

"The Valtorak," Ilithranda concluded, the grand title striking Daijen like cold steel.

On the heels of her words, a distant call drew all eyes up to Ka'vairn, where a dark speck was parting from the ramparts and crossing the sky. It had launched like a bolt from the heavens before changing direction. The speck then grew in detail, revealing fanned wings. It was only seconds before another Aegre cleared the tops of the trees and landed on the other side of the group, blocking the path that rose up to Ka'vairn.

Daijen immediately noted the differences between the great eagles. This new Aegre was older, its body of feathers greying with large patches of white. Its pale appearance did nothing to conceal the scars that marred so many of its features. Terrible grooves had been gouged into its side from neck to feathered tail. One of its eyes was divided by a jagged strip of grey that continued in the form of a scar both above and below the yellow orb. Unlike Strix, this Aegre wore no armour, its golden beak, chipped and pitted, there to see.

The most obvious difference was related to the legs upon which it stood. The front left limb was entirely missing, a rounded stump in its place. Like Strix, it frowned at the newcomers, its hooked beak snapping once at Daijen.

The snow gave way to the Aegre's rider, who climbed down with a touch more control than the previous Vahlken. From his saddle, he removed a tall staff of curved wood, each end carved smoothly but angled.

The other Vahlken dropped to one knee a fraction of a second before Ilithranda and Elivar followed suit. Daijen met The Valtorak's eyes a moment before he too genuflected. Keeping his head bowed and gaze on the snow, one hand gripped to his horse's reins, Daijen held on to the image of the violet eyes that had just looked through him.

The Valtorak moved between them, his staff crunching through the snow before his right boot. "Thank you, Kastiek," he croaked, accepting the scroll.

They all remained on one knee while The Valtorak perused the Paragon's words. Daijen used the spare moment to find Elivar. The warrior's expression was blank, if focused, giving nothing of his thoughts away. Beyond him, Ilithranda's face was hidden behind a curtain of white hair.

"That will be all, Kastiek," The Valtorak said by way of a dismissal.

"Master." The Vahlken rose from his knee and disappeared from sight.

Daijen was tempted to turn and watch him mount the Aegre, but to do so felt disrespectful in the presence of The Valtorak. They were all buffeted by Strix's wings and sprinkled by a light fall of snow as the creature took to the sky.

"Ilithranda," The Valtorak, said, reading from the parchment.

Rising before the master of Ka'vairn, Ilithranda stood tall and said nothing.

"Elivar," he continued, bringing the warrior to his feet. "Rondir," he said lastly.

Daijen hesitated. It had been weeks since he had heard his predecessor's name. Even Ilithranda and Elivar hadn't spoken of him, though he recalled a flippant comment from one of them that Rondir had come from a different legion.

Feeling eyes on him, Daijen could but stand. Never in his life had he required courage to look at someone, but it took every ounce of his bravery to meet The Valtorak's gaze. He saw the aged

Andaren in his entirety now. The angles of his face were harsh, weathered even, with crow's feet about his eyes. He had to be somewhere between four and five hundred years old to display such ageing.

Like his Aegre, The Valtorak showed signs of a life forged through war. His most prominent scar was a jagged grey line that started somewhere beyond his hairline and tracked diagonally through his eyebrow, over his crooked nose, and down to his jaw. There were other scars about his lips and prominent cheek bones, all a testament to his time on the battlefield, be that on the ground or in the air.

Like Kastiek, he wore a fur cloak—his a deep black speckled with snow. The Valtorak's cuirass was also identical, if more heavily cratered by battle and adorned by various personal trinkets. Curiously, he wielded no sabre as Kastiek had. Something told Daijen that The Valtorak had little need of a sword should he face his enemy.

"The Dain'duil has been known to rob many of their name," the ancient voice declared, speaking over Daijen. "But never from the Path of Handuin, so tame is the weathered road."

Daijen made to speak but his throat and lips were dry. "Forgive me," he managed, his voice a rasp. "Master," he added a second later. "I am not Rondir," he went on to confess.

The Valtorak's expression remained impassive. "Then who are you? Those chosen to follow in Handuin's footsteps should not require an escort."

"I am Daijen Saeth," he declared, after licking his frozen lips. "I am not an escort," he explained. "I was," he elaborated needlessly. "I was a messenger guard..." The words trailed off when he noted the embarrassment Elivar emoted on his behalf.

"A messenger guard," The Valtorak mused.

"He saved our lives, Master." It had been Ilithranda who had spoken up, turning all towards her. "We were fighting at Harendun. A catapult struck The Rune Tower—brought the roof down. Elivar and I would have been crushed beneath it had he not come to our aid."

"Rondir died in the tower," Elivar added.

"So Paragon Sorn decided to send you in Rondir's stead," The Valtorak surmised, his expression turning to stone. "A messenger guard," he repeated with exasperation. "And am I supposed to be impressed by you two? You who needed *saving* by a messenger guard." He let the scroll go, there to be taken by the breeze. "It has been eleven years since any were considered worthy of this path. Four they sent. Four we buried. Now they send me you three. Perhaps I should have Kastiek dig your graves now."

"We *will* survive the trials," Ilithranda insisted.

"Silence!" The Valtorak snapped, biting the word off. He stalked towards her, head tilted in analysis. "Ah," he voiced softly in recognition. "Your imperial blood has a voice of its own, I see."

Daijen blinked in confusion and looked to Elivar, who subtly shook his head in response, a gesture that relayed the need to keep his mouth shut.

"It means little between these mountains," The Valtorak went on. "Even less inside those walls. And should you survive the process," he said quietly, his eyes looking past Ilithranda to spy Elivar and Daijen, "your blood will be forever changed." Quite dramatically, he pivoted away and strode towards his Aegre. "Keep to the trail," he called out, gesturing at the rising path. "But know this: when you reach the gates, you leave everything that you once were behind. Should you cling to any of it, even your *blood*," he intoned, looking pointedly at Ilithranda, "you will never leave Ka'vairn."

Within seconds, The Valtorak was seated in his saddle, his staff secured. "Aramis, fly!" The battle-scarred Aramis spread his wings, bent all three of his legs, and launched into the sky.

Daijen managed to steady himself and avoid being bowled over by the powerful departure. Again, the horses required input from their riders lest their aggression get the better of them.

"Easy," Daijen bade, stroking the mount's muscled neck. By the time he looked back at Elivar and Ilithranda, The Valtorak and Aramis were distant spots against the fading blue. "What was he talking about?" he asked them collectively, though his eyes were naturally drawn to Ilithranda.

Again, Elivar was shaking his head. "Leave it be," he uttered.

"He said *imperial blood*," Daijen felt compelled to point out.

"Valtorak," Ilithranda said firmly. "Or master. Call him anything else at your own peril."

Daijen watched her guide her horse towards the slope, ignoring the details of his comment. Again, he looked to Elivar for enlightenment. The warrior gripped his mount's reins and paused, checking that Ilithranda was still making her way towards the final, mountainous, leg of their path. Over one shoulder, he met Daijen's eyes and glanced at something on the ground, beyond them both.

Daijen turned around, his brow furrowed with increasing confusion. The parchment stood out in the evening light, the scroll caught in the snow. By the time he had retrieved it, Elivar was on the rise behind Ilithranda.

The parchment rustled as he straightened it out between his icy fingers and thumbs. The scrawl was that of Paragon Sorn, his calligraphy typically styled with the flourishes of a highborn. Daijen didn't even bother reading the instructions the Paragon had written out, his attention moving down to the three names listed at the bottom.

Elivar of House T'saren.

Rondir of House Jovuhn.

Ilithranda of House...

Daijen's mind stumbled over the last word on the parchment: the name. It wasn't *just* a name. It was *the* name. Daijen had heard it all his life. More so, like every Andaren, he had been born into loyalty to that name, to House *Lhoris*.

7
HOLLOW VICTORY

THE BEACH WAS CLUTTERED WITH NUMEROUS CAMPS AND SUPPLIES, MOST of which had been abandoned in favour of new dwellings inside the city walls. Gallien navigated the debris, including the gulls that picked at it all, until he found the path that led up and round to the Sea Gate: not that there was much left of it now. The battering ram still lay on the ground, along with a handful of bodies that had never made it inside.

Stepping under the arch and into Harendun for the third time in his life, the smuggler struggled to see much of it. The pale blue of the dawning sky did little to bring definition to the city of smoke and ash. Gallien wafted it from his face and pressed on, relying on his memory to guide him.

The number of corpses littering the streets brought him to a slow stop. It had been years since he had witnessed such a sight. There had been a time when this had been all he knew. At the end of his soldiering career, he hadn't even noticed the bodies they had piled up, be they humans or Andarens.

War was an unthinking machine, he knew, a beast that only moved in one direction and cared nothing for what it left in its wake. For a long time that had suited him, but every man has their limit, their fill of blood and death before the rot sets in, tarnishing the soul. Most never reach that point, but Gallien had pushed himself again and again, throwing himself into countless campaigns.

Now it sickened him.

Pausing by the corner of a building that had been struck by a catapult, the smuggler observed the broken stone. It had been a long time since he had seen Andaren magic in practice, but there it was, laced into the very fabric of the city's architecture. Though it would take days, perhaps weeks even, the stonework would continue to grow back into its original form. Then the city would be made whole again, ready to be reclaimed by its makers before Erador saw fit to seize it again. Round and round the wheel turned.

Gallien brought his fingers to the broken corner, where the stone continued to rise out of itself, and thought better of touching it. He might be far from the streets of his own civilisation, but he could still hear the priests of The Gilded in the halls of his memory. They would take to any corner where they might amass a mob and shout their warnings of *unnatural magic* or *a perversion of nature itself*, and always with the powerful Jainus standing behind them, lending weight to their rhetoric.

The smuggler was suddenly filled with visions of touching the healing stone, only for it to spread from his finger to his whole body, turning *him* to stone. He retracted his curious hand and moved on.

He made it no more than a step before he was forced to dive aside. Pounding hooves thudded down the street, the distorted and unnatural neigh of a horse reverberating in its wake. From the ground, Gallien looked up to see the Andaren war horse as it raced away, fleeing on all six of its legs and trailed by its forked tail.

More Andaren magic. Though, in truth, Drakalis saw beauty in the creatures that had once been ordinary horses. They were magnificent and strong with unmatchable speed where Erador's horses were concerned. Of course, to ever voice such an opinion would be to bring The Gilded down upon him. The Jainus would soon follow, a thought that sent a chill down his spine.

Standing up and dusting himself off, Gallien rounded the next block, where he was reunited with the same company who had departed The Raven. They had been brought to a stop by a marshal commander and were all sweating despite the morning chill. The smuggler took a step back and concealed himself behind the remains of a broken wall.

Waiting, he listened to what he could over the sound of crackling fires and distant shouting. It seemed they were being given new orders to sweep the streets and search for Andarens who might be hiding. There came more than a few groans from the company, who now saw their tedious part in the war.

Deciding that his presence would raise too many questions among the invading force, Drakalis chose a more obscure path to his destination. More than once, however, he was forced to adapt his route and avoid the patrols. He was again compelled to seek out shelter when he came across one of the public squares, where a pitched battle had clearly taken place.

"Just spear 'em all!" one of the captains yelled.

As commanded, the dozen or so of the king's weary men made their way across the square, stabbing every body they stepped over.

Gallien watched for a moment, wondering if one of the prone Andarens would rise at the last second and make a run for it. The dead did not rise and soon the men had swept from one side to the other, ensuring they stayed that way. How many years of life lay dead in that square? the smuggler wondered. Hundreds? Thousands? He couldn't imagine living the many centuries of an Andaren only to die a bloody death in some public square.

After they had moved on, Gallien crossed the square himself, careful to step over and around the dead. He tried not to dwell for long on the bodies *he* had left on the same cold stone, years earlier. The thought of it brought one hand to the hilt of the broadsword on his hip, the scabbard resting between the flaps of his longcoat. It was a reflex, he knew, but a reflex that lent him some courage.

To avoid another patrol he was forced to move through the building on his right. He stepped over the partially shattered door and continued through the cramped rooms until he discovered a back door that led onto the next street.

Movement caught the corner of his eye. The smuggler froze.

With fingers clasping the door handle, Gallien slowly turned to see what had captured his attention. He let go of the door and slipped both hands into the air—a sign of peace.

"*Hello,*" he whispered in Andarneese.

The family of three stared at him from the cluttered corner of the room, the parents ensuring their son was safe between them. It was impossible to discern the age of an Andaren, but their children grew up at the same rate as any human, meaning the small boy was no more than six years old.

"*I'm not a soldier,*" he uttered, and how glad of that he was.

The father glanced at the sword on Gallien's hip.

The smuggler had a reply for that but the shadow of a patrol crossed the ash-covered window. Drakalis stepped sideways and pressed his back to a wall, his fingers flexing to direct the family to do the same.

After a tense moment, the soldiers were gone, likely too tired to actually search every building they passed. Gallien took a breath. He wasn't entirely sure what he would have done had the soldiers found their way inside. He liked to think that he would have kindled his blade and killed to defend the innocent family, whose only crime was to have been born Andarens. Or would he have slunk into the shadows and let the men take them away? Or worse.

In their absence it was a question that didn't need answering and his sword remained where it was. "*You can't stay here,*" he warned them in hushed tones. "*They will find you.*"

The father slowly rose, purposefully putting himself between his family and the smuggler. "*You... You are human,*" he stated, his tone a mix of curiosity and fear.

"*That doesn't always have to mean we're bad,*" Drakalis replied earnestly.

"*That is not my experience,*" the Andaren told him.

"*I understand,*" the smuggler said, for what else could he say?

There was a good chance this Andaren had seen *every* siege of Harendun.

"*We will leave,*" the father eventually declared, ushering his family to their feet. "*There is a way,*" he said cryptically.

"*The Orsindil Mountains?*" Gallien enquired, drawing a frown from the Andaren. "*We discovered those tunnels years ago. You cannot take that path.*"

"*All the fighting has moved to the north,*" the father complained. "*We would never reach The Sael Road.*"

Gallien's smuggler mind, ever at the forefront of his thinking, assumed command. "You need to reach Yalafar," he reasoned, his thoughts sprouting from his mouth, and in the common tongue of man. "*The Sea Gate,*" he announced, his words returning to Andarneese. "*The beach is all but empty. If you're careful—and* slow *—you might reach those sands. There are any number of row boats. Take one and follow the coast north to Yalafar.*"

The father absorbed the directions, eyeing Gallien all the while with suspicion. He eventually nodded his head and directed his family to give the smuggler a wide berth as they slipped from the room. He offered no thanks but a simple nod of appreciation. He also never turned his back on Gallien. Smart Andaren, he thought.

The smuggler was soon on his way again, darting from corner to corner. He didn't get far, however, before the sound of clashing swords filled the air. It wasn't many he ascertained, catching sight of four human soldiers, each wielding a sword and shield. Gallien moved closer to see the opposing force that withstood the armoured warriors.

Stepping over bodies from both sides, Drakalis crouched behind a stack of crates and observed the unfolding fight. He had been wrong. There was no opposing force. There was just one.

He moved like a dancer, his blade rounding in swift but delicate arcs that found the gaps between every plate of armour. He dropped one before leaping off a wall to come down on another, his sword slicing neatly through a man's throat. Here was an Andaren no soldier wished to face, an Andaren who had seen many lives of men and taken twice as many.

A Vahlken.

The long war had inevitably robbed Andara of many such warriors, but they were still out there, amidst their kin. His fur cloak and leather cuirass were another badge of his station, his *mutation*. It was said the Vahlken didn't need armoured plate, that their skin was as hard as iron. A fable, Gallien knew. If it were true, their numbers would not have dwindled so.

Ducking under a sweeping blade of man-made steel, the Andaren emerged to thrust his scimitar up and under his foe's cuirass—a mortal blow. The last among the humans swung his sword in both hands, a chopping blow that would stagger any foe. The Vahlken raised a single hand, in which he wielded a short-sword, and blocked the incoming steel with seemingly minimal effort. A swift side-kick sent the soldier from his feet and into the nearest wall, his fight at an end.

A shadow swept over the street.

An instinct born of ancient time saw Gallien retreat further.

The smuggler caught naught but a dark blur falling from the sky before the stack of crates robbed him of the view. He heard the landing, however, as if Kaliban had hurled a bolt from the heavens. Daring to peer over the rim of the crate, there was no doubt in his mind that he was looking at a Dragon Rider.

Tall, though not as tall as the Vahlken, the Rider's dusty cloak blew in the breeze, revealing glimpses of his black armour. Each piece appeared moulded to his form, as if he wore a second skin of dark plate. It was contrasted by a topknot of blond hair that felt nothing of the wind, each strand as tightly bound as the legendary armour.

The two warriors were slowly circling each other, blades drawn and already dripping with blood. Who could say how many Andarens had fallen to the Rider since the invasion had begun?

"Your wretched mount is dead," the Rider taunted. "Its meat shall fill my dragon's belly for days."

"Your dragon will taste my slaiken blade," the Vahlken replied venomously, his command of man's language far superior to Gallien's attempts at Andarneese.

The Dragon Rider laughed at the threat. "Your *slaiken blade*," he said mockingly. "Would that be the same blade you dropped three days ago? Perhaps you don't recall. You were *fleeing* after all."

The Vahlken's features creased into anger before he lunged. One after the other, his scimitar and short-sword were thrust at the Rider, forcing the human back a step with each attack.

When the Rider initiated his counterattack it was nimble and decisive. He weaved between blows and slashed his sword from left to right, the angle low so as to slice his enemy's leg, just above the knee. The strike was perfectly executed, for had it been an inch higher the blade would have met the resistance of the Vahlken's tasset, and an inch lower it would have scraped the kneepad.

Blood was drawn and an injury delivered, the latter dropping the Andaren warrior to one knee. There he would have met his end had he not turned his fall into a roll and ducked beneath the Rider's swinging blade. The Vahlken came up with an unfurling arm, the end of which released his short-sword. The weapon spun for no more than a second before finding the Rider's chest.

Again, these gods of the earth defied death. The Rider was pushed back by the blow but the steel—and the considerable force behind it—failed to pierce the dark armour. Instead, the weapon clattered to the ground, where the Rider swept it aside with the tip of his broadsword.

"You should have aimed a little higher," the Dragon Rider shamed.

The Vahlken rose to his full height, his jaw gripped by determination. He said nothing, his response made by action alone. The two collided in a flurry of steel that took them from one side of the street to the other, each careful to navigate the corpses the Vahlken had left. Gallien blinked and missed the particular exchange that resulted in the Rider's head snapping back and a splash of blood arcing into the air. There was no missing the boot planted in his chest, however.

The Rider tumbled over himself, his sandy cloak wrapping about him with abandon, until he was stopped by one of the bodies. He was quick to rise—quicker than any ordinary man might boast—but it wasn't before the Vahlken stepped in and slammed his foot up into his ribs. Up and round the Rider spun, his trajectory taking him into the adjacent wall.

"Do you need to catch your breath?" the mutated Andaren asked, his free hand snatching at the Rider's throat. It was with an extraordinary feat of strength that he picked the Rider up to his toes and pinned him to the wall.

The Dragon Rider responded as the Vahlken had—with action.

His right hand shot out as if to push the Vahlken away but his palm never touched the Andaren warrior. Instead, a burst of light and a *crack* of thunder exploded from his hand and slammed the Vahlken in the chest, launching him back at speed until his bulk fractured the adjacent wall.

Magic...

Gallien instinctively hid from it, dropping below the crates. Like all men, he associated magic with danger, an element of nature that only The Jainus and the Dragon Riders dared touch. He had seen it used but once before, as a young soldier. He could still recall The Jainus wizard in the streets of Thedaria, brought to the city to show what happened to captured deserters. A line of them there had been, all brought to their knees and bound. One by one, they succumbed to the ice that froze their blood and burnt their skin; and all from the fingertips of the wizard.

Not only had he seen it again this day, but the smuggler had felt the withered edges of the concussive wave from the Rider's spell.

Some of his nerve recovered, Gallien returned to the view.

The Dragon Rider paused in his advance to throw a slender dagger at the rising Andaren. Impossibly, the Vahlken batted it away with the edge of his scimitar. Whether by design or opportunity, the Rider then kicked out, targeting his opponent's wounded leg. The Vahlken went down to one knee again and the Rider leapt, sword angled down to take his enemy in the neck.

Reflexes beyond Gallien's understanding allowed the Andaren to tilt his head and avoid the plunging blade while his free hand snatched at the Rider's sword arm, fingers wrapping around his wrist. At the same time, the Vahlken was bringing his scimitar up to gut the human. It was then that they became locked in a battle of wills, his sword-arm blocked by the Rider.

Their arms and faces shook with exertion, the edges of their fine blades slowly pressing into the cuirass of the other. Gallien's eyes narrowed as he glimpsed movement beyond the Andaren.

For all his skill and experience, the Vahlken didn't have eyes in the back of his head. Thus, the blow delivered unto the lone warrior was also a mortal one, the human sword driven through the back of his head and out through his mouth. There was no honour in the kill, but the previously discarded soldier cared little for such things.

The fight was over in that instant. The Eradoran soldier, exhausted and chest heaving, yanked his sword free. The Dragon Rider stepped back, his momentary surprise melting into a frown, as the Vahlken's body fell in a heap at his feet. The soldier stared at his great deed—the death of a Vahlken! But there was no elation about him, no epiphany. Victory was a hollow thing when you were standing amongst corpses, amongst men he had likely called friends, brothers even. He spared them a moment, a prayer perhaps, before walking away, his sword dragging behind him.

"Soldier," the Rider called, halting the man in his tracks. "You just slew a Vahlken warrior." He stretched out his arm to the man, revealing a vambrace of layered red scales. "I would shake your hand."

Gallien continued to watch, his breath shallow. He couldn't imagine a Dragon Rider asking to shake his hand—the honour of it.

The Eradoran soldier turned fully to face the Rider. Something about his expression perked up, defying the blood and death that surrounded them. Closing the gap, he extended his hand until the Rider clasped his forearm and pulled him in to a warriors' embrace. So close were they, that the soldier didn't even see the Rider's broadsword when it slipped through the gap between his cuirass and his arm. Shock and pain mixed together as they ruled his features and his limbs stiffened. He was eye to eye with the blond Dragon Rider when his shock of pain turned into a questioning frown. There was no time for answers, however, and the Rider wasn't offering any. He simply withdrew his blade and let the man fall dead amongst his brothers.

Crouching down, the Rider used the cloak of that same soldier to wipe his sword clean before returning it to the scabbard on his hip, its red hilt exaggerated against his black armour. Gallien knew he should have run away several minutes ago but he was enthralled by the scene playing out in front of him. They were supposed to be the great protectors of the realm, the champions of the king, and the heroes of Erador. How could they so easily snuff out a human life for taking their kill?

The Rider paused before departing the street, stealing Gallien's attention once again. He retrieved something from the ground and held it up for inspection—the Vahlken's short-sword. He turned it over, inspecting the weapon from all sides, before securing it on his belt. Proof of the kill, perhaps. A trophy? Who could say how immortals thought?

It could have been the smuggler in Gallien, a sixth sense, that informed him he was about to get caught and saw him drop beneath the rim of the crate. He was sure the Rider had been turning towards him only a second before he ducked. He didn't dare look back. He didn't dare move either. Instead, he waited for what felt like a nerve-racking eternity. When, finally, he found the courage to set eyes on the street ahead, there was naught but corpses caught in the morning sun.

Fearing he was behind schedule now, Gallien parted from the crates and moved up the street. He couldn't help but pause to look upon the dead Vahlken and the man who had killed him, both side by side in death. Gallien had seen Vahlkens from afar, astride their Aegres as they streaked across the sky. To see one up close, and dead no less, was... underwhelming. Absent life, the mutated warrior was just like everyone else. Gallien offered no prayer of his own. Whatever the species, he had seen enough war and death to know that the great Kaliban didn't care.

Attempting to move on again, his boot trod on something

small that refused to give way to his weight. Lifting his boot revealed a red stone that nurtured his curiosity. Picking it up, he soon realised it was rather flat and curved, the object fitting easily in the palm of his hand. Recalling the Rider's vambraces and, more specifically, the blow to his chest, Gallien's eyes widened with revelation.

It was a single dragon scale.

The smuggler had heard the tales of the so-called scale mail worn beneath their dark armour. Like so much he had heard, Gallien had lent the notion little credence. Until now. He ran one finger over the scale before squeezing it as hard as he could. It might as well have been stone. Looking about, he slipped the red scale into the inside pocket of his long coat and darted away from the street.

He was nearly there now.

Just east of the city's heart, where Harendun's greatest spire rose to challenge the mountains in the north, there sat a quiet courtyard, its walls covered in trellises of honeysuckle that defied the winter. Andaren magic was everywhere it seemed, interwoven like the threads of any fabric. Gallien ignored it, just as he had the first time he had entered the courtyard. Back then, of course, he had not entered alone, but with his brother beside him.

How long would it be, he wondered, before Corben's image completely faded in his memory? Even now Gallien struggled to recall which side of his brother's mouth bore the small scar he had inflicted upon him when they were children.

The courtyard itself was intact, untouched by the current invasion. When last he and Corben had investigated the area, the adjacent building had been struck by a devastating spell, hurled upon the city by a Jainus wizard. It had rained enough debris upon the site to shatter the walls. Of course, it had all grown back since then.

Gallien stood over a particular patch where one intricate pattern, that had been artistically carved into the stone, met another, creating a larger mosaic. It was there, on that very spot, where Corben had fallen victim to the same debris that had demolished so much of the courtyard.

Drakalis crouched and ran his fingers over the stone, feeling naught but the engravings. There was no trace of the blood that had once spread across the ground. There were no last words to recall. No farewell. Corben had sputtered blood, his breathing shallow until it wasn't there at all.

Gallien stood up and adjusted the satchel strap across his chest. "I hope you're right about this place, brother. I could really do with a *win*."

Moving away from the spot, he made for the corner of the yard, where a circle was carved into the stone, a pattern all of its own filling the space inside. There were three others, one in each corner, but it had been this specific one, in the north-west corner, that Corben had made note of.

"*Harendun is a city built upon a city,*" Corben had said that fateful day.

Gallien crouched again, his back now resting against the wall. He waited. And he hoped. If Kit didn't appear, then it had all been for naught, and he would be left in a city under siege with no way of returning to Erador that wasn't in The Raven's brig. Beyond that, he would be delivered into the hands of Thedaria's Padoshi, its highest of criminal lords.

Better to die in Harendun.

8
AMONG GIANTS

80 Years Ago...

The ancient Hellion stone rumbled beneath Daijen's feet as great counterweights dropped on thick chains, levering Ka'vairn's hulking gates apart. The young master of House Saeth should have been fixed on the growing gap, spying whatever he could of the legendary fortress and his new home, yet still—even after trekking up the rise—his gaze was drawn to the back of Ilithranda's head.

Vast was the imperial family, their numbers able to swell within the safety of Aran'saur's thick walls, well beyond The Gap and humanity's reach. Ilithranda could be removed from the throne by as many as two hundred places and be no more than a second cousin to the true line. Whatever her place in that most elevated of families, she was still a Lhoris. Why she had ever been east of The Gap or allowed within the ranks of the army was such a mystery to Daijen it bordered on concerning.

Nevertheless, his gaze was inevitably torn away by the approaching figures from within Ka'vairn's courtyard. Six of them there were, tall and lithe, their exposed arms displaying muscles that might have been sculpted from marble. Their forms were easily seen as the mountain wind pushed their loose clothing about their limbs and torsos.

Of the six, one stood out more than the others and not because of his bald scalp—a most unpopular appearance amongst their people. It was his hungry smile. Could the monsters of the world mimic such an affectation, they would undoubtedly look exactly like the bald initiate. Where the others stopped at the threshold, he continued to stalk forward and round the trio, a predator circling its prey.

He passed Daijen, revealing his superior height and golden eyes. It seemed to Daijen that there was something missing behind those eyes. Warmth, perhaps. The hint of a soul.

Monster indeed.

"What do you think, Slait?" Of the six, three were female, though Daijen couldn't guess which one had voiced the question. Still, the circling beast now had a name.

Slait came to a lazy stop between the trio and the gates, his brothers and sisters at his back. "I think it's time to get the shovels out again," he replied, with a sharp smirk cutting up one cheek.

A piercing cry made the trio alone flinch, though all in the snow turned their gaze up to the Aegre perched upon Ka'vairn's ramparts, its scarred beak pointed down at them. A moment later, the six parted for The Valtorak to stand upon the threshold, his curved staff planted beside him.

"Initiates." The Valtorak's voice cut through any tension and brought the bald one to heel beside him. "Slait. Take their horses to the stables."

Slait's jaw firmed up and his golden eyes flitted to the newcomers before settling on his master again. "They can tend to their own mounts," he replied insolently.

The Valtorak pushed out his arm until the curved edge of his staff was resting neatly against Slait's neck. "It seems the wind caught your words. What did you say to me?"

At last Daijen saw something behind Slait's eyes—a caged

animal. It raged behind those golden orbs, flaring like new flames. "I will see to the mounts," he said through gritted teeth.

Of the three war horses, Daijen's alone protested Slait's control of his reins. Daijen expected the bald initiate to get tugged off his feet, his strength no match for the mutated mount, yet one pull on the reins brought the horse's head to bow. Looking over the six initiates again, Daijen decided there was more to their advanced height than mere coincidence.

"Come," The Valtorak commanded, leading them all into the courtyard before Slait could tow the horses.

Daijen felt himself being swallowed up as he passed through the gates and into the shadow of high walls. The courtyard was the maw of some mighty beast that could easily have swallowed three hundred Andarens whole. Around its edges were areas designated to different types of training, be it archery, axe-throwing, swordsmanship or tackling various pieces of equipment. All were coated in snow, their surfaces crusted with ice.

Quite naturally, Daijen's attention was drawn to the fires inside Ka'vairn, their hot glow filling narrow windows and the gap that separated the looming doors. He was desperate to feel his toes and hands again, and the thought of sleep under a roof, beside a fire, was all-consuming. Along with Ilithranda and Elivar, who appeared to be thinking along the same lines, he began walking towards the promise of shelter.

The Valtorak cleared his throat.

The ancient master swiped his foot in an arcing motion, piling the snow up. He tapped his staff into the ground beneath and struck not dirt but stone. Daijen could see now the outline of a circle beneath the snow, a ring of stone. There was no understanding The Valtorak's meaning in exposing it, but the smile on every initiate's face filled Daijen with dread.

"You are all quick to find rest," The Valtorak observed. "Did you not come here to train as a Vahlken?"

Sensing the question was rhetorical, the trio kept shoulder to shoulder, lips sealed.

"This is a duelling ring," The Valtorak continued, his staff tracing the circle in the air. "Once you step inside, you are fated to find victory or defeat. Step out or be forced out and you will find the latter."

With no command, invitation or even a hint of what they should do next, the newcomers continued to stand side by side, looking from The Valtorak to the duelling ring.

"Interesting," The Valtorak remarked, both hands coming to grip his staff at the shoulder. "I would have expected any who wish to become a Vahlken to volunteer."

"You want us to fight?" Ilithranda asked, and she suddenly seemed so much smaller than before. "Now?"

The first sign of a smile flashed across The Valtorak's face. "You would prefer to sleep, I suppose."

The initiates chuckled to themselves at his back, including Slait upon his return from the humble stables in the south corner. "I was first to step inside the ring," he boasted, one fist coming up to slam into his own chest.

"I would get the measure of you before the trials," The Valtorak said, taking command again.

Elivar stepped forwards, his easy smile displaying some species of arrogance. "You want to see if we can fight?" In one smooth motion, he unclipped his cloak and furs and stood defiant in the blistering cold, one hand coiled around the hilt on his hip.

"You *can't* fight," The Valtorak told him bluntly. "But there are other things I can learn from watching you bleed."

If Elivar was put off by the statement he showed no sign of it. He stepped inside the belt of stone and drew his scimitar. Slait flashed his teeth as he made to step inside himself, but the curved staff of The Valtorak barred his way.

"Laif." The name snapped from The Valtorak's lips and one of the male initiates stepped inside.

Like the others, Laif was a head taller than Elivar, his shoulders slightly broader, though not by much. He knotted his fists before rolling them at the wrist.

Elivar frowned. "No blades?" he questioned, ready to toss his own aside.

Laif held up a hand to stop him. "Keep it," he instructed. "You're going to need it."

Elivar looked to The Valtorak for reassurance, to which the master of Ka'vairn tapped his staff into the ground. "Begin."

At a thrust, steel whistled through the air, spearing towards Laif's right cheek. It seemed impossibly quick to Daijen, who felt the cold and exhaustion seizing his joints and slowing his mind, but Elivar sprang like an uncoiling snake.

And yet...

Laif had moved—though *when* was hard to say exactly. The sword pierced naught but air and the initiate came at Elivar from his right, a single fist rushing in to meet his jaw. The snow was displaced beneath Elivar as he struck the ground, his weapon released to clatter over the edge of the stone ring.

The other initiates filled the air with their laughter, a sound that set Daijen's blood on fire. The temptation to step inside the ring and aid Elivar shocked him, even if he didn't act on the thought.

A groan on his lips to accompany the blood that trailed there, Elivar picked himself up, pausing only to grip the hilt that remained inside the ring. On his feet again, the warrior spat blood at the ground between him and his opponent and crouched into a fighting stance, his blade horizontal to his face.

While the others grinned and whispered between themselves, Laif remained a pillar of discipline within the circle. His vibrant blue eyes never strayed from Elivar, even when his mane of white hair blew across his face. As it became apparent that Elivar wasn't attacking this time, Laif advanced at no more than a steady step.

Elivar reacted swiftly, his scimitar rolling up one way then the next. It was a blur of steel few could have evaded, and something just as few would have struggled to deflect had they a sword of their own. Laif—weaponless—dodged the edge of the blade with no more than a slight pivot in his shoulders, his every step bringing him closer.

Changing his attack in an instant, Elivar lashed out low, intending to swipe at Laif's left leg. The tall initiate simply raised his leg and allowed the scimitar to sweep beneath his bare foot by an inch. Keeping his movements fluid, Elivar brought his weapon back into the fray with a darting thrust that would have gutted any foe.

But Laif, it seemed, was not just any foe.

The initiate clapped his hands and trapped the blade between his palms—an impossible defence against Elivar's impressive speed. A battle of raw strength followed, each exerting upon the other to push the sword away from themselves. Slowly, the curved tip of the scimitar came up until it was pointed at Laif's jaw, yet still it remained exactly where the initiate wished it. By now, Elivar was growling with strain, his pale cheeks flushing grey. By comparison, Laif displayed minimal effort as he steered the sword out over his shoulder.

Using his superior height to his advantage, the initiate kicked out and caught Elivar inside his right leg, dropping him down and back. At the same time, the scimitar was yanked from his grip and deftly flipped so the hilt landed neatly in Laif's hand as Elivar met the ground once again.

"If you get up," Laif threatened, "I'll put you down twice as hard."

Elivar glared up at the initiate, defiance in his eyes. Sure enough, the warrior stood up and shrugged off the embarrassment of being disarmed. From the back of his belt, he drew a slender dagger that matched the curve of his scimitar, the pommel shaped into an eagle's head—a popular style among Andarens.

"I have learned all I need to," The Valtorak announced, and softly so.

Laif took it as a command.

Elivar never got the chance to use his dagger. His own scimitar was brought against him in a twisting motion that disarmed the warrior again. While the small blade spun high, free of its master, Laif advanced a step and brought the scimitar's pommel round in a swift arc. Elivar's right temple took the brunt of the blow, which immediately robbed him of consciousness.

Daijen could but watch as his companion impacted the ground

with all the finesse of a weighted sack. One of the other initiates, a female Daijen couldn't name, stepped in and dragged Elivar out of the ring by one of his wrists. Laif spared a moment to examine the scimitar he had claimed, his expression one of dissatisfaction. Compounding his opinion of the blade, he tossed it away, across the courtyard with flippant regard. At least it had appeared that way. The weapon flew further than Daijen would have expected and the edge bit firmly into a wooden pell already scarred by practice.

Casting the feat aside, Daijen rounded the circle of stone—against Ilithranda's quiet objection—and crouched by Elivar's side. He was alive and breathing, if unaware of the world around him. His temple was bruised already, but he had suffered no blood loss.

"What are you doing?" The Valtorak demanded sternly.

Daijen looked up to discover all eyes were on him. He swallowed. "Making certain he's alive," he finally answered.

The Valtorak eyed him a moment longer, his thoughts his own. "Leave him be," he ordered.

Daijen sensed pain would follow if he failed to obey, and so he resumed his height and backed off, returning to Ilithranda's side. They were together for no more than a second before Ilithranda willingly stepped inside the duelling ring. Like Elivar, she let her cloak and furs drop to the ground at her heels. Adding to the pile, she removed her sword belt and dropped it with the weapon still sheathed.

"This one's bold," Laif remarked, arms folded as he stood amongst his kin again.

"Foolish," Slait put in with a sneer.

"Kovun," The Valtorak said, his violet eyes darting to the broadest of the initiates.

Before Kovun could advance into the ring, one of the females stepped forward. "I would test this one, Master." Despite her words, her tone implied a question.

"You will get your chance, Soyra," The Valtorak promised, his head gesturing for Kovun to advance as originally directed.

Kovun shoved past Soyra with glee as he entered the duelling ring. Shoulders squared, he looked down on Ilithranda as he cracked all the knuckles in his right hand. “Do you have what it takes to be a Vahlken?” he asked bluntly.

Ilithranda said nothing, her impassive expression never wavering.

“Begin,” came the order.

Where Laif had stood his ground and waited for Elivar to strike, Kovun darted forward with that right fist of his. Ilithranda sidestepped, attempting to evade along the outside of his arm, but Kovun’s speed could not be denied, and the knotted fist caught her in the shoulder. Her footing adapted to keep her balanced and she even moved in with a counterattack that batted his arm away and exposed his side. Defying her fatigue, Ilithranda landed three successive blows to his right kidney before jumping up to land a fourth across his jaw.

Kovun moved with the last punch, pivoting on his heel. It seemed no more than a blink of the eye before his elbow was smashing into Ilithranda’s face. Both force and surprise took her from her feet and sent her sprawling in the muddy snow. Daijen had taken an instinctual step towards her, moved, perhaps, by his training as a messenger guard. His duty was to *protect.* The Valtorak’s steely gaze, however, was enough to keep him outside the duelling ring.

Blood oozing from mouth and nose, Ilithranda sighed and tried to stand. The elbow to the face had left her so dazed that she required her hands to keep herself from falling again.

“Well, that didn’t last very long,” one of the unnamed initiates commented with a broad grin on her face.

“She isn’t down yet,” Daijen argued. He met the initiate’s cold eyes—cobalt as his own—and found he couldn’t maintain their silent duel. There was something inherently predatory about the initiates, as if they were more monster than Andaren. It was enough to send a shiver of cold dread down Daijen’s spine.

Ilithranda grunted and took a deep breath as she finally stood upright. Her head tilted to the left, she audibly cracked the bones in her neck. Determination about her, she hunched her shoulders and raised her arms, hands open as if to grab her opponent. Slowly, she began to follow the stone circle, a movement that Kovun mimicked. They struck simultaneously. Their hands deflected one another's, scoring no more than a disorientating slap here or a push there.

Light on her feet, Ilithranda danced about Kovun, ducking and weaving his fists and sweeping feet.

"He's messing with her," Laif observed, a soft chuckle on his lips.

"Sealed lips and open eyes," The Valtorak voiced, the words produced like a mantra that saw the initiates stand a little straighter. "Observe her style," the master went on. "There is but one fighting force in all of Verda known to use it."

The initiates took a quiet moment to watch Ilithranda as she scored no more than a couple of punches to Kovun's midriff—though she might as well have been hitting a tree. "The Praetorian Guard," one of the females declared, revelation in her tone.

"Very good, Naelin," The Valtorak replied evenly.

"Impossible," Slait grunted, one hand cupping his square jaw. "The Praetorians kill themselves when they're no longer fit to serve."

At that moment, Kovun backhanded Ilithranda and sent her sprawling across the duelling ring. Her sudden yelp cut through their discussion and set Daijen's heart racing.

The Valtorak crouched, with an ease that displayed his youthful dexterity, and tilted his head to better see Ilithranda as she tried hopelessly to rise. "Then how does she know their ways?" he asked.

Daijen looked from Ka'vairn's master to its six initiates: he was testing them. Knowing Ilithranda's heritage already, The Valtorak knew she was part of the Imperial family. It seemed the initiates weren't only to be warriors on a battlefield but keen investigators, their minds just as sharp as everything else about them.

"A daughter perhaps?" Laif posed.

Naelin was shaking her head. "The Praetorian Guard are forbidden from siring children."

"An adopted daughter," Laif countered.

"A drop out," Soyra contributed, looking down her nose at Ilithranda. "She learnt some of their ways but not everything."

"A palace guard," said the only female—and only initiate—to have remained silent thus far. "She might have merely observed them training from afar."

The Valtorak stood up, proving his height to be an inch above the rest. "A good hypothesis, Yendi, though not the correct one."

Slait narrowed his eyes on Ilithranda. "She's..." He grinned wickedly. "She's imperial blood!"

Ilithranda managed to look up at the bald initiate, her frown darkened by a fresh bruise.

Slait was laughing to himself. "Well, what do you know? Their blood runs just as red as the rest of us. I thought for sure it must be gold," he jabbed, leaning down imperiously.

Ilithranda sneered before spitting a mouthful of blood in his face. "Does it taste like gold?"

Taken aback, Slait snapped his head away and spat on the ground, one hand coming up to smear her blood across his white cheeks. Then came the rage he had been keeping in check, his bare foot rising to stamp on Ilithranda's head. He might have crushed her skull too had The Valtorak not intervened and shoved him away with a flick of his staff.

Using the distraction—and what burst of energy she could muster—Ilithranda flipped her body and kicked out, her boot catching Kovun across the jaw. In the same fluid movement, she found her way back to her feet, hands up to mimic the Praetorian Guard again. It mattered little. Kovun had recovered from the blow before Ilithranda was even upright. His fist cut through the gap between her hands and slammed into her left eye.

After that, his knuckles came away with more imperial blood and his opponent lay still on the ground.

Like Elivar, Ilithranda was unceremoniously dragged from the ring and left in the cold snow. Daijen turned from his unconscious companions to the six initiates and their master, all of whom were looking at him. Knowing what was expected of him did little to help him take the necessary steps.

"There is no honour in being forced," The Valtorak intoned.

Daijen took a steadying breath, all too aware of the fatigue in his legs and the stiffness in his joints. Still, he removed his cloak and furs and pulled his blade from its scabbard. The moment his feet were firmly planted inside the duelling ring, The Valtorak called for Slait to join him. The initiate's bubbling rage quickly turned to glee as he stepped inside the stone.

For just a second, Daijen Saeth wondered if he had made a mistake drawing his scimitar. How quickly would Slait take it and use it against him?

"Begin."

Slait was all aggression. He advanced without a care for the steel in Daijen's hand. Indeed, the blade was immobilised almost immediately when the bald Andaren snatched Daijen's wrist and bent it into pain. The weapon slipped from his paralysed grip and fell smoothly into Slait's waiting hand. The scimitar was no more than a blur as the initiate whipped it backhand across the shoulder straps that kept Daijen's cuirass tight to his chest.

The plate and its imprinted sunburst fell open, exposing the padded shirt beneath. Swift as he was, Slait gave him no time to do anything but feel the pain from the pommel being thrust into his sternum. The air was forced from his lungs and his chest racked with pain; a precursor to the hammering punch that Slait landed in the side of Daijen's face.

The numbing mist that enveloped his mind was brief, and he returned to his senses on the ground, face plastered with mud. The initiates were laughing again. The sound of their amusement sent tendrils of anger through Daijen, pushing down his pain as he held on to his humiliation instead.

Pushing up from the ground, his hanging cuirass dragged across his legs. He never stood up of course. Slait was upon him, one hand coiled about Daijen's throat, and all his strength forcing the young Andaren onto his back. Now, with an arm pinned beneath Slait's knee, he had but one hand to prise away the fingers that constricted his air pipe. He might as well have been scraping at the bark of a tree, for it seemed those pale fingers were fused to his skin.

The world about him began to blur, narrowing on Slait's face and framing his exhilaration.

"Enough." The command came short and sharp, despite sounding terribly distant.

There came no relief.

Slait appeared caught in a world of his own, where Daijen was no more than an ant. He squeezed all the tighter, his golden eyes watering as he stared at what life remained in Daijen. Enraptured, he was waiting to see it ebb from his opponent, to see that moment when the stillness of death replaced the thrashing of life.

"Slait." The Valtorak's voice was brimming with authority now.

It was enough to break the spell upon Slait but not enough to satiate his hunger for death. Releasing his throat with one hand, he raised the scimitar in the other. As the world continued to darken for Daijen Saeth, the last thing he saw was the edge of his own weapon gleaming in the moonlight, the steel whistling towards him.

9
WHERE GODS LIE

KITRANA GROANED AS SHE PUSHED UP, HER SHOULDER AND HEAD ADDED TO the strength of one arm as she heaved the circular port from its fixings. Once a portion of the lip was above Harendun's street level, Gallien curled his fingers underneath and helped the Nimean to move it aside.

"You're a sight for sore eyes," the smuggler commented.

"I could say the same," Kit replied, her breath laboured. "Gallien," she uttered, drawing his blue eyes to hers. "You're not going to believe what's down here."

Drakalis smiled, his grin so broad it flashed his teeth and spoke of a child-like excitement swelling within. "I knew it!" he hissed. "Let's be going then," he added, glancing over one shoulder. "I'd not linger up here any longer than I need to."

Kitrana considered the creatures that had given her chase. "It's not much better down here," she muttered, retracing her steps.

Climbing down through the highest level, past the square grill she had already moved aside, the two companions were soon standing in the chamber that had been sealed by the portcullis. The darkness that had occupied the ruins for centuries was now replaced by a thick gloom due to the light provided by the shaft that led up to Harendun's streets. Still, what little light there was found the floating droplets and steeped the chamber in glistening stars.

Gallien's nose crinkled into his frown. "Now that's a smell," he remarked, discovering the damp mustiness that filled the room. "What *is* this?" he soon asked, noting the droplets around him. In a human clumsy-like way, the smuggler waved his arm through a portion of the suspended water, dispersing the droplets around his hand and sleeve.

Impatient, Kitrana looked from her discovery to the smuggler and his inferior eyes. "Did you bring torches?" she asked, eager for him to see what lay hidden in shadow.

"Aye," he said, poking one of the droplets. "What in the hells have you found, Kit?"

"The torches," she repeated, her tone clipped.

Crouching, Gallien retrieved a pair of small torches from his satchel. After striking some flint, he was able to stand and offer her one. While the Nimean did not require it, she knew exactly what to do with it, and tossed the torch into the middle of her discovery.

Mirroring Kitrana's earlier reaction, Gallien's lips parted and his jaw fell open. He craned his neck to take it all in.

"What is this, Gallien? You said there would be *relics*. This is something else entirely."

Gallien didn't respond, his previous excitement apparently replaced by pure wonderment. He continued to stare at it, his eyes roaming over every inch that the light dared to touch.

"Gallien," she prompted.

"It's a *god*."

His voice was half a rasp, as if that too had been ensnared by the giant skeleton that sat slumped against the chamber wall.

"A god?" Kit echoed, her disbelief audible. Like Gallien, she looked upon the humanoid skeleton. It required little scrutiny to see the four arms protruding from the ribs or the abnormal skull that sloped back and high.

"I've only ever seen drawings of these," Drakalis muttered, lost in thought.

"You're going to have to do better than tell me it's a god," Kit said. "Even my people have gods, Gallien, and they don't amount to a pile of bones."

"You've heard of the Andarens' gods, aye?"

Her time blending in amongst the people of Erador meant she was better versed in their religion and history, but still she nodded. "They believe their gods died eons ago or some such." Even as she said it, she looked at the skeleton with a degree of revelation.

"Not died—*killed*." Gallien moved about to see it from other angles.

"That's still not a good argument for a god," Kit remarked. "And I thought this was Corben's area of expertise."

"Oh aye, it was. But the Andaren faith is damned outlandish; hard to forget. There's eh..." The smuggler began counting on his fingers. "There's four of them! *Four gods for each corner of the realm*," he began reciting before losing interest. "They believe their gods actually walked the earth, and that they died defeating... some *evil*. You've heard them curse, aye? *Black Abyss!*" he mimicked dramatically. "They think that's all that awaits them in the afterlife—no gods, no paradise."

"That doesn't sound like a great foundation for a religion," Kitrana opined.

Gallien shrugged with indifference. "True or not, the important part is that they *believe* it. That belief lends value to this. *Great* value."

Kit could hear the hungry opportunist in his voice. "This is not what I was looking for," she said dourly.

Gallien looked as if he had been struck. "Did you not hear what I said? The Andarens have dig sites *everywhere* looking for these," he reported, his voice still soft on the air, as if he might disturb the dead thing. "They would give us all the gems in Andara for this."

"They would *kill* us for this," Kit corrected. "Hells, if you're right, they would kill us just for knowing we'd looked at it."

"They'd kill us for not being Andaren," Gallien said morbidly.

He waved the conversation away. "There's only one of these in all of Verda. *One!* And we just found a *second*."

"There's another?" Only after voicing her question did she recall Drakalis's comment concerning a sketch.

"These," Gallien replied, gesturing at the hulking skeleton, "are the entire reason Andara has its religion. They found one in..." The smuggler clicked his fingers a couple of times. "God Fall," he conjured. "It's somewhere far west of The Gap, deep into Andaren territory," he added as an afterthought. "They literally worship these."

It was clear from his tone that Gallien was already seeing coffers of precious gems and all the marks he could ever dream of.

"How do you know this one is the same as the one they found in God Fall?" she enquired sceptically.

"I've seen the drawings," he reminded.

"*Exactly* like this? Where?"

Gallien shrugged. "I think I was in a tavern in Warth."

"Of course," Kit said sarcastically. "You spend half your life in taverns. Why wouldn't you be getting most of your information from *bards*?"

"Never underestimate a bard," Gallien countered with a cheeky smile. "And you asked *where*," he pointed out. "It was Corben who showed it to me."

Kit's scepticism continued to thrive. "So you haven't actually seen this other *god*," she concluded. "Just sketches."

"Aye," he reaffirmed, finally daring to approach the skeletal remains, his boots treading over the tarpaulin. "I couldn't reach God Fall with an army at my back." He snorted. "How many kings have tried just that?"

"And how did you get your hands on a sketch of something coveted by the Andarens?"

"I'm a Drakalis boy, remember?" he quipped, finally tearing his gaze from the skeleton to flash Kit a cocky grin.

"Corben sketched it?" Kitrana guessed, determined to follow the lead through to its end.

Gallien was shaking his head. "He said it was my father's. How *he* got it, I have no idea," he caveated before she could bombard him with follow-up questions. "What matters is that *this* is definitely one of *them*."

Kitrana crossed her arms and scrutinised the remains. "You're sure?"

Drakalis crouched, bringing the flames of his torch closer to one of the shin bones. "There was a separate sketch, a detailed one of a single bone. It looked *just* like that."

Kit dropped beside the smuggler to better see what he was talking about. It was an intricacy she had failed to see before. The shin bone, like every bone that made up the skeleton, was decorated with small carvings. "What are they?" she asked, head tilting to line them up with her sight.

"Hells if I know," Gallien replied gruffly. "Corben thought they were glyphs of some kind."

"Like a language?"

Drakalis shrugged. "Perhaps. I was always too interested in the value of something to take note of its meaning." Gallien reached out and ran a hand over the nearest bone, his fingers tracing the grooves of the individual glyphs.

"And the water?" Kit pressed. "I've never seen anything like this."

Gallien glanced about, observing the suspended droplets. "Must be the big fella," he surmised.

Kitrana narrowed her eyes and sighed—there would be no convincing her. "It's just a Giant, Gallien. Or, some cousin to that end."

"Like I said: it doesn't matter whether it's true or not. The Andarens believe this is a god, so we *sell* them a god."

Kit's disbelief found new heights. "Sell it to them? What are you going to do? Carry each bone out of here and cart them off to The Saible? You'd be killed a thousand times over before you made it that far. Hells, you'd die just trying to extract the bones from down here. Look at the size of them!"

"We can't leave them here," Gallien protested. "This is the find of a lifetime!"

"It's not the find I'm interested in," Kit said definitively.

"Oh damn your bloody sword!" the smuggler yelled. "This *has* to be more important than some broken blade..." Gallien's voice trailed, as did his eyes.

"Damn the sword?" she repeated, as if the words were a blasphemy. "You can be sure you don't want anyone but *me* to find it." Kitrana groaned in frustration. "You have no idea how important the sword is. What it means to my people. Do you think I would be on this dry godsforsaken earth if I didn't—"

"Kit." Her name was short and sharp as it left the smuggler's mouth.

She followed his gaze down and to herself, where the sword in question rested on her hip. There she discovered an orange hue about the broken blade, as if the steel had trapped some of Gallien's torchlight. Both curious and concerned, Kit lifted the blade an inch until the light caught the rune carved into the centre of the hilt—a vertical line with two four-sided diamonds cutting through the middle of it. While there were numerous legends about the meaning behind the symbol, to Kitrana, it was the sigil of her order, the sigil of the *Battle Maidens*.

Before dark memories could take hold, Kit pushed on and drew the half blade, its jagged tip rising to one side as she held it aloft.

"Has it ever done that before?" Gallien asked.

"No," she answered absently.

Turning the weapon over, she could see that the fiery light was coming from fine shards that had previously been concealed in the steel. It was beautiful, reminding Kit of the luminous trill grass that covered the mountains of the deep.

But there was another light.

A sharp, if slight, turn of her head redirected Gallien to the violet glow behind him. "What is that?" she asked.

The smuggler was the first to reach it, stepping over one of the skeletal legs. He pulled back the leather tarpaulin masking most of the new phenomenon, the flames of his torch clashing with the violet hue. Moving round the leg, Kit was unable to discern the object until Gallien turned around with it in his hand.

"It's an axe," he announced, his voice reflecting his surprise.

"I can see that," the Nimean informed, before sparing a second to inspect the area from which it had been retrieved. "It looks..."

"Newly-forged," Gallien finished, his lips curling into his easy smile.

Kitrana had to agree, her eyes absorbing the weapon's exquisite details. It was certainly unlike any axe she had ever seen. Though easily wielded in one hand, it had the grip space for two, the haft being a little longer than a typical two-handed sword hilt. It looked to be forged from steel but be bound within a snaking coil of bronze. The blade itself was elegant in design, with slender curves and dips, making it deadly from several angles. Like the handle, much of the blade edge was coated in the same bronze with just a hint of gold inlaid to the silver face. Interestingly, there was a grip space in the middle of the axe head, where the haft could be taken in hand for a different style of combat.

It looked too fine a weapon in the hands of a lowly smuggler like Gallien Drakalis, who foolishly sliced his thumb on the blade. "Goddamn it," he cursed, wagging his injured thumb in the air. "It's damned sharp," he grumbled.

"It's the *same*," Kit declared, noticing the smaller details now. "Look." The Nimean pointed out the delicate shards of violet light that danced across the smooth silver and bronze of the axe head.

His bleeding thumb forgotten, Gallien looked from axe to kindred sword. "Maybe it's time you told me about that broken blade of yours."

Kitrana swallowed. That was a tale she had deliberately held back, never offering more than a snippet here and there, and often only after a day in a tavern. "It's a long and... complicated story," she began reluctantly.

Gallien hefted the glowing axe by way of a response.

The Nimean sighed. Whatever their friendship, it had always felt like too much that the smuggler knew she was from the seas, a secret her people had killed many humans to keep over the centuries. She opened her mouth to respond, even though she didn't know where to begin, when a distant *hiss* reverberated down the passage. The dark could not hide the three Vorge slithering towards the portcullis. Their presence known, the creatures bolted for the iron gate, bringing their monstrous features into the light of Gallien's torch.

The portcullis bucked under the force of the trio, raining dust and debris down into the chamber. Their shrieks were that of eagerness, though the fiend with the wounded eye sounded distinctly angry, its rage bubbling over.

The smuggler naturally jumped back, his arm rising to give the axe some elevation. "Friends of yours?"

Kit's only reply was to bend her knees and raise the broken sword to eye level, the blade held in reverse. There was no training for conflict on land, a fact that had cost her numerous fights during her earliest days on her feet. With years under her belt now, however, Kitrana Voden knew exactly how to put her aquatic attributes to best use.

Inevitably, the portcullis gave way—that is, its ancient fixings were torn free of the stone. With a mighty crash it hammered into the floor, sending a wave of vibrations up Kit's legs. Those same legs sprang the Nimean from where she stood and sent her diving into the gap between her enemies. Being more flexible than a human's, Kitrana's bones and joints could overextend without fracture or dislocation, allowing her to twist into the most unorthodox position mid-air.

With one boot, she clipped the head of the Vorge on the left, while her arm rotated round to slice the edge of the broken blade across the central Vorge's face. The fiends parted with speed and force, knocking the Vorge on the right from its path, and saving Gallien from being rammed.

Her momentum at an end, Kit rolled across the floor and came up in a fighting stance. There she faltered, like all else in that long-forgotten chamber. All eyes, be they blue or wholly black, were on the central Vorge that had been slashed by the broken blade. Brighter than the flames of the torches, the creature's body flared up and burnt into cinders and ash.

Kit looked down at the weapon in her hand, the blade still

illuminated by the fiery shards. For a second, and no more, she held her gaze with Gallien, each as stunned as the other.

The Vorge recovered far quicker.

One slithered towards Drakalis while the other used the wall to gain some height and dive down on Kitrana. The Nimean dived aside, avoiding the terrible bulk and deadly claws at the same time. Gallien was more strength than agility and, as always, relied on the closest weapon. The extraordinary axe he had only just taken in hand was let loose from his grip. Accurate though his throw was, he couldn't hope to match the speed of a Vorge.

The creature coiled its body as it propelled itself forwards, avoiding the blade of the axe by inches. Down came its lashing arm, its five fingers splayed to maximise the range of its curved claws. Kitrana called out, naming Gallien by way of a warning, but there was nothing she could do, the distance between them too great. She could but watch those claws rake across the smuggler's face, if not his throat.

And yet, such a tragedy did not come to pass.

The instinct to protect his eyes saw Gallien raise his free hand to meet that of the Vorge's. There was an instance, however, a single heartbeat in time before those claws met flesh, when the smuggler's hand went from being alone and exposed, to once again wielding the remarkable axe. His grip was wrapped around the haft and high, where the blade's interior arched to accept a single hand.

The Vorge lost all four fingers and the majority of its palm when it struck the axe instead. Both Gallien and the Vorge were taken by surprise at the turn in events, but still the creature was quicker to respond, its pain yet to strike hot. And so the smuggler was shoved by the fiend's whipping tail and flung into the bones.

Stunned by the extraordinary feat of magic, Kit lost track of her own foe, which had curled around on its powerful snaking body to face her. Merciless claws raked at the stone where she had been crouching, her instinctive evasion just enough to see her avoid injury. Still, the creature came again and again, slashing at the air about her, forcing the Nimean into the curved wall.

The blade still aglow, Kitrana thrust it at her enemy. Fearing its devastating edge, the monster of the deep retreated, its upper body arching back while its tail whipped around to strike Kit's sword arm.

The blade was lost.

It clattered across the floor, far from reach. For one precious moment, Kitrana watched the broken weapon skid across the stone, wondering—hoping—that it would reappear in her waiting hand as Gallien's axe had. But there it remained, just as isolated as she was.

In a blur of dark scales, the Vorge grabbed her with its strong arms and yanked her off her feet towards the passage. Kitrana reached out hopelessly for the blade she had carried for so long, the blade she had killed to possess in the first place, and screamed in defiance. There was little she could do, however, against the sheer force of a fully grown Vorge. With abandon it hurtled into the passage, intending to take her back to the water.

"Gallien!" she cried, spying the smuggler as he clambered out of the godly bones.

"Kit!" he yelled back.

He tried to run towards her but found his way blocked by the Vorge. The smuggler waved both the axe and broken sword to keep the creature at bay. It was the last she saw of Gallien Drakalis before the chamber and all inside were gone from her view.

Kitrana landed blow after blow into the monster that gripped her but it counted for naught. Instead, she threw her weight about and unbalanced the fiend, sending them both into the wall. Again, it counted for naught, the Vorge's thick tail capable of pushing them back on track.

Plunged into the underwater ruins, her body transitioned as it would, bringing the Nimean into harmony with the water. It was there, where she was better versed in aquatic combat, that she let muscle memory and flexible bones guide her counterattack.

After diving beneath the spiral of broken stairs, where the jagged crevice lay waiting in the wall of the ancient tower, Kitrana kicked her legs out to increase their already impressive speed.

Then she twisted her hips while driving the blade of her hand into the side of the Vorge's head, where its injured eye had been partially blinded. The creature was sent off course and unable to prevent the Nimean from forcing it beneath her.

Changing tack, she decided to show the fiend a display of *real* speed.

Like a spear launched from the hand of Atradon Herself—the goddess of the seas—Kitrana Voden rammed the Vorge into the rubble of broken stone at the base of the ruined chamber. The creature involuntarily spat blood into the water as it was used to push through and into the rest of the tower below. Unable to see past the Vorge, Kit forced her foe into a shelf of stone that instantly parted them with a shock of pain.

Momentarily dazed, Kit floated towards the other side of the tower until her head lightly knocked against an intrusion of natural rock. Her view sharpened in time to see the Vorge diving towards her, its rows of teeth bared. Kicking off from the stone, the Nimean evaded that hungry maw and swam over it before rushing down, past the fiend.

Navigating the ruins at speed, Kit could hear and feel the shrieks that stalked her. Here and there, where the corners were sharp, the beast nearly collided with her, its claws—just once—streaking down her cloak.

When, at last, she was free of the tower and returned to old Harendun, she dived for the entrance that connected the ruined city to the ocean.

But the Vorge was just behind her.

With no weapon, fighting the creature with her bare hands was going to be brutal and would likely leave her bleeding out in the water, where she would only attract more predators. Her only chance was to outswim it.

Clearing the cave and the cliff face altogether, the Nimean made for open water. Rays of sunlight pierced the ocean's surface, lending a majestic hue to the vista. The Vorge's ugly form was the antithesis of that majesty. Its partially scaled skin and half humanoid body were something from nightmares when coupled with its black eyes and bristling claws.

Heading towards that dark wall of deep sea, Kitrana began to think of the broken blade she had left behind—even more so than she thought of Gallien. The smuggler had led a life on the edge of death for as long as she had known him, but that weapon meant *everything* to her people and their way of life. She knew then that she must turn back. She would have to kill the Vorge in pursuit, whatever the cost, and return to that chamber.

Turning her momentum into a quick spin, the Nimean now faced her oncoming foe with renewed determination. She had no idea how she was going to put the creature down, but she knew she would.

Kitrana flinched as a length of siden steel rushed past her ear, hurled from the deep behind her. The spear cut through the water, its haft glistening in the columns of sunlight, before finding its end in the Vorge's head. The beast continued forwards as its body flipped backwards end over end.

A sinking feeling took root in Kit's stomach.

Turning around, her feet hanging beneath her, Kitrana looked upon a phalanx of Merdian soldiers, cousins to her own people. They quickly spread out, creating a semi-circle that guarded her against the deep. Encased in armour of whale bone, they wielded swords and spears of dull siden steel. Beyond them, almost faded from sight, were their mounts, the saddled Karathasaurs.

Judging by the supplies tethered in seaweed nets to the distant Karathasaurs, Kit guessed the group of soldiers to be scouts from Atlas. They had likely come to watch the invasion above—a source of entertainment to all ocean dwellers.

Of the group, the only female advanced, a predatory grin on her face. Like all her people, the Merdian was metallic bronze of skin and bald beneath her sloping helm. "What do we have here?" she signed.

"She's Nimean," one of the males in the group pointed out, his eyes having found some of the thick blue tattoos that poked out of Kit's sleeves and trousers.

"Nimean," the leader echoed, her grin somehow finding room to broaden all the more. "We really have scattered you to the darkest corners of the seas," she went on.

"Look at her clothes," another remarked, his fingers cutting through the water. "She has taken refuge among the mud walkers."

Kitrana wanted to interject, to give them her name and title—a title she had hard earned and should have been respected by all ocean dwellers. But she could expect something worse than death if she did. They would peel flesh from bone to get answers out of her. To get the blade...

The blade!

It was gone, lost to her in the tomb. A great weight of hopelessness overcame her, a shadow that stung with barbs of shame for her carelessness.

She had failed.

No. Kitrana refused to let that sink in, to face defeat. She was a battle maiden of the Swordsworn—she was the line that could not be crossed. It wasn't over until she had the sword made whole and her people with it. One hand began to clench by her side as she formulated a very rough plan to see her returned to the tomb. The odds were against her, and obviously so, but she was able to quieten the alarm in her mind and replace it with grit.

The lead Merdian swam around the interior of her soldiers' line, her eyes never leaving Kitrana. Her proximity evoked fear in each of the soldiers as she passed them, their muscles tensing to keep them perfectly still. Kit had seen as much before, well aware that the Merdian matriarchy was a brutal one compared to her own culture. Indeed, she could see scars that laced the arms and face of every scout.

"What is your name, surface lover?" the Merdian female demanded, floating directly in front of her now.

"My name is Kitrana Voden," she declared with her hands, chin raised and posture rigid.

"Well, Kitrana Voden, you are my prisoner now." That wicked smile was so quick to return. "You should have stayed up there."

Kit visualised the blow she intended to land across the Merdian's jaw. It wouldn't be enough to take her out of the fight, but it would daze her long enough to claim the trident she wielded. The others would attack, of course, but one of them would feel the three-pronged bite of Kit's new weapon and the others would struggle to get their aim past their leader—they wouldn't dare risk injuring her to kill Kitrana. More of the imminent battle would have come together in the Nimean's mind had the Merdian not continued.

"Perhaps you would have been better to stay in Nimala and die with the rest of your people. You would certainly have suffered less," she added menacingly.

Her plan scattered like fish in a shadow. The statement simply stumped her.

The female Merdian scrutinised her expression before revelation illuminated her sharp features. "You don't know," she surmised with amusement. "How long have you been in such shallow waters, little Nimean?"

"You're lying," Kit managed with one hand.

The Merdian looked elated, one hand raising to sign to the others. "She doesn't know!" The water about the scouts vibrated with their laughter.

"You're lying!" Kit accused again, a snarl forming about her lips.

The Merdian whipped up her trident, its arrow heads now levelled at Kitrana's throat. "The war is over. It ended when the Light Lord of Atlas brought one of the deep dragons to your gates."

"Impossible," Voden snapped, with no care for the silvyr tips at her throat. "They cannot be tamed."

"*We* tamed one," the Merdian boasted.

Kitrana felt those words as she might have a physical blow, and her hopelessness returned tenfold. She felt sick, disorientated. She was hardly aware that the Merdians were forming a sphere around her.

Her senses only returned in time to register the trident's ferrule hammering onto her head.

Then there was nothing.

10
NO CHOICE AT ALL

80 Years Ago...

Daijen awoke to the sound of thunder.

His eyes snapped open in the gloom of a small chamber. The pain was immediate, like waves crashing against the inside of his skull. Disorientated, he rolled to one side and fell off the edge of a narrow cot. He landed on cold wet stone as a new shock of pain ran through his knees and hands.

Looking up, through the strands of white hair that masked his face, he could see that the dawn had broken but its light was struggling to pierce the storm that raged outside. The rain showered his floor, finding its way in through the slitted window beside his cot. There was no glass to shut it out or the cold wind that had Daijen searching for his cloak and furs.

The chamber was just large enough to fit the cot from wall to wall and so he soon found his belongings dumped unceremoniously beside the door. A wave of nausea tried to overthrow him as he stood to don his cloak and furs. Running a hand over his face and head, Daijen was sure he would find a serious injury or trace of blood.

What he found was a memory.

The bald initiate... Slait. Daijen closed his eyes and saw the brute pressed on top of him, hands around his throat. Without thinking, he rubbed his sore neck and tilted his head tentatively one way then the next.

Two heavy knocks against the door jolted him and he naturally reached for the sword that wasn't on his hip. "If I have to knock a third time," an abrasive voice warned, "the door's coming off its hinges."

Daijen licked his lips and squared his shoulders, though it wouldn't help him to appear any taller next to one of the initiates. Opening the door that he had half expected to be locked from the outside, he was met by a fellow Andaren who filled most of the frame.

"Look at you on your feet," the initiate said mockingly. "You're lucky the master stepped in when he did or you'd be in two different places by now."

"Laif." The name came out of Daijen almost involuntary.

Laif raised one thick white eyebrow. "You still have some sense about you. Good. Kovun was sure you'd wake up without your own name." The initiate barked a laugh. "Follow me," he bade.

Afraid he would get lost, Daijen didn't even give his chamber a second look before falling in behind the tall Andaren. Torches fixed to the walls illuminated the way. There were many doors, all closed to maintain the fortress's secrets, and many passages that Laif ignored.

"It's a labyrinth," Daijen uttered.

Laif glanced one eye over his shoulder. "Ka'vairn is an ancient beast of blood and stone. It will devour you if you let it."

Those deeply unsettling words didn't have chance to take root before the initiate pushed open a set of double doors, flooding the passage with natural light. Daijen squinted before adapting, his head still protesting life itself. Sheets of rain fell from the stormy heavens and bathed the balcony in cold water.

The weather didn't appear to bother Laif, who strolled out onto the balcony, head upturned to the dark clouds with a smile on his face. When Daijen didn't immediately trail him, the initiate gestured for him to step into the rain and accompany him to the rail. Raising his hood against the rain, he joined Laif by the edge, where the rail was visibly chipped and in a state of disrepair. Indeed, it seemed much of Ka'vairn was in need of reconstruction. In the north, where the fortress rose up into a collection of towers, he could see a web of scaffolding that had been erected to do just that, but even the scaffolding looked to have been long abandoned.

Laif regarded him, taking particular note of his hood, and chuckled lightly to himself. "If you survive the day, you'll come to enjoy this as much as I do."

Daijen was both unnerved and confused by the statement, but his head still hurt too much to make conversation of it. Instead, he let his vision drift out, taking temporary solace in the folds of his hood.

While the valley and forest beyond Ka'vairn were hidden behind a grey mist of rain, Daijen could see the courtyard below and the duelling circle at its centre. The ring held his gaze a moment longer, as if he was looking to make certain that neither Ilithranda nor Elivar were still lying flat on the stone.

"They survived as you did," Laif declared. "It's tradition."

Daijen turned his head to see the initiate past his hood. "Tradition?"

"No one passes through the doors of Ka'vairn for the first time with their wits about them. I myself stepped into that ring and was carried inside, bleeding and broken."

Feeling the dull ache in his head, Daijen was less than impressed. "Brutal tradition," he commented.

Laif let loose a hearty laugh. "You don't know what brutal is. There were no initiates here when I arrived. I stepped into that ring with *Kastiek*."

Daijen thought of the Vahlken and his Aegre, Strix, conjuring the image of the two sweeping over the trees of The Dain'duil to confront the trio the previous day. Kastiek had possessed a quietude about him that suggested he was dangerous. Daijen would have volunteered to fight all of the initiates before stepping into the duelling ring with him.

Laif looked down on him. "Survive the pits and you will taste his steel before long," he said ominously.

One word opened a chasm in Daijen's stomach. "Pits?"

Laif clapped him on the back. "Follow me."

No sooner had they entered the fortress than Elivar appeared, and in the company of Soyra who, being a head taller than Elivar, made the warrior appear somewhat diminutive.

"Daijen!" Elivar exclaimed, genuinely happy to see him.

"This one talks a lot," Soyra asserted, her tone more than enough to convey her annoyance.

"I think Slait might have choked a few words out of this one," Laif quipped.

Elivar stepped in beside Daijen. "You fought Slait?" He sounded somewhere between impressed and concerned.

"I *survived* Slait," Daijen corrected.

Elivar landed a heavy but reassuring hand on his shoulder. "He'll survive *you* next time."

Soyra snickered in front. "Slait will *kill* him next time."

"That's if the pits don't kill them first," Laif reminded.

Elivar looked to Daijen and mouthed the word *pits* to him, his expression a question. Daijen could only shake his head and keep his feet moving one after the other. If he stopped to really think about everything the initiates had said, he would realise that today might be his very last.

After descending numerous floors, the passages began to open up and the hallways took on grander heights. Entering the largest of these, the ceiling so high it could have accommodated a catapult, Daijen noted that, to his right, one of the tall doors was partially open, revealing a sliver of the courtyard and rain outside. To his left, the direction in which they all turned, was an identical set of double doors. They were so large it seemed an impossibility that anyone could open them, yet Soyra and Laif each pulled one of the wooden slabs with a single hand.

The palatial chamber therein looked to have once been awe-inspiring, monumental even, but it knew as much ruination as the fortress's exterior. It was crowded with shadows, and the tall and slender windows rattled as they were assaulted by the torrential rain. The four supporting pillars still stood strong but they did not stand proud, their surfaces streaked with grime. Mud, dust, and all manner of debris blanketed the stone floor, concealing much of the pattern that had been mosaicked into it.

So vast was the chamber that the ringed table at its heart, and accompanying chairs scattered about it, seemed inconsequential. Indeed, Daijen might not have noticed them had Laif and Soyra not been leading them towards them. Further still, and almost wholly steeped in shadow, was a dais that housed a squat and empty throne.

"The Hall of Handuin," Elivar uttered, his eyes cast high.

Daijen followed his gaze and realised he was inside one of the many stories he had grown up hearing about. It was humbling as much as it was terrifying.

By the time they reached the circular table, Ilithranda was entering the chamber behind them, and with Kovun in step beside her. Daijen offered her a warm smile even though he knew it would not be returned. Seeing her face, however, he wasn't sure she *could* smile.

Kovun had delivered quite the beating before exacting Ka'vairn's tradition, leaving Ilithranda with a cut and swollen lip, a bruised left eye, and a scuff across her right cheek. Her chin still remained raised, however, lending her a regal appearance that made much more sense in light of her name.

The trio were only together for a handful of seconds before The Valtorak entered via the same doors, his tall staff in step with him. As he approached, the three initiates departed, passing their master with a subtle bow of the head.

"You will follow me now," The Valtorak commanded, his step never pausing.

Elivar and Daijen shared a moment of apprehension while Ilithranda immediately followed the master of Ka'vairn. He led the trio past the squat and neglected throne, where an unassuming door waited in the shadows. Its creaking hinges were exaggerated by the cavernous hall, but they soon left it all behind, taking to the labyrinth once again.

They walked in silence for several minutes, until Daijen was sure he could never find his way back and up, for they descended all the more, seemingly into the mountain.

When, at last, they arrived in what appeared to be an antechamber, The Valtorak moved aside so they might see the circular door of black iron that sat in the natural rock of The Hellion Mountains. Upon its dark face was an eagle's claw, the sigil of the Vahlkens and the long dead house of Handuin himself.

The Valtorak gripped his staff with both hands and held it close to his chest. "What you know of this order is naught but myths built upon facts, mere rumours that pass between soldiers, and the suspicions of highborns. Even the emperor does not know how Vahlkens come into being. The magic that Handuin commanded was his own, a mystery to even the grand clerics and their alchemy. Before his death, Handuin passed on his knowledge to one, a tradition that brings that exalted line to me. While you have slumbered, I have brewed that which will test your very soul."

His speech at an end, The Valtorak rested his staff against the wall and pulled open the iron slab with both hands, revealing a door as thick as a man's torso. Like the others, Daijen's attention was drawn to that which lay beyond.

The cavern was half the size of Handuin's grand hall, its arching ceiling jagged with glistening stalactites. It was illuminated by a large and central pit that housed a pool of luminous liquid, its surface radiating a myriad of colours. Indeed, it was hard to look directly at the pool within, so bright that it outshone the torches fixed to the walls of the ante-chamber.

Staff in hand again, The Valtorak gestured for them to enter first. Even Ilithranda hesitated, a fact that seemed to keep all three of them rooted for a moment. "Honour cannot be forced upon one," the master said. "It must be *taken*."

Elivar took a breath and was the first to step over the rounded lip and enter the cavern. Daijen followed Ilithranda before watching The Valtorak swing the door back into place, sealing them all inside. Laif's words came back to Daijen, reminding him that Ka'vairn was a beast of blood and stone. Those words, at least, made him understand why he felt like he *was* in the belly of some creature.

The master of Ka'vairn slowly navigated the uneven floor of the cavern until he was able to make his way around the central pool. "What do you know of Handuin?" he asked, his own gaze taken by the shimmering water.

Daijen knew the answer to his question but his attention was stolen by a small alcove dug out of the wall on his right. It wasn't well constructed, the edges hewn and rounded, but its overall shape was somewhere between a circle and a square.

It was the contents, of course, that truly captured Daijen's mind. Was it a bone? It looked like a bone, though from which part of the body he couldn't guess. Nor could he guess who or what it once belonged to, being easily as long as his leg.

From end to end, all the way around, it appeared to be inscribed with runes he couldn't begin to understand. He was equally puzzled by its significance, though its status inside the alcove, displayed horizontally on a pedestal, suggested it was of great importance.

"He was the first Vahlken," Elivar answered, breaking his momentary reverie.

"And before that?" The Valtorak pressed.

Elivar opened his mouth reflexively but had no response.

"He was a grand cleric," Ilithranda stated, though her confidence faltered under the master's sudden scrutiny. "He had to be," she went on, defending her deduction. "Only the grand clerics have knowledge of magic."

"And from whom," The Valtorak probed, "do the grand clerics learn their potion mastery?"

Revelation struck Ilithranda first. "The warlocks," she said.

The name sharpened Daijen's attention, as it did Elivar's. The warlocks, their great works recorded in the scriptures of the

Arkalon, were as much a mystery to the world as the Vahlken themselves. Though he had given them little thought during his short life, Daijen knew they were revered at the very top of their divine order: they who lived in deep seclusion, where they might unravel the secrets of magic imparted by the very bones of the gods.

"Yes," The Valtorak confirmed. "Handuin was a warlock. In his absence, their holy circle was reduced from four to three. Walking away from his sacred duty was punishable by death, but he knew the great Ahnir had instructed him to do so. Can you imagine such a thing? To hear the voice of a god whisper in your ear."

Ahnir be raised, Daijen prayed inwardly, the words coming to him as instinctively as breathing. Was there any Andaren who could hear that name and not offer up that prayer? A prayer that those dry bones find new life and restore the heavens. He even noticed Ilithranda and Elivar make a similar head movement, their eyes closing longer than an average blink.

Though he did not answer The Valtorak's question, the answer was unequivocally *no*. In truth, he found it hard to imagine any of the four gods actually speaking to a person. Leaving his faith where it was for the time being, Daijen focused once again on the master of Ka'vairn.

"Should you survive these waters," The Valtorak continued, "I will tell you why he established this order. I will tell you *why* the Vahlken are needed in this world."

Daijen looked at the luminous water again, trepidation creeping through his bones. "We have to go in there?" he asked, a lamb before the jaws of a lion.

Having rounded the pit, The Valtorak came to a stop directly in front of him, his violet eyes following the arch of his hooked nose. "One way or another, Daijen Saeth, you face death. Will you risk the Black Abyss in those waters? Or will you turn back and meet your end on Kastiek's blade? It is his sworn duty to protect Ka'vairn for all his days. He will not let you leave with all that you have seen and heard in these walls." The master straightened up, his stark gaze still fixed on Daijen. "If it aids in your decision, know this: Kastiek will kill you quickly. The pit will not be so merciful."

Daijen felt dizzy with such bleak choices. Either way, The Valtorak's words had silenced him.

"You are to enter in the same order you entered the duelling ring," the master explained, continuing as if he hadn't just told the trio that they stood on the precipice of death, on the very edge of that Black Abyss. "Elivar of House T'saren, you are to be the first."

Elivar's usual bravado was notably absent. "I just... I just get in?"

"First, you must be harnessed." The Valtorak used the end of his staff to indicate the leather straps and chain that had lain unnoticed beside the pool.

Elivar picked it up, holding it high to better see the contraption. "Why do I need a..." The Andaren warrior stopped himself from asking the question when the grim answer came to him. "I see," he muttered, glancing at Daijen.

"Remove your clothes," The Valtorak said bluntly.

Elivar was taken aback but for no more than a couple of seconds before he adopted the hard expression of a seasoned veteran. Without a word, he stripped down to his silvery skin and fastened the harness about his thighs and waist.

The Valtorak took a long and deliberate breath as he watched Elivar stand upon the raised edge of the pit, his toes bathing in flickering colours. "From these waters you will be reborn a Vahlken. Or you will *perish*," he added as a matter of fact. "There is nothing you can do to sway what happens next. Your fate is already written."

Elivar gave no sign that he had heard the master's words, his focus drawn in to a point now. It seemed a lifetime that he stood there, staring down at the waters. Daijen had come to enjoy Elivar's company, and would even call him a friend after their time together, but he couldn't fathom what thoughts were passing through his mind. Whatever they were, they found a crack in that honed focus and allowed him to flash that easy confident smile at Daijen.

He stepped in.

Whether he thought it was shallow or not, the pit accepted Elivar whole, taking him from sight. Only the chain remained, tethering him to the outside world. Daijen and Ilithranda moved to the edge and peered in while The Valtorak remained somewhat removed, aloof even, as he circled and watched.

Then they waited.

It seemed that time had come to a stop. Seconds felt like minutes and minutes stretched into hours. The only thing Daijen knew for sure was that Elivar had been without air for a deadly amount of time.

When his anxiety bubbled over, he looked to the master for guidance and blurted, "What do we do?"

"Handuin's magic will do as it will," The Valtorak replied unhelpfully. "He could be under there for hours, days even. Soyra was down there for near on a week. For me, it was mere minutes. It is said that Handuin was submerged for *years*."

"Years..." The word escaped Daijen and took any last shreds of hope with it. He was going to die in that pit.

"What's happening?" Ilithranda's dire tone turned all eyes back to the waters.

The pit bubbled here and there, disturbing the myriad lights that played across its glassy surface. Then it began to fade, its innate glow ebbing away. More so, the water began to darken from within, the white streaked with black veins. The bubbling increased, spilling some of the water over the edge.

"What's happening?" Ilithranda demanded.

The Valtorak sighed, his violet eyes narrowed in disappointment. "The chain," he rasped. In their hesitation, his gaze snapped to them. "Pull him out," he barked.

Ilithranda gripped the chain behind Daijen and together they began to heave Elivar from the pit. Using some of the strain to fight his mounting fear, Daijen gritted his teeth and focused on the single task of retrieving his friend, the first of his kin to show him any kindness in many years. Try as he might to scrub those thoughts and feelings away, they gnawed at him, bringing tears to his eyes.

Upon breaking the surface, Elivar's appearance renewed their strength and they pulled with all they had. When, at last, he was partially laid over the lip of the pit, Daijen and Ilithranda hurried to finish the job by gripping his arms. Laying him on his back, Daijen already knew the worst had happened, for Elivar's skin, so cold it could have been mistaken for the mountain stone, had dulled to a deathly grey.

Yet he blinked.

"He's alive!" Daijen exclaimed, his hope burning bright. "Elivar!"

The Andaren offered no response to his name.

"Elivar?" Ilithranda tried.

Daijen tapped his friend's cheek a few times. "Elivar, it's me."

He blinked again, his vacant stare directed at the cavern above.

"I don't understand," Daijen muttered, his hope freezing over.

"Is this part of the process?" Ilithranda asked, turning to The Valtorak.

The violet gaze of Ka'vairn's master found only Elivar at his feet. "He is dead."

So absolute was his tone and so bold his response that Daijen and Ilithranda could only look at The Valtorak in shock. His statement given, The Valtorak turned around where he might focus on the pit instead.

Daijen looked from Elivar to The Valtorak's back. "Dead?" he echoed incredulously. "He's *alive*," Daijen insisted.

The Valtorak crouched to inspect the waters up close. "His heart is still beating, yes, and he retains enough brain function to blink, but that is all Elivar of House T'saren now boasts."

"How can you say that?" Daijen spat. "He's alive! We need to help him!"

"Daijen," Ilithranda cautioned.

"He needs help," Daijen urged, doubling down. "There must be something you can do. Some magic. Anything!"

The Valtorak responded with no more than a glance before the pit took his attention again. The cruel disregard irked Daijen, lancing him like a spear. As it had in Lornak's office at The Saible, the quietude that had long dwelled in Daijen snapped, forcing him to his feet in a spate of righteous anger.

Daijen had intended to turn the master around and make him look upon Elivar's ruin, but his conviction lacked the strength and skill to see it done. The Valtorak rose sharply and shrugged his hand off. In the same motion, he shot a closed fist into Daijen's chest, taking him from his feet.

"Touch me again, Daijen Saeth, and you will share his fate," the master warned.

Ilithranda remained by Elivar's side while Daijen recovered, one hand pressed to the pain in his chest. He watched, a cold dread sinking into his bones, as The Valtorak came to tower over him.

"Do not think me cruel nor uncaring. I know what he has been through, what he has *lived* through in those waters. It is a mercy to consider him one with the dead. Though it offers little solace for myself, for it is *I* who must see him to the Black Abyss. Not *you*."

"What he's lived through?" Ilithranda voiced, her words catching.

The Valtorak held her gaze a moment before answering. "To you and me, it has been mere minutes. But Elivar has seen *eons* beneath that surface."

Eons... The word blanketed Daijen's mind, subduing his thoughts.

"It will be the same for you," the master informed coldly. "It will either transform you, or *break* your mind."

Daijen returned to his crouch over Elivar, seeing him differently now. Those eyes, so distant and glazed, had seen millennia piled upon millennia. He could see now that his friend was gone, that Elivar had been cleaved from his own body. He *was* dead.

Ilithranda saw it too, a single tear streaking her face.

Daijen considered a comforting hand, and even raised one to offer, but withheld it after seeing her eyes slide towards him. Upset or not, he could still detect the barbs behind those eyes and knew she would reject any solace he might offer. Instead, he turned back to the master of Ka'vairn.

"He's gone then," Daijen accepted reluctantly, blinking his own tears into existence.

Slowly, the master's eyes slid across and down to Elivar. From his belt, The Valtorak retrieved a straight-edged blade, the pommel a rounded ball in the clutches of an eagle's talon. Without a word, he crouched beside Elivar, his free hand moving to shade the warrior's eyes.

"Rest now," he uttered.

As the blade sank quietly into his chalky flesh, biting through his chest and heart, The Valtorak ran his free hand down Elivar's face, closing his eyes for evermore. Daijen could hardly spare a gasp. Instead, he watched wide-eyed as his friend truly slipped from the world of the living.

"Now begone," the master ordered, rising to his superior height. "And take his body with you. I must begin again," he added with irritation, his focus already returning to the spoiled waters.

While some of Daijen's ire had been knocked out of him, there was still enough left in his boiling blood to see him rise to his feet and try again. Only Ilithranda stopped him, one arm whipping out to catch him across the chest.

She brought her lips close to his ear. "Hold on to it." Her directive was firm and, perhaps spoken for herself as well. "Keep it here," she instructed, knotting her fist into his chest. "Let it go at the right time."

Daijen took a long and calming breath, his eyes still fixed on The Valtorak's back.

"Help me with Elivar," Ilithranda said, her voice helping to cut through his fury.

It seemed so undignified, so unbefitting of a warrior of Elivar's station, yet they had no choice but to release him from the harness and carry him out, arms over shoulders.

It would be a long walk back.

11
STRANDED

GALLIEN DESPERATELY DRAGGED THE CIRCULAR COVER INTO PLACE, BUT HE failed to do so before the creature's only remaining hand reached out of the port, its claws searching for him. The smuggler pressed the cover into the arm, trapping it in place, but the fiend was strong and determined to bring him back down into the dark.

While the threat of the broken sword had kept the sea monster at bay long enough to ascend the rungs, Gallien had abandoned the blade the second he reached the top of the ladder, his grip required to pull him over the edge. Now, when disintegrating the creature would save his life, it remained too far to retrieve.

It was then that he registered the cool haft of the axe in his other hand, as if the weapon knew he was in need of it. He didn't hesitate to chop down and cut off the beast's arm, just below the elbow. It screeched in agony, now bereft of both hands, and fell into the gloom below.

The circular slab fell into place, sealing the tomb, and Drakalis lay over it, his eyes cast to the blue above. His chest heaved with exhaustion and new injuries began to make themselves known. He ignored it all, thinking only of Kit.

He relived the scene, watching her as the monster hauled her into the darkness. Alive or dead, she had gone where he could not follow.

He knocked his head back into the ground, his frustration and anger bubbling over until pain alone could focus his thoughts.

Kit was gone.

The smuggler told himself—reminded himself—that any emotions he had felt for her were simply convenient. And the Nimean certainly knew the risks that came with their line of work.

Lies, of course. But they would patch the wound for a time.

"Get up, Drakalis," he muttered to himself. "Get up."

When, finally, he found the energy to sit up, he hefted the axe. There wasn't a single attribute about the weapon that he could explain. Why was it in such pristine condition after eons down there? Why or how was it able to disappear and instantly reappear in his hand? Why did it glow in the presence of Kit's broken sword?

The last question directed his attention to the blade. Putting the axe down, he stood up and retrieved the broken weapon. The smuggler held it for no more than a few seconds before the orange embers scattered across the blade faded to nothing. Confused, he turned it over and found the ordinary steel of an ordinary blade.

Wondering if the violet shards had similarly faded in the blade of the axe, Gallien turned back to examine it. It was gone. He looked around—though there wasn't much of an area to search—and, despite being alone in the courtyard, it was simply gone. In its absence, it seemed Kit's blade could not hold its glow. He had to wonder if its ability to disintegrate its foes was also gone; a theory he couldn't test.

Drakalis was brought firmly into the present as he heard the ringing of a large and heavy bell. He had last heard that bell as a soldier of the king, when they had previously seized Harendun. Like then, the ringing was followed by a chorus of cheers and hollers.

The city had been taken.

In the coming days and weeks it would be turned into a foothold from which the human army would spread across eastern Andara and work its way north, towards The Gap. From there, they would lay siege to The Saible—a fortress that had never been claimed.

Gallien dismissed it all at once. In the coming days and weeks, while the Eradoran forces were *planning* their easterly march, the Andarens would come down on them like a hammer on an anvil. The smuggler had no intention of being in Harendun when that happened.

He placed the broken blade in his satchel and gave the courtyard one last look over before departing, the axe remaining elusive. With naught but a broken blade—and no means to prove its magical properties—he left the area absent any treasure or relic.

And he left without Kit.

In something of a daze, a pall of depression coming over him, Gallien wandered through the streets, barely aware of the Eradoran soldiers who sang and celebrated about him. They too hardly seemed to notice him, who walked amongst them absent any trappings of a soldier. It soon became apparent that he was one among many who now walked Harendun's streets without the king's iron about them. The sailors, who had brought so many from shore to shore, now took to pillaging the city as much as any who bore the scale-patterned sword of the king.

Seeing marauders who called themselves sailors streaming through the city, Gallien was forced to consider one pirate in particular. He had nothing to offer Captain Addison of The Raven. His old mentor—the wretch that he was—would, instead, get his coin by delivering him bound and gagged to the Padoshi of Thedaria.

In a bid to avoid a raucous group of soldiers, Gallien ducked down a side street and ascended a set of narrow steps that led up to a small balcony offering a view over the city walls and the beach. There he saw the fleet of ships that had set sail from Caster Hold and brought the armies of Erador to Andara's shore.

His options were few.

There wasn't a ship in the king's navy that would grant him passage and he didn't have nearly enough marks to pay his way onto one of the privately owned vessels. He could offer to aid in crewing any ship of course, but Captain Addison had allies everywhere, and where he lacked allies he had those indebted to him.

The smuggler almost laughed at the idea of walking back to Erador. Even if he survived beyond Harendun and the trek north, he would never make it past The Tower of Argunsuun and no-man's-land.

His depression growing, Gallien abandoned the high perch and found his way back to the streets. No one seemed to care about the bodies that littered the ground or the homes that had been invaded or torched. Everywhere Drakalis looked he saw the remains of peoples' lives, lives that had been destroyed in so few days.

Not far from the Sea Gate, the smuggler found his way blocked by the sheer number of soldiers crammed between the buildings. Though he wished to see what had drawn so many to the spot, he didn't need an elevated position to see the red dragon that blotted out the sun. Four strong legs put the rubble of Harendun to the test, its barbed tail curled up and round the remains of a shattered tower. Its head, however, remained bowed, below the sea of sloping helmets and upright spears.

An ounce of determination was all his curiosity needed to set him to climb a stack of crates and see for himself what was happening. He almost immediately wished he hadn't.

The dragon's head was low for a reason. Its jaw—comparable in size to a shire horse—was steadily tearing through the body of an Aegre. The eagle's blood coated most of the dragon's face, shading its red scales. Soldiers watched from all sides, though their attention was arrested by the dragon's rider, who appeared from the other side of the dead mutated bird. Gallien naturally pressed himself into the wall and crouched to make himself small.

Twice now he had seen this Rider, his blond hair still knotted high on his crown and highlighted against the red scales that layered his vambraces and pauldrons. His dusty cloak hung limp about him, touching his heels, and his sword remained sheathed on his hip. Satisfied that all eyes were on him, he thrust one hand high into the air and presented the crowd with the bronze-coloured short-sword he had taken from the dead Vahlken.

The soldiers let loose a roar that might have rivalled a dragon's had the dragon itself not paused in its feast and cracked the air with its thunderous voice. It was enough to silence the revelry and give the Rider the attention he required.

"Harendun is ours!" he bellowed, exciting the masses for a moment. "It is with our blood and steel that the enemy has been pushed back from their own lands! Their *precious* Vahlken," he said mockingly. "My sword thirsts for their blood! And their *ferocious* Aegres? My dragon will scorch them down to the bone!"

The soldiers lapped it up, their confidence and loyalty in the palm of his hand. "VANDER! VANDER! VANDER!" they chanted, the name coming to Gallien like an old memory.

With a satiated smile, the Rider batted the air with his hands. "Herragax. If you would..."

Gore hanging from its jaws, the red dragon stretched its neck and sank its fangs into the Aegre's throat. Even at the back of the crowd, Drakalis heard the bones break and the flesh tear as the eagle's head came free of its body. It seemed too gentle for such a creature as a dragon, but Herragax released the head without destroying it, leaving it at Vander's feet.

"Spear!" the Dragon Rider snapped, his hand already out and waiting.

The closest soldier obliged, if fearfully so, and hurried to offer his spear. Taking it in hand, Vander thrust it into the Aegre's exposed throat and up into its skull. It was with a strength no ordinary man could attain that the Dragon Rider then raised the severed head into the air, displaying it as he had the short-sword.

"For Erador!" he shouted.

Gallien used the ensuing celebration to retreat from the scene. This was everything he remembered about war, and more. He had seen dragons and their Riders fly into battle before, but they were few and far between, with most battles being won by numbers and strategy. Still, he had always thought of them as heroes: recalled them as heroes even. There seemed nothing heroic about what he had just seen, or what he had seen when that same Rider had killed an Eradoran soldier for taking his kill.

His mood having struck rock bottom now, Gallien Drakalis decided there was only one thing left to do.

He went in search of a strong drink.

12
PROTECTING DESTINY

"Damn you, Daijen Saeth." The words might have left Androma pitched at a whisper, but they were emphasised by the stamping of her staff into the hard earth.

For the second day in a row, she had departed Harendun and made for the hills that rolled across the base of The Orsindil Mountains. Had she still her sight, she would have been looking out on Andara's eastern coast and the many Eradoran warships docked there. Instead, she inhaled the sea air that carried the scent of Harendun's ruin. Androma knew the scent well; a city brought down by dragon fire.

Thinking of Herragax, the old Rider had to wonder if the dragon's continued presence was the cause of Daijen's absence. While possible, it seemed unlikely that Daijen was avoiding a fight. Something *else* had detained him.

Feeling the weight of time against her, Androma began the slow trek back down the slopes, her staff tapping the ground from left to right in front of her. Upon finding the coastal path, the route she had used to reach the hills, the old Dragon Rider made her return, if reluctantly, to the city.

The noise of it all was immediate, attacking her most

important sense. Then there was the baby to consider. Joran was pressed into her chest, his small body swaddled against the cold and bound to her own.

He was sleeping, for now. Androma's experience of newborns amounted to naught, just as it did with children of any age. What she did know, however, was that they were *loud.* He couldn't be kept a secret for much longer and there were none in all of Harendun who would tolerate a baby of both worlds. Joran's pink flesh, pointed ears, and white hair would mark him for death.

Androma would die first, she knew. Her and a few others.

Besides being the definition of innocence, a fact that spoke to every ounce of her virtue, and whatever fate had in store for him, he was Ilithranda's boy. He was to be protected at all costs, so he could live up to her legacy and that which destiny intended.

In Daijen's Saeth's absence, that was to be all the harder. Androma considered her intended destination and the limited choices that would get her there. Erador was three days by ship, and all the ships were commanded by the king's men or the very worst of men. Though many of the vessels had brought women along for post-invasion entertainment, none were blind old women with five hundred years under their belt. Nor did any of them have a baby bound to them.

Androma paused by the corner of a building, one hand continuously patting Joran's bottom. She could hear heavy wagons, all laden with stolen wares—the spoils of war—as they were transported through the streets. The pirates and marauders were always bound to double, if not triple, their fee with all that they claimed in the aftermath. Then there were the soldiers, the king's men who searched for trophies or means to increase their wages. Androma heard sacks of metallic goods slung over iron pauldrons, their plundered treasure to be stored in the ships before their commanders caught them.

A sigh of disappointment escaped Androma's dry lips, like a warm summer breeze passing between two branches of a very old tree. This wasn't the war she remembered.

The loud, but distinct, clip-clip-clopping of a horse's hooves sounded in her ears before she heard its deep-throated neigh. Androma pressed herself into the arch of a doorway and wrapped her arms protectively around Joran. The horse rounded the corner, informing the old Rider that it was significantly taller than an average horse and it possessed an extra pair of hooves. The swishing of its long and slender tail followed in its wake. Androma was sure to keep to her small alcove, lest she startle the Andaren war horse.

By the sound of its hooves, the horse was faltering as it entered the street. A sharp sigh was forced from its many nostrils before its considerable bulk dropped to the ground, sending a subtle vibration through Androma's feet. Using her stick, the old Rider found her way to the mutated animal. With an outstretched hand, she probed the air in front of her and above the war horse. The haft of a protruding spear was soon in her grip.

The memory it conjured was inevitable and she tightened her grip until it hurt.

Don't think about him, she urged herself, yet her knees were bending as she followed the spear down to the war horse. From the haft, her hand roamed over the saddle until she was touching the short hairs of its hide. It was still alive, the creature's ribs moving with its last breaths.

If only she had been with *him* in his final moments, all those years ago.

Had her tear ducts not been melted with her eyes, Androma would have cried in that moment, her grief a burning fire that was slow to die out.

The animal dead, the old Rider stood up and walked away before the carcass attracted others.

"You there!"

Too late.

Androma didn't have to see to know that hail had been directed at her. Keeping her staff swaying, she returned to the previous wall and continued along it. When she felt the corner from which the horse had arrived the old Rider turned down the next street, all-too aware of the clattering armour that pursued her.

"I said stop!" the soldier barked, despite having said no such thing.

Androma cocked her head, listening for others on that same street. Her staff resounded with every tap of the wall, informing her that the adjacent wall was closer than the size of an average street. An alleyway then. And an empty one.

"You!" The soldier had entered behind her. His accent caught in her ear and she knew immediately that he was from Sunhold, outside of Freygard.

Aware of how this was likely to end, Androma pushed it away. He wasn't a man from Sunhold, the son of a fisherman, husband to a good wife, and father to who knows how many children that all awaited his return. He was a direct threat to Joran. There was no room for him to be anything else.

His armour clattered as he broke into a quick jog to catch her. His hand hooked around the back of her arm, his fingers pinching into a vice as he turned her about. Hoping that words might prevail, Androma let the soldier handle her and see the tattered blindfold that covered her eyes. If nothing else, it would disarm him and make the fool believe he was entirely in control.

"You..." he stumbled over his command. "You stop when a soldier of the king tells you to."

"Begging your pardon, sir," she replied meekly, one hand scooped under Joran.

The soldier paused, likely having noticed the babe locked against her chest. "Who are you? Who did you sail with?"

I didn't come to these lands by sea, she thought. "The Delly Maid," Androma said instead, recalling a ship she had once set sail on—long before the soldier had been born.

He didn't respond right away, clearly taken aback by an old blind woman and a baby on what had, until very recently, been a battlefield. Of all the folk who had come ashore, she didn't belong and he knew it.

"What are you doing here?" he demanded.

"I'm trying to find my way back to my ship," the old Rider lied, stooping her shoulders to appear all the weaker.

"What are you doing *here*?" he emphasised this time. "Why are you in Harendun? Hells, why are you in Andara? This is no place for the blind or a babe."

"The Delly Maid, sir," Androma began. "'Tis a... well, a *ladies'* vessel, if you understand my meaning."

The soldier sniffed and his words came through an amused grin. "You are *not* from a pleasure ship," he insisted.

Androma attempted a small laugh. "My role has certainly changed, sir. Now I am only fit to care for the seeded babes." Here, the old Rider indicated Joran, hoping now that her lie and the baby's presence would be enough for the soldier to let it go.

"Being out here ain't caring for any babe," he stated. "There could still be Andarens lurking about. Hells, you nearly got flattened by one of their ghoulish horses back there."

"I just needed to feel the earth beneath my feet for a while." Even as she said it, Androma was turning away.

"I'll escort you back," he said.

"Oh, there's really no need—"

"The Delly Maid, you said?" He spoke over her, his hand coming up to take her by the arm again.

The imminent future came to Androma as clearly as it had when she possessed her sight. They would reach the sands beyond the Sea Gate and the lack of any Delly Maid would reveal her lies. Worse, it would do so in front of witnesses. The conclusion was obvious, if brutal.

Then there was the other option, a far darker reality unfolding around her. He was one of *them*. *Trust no one, suspect everyone.* They had been Daijen's words, a warning from decades earlier that had always stuck with the old Rider. They could be anyone, she knew. If that was the case, this common soldier was no such thing. It meant he was hunting the boy. Worse, he had *found* the boy.

Whether he was an extension of such evil or, in fact, a mere soldier of Erador, it didn't change his fate.

Androma whipped up her staff and twisted it to press against the back of his cuirass. In the same motion, taking it in both hands, she shoved him hard into the nearest wall. He hardly bounced off the stone, but it was enough that when she cracked him round the back of the head, his face slammed into the stone once more. A second strike took him in the back of the knee, dropping him to waist height. A third and final blow hammered him on the left ear and sent him to the ground.

He didn't get back up. He didn't so much as stir. But neither of those facts meant this soldier of the king was no longer a threat to the boy.

Androma crouched down and located the back of his neck before finding his mouth. He was still breathing. When he awoke, and he would, he would search everywhere for the blind woman who had assaulted a king's man. It was more than likely that he would muster others to aid him and then moving about the city would be even harder than it already was.

Again, Androma followed the chain of events through to their logical conclusion and knew that Joran would be in peril.

She had to end the threat.

Placing her staff on the ground, Androma retrieved the curved dagger from her belt, the weapon previously concealed within the folds of her rags. She again located the base of his neck and pushed down the collar of his undershirt to make space for the tip of her blade. In that moment, the old Rider recalled his accent in her mind and conjured that life she had imagined for him.

Her knuckles paled around the hilt.

She could feel her heart racing. How she longed to hear that other voice in her mind, to hear *his* voice. Androma knew, of course, what the dragon would have done—and without hesitation. He would have swallowed the soldier whole to protect Joran.

Such little pressure was required to push the blade through his spine and even less to continue through to the other side. Death was instantaneous. Painless. Absolute.

Pulling the dagger free, Androma used the soldier's own clothes to wipe some of the blood away before returning it to the shadows of her attire. Joran was made safe a little longer. That would have to do.

Staff in hand again, the old Rider left her victim where he lay and hurried from the alley. She left it, however, with the same problems she had entered it with: how to find a way to smuggle a baby across The Drifting Sea, to the shores of Erador. She could pick-pocket her way to the nearest ship and try to pay her way, but how much would it cost to travel without questions? How much would it cost to ensure privacy on the ship and safe departure once they arrived at Caster Hold?

Androma didn't have any of the answers, but she also knew she couldn't pick-pocket that many marks. Frustrated, the old Rider paused to drink some water from the skin on her belt and was frustrated all the more to find it as dry as her lips.

"Damn you, Daijen Saeth."

13
REBIRTH

80 Years Ago...

Elevated upon Ka'vairn's eastern ramparts, Elivar's body succumbed to the flames of his pyre. Yendi and Naelin had aided the uninitiated pair to build it, stating that it wasn't the first pyre they had built on the ancient wall. Laif stood sentinel on the western rampart, Kovun and Soyra beside him, watching the fire burn.

Slait seemed not to notice. In the wake of the storm, he remained in the courtyard where he might practise his swordplay against one of the wooden dummies. He was hacking it to pieces all the while Elivar was being consumed by flames. The sound of his blade chopping into the wood and the exertion that came with it had a similar, all-consuming, effect on Daijen.

The young Andaren regularly looked over his shoulder to spy the bald initiate below. The anger he had quashed in the cavern was quick to rise to the surface and with it came the recollection of the man he had killed in Harendun.

All at once, he craved that god-like feeling again and wished to let loose his rage upon Slait.

"That would be a mistake," Ilithranda told him, her words almost swallowed by the crackling of the flames. Daijen looked at her but she maintained her steely gaze, her violet eyes never wavering from Elivar's pyre. "Your anger burns brighter than the flames. It speaks of your intent. You must learn to control it or be controlled by it. Choose the latter, and Slait will cave your head in and then we'll have to build another pyre."

"He's being disrespectful," Daijen insisted.

"He's baiting you," Ilithranda informed. "That's his way. Rise above it or be buried beneath it, because he *will* bury you. Slait survived the pit. He's a testament to Handuin's magic now. Until you can say the same, accept the differences between you and adapt."

Daijen let the reaching flames hypnotise him for the moment. He soon came to realise, as he had back at The Saible, that Ilithranda was trying to save his life again.

Doing his best to ignore Slait, Daijen turned his head to Ilithranda, head slightly bowed. "How long did you know him?"

Ilithranda stood motionless for a while, her chin somewhat elevated. It reminded Daijen all the more that she was from the purest imperial stock. In all his years in the army, he had never come across a soldier—whatever their title—who held themselves so regally without thought.

"I was posted in his battalion after The Battle of The Triden. He had been fighting for a couple of years by then. He didn't need to see my name on a piece of parchment to know who I was. Or... where I had come from," she specified. "Elivar was always perceptive. It's one of the reasons he was such a great fighter. Why he was chosen for this... *honour*."

Daijen considered all that they had seen together, but there was only one thing he was truly curious about. "You both knew a time before the war," he commented, shaking his head. "I cannot imagine it."

Ilithranda gave an almost imperceptible laugh. "Elivar would have told you it was boring."

Daijen shared something of her laugh. "Was it peaceful?" he asked, imagining his people going about their daily lives without threat of invasion or call to war.

"What it *was* doesn't really matter anymore. We're not fighting for what we've lost—I don't think we *ever* were."

The remark struck Daijen as odd, if somehow insightful. "Then what *are* we fighting for?"

Ilithranda finally turned to look at him. Daijen quickly became uncomfortable under her scrutiny, sure that she knew of some mystical way to see into his heart and mind.

Something in her expression, however, suggested that she had found Daijen wanting. "The same thing everyone fights for..." She paused, albeit momentarily, before deciding upon, "*More.*"

Despite sensing her omission, Daijen could hear some semblance of truth in her voice. "I'm not sure that's the purpose of the Vahlken," he replied.

"No," Ilithranda agreed, her eyes led back to the flames once more. "The Vahlken are two things and I intend to harness both." When she gave no further explanation, Daijen was forced to enquire, to which she simply responded, "Freedom... and *power*."

Those two words sat with Daijen for the remainder of Elivar's unassuming funeral. They were two things he had never considered beyond the dreams of a young boy, but he found his curiosity truly ignited by Ilithranda's desire for them. Freedom and power were surely the foundations underpinning the imperial family, setting them apart from the lowborns and highborns alike. Why would she willingly go through all this to attain them? The answer most likely lay with the reason for her being in the army to begin with.

Seeing Elivar's body through the flames, Daijen cast his thoughts and questions aside and quietened his mind out of respect. When the fire died down, they would collect what remained of his bones and bury him on the edges of The Dain'duil.

Daijen couldn't help but wonder if he would soon join him there.

A thunderous knock brought the sole heir of House Saeth to his senses, rousing him from his cot. He opened his door expecting to see Laif again. He was somewhat disturbed to find Slait in his stead. The bald initiate was leaning against the doorframe, his hands out to support a thick leather-bound book in his hands.

The Arkalon.

Daijen would know the holy book anywhere, though seeing it in Slait's hands was the last place he expected to see it.

Slait licked his lips. "*And the last of the Leviathans was hastened from the land,*" he began. "*Yet still, their masters stood defiant against the gods. Their Leviathans defeated, the Dark Ones unleashed new hell on earth, releasing the human scourge from their demonic flesh. This new enemy, whose image was made in mockery of all Andarens, was set to infect the world with malice and darkness. As one, this new enemy stood at the backs of their masters and war was renewed upon Verda—*"

"I've read this before," Daijen cut in.

There was violence in the gaze that Slait brought upon him. "Shh," he bade. "I'm getting to the best part." The initiate turned one delicate page. "*War was death to us all,*" he continued, "*past, present, and future. One by one, the gods gave their lives on Verda to quash the Dark Ones and their human horde. Only Ahnir remained, the god who had seen The End. What evil He had slain. What heroes He had made. But sacrifice was His end. And with His end came the fall of the heavens and all those who dwelled therein. There now reigns a Black Abyss, a crushing darkness. Until the day of Reclamation, all are fated to this vast chasm between worlds.*"

Slait closed the book with a *snap*. "I've read this book more times than I've wielded a sword," he admitted, offering Daijen an unexpected insight. "It comforts me. Emboldens me. Reminds me why we fight the human scum. But I'm always left with that Black Abyss. Have you ever thought about it?" he questioned. "I mean, *really* thought about it? We can't be the only ones condemned to it until Reclamation. Do you want to know what I think?" he asked, an impish grin on his face. "I don't think it's an abyss at all. I think it's *full.* Packed to the walls! I think the Leviathans are there. The Dark Ones too. All that have been slain, good or bad, now dwell in the Black Abyss, writhing and feasting. And I think that's where *you're* going this very day. Perhaps you'll see Elivar down there, trapped in the jaws of a Leviathan—"

"Slait!" Laif's voice dominated the passage outside Daijen's room and simultaneously cut through his mounting rage. "The master does not like to be kept waiting," he reminded sternly.

"So he doesn't," Slait agreed, his eyes never leaving Daijen. "And neither does the Abyss." The initiate stepped aside and gestured for Daijen to follow Laif.

"This way," he instructed upon sighting the uninitiated.

Slait was left behind, and with an air of amusement about him, as they made their way back to the Hall of Handuin. There, Daijen was reunited with Ilithranda, who was towered over by Soyra. There was no sign of The Valtorak, nor did they wait for him, and the pair were escorted through the maze and, inevitably, into the ante-chamber.

The rounded door was already open, revealing The Valtorak inside. His staff remained propped up against the far wall while he used a similarly long stick to stir the mysterious waters inside the pit. Daijen hesitated to step inside the cavern, as if that circular door itself was the entrance to the Black Abyss. He glanced back to spy Laif and Soyra but both had vanished, departing without a sound.

A cool hand gripped his wrist, turning him to Ilithranda. "Freedom and power," she whispered. With that, she released him and entered the cavern.

Daijen swallowed, unsure now what his reasons were for being in that doorway. Why had he left The Saible? Why had he believed there was to be glory in this path? His mind drew a blank. He faced death, right here and now and he couldn't say why. Had he remained a messenger guard and skirted the frontlines, he could have lived for another five centuries. Now, with only thirty-five winters under his belt, he was to become just another pyre on Ka'vairn's walls.

"The choice you had yesterday, Daijen Saeth, remains the same today." The Valtorak wasn't even looking at him, his hands still stirring the pit. "Should you choose to stay, I would ask that you close the door behind you."

Daijen commanded himself to act without thought and, as always, move forward. With one hand, he gripped the vertical handle on the inside of the door and immediately realised he didn't possess the strength in one arm to pull it closed. Taking it in two hands, he heaved the iron slab, his back straining with the effort. The rounded slab pivoted on its hinges and slotted into place, leaving Daijen with sore hands.

When he finally joined them by the pit, Ilithranda had already removed her clothes and donned the straps and chain of the harness. Daijen glanced at her nakedness before adopting some manner of discipline. For all her beauty, and the way her skin clung to every muscle group, his gaze had been drawn to the scars she bore, each one a mark of her heroic efforts and the culmination of why she had been picked for this honour. But she was also on the precipice of death, just as Elivar had been.

It felt all too quick to Daijen, who thought there should have been more time to say something, for any of them to say something, but Ilithranda stepped in without hesitation and disappeared beneath the shining water. The chain rattled as it followed her in, an iron snake taking refuge beneath the surface.

"Stand back," The Valtorak warned, his staff—back in hand—forcing Daijen away from the edge.

Daijen frowned, unsure what the master was seeing in the water that he was not. His guts however, churned with fear for her. He watched the water's surface closely, waiting for the bubbles to form and the dark veins to lay their web.

But the light only brightened.

Soon, Daijen was narrowing his eyes to see the pit. "What's happening?" he blurted.

"Rebirth," The Valtorak stated.

Ilithranda emerged without warning, breaking the water with dramatic effect. Her head flicked up and her white hair whipped around to find her back. Her eyes snapped open, adding shards of violet to the countless colours that sparkled around her. Daijen was too stunned to move and offer aid, though she proved not to require it as she climbed out of the pit with ease.

Tall she stood—taller than Daijen now. Her muscles were more defined than before, and larger too. Her chest heaved with laboured breath, as if she had been fighting for her life in the few seconds that she had been submerged. The harness's straps were stretched almost beyond their limits, the buckles on the verge of breaking before she removed it.

"Ilithranda of House Lhoris," The Valtorak announced officially. "Welcome to the order of the Vahlken."

Ilithranda continued to stand naked but proud, her pale skin dripping the brewed water onto the cold floor. Then she faltered. Her expression cracked. Daijen moved, his arms already coming up, but she fell to the ground and crumpled in a heap at his feet.

"What's happening?" Daijen spat, seeing Elivar's death all over again.

Turning her over, there was confusion behind those beautiful eyes. She attempted to speak but produced little more than gibberish.

"This is normal," The Valtorak said at last, his words a soothing balm. "Her disorientation will fade. She must rest now." Ka'vairn's master fanned out a long cloak shouldered with dark fur and draped it over her naked form.

"She was only under for seconds," Daijen remarked.

"It means nothing," The Valtorak informed him. "Yendi was under just as long and half a dozen others besides."

Daijen brushed a few strands of hair from her face and saw that Ilithranda was already asleep on the hard ground. "She looked so... *powerful*," he observed, noting how much bigger her hands were compared to his.

"Power," The Valtorak stated, "is attained through practice and discipline. *Freedom*, however, is considerably harder to come by."

Daijen felt a short and sudden drop in his stomach. Had the master heard Ilithranda's whispered words from across the cavern? Impossible. But surely not a coincidence.

"There is one yet to be tested," The Valtorak went on, his gaze falling on Daijen. "What will you do, messenger guard? Was it a twist of fate that saw you replace Rondir of House Jovuhn? Or was it merely a foolish and regrettable act of heroism?"

Caught in those unforgiving sights, Daijen Saeth grabbed hold of the tenuous thread that was his bravery. Burying what thoughts he could, lest they shatter his nerve, he quickly stripped off his clothes and marched to the edge of the pit. He had intended to simply step in, as Ilithranda had, but now found himself balanced on the lip, hesitation in his bones.

"The harness, Daijen," The Valtorak reminded.

Doubt. It was *doubt* that had brought those words to the master's lips. And he had heard them before, if not those exact words. How many people—how many superiors and mentors—had voiced something similar? He had been doubted his entire life. He had been held back, put down, and made a mockery of.

Not today.

Forsaking the harness, Daijen stepped into the pit and fell beneath the water.

Into eternity.

14
THE NEGOTIATION

Gallien Drakalis sat snug in the tavern booth, his feet propped up on a chair, and his head resting back so he might take in the intricate pattern laced into the ceiling. It ended, of course, in the centre of the tavern, where the roof had been caved in by a catapult. The late afternoon sun now shone through that jagged hole, illuminating the burnt crater and surrounding debris.

Every table and chair not destroyed by the invasion was taken by the numerous sailors, marauders, and pirates who now claimed all that they could see. There wasn't a man without a bottle in his hand or cheer in his spirit. Today was a good day as far as they were all concerned. *They* hadn't failed to find any valuable relics. *They* hadn't lost their only way of getting home. And, most of all, *they* hadn't watched an old friend and lover be taken by some monster of the sea.

The bottle soon found his waiting lips again. The sweet honey ale was most welcome, even if it wasn't enough to dull his depression. "Say what you will about Andarens," he said to no-one and everyone, "they make damn good liquor!" Some cheered in agreement, but most continued with their own merriment.

And again, Gallien was left to his dark thoughts. He faced death

—there was no getting around it. Returning empty-handed to The Raven and its Captain was death at the hands of Thedaria's Padoshi. Stay in Harendun and he would face the wrath of the Andarens when they exacted revenge.

He took another swig of the bottle, pausing only to watch as a hooded figure navigated the wreckage and the people. Drakalis slowly lowered the bottle from his lips and scrutinised the newcomer. Despite the layered rags and hood, he knew it to be a woman. It was all the more interesting to see her use a staff to find every object at her feet. The smuggler's curiosity was piqued when he glimpsed the blindfold within the shadow of her hood.

Her short journey came to an end when she discovered the bar between her and a wall of half-empty shelves. Gallien continued to watch her, amazed really that she had moved without being noticed by the others—as if this blind woman knew how to step in the blind spots of others. The stranger rested her staff against the bar and rummaged for something beneath her rags, on a belt perhaps.

A glimpse of brilliant bronze caught the smuggler's eye and stopped him from taking a further sip. Not only had he seen bronze, but the bronze of a curved short-sword. He might have let it go as no more than the fascination of a man attracted to shiny things, but he had seen that weapon this very day. This blind woman—whoever she was—possessed a Vahlken's blade.

Having last seen it in the hand of the Dragon Rider—raised for all to see—Gallien had to assume this was not that same weapon. Such a conclusion only intrigued him more. And he would be lying if he hadn't already estimated the worth of a genuine Vahlken short-sword.

The stranger ran a hand along the bar, until she found the gap in the end, and rounded it to find a suitable drink. There wasn't much left, but she happily picked up and sniffed what Gallien knew to be a carafe of water. Taking one of the cups she clipped with the back of her hand, the blind woman retraced her steps to the other side of the bar and began pouring herself a drink, one finger hooked over the rim to ensure she didn't pour too much. She knocked it back like a stray sailor hauled in from the sea before pouring herself another one.

Somewhat bemused, Gallien continued to observe quietly from his booth, saying nothing as she made her way towards him. When her staff located the end of the curved bench, she assumed the edge of the seat and placed the carafe on the table. She sighed and pushed back her hood to reveal a head of short greying hair, her fringe spilling over one side of her blindfold. Still, the smuggler dared not make a sound, enraptured by the aged blind woman and her Vahlken weapon.

Her nose twitched. Then her head tilted towards Gallien and she sniffed again. "Apologies," she breathed, making to stand and leave.

"Don't leave on my account," he replied, resisting the urge to sniff his armpits. "Is that a baby?" The question forced itself from his lips—how could it not after seeing the tiny arm and hand protruding from within her rags?

Quicker than he could have anticipated, the woman fell back into her seat opposite him and he felt the tip of a dagger intruding between his legs. "One more word," she threatened, her voice low and commanding, "and I'll make you less of a man."

Drakalis held up his hands even though the gesture went unseen. "Easy," he breathed, feeling the dagger's edge press a little harder into his thigh. "So, the baby's a secret then," the smuggler concluded, if quietly so. He was also sure to keep his tone light, making himself seem less of a threat.

"I'm going to walk out of here," the stranger told him. "Keep quiet and you keep your life," she added simply enough.

"That's quite the threat coming from a blind woman," he quipped and then quickly regretted doing so. "Easy," he hissed, the tip of the blade moving dangerously up his thigh.

"This *blind woman* could find your stench across any room. Then you *would* find my aim to be true."

"Fair enough," he said, happy to feel the dagger inch away. "But where are you going exactly?" he just had to ask. "I mean, you say you're walking out of here, but do you know where *here* is?

You're a blind woman with a baby strapped to her chest in the middle of Harendun. You don't exactly belong here."

"None of us belong here," she reminded him darkly.

"True," he conceded. "But you less so than... well, *everyone*. Why would you come here? *How* did you even get here? Old maids and their young babes aren't the usual type to be brought along for ship's entertainment."

The stranger spoke with her dagger first, quick to slip it all the way into the crease of his groin, sending Gallien up his seat slightly. "I killed the last man who asked me those questions." Something about the way she delivered the response informed Drakalis that she wasn't exaggerating.

"Maybe that's because he couldn't get you out of here," he said swiftly, if tonally off-kilter.

His reply hung between them, filling the air with tension. The stranger frowned behind her blindfold and tilted her head, as if assessing some hidden part of him. "Why would you say that?"

Gallien licked his lips—the most powerful tool he had ever possessed. "You clearly don't belong in Harendun," he began. "And judging by your reaction when I noticed the baby, I'd say you don't *want* to be here either. That means you're looking for a way out, back to Erador. Now, I don't know how you got here in the first place but, if I was to guess, I would say you can't get back the same way. Bad ship perhaps. Bad captain. Bad crew. Hells, maybe all three—Kaliban knows I've sailed on a few of those."

"You have a ship?" she questioned, her dagger yet to relent.

"The Raven."

The stranger absorbed his answer. "That doesn't sound like a navy ship."

"That's because it's not."

"Pirate then," she surmised dourly.

"Pirates," Gallien echoed, his tone suggesting he agreed with her estimations. "But," he caveated, "they're on the better side of bad. Negotiate the right price and they'll take you back to Caster Hold."

The woman was already shaking her head. "Negotiating with pirates is like trying to catch smoke with your hands."

Drakalis raised a finger in victory. "So we've established that you *do* need to get out of here, you just need someone who can speak *pirate*."

The dagger retracted a notch. "I'll take my chances with one of the king's ships," she stated, a touch of defeat mixing with her tone of tired irritation.

"No you won't," Gallien told her confidently. "Soldiers ask more questions than pirates, and when a blind woman with a baby arrives on their deck, they're going to..." A thought occurred to the smuggler, dark as it was. He glanced at what now seemed like an obvious lump on her torso and cleared his throat. "That is a... *human* baby, aye?"

"You think I would journey into a siege to steal an Andaren baby?"

"I think you wouldn't be the first," Gallien remarked, having seen just such a thing.

"I am not some grieving mother come to snatch a fresh orphan. And *yes*, he is human. And yes," she added, "I do need to get out of here. So, unless you can actually help me, I'll be on my way."

Drakalis watched her stand and, thankfully, take her dagger with her, but he also watched his best chance of getting back to Erador leave with her. "I can get you on The Raven," he said reassuringly. "For the right price, I might even be able to convince Captain Addison to depart this very night."

The stranger paused, two out-stretched fingers still pressed into the table top. "This very night?" she echoed incredulously.

Gallien made a face to suggest he was weighing up his own words. "I've been in this city for... two days? Maybe three. That's two or three days more than any privateer wants to be harboured on Andara's shore. At this point, we're just *waiting* for the Andarens to mount their counterattack. When that happens, like it *always* does, the soldiers will fight until they realise they've lost too many men to win. Then, and *only* then, will they retreat to the beach and seek out the nearest ship. That puts a lot of ships and their crews at risk."

Turning to face him again, the older stranger raised an eyebrow above her blindfold. "You use ten words where one would suffice."

Gallien shrugged. "I've not had a lot of people to talk to of late." The smuggler thought of Kit Voden again and he saw her dragged into darkness.

Surprising him—and turning his mind from Kit's fate—the stranger assumed her seat again. "And what is the right price exactly?" she asked, full of suspicion.

"Well, even between us, I'd say neither of us have enough coin to book passage home. So we're going to need something *worth* the coin."

The woman sat back, one hand coming round to find the baby's back. "*Worth* the coin?" she repeated. "I might be blind, but even I know I am past the point of enticing pirates. And I swear to Kaliban, I will open the throat of any man who even *thinks* about touching the boy."

Gallien reactively raised his hands. "The crew of The Raven are bad, but they're not that bad. And I'm not suggesting you sell yourself for passage. No, no, no. I'm asking about the..." The smuggler mouthed his next words before remembering his companion was blind. "The Vahlken blade," he whispered.

It was all too obvious that the stranger had become unnervingly still. "What Vahlken blade?" she enquired evenly.

"The one you flashed when you were reaching for your belt," he explained as a matter of fact.

She said nothing.

Gallien pursed his lips, wondering if he had erred in his wordplay. He had been sure that was the right moment to bring it up, his timing always calculated to ensure the best negotiation. Now he felt threatened, and by a blind woman of all things. While one part of his mind informed him he could best her with ease, another, more instinctual, part of his mind knew she was no ordinary opponent. He glanced at the satchel on the bench beside him and wondered if he could remove Kit's broken sword without notice. Then there was his sword, standing up against the booth and utterly useless inside its scabbard.

Under the table, he grabbed at the air, hoping the axe might return to him as it had in his moment of need. Nothing. As usual, he was left with words alone to keep him alive.

"You would try and take it from me?" the stranger finally spoke.

"I only take things that are already lost," Gallien told her.

"A treasure hunter then," she concluded derisively. "And not a good one if a burnt-out city, bereft of its people, are where you hunt. I think they call that easy pickings."

"Says the blind woman with a Vahlken blade hanging from her belt," he quipped. "Did you even know the body you were tripping over was a Vahlken?" he sniggered. "Where did you get it anyway? I saw the Vahlken defending this city die with my own eyes, so I *know* it isn't his."

"Where I got it is none of your business."

Again, Gallien raised his hands, in meaningless apology this time. "For the right price, even I won't ask any questions."

"I doubt that, though I would very much like to know the price."

"Easy," he replied with a smile behind the word. "*When* I negotiate your safe return to Caster Hold, your offer to Captain Addison includes my own safe return."

"I see," the woman drawled, an unlikely, if knowing, grin crossing her face. "You need to get out of here as much as I do."

"Maybe, but I'm not a blind woman with a baby strapped to my chest, so my odds are a little better."

"I'm starting to wonder if I need you at all," she said.

"Negotiating with pirates and their ilk is but one of my skills," he was quick to boast. "As well as the... *procurement* of certain items, I also specialise in moving them from place to place... *discreetly*."

"You're a smuggler," she stated bluntly.

"A damn *good* smuggler," he was sure to point out. "Which is something you could benefit from when we arrive at Caster Hold. Nothing comes and goes through that port without questions."

Again, the woman sat back and said nothing for a time, though she did begin to gently sway and pat the baby's back. "It's not for sale," she told him flatly.

Gallien frowned and adjusted himself in his seat. "You might not know this, but that blade's complexion is bronze from pommel to tip and curved like an Andaren scimitar. *Everyone* knows it's a Vahlken short-sword. If you hold on to it, someone will kill you to possess it."

"It's an *atori* blade," the woman told him. "And let them *try*," she added.

Drakalis pinched his eyes with finger and thumb. "I don't know what that blade means to you, but I'll tell you what it could mean: *home*. Vahlken weaponry is worth a small fortune. Part with it and, in three days' time, you and the babe walk on Eradoran soil."

"I said it's not for sale."

Sitting back in the booth, Gallien sighed as his frustration mounted. He could see in his mind the shores of Erador shrinking into the horizon. "I thought you wanted—*needed*—to get back to Erador."

"It sounds like *you* need to get back to Erador," she returned.

"I've seen this play out before," Gallien told her, an air of dark prophecy about him. "We have days, maybe weeks, before The Saible opens its iron jaws and unleashes Andaren hell on this city. I'm not a soldier and I have no ship to call my own, so aye, getting back to Erador is something of a *need* for me."

"History doesn't always repeat itself," the stranger opined. "Erador has invaded with a dragon this time."

Gallien gave a mirthless laugh. "If dragons couldn't be killed, this war would've been over centuries ago."

Something about the woman went rigid, her jaw tense and lips thinned to a straight line. One hand gripped the edge of the table until the knuckles paled. She swallowed and regained a measure of previous composure. "True enough," she uttered.

"So what's it to be?" he began again, pushing her now. "Want to stay and see if you and a baby can survive the next battle for Harendun? Or will you trade a sword for *all* our lives?"

The stranger cupped the back of the baby's head—concealed within her rags—and held him even closer for a moment. "Trade," she eventually rasped.

Gallien was glad she couldn't see the relief in his expression.

"What is your name?" she asked, jolting him back to the booth.

He cleared his throat. "Gallien Drakalis."

The woman held out a single hand, palm up, on the table. When he didn't react, she flexed her fingers. "Give me your hand," she insisted.

Gallien thought of that dagger again. "Why?"

"Names can change like the shifting sands, but our hands never lie."

The smuggler didn't know what to make of that, but he also didn't see any better way forward. The moment his hand clapped hers, the stranger began to explore his skin and the creases in his palm and between his fingers. Seeking out every inch, she roamed over his calluses and knuckles.

"You have lived many lives, Gallien Drakalis," she declared. "You've spent time on a ship. You've also worked the land. Hmm. You said you're not a soldier but I'd say you were. A swordsman in fact." She ran one thumb over his knuckles. "You've seen your share of tavern brawls too."

"Who hasn't?" he replied lightly.

Her grasp changed in an instant and he suddenly knew pain as he was tugged slightly across the table by his thumb. He could feel the pressure in several joints around his hand and knew he was on the verge of suffering multiple fractures. "What the hell, lady!"

The stranger leaned in. "The very second it comes to light that you are double-crossing me, Mr Drakalis, I will end your miserable life without hesitation."

Gallien's frown deepened. "Miserable?" A degree of extra pressure was applied, forcing a wince out of him. "I think we understand each other."

"Good." The woman released his thumb and sat back.

The smuggler massaged his sore thumb as he scrutinised this stranger all the more. He had so many questions—one of which concerned the dangers of throwing his lot in with such a volatile individual—but passage across The Drifting Sea would keep his mouth shut.

"Since we're sharing," he voiced, "what's *your* name?"

The stranger poured herself another cup of water and downed it all before answering. "My name is Androma."

Gallien blinked. "That's it? No blood name?"

"I am the last of my blood," she said, and without a trace of emotion. "Since I have no intention of extending my line, the name means nothing."

The smuggler was nodding along, sure now that the baby wasn't hers. "Does *he* have a name?"

"He does, though it need not concern you." With that, Androma slid out of the booth and moved one hand along the wall until she collected her staff. "I wish to set sail as soon as possible."

Drakalis thought of Captain Addison and wondered if he had overestimated himself. "To The Raven then."

15
TRADITION

80 Years Ago…

What depths lay hidden below those shining waters. Depths that had long shrugged off the shackles of time. Depths that did not need the world and its ways. There was only fire and ice. Ice and fire. Daijen Saeth succumbed to both, his body and soul burning and freezing. Freezing and burning. Over and over the process tormented him. *Transformed* him.

At the same time, and despite the constant agony, Daijen's body seemed lost to him, intangible. His consciousness was moving through a void streaked with light and stars and at a speed only the gods could have boasted. Any thought that occurred to him was soon left behind, as if his mind couldn't keep up with his momentum.

He simply *was*.

And there he remained, ever moving, ever in pain. Eons could have passed him by, the world to die and be reborn, before he rose from the depths of Handuin's magic.

If he rose…

For all the thoughts that fled his mind, there was one constant that returned again and again to haunt his eternal journey.

Was this the path to the Black Abyss?

The thought that this journey would end in such a dark place would have put ice in the veins of the young Andaren who stepped into the pit. But that Andaren was gone already. In place of fear, the prevailing emotion was naught but pure determination. An iron will that he grasped in the seconds before plunging into the pit. Whatever awaited him, Daijen Saeth knew he would be ready for it. How he knew that he could not say. He couldn't really explain anything about who he was or, indeed, where he was.

How could he, being no more than a speck of dust moving through the untold depths of raw reality?

There seemed years, centuries even, where he lived through every moment of his life again. Memories emerged from a time when his mind was immature, showing him his childhood in Taranathen. Again and again he said farewell to his mother and father as they took up the call to arms, the call to defend their country against the humans. Again and again he lived through the moment in which his uncle told him they weren't coming back, their lives taken by a storm while travelling at sea.

"You are my burden now, boy," his uncle had said in his gruff voice. "Your parents never made it to the front," he stated bluntly, "and nor shall you. However bloody, this war will be a footnote in our history. I shall not see it claim the only heir to our name. Come. I'm to make a fisherman out of you."

Eternity continued to corkscrew from there, dragging him through every conversation he had ever had, every emotion he had ever experienced, and every person he had ever met. Inevitably, Daijen came to know every word that had been voiced about him, as if his life was a play and he held the script.

The pain seared every moment of it into his soul.

"People spit at me!" Daijen blurted, his teenage body tall and lithe as he stood defiantly in Taranathen's port. "They say I have no honour!"

"There's no honour to be found out there," his uncle had

replied, his chronic limp bringing him a step closer. "It's just *war*, boy! It churns and it churns and broken bodies come out the other end. That's it. Two centuries of fighting and all we've got to show for it is enough spilt blood to fill The Vallen twice over! I'm saving your life, you foolish boy!"

"You're not saving me," Daijen argued. "You're keeping me prisoner! Everyone else heeds the call. Everyone else is bound for The Saible. Not me. I'm here catching *fish* in a net."

"You're all that's left of us," his uncle protested. "Look at me, Daijen. I've no children. No wife. The House of Saeth lives and dies with you. You're all we've got left. All I've got left."

How many times had Daijen watched this scene play out? It hurt every time. Despite how real it felt, he was helpless to change it, the past already carved into time.

"You're not all *I've* got left," he said with venom. "I've got centuries ahead of me. I'll not spend them fishing while everyone else fights."

That was the last time he saw his uncle, his image and voice never to appear again as Daijen collided with memory after memory.

There came no warning when he was born again. One moment, he was travelling through an endless tunnel of striated light and, the next, he was gulping on air amid splashing water. He blinked the water from his eyes and beheld a blurry world of gloom and shadow. Something moved in the haze but, like so much that had surrounded him inside the pit, he gave it little attention.

His instincts told him to get out of the water and so he moved for the edge, finding his limbs for the first time in eons. One hand after the other clawed at the hard stone around the water and dragged him from the pit. His naked body felt the cool air settle over his silvery skin before a warm hand touched his shoulder.

After inhabiting a realm devoid of anything physical, the

harmless encounter set off every warning in Daijen's mind. He hardly recalled his reaction he moved so fast.

On his feet now, he grasped someone's wrist in his hand, his fingers locked like a vice, as he kept the stranger at bay.

Her vivacity struck him first. Then his mind was quietened by the strength in her violet eyes. There was fortitude in them, a source of stability if not vitality. Then his mind shifted dramatically, taking him from reality.

It seemed in the blink of an eye that the stranger was strewn across the ground and he was rocketing through a larger circular door. Though thick and obviously heavy, he moved it aside with ease and continued to barrel down the hall.

"Daijen!"

The cry followed him down the passage, though he could not make sense of the word. He didn't know who he was or where he was. He possessed only the singular belief that his life was in danger. And so he ran. His speed, however, quickly proved to be his own undoing. Wall after wall, he ploughed into hard stone as he failed to make the corner until, eventually, he rammed his way through a door and found himself on the floor of a grand hall.

"Daijen!" came the call again, hounding him.

A harsh and rasping laugh turned him to the enormous doors on the other side of the hall, where a bald man was strolling towards him.

"Kovun!" he shouted over his shoulder. "Come and get a look at this one! We've not had a runner in years!"

Scrambling to his feet, he put the round table between him and the approaching stranger. There was something about that hungry smile that emboldened his belief that he was in peril. Then more Giants came in behind the bald one, pushing him back towards the towering steps and the apparent throne.

"Daijen."

The voice was close now, turning him to the stranger who had greeted him in the gloom. She stood in the shattered doorway from which he had burst.

"It's me," she said, one hand coming up. "Ilithranda."

The name assaulted him, breaking the dam that had kept him from his memories.

"Ilithranda," he muttered, before darkness crept into his vision, narrowing it to a single point.

Then there was naught.

The world came back to Daijen with such clarity he wasn't sure he had ever been asleep. His body rose from the cot with a vitality he had not known, as if the dregs of sleep could not hold him as they once had.

He might have noticed other aspects of his new body had Ilithranda not stood up from her chair in the corner of the room.

There was an air of disbelief about her as she looked him over. Perhaps even a hint of awe, though he couldn't rightly say. He only then noticed that he was wearing naught but a pair of trousers.

"Do you know who you are?" she asked, her eyes level with his again.

Daijen nodded, a bemused grin cutting his lips. "And who you are," he replied.

"They're new," she said, glancing at his trousers. "You're old clothes don't fit you anymore."

"How... How long was I..."

Ilithranda's eyes traced the new muscles in his arm as she collected a small pile of clothes with a cloak and handed them to him. "You were down there for a month," she said, robbing Daijen of clear thought.

"A... A *month*?" he repeated, struggling with the buckles on his boots, his fingers clumsy and stronger than he recalled.

"A little over, in fact," she specified, moving for the door. "We all took it in shifts to be there."

Daijen tried to make sense of it and failed. While it seemed an unbelievably long time, he might have better believed her had she told him he had been down there for millennia. In his confusion and frustration, he clenched his hands within the folds of his new cloak. They felt bigger, each fist a knot of swollen iron.

"Come," Ilithranda bade.

"Was it the same for you?" he enquired.

"Yes, though I didn't burst into The Hall of Handuin like a naked mad man."

Daijen tried to laugh off her comment, despite the embarrassment he felt. Following her into the hallways of Ka'vairn, he couldn't help but note the prominent veins that wormed over the top of the muscles in his forearms. Inquisitively, he moved one hand to roam his torso, feeling the ridges and contours of newly-defined muscles.

"I know," Ilithranda voiced, observing him. "Everything's different now."

The pair continued across the vast entrance hall until Ilithranda opened one of the main doors, piercing the fortress's shadows with a pillar of golden light. Daijen instinctively moved to raise a hand to shield his eyes, but quickly discovered there was no need. His cobalt eyes adjusted immediately to the change in brightness, keeping his vision sharp so as to hold on to every detail about him.

A blast of mountain air fell upon them both and threatened to rob Daijen of the cloak that enveloped his body. Even so, the freezing wind washed over his skin as no more than an autumn breeze might. The wind then swirled about him, seeking its way inside the open door, and blew out his wild mane of white hair, and still his skin felt no more than its cool pressure.

Having shrugged off the cold, Ilithranda directed him to the steps of the ramparts. They were soon walking along Ka'vairn's battlements where the entire valley opened up before them. The Dain'duil was an expanse of green that carpeted the valley floor and reached up to the base of the surrounding mountains.

It was those distant mountains, however, that drew Daijen's attention. The sun was rising in the east, its early light just topping the crest of The Morthil Mountains, where wisps of curling cloud clung to the high stone. Touched by the orange light of dawn, those same clouds looked like the flames of a great torch, as if the mountains wore a crown of fire. It was befitting, perhaps, for the mountains claimed by the dwarves.

Without intention, Daijen's eyes focused on the flaming clouds and closed the distance between them. His vision was crisp despite the miles that stretched out from Hellion stone to Morthil stone. Taken aback, and naturally disorientated by the lack of peripheral vision, he backed away until Ilithranda's hand halted him.

"Close your eyes," she instructed.

He shut them tight and tried to ground himself on the battlements.

"Look again," she said.

Opening his eyes now, the mountains remained firmly in the east and The Dain'duil returned to his vision. "What was that?" he asked, afraid to take in the distance.

"Just the beginning," Ilithranda replied cryptically.

"Daijen of House Saeth!" The booming call turned both to the courtyard below and behind, where The Valtorak and the initiates stood as ashen pillars. "Welcome to the order of the Vahlken!"

Daijen heard the mighty wings before the Aegre soared over his head, its talons barely missing the ramparts. Still, the proximity and sheer noise in his sensitive ears saw him stumble and fall from the interior edge of the battlements. The courtyard rushed up to greet him, the drop more than enough to shatter bones.

Somewhere mid-fall, Daijen's sense of balance corrected his angle of descent and he twisted in the air. A second later and he landed in a crouch, unharmed. Bewildered, he rose and resumed his new height.

Putting his fall to shame, Kastiek leapt from Strix's saddle and plummeted forty feet before landing in the centre of the duelling ring. His fur cloak lent him the look of a bear as he unfurled from his own crouch.

Landing beside Daijen, Ilithranda made hardly a sound, a cat in Andaren form. "Brace yourself," she warned.

"Daijen Saeth!" The Valtorak called, one arm stretching to indicate the duelling ring. "Prepare to fight Kastiek."

The master's last two words lodged themselves in Daijen's brain, holding him fast. He looked at Kastiek, who waited patiently inside the ring of stone. His golden eyes never wavered, reminding Daijen again of the Vahlken's Aegre.

"I gave you a command!" The Valtorak barked.

With a glance at Ilithranda, Daijen made his way to the duelling ring with a lump in his throat. He was stopped when the master of Ka'vairn thrust out his staff at an angle.

"I see fear in you," The Valtorak noted. "In your eyes. In your very step."

Daijen's body language immediately changed in an attempt to combat the weakness. His chest puffed out and his back straightened. His hands clumped into fists and he took a steadying breath before tensing his jaw.

"You cannot shed fear," the master told him. "Every living creature in Verda feels fear. Even *dragons*," he added, circling Daijen. "Fear cannot be dispelled. You cannot quash that which dwells in your very bones. But you can conquer it, as every Vahlken must. Embrace your fear and you will master it. This cannot be done without training, and it is here that your training begins."

Stepping aside, Kastiek was revealed again, absent his cloak now. The Vahlken went on to remove his belt, his sabre and short-sword going with it, all to be collected by Yendi. There was almost a ceremony to it, as he continued to part with the sandy leather cuirass and pauldrons before removing his vambraces. In his trousers and boots, Kastiek now stood a monument to war. His slab-like chest and rippled stomach were marred with a patchwork of scars far worse than anything his cuirass displayed.

The Valtorak caught Daijen staring at the tapestry. "It might trouble you to know that Kastiek came by most of his scars inside these very walls. Trust me, Daijen Saeth, when I tell you: you *will* bleed before you call yourself a Vahlken."

Daijen accepted the words, absorbing them for later, when he didn't feel so raw and exposed. "Why must I fight him?" he asked evenly.

The master eyed him, curiously. "Your instinct is to ask

questions first," he remarked, though his words were no more than an observation apparently. "Tradition," he answered simply.

Daijen sighed inwardly at the word he was already coming to loathe.

"Think of Kastiek as a gatekeeper," The Valtorak began. "Not only is it his duty to keep people *out* of Ka'vairn, but also to keep them *in*. When Kastiek deems you fit, you may receive a Vahlken's sabre and atori blade. There is a difference, however, in having the skill to wield such weapons and wielding them as a Vahlken should. Only *I* can deem you fit for the latter."

Daijen nodded along. "What are the rules?" he asked, setting loose a ripple of amusement through the initiates.

"The rules are simple," the master replied. "Beat Kastiek in hand-to-hand combat and you will receive your sabre this very day."

Daijen's eyes narrows momentarily. "And what does *beating* him look like? First blood? First on their back?"

A sharp smile cut The Valtorak's face. "Don't worry, Daijen of House Saeth, Kastiek will teach you what it is to be beaten."

It was then, before he had even stepped inside the duelling ring, that Kastiek's boot imprinted upon Daijen's chest. He slammed onto the stone before skidding across the courtyard at speed. Coughing and in pain, he tried to pick himself up as quickly as possible, his peripheral vision informing him that Kastiek was fast approaching.

On his feet again, Daijen had just enough time to raise his left hand and push aside the incoming punch. His left hand, however, moved significantly faster than he knew it could and he pushed naught but air aside. A fraction too early, he now suffered the fist he had tried to deflect, taking it across the jaw. Again, he was taken from his feet and launched back until he crashed through a portion of the stable's wooden wall. He heard the horses move and neigh in disturbance but he never even glimpsed the animals before Kastiek lifted a boot into his gut and sent him across the courtyard again.

Getting up, his ribs crying out in pain, Daijen misused his new-found strength and propelled himself from his feet and back to his hands and knees. He was scrambling across the stone when Kastiek caught up with him and hammered his face into the ground. Before he could recover, blood drooling from his mouth, rough hands picked him up and threw him into one of the training dummies.

Amidst splintered wood and tufts of straw, Daijen spied his opponent rounding the debris to reach him. Be it pain or humiliation, something snapped inside of the younger warrior. Now his blood was boiling with wrath. A burning anger demanded his attention, demanded that he unleash pure savagery upon his foe.

Daijen exploded from the debris at speed, one fist rising and determined to meet Kastiek's face. But damned if his feet weren't moving fast. Daijen covered more ground than he could ever have believed possible in such a short time and he quickly dashed past Kastiek. By the time he thought about stopping it was too late and he crashed into the archery range.

Slait's hearty laughter was exaggerated in Daijen's ears. "He's going to beat *himself* to death!"

On his hands and knees, blood trickling from his right eyebrow, Daijen caught sight of Ilithranda, standing apart from the other initiates. Her features remained as impassive as The Valtorak's. Nevertheless, just having her watch him increased the humiliation as well as increasing his need to impress her. And so he found the strength to rise again.

Kastiek was coming for him, his strides that of a war horse that knew it could not be tempered. Daijen reached for the nearest piece of debris—a broken target board—and hurled it at the Vahlken. Though he possessed the ability to evade the missile, Kastiek threw his fist into it, creating a shower of wooden splinters and dust.

The latter might have clouded the Vahlken's vision for little more than a second but, with Handuin's magic coursing through his veins, Daijen was able to dive at his opponent and cross the gap in that precious moment. He wrapped his arms around Kastiek's waist as his shoulder, all his weight behind it, slammed into the Vahlken's midriff.

Yet it was not enough to tip the fight, nor even push Kastiek back a step.

The Vahlken absorbed the blow while simultaneously pivoting and grabbing Daijen by his clothes. When his twist was complete, he merely tossed Daijen away, using his own momentum to send him spinning across the courtyard.

The fight would have long been over for the Daijen Saeth who entered the pit of gleaming water, but as he was, rebuilt by ancient magic, the young Andaren managed to find his feet and spit a mouthful of blood onto the ground. He realised, if only for a brief moment, that he wasn't out of breath as he had expected to be. He still knew pain though. It seemed there was no cure for such a thing, even if he was able to bear it.

Kastiek came at him again, a slab of Andaren carved from the whitest marble. He gave no outward sign as to what he was going to do, forcing Daijen to rely on his reactions. It was no use. Though he succeeded in batting away two or three of the incoming fists and evading what could have been a devastating kick, the Vahlken was simply the superior fighter. He found the gaps and took advantage of Daijen's inability to coordinate his newborn body.

Where three or four blows would have sufficed, and ended the fight, Kastiek deliberately kept Daijen on his feet until he had delivered near on a dozen blows to his body and face. Then, and only then, was Daijen allowed to fall back and greet the edge of the duelling ring. He looked up at the many faces that peered down at him, their features slowly fading to shadow.

The Valtorak towered over him until the tunnel of darkness framed his face alone. "You are beaten, Daijen Saeth."

16

ACROSS THE DRIFTING SEA

HAVING MADE A BRIEF STOP ON HARENDUN'S SOUTHERN OUTSKIRTS, WHERE a small herd of milk-rich cows still remained inside their pen, Androma fed Joran what she could before putting him back to sleep on the walk to the beach. The old Rider kept close to the smuggler, her staff swaying steadily to keep her from tripping over so much debris.

Now, on the deck of The Raven, Gallien Drakalis put his mouth to good use. "It has to be tonight," he was saying to the ship's captain, one Bail Addison.

"Tonight?" the captain echoed incredulously, his voice on Androma's right and his salty musk in her nose. "You must've hit your head in there, Drakalis. I can't leave tonight! I've been paid to ferry both ways."

"Both ways?" Gallien questioned from her left.

"Aye! Soldiers here and prisoners back." With his answer, Captain Addison stamped on the decking. "We've already got two dozen below. Waiting on ten more apparently—not finished questioning them yet, I imagine."

"You're taking *prisoners* back to Erador?" There was a touch of horror in Gallien's disbelief.

Addison responded with a mirthless laugh. "Things have changed a bit since your days in the king's colours. There ain't no more trading of prisoners and the like. They all go back to Erador. They make damned good farm hands by all accounts." The captain's leathers creaked as he leaned towards the smuggler. "I wonder what the Padoshi will make of *you*?" he pondered menacingly.

Andaren prisoners came as no surprise to Androma, but she was interested to learn more about her travel companion. Now she knew for certain that he had once been a soldier, a fact that informed her of several things where his attributes were concerned. The other was more concerning.

"Padoshi?" she questioned. "Which one?"

"Thedaria's," the captain replied. "Who are you again? Who *is* she? And why is she on *my* ship?"

"You're in trouble with the Padoshi of Thedaria?" Androma aimed her voice at the smuggler. "His reputation would suggest he's the worst of them all," she pointed out.

"True enough," Gallien said, exasperated already. "She's with me. The babe too."

"Babe?" the captain spat.

Androma's heart was immediately set to racing and she whipped her head around. "I warned you, smuggler." Her voice was laden with threat as one hand came protectively around Joran's back. The other felt for the hilt of the dagger through her rags.

"The journey's three days," Gallien was speaking quickly now. "Captain Addison doesn't take kindly to secrets on his ship and there's no chance in hell you're keeping a baby secret all that time. He needs to know. He also needs to know..." Judging by Drakalis's voice, he had turned his back to The Raven's captain. "... we can pay our way."

"I highly doubt that," Addison replied dourly. "Not with what you're demanding. Leaving tonight, without the rest of the prisoners will spark their ire. And I know for a fact that my crew aren't going to take kindly to a baby on board."

"Take the prisoners to Caster Hold," Gallien told him. "Tell them that's all they gave you and take the coin for services rendered. We both know you'll have changed the ship's name before word can get back from here. As for your crew: they're *your* crew, aye? They'll do as you tell them and get on with it."

Again, Addison's leathers creaked about his chest, suggesting he had folded his arms. "Well haven't you got it all figured out. Go on then, impress me, Drakalis. What could you have that will set wind to my sails?"

Gallien said nothing, leaving Androma to assume that he was looking to her. She sighed in defeat, ashamed to have found herself in this position. Reaching for the atori blade that Ilithranda had wielded for so long, she held it between the three of them and waited for one of them to claim it. The direction of the hand told her that Addison had taken it from her grip. In so doing, she felt some of Joran's inheritance go with it.

"Gallien..." The captain's voice was little more than a quiet rasp. "Is this..."

"Aye," the smuggler confirmed, a broad grin behind his voice. "It's a Vahlken short-sword. An *atori* blade," he added, using what knowledge Androma had imparted.

"The blade," Addison commented. "It's so rough."

"Silk of The Weavers," Androma stated flatly. "It's bonded over the steel: gives it a look of bronze."

"Silk of the what?" The Raven's captain reminded Androma that she was privileged to know such secrets of the Vahlken.

"Never mind," she said dismissively. "It's the real thing. You'll note the stamp on the pommel."

Addison said nothing while he tipped the blade down, where he might see the taloned foot of an eagle. "How in the hells did you..." The pirate faltered. "Something tells me, boy, this isn't what you came looking for. Hells, this ain't even the woman you came here with. What are you getting mixed up in now? What are you getting *me* mixed up in? I can't shift this! It'll raise too many questions and point too many fingers back at me."

"I have a contact in Caster Hold," Gallien blurted. "You can sell anything to anyone through him. He's discreet. Trust me, Captain. I've sold relics to Blood Lords in Elderhall and Hemon through him. Do you have any idea how much you could sell this for? A real Vahlken weapon. There isn't a highborn in Erador who wouldn't want that on their mantel. And they won't care where it came from."

Addison groaned as his greed and concern clashed. "Damn you to the hells, Gallien Drakalis. You'll be the death of me. Mr Gibbons!"

Androma heard rushing footsteps heading towards them. "Captain?" came a man's voice, maybe four paces away.

"Quick and quiet, get the crew aboard. Come nightfall, we're putting this place to our rudders. Got it?"

"Aye, Captain," was Gibbons' response, before hurrying to his work.

Addison's breath, clouded with ale, assaulted Androma. "As for you two," he said, "it's going to be a cramped journey. Nothing I can do about that. There might be a couple of bunks next to the galley. As for the baby..." The pirate sighed. "This ain't no place for a babe. Hells, it ain't no place for the blind neither. If it gets choppy, stay away from the rails; ain't no one going in after you. That goes for the babe too. Oh, and don't let it go waking the men up. Life at sea with pirates is one thing, but life at sea with pirates that ain't slept puts us all in danger."

"While we're laying out the rules," Androma asserted, "let it be known, *Captain*: any man who tries to touch me or the baby will never see home. Also, I will not tolerate questions of any kind. My business is my own."

Addison had no immediate response, though Androma heard the atori blade twisting in his grip. "Aye, that seems fair."

"To be clear," Gallien said, reinserting himself, "this pays for both of us."

"Hmm," the captain pondered. "So it does. But you're going to tell me everything about this contact of yours. You won't take one foot off this deck until I'm satisfied."

"Excellent!" Drakalis exclaimed, clapping the captain on the arm. "You wouldn't happen to have already loaded any Andaren cider, would you?"

Had Androma any eyes beneath her blindfold, she would have rolled them.

It was with no small amount of relief that Harendun was left behind. Though she had seen her last sunset, the old Rider had felt its heat fade and the cool of night come on before departure. And so, it was under the cover of night that they fled. The deck had been all whispers and the sailors' work slow and quiet, but The Raven had set sail from Andara's shores with ne'er an alarm.

A wave of terrible regret and grief overcame Androma, her thoughts cast back to Ilithranda, left in the bed amidst a city in ruin. It was undignified. It was not what she deserved. What did war and destiny care of such things? They were all but pawns—Ilithranda included—in a game being played by the powers of Fate itself.

All she could do now was keep the child safe so he might see the prophecy through.

Feeling the increased chill that came with the sea breeze, Androma planted a soft kiss on Joran's head and retired to the lower decks. She still had a long way to go.

The next two days and nights became one long stretch of combating seasickness. Androma had hardly slept and, when she did, it was always with a bucket beside her hammock. On the third and final day of crossing The Drifting Sea, the old Rider pressed herself against the starboard rail and, once more, retched into the water.

Feeling the sun on her left cheek, she knew the dawn was cresting the eastern horizon, bringing a new day to Erador. How she craved to be up there with the sun. Vivid were her memories, bringing back the clouds and heavens above to her imagination. What she wouldn't give to soar through it all again. Up there was where she belonged.

With *him*.

Joran began crying, jolting her from the reverie. The thought of walking up and down the deck and patting him back to sleep was almost enough to make her vomit again. "There, there," she managed, rubbing his back uselessly.

"It seems you have no career in sailing." The comment strayed from Gallien's mouth, the rising sun behind him.

"My stomach wasn't made for the water," she agreed.

"You haven't slept since we left Harendun," the smuggler pointed out. "And I've been eating most of your food so I know you haven't eaten. And what you have eaten..." His voice drifted over the railing. "Well, the fish are eating it now."

"What's your point?" she rasped, her irritation rising dramatically with Joran's insistent cry.

Drakalis either didn't have a point or he was hesitating. "My point is... Well, I could help with... with the *babe*. I could take a turn. Walk him up and down."

"Out of the question," Androma blurted, her grip tightening around the rail as another wave of nausea came over her.

"I've been watching you," he said. "I've seen what you do—it doesn't look that hard."

Androma would have sniggered if it didn't mean more vomiting. "Your back will disagree."

"Where am I going to go?" he asked. "We've another day ahead of us."

Androma was nearly sick just hearing that.

"Let me take him for a time," Gallien persisted. "You rest. Or at least try and rest."

Still suspicious, Androma demanded to know why he would show such kindness. "I have no more to offer you," she added.

"I'm not one of them," he told her, his voice moving as he looked to the ambling crew.

The old Rider, her hood resting on her shoulders, raised an eyebrow. "Not anymore, you mean. I have heard your patter while talking to them. This was your life once."

"I've lived a few lives, I'll admit. I'm happy to say I didn't bring harm to a child in any of them."

Androma took deep breaths. "I find that hard to believe. The king's colours, he said. One of those lives was that of a soldier."

"Aye, it was," he confirmed. "And my statement still stands."

"How many Andaren children will never see their mother or father again because you swung your sword?" she countered, her irritation morphing into outright anger.

Gallien said nothing for a time. "Very well," he eventually replied, his offence articulated by his voice. "I was only trying to... It doesn't matter." He was turning to leave.

"Wait," she commanded, one hand reaching out to find naught but air. "I... Whatever your answer, my own would have dwarfed it," she assured, her shame and guilt enough to drown out her anger.

"Who *are* you?" the smuggler asked, a frown behind his question.

"The answer to that won't make your life any less complicated." Feeling another spasm reaching up for her throat, Androma decided to do what was best for Joran. "Here," she said, untying the fabric that kept the baby strapped to her chest. "Keep him close. Patting seems to work."

The moment she was free of Joran's weight the old Rider heaved again, drawing a chuckle from one of the passing crew. The journey couldn't be over soon enough.

"Have you done it?" she eventually asked, hearing Joran's muffled cries.

"Just about. Get some rest. He's safe with me."

"Trust me, smuggler," Androma intoned, "that boy will never be safe."

17
WHY WE FIGHT

80 Years Ago...

The world came back to the newly initiated while the morning was still young. The dawning sun was warm on his face as it topped the mountains and brought light to the valley. Daijen soon realised he was lying exactly where he had fallen.

Cautious of his injuries, he was slow to sit up. He was pleasantly surprised to find there were no lingering wounds save the subtle ache in his left ribs. One finger explored his lips where there should have been obvious splits but found no such thing. This startling revelation—making him feel near invincible—would have seen him leap with excitement were it not for those he shared the courtyard with.

The other initiates, Ilithranda included, were dotted around the interior walls, each focused on the demands of various routines. Laif was in the archery range, a bow raised and arrow nocked at his impressive jawline. Naelin and Yendi danced across the ramparts as they collided with swords and fury. Kovun similarly wielded a sword, though he brought it to bear against all five of the stuffed dummies that surrounded him. Soyra was the closest to Daijen, her body upside down as she balanced on an upturned log and using one hand no less.

Slait stood out, as he always did.

Rather than his fiery temper or severe scalp, the initiate stood out for his lack of activity. He sat with his back against the battlements and knees up to support the leather-bound book in his hands. The book might have remained obscure to Daijen had his eyes not closed the gap and found the glyphs along the spine. Slait was reading the Arkalon again, consumed by it.

Hoping to avoid Slait's notice, Daijen stood up and immediately made for Ilithranda, who was hurling spears in the south-west corner. The latest spear to leave her grip went wild by several feet and struck Ka'vairn's unyielding stone. The weapon snapped and Ilithranda swore under her breath. Daijen couldn't help but smile, though not in light of her struggles, but because he had heard her so clearly and from so far away.

"Daijen Saeth."

If hearing his name wasn't enough to halt him in his tracks then The Valtorak's voice certainly was. The master of Ka'vairn was standing by the main doors, his curved staff gripped in both hands and close to his chest. His violet eyes arrested Daijen and would have drawn him in regardless of any spoken word.

"Master." Daijen hadn't even registered the steps taken to put him in front of The Valtorak.

Ka'vairn's stoical master said nothing as he retreated into the fortress. Daijen couldn't help but get swept up in his wake and so followed The Valtorak inside. They walked through the labyrinth, one behind the other, in silence, the only sound from their footsteps and the master's trailing robe. As they rose ever higher, he was tempted to ask where they were going but decided against voicing any questions. If The Valtorak wanted him to know, he would know.

At last, the pair arrived at a short hall that housed a single door. The Valtorak inserted a key, retrieved from within the shadows of his cerulean robes, and pushed his way through.

Daijen's attention was naturally drawn up, for the humble office was crafted with four pillars, partially buried in the walls, that rose to a domed ceiling. There might have been an image painted inside the dome, but it was so faded, cracked, and layered in dust that its beauty would be forever lost.

The heart of the sanctum was dominated by a thick desk of dark oak, the foundation of a small fortress made entirely of parchments and scrolls. Books lined the walls between the pillars: volumes and collections that spanned Andara's history, laws, and ancient geography. The morning sun found its way in through narrow slits set high into the walls.

"You survived the waters," the master began, rounding his desk. "It is never a sure thing, though I believed it less so in your case."

"Why did *I* survive?" he asked, his thoughts dwelling on Elivar.

"No one knows why some survive and others do not. You saw yourself how the pit rejected Elivar, a warrior of renown and worthy of Handuin's path, yet it has imbued *you* with great power. You should know, Daijen Saeth, it has also burdened you with *honour*. Do you know what that is?"

Daijen hadn't been expecting the question and was therefore slow to answer. "To be good." He cleared his throat. "To be good in all things."

The Valtorak kept him firmly in his violet gaze. "Good and bad. Right and wrong. Most people in this world know what the right thing is. What it is to be *good*. I say it is not enough to *know* what is right, what is good. As a Vahlken, it is your duty to *do* the right thing. In time, you will come to see that the laws and ways of Andara do not always align with the right thing. With the *good*. In time," he echoed, "you will come to see that *you* are the line that stands *between* right and wrong. Goodness and evil. Do you see the distinction now? The difference between mere soldier and Vahlken?"

Daijen cleared his throat. "I think so."

"Then say it."

"As a Vahlken," he replied, "I am to show a quality that sees me rise above the laws and rules of our people, if for their own good."

"Not above," The Valtorak corrected. "*Outside*. Handuin created this order to fight for Andara's people. Not Andara. Not Andara's emperor. Not Andara's interests. For its *people*. Without them there is nothing worth fighting for. We do not answer to the imperial line. We are not beholden to the grand clerics and their religious law. We are the guardians of every Andaren man, woman, and child. There is no force, be it magic or weapon, that can stop us from being that. And," he pointed out, "as long as we vow to be just that, we will maintain the support of the people. That is something the emperor cannot ignore."

Daijen spared himself a moment to absorb his master's words and try, as he might, to align them with all that he knew—all that he had been told. "But," he finally responded, "Vahlkens fight in the war. They've led entire armies," he added, thinking of the famous battle that had ravaged The Plains of Pelun centuries ago.

"Do not mistake our aid for *service*," The Valtorak said bluntly. "We rise to defend the people when they are under threat. That includes the men and women who serve in the emperor's armies. And *dragons*," he specified, "qualify as a threat to us all. More so, the war is a threat we cannot ignore. So yes, we fly into battle and the armies of Emperor Qeledred follow us. We do not *lead* them, though it may look that way. It may even be *recorded* that way. But written history is seldom the same as history itself."

Daijen was shaking his head. "I have grown up on stories of the Vahlken, of Handuin. How could I not know this?"

The Valtorak moved for the first time since he began speaking, moving to the nearest window where he might look out on the battlements and valley beyond. "We protect the people. We do not educate them. It has long been the opinion of the emperor, and those who counsel the Empyreal Throne, that such distinctions remain quiet, lest the people discover that there are *any* who are permitted to dwell outside of the law."

The sacred words of the Arkalon came to Daijen in response. "The house of Lhoris is written in scripture, their rule decreed by the gods before The Fall. All are to bow to their line. Any who do not are punishable—"

"By death," The Valtorak finished. "So it is written. And indeed they tried. Ka'vairn still wears the scars of those early battles."

Moving to the adjacent window, Daijen couldn't help but search for those scars. "Our own people attacked Ka'vairn?"

"The emperor of the time wanted Handuin's head to adorn the gates of Aran'saur. Remember, Handuin had not only positioned himself outside of the law, he had also abandoned his duty as a warlock. He drew the ire of emperor and cleric alike."

Looking out at the fortress with new eyes, Daijen almost imagined the siege taking place. "But they found peace," he said, stating the obvious.

"An uneasy one but, yes, *peace*. And not with the emperor but his successor, Empress Venya. While her father would have been happy to send battalion after battalion, she saw the futility in waging war with an enemy who held the better vantage and with naught but a narrow path to reach it. Then there was Handuin's Aegre, of course."

"Ronyn," Daijen blurted, the fabled name never far from memory.

The Valtorak was nodding. "The ways of our order were established in the aftermath of that conflict and have continued through the millennia without too much friction. More often, the emperor will call on us for advice, though I, and many before me, have suspected our counsel is not wanted so much as our presence in the capital from time to time."

Though The Valtorak had spoken at length, Daijen still felt the central question remained unanswered. "Why?" he asked. "Why would the gods—*Ahnir*—instruct Handuin to establish the Vahlken, to create Aegres? Why would they put the house of Lhoris on the throne and then order others to stand apart?"

"Those questions have been asked inside this room more times than the sun has risen over The Morthil Mountains. Until the gods are reborn and the heavens reforged, we can but debate and speculate." The master's attention was taken again but not by the view but the past, his violet eyes fixed on the spot beside Daijen. "I too asked those questions when I was brought here."

Hungry to know more, Daijen stepped forward. "And what were you told?"

"The Valtorak of my time was better read where the Arkalon is concerned. Her answers would often refer to its words and teachings. She said..." The master hesitated, licking his lips before starting again. "She said the Vahlken would be needed when the empire was blinded by its own pursuits. That we, who stood apart, would be the only ones who saw it coming."

"Saw what?"

"The *End*. The return of the Dark Ones." The Valtorak tapped his staff twice into the stone at his feet, missing one of the rugs that lined the floor. "You may determine your own interpretation. Though, I warn you, trying to understand the machinations of the gods will trap your mind in the future. You will better serve the people of these lands if you keep yourself grounded in the present. Understood?"

Daijen missed a beat while taking on so much. "Yes, Master."

"Good. Adhere to Kastiek's training as you do the rules of this order and you will rise above any accolade The Saible might have bestowed upon you. This is your opportunity, Daijen Saeth, to do something with your life. Give it everything you have—your duty demands nothing less."

The initiate bowed his head. "I will, Master."

"I should say," The Valtorak added, "that if you fail in your training or break the rules of Ka'vairn, your life will be forfeited. Surviving the pits does not entitle you to the rank of Vahlken; it merely gives one the tools to *try*."

"I understand, Master."

"I hope you do," The Valtorak replied. "Fewer and fewer are chosen for this path. You may yet be the last of our order. The last hope against the coming dark," he muttered, moving for his chair. "Now be gone. I have imparted all that you need to know. For now. Return to the courtyard. Kastiek will inform you."

Daijen bowed his head. "Thank you, Master."

Atop the northern ramparts, his hair swept out by the mountain wind, Daijen felt laid bare under the scrutinising gaze of Kastiek. His golden eyes glanced up at the domed tower from where Daijen had come.

"You have spoken with The Valtorak," he said, the timbre of his voice too soft for one who commanded death.

"I have. I know *why* we fight."

Kastiek laughed without making a sound. "You don't get to know the *why* until you know *how*," he said, his words in contradiction to their shared master. "Do you know *how* to fight, Daijen?" the Vahlken asked, his tone almost mocking.

Daijen wanted to argue the point and remind Kastiek that he had been through the same training as every soldier in the emperor's army. That he had fought humans in the streets of Harendun and even killed one. But Kastiek had beaten him with his bare hands only hours ago, and so he kept his mouth shut.

"You don't even know how to run," the Vahlken continued. "Right now, muscle memory is your greatest enemy. That is to say: *you* are your greatest enemy. Over the next decade you will have to unlearn everything and retrain your new body and senses—"

"Decade!" The word forced its way from Daijen's lips.

Kastiek's hand lashed out and clipped the initiate around the head. "You are to listen, learn, and adapt. Interrupt me again and I'll clip you with *steel*."

"Sorry, Master," Daijen offered with a short bow.

He hardly registered Kastiek's hand before he felt the sting of it whipping the back of his head again.

"I am not your master," the Vahlken told him. "I am not your castellan or your paragon or your justiciar. I am simply your *better*. You will bend to my will because you are incapable of doing otherwise. Should there come a day when you find yourself capable of beating me—or even stopping *me* from beating *you*—then, and only then, will you be truly free."

His speech delivered, Kastiek moved away so he might better

see the other initiates training in the courtyard below. "Look," he instructed, having Daijen join him by the edge. "They have spent years in these walls. Watch how they move, the control they employ. It is only with time that they have all known such command over their actions. When they emerged from the pits, they all looked like *that*."

Daijen followed the Vahlken's gaze to Ilithranda. She was all the easier to spot while training alongside Naelin, the two having ascended the upturned logs that formed a grid pattern. Naelin danced across the logs, her sword flashing to slice every one of the small pouches of sand thrown up by Yendi. Ilithranda missed all of her targets and was notably slow at transitioning from log end to log end. It seemed inevitable that she would fall and she soon did just that, her right foot overstepping and finding naught but air.

Slait's laughter cut through the courtyard.

Caked in mud and sweat and bristling from head to toe, Ilithranda picked herself up and immediately began marching towards him. Her sword was still in hand. Daijen took a step, seeing the fight to come, but was halted by Kastiek's arm.

Daijen looked from the Vahlken to Slait, who appeared only too happy to see Ilithranda coming for him. "What are you doing?" he asked urgently.

"This isn't the first time," Kastiek replied evenly. "I intervened then. Now she's on her own."

Slait was casually tossing and catching a single-handed axe as she approached. "Come on then, little princess," he goaded.

Ilithranda broke into a run and closed the gap at incredible speed. Slait, it seemed, had been anticipating as much and launched his axe, sending the weapon into the hard ground at her feet. Ilithranda was forced to leap over the axe but, as Daijen had in his fight with Kastiek, she used more strength than was necessary. Instead of merely clearing the weapon, she bounded over Slait's head and impacted the edge of the hard canopy that covered the axe range. Her body twisted at an awkward angle and she hit the ground on her side.

Slait was waiting for her.

The bald initiate picked her up by the back of her neck and slammed a tight fist into her face and a second into her gut, doubling her over. Still holding her by the back of the neck, he then tossed her aside like a rag doll, a fresh laugh on his lips.

It was then that Daijen's fist met Slait's jaw.

How Daijen had got to that point was a blur, his body moving with a swiftness he had never known. Even Kastiek had failed to react in time and prevent him from dropping off the ramparts. Now, taken by surprise and unbridled strength, Slait was launched from his feet and sent sprawling across the courtyard.

No one moved.

The other initiates watched intently.

Daijen might have been amazed—shocked even—with his actions had his blood not still been boiling under his skin. He stood with hands clenched, waiting for Slait to get up so he might strike again. Inevitably, he did. A deep scowl ruled his expression and he spat blood on the ground. Daijen gritted his teeth, preparing for the fight coming his way. And so it came, but not from Slait's direction.

Ilithranda shoved Daijen's shoulder so he might face her—if only for a moment. Her fist shot out like a ballista bolt and took Daijen in the chest. Like him, her strength was beyond control, the blow throwing him back into the axe range and through one of the wooden targets.

The pain was overwhelming, distracting even, but it subsided at supernatural speed, allowing Daijen to prop himself up on his elbows. Kastiek was in the courtyard now, his considerable frame between Slait and all else. It seemed Slait's anger had bubbled over and taken his sense with it, for he assaulted Kastiek to reach the axe range. At least he tried.

Kastiek raised one arm and pointed his elbow at Slait's incoming fist, a defence that broke at least one of the initiate's knuckles. The Vahlken's hand shot up in a blur of white and caught Slait across the throat, cutting through the pain in his hand and giving him an entirely new problem. Choking and spluttering, and down to one working hand, Slait was powerless to stop Kastiek from flipping him onto his back and dragging him away by one ankle.

By then, Ilithranda was standing over Daijen. She looked down on him with a split lip and contempt behind her violet eyes. "Fight for me again, and I will put you down myself."

Daijen hoped that the hurt he felt didn't reveal itself in his breaking expression. He simply nodded in response as it dawned on him how alone he was going to be in this cold place.

Still, Ilithranda's open hand appeared in front of him, turning his attention back up to her. The contempt was gone, softened to something close to appreciation. Daijen took her hand and accepted the help to stand.

"And thank you," she said, eye to eye again.

Unsure what to say to that, Daijen could only nod sheepishly. "I really don't like him," he remarked, glancing at Slait as he was unceremoniously dragged inside the keep.

"That's something we *all* have in common," Ilithranda replied.

"Did Kastiek tell you how long we're to train for?" he asked.

"He told me it would take ten years to learn how to control my body," she answered. "I have a feeling our *training* will take much longer than that."

"Longer?" Daijen was looking past her now, to the initiates.

"I've been here for a month, Daijen. None of them have received training in the ways of the Vahlken. *None.* I don't think any of that begins until we've mastered our new selves."

Daijen now saw the decades rolling out in front of him. Decades in which he would be trapped in these walls, and with Slait no less. He thought of the foolish and weaker young man who had stepped into the pits without so much as a harness. Had he proved his point? Had the eternity of pain been worth it? The eons of fire and ice, the agony of it?

No was the simple answer.

He had proved nothing. *Yet.* Damned if he had gone through all that to remain overlooked, underestimated, and discarded. He would see this to its end, to glory and honour. To power and freedom.

He looked at Ilithranda, walking away now. Power and freedom, she had said, planting those ideas, those dreams, in his head. He was sure they didn't mean the same thing to him. Ilithranda, he felt, wished to leave, to leave it *all*. She would take her power and freedom and put Andara and the war behind her. For Daijen, power and freedom were the two things he would give back to his people.

When he was ready, he would return to the war that had raged for so long without him. On that day, he vowed, the earth would tremble.

18
RETURNING IN DARKNESS

As always, Androma awoke to the same darkness she had fallen asleep to. Though she would never admit such a thing, it was always fear-inducing. On this occasion, her fear was amplified when she remembered leaving Joran with the smuggler.

The old Rider sat up immediately and began reaching out to feel her surroundings. "Gallien?" she called, claiming her staff. "Gallien?"

Cramped though the quarters were, on her feet she realised her nausea had passed. More so, The Raven was stationary. Fear and adrenaline put her to action and she retraced her steps to the main deck. By the temperature on her skin she guessed it to be dusk, which meant she had slept most of the day away.

Then there were the sounds that engulfed the old Rider.

The noise was well beyond anything the ship's crew were capable of. It was the general hubbub of a populated area. The various calls that cut through the buzz suggested they were in a port. That could only mean one thing.

They had arrived at Caster Hold.

"Gallien?" she shouted over the din.

Her heart was in her throat now, her blood pounding in her

ears. What had she been thinking? How could she have just handed Joran over? And to a man she had known for little more than two days! Ilithranda's image and berating voice came to her, reminding Androma of the vow she had made to protect her son.

Moving across the deck, she was inevitably knocked and jolted by the busy crew. She grabbed the second to clip her and forced him to turn about. "Where is Gallien Drakalis?" she demanded.

"Easy!" The very same smuggler's voice came from behind. "Let's not harm the crew *now*."

Androma swivelled, forgetting the sailor altogether. "You have Joran?" she burst out with.

"He's right here." Gallien took her by the wrist and gently guided her hand to the baby's head. "You've been out of it all day," he explained, before pulling her in so his mouth was closer to her ear. "You *lied*," he accused through gritted teeth. "The boy's half *Andaren*."

Androma froze—if only for a second—after taking the babe in her arms. Of course he had discovered the truth. How could he not have? His eyes alone betrayed his heritage. For centuries she had fought and survived the worst of times, yet seasickness was enough to make her lose all sense apparently. She ran a hand over the boy's head and discovered the tight wrap she had previously secured to hide his pointed ears and ashen hair.

"I put it back on," Gallien explained.

The old Rider proceeded to strap him to her chest. "Who else knows?" she demanded, wondering how many people would have to die.

"No one," the smuggler answered, and with truth in his voice. "Addison would..." Gallien paused as a handful of the crew walked past. Before starting again, he took Androma by the arm and she allowed him to guide her across the deck. "If anyone had seen him, you can be sure Addison would've had Gibson throw the boy overboard."

The old Rider gripped his forearm. "You're sure he remains a secret?"

"Yes," he hissed, almost dismissively. "Do you have any idea what would happen if a *half blood* was discovered on this ship? This is Caster Hold! It's an army town wrapped around a fortress! Even The Gilded have a temple here. Set them off and The Jainus will come down on us. The Jainus," he repeated, as if he had only just considered the complication and danger of wizards. "They'd seize the whole damn port with their *magic*. We'd all be stripped of our skin before the dawn."

"Calm yourself, lest you give us away," Androma directed.

"*Us?*" the smuggler instantly questioned.

"Us," she reminded. "Was it not you who talked *us* onto The Raven? Have the crew not seen *you* walking up and down the ship with the boy? Make no mistake, Smuggler, your life is tied to his now. You had best see us safely away from Caster Hold as you promised."

"I'll hold up my end," Gallien assured. "But how in the hells have you come by a half blood? They're forbidden in both realms. *Highly* forbidden," he stressed. "Do you know what that means? You don't just face execution, you face an excruciatingly *slow* execution."

"We agreed no questions," Androma reminded.

"That was before I had to smuggle a baby with pointy ears and white hair," he seethed.

"Can you do it or not?" she asked bluntly.

The smuggler leaned against the port side railing and sighed before turning back to her. "I can do it," he stated. "But violet eyes aren't going to help. You need to keep him wrapped up tight."

"Joran is safe with me," she said. "You should worry about those who challenge that."

Gallien sighed again. "Let's try and keep the dagger on your belt."

Hearing the smuggler move away, Androma enquired, "What about Captain Addison?"

"I've squared things with him," Drakalis reported. "He's already sent Gibson to meet my contact."

"So it is gone then," she lamented. "The blade..."

"It's *us* who should be gone," Gallien insisted. "We're the first ship back—there's going to be a lot of eyes on The Raven soon. Our best chance to pass through is while they're unloading the prisoners."

With no choice but to continue trusting the smuggler, Androma kept one hand hooked under his arm as they crossed the ship and descended to the docks. She could hear the chains of Erador's new work force and the padding of their bare feet on the damp wood. Among them were the stomping of heavy boots and rough calls to keep everyone quiet and in line.

"Fresh batch!" one man called from inland.

She heard others spitting and hollering insults. There would be no getting away from the generational hate they would experience in the east. There wasn't an ordinary human alive who had seen the start of the war. As far as these onlookers were concerned, the Andarens were the reason they had lost loved ones and suffered under harsh taxes.

Navigating the docks to reach hard ground, a new voice soon drowned out all others, and pitched from an elevated platform. "The great Kaliban sees all and judges all! He will deliver the faithful unto paradise and He will smite the enemy upon the stone of justice!"

The Gilded.

It was with considerable derision that the name came to Androma. Though she couldn't see the priestling, she knew well from memory that he would be towering over the docks, where he might speak his rhetoric at the approaching Andarens. The lowest of their order, he would be attired in black robes, his head shaved so all could see the three stars tattooed on his forehead.

"This way," Gallien whispered, leading them away from the booming voice.

They travelled across the docks rather than directly to the mainland. Vast as the port was, they could no longer hear the priestling by the time Drakalis instructed her to wait by a post he placed her hand on. She heard him move off and enter a quiet conversation with a stranger. Then there was the distinct sound of metallic marks crossing hands.

"Right," he said upon his return. "Follow me."

"Hold on," the stranger said, his footsteps heard on the wooden boards. "I've got to check you both first."

"What?" Gallien spat. "The whole point of me paying you was so you don't have to check us."

"You paid me not to register your arrival," the stranger specified. "But I've still got to make sure you pose no threat. There's word of pale spies about these parts."

"Do we look like Andarens to you?" the smuggler retorted.

"I can't even see that one?" came the official's response.

Gallien paused, one hand wiping down his face. "Pull your hood down," he said, voice directed at Androma.

Wishing to be done with this, the old Rider complied, revealing her greying hair and tattered blindfold.

"Does she look like a *threat*?" Drakalis fired at the official. The smuggler's voice had begun to trail off at the end, his tone laced with concern.

"What is it?" she asked.

"Soldiers," he informed her, voice tight.

"Where?"

"Walking along the sea wall," he said, "making their way to the dock entrance."

"How many?"

"Three," the smuggler noted.

"Have they seen us?"

"I'd say so—they look damned interested."

"Hang about," the official interrupted. "What is this? You in some kind of trouble with the law?"

"Listen," the smuggler tried before the official spoke over him.

"No, you listen, *mate*. I don't mind letting a few folk slip by here and there, so long as they're not up to no good. I can't be letting troublemakers move about unregistered—I've got family in this town. Is that... Is that a baby?" he questioned with deep suspicion. The official moved back a step, perhaps to alert the soldiers that their hunch was correct.

"Gallien." Androma put all of her distress into the smuggler's name.

"Goddamn it," Drakalis cursed under his breath.

Though incapable of seeing what happened next, Androma knew the sound of one man's head colliding with another. It seemed the smuggler then hurried to catch the official before he fell into the water.

"The soldiers?" she questioned, satisfied with Drakalis's actions.

"I can't see them past the ships, but they were still coming this way," he said, voice strained and low to the dock now.

"What are you doing?"

"Those were my last coins," he replied by way of an explanation.

"We don't have time for that," she chastised. "Prepare for battle."

"Battle?" he echoed with half a laugh. "I don't know who you are, lady, but that begs a *lot* of questions."

"Draw your sword," she commanded, her staff braced in both hands.

"Fighting will only bring more," he warned, rising from the unconscious official. "There's another way. Quickly!"

With one hand firmly fixed on the smuggler's shoulder, Androma followed her companion ever southward, through the maze of docks. She soon heard, however, the sound of scraping armour amidst the gentle splashing of the lapping waves. There came a call to halt but the pair continued their escape.

"They are pursuing," she reported.

"You don't say." Gallien sounded distracted, his head turning left and right as they arrived at new junctions.

"You said you could get us through the harbour safely," Androma reminded.

"It was a different guard," he said in his defence. "And," he pointed out, "no harm has come to you, so I'd say I'm delivering as promised. This way!"

The old Rider heard their rushing footsteps resounding off the larger ships that they passed between. There was a fight coming. She could feel it.

"Can you climb?" the smuggler asked.

"That depends on what I'm climbing," she cracked dryly.

"It's just the sea wall. We can get lost in the streets above."

Androma felt Gallien slow down as they left the boards of the harbour and stepped onto the narrow path that ran along the base of the sea wall. Using one exploratory hand, the old Rider soon touched the wall itself, her fingers feeling out the rough stone and potential handholds.

"Throw it up," she snapped, thrusting her staff into Drakalis's chest.

After hearing the length of wood clatter above, Androma set herself to the climb. "How high?"

"Thirty foot maybe," Gallien replied, his exertion weighing on his voice.

Androma soon left the smuggler behind, ascending the wall with enviable speed. She heard the soldiers again before reaching the top, their boots hurrying down the dock to meet the sea wall.

"You!" one of them cried. "Stop! Oi! Stop!"

The old Rider climbed over the lip and rolled away. Staying low, she swept the ground with her hands until the staff was returned to her grip.

"You're both under arrest!" the soldiers yelled.

By the sound of it, one of them even attempted to wound Gallien by throwing his sword up the wall. The steel *clanged* harmlessly against the stone and fell back to the narrow path as the smuggler topped the wall.

Androma hooked one hand under his arm and aided him to his feet. "What are they doing?" she asked, hearing them retreat.

"They'll not risk that way up," Gallien explained, his breath laboured. "They'll have to circle back to the entrance."

"Then we had best not be here when they return," she suggested.

"I know somewhere," the smuggler said wearily.

Androma kept a mental note of the various turns Gallien led

them down, her mind building a picture of Caster Hold. Having ascended the sea wall in the south, they were on the outskirts of the town that had developed around the keep.

A clap of thunder preceded a light drizzle of rain that wasted no time in becoming a torrent. Androma hated the rain and had done so since losing her sight. It created a racket everywhere it touched and dampened the world about her, robbing the old Rider of a vital sense.

"Over here," the smuggler bade, guiding her by the arm.

"Where are we?" she asked when their journey came to an end.

"Shh."

Androma wanted to scold the man for treating her like a child, she who had ridden on dragon back and touched the top of the sky. She who had saved hundreds of lives in The Battle of the Pelun Plains and broken the lines that defended The Triden.

Her shoulders sagged as she leaned against the wall. It was like remembering a story she had been told. They were memories, she knew, but, without that most extraordinary of bonds, her memory was steadily fading, just as her immortality had withered, numbering the days she had left in Verda.

"Got it," Gallien reported, the sound of small metallic objects in his hand. "Get inside."

"Inside where?"

The smuggler guided her through the door whose lock he had just picked. The overwhelming smell of horses washed over Androma and, free of the rain, she heard a couple of the animals breathing heavily at their intrusion.

"Easy," Drakalis said soothingly, though apparently not to her. He had quickly and quietly moved away—to the nearest stall, perhaps—and was addressing one of the horses. "Good girl," he whispered.

Androma sighed, feeling her fatigue now that they had stopped. She also took the opportunity to relieve herself of Joran's weight and give him a much-needed feed before the crying began.

"Here," Gallien offered, handling the container of stored milk she had removed from her satchel. "Damn that's cold," he remarked. "How in the hells have you kept them so cold?"

Androma motioned with her fingers for him to hand it over. "Cold milk should be the least of your concerns," she replied, quick to shut the line of questioning down. "Should these horses take umbrage with our presence they will alert their master."

"Don't worry about them," he said reassuringly, a hint of affection in his voice. "They already like me."

"You're good with them," she commented off-handedly.

"I hope *you're* good with them," he quipped. "The Beggar's Path is the only road out of here and it's a long one to Farnfoss. We're going to need to steal one of these."

"I don't need to get to Farnfoss," Androma said, positioning the baby in her arms as she sat atop a small stool. "My destination is..." The old Rider stopped herself.

Gallien gave a breathy laugh. "You still don't trust me? Fair enough."

"You're a smuggler and likely worse considering the Padoshi of Thedaria wants your head. Joran is too important."

"What I am," Drakalis replied boldly, "is the man who got you from Harendun to Caster Hold. *Safely*," he added, and pointedly so.

"Thank you," Androma spouted, cutting through the obvious offence she had caused.

The smuggler said nothing for the moment. "You're welcome," he uttered.

Androma nodded along solemnly. Indeed, this apparent scoundrel had done exactly as he said he would, a refreshing fact in itself. He could have left her and Joran on the docks, his own goal of reaching Erador achieved. And there certainly existed a gentle side to the man, for there weren't many who would look after a baby without reward.

"I'm sorry the price was so high," Gallien said, still beside the horse.

In a bid to push aside her memories of Ilithranda, she replied, "There is no price too high to keep Joran safe." And she truly meant it.

"If you want to keep him safe, you can't stay in Caster Hold. Too much suspicion here. It wouldn't take more than a glance to see the truth of him."

Androma agreed. She had never intended to return to Erador via the coastal fortress. "And what would a *damn good* smuggler suggest?"

"Good girl," he muttered to the horse again, before sitting on the edge of a hay bale. "There'll be a shift change when the moon begins to wane. Just before that, when all the patrols are tired and making their way back up to the keep, we saddle one of these horses and make for the road east. It's a little over a week to Farnfoss but you can resupply there before crossing the bridge. From there, you can just follow the road all the way to Thedaria. After that you can go, well... wherever it is you need to."

"You're not crossing the bridge?"

"Oh," Drakalis began with half a laugh, "I have no intention of stepping on the other side of that river. There's only one road and it leads straight to Thedaria. I won't be going within ten miles of that city. No. I'll catch a boat at Farnfoss, head down to Broadcastle and find work there."

"Work?" Androma questioned. "Or trouble?"

"Aren't they the same thing?" he said, with what she suspected was a cocky grin.

A genuine, if quiet, laugh made its way out of the old Rider. "I have lived a similar life," she said wistfully. Sensing some bond of familiarity forming between them, however tenuous, Daijen's warnings returned swiftly to the forefront of her mind. "Why would you come with me?" she was compelled to ask.

"Why? What happened to *us*? I thought we were in this together now."

"I said that so you would feel motivated to get us out of the harbour," Androma explained as a matter of fact. "Now that we are both on home soil, you could easily have lost me in the streets by now, left us to find our own way. Yet here we are. I would know why, when there is work and trouble aplenty in Caster Hold, especially for a smuggler. Those soldiers wouldn't have got a good look at you."

Gallien didn't respond immediately—his expression unknown to her—but, when he did, his voice was weary. "What is a man if he can't at least live by his word?"

Androma frowned inside her hood. "You don't strike me as a man who lives by his word. Aren't you a liar by trade?" Though she couldn't see him, the old Rider detected a heavy air about his demeanour.

"True enough," he breathed. "But I did once. Sometimes I remember that man. Thinking like him can be just as dangerous it seems."

Androma considered his words far more than she intended to. "Sometimes, holding on to who we were is all we have left." She hadn't meant to say it aloud, a truth the old Rider could hardly stand. Uncomfortable, and sensing the smuggler had a response, she adjusted her position on the stool.

"So who were you?" he asked anyway.

Androma replied with the only answer she could truly give. "I was alive." Damned if the man wasn't easy to talk to, an inherent skill he likely employed everywhere he went. Deciding to hold firm to Daijen's imparted caution, she cleared her throat and said, "You have done as you agreed—one way or another. You need not throw your lot in with us any longer."

Gallien made some kind of movement, a shrug possibly. "We both need to get out of Caster Hold and there's only one road to follow. We might as well continue... whatever *this is*."

"I don't require your charity," she told him sharply. "I have walked this earth without sight for many years and I will continue to do so for many more."

Something of a nervous laugh escaped the smuggler. "You're talking to the man who can still feel the dagger between his legs. I believe you."

"I have nothing of value left to offer you," Androma continued, baffled that the man would travel with them. "And I would have thought, given the child's heritage, that you wouldn't want to be anywhere near us."

"I have no hidden agenda," Gallien assured. "We both need to get out of here and we're both going the same way. That's it. Though, I think you might have lost your mind taking the boy further into Erador. There's nowhere he can grow up or find a life without his Andaren half being noticed. I mean, he could get away with the white hair, but the pointy ears and violet eyes... You were right when you said it: he won't be safe anywhere."

"I was wrong actually," Androma admitted, after a moment's thought. "There is one place. He would be safe there. None would dare come for him."

Drakalis shuffled on his hay bale. "Where?" he asked intently. When Androma purposefully gave no response, Gallien dragged a hand down through his beard and rose from his seat. "One step at a time then," he concluded. "Let's just reach Farnfoss. Get some rest," he advised. "It's going to be a *long* week."

It would be the smuggler's *last* week, Androma thought, one hand resting on the pommel of her slender dagger, its blade already crusted with blood.

19

THE BOUND AND THE BROKEN

Again, Kitrana Voden was awoken by the sharp pain in her wrists. The Karathasaur had only to speed up a notch and the increased drag caused the manacles to bite into her flesh. For untold days and nights the creature had towed her through the ocean, taking her ever deeper. She had pondered on the passage of time, her mind still working like a human's. They had journeyed so far down now that the sun couldn't hope to pierce the world of water that sat between Kit and the surface. Day and night had no hold where they were going.

Tilting her head back, she could see all but one of the scouts that had taken her prisoner, the Merdians riding their mounts in an arrow formation. Putting her chin to her chest, she laid eyes on the soldier guarding the rear. He seemed so small astride his mighty Karathasaur.

Looking to her left, Kitrana expected to see the indomitable wall of Erador's western foundations, for the Merdians had been taking her south, following the wall, since capturing her outside Harendun. But it wasn't there. Her eyes strained to see through the dark soup but succeeded only in spying the minuscule particles that littered the water. That meant they were somewhere in the open waters of The Drifting Sea.

They were nearing Atlas.

That was not a city she wished to see, a sentiment shared by all her people. It was then that the Merdian's words came back to her and the Nimean felt the blow all over again. Not only had she missed the war on her crusade but she hadn't been there at the end, to see it through beside her people. Kitrana couldn't even imagine the nightmare that had beset Nimala—a deep dragon with a Merdian army at its back.

Through the black mood that shadowed her thoughts, Kit thought of the broken blade, recalling how it had reduced the Vorge to sparks and ash. Seeing it perform as the legends said was a source of unimaginable relief, but now it only salted the wound to know that, had she succeeded in her quest long ago, she might have saved her people and her home.

In her misery, Kit's head once again sank into her chest. With their arrival in Atlas, she would come to know a new form of torment. To accompany the physical suffering, she would have to live with the knowledge that the broken blade had been lost on her watch. If the Atradon—the Water Maiden—knew any mercy, She would see that Kitrana endured a swift execution. Beyond death, however, she would face The Hag. How would she convince the spiteful being to grant her passage to the Eternal Waters now? Without deed or honour there would be naught but The Devourer to greet her.

As her mind drifted into a bleak future, she looked again to the rear scout. She envisioned her bindings breaking and the trailing Karathasaur opening its jaws to swallow her whole.

But it was not there.

Kit twisted her body to better see the waters behind them, but still the scout and its grim mount were nowhere to be seen. She then felt a sudden tug on her bindings and looked back to the Karathasaur pulling her through the stygian waters. The siden silk weed that had tethered her to the mount was now floating aimlessly in the water ahead, though her momentum soon brought the two together.

In the distance, the remaining Karathasaurs continued unaware until they faded into the deep. Kit grabbed the end of the silk weed, noting how the threads had been *sliced*. The answer soon came, and in the form of dark figures ascending from the depths.

Her sensitive skin felt movement in the water above her, turning her gaze from the approaching shades. There, floating above her like one of the reef angels of old, was a Nimean lance defender, her trident in hand. Her blonde hair rippled in the currents beside her angular face, a face marred by battle scars. Kitrana was soon surrounded by more of her people as the depths released more Nimeans. A mix of men and women, all weary and worn down by the war they had lost, swam into view, their blue tattoos worn proudly.

"Come, sister," the lance defender signed, before severing Kit's bindings. "The Merdians will soon be upon us if we linger."

Without any further word, the blonde Nimean dived for the ocean floor, the ragtag group of rebels around her. Kitrana wasted no time accompanying them into the darkest dark.

The pressure exerted on her body increased to limits that would have reduced any human to paste. Still she descended, the small gaps in her skull adjusting to harmonise with the new pressures.

Kit's eyes discovered the sea floor before her fellow Nimeans could reach it.

The Ruins of Ilthor stretched across the uneven earth, its towers shattered or strewn across the ground. No building or temple, nor even the great arches, remained intact, the ancient settlement little more than a ragged scar at the bottom of the world. Kitrana hadn't seen the ruins since her childhood, though her mother had taken her no further than the city's northern border. Now, she was passing mounded rock and stone and swimming through those long-deserted streets.

The lance defender tucked her trident in and slipped between a narrow gap in what appeared to be the pock-marked remains of a temple that had once been devoted to the worship of the Water Maiden. Kit paused before entering, her attention having wandered just enough to spot the dead Karathasaur not far from the temple, its humungous corpse atop the rubble of a fallen tower.

The lance defender appeared in the narrow crack. "This way," she urged, her eyes darting to the waters above.

After entering the temple, Kit's eyes adjusted again to the deeper gloom. Beneath that domed roof were the many faces of her people, watching her descend. Among them were whole families or, at least, families stitched together in the wake of war and death. Scattered between were soldiers, be they lance defenders, cleavers or hunter scouts. Kit even noticed a trio of guardian knights, their white cloaks flowing out behind them. It was there, behind the protection of the knights, that she laid eyes on a familiar face.

Kitrana darted down, her speed enough to see the masses part and create a path that led directly to the exalted princess. The trio of knights didn't budge an inch at her approach, the bladed tridents ready to whip up. Kit respected their line of authority and simply floated to the floor before them, her head bowed. "Lady Helaina," she signed, her fingers flowing in the more elegant style of the palatine caste.

The princess was slow to advance, though her movement was still enough to part the knights protecting her. Gone was her radiance, the so-called Starlight of The Deep. Destined to replace her mother as queen one day, Helaina had been afforded the finest of attire and jewellery. She had lived in a palace surrounded by admirers, where her every need was attended to by servants.

Had Kit's memory not recalled her face, the princess might have blended in with everyone else. Her dress appeared to be made of the same qelroot most others wore and her fingers and neck were bare without the touch of silvyr rings or coloured siden steel.

"I know your face," the princess signed in return. Revelation soon flashed behind her large green eyes. "You are a battle maiden of the Swordsworn." The declaration sent a ripple throughout the crowd, turning the attention of all upon Kit.

"My name is Kitrana Voden," she announced, still genuflecting.

"Yes. I was there for your ceremony," the princess recalled. "We thought you dead, Maiden. The Sanctum was destroyed by our foes so early in the invasion. Perhaps," she went on, her gaze soaring over her people, "there is hope after all!" Her regal eyes fell over Kit once again. "You have the ancient blade of Skara?"

It was with a mere expression that Kitrana conveyed her answer.

Princess Helaina maintained her own expression before motioning for the battle maiden to accompany her. At the same time she made a gesture of peace to the masses, suggesting they return to their business while she took Kit into her royal, and private, company.

"Swim with me," the princess instructed, taking what was left of a wide passage through the temple. The trio of guardian knights swept in behind them as if they were physically tethered to Helaina. "You do not have the blade," she concluded when they had passed from the sight of all others.

"No, Princess." It was with great shame that Kit replied with those words, and after so long keeping it safe on the surface world.

Helaina gave a mirthless laugh. "Such formality," she remarked. "We have been fighting and hiding for so long. I cannot blame them for their irreverence."

Kitrana frowned. "If I may... where is the *Queen*?"

Helaina nodded solemnly, as if she had been aware that very question was forthcoming. "Where indeed?" she echoed, her sign language slipping here and there into the more colloquial form used by the commoners. "I do not know where my mother is. Nor my sisters or cousins. The family was broken up when..." The princess had to make a conscious effort to push through her violent memories. "There was such chaos that day," she eventually continued. "I had never seen one of the deep dragons before. It was more terrible than the stories would have you believe. We had no defence against it. The Merdians made it their priority to hunt down my family. We have only succeeded in evading them for so long by living like this, in pockets, our people scattered like fish. We have tried to coordinate our counterattack..."

Kitrana could feel her shame trying to avert her eyes, to drag her face down where the princess might not look upon it. "I should have been there," she signed miserably.

"It was never your place to safeguard Nimala," Helaina pointed out. "You shed such responsibility the day you took your oath outside The Sanctum. Yours is only to protect the sword."

Kit could hardly bear the green eyes that bored into her. "I have failed in my duty," she finally put into words, unable to hold on to her fortitude.

"Where is it now?" the princess asked gravely. "Do the Merdians have it?"

Kitrana shook her head. "It's on the surface."

Concern cracked Helaina's visage. "The surface! It was broken for a reason, Maiden! It was to remain beneath the waves for the safety of us all!"

Kit was nodding along, her guilt strangling her features. Small was the voice in her mind, a voice that reminded her that battle maidens existed outside of all hierarchies. Still, she accepted the lambasting from her once princess. After all, she wasn't wrong.

"They all died," Kitrana explained, her flint words enough to momentarily calm Helaina. "The Merdians attacked The Sanctum in numbers we could not stand against. The other battle maidens died defending it. Even the Merdian's tribute. They died fighting so I could get away with the hilt."

"But why would you take it to the surface world?" the princess demanded. "To be so close to its blade is to risk everything. You know this better than I."

Again, Kit was nodding along. "I thought..." It seemed so foolish to say it out loud, even if she believed in her path. "I thought if I could reforge the sword—make it whole again—I could use its power to fight for Nimala."

The princess surged forwards and gripped Kitrana's forearms.

"It cannot be reforged," she warned. "They want it," she said simply.

"The Merdians?"

"Yes, the Merdians," Helaina replied impatiently. "Why do you think they attacked The Sanctum before Nimala? The Dread Queen wants the blade of Skara."

Kit was shaking her head in disbelief. "No," she replied. "The Merdians swore to never wield it—every race did! All but the Vorge have always offered a tribute."

"Is it so unbelievable?" Helaina countered, releasing her grip on Kitrana. "You yourself wished to make it whole and use it in the defence of Nimala. The Dread Queen wishes to use it to attack, to wield it as a symbol of her right to reign over all the seas."

"She already possesses a deep dragon," Kit protested. "What greed could drive her to need more than that?"

The princess was shaking her head. "The Jinn and the Kells have formed an alliance in response to Nimala's demise. Even a deep dragon could not hope to bring down their combined force."

Kit thought of the power she had seen in the broken blade, its ability to reduce life to ash with a single cut. Mighty though it obviously was—and, she assumed, she had witnessed but a portion of its potential—one sword of power would not be enough to bring the other water realms under her banner. It made no sense.

"What of the Adakii?" Kit asked.

The princess shrugged—another mannerism she had adopted from her time living among the commoners. "The Adakii?" she repeated. "Who can say? Besides their tribute, have you ever met another of their people?"

Kit could only shake her head. Guwain had been her name. She had offered little about her people and their ways, they who had sought seclusion after the Merdians expanded their empire centuries past.

"Their fate is to be our own," Helaina deplored. "You know where we are, yes? The Ruins of Ilthor. A great city it was called.

When the Adakii lived here. The same will be said of Nimala in time."

The battle maiden in Kitrana swelled in her chest. "Nimala will have its time again," she avowed. "My Lady, I *will* return to the surface world and I *will* reclaim the hilt—I have seen its power with my own eyes. I will discover the blade, I swear it. We can avenge the fallen and rebuild."

"No," the princess insisted. "Leave the hilt where it is. At least up there it will remain out of the Dread Queen's reach." Something about Helaina's demeanour changed and she was somehow able to grow more serious in that moment. "There is another reason the Merdians may desire the blade." Her eyes flickered to the guardian knights at Kit's back. "We have heard rumours on the currents, though I dare not believe them."

Kitrana fanned her hands, bringing her closer to Helaina. "What rumours?"

The princess brought up her hands to respond but it was another who spoke first, and literally so. The banshee-like shrill penetrated the passage and bombarded their ears, turning them back towards the temple's main chamber. There, floating in the threshold was the same lance defender who had rescued Kitrana. Again, she opened her mouth and produced the deafening alarm. Behind her, clearly panicked, the Nimeans were scattering in every direction.

Kit grabbed one of the guardian knights by the shoulder and turned her about. "Get the princess to safety!" she signed in shorthand.

As the knights rushed the princess further down the passage, Kit propelled herself back towards the temple chamber. The lance defender drew a one-handed sword from over her shoulder and tossed it into the space between them. Voden scooped it up with ease as she brought herself shoulder to shoulder with the Nimean warrior.

"Merdians?" she questioned, half watching her people scurry through every crack they could fit through.

"I think you were bait," the lance defender replied, her expression grave.

On the other side of the domed chamber, cleavers and hunter scouts darted for the largest entrance in the ceiling to stem the Merdians that began to enter.

The lance defender hefted her silvyr trident with vengeance in her veins. "For Nimala!"

The blonde Nimean disappeared like a ballista bolt. Her aim true, the warrior struck the mass of Merdians trident first. The force of her charge was enough to see them and her back through the jagged hole and into open water, and all in a dark cloud of blood. The cleavers and hunter scouts followed her through, adding their blades to the fight.

Kit would have been right behind them had she not noticed a family backing up from their escape tunnel, the children and father taking shelter behind the mother. They had been forced back inside by a Merdian, her bronze skin complemented by a spear of the same shade. It was not her weapon, however, that kept the family inside the chamber. It was the Vorge she had on a chained leash.

Link by link, the Merdian gave the Vorge more slack. It advanced with mouth ajar, its fangs bared, and bulging black eyes fixed on its next meal. All the while, its master was grinning with bloodthirsty glee.

To the Vorge, the battle maiden would have appeared from nowhere as she arced over the top of the family and came down with a thrust. The tip of her blade skewered the Vorge through the neck and down into its body until the siden steel pierced its back. Pushing off from its rapidly dying body, Kitrana gripped the chain and launched towards the Merdian on the other end. The bronze warrior attempted to counter with her spear but found naught but water when Kit coiled around the blow.

The fight came to a swift end when the Nimean wrapped the chain around the Merdian's neck and pulled her into the waiting sword. Blood clouded the water, adding to the Vorge's.

"Go!" Kit signed, urging the family to take the tunnel.

To ensure they departed the temple without threat, Voden accompanied them, and with the Merdian's spear added to her arsenal.

Open water soon greeted them and the ruins beyond. So too did a Merdian battalion. The battle maiden craned her neck to see them all descending from higher waters. Most were astride Karathasaurs, their thick tails swishing gently to bring their riders into the chaos. Others were simply brought into the ruins by holding on to the leashed Vorge, who surged down in their harnesses of chains.

Kit got the attention of the family's mother and pointed down the nearest street. "That way!"

No sooner had they taken off than a group of Merdians took to the pursuit. Kitrana put herself between them, spearing one of the four with a levelled throw. She batted away the sword of another and opened his throat with the blade given to her by the lance defender. The two remaining rushed her from both sides, forcing Kit to swim forwards, out of the pincer attack. A strong yank of the spear freed it from the chest of the dead Merdian and put the weapon back in her control.

The Merdians snarled, their white teeth a stark contrast against their dark bronze skin. Kit looked over their shoulder to make certain the family of four had escaped further harassment. Unable to locate them she assumed they had found their own way out of the ruins or, at least, found shelter where the Merdians couldn't find them.

The battle maiden didn't wait for them to attack her. She swam towards them, weapons bristling. They succeeded in evading her first swipe of the sword and thrust of the spear, but they did not survive her bare hands.

Dropping both weapons, Kit twisted around one of her foes and appeared behind them, where she was able to snap their neck in one precise and sudden movement. The only one left came in with her own trident but found only her dead comrade, the body shoved in its way. Kitrana then rushed her opponent, barrelling her into the temple wall. Not one, but two slams of the head into the stone were enough to crack the Merdian's skull and end the battle.

Killing a handful of enemies, however, would not be enough.

Kitrana Voden turned away from the temple and looked upon a knot of Merdians crowding the waters about her. Among them were Karathasaurs and captured Vorge. Beyond them, she witnessed so many of her people being rounded up, executed, or eaten by the Merdians' mounts. There was so much blood in the water now that The Ruins of Ilthor were becoming veiled.

Of the Merdians who had boxed Kit in, one emerged to face the Nimean alone. It was the same scout that had taken her from Harendun's waters, that same wicked smile pushing at her cheeks. "You have some fight in you," she complimented. "That's good. I know exactly where to put all that *spirit*." The scout held up a hand for the others to see. "Take this one alive," she commanded.

The battle maiden braced herself, ready for the fight of her life. But there was no fight. How could any one fight so many? The wall of Merdians descended on her like a tidal wave, bringing pain and oblivion.

For days, Kitrana endured the same bindings that had returned her to the depths of The Drifting Sea. So too did the survivors, each bound and dragged on varying lengths of siden silk weed in the wake of numerous Karathasaurs. Only one among them was bound and secured to one of the saddles, where the rider could keep a close eye on them.

Princess Helaina had been captured like so many others. Word had come to Kitrana along their journey that the guardian knights had all been executed, their bodies given over to feed the Vorge. Despite her swollen eye, the battle maiden had watched the back of the princess for much of their time crossing the open waters. Swordsworn or not, it pained her to see how low her people had been brought, their monarch battered and broken.

She dreamed of wielding the blade of Skara again, of watching the Merdians disintegrate into ash and sparks.

That dream died when they finally arrived at their destination. For days, the prisoners had speculated about the Merdians' intentions, with most believing they were being taken to Atlas to live out their days in the thrall of their captors. But they had not been taken to Atlas.

The Karathasaurs' formation broke apart and the battalion of Merdians scattered to reveal the daunting truth. They had travelled north, as if to return to Harendun, but not so far. They had rounded the tip of Agandavael, the largest island that sat within Andara's borders, where they might enter a significant bay set into the continent's foundations. It was a place every creature in every sea knew of, and a place every creature in every sea keenly avoided.

Before the battle maiden now was a sheer wall of rock that disappeared up into the haze of ocean. Of course, it wasn't the rocky face of the bay nor its unfathomable size that gripped Kitrana's heart with cold dread. It was the truly enormous cavern at its base and the inky chasm within, a place even her eyes couldn't penetrate. As she feared, the Merdians continued their journey, forcing the Nimeans inside the cavern, where they might swim beneath Andara.

Kitrana tried not to think of herself entering the maw of some great monster.

The darkness inside was oppressive, and it seemed no matter how far they travelled the blackness continued ever onwards, the ancient tunnel winding through the rock. For the first few days of their swim through the rocky bones of Andara, the Nimeans would talk discreetly between themselves, their fears adding to the dread that awaited them at the end. After two weeks of swimming, however, the prisoners had ceased much of their conjecture and settled into numbness. They were to swim through the dark—nothing more.

They were well and truly beneath Andara now, having passed beneath and through so many of its rivers and mountains. It was as if they had followed the path of some god-like snake that had once burrowed through the world. Kit considered where the tunnel ended and realised that might not be too far from the truth.

The truth, as it was, struck every Nimean upon reaching their final destination.

The Black Vault.

After their nearly sightless journey, however, the phosphorescent glow seemed to negate its title. Still, all the fear that had been bubbling up between the prisoners was given new life in the face of the hulking doors. Those doors sat on the far side of a cavern that might have swallowed Andara's capital of Aran'saur. And still the doors stood out, their size suggesting they had been made for nothing smaller than a god.

At its centre, connecting the two mighty slabs of siden steel, was the fabled knot of pure silvyr said to be several feet thick—an impenetrable lock that kept The Black Vault sealed.

Surrounding the edge of the great doors was a series of deep excavations where it seemed thousands upon thousands of workers were slowly tunnelling their way through the bedrock. Not just workers, Kit realised. Nimeans. It made her sick to see her people put to the lash, their days spent digging through the rock of hell itself.

It was then that the princess crossed her path and Kitrana met Helaina's eyes for one precious moment. A portion of her fears passed through the water and settled over the battle maiden, bringing with it new revelation. The rumour Helaina had spoken of, the reason why the Dread Queen desired the blade of Skara so...

Kitrana tore her eyes from the princess and stared at The Black Vault. Now she knew exactly why the Merdians wanted the sword.

They would unleash doom itself.

20
LEFT OR RIGHT

For five days, Gallien Drakalis had felt little but the hard leather of a saddle between his legs. Pressed into his chest, Androma shared that same saddle with the added weight of Joran, the trio putting mile after mile behind them.

Putting Caster Hold behind them.

For most of their journey, The Beggar's Pass had hugged the coastline, the road shared with many a merchant and supplier who traded in the military town. Besides them, they passed groups and the occasional mass of soldiers on their way to reinforce or replace the ranks holding Harendun.

It was upon meeting these caravans that Gallien considered his own appearance and that of his companion. Though the soldiers might not consider their being together as suspicious, it would be reasonable to question how they had come by such a fine horse and saddle.

Androma required little persuading to divert from the road and head north, into The Edda Highlands, where they could continue their journey east beyond notice. Unfortunately, it added another day to their expedition and another day of testing Gallien's hunting skills. Without a bow, he was forced to make traps, where he soon discovered a gap in his knowledge. Fortunately, Androma appeared well-versed in that area, allowing them to eat every evening.

There was, however, only so much eating and riding in silence that the smuggler could take before madness began to set in.

"You said *the child's heritage*." He hadn't even meant to speak the words but they had sprouted from his lips nonetheless. He caught a subtle twitch in the back of Androma's head, which remained hooded and resting at his chin level while they rode through the highlands. "Back at Caster Hold," he specified. "You thought I wouldn't want to travel with you because of the child's—"

"I know what I said," Androma cut in, her tone heavy enough to halt any further questions.

At least it would have, were Gallien a man who knew what was best for him. "That's not how a mother refers to her son," he opined.

"I suppose not," she replied, her voice still barbed.

"If the boy's not yours," he continued, and blindly so, "whose is he? He's a half blood, so I'm assuming we left the mother or father behind in Harendun. Where's his human parent? Is that where you're going?"

"We agreed no questions," Androma reminded him.

"That was to get you into Caster Hold," he was quick to counter. "We're well beyond *that* negotiation."

"Then, perhaps, we should enter into a new one," Androma proposed. "Between here and Farnfoss, we agree to learn no more about each other and to ride in silence where possible."

Gallien was slow to blink and held nothing of his sigh back. "Agreed," he said reluctantly.

Indeed, they weaved through the rolling highlands for three more days in relative silence, and without seeing another soul. Their camps had been small and the suppers rationed to provide some kind of breakfast the next day. Sleep had been a brief affair, always broken by Joran's routine cries and need for milk. Gallien had enquired only once about the supply of milk before Androma had assured him, and sharply so, she had enough inside that strange satchel of hers.

Since she was not immune to exhaustion, Androma had allowed Gallien to take the baby's weight now and then and aid in the boy's sporadic sleeps. It was on the eighth night of their journey together that the smuggler was afforded some time with Joran while the babe was actually awake and happy. Androma sat opposite the fire, the lines of her face made all the more defined in the dancing shadows.

"You are sure about the crossing?" she asked, breaking the crackle of the flames that cooked the squirrel.

"I've smuggled all sorts through these lands," he said reassuringly. "You wouldn't believe the things a battalion of bored soldiers are willing to pay for." Gallien glanced at the fire. "Are you sure you can cook that thing?"

"You don't need eyes for everything," she told him.

Gallien recognised that same tone she always used to end a conversation before it got started. He was only too happy to return his attention to Joran. Damned if his eyes weren't the most mesmerising thing he had ever seen. So big and round, like pools of glistening violet. And he might have had the ears of the enemy, but they were cute when framing the chubby face of a newborn with a halo of white hair.

It was an old memory, but it hit Gallien with a vividness that held him fast. He recalled, so many years earlier, holding Corben just as he did Joran. He was just a child himself but his parents had encouraged him to hold his newborn brother. There and then a bond had been forged that he thought Kaliban Himself couldn't sunder. He had been wrong.

Before old scars of grief could resurface and drag him down, the smuggler centred himself in the present again, focusing on Joran rather than Corben. "His skin is so soft," he uttered, if only to hear something other than the fire, and even if it was his own voice. "I knew a woman with skin like yours," he whispered to the boy, one finger stroking down his rounded cheek. "Though, yours might be *softer*."

"Is this the same woman you travelled to Harendun with?"

The question took Gallien by surprise, as well as so many words spilling from Androma's mouth. "I thought you said we were to travel in silence."

"I said *ride* in silence."

Gallien nodded along, recalling the distinction. "You also said we weren't to learn any more about each other."

Androma stoked the fire. "As you wish."

Drakalis remained cross-legged with the boy in his lap, wondering all the while if the opportunity to speak was worth opening the wound. "Yes," he finally answered. "Her name was Kit."

"Kit?" Androma questioned, her tone emphasising the unusualness of the name.

"Kitrana Voden," Gallien replied. "She's..." The smuggler stopped himself from saying exactly where Kit came from, a fact that would overly complicate their conversation. "She was like me, a... how did you put it? A *treasure hunter*. Kit was a *real* treasure hunter. Give the woman enough time and she'd peel the world back to its beginning."

"What happened to her?"

Gallien watched Kit disappear into darkness again, taken from her feet in the grasp of a monster.

"Not everything that's lost wants to be found," he muttered, using Corben's words. "There are dark corners of this world that don't like to be disturbed," he said a little louder, tracing a line down Joran's nose. "We found a particularly dark corner in Harendun. Kit didn't come out." Despite his companion's blindness, Gallien still felt too vulnerable to look at her.

"What were you searching for?" Androma asked.

The smuggler couldn't help but think of the axe. It wasn't the treasure he had been seeking but it was, perhaps, the most valuable item he had ever recovered from a site. Not that he still possessed it. How many times had he flexed his hands on the ride, willing the weapon to appear in his grip? He might have thought he imagined the axe altogether had Kit's broken sword not been in his satchel. What connected the weapons was well and truly beyond him.

Rather than explain an axe that could disappear and reappear, Gallien shrugged, discovering a tear in the seam of his coat's left shoulder at the same time. "Anything," he admitted, sounding somewhat desperate. "I knew of the site and thought there had to be something worth a mark or two. I have *debts* to pay."

"Ah, the *Padoshi*."

"The Padoshi," Gallien repeated wearily. Even Joran couldn't keep the smuggler's expression from dropping.

"What did you do?"

"I did a *lot* for him. It's what I *didn't* do." Drakalis took a breath, wondering whether he should say any more. "He... He wanted me to smuggle children," he said simply enough. "From Thedaria to Freygard. Orphans mostly, taken off the streets by his thugs. I wanted to say no but... you don't say *no* to a Padoshi."

"I see." Androma had stopped tending to the squirrel, her seated form still and rigid.

"I took them as far as Valgala," he said. "They won't have the best life but it'll be better than whatever the Padoshi was selling them into."

Something about the woman relaxed a notch. "So now you owe him," she surmised.

Gallien laughed quietly to himself as he noted the fog creeping out of the dark to touch the light of their fire. "To put it mildly. He wants to make an example out of me. That's why I was foolish enough to wade into a siege in the hope of finding something worth my life. Instead, I lost a friend and found nothing," he lamented with fake bravado.

Androma was nodding slowly. "You are not a good man, Gallien Drakalis," she declared. "But you are not a bad man either."

"You have a wonderful way with words," he quipped.

"I did not mean it as an insult. There is always more potential in the *grey*."

Gallien would have dwelled on that had the woman not instructed him then to wrap Joran in the blankets, just off from the fire. The boy looked up at him blankly, unable to move now inside his cocoon. Again, he saw Corben, not Joran, looking up at him.

"Tell me more about this crossing," Androma said, the usual harshness returned to her voice. "How far is it from here?

"Not far at all," Gallien told her, wondering where the fresh line of questioning had come from. "We have to keep these hills on our right."

"There is a bridge?"

"No. It's... Well, it's a few logs strapped together and a rope to pull yourself across." He shrugged. "It's simple... and *old*, but it'll get us over. The horse too."

"I thought you weren't going to step one foot over the river," Androma commented.

Gallien walked around the fire as the fog crept ever closer. "If there's anything in this world that I'm really good at, it's saying one thing and doing another." He tugged free one of the blankets they had taken from the stables. "I'll get you over the river and put the horse on an easterly heading. I'll go on foot. Follow the river to Farnfoss."

Androma said nothing, though her shoulders sagged and her head sank ever lower, masking her face inside the hood. She let out a gentle sigh and Gallien noticed for the first time her dagger was in hand, the blade resting in her lap.

"I'm sorry, Gallien," she uttered, a note of genuine emotion in her voice. "Whatever your past, you have done naught but aid me. You have done nothing to deserve this, but still it must be done."

If there was ever one thing Gallien Drakalis just knew, it was when his life was in danger. He looked to his sword, still housed in its scabbard, on the other side of the fire. Beside it was his satchel with Kit's broken blade inside. As always, he fell on his words to buy him precious time, if not his life.

"What are you talking about?" he asked, one foot creeping after the other to see him round the fire.

"Joran's too important," Androma said, her three favourite words. "I can't risk you telling anyone about him. I'm sorry you will have to die knowing no more than that."

Gallien glanced at the boy, wondering what in the hells could be so damned important about a baby that had done absolutely nothing. "Well," he began, as if he hadn't just been threatened, "how about nobody dies and we go our separate ways with a good old fashioned oath of silence?"

"Creeping is pointless if you're *speaking*," Androma stated, bringing the smuggler to a halt. "You're going for your sword, yes? Retrieve it if you must. I will grant you the dignity of killing you with your weapon in hand."

It was her absolute confidence that unnerved him. How could she believe herself capable of defeating him, a veteran of the war, in combat? Yet she clearly did believe it, and that belief was beginning to make Gallien believe it too.

"I should say," Androma added, as he made two more steps towards his sword, "if you approach Joran you will be dead before the blade leaves its scabbard."

"Who in the hells *are* you?"

"I told you; I'm already dead."

Disliking her answer as much as her stone-cold belief, Gallien dashed for his sword. His short roll across the ground saw him collect the weapon and draw it before resuming his full height. He still wasn't ready for the Banshee that was already mid leap, crossing the fire in a single bound. Her curved dagger came down at an angle that would have cut the smuggler from shoulder to groin had he not deflected it at the last second.

Her first attack, however, blended seamlessly into the second. Following the downward angle of her blade, Androma folded into an unorthodox bow and brought her elbow up to smash into Gallien's nose, whipping his head back. A short jump and her boot was levelled perfectly with his chest, taking him from his feet.

"This is madness," he groaned from his back.

"This is necessary," Androma replied as a matter of fact. "Do you wish to die on your back or on your feet?"

The question shot a dose of rage through Gallien's veins, spurring him back to his feet. He did so with another weapon in his hand. Drakalis looked down and marvelled at the axe in his grip, its coil of bronze shining in the firelight. Where it had come from—or where it had been—he could not say, but he was happy to see it returned to him.

He came at the blind woman with a one-handed thrust of the sword and pierced only air as she pivoted away and scored a bloody line across the top of his arm. The pain was like a hand squeezing his rage and he used his cry to come back at her with a swing of the axe. Again, Androma evaded with no more than a mere step, leaving the axe to lash out wildly at nothing.

"You have a second weapon," she remarked, a subtle hint of astonishment in her voice.

"It appears I do," he said, just as surprised as she was.

"You know how to fight," Androma complimented, standing perfectly still. "You just don't know how to fight someone like me."

"Trust me, lady, I've been fighting everyone since I could walk."

Androma bandied no more words, her dagger drawn back into the fray. Gallien blocked it twice with his sword and countered once with the axe. The low strike was avoided by a sharp lift of her leg and his follow-up sword attack was parried with seeming ease. Like a snake coiling around its prey, Androma pivoted and danced about his attempts to score a blow until she was able to slice the edge of her dagger across his leg.

The smuggler growled in more pain and mounting frustration. "Why do I get the feeling you're toying with me?" he asked, chest heaving.

"I'm giving you the best death I can," she told him, her posture irritatingly calm.

Deciding the axe was doing naught but muddle his fighting style, Gallien tossed it away and gripped his sword in two hands. Woman or not, blind or not, he meant to cut her down.

A barking laugh cleaved through the night, securing both fighters where they stood. The voice that followed could have been the crisp voice of death itself. "*There's only one thing I enjoy more than watching humans kill each other, and that's killing them myself.*"

Gallien's mind, so recently focused on survival, took an extra second to realise the words had been Andarneese. A cold and unsettling pit then opened inside the smuggler. What had the docks' official said upon their arrival?

"There's word of pale spies about these parts."

It seemed an impossibility that any Andarens were out there in the shadows, but Gallien had believed something similar of Androma's abilities to kill him.

Proving that the world had truly turned upside down, not one but seven figures took shape on the edges of the firelight. Andarens all. They stood robed and cloaked in white and red, each encased in armour of the same colours, including a high collar of steel to protect their necks. About the hard collars draped their hoods, which did little to conceal the streams of ashen hair that flowed over their waxen cuirasses.

Of the seven, one stood out against the rest, his height lending him an extra foot. He was also absent a cloak. He stood easy, one thumb hooked into his belt while the other hand rested on the hilt of a scimitar. The shadows of his hood concealed much of his face, but Gallien was still able to make out the grey scars that cut across his mouth and up his jaw.

Androma had fully turned away from Drakalis now, their fight at an end in the face of this new threat. "How many?" she questioned so only Gallien could hear.

"*Too many*," the tall Andaren answered nonetheless, a wicked smile appearing within his hood.

"Seven," the smuggler reported, wondering if he had lived his whole life without knowing that Andarens had superior hearing. "The chatty one's damned big though."

"Strap Joran to your chest," Androma instructed sharply, all memory of their fight forgotten.

"What?" Gallien retorted, believing he must have misheard her.

"Strap him to your chest *right-now*."

His sword still out in front of him, Gallien replied, "That's going to make fighting a lot harder."

"You're not fighting," Androma told him. "I am."

She slowly, but quite deliberately, crossed their little camp, likely using the heat and sound of the fire to navigate her way back to her staff. Rolling it with her foot, she flicked it up into the air and wielded it alongside her dagger.

"I had hoped it was you," the tall Andaren announced in his native tongue. *"I would have no other claim your life."*

Androma sheathed her dagger and twisted her staff as she part-buried the end in the soft earth, where it might stand unaided. Her hands free, she unclipped her rags, pulled back her hood, and dropped them at her feet, disturbing the growing fog.

Gallien paused in his effort to strap Joran to his chest, sure that his eyes now deceived him.

From neck to toe, Androma was garbed in the tight-fitting body armour of a *Dragon Rider*. Like Vander's had been in Harendun, hers was layered in overlapping dark plates with hints of fabric between all the joints. Her vambraces, previously hidden within the folds of her rags, displayed overlying dragon scales no bigger than a thumbnail and all a deep shade of blue.

The Andaren laughed again, filling the night with his menacing amusement. *"That fancy armour won't stop me from cleaving you in two, Witch."*

"The Dancing Sword of the Dawn," Androma replied, slowly articulating every word in Andarneese. *"It's a little ostentatious for my liking."*

"Like all heroes of the empire," the behemoth continued, *"I earned the title."*

"You're hero to no-one," Androma retorted venomously, her dagger returned to hand. *"You're just another butcher for The Skaramangians."*

The Andaren tilted his head a fraction. *"There are few who would speak that name so freely, even among those who bear the mark. You are bold for a Rider without her dragon."*

Androma presented the Andarens with her left vambrace and dragged the blade down the blue scales. *"Who says I am without my dragon?"*

Gallien finished tying the various knots that would keep Joran secured to his chest. By then, he had already placed the sword in its scabbard and returned it to his belt, leaving him to glance about for the axe he had tossed away. He thought the damned weapon had vanished again until he discovered it not far from the horse, its coil of bronze catching the light through the fog. In the same instant he considered it too far to reach, the axe appeared in his waiting hand.

"*Had you your dragon, I might not have tracked you so easily,*" the Andaren taunted. "*Though, I must admit, I had hoped to find you in the company of Ilithranda. I can only assume birthing the abomination was too costly, else she would not be parted from her precious child.*"

Androma took her staff in hand and flicked the dagger so the blade pointed up her arm. "*Should her name leave your lips again, monster, I will kill you slowly.*"

The Andaren laughed again. "*The arrogance of a Rider. How long have you been bereft of your beast? I see your pathetic life span is already catching up with you. Do you still possess your magic? Even an ounce?*"

The Dragon Rider held her ground, drawing out another grin from The Dancing Sword of the Dawn.

"*I'll take that as a no.*"

Androma adjusted her stance to that of a fighter, the staff now resting over one shoulder and the blade raised to eye level. "*You'll take it alright,*" she promised.

As one, the Andaren assassins retrieved the sabres from their belts and began to slowly widen the semi-circle they had formed. The Dawn Sword flashed his own blade, the razored steel drinking in the firelight.

"Androma?" Gallien didn't know what to do, the babe strapped to his chest and one hand holding tight to the horse's reins.

The Rider turned her mouth over one shoulder. "Riverwatch," she said, the name snapping out of her mouth. "Go to The Tallow Inn. The Green Leaf will find you there."

Gallien was shaking his head before she had even finished delivering her cryptic command. "The *what* will find me?"

"Go," she hissed. "*Now!*"

A wave of white and red and bristling steel rushed forwards, converging on Androma.

All but one.

A single Andaren peeled away from the end of their formation and came for the smuggler. No. He was coming for the boy. Gallien was already directing the horse away and towards the river when he let fly the axe. Silver and bronze flashed from hand to chest, the sleek curves of the blade making short work of the Andaren's cuirass before sinking deep into his chest and flinging him from his feet. By the time Drakalis had climbed onto the already moving horse, the weapon was returned to his hand, absent any blood. The smuggler looked back as the horse broke into a gallop, wondering if he had imagined the kill, yet the assassin remained on the ground, his white armour splattered with blood as the fog edged over his corpse.

Further still, Androma was unleashed, for there were already two Andarens dead at her feet and Gallien watched as a third fell beside her, his body displacing the fog as he met the ground. Her staff whipped side to side and flipped deftly in her hands before she cartwheeled over one of the bodies and retrieved her bloody dagger. Upon rising, she hammered the end of her staff into the earth and a brilliant flash, brighter than the fire, expelled the night. It also expelled the surrounding assassins, the big one included. They were flung wide, granting the Dragon Rider a moment to catch her breath and crouch into a new fighting stance.

Then she was gone from sight, the violent scene masked by fog before the horse rounded a sloping curve in the hills.

Eyes ahead, Gallien tried to see through the wall of vapour. Branches materialised from nowhere and threatened to snatch him from the saddle, though most succeeded in simply scratching his hands and face. The sound of rushing water soon pierced the thundering of hooves.

The Edda River.

It had been a couple of years since he had used the trail through the highlands but, thankfully, the path was flat enough for the horse to follow with minimal guidance. A terrible thought then occurred to the smuggler. What if the raft was on the other side of the river?

It was at that point Joran began to cry profusely. It was like a warning bell that consumed Gallien's thoughts and set his heart racing. It took his attention from the path, but with the reins in one hand and the axe in the other there was little he could do to comfort the boy.

Without warning, the horse skidded to a stop and reared up. "Whoa!" Gallien called, trying to calm the animal. "Easy!"

They had reached the short rise that overlooked the western riverbank. Desperately, he urged the mount to turn south and hug the edge of the rise while he narrowed his eyes to find the slope through the fog.

He heard the raft before he saw it, the sound of wood rhythmically knocking together. It was loosely fastened to a mooring point on the western banks, like the hand of a god waiting to take them to safety.

Then there came another sound. Running.

The smuggler didn't even bother to look back, his heels already urging the horse to hurry. He almost missed the slope that ran back along the ridge and he was forced to bring the horse into a tight turn. Again, he urged the mount to make all haste and dash down to the shore.

The smuggler climbed down and guided the horse at a run. He glanced up at the rise every few seconds expecting to see the Andarens upon him.

He bolted from the horse, buried the axe in the boards, and scooped up the long sweep oar that had been left on the shore by the previous smuggler. Such was his haste that he barely checked the suspended rope was intact and that it fed correctly through the metal hoops fixed into the raft's posts. All he had to do now was slide the oar into the oarlock.

That same feeling came back to him. Danger was closing in.

The smuggler wasted no time shoving the barge fully into the river and guiding the horse to splash through the shallows and step aboard with him. At about ten feet out, his hands were aching already from the firm grip needed to drive the raft across the current. Wondering if he needn't be so hasty, Gallien looked back at the western shore.

The sight of the behemoth took his breath away.

The tallest of the Andarens stood on the lip of the rise, his features veiled by fog but the white of his attire and armour were highlighted in the little light there was. So too did his razored blade catch the natural light, as if the weapon had winked a promise of death at the smuggler.

Gallien continued to sweep the oar and increase the gap, but the speed of the river made it slow and hard work. And it was with speed and ease, apparently, that the deadly Andaren leapt from the rise and landed on the stony shore. Drakalis blinked, sure that such a fall would break the legs of any creature.

Determined strides then brought The Dawn Sword into the shallows. He was soon up to his waist and closing the gap. When the water began to meet his chest, the Andaren gripped the rope that ran over the river and used it to pull himself even closer. Despite every warning in his mind urging him to speed up, Gallien didn't hesitate to abandon the oar and retrieve the axe he had part-buried in the boards.

Disbelief gripped Drakalis as firmly as he had gripped the axe.

Though the distance had been short and the force of his throw had been considerable, the Andaren caught the axe mid-air. An impossible catch. Since it had been a day of impossibilities, Gallien simply swore at the top of his voice and reached for the sword on his belt. He might have taken the hilt in hand too, were his grip not occupied.

The axe had returned to him.

Seeing The Dawn Sword's hand reaching for the edge of the planking, Gallien swung the axe down, cutting easily through the rope that prevented them from being taken by the river. Instantly slack, the raft was cast loose, a slave to the strong currents. Gallien braced himself and gripped the side of the horse as the craft swivelled and slipped through the fog. More importantly, it slipped away from the Andaren.

Leaving the assassin, his image quickly fading, the smuggler could barely register the constant cries of the baby for all the blood pounding in his ears. When, at last, he did consider the boy, Gallien began to pat his back and shush him as he had seen Androma do countless times in the last week.

Androma...

Gallien looked back, though the shore and the rise beyond it were completely concealed behind a wall of fog now. Not that he had expected to see her. The appearance of The Dawn Sword told him everything he needed to know about her fate. Her. A Dragon Rider. In what world had he, Gallien Drakalis—smuggler—been companion to a Dragon Rider? That question spiralled into dozens of others that he didn't have the energy to face.

Seated on the damp boards beside the horse, he continued to pat Joran against his chest while his free hand roamed about inside Androma's satchel. He needed milk.

"It's alright," he was saying soothingly, his fingers rummaging through the contents.

The smuggler was utterly dumbfounded when he retrieved a handful of crushed ice. Indeed, the satchel's interior was freezing and all of its contents cold to the touch. Diving one hand back inside, he discovered one of the containers Androma had been storing milk inside.

That was not all he discovered. Quite impossibly, Gallien was able to sink his entire arm inside the satchel, defying the physical space it occupied.

Magic.

Gallien pulled his arm out and stared at the satchel with suspicion. Dragon Rider magic. It was just as mysterious as the magic commanded by The Jainus, which meant it was just as dangerous.

The smuggler in him, however, couldn't help but imagine the advantages in his line of work. That thought trailed off, its ends singed by the reality of his situation. How was he to work exactly? What was he to do with a baby? How could he evade Andaren assassins?

Plagued by more questions, Gallien's exhausted mind boiled them all down to just one.

What in the hells was he going to do now?

That same question still plagued him six days later. Having abandoned the raft on the eastern bank a mere hour after their escape, the smuggler had taken to The Crooked Road on horseback.

For six days he had fed Joran from the enchanted satchel, changed his soiled wrappings, and kept him warm against the bitter chill. For six days he had looked back over his shoulder, expecting to see the red and white of Andaren assassins.

Now, standing to the side of a busy crossroad, Gallien Drakalis had to finally answer that question.

Before him was the last place he wanted to be: Thedaria.

The city dominated the flatland. At just over a day's journey from the nearest coast, the city boasted no harbour but did benefit from the The Treeling, a vast river that branched throughout Erador's western lands. Even now, as Gallien stood indecisively, the river carried great ships, importing and exporting, like veins carrying nutrients around the body. The smuggler looked over the makeshift villages that lined the river until his gaze settled on Thedaria's high walls and towering spires therein.

He swallowed, fingers tapping incessantly on his leg.

Gallien knew he risked everything just by standing on the crossing, where so many merchants trundled by. The Padoshi had eyes and ears everywhere, his reach extending beyond Thedaria's walls. He couldn't stay. The best he could do was sell the horse and use the marks to buy enough supplies to see them on.

To his left, The Misted Road cut to the north and promised to take any traveller through The Spine of Erador and into the heartlands. From there he would reach Valgala, the white city and gleaming capital, before going on to Riverwatch in the east. It would take weeks, months even if the mountain pass was blocked or the trail had simply succumbed to winter. Joran would slow him down too, the baby requiring numerous breaks.

"*Go to The Tallow Inn,*" Androma had said. "*The Green Leaf will find you there.*"

Gallien wasn't familiar with The Tallow Inn and he had no idea what to make of The Green Leaf. Was that even a person? And what would they do with the boy? As kind and mothering as Androma had been to the child, she was a Dragon Rider, a harsh breed of warrior built to kill and lead armies into war. How did he know her designs for Joran weren't as nefarious as the Andarens who had called him an abomination?

Those same Andarens might also have heard her instructions to go to The Tallow Inn. If that were so, they might already be there waiting for them.

The smuggler looked to his right, where a signpost read: The Weslan Highway. It was a long stretch of road that would take him to Broadcastle, another coastal fortress equal in size to Caster Hold. He had no desire to enter another hold under the king's banner, but from there he could avoid the mountains altogether and go north again, where the world would open up to him.

Since forwards wasn't an option, it was to be left or right.

Drakalis sighed, the baby in his arms now, his violet eyes looking up at him. "I have no idea what to do with you," he said, his words making it no further than Joran's pointed ears. "I don't know anything about babies," he confessed. "It's a damned miracle I've got you this far, lad."

The smuggler looked up at his options again. Left, and he could hand the boy over to whomever was expecting him—a choice that would see him free of the burden. Right, and he knew he would have to take the boy with him, there to get lost in the realm where Andarens and Dragon Riders couldn't harm him.

There was a third option, of course, an option that allowed him to still go right but without the burden. Without *Joran*. He could pick any of the houses that lined the river and simply leave the boy at someone's door. He could be gone before they found him and then he would be...

Gallien met Joran's eyes again. His *Andaren* eyes. He wouldn't just be someone else's problem. No one would take in a half blood. To leave him anywhere was a death sentence. But, to be caught with him was a death sentence for both of them. The survivor in him urged him to abandon the babe and return to his easy life.

But he soon found himself thinking like that man again. The man he used to be.

That man couldn't leave any child to die.

He looked down at Joran again, who was now sucking on the end of his little finger—a trick he had discovered to keep the boy from crying. The smuggler groaned, already aware of what he was going to do.

"I've no right to take you, boy. You're not mine. Hells, you weren't even Androma's." Gallien was shaking his head, wondering how he had found himself in such a desperate situation. "Come on then, lad," he said wearily. "Let's get lost."

PART TWO

21
THE STONE BONES

16 Years Later...

Deep beneath the earth, where the ancient stone had long been hewn, the great halls of The Morthil Mountains reverberated with the roar of dwarves.

It was a thunderous cacophony that drew in spectators from every tier and bridge that overlooked the would-be battlefield. Resounding drums beat in the deep, as if the very heart of the mountains thrummed with anticipation.

Upon reaching its crescendo, the drums stopped and battle commenced.

From the north of the field, the Redbraids charged under the banner of the axe and cleaver, the weapons sewn together by scarlet threading.

From the south, the Ironguards surged to meet them, the chained fist of their guild seared into their chests.

The two sides crashed into each other, meeting like hammer on anvil. Steel and silvyr were exchanged, be it in whatever form of weaponry their owner preferred.

The first row of each guild was killed almost instantly, crushed by the weight of those piling in from behind. The immediate dwarves that followed tripped over the fallen dead and quickly joined them, trampled by their battle-focused kin. The Ironguards and their spiked shields were the first to advance beyond the line of corpses and penetrate Redbraid ground.

It wasn't long before they were all slipping on blood, there to meet the fall of some warhammer or sundering axe. The Redbraids weren't without fire in their veins. Those who lost their weapon picked up severed limbs and decapitated heads to beat back their enemy. Still, the Ironguards advanced, carpeting the cavern floor with those who wore a single braid of red in their beards.

It was guild warfare at its worst.

Like so many others, Grarfath watched from a lofty vantage. The ruby apple he put to his lips crunched like broken bone between his teeth. He shook his head at the mayhem, and not just below. The onlookers cheered and hollered, the death of their kin no more than entertainment. Even among the spectators, small fights broke out here and there where disputes had bubbled over.

"An' they call this a golden age," he muttered to himself, before being jostled by the two dwarves leaning over the rail beside him.

"I've got five spurns says the Ironguards claim victory," one of them bet.

Shaking his bald head, the second dwarf—a Boldbane by his thick tattoos—replied, "Ten *kronums* says the Redbraids take it."

"Kronums?" the first questioned, his bushy eyebrows knotting into one. "Aye, go on then! Ten kronums it is!"

"Ye want in?" the bald dwarf asked.

It took Grarfath a moment to realise the question had been directed at him. He looked over the Boldbane and guessed that the dwarf didn't have the kronums to pay either way. In fact, if Grarfath was to place a bet, it would be to wager their private gamble ended in violence.

"Kronums are a little rich for me blood, fellas," he told them, and honestly so. In fact, he might have struggled to place a bet concerning mere spurns.

"Suit yerself, lad."

Grarfath took another bite of his apple and watched the bloodshed a while longer. "Do ye reckon the High King knows abou' this?" he asked, his question sent in the direction of the wagering dwarves.

"The way I heard it," the red-headed Frostbeard said, "the High King *encouraged* it. Told 'em to sort out their differences with steel."

Were it not for the battle they might have heard Grarfath gasp. What madness could drive the High King to break the guild laws? *His* laws. It was those very laws that maintained the peace that allowed the Boldbane and Frostbeard beside him to call each other friend.

The battle shifted below. The Redbraids closest to the Ironguards dropped to the ground and pressed themselves as flat as their armour would allow. From somewhere in the middle of their ranks, a long bar was picked up by the wings of their dense force. The bar was bristling with spikes. Those who had picked it up charged forwards, carrying the deadly bar over the prone bodies and corpses, until they met the Ironguards.

The Redbraids were already picking themselves up and hurtling after the bar that was now flattening their foes. Any who survived the spikes were promptly speared or hammered to death. After penetrating the Ironguards' ranks by a dozen rows, the Redbraids were finally halted by sheer numbers and the fighting resumed.

"What's the dispute?" Grarfath enquired.

The Boldbane shrugged his round shoulders. "Who knows?"

"I heard it was a trade dispute," the well-informed Frostbeard chipped in.

Grarfath whipped his head around. "A trade dispute? They're killin' each other in droves over a trade dispute?"

The Boldbane frowned and gave Grarfath a suspicious look. "Well o' course," he said. "Any upheaval in trade affects the profit margins."

When Grarfath didn't respond with enough reverence at the

mention of *profit*, the Boldbane scrutinised him all the more. He elbowed the Frostbeard who tore his gaze from the fighting just long enough to hear whatever his bald friend was whispering in his ear.

"Hang abou'!" the Frostbeard snapped, stepping away from the railing. "I thought I recognised ye. Ye're Mordrith's boy."

"Careful," Grarfath warned.

"Who?" the Boldbane asked.

"Mordrith," the red-headed dwarf reiterated. "That loud-mouthed miner from the Underborns."

Grarfath too stepped away from the railing. "I'm warnin' ye."

The Frostbeard pointed one stubby finger at him. "He's un-guilded," he accused.

"I ain' un-guilded," Grarfath spat. "I'm an Underborn."

"Liar," the Frostbeard retorted. "I heard some o' the rubbish yer mother were spoutin'. Anti-profit this an' anti-profit that!" The dwarf thumbed over his shoulder at a distant group waving banners and shouting in unison. "An' look what she's started."

The shouts couldn't be heard due to the battle below, but Grarfath knew they were deploring the profits made from selling weapons and armour to both the humans and the Andarens during their war. Mordrith Underborn would have been at home amongst them.

The Frostbeard pressed a strong finger into Grarfath's chest. "She should o' stayed in the mine an' kept her mouth—"

Shut is exactly what Grarfath ensured, only it was the Frostbeard who would spend the next few months struggling to open his broken jaw. He hit the floor with all the grace of a boulder while his friend, the Boldbane, yelled in surprise and braced himself, fists rising into knots. It wouldn't matter. He faced a smith, whose arms commanded the power to shape silvyr.

"Don' do it, laddy," Grarfath cautioned him wearily, the fire in his blood having cooled the moment the Frostbeard went down.

The Boldbane licked his lips and glanced at his unconscious companion. There was still time for him to back off but he had made a show of himself now, fists up and ready to throw. He had only to take note of the few onlookers and he succumbed to the expectation of strangers.

Grarfath tossed his apple into the dwarf's face, staggering his lunge and partially blinding him. The smith then launched a fist of his own, using the Boldbane's forward momentum against him. The blow robbed the dwarf of his front teeth, cracked his cheek bone, and shattered his nose. That was all before his head hit the floor, adding one last injury to the list.

The smith was left standing over them, his fingers flexing by his side. Those who had been watching the altercation had already grown bored, their attention returned to the carnage below. Having had far more excitement than he had bargained for, Grarfath stepped over the two fools and departed the area altogether.

He had to travel for some time to get away from the sound of battle, if not the haunting presence his mother still had on his life. Following the maze of tunnels and winding paths, he passed through the many districts, crossing bridges that would confound human and Andaren engineers alike, allowing him to traverse chasms that could comfortably house entire kingdoms from the surface. For hours he trekked, making the journey to the hallowed halls. The smith craned his neck to see the towering heights of those chambers, each supported by pillars twenty dwarves abreast.

Almost every available space between was crowded with overshadowing statues: kings, queens, and lords of old, that had been granted their immortality in the stone by no more than birthright and the wealth that came with it. With each descending size of statue or monument, the figure entombed within had boasted less and less profit.

That brought Grarfath to one of the smaller statues, situated in the far right corner of the smallest hall. "Hello, Pa," he began, suddenly conscious of the blood on his knuckles. "Five years to the day," he lamented. "I had hoped to afford ye a better place by now. A bigger stone too. But..." The smith struggled to voice his failures, especially in The Immortal Halls of Success. He would be lucky if he got anything more than a plaque on the wall. Though who would put it there he couldn't guess.

Rather than say any more, he retrieved the rag and small pot of polish from his laden belt and went about cleaning the statue. He was sure to get a finger inside the creases and lines that had been fashioned to bring out his father's expression and full beard. He soon found his father's eyes looking down at him. In life, Thronghir, son of Enghir, had possessed kind eyes of hazelnut. Immortalised in stone, they seemed cold and unforgiving, as if they were to judge his son on all his deeds.

Grarfath polished them all the same before sitting on the corner plinth to enjoy the pork sandwich he had prepared. "I'll be off then, Pa," he finally announced, sure that the time and the sojourn he had taken to be there would absolve him of any potential guilt. He patted the stone one last time. "See ye next year."

By the time he had retraced his steps and found himself returned to the Gendel District, the two dwarves he had knocked down were gone and the battle between the Redbraids and Ironguards had come to an end. Peering over the edge of the rail, he spied the many corpses being loaded onto carts and the scattered weapons being collected likewise. Regardless of the death that surrounded them, the Redbraids and Ironguards held no animosity towards each other as they scoured through the dead and cleared up the bloody mess. And why would they? The battle had been no more than a negotiation of new terms between the two guilds.

Grarfath tried to put it from his mind as he returned to his little corner of the world. If he dwelt on the politicking of his people for too long, he quickly discovered his way of thinking mirrored his mother's. He simply wouldn't allow himself to do that. What he did allow himself was a smile at the workshop he had called home for the last century. It was crowded by a street of similar smiths, all of differing skill levels, along with a handful of masons, a couple of tanning workshops and a particularly good bakery.

And it was always damned loud.

The sound of clanging metal and hissing water, hammers on steel, and forges roaring in hollowed stone was nothing if not the melody of home. Familiar and soothing as it was, Grarfath was unable to maintain a smile. The Banking Federation, a guild unto themselves, had sent Dobrin, son of Gouser, again, only this time he was nailing a piece of parchment to the workshop doors.

"Oi!" Grarfath yelled, dashing between the passers-by. "Dobrin!"

The banking agent was already turning to leave when the smith reached his door. The parchment was lined with thick dwarven glyphs, dictating to Grarfath that he was now on a countdown of mere days before the workshop would be reclaimed by the federation.

"What's this?" he raged, tearing the sign down.

The squat and balding dwarf barely pivoted to regard the smith. "It's exactly what it looks like, son o' Thronghir. Ye've six days. Anythin' ye leave inside after that will be property o' the Bankin' Federation."

"I've been payin'!" he protested.

"Not nearly enough," the son of Gouser countered. "And not for months, I'd add. Six days!" he repeated, making to leave again.

"Ye can' do this! It's mine! Has been for a hundred years!"

"Ye should o' told yer father that when he took out the loan to pay for it. Good day, son o' Thronghir!"

Grarfath watched the banking agent disappear into the crowds and caught sight of a few neighbours in the process. They pitied him. As a guild, The Underborns had held his skills, and his father's before him, above all other smiths, but those surrounding neighbours had watched his workshop fall into ruin over a number of years, decaying from its once lofty heights. He recalled the beginning of that steep decline and thought again about what the Frostbeard had said about his mother.

The smith crumpled the parchment and let it fall from his hand before unlocking the workshop and taking solace inside. It struck him, as it often had of late, how bare the interior was, absent the numerous materials required for a variety of jobs. There had even been a time when their business thrived enough to employ other smiths and assistants.

What a shadow it was now.

Like a ghost drifting through empty halls, the dwarf donned his apron and made his way to the primary workbench. He picked up and put down the broken Warhog stirrups that he had left there, his only job in days. It was just so pitiful. Worse, the fee wouldn't cover the next instalment he owed the Banking Federation. His eyes were drawn to the circular safe built into the far wall. He had just enough coin scraped together to pay the Guild Lord for his membership of the Underborns.

Grarfath seemed hardly aware that his fists were clenching atop the workbench. He was consumed in that moment by the corner he found himself in. Pay the Banking Federation and keep the workshop a while longer—perhaps long enough to drum up some real work—or pay for his membership and retain the Underborn name. If he didn't choose the latter, however, no one would come to an un-guilded smith, but retaining the Underborn name would do him little good if he didn't have somewhere to ply his trade.

Those fists of unyielding dwarven bone whipped up before slamming into the workbench. He was glad in that moment that his father wasn't there to see the tears welling in his dark eyes. How could such a bleak future lie before him? How could he have fallen so far, he who had crafted armour for Guild Lords and trinkets for royalty?

He was again reminded of his mother, taking his gaze to the small portrait above the workbench. He would have taken it down years ago himself, but his father wouldn't have it. For all the ruin she had brought upon them, Thronghir son of Enghir had loved his wife with a passion that could outshine even the High King's forges.

Grarfath was of a mind to swipe the portrait from the wall when he heard the shop door open. For just a second, he believed the banking agent had returned with enforcers, there to begin taking his belongings ahead of schedule. Before his anger could rise any higher, though, he noted four unfamiliar faces enter his home.

Customers!

His ire was dashed and hope rekindled. He quickly presumed the job to be of considerable size for so many to have come to him. The son of Thronghir brushed his apron down and raised his chin before moving to greet the newcomers.

"Welcome, friends!" he declared in his rich baritone. "Be it steel or silvyr, Grarfath Underborn's the smith ye need! What can I do for ye?"

Of the group, one appeared to be in charge. His thick mane of silver-white hair flowed down into a full beard of the same colour. Deep were the crevices of his face, framing his eyes of chipped blue, putting his age somewhere between eight hundred and a thousand years under the Morthil stone. His soft robes of black and gold spoke of wealth and power, the pair intrinsically linked. The old dwarf even wore gloves of the same material, and with exquisite gems decorating his fingers and thumbs.

The remaining three required only a glance to see the disparity that lay between them and their leader. Grarfath saw now that they were likely the dwarf's security if not underlings awaiting their master's bidding.

The smith struggled, however, to identify their guild. Of the beards they all sported, none wore a red braid. Neither had they bound them into a single column as the Frostbeards did. If they were Ironguards they would have a hole cut into their clothes to display the chained fist burned into their flesh. Boldbanes were always sure to wear attire that revealed some portion of their thick tattoos.

A cursory glance at their wrists was all Grarfath needed to know they weren't Underborn. Had they been, they would have worn the beaded bracelet of stone, the fragments taken from the very slab of Morthil upon which they were born. It had been his father who had chipped the stone and worked the fragments into smooth spheres that were then threaded with leather. The thought of it caused a notch of guilt to seep into his bones—he should have spent longer in The Immortal Halls of Success.

Shrugging off his emotions as he might a cloak, the smith clapped his hands and put aside any thought of his parents. He also looked past the fact that he couldn't identify the guild from which these four dwarves had been sent. What mattered was the job they were bringing to his door. That and the coin that would follow. How he needed that coin.

The dominant dwarf began to slowly walk around the central forge, his eyes roaming over the stations and tools that lined the walls. His lack of response was unnerving, though not nearly as disturbing as the level gaze set upon him by the other three. So intent was their stare that Grarfath felt himself no more than a piece of meat before a pack of hungry dogs.

"Ye've need o' somethin' discreet, perhaps?" the smith posed. "I've completed many a job that holds me to secrecy." Still there came no word from the wealthy dwarf. "Oh," he said with revelation. "If ye're 'ere to scout yer new investment ye can clear off. The Banking Federation won't be takin' this place, I can tell ye that. They won' be sellin' it an' nor am I."

"I haven' come all this way to buy yer shop," the lead dwarf finally replied.

Grarfath saw a hint of disgust cross the dwarf's face as he cast a glance about the walls. "Then... ye're a customer?" The smith could already see all those coins he was set to earn falling through his fingers.

The dwarf came to a stop, forcing Grarfath to turn his back on the three guards. "No, son o' Mordrith, I am not a customer."

The smith was about to reply when the dwarf's response caught up with him. There were none, whatever their guild, who named another by way of their mother, however true the statement remained.

"Who *are* ye?" he asked seriously.

"A friend," he said cryptically. "At least, yer mother called me so."

"Ye know me mother?" It wasn't an impossibility, Grarfath realised. His mother had been a miner for centuries before he was even born, and a damned good one by all accounts. How many times had his father recounted the tale of her discovering a fresh deposit of silvyr in the depths of the earth? She had known fame after that for many years though, again, that had been before Grarfath's time.

"For a time," the dwarf answered, his words guarded again. "I've never known one to wield such strength as her. Combined with her ingenuity, ye 'ave yerself an irreplaceable dwarf."

Grarfath was taken aback, and not just because his mother's name had come from the lips of two separate dwarves in a single day. He couldn't count the years since he had heard any but his father speak so highly of Mordrith, daughter of Andal. "Ye've seen her?" he couldn't help but ask. "Recently?"

"Oh aye," came the enthusiastic response, though it did not come from the mysterious dwarf. "O' course he's seen her," the female voice went on, turning all to the woman leaning against the frame of the open door, her thick arms folded across her chest. "Why don' ye tell 'im, Tharg. Tell 'im what happened when last ye saw his mother?"

"Ye." The word left Tharg's mouth with blunt disdain. Those chipped blue eyes dashed to Grarfath. "Ye cannot trust this *kud*," he warned, edging towards him as an ally might. "She will claim to know yer mother an' exploit ye in the process. I advise ye stand back, smith, an' let us take care o' this. We may continue our business in her wake."

With something of a hungry smile on her face, the woman stepped fully into the workshop and deliberately closed the door to seal them all inside. It was then that Grarfath noticed the brass knuckle-dusters she wore on both hands, their colour matching the coppery hair that ran high over her scalp, before cascading down her back in a combination of coils and interwoven braids. It was an intricate masterpiece compared to the black dreadlocks that Grarfath kept knotted at the back of his head. So too did her pale complexion and sprinkling of freckles contrast with his smooth dark skin.

Most unusual was her beard, or lack thereof. It had long been fashionable for the women of The Morthil Mountains to grow their beards, longer even than their male counterparts, yet this woman had little more than a thin coating of ruddy stubble.

Emerald eyes assessed each of Tharg's escort, flicking from one dwarf to the next as her fingers disappeared inside clenched fists. "I love breakin' ye idiots."

Grarfath might have been utterly perplexed by what was playing out inside his workshop, but it quickly turned to astonishment, if not outright bewilderment, when the fighting began. The first of the trio to advance went down with no more than a grunt, his face punched just the once, and sufficiently so, by a single knuckle-duster.

The second came at her with a dagger drawn from his belt. He lashed it from left to right but the woman ducked under the arm and delivered a rib-breaking blow to his side. Having dropped to one knee, he soon found his hand snatched at the wrist and pressed onto a workbench. Grarfath winced when the woman's fist hammered down and crushed every bone that gripped the dagger.

The third darted within arm's reach. Grarfath hadn't seen him produce a hammer but still he swung it at the woman. However certain that blow had seemed, the weapon struck the dwarf's companion, who had been yanked from his crouch and thrust into the hammer's path. Within seconds, two of the three were out of the fight, their bodies prone, bloodied, and still.

Undeterred, that third and final guard came at the woman again. She weaved between his swipes until his arm was outstretched and locked in her grip. Like a piston, her fist ploughed through the back of his elbow and snapped the bone. The dwarf let loose an animal screech of pain. His cry was cut short when the woman turned him about and slammed her head into his nose. A third body was then added to the rest that lay at her feet.

Her chest heaving, the woman levelled her gaze on the smith. Grarfath couldn't say exactly when, but he had picked up one of the iron bars he used to adjust the forge's interior. Meeting those emerald eyes now, he raised the bar a notch higher.

"Come any closer," he cautioned, "an' I'll add ye to the others."

"O' course ye will," she replied dryly. "Wait." The violent stranger pivoted to take in every corner of the workshop and groaned in frustration. "By the All-Fathers I will have that kud's head!" she vowed.

Indeed, Grarfath also failed to locate Tharg. Aged and illustrious as he had appeared, the dwarf had been wily enough to slip away at the perfect moment. "*What* is goin' on 'ere?" he demanded, not confident enough to lower the iron bar. "Who are *ye*? Who was *he*?"

"There isn' nearly enough time to answer any o' that," she told him firmly, moving to peer between the shutters. "All ye need to know is: he'll be back, an' *soon*. Ye can bet he'll come back with a lot more o' these fools an' all." The woman turned around and began walking towards Grarfath, though her attention had wandered over him to the doors that led off to his personal quarters. "Ye've got two minutes to pack whatever ye need, but pack *light*."

The smith made sure to exaggerate his frown. "What are ye talkin' abou'?" he fumed. "Ye've damn near killed three people in me home! I'm not takin' orders from ye! An' I'm especially not followin' ye anywhere!"

"We don' 'ave time for this, Grarfath. I won' be able to stop 'em next time." The dwarf paused, glancing back at the trio on the floor. "An' only *one* o' 'em's dead," she remarked flippantly.

Her last statement made the smith trip over his response. It seemed obvious now that one of them was dead, his head having been caved in by his companion's hammer. "Who's... who's *them*? An' how do ye know me name?"

"Answers later," she replied sharply. "Get yer things. An' put that down before ye hurt yerself."

Grarfath licked his lips and lowered the iron bar. "He said I wasn' to trust ye," he pointed out, as she rummaged through the belts of the trio. "That ye'd use me mother."

The stranger stood up, taking three coin purses with her. "Ye mean like *he* was?" she countered. "Tharg's a smart one. Doesn' like to get blood on his hands."

"He said—"

"I heard what the kud said," she cut in. "He can keep his fancy words where yer mother's concerned. Mordrith was a stubborn Warhog with a mean swing."

It was a short sharp description of his mother, but damned if it wasn't on point, bringing back more memories of the cantankerous woman. "Wait," he said, his mind slowly pulling her choice of words apart. "Ye said... *was*." His words hung in the air, a question that hadn't been asked.

At last, something of her hard exterior melted away, allowing the smith to see something of a person behind the brutal warrior who had barged into his life. "Mordrith was murdered," she revealed bluntly. "I'm sorry."

Grarfath physically swallowed as he absorbed the information, and on today of all days. "Murdered?" he managed, lips dry. "When? Who by?"

"Nearin' a month ago. An' I don't know who killed her. But I know the order came from the kud ye were jus' talkin' to."

It felt a double blow to hear that. If it were true that is...

"How do I know ye're not lyin'?" he asked, the iron bar rising in his hand again. "How do I know ye're not usin' her death to *exploit* me?" he questioned, using Tharg's own words.

The stranger sighed. "We don' 'ave time for this, Grarfath. We need to leave *now*."

The smith pointed his iron bar at her all the more.

She huffed, shrugging the chunky pauldrons on her shoulders. "Fine," she conceded, her attention wandering while she sifted through memories. "She would always sing the same damn song. Always while she was cleanin', be it pots or blades. The Ballad o'... The Ballad o' Sunstruck."

"The Ballad o' *Sunstrun*," Grarfath corrected quietly, the ancient hero's name bringing with it a wave of grief. He had heard his mother sing that song all his life. And, true to her recounting, always in the process of cleaning something, anything.

"Aye, that's the one. Damned earwig it was. An' she couldn' hold a tune neither."

The smith turned so his face was hidden. Tumultuous as his emotions were where his mother was concerned, word of her death—her *murder*—shook him to his core.

"Grarfath." Her voice was lower now, the edges of her tone smoothed out. "I know this is a lot, an' by all the stone in Verda this isn' how I wanted to tell ye, but they found ye *first*. I knew yer mother. I called her friend. Ye 'ave to come with me. Please."

The smith scrunched his eyes tight for a moment before he turned back to face her. "Where are we goin'?" he asked, sparking a flame of hope in the stranger.

"Far from 'ere."

Grarfath was slowly nodding his head. "Wait. What's yer name? Give me that at least."

The stranger paused on her way to the main door and looked back, sending her braids and wild curls over one shoulder. "My name is Yamnomora."

22
THE BLACK VAULT

Despair was a bottomless well, a pit that knew no end and dragged everything down to crushing depths. For sixteen years, Kitrana Voden had desperately tried to climb out of that black hole, to hold on to who she was. The oath of the Swordsworn had been a mantra that kept the fight in her bones—for the first few years, at least.

Now it only served to remind her of what she had lost. What they had *all* lost.

Today, they were going to lose something more. The rhythmic hammering of siden batons resounded throughout the network of tunnels, bringing an abrupt end to the extensive excavation about The Black Vault.

Kit let her tools fall to the cave floor before joining the line of imprisoned Nimeans that shared her tunnel. The Merdian guard that patrolled their site thrust her trident towards the distant entrance and the prisoners steadily flowed out one after the other, weaving between the struts that supported the long tunnel.

The cavern opened up beyond the excavation site, revealing the distant tunnel that led back to open waters. Kitrana turned her head from it, from the dream of freedom it offered. Today was the day they would suffer the price for succumbing to that temptation.

As they had done for millennia untold, the hulking doors of The Black Vault stood resolute, firmly shut within the heart of Andara's bedrock. On the far side, Kit could make out the other Nimeans—thousands of them—as they too were escorted from their sites and formed into rows facing the doors. Karathasaurs swam up and down, their riders watching for any signs of rebellion.

Sorted into her own line, the once proud battle maiden was turned with the others to watch a single Karathasaur descend, following the central line that divided both doors. It was considerably larger than the other Karathasaurs that maintained the site's security.

A female then.

Though not nearly as difficult to tame as the legendary deep dragons, female Karathasaurs were notorious for eating their handlers. What few they managed to wrangle were reserved for the upper echelons of the Merdian hierarchy.

"It's her," signed so many of the Nimeans, their fingers moving discreetly by their sides.

As fear spread through the rows of mer-folk, Kitrana Voden felt her despair melt away to be replaced by a sharpened sense of righteous fury. In that moment, the battle maiden within was reborn as a single spark might illuminate the dark.

The same pale face that had taken her from Harendun's waters, and then again from the Ruins of Ilthor, came into view as her mighty Karathasaur levelled out half way down the doors. Her bald head was hidden by the sloping helm of spikes, each one styled after the claws of a deep dragon. No longer did she wear the common attire of a scout, her accolades having elevated her such that she now wore plated silvyr that had been tinted rose-gold—the colour of *bright commander*. In one hand, she wielded a trident, a weapon of siden steel coated in silvyr. Were she a member of the royal family, she would have been permitted a weapon of pure silvyr.

It was still a deadly weapon. More so in the hands of Gelka Ornst.

Years had passed since Gelka had overseen the site—her first promotion after orchestrating the capture of so many in the Ruins of Ilthor, including Princess Helaina. That promotion was short-lived, however, when the Dread Queen decided something grander was in order. She had been recalled to Atlas, where the princess might be paraded. It had come as a blessing to the Nimean prisoners, who had suffered horribly under Gelka's watch. Now she returned a bright commander, and riding a worthy mount.

Quite gracefully, Gelka rose from her saddle and pushed off to acquire some space from the Karathasaur. The creature quietly descended to the sea floor, where its rough hide gave it the appearance of just another rock formation. That left the bright commander floating before the masses, a living extension of the Dread Queen herself.

Gelka was soon joined by another of her pale caste. Kitrana recognised her as Reso Huk, who had assumed oversight of the prisoners in Gelka's stead. While she hadn't shied away from punishing prisoners who broke the rules, she hadn't performed regular culling as Gelka had. The bright commander had enjoyed rounding up the weakest among them, those who struggled with the physical task of digging through the solid rock around the doors. She had also taken great pleasure in using the male Nimeans as sport.

"Your existence is simple," Gelka announced, her signing hands drawing in the sharp eyes of every prisoner. "Why must you complicate it? Try to escape and you die. Try to aid someone in escaping and you die. You have been warned again and again. How many more must face execution?" The bright commander let the rhetorical question linger before going on.

"I have returned because some of you believe there is yet hope. Hope that you might defy your fate. Hope that you might know life beyond your toil. I am here to remind you that Nimala is *gone*. The Nimean people are *gone*. You are the property of Queen Yilda, Light Lord of Atlas. Nothing more."

Again, the bright commander let her decree settle over the

prisoners. "I understand, however, that my words might fail to shadow your hope."

Kitrana knew what was coming—they all did. The last escape attempt was only weeks ago and, since then, there had been repercussions beyond the executions of those who had tried to flee. But there were always repercussions for everyone else. It was the only way to truly dissuade others from trying the same. The only question was: how many of them were about to lose their heads?

The battle maiden was just as shocked as everyone else when the first head to be parted from their body belonged to Reso Huk. The razored edge of Gelka's trident had swept out in one smooth motion, drawing a silvyr line across her neck. That line was soon clouded with dark blood that plumed to conceal her falling head. Slowly, Reso's body accompanied it, trailing down to the sea floor.

"Until we find a way through this rock," Gelka continued, her trident swinging out again to indicate the mountain wall, "I will again hold rule over you all. There will be no more fighting back. You will dig, eat, and sleep. Nothing else is permitted. Should you forget this, look to your brand as a reminder."

Unable to see her own brand, Kitrana looked to the Nimean in front of her. It was identical to the one that had been seared into her flesh—a ring of foreign glyphs that meant nothing to the battle maiden. Though the glyphs remained unintelligible, the meaning behind them was just as clear as Gelka's words: they were property.

"As for your precious *hope*," the bright commander went on, "I will see it quashed right here and now."

Slowly but surely, all eyes were diverted to the small procession making its way through the middle of the Nimean ranks, brought into their space from the cavern beyond. A cold pit formed in Kit's chest as she finally saw past her kin.

Princess Helaina.

Her wrists were bound in manacles, each chain in the hands of a male Merdian as they pulled her through the water. Appearing no more than a lifeless doll, Helaina was paraded through her people and presented to the bright commander, where her demeanour and attire were all the more contrasted. Where Gelka floated tall and proud, her armour gleaming around her strong form, the princess existed in a swirl of filthy colourless rags, her golden hair reduced to patches and tufts. Much of her skin was on show, there to display the patchwork of scars and bruises.

The Starlight of the Deep. Her future had been as bright as Nimala's. But everything, it seemed, wilted and died in the shadow of the Merdians and their Dread Queen.

The male Merdians moved further apart, stretching Helaina's arms out wide. The princess looked pained but the guards were unsparing while Gelka circled all three of them.

Facing the prisoners once again, the bright commander raised her hand to address her captive audience. "No one is coming for you. There are no heroes." Her short sharp message delivered, Gelka lowered her hand and opened her mouth.

The numerous vocal flaps inside her throat began to collide at speed, vibrating the water at a specific pitch. It was then that the power behind every matriarchy under the sea was brought to bear.

In Kitrana's experience, that power was comparable to humans' ability to sing— everyone could, but some were better than others. It seemed Gelka Ornst was exceptional.

From the lowest depths, the gigantic Karathasaur heeded its master's call. The female wasn't the only one. The male Karathasaurs that patrolled the area turned from their routes and angled towards the bright commander, fighting against their riders. Were the terrifying beasts not present—and in such numbers—Gelka's call would have even drawn in the predators that knew to stay well away.

Before the males could get much closer, Gelka closed her mouth and ended the hypnotic effect. It was all the female Karathasaur required, apparently, for the beast approached with its jaws open. It was all so horrifically slow, giving every Nimean time to watch and understand what was about to happen. Princess Helaina didn't even struggle—was she even aware of what was unfolding? It seemed there was nothing left of her mind but a hollow shell.

When, at last, that dreadful moment arrived, it was worse than Kitrana could have imagined. The Karathasaur's tail ceased its rhythmic swaying and it finished its journey on momentum alone. So perfectly timed were the creature's movements, that Helaina's lower body slipped easily inside its mouth before it began to sink again.

From the waist down, the princess was gone.

Blood plumed into the water as Reso's had, spoiling the deep blue. Helaina didn't so much as twitch, as if she were already dead before the monster tore her in half. New waves of heartache rippled throughout the Nimean prisoners.

The Karathasaur returned with an insatiable hunger. The two male guards still holding the princess's torso aloft didn't have time to register what was happening before they were swallowed whole. As Helaina's remains drifted down, chaos reigned amidst the ranks of Nimeans, who feared the beast would turn towards them. The anarchy was swiftly quashed by the patrolling guards, their tridents and swords brought down on those who swam from their line.

When nearly a dozen more were added to the graveyard below, the Nimean prisoners managed to huddle together in the water and maintain some kind of formation. The female Karathasaur was already back under the control of Gelka and her powerful voice.

"Back to work," the bright commander signed as she rode past, oblivious to the battle maiden she had captured years earlier.

Kitrana Voden had hardly taken notice of The Black Vault's new master. She was tracking Princess Helaina's torso as it fell to the bottom of the ocean. Hers was the first to reach the sand, her open eyes bearing witness to the bodies that rained down around her. She had been but one woman, but her death seemed to take so much of their culture with it. That much could be seen in the Nimeans about the battle maiden.

As one people, they discovered new depths to their despair.

The days and weeks that followed were darker than all that had gone before. Gelka Ornst hadn't shied away from daily executions and the male Nimeans were, once again, picked at random for sport. Kitrana had heard they offered them freedom if they could make the journey back to open waters. Of course, none among the prisoners could outpace their Merdian captors, who ate better, slept well, and didn't spend every day mining hard rock.

Then, one day, two words found Kitrana Voden that she hadn't seen in years: *battle maiden.*

Kit glanced down the tunnel, making certain the guards were facing away from her. "What are you talking about?" she asked of the two mining beside her.

"The bright commander," the closest replied, fear flashing in her eyes as she signed the title. "Apparently she was torturing someone from the lower tunnels."

"Why?"

The Nimean shrugged. "Amusement?" she posed. "But they told her about the battle maiden who works in the tunnels."

Dark thoughts crept into Kit's mind. As a battle maiden of the Swordsworn, it was logical to assume that she would possess knowledge concerning the blade of Skara—the Dread Queen's most desired object. What would Gelka Ornst do to be the one who delivered it into the hands of the Light Lord of Atlas?

Those dark thoughts were given credence only a day later, when word reached Kitrana's tunnel that the bright commander was personally inspecting every site. Would she remember the face of a single Nimean she had captured as long as sixteen years ago? Even if she didn't, Gelka had only to apply pressure and Kit would be singled out by those around her. What pain would follow. Worse, in Kitrana's eyes, what oaths she would be forced to break. There were only so many body parts a person could lose before their absolute vows meant very little. And, after so long working the stone about The Black Vault, Kit's resolve was not what it used to be.

In the days that followed, Kitrana did the only thing she could do: she mined. Without thought, her siden pick chipped away at the rock, her station placing her at the very head of the tunnel. How many years had she looked upon that wall? For every inch they broke away, they were simply left with more of the same.

Like so many times before, Kit swung her pick and gave the rock everything she had. The siden tip became lodged, forcing the Nimean to adjust her grip and yank it free.

Warm water began flowing into the tunnel.

Astonished, Voden considered how far past the doors they had mined. It was entirely conceivable that their tunnel had found the blackest of dungeons beyond.

Her focus was shattered at the sound of siden batons hammering down the length of the tunnel. That specific beat informed the prisoners that they were to cease mining and line the walls of the tunnel.

Kitrana remained frozen in front of the small hole.

"She's here." The words rippled down the tunnel at speed, driven by terror.

She didn't know what to do. There was every chance that Gelka Ornst would, indeed, recognise her. Torture would follow, and this very hour. Beyond that, who could say? Would her interrogation ultimately lead to the Dread Queen wielding the blade of Skara? The answer had to be yes. With that firm belief came an old resolve, one that had been quieted by brutal subjugation.

Suicide was her first thought. If she was dead they could never learn of the hilt's last known location. Did she have the will to carry out such a bleak plan? Could she take her pick and thrust it into her chest? That led Kit to the next option: death by fighting. She could attack the Merdians and try to kill as many as she could before one of them delivered that final blow.

Even that was flawed.

Kitrana couldn't deny the possibility that they would simply overpower her and keep her alive. There was one, however, in those hellish depths that would kill her without hesitation. That creature lay on the other side of the small hole she had just made.

While her fellow Nimeans lined the walls, Kitrana Voden heaved her siden pick and slammed it into the rock again and again. When she came across a stubborn piece, she levered the rock and prised it away, exposing more of the void. Her continued work naturally drew the attention of the closest Merdian, who swam towards her, sword in hand.

Kit's next swing was interrupted when she was forcibly turned around. Unfortunately for the Merdian, the battle maiden used her turn to drive the head of her pick into their neck. As blood mixed with the water, Kit pinned the bronze guard to the wall by the point of siden steel. Shock and horror split the Merdian's expression, but it only lasted until Kitrana claimed the sword and thrust it through the guard's chest.

Leaving the sword where it was, Kit yanked the pick from her foe's neck and returned to mining the wall. Of course, her brash actions had sent a tidal wave of Nimean signs down the tunnel. Those closest to the battle maiden instinctively backed away, sure that death would come to any in her vicinity when the Merdians arrived in force. And that wouldn't be long.

Strike after strike, Kitrana widened the hole until she was confident she could just fit through. Looking back, shadows were beginning to take shape down the tunnel. Gelka was coming. Kit's eyes slid sideways to the cylindrical strut that had very recently been fitted into place between floor and roof. The battle maiden wasn't really thinking anymore, her mind having switched to a more instinctual survival pattern.

Pushing off from the head of the tunnel, the Nimean rammed into the strut with all her strength. When that wasn't enough, she began knocking the end of her pick into it.

Time was running down.

Gelka and her entourage of soldiers were well defined in Kit's sharp eyes now. Still the battle maiden hammered away. It was feeling unstable now, the bolts of siden steel losing their place in the stone. Small fissures began to open above and below. Nearly there. The same could be said of the bright commander.

With no more time on her side, Kitrana dropped the pick and brought her knees up, so her feet could be placed against the strut. Her face turned to the hole she had made, Kit pushed off with all her might and speared towards the void beyond. It was enough to finally dislodge the strut. So violent was its removal that it disturbed the rock above, causing the head of the tunnel to cave in as the Nimean shot through the hole.

Through darkness she drifted.

The Water Maiden had delivered her from the clutches of Gelka Ornst, but had she brought her to the lair of The Hag itself?

There was nothing to be seen inside The Black Vault. For the first time in her life, Kit's eyes couldn't make sense of the dark, even that which lay in front of her nose.

What had initially felt like pleasantly warm waters was beginning to heat up to uncomfortable temperatures. Was she to be boiled alive in the abyss? The battle maiden had imagined, however briefly, that she would simply be consumed by the nightmare that had long been buried under the world.

As the water continued to heat up, the sound of cracking stone reached Kitrana's ears, though it came from all over. So distant was some of it that she had to assume the space she now occupied was cavernous.

Strong currents arrived from nowhere and carried her through the pitch black. They pushed her up and dragged her down, as if a storm had taken shape inside the ancient prison. The sound of breaking rock was suddenly amplified—coming from above. The currents were immediately exaggerated in the wake of that sound.

Disorientating as it was, Kitrana came to realise that she was being swept towards the loudest sounds of the breaking rock. She pictured it in her mind's eye; a fissure opening up and being enlarged by the torrent of water that now flowed through it at force.

Or...

The battle maiden could also imagine it to be the maw of some hungry monster, sucking in the water to find its new prey. The sound of breaking stone could be its teeth grinding or the bones in its jaw opening for the first time in millennia. She had no way of knowing, her body a slave to the currents that jostled her in the dark.

Hearing the increasing roar of gushing water, Kitrana knew she was nearing whatever it was that drew in the ocean. It was only then, as she raced between the cavern and whatever lay beyond the fissure, that her eyes were able to make sense of what was happening, of what she *shared* the cavern with.

The creature shifted in its prison, but so big was it that its black hide had concealed all, giving the impression of total darkness.

It was colossal.

Its scale was such that Kit failed to discern its exact shape. It was just a mass of black that was barely contained inside the prison. That's what had caused so much of the rock to crack, including the roof above it, where she could now, at last, see the fissure.

She hardly had time to comprehend any of it before the current rushing through that very same fissure sucked her up. The battle maiden was swept away, cast from the prison at speed.

The encounter, and her sudden exit, paralysed her thoughts. Only the monster's name came to her, a resounding echo from the tales she had heard as a child.

The Leviathan.

23
THE BOTTOM OF THE WORLD

RUN!" YAMNOMORA URGED, SHOVING HER FELLOW DWARVES ASIDE.

"I am runnin'!" Grarfath countered, his overly-stuffed backpack digging into his hips.

"I told ye to pack light!" the surly warrior called back, taking a sharp turn down Kelig Street.

"I did pack light!" the smith protested.

"Ye could set up a new workshop with all that!" Yamnomora complained, her armoured shoulder ramming through the knotted groups.

Grarfath came to a much-needed stop, his hands coming to rest on his knees. "Why are we runnin' anyway? There ain' no one after us!"

Yamnomora doubled back on herself to join the smith. She offered him little more than a glance before her eyes wandered over the busy streets behind them. Those emerald orbs settled on one patch in particular. "Run," she hissed, turning on her heel.

Grarfath frowned and straightened up so he might see as she had. Amidst the river of heads and beards, a handful stood out as they bobbed above the rest. Seven, perhaps eight, dwarves were barging their way through in pursuit. The smith swore and turned about.

"This way!" Yamnomora yelled, waving him towards her.

Together, they descended the zig-zagging stairs built into The Wall of a Thousand Shields. With no railing, it was all too easy for the quick-footed to miss a step and fall over the edge. That was made even easier when that same dwarf was over-laden with sundries. Grarfath yelped as he attempted the u-turn at speed and began to topple over the lip. Yamnomora whipped out a hand as he had no more than a single heel on the stone, and grabbed the smith by the strap of his backpack.

"Move as I move," she suggested before taking off again.

Indeed, he watched as Yamnomora never reached the flat landing that connected the many stairs. Instead, the dwarf cut out the bottom two steps, dropped into a crouch, and hopped down onto the top of the next set. Grarfath sighed, but he mimicked her exactly and removed the danger of slipping over the edge every time.

The smith was thinking of another break when they finally reached the bottom, but Yamnomora was already running between the gargantuan pillars that supported Galadin's Floor. Though the cavernous area offered an immense amount of space, the best of dwarves had consumed much of it with their palatial homes, some of which were better described as fortresses. Grand as they all were, none could boast the height of Galadin's pillars—a hundred blocks of stone that kept the mountain roof at bay.

"What are we doin' 'ere?" Grarfath questioned.

"We need speed," Yamnomora told him, her own speed yet to let up.

The smith followed her as she navigated the grid system, their path taking them towards the outer edge of Galadin's Floor. After jogging the last hundred yards, they arrived at a building that blended in with the stone walls more than it did the gilded homes. So too did all the buildings in that same row.

"What's this abou' then?" he asked.

Yamnomora stopped in front of a double gate and produced a key to the padlock. "The servants 'ave to live somewhere," she quipped, nodding her head at the stately homes behind.

"Do *ye* live 'ere?"

The dwarf snorted. "No. A friend does though. He lets me keep Bludgeon 'ere."

Grarfath blinked. "Bludgeon?"

Yamnomora opened the gate to reveal a small pen littered with straw and a trough of water. "Bludgeon!" she repeated with a broad smile.

The Warhog squealed and moved to meet the dwarven warrior. Yamnomora playfully jostled his tusks before going on to saddle the beast.

"Is he yers?"

The pig's thick head turned towards the smith, its body bristling as it stamped one of its hooves.

Yamnomora winced before she grinned. "I don' think he likes ye."

Grarfath circled the mount, wary of the beast usually reserved for the high king's personal army. "Where'd ye get a Warhog from?"

"I won 'im in a bet," she informed, retrieving two previously unseen axes from the corner.

The smith couldn't help but closely examine the weapons as she strapped them to the side of the saddle. They were each two-handed and of their own design. Where one was a solid haft of wood with a large and single curving blade at its head, the other was steel from top to bulbous pommel, and the head boasted a blade on both sides of the haft. They were considerable weapons that went well with a Warhog draped in chainmail, its tusks tipped with steel points.

"Hop on," she instructed, a sense of urgency in her voice again.

Bludgeon moved restlessly as the smith climbed on, but it gave no violent protest. Nor did it resist when Yamnomora had it charge from the humble stable at speed. Grarfath held on tightly, his hands clasped around Yamnomora's waist and his cheek pressed against her back, where her swept-back mane of copper ringlets tickled his face.

They were soon departing Galadin's Floor and descending the ramp into The Spokes, a vast canyon of bridges and waterfalls that connected numerous districts. Both canyon walls were layered with scaffolding and platforms that allowed the lift system to transport heavy goods or even crowds of dwarves up and down the cliffs. At the base, where the water collected and ran through the stone, great wheels churned, using the strong currents to generate power.

Yamnomora brought Bludgeon to a stop before they crossed the first bridge. She turned the beast so she could see the way they had come.

"Did we lose 'em?" he asked.

"Ye never lose 'em. Ye can only hope to stay ahead o' 'em." Yamnomora turned her attention on the network of bridges and lifts. "Where to?"

Her question threw Grarfath. "Ye're askin' me?"

"Before she died, yer mother hid somethin'—the same thing Tharg an' his ilk are after."

The smith scowled and shrugged his rounded shoulders. "How am I supposed to know where me mother hid anythin'?" he interjected.

Yamnomora turned her face over one shoulder. "Mordrith used her last breath to speak yer name."

Though the dwarven warrior went on, Grarfath heard not a word. He was, instead, imagining his mother's final moments. He knew nothing of the circumstances, but he well envisioned her looking up at Yamnomora and uttering his name. Whatever he held against her, the smith wished more than anything that he could have been there at the end.

"Well?"

Again, the question threw Grarfath. "What did ye say?"

Yamnomora's patience was visibly wearing thin. "She said ye

would know where she hid it. Only ye. So if Mordrith was to hide somethin', where would she go?"

Grarfath blinked. There was a part of his mind that knew exactly where his mother would hide something valuable. At the same time, he had long convinced himself that he didn't really know his mother—that he never had—and so how could he begin to fathom such a thing? The fact that she had voiced his name, however, suggested that his initial suspicion was likely correct.

Yamnomora groaned, though her ire was not directed at the smith. "We need to go," she urged, spurring Bludgeon into a fresh sprint.

Grarfath managed to look back before the Warhog took off across the nearest bridge. Tharg himself was leading the party of thugs, and all astride ponies to lend them speed. Bludgeon's hooves clopped loudly as they traversed the stone and passed over the circular platform that served as a meeting point for six of the bridges.

"No, no, no!" Grarfath yelled in Yamnomora's ear. "That way! Go *that* way!"

The dwarf noted his pointing finger and put Bludgeon into a tight turn. A handful of pedestrians were forced to dive aside, their fists rising threateningly from the ground. Yamnomora shouted an apology despite the broad smile that adorned her face.

"Turn right!" the smith instructed.

Bludgeon crossed the next bridge and turned right after reaching the opposing canyon wall. From there, Grarfath directed them ever downwards. In order to put as much distance between them and Tharg's lot as possible, Yamnomora had Bludgeon leap onto one of the descending lifts only moments after it had departed. Grarfath felt his stomach rise uncomfortably into his chest before the Warhog touched down. Their sudden presence startled the merchants transporting their laden carts, but one look from Yamnomora kept them quiet and their thoughts to themselves.

Craning his neck, Grarfath located Tharg, the older dwarf

looking down on them from his saddle. The jump was death to them, forcing their group to turn and find another way down.

"So," Yamnomora said. "Where are we goin' exactly?"

The smith took a breath and consulted his memory one last time. "Ye knew me mother was a miner, aye? She was a damned good one. It was years ago now, but she were the one who discovered them ancient minin' shafts down in The Well."

"The Well?" Yamnomora echoed incredulously. "That's as far down as ye can go," she remarked.

"Aye," Grarfath agreed. "She thought they might lead to new silvyr deposits, ones that had been abandoned by our ancestors when our craft was crude. Or so she would say."

"I heard they collapsed," Yamnomora commented.

Grarfath nodded dourly. "Some of 'em did, aye. Killed two dozen miners. Me mother always felt responsible. They shut down the whole site after that—too dangerous. When it weighed her down, she would take herself off to walk the mines again. Me Pa never knew, but I followed her once. She made me promise not to tell 'im. She didn' want 'im to worry."

"An' ye think that's where Mordrith'd hide somethin'?"

Grarfath shrugged. "Where better? Those mines are dead an' they lead nowhere. No one would even stumble upon... Wait, what is it she's supposed to 'ave hidden?"

Ignoring his question, Yamnomora had Bludgeon leap the remaining few feet, beating the lift by a couple of seconds to touch down. With a burst of speed, the beast set to a new path that took them along the river and streams.

Though they now traversed the lowest depths of The Morthil Mountains, they were by no means alone. The undercity thrived nearly as much as those who dwelled on the higher levels.

Lacking the grandeur of lofty halls and towering statues, the undercity was stacked from floor to ceiling, buildings built atop each other like cubes upon cubes. Torches and braziers illuminated the domed cavern, revealing the busy markets and workshops. While Bludgeon could have made short work crossing the undercity, Yamnomora slowed the animal to a natural walk, lest they leave a trail of bodies for their pursuers to follow.

Grarfath was hit by waves of heat from forges and the aromatic spices from the various food stalls. Children dashed about in tight groups before scattering to abide by the rules of their games. For all the chaos, Yamnomora weaved through it all like a leaf floating atop a stream.

"Ye seem to know yer way abou'," the smith observed.

"I grew up down 'ere," she replied. "Ye would have too," she added, glancing over one shoulder, "had yer father's work not elevated yer family beyond Galadin's Floor."

Grarfath wished to protest that in some way, but every word had been true. The Underborns—his guild—heralded from this very stone. Every dwarf about them called themselves Underborn, and proudly so. Perhaps more proudly than he ever had. His father's smith-work, however, had seen them rise above the crowded streets, where the richest of the guilds might call upon his skill without having to descend into the undercity.

It made him feel privileged, which jarred with the struggles he had faced in recent years.

They eventually concluded their journey across the undercity and found themselves at Torlin's Doors. The pair drew curious eyes from passers-by as they worked together to open the heavy doors, long abandoned. Beyond was the bridge that stretched on from the threshold to overcome a significant dip in the rock. With Bludgeon's reins in hand, Yamnomora led the way on foot, bringing them to the other side, where the ground levelled out.

"Which one?" she asked, gesturing loosely at the four tunnels that branched from the central foyer.

Grarfath consulted distant memory and landed on the tunnel second in from the right. "That one."

Together, with torches they had taken from the undercity, they passed through that tunnel and followed its winding path.

"How deep does it go?" Yamnomora asked.

"Not far. It wasn' too long after they reopened the mines that the trouble started. This one," he said, indicating the stone about them, "was one o' the older tunnels."

As the smith had said, it wasn't long before the pair were standing inside a new expanse of ancient stone. Unlike the domed roof of the undercity, the cave sloped up to an unaligned point, its true height beyond the touch of their torchlight.

Grarfath walked a few steps ahead before coming to a stop. "This is where she would come to be alone."

Yamnomora looked around and nodded her head. "That seems abou' right for Mordrith."

The smith felt a cold shiver run through him. It was unusual to be back in that place, as if he had stepped into memory. "So, ye're sayin' she might 'ave been 'ere jus' before she died?"

Yamnomora opened her mouth but seemed to struggle to find the right response. "Not exactly," she managed, if cryptically so.

"Well she must 'ave been if she hid somethin' 'ere. What *did* she hide?"

Yamnomora walked slowly around the edge of the jagged chamber, her eyes cast low to the floor. "Ye would know it if ye saw it," she told him unhelpfully.

Frayed by the day that had unravelled about him, Grarfath sighed and guided his torch to the cave floor. There weren't even any tools left behind, nor a single piece of equipment used to excavate the rock from the chamber. What he did find, however, was an obviously *empty* space.

"Somethin' was 'ere," he called out, bringing his torch up to illuminate the rocks and the deep impression that marked them. "Somethin' *big*," he specified. The smith couldn't discern the truth of the shape, only that it was ten to twelve feet in length and with three or four extensions coming out of the middle.

"It were the skeleton," Yamnomora said offhandedly, not even bothering to join him.

"A skeleton?" the smith echoed scrutinising the huge space again. "A skeleton o' what?"

"It don' matter. Jus' keep lookin."

"I don' know what I'm lookin' for," he complained.

"I told ye: ye'll know it when ye see it!"

Grarfath turned from the unusual excavation to face his irritating companion. "Ye've spent too long with no one to talk to but that bloody pig. An' how is it that *I'm* not the one to be trusted? *Ye* came to *me*!"

Yamnomora lifted her torch to eye level. "Trust no one," she perfectly enunciated. "Those three words are the only words to live by an' ye'll..." The dwarf trailed off upon seeing Grarfath's attention move past her.

The smith crossed the chamber as Yamnomora turned around. Side by side, they frowned at the partial tree resting against the cave wall. Only in torchlight had it been revealed, its bark too similar to the natural rock in the darkness.

"That's a tree," Grarfath stated, dumbfounded.

Yamnomora ran her torch low and discovered the torn roots and soil that lay on the cold stone. "It's 'ere," she whispered, anticipation in her voice.

"What's 'ere? An' why is there an uprooted tree in The Well?"

The dwarven warrior was already moving her torch to inspect the area. "That," she announced, pointing at the mysterious tree, "and these," she added, using her torch to reveal dried up flora and splinters of broken trees on the floor, "are from The Swamps o' Morthil."

Grarfath ran his fingers over the narrow tree and pinched his finger and thumb to snap off one of the delicate branches. "How can ye tell?"

Yamnomora paused in her investigation and faced the smith. "Yer mother was killed in those swamps."

It felt another blow to Grarfath's senses. The Swamps of Morthil were no place to die. It was unbefitting of any dwarf, but it seemed somehow worse for it to have been his mother's final resting place. Still, the smith swallowed the lump in his throat and absorbed the information as he had everything else since Yamnomora walked into his life.

"Wait," he said, reason and logic catching up with him. "What does her dyin' there 'ave to do with bits o' the swamp bein' down 'ere?"

Yamnomora ceased her investigation so she might display her best interpretation of exasperation. "All o' yer questions could do with waitin' until we find the..." For the second time that day, her words faded to nothing, only it was Grarfath now who followed her distant gaze.

Looking over his left shoulder, the smith was slowly turned around by what his companion had first discovered. He raised his torch, sure that his eyes deceived him. "Is that a..."

"Hammer!" Yamnomora declared, a hungry grin on her face.

Grarfath moved closer to the hammer, its head mostly buried in the cave wall. Even so, he could see that it was of exquisite craftsmanship. The steel haft was loosely coiled in bronze; the effect ending in an angled pommel. He couldn't help himself, his hands instinctively reaching for the hammer. It took some strength to yank it from the rock, but Grarfath Underborn had never been without such power.

With a crack of stone, the weapon came free. He held it aloft and bathed the head in torchlight. What magnificent work had gone into its forging! The golden head, a block of rectangular steel, was trimmed with lines of bronze that connected to the coil wrapped around the haft. It was the finest piece of smith work he had ever laid eyes upon.

Judging by Yamnomora's intense gaze, Grarfath assumed the hammer to be the very thing they had been searching for. "Me mother died over a hammer," he concluded dryly, his disbelief more than evident.

Yamnomora's expression dropped. "It ain' jus' a *hammer*. It's *The Anther*."

Grarfath blinked. "The Anther?" he scoffed. "Ye're talkin' abou' a legend. A myth!"

The dwarven warrior gave a mirthless laugh. "An' I suppose ye think Duun, son o' Darl, was a myth too."

"*Aye*. Because he was."

"The Hammerhold was jus' as real as ye an' me," Yamnomora

asserted, referring to the ancient dwarf by his title. "The proof o' it's in yer very hand."

"Me Pa used to tell me stories o' Duun when I were jus' a pup. That's all they are: *stories*."

The warrior placed her hands on her hips and huffed. "I'm to be killin' ye meself for sure. Ye need to understand one simple thing: ye 'ave no idea what world ye're livin' in."

The smith scowled. "A'right. I've had abou' as much o' this as I can take." He lowered the hammer, purposefully concealing it behind his stance. "This Tharg fella wants to kill me. Ye're *talkin'* abou' killin' me, an' me mother has actually *been* killed. Not to mention the fact that ye've had me run from me home, an' to the bottom o' the world at that. What is goin' on? What am I in the middle o'?"

Yamnomora adopted a serious demeanour and she ran one hand down her thick stubble. "I have to assume," she began, gesturing to the hammer she couldn't see, "that Mordrith wanted to bring ye in to all this. Though ye might not thank her for it."

Grarfath ignored her last statement. "Bring me into what?"

The dwarven warrior licked her lips and took a breath—she even glanced about the darkened cave as if they might be overheard. "Yer mother was a *Skaramangian*."

A moment of silence held sway.

"Stop with the made-up words," the smith pleaded, "an jus' tell me what ye're talkin' abou'."

Yamnomora's expression scrunched up into frustration. "Ye're askin' me to explain somethin' that's older than civilisation. We really don' 'ave time for it. We've got The Anther. Now we need to get out o' 'ere before Tharg an' the others find us. An' when I say out o' 'ere," she clarified, "I do mean out o' The Morthil Mountains."

The smith refused to budge. "Who in the hells *is* Tharg?" he demanded. "What's he got to do with me mother? An' why would he 'ave her killed for a damned hammer?"

Yamnomora groaned as she tried to make for the exit with Bludgeon. "Tharg is a Skaramangian," she said as a matter of fact.

"The others too. An' they *will* kill ye, Grarfath. They've eyes an' ears everywhere. The Morthil Mountains ain' safe for ye no more."

The smith skipped over his own questions for the moment and focused on what had been said to him. "Well, why don' *ye* take it then," he suggested offering her the hammer. "Ye seem to enjoy this life. Why don' ye take it an' run. They'll see I don' 'ave it an' leave me be."

An almost sad expression overcame Yamnomora's features. "It's too late for that now. Ye've seen 'em. Ye know Tharg's name. Hells, ye fled with *me*. That's all they need to know. An' besides," she added, looking at the hammer, "Mordrith wanted ye to 'ave it. I'll not deny the woman her dyin' wish."

The smith lowered the hammer again, and with it he felt his life and all that he had known be dragged down with it. He opened his mouth to speak when a violent tremor rocked the floor beneath his feet.

"Is that normal?" Yamnomora enquired.

Grarfath looked down at the cave floor, his torch brought low to see the small rocks rattling about. "No," he said at length.

Another quake tore through the mountain and the dwarves were nearly taken from their feet. Bludgeon staggered about and snorted in protest.

"What's happenin'? Is this a cave-in?"

Grarfath was shaking his head. "It's comin' from below," he replied in disbelief.

Again, the mountain shuddered. The stone around them began to crack, though not nearly so much as the cave floor. The fourth tremor caused parts of the floor to rise and the dwarves found themselves lifted several feet with it.

Yamnomora slapped a hand on the smith's shoulder. "We need to get out o' 'ere *now*!"

The next quake ripped through the cave floor and prevented the dwarves from going anywhere, the force of it enough to cast them from their feet. Before they hit the hard stone, a jet of water erupted from below and formed a liquid pillar as it slammed into the roof.

Grarfath looked up from the cave floor, his face bombarded by salty water, as if it were raining under the mountain. For the second time in as many minutes, he couldn't believe his eyes.

Not far from where he lay, Yamnomora was yelling his name over the deafening sound of the water. "We need to get out o' 'ere!"

Of their torches, only one had maintained its flames and the smith was sure to scoop it up on his way to his companion's side. He tripped and nearly fell again, drawing his attention to his feet. More cracks were sundering the stone and water was already bubbling up in new places.

Determined to flee the mines before he drowned, Grarfath steadied himself against the next tremor and made for the exit behind Yamnomora.

He would have made it too had he not heard the distressed cry of a woman.

The smith turned back and raised his torch just in time to see a person falling from the cave roof, her body apparently ejected from the forceful gush of water.

"What in the hells?" he muttered, his feet slowly taking him towards the prone woman.

"Grarfath!" Yamnomora shouted before landing a heavy hand on his shoulder. "We're goin' to..." Her eyes found that same woman. "Where did she come from?"

At the question, the stranger steadily picked herself up and proceeded to vomit an awful amount of water. For every bit of height she eventually gained, the jaws of both Grarfath and Yamnomora slowly dropped. She had at least two feet on them both. Her pale skin was contrasted by vibrant blue eyes and raven hair that framed her angelic features. Her beauty was so sharp it lent her a dangerous look in Grarfath's opinion.

"She's a human!" Yamnomora spat.

The strange woman shook off her disorientation and assumed a level of alarm that seemed fitting for their situation. "*Run!*" she exclaimed in the human tongue.

There was no time to ask questions—the sea water was quickly rising. With Bludgeon by their side, the unusual trio ran from the cave and followed the winding mine back to the platform that offered several entrances. They ignored them all and made for the bridge with all haste. The damned thing hadn't seemed so long coming from the other way.

"No!" Yamnomora was calling out, for she had seen their calamity first.

"Wait!" Grarfath added his own voice, desperate for the folk of the undercity to hear him.

Not only did they see the approaching group, but they must also have heard them. It made no difference. The Underborns, having no doubt felt the earthquakes, were working together to seal the heavy doors of Torlin. The trio ran as fast as they could while watching their salvation narrow to a sliver of light and heaving dwarves.

Thoom!

Torlin's Doors came together only a moment before Grarfath's hand slapped against the iron. "Open the doors!" he growled.

Yamnomora was incessantly patting his arm. "Grarfath," she muttered.

The smith turned back to face the mines. The rock above the tunnel entrances was visibly cracking, the sound of it just audible over the rushing water. Chunks of dark stone, laid down millennia ago, were being forced apart.

The ocean was coming for them.

"Quickly," Yamnomora urged. "Use the hammer!"

Grarfath looked at his fellow dwarf as if she had lost her mind. "I couldn' get these doors open with all the hammers in Verda!"

"No!" she retorted. "Strike the floor! The floor!"

"What are ye talkin' abou'?"

"It's the only way we're gettin' out o' 'ere! Ye need to hit the floor with all yer strength!"

The tunnel from which they had come exploded with water, the force of it bringing down much of the rock surrounding the other entrances. The water reached out for every inch of ground, seeking out the crevices and pitfalls. The damage wrought rippled up through the chamber and began to threaten the high roof above them.

"Do it now!" Yamnomora yelled.

Frustration, fear, and anger brought out a roar from the smith. He raised the hammer in one hand and slammed it into the ground at his feet if for no other reason than to shut Yamnomora up.

The gold and bronze head struck the stone with a resounding knock. But that was not all. Grarfath was taken aback by the ripple of distorted air that exploded from the point of impact.

"What was that?"

"Again!" Yamnomora insisted, as a slab of rock came loose from the cavern roof and broke apart only a few feet away from them. "Again! Use all yer strength!"

The smith brought the hammer down a second time and, again, the air rippled out from the impact.

Yamnomora grabbed him by his shirt. "Ye have to think o' somewhere! Anywhere but 'ere!"

Grarfath glanced at the ruined mines and torrent of water rushing out towards them, filling the chamber up. He did as she instructed and slammed the hammer down onto the bridge. This time, the ripple effect was cut with another environment, as if two places were beginning to overlap.

"*What is that?*" the tall stranger demanded.

Yamnomora waved her question away and focused on the smith. "Keep thinkin' o' that place an' hit the floor with *all* yer strength. Both hands!"

At the last second, Grarfath took the hammer in two hands and thundered it into the stone bridge. That same environment flashed around them, bringing trees and yellow grass into the rocky chamber. Then it was gone, as if it had been no more than a mirage. The water, however, was not a mirage and had found its way to the bridge where it was quickly filling up the shallow basin below.

"Again!" Yamnomora bellowed.

A new surge of sea water burst from the mines. It was too much for the surrounding stone. Huge swathes of rock were pushed away from the walls and roof, destroying the other end of a bridge that had stood for thousands of years. They had precious few seconds before the entire chamber imploded.

Grarfath's back arched under the strain of raising the hammer so far over his head. He gritted his teeth.

The hammer struck stone.

24
GOD FALL

The Ahnir'duil, a forest so named for the god who fell dead in the heart of it, was a leafy paradise. The trees were strong and wide, their roots nourished by soil that had greeted the mighty Ahnir upon his last breath. Their branches stretched far and wide, offering natural bridges from one tree to another. The leaves, of which there were millions, appeared a different colour depending on the angle from which they were viewed. Though thick, the canopy allowed a generous amount of speckled sunlight to touch the forest floor, illuminating the hallowed path to the catacombs.

Teeming with wildlife, The Ahnir'duil's animal population was nevertheless carefully controlled; a measure taken to ensure its greatest treasure remained undisturbed. It was controlled by the same people who watched The Eldan and his massive entourage parade through the forest.

Through the slits of his sloping iron mask, The Eldan glimpsed the forest guardians as they observed from the tree tops. He had to look for them, they who blended in with the trunks, branches, and colourful leaves. All had forsaken their white hair, shaving their scalps so they might better camouflage themselves. So they might better protect Ahnir.

Of course, these guardians did not look down on *The Eldan*. To their eyes, he approached as none other than the highest of grand clerics—the *master cleric*. Unlike the grand clerics, his robes were more black than red and his helm branched out and up in the style of wings. If his attire wasn't enough to identify him, the two hundred souls in his wake would suffice. From a retinue of attendants and advisors, to fellow clerics and guarding soldiers, The Eldan travelled as well as the emperor himself.

Since the pilgrimage to the holy site was only permitted on foot, The Eldan and his entourage had taken the River Illisar, setting off from Aran'saur without a single mount. After a day of walking and one night of camping, the entrance to the catacombs was finally in sight.

A simple door of stone, its walls sloping down into the earth, it appeared a humble entryway in place of what could have been something akin to the gates of paradise. Though The Eldan couldn't see it from the doorway, he knew that half a mile from the modest entrance sat a large dome of the same stone. His destination lay beneath it.

Since no guardian descended from their leafy perch to prohibit him, The Eldan stood and waited for two of his strongest soldiers to step forward and heave open the thick door. His orders previously given, no command was required to separate himself and three others from the entourage as they alone descended the steps beyond.

The catacombs beneath The Ahnir'duil were well lit by torches fixed to the walls, each bringing light to the stream of carvings that flowed along the stone. They told a story, of course, detailing the first Andarens to have found Ahnir's resting place and His helm beside Him. Since then, the forest had become the most protected place in all of Andara, surpassing even the palace.

The Eldan paid the stone tapestry little regard. He was well-versed in the scripture, able to recount it verbatim. A story for the masses, he always thought, the narrative created by his predecessors eons past.

Soon the lie, and all the lies it had spawned, would come to a crashing end.

The truth would free them all.

Following the catacombs for a little over half a mile, where the tunnel weaved and branched into various chambers, The Eldan and his three closest attendants arrived at an enormous circular wall. It was, in fact, another impenetrable door. This one, however, could not be opened by any soldiers or even the attendants.

The Eldan didn't even bother looking up at the monstrous figure that stood between them and the door. He had seen it before and had no intention of spoiling his breakfast by taking in its atrocious and grotesque features again. He simply waited, as he had before. Though little more than a beast, the towering guard knew the master cleric stood before it and knew better than to make him wait.

Two monstrous arms of charcoal black, bulging with muscle and overlain with veins, reached out for the door. The creature groaned with exertion as it rolled the door to one side, the stone grinding with every inch of movement. The way cleared, the dreadful creation pressed itself to the wall so as not to get in the way.

The Eldan stepped over the threshold with his attendants and, again, waited until the circular door was rolled back into place, securing them inside the antechamber. On the other side, a pair of ancient doors were soon opened to reveal the vast cavity that sat beneath the stone dome.

"Greetings, master cleric."

The Eldan regarded the warlock. He was one of three, the fourth never to be replaced after Handuin's betrayal, so many centuries ago. Like his fellow warlocks, the one greeting them had no name, his life given over to the brotherhood. Now, he was identified by no more than a tattoo that marked his right cheek; a vertical line interrupted by two four-sided diamonds. It was a symbol of his true allegiance. It was also the same symbol that could be found on The Eldan's gold ring, situated on a finger hidden inside one of the leather gloves he wore.

"Let this site remain a place of truth, warlock." With this decree, The Eldan removed his bronze helm and mask, his bright eyes a set of golden orbs against his pale face.

One of the attendants accepted the helm and retreated with the other two, the trio to wait by the door.

The warlock bowed his head. "Greetings, *Eldan*," he said. "Welcome back to God Fall."

How much more powerful he felt being called his true title. While Clerics, and even those grand clerics who had yet to enter the inner circles, coveted the title of master cleric, it felt no more significant than the fiction they spouted as scripture. As master cleric, his station served to steer the masses, and even the imperial family, like sheep. As The Eldan, his station served to steer tidal events across all of Verda. More so, it was a position that allowed him to forge the future.

A Skaramangian future.

The warlock's crooked back kept him in a bowed posture, forcing his neck to work all the harder so he might look up at The Eldan. He was one of very few in all the realm who had seen his actual face. To most, including Emperor Qeledred, he was a pair of golden eyes inside a bronze mask.

"You need not have come so far," the warlock told him, turning to guide them further into the main chamber. "We could have sent word of our progress."

"My presence here is expected," The Eldan replied, following in the warlock's wake. "We must keep up pretences until the final hour is upon us. Besides, I would see the two together," he added hungrily. How many Eldans before him had only dreamed of bringing two skeletons together?

Two *gods*. A bemused smile curled his cheeks.

The warlock gestured to the chamber at large. "Come then. We have only recently assembled the new arrival."

The circular chamber was lined with workstations, atop which lay a plethora of equipment from alchemical instruments to excavation tools. Shelves had been dug into the surrounding stone, so that hundreds of books could be stored and called upon at a moment's notice. In between these stations were doors that led to smaller rooms, each providing space for experimentation while keeping the bones safe from harm. Though he had never seen it, The Eldan had to assume there was somewhere for the warlocks to sleep.

"Where are your brothers?" he asked, hearing the distant screams of terror and agony that begged for attention.

The warlock's faded blue eyes shifted momentarily to one of the doors. "Seeing to the great work, of course."

"And their apprentices?" The Eldan checked, aware that the warlocks were nearing the end of their many centuries—the very reason he had sent them worthy candidates.

"They will be ready to assume their duty when the time comes, though we would see our master's return before we are replaced."

His hands clasped neatly behind his back, The Eldan gave the comment little thought. After all, how many before them had dreamt of such a thing and died of old age?

The Eldan stopped by the edge of the pit in the very heart of the cavity. Looking down, he was always drawn first to the dark pits of Ahnir's eye sockets—all four of them. *To have seen what they have seen*, he thought. To have seen *Him*.

When he was finally able to break away from the skull and its sloping point, his gaze wandered over the long skeleton, its four arms, and the lines of runes and glyphs etched into every bone.

As there had ever been, the right femur bone was absent, presenting a break in the skeleton's flow. The magic inscribed on the missing bone had been enough for Handuin to make his Vahlken, though by a flawed and incomplete method that killed more than it transformed.

Then there was the second skeleton, its bones displayed on a slab set to a forty-five degree angle on the other side of the pit. Every bone fitted perfectly into the stone that had been carved to house it, preventing the skeleton from losing its shape on the incline. It was identical to Ahnir in every way except for its most important distinction—different glyphs.

For sixty years the skeleton had been moved from location to location, dogged all the while by the tenacious Vahlken. Astride their Aegres, Handuin's legacy had begun tracking the bones not long after they had departed The Morthil Mountains. Ever since, they had prevented them from being transported to God Fall. Their constant interference had cost the Skaramangians time and stopped the warlocks from examining the skeleton first-hand and side by side with Ahnir.

But now, at last, they had circumvented the Vahlken and reassembled the bones where they were needed most. The warlocks' previously piecemeal investigation could now begin in earnest and without interruption.

"How goes the war?"

The Eldan glanced at the smaller Andaren. "Which one?"

The warlock gave a wry smile. "The only one that has ever mattered."

"The Vahlken still pursue us, though their numbers are so few that most are stuck guarding the borders against the humans."

The warlock chuckled to himself. "After all this time, they still have no idea what we're trying to do."

That only remained a fact, The Eldan knew, because so many Skaramangians were kept in the dark as to the order's true purpose. How many believed they were doing the gods' work? How many did his bidding because it provided them with wealth or offered them power?

"Whether they know or not, Handuin's children remain a thorn in our side. Thankfully, they have cut down enough of the Dragon Riders to be useful."

The warlock spat on the floor in disgust. "Filthy beasts," he cursed, as he always had at the mention of dragons. "I should like to be there for the demise of their last," he said, grinning.

"Alas," The Eldan replied, "it is your work here that will see to that." *That's if the Dragon Riders don't annihilate themselves in the meantime*, he thought.

"Fear not, old friend," the warlock went on. "My brothers and I will make sure the wretched dragons do not interfere as they did so long ago. They will all perish. Even the wild ones."

The Eldan took little notice of such conviction. They had started the war with Erador to ensure they would face no opposition from the dragons in the crowning hour. Unlike the rest of the world, the Skaramangians knew their history, and they had no intention of seeing it repeated. The final victory would be theirs this time.

"It would help if we possessed The Anther," the warlock remarked, a single eye managing to find The Eldan's face.

Thinking of the hammer and its ancient name, The Eldan stared into the empty eye sockets of the new skeleton. Found beneath The Morthil Mountains, and with The Anther no less, there could be no mistaking the skeleton's identity. They had found the indomitable *Govhul*. If only it were so.

"Soon," The Eldan answered. "It recently eluded us," he elaborated. "Tharg has assured me results."

"Never trust a dwarf," the warlock remarked.

"He is a Skaramangian first," The Eldan reminded.

"Not like us," came the response. "Dwarves think only of themselves. The Anther may need prising from his grasp should he retrieve it."

"Leave it to me," The Eldan instructed.

The warlock licked his lips, his old eyes shifting round and up to find his master. "And what of the vambrace," he enquired, much to The Eldan's irritation. "When we find him," the warlock continued, "our work will stall without it. Of all the weapons of power, we need that one the most."

"The wizard still eludes us," The Elden reported, his words clipped. "What of your own work?" he demanded.

The warlock navigated the rounded edge of Ahnir's pit until he was standing beside Govhul's bones. "For decades we have learned what we can from the segments we received—"

"I am aware of your previous breakthroughs," The Eldan interrupted, the new spells they had gleaned already in use and at his disposal. "But you have complained for years that you needed them *together*." He gestured at the skeletons. "What have you learned?"

The warlock hesitated, perhaps having hoped to talk a while longer about their meagre successes over the last sixty years. "There is a page missing," he admitted, his voice a croaking whisper.

So used to wearing a mask, The Eldan failed to frown despite his confusion. "What does that mean?" he asked, his voice enough to convey his emotions.

"They are like the pages of a book," the warlock explained, his long fingernails gliding over Govhul. "They are each a page, and each filled with a language of magic."

The Eldan's gaze was drawn down to the smaller Andaren. "But?"

"It seems Govhul does not follow after Ahnir," the warlock confessed. "We believe Meliax or Yohem sits between them. Possibly *both*," he added. "I have read the grimoire thoroughly over the centuries. It states that Ahnir was the first of the four, but there is no record of which one came next. I only know it wasn't Govhul. Were we to possess Meliax," he said provocatively, "we would have two consecutive pages, so to speak. We might even learn magic that allows us to locate the fourth, wherever Yohem slumbers. I don't need to tell you what we can do with all four."

Of course The Eldan knew. Along with the warlocks, he was at the end of a very long line who had dreamed of nothing but bringing the four together. Only then, with the secrets of the magic realm laid bare, could they find *Him*.

The Timeless One.

The Eldan resisted the shiver that ran up his spine, thankful that his robes concealed the hairs standing along his arms. The Eldan knew it would be him—no other! He would be the one to fulfil the very meaning of the Skaramangian order.

He turned back to look at Ahnir's resting bones. How many millennia had they been searching for another? How many lifetimes spent to no avail? Now, when they finally had another in their possession, they were still no closer than they were a thousand years ago. It would slip through his fingers if he didn't escalate things, if he didn't use the full weight of the power he and his predecessors had worked so hard to secure.

"That is not to say," the warlock caveated, "that Govhul's bones won't propel our efforts."

The Eldan held up a hand to silence him. He needed to think. *No.* He needed to accept the only path left to him. He had been holding back, biding his time while they further infiltrated The Jainus, but progress was slower than he liked. Slower than they could afford.

After all, it had been *seen.*

A Time of Dragons loomed over them, a shadow that promised an end to thousands of years of sacrifice. The light was rising to meet the darkness. It only encouraged The Eldan, convincing him that they were getting closer to their ultimate imperative.

The Eldan's thoughts swirled to a point. The abomination.

Pendain.

The name was a venom in his mind, for he knew the translation. What he could not fathom was how such archaic words were still in the mouths of any humans, no matter how witless they were. It was unthinkable that any, even an Andaren, would belong to the ancient name. It was a worrisome conundrum that wormed beneath his skin.

Without thinking, he reached into his robes and felt for the small box that hung from his belt. He retrieved it, pausing before opening the lid.

"Leave me," he commanded, sending the warlock slinking towards the nearest workstation.

The Eldan proceeded to remove his right glove, where his eyes lingered for a second on the gold ring and the sigil of his order. He was the forty-first Eldan to wear it. He was determined to be the last.

Opening the small box, he regarded the black sphere nestled inside. Facing up was a small circle that had been sliced out of the orb, where he might place his thumb. Waiting for his thumb was a fine needle.

The Eldan removed the sphere entirely and pushed his thumb

onto its point. The orb drank from him, taking in his blood. His hand soon grew cold. Then his arm. Eventually, the numbing sensation spread throughout his body until it reached his eyes, forcing them closed.

Though the world about him was gone, a new world was revealed in its absence.

In shadow and smoke, he waited.

Thousands of miles away, an identical orb was alerting its owner, bidding him to offer blood. When, at last, he complied, a new form took shape from the smoke, filling the ethereal void with another consciousness.

"Master," came the usual greeting.

Troubled as he was, The Eldan made a point to reinforce his air of command and control—how else would one maintain authority over a wild dog? "My Dancing Sword of the Dawn," he replied lovingly, sure to use the title he had personally bestowed—a title taken right out of the Arkalon. "I am in God Fall," he informed, using the holy site as a reminder that he was the closest thing the gods had to a voice.

"I pray that one day I will be worthy to return," the servant responded.

The Eldan recalled the first and only time he had brought The Dancing Sword of the Dawn to God Fall. It had solidified his servitude and loyalty. It had also blinded the fool to the truth. Like so many others, The Dawn Sword believed he was working towards the blessed day of Reclamation, that he was a tool of the gods. He was a Skaramangian in name only.

That didn't mean The Eldan could be careless with him. He was one of the greatest weapons at their disposal, if a double-edged one. If mishandled, he could draw blood from their order, becoming a problem that would drain valuable resources to put down. If that was even possible.

But if manipulation was an art form then The Eldan was an artist unlike any other. "Have faith, my friend. With you at the tip of our spear there can be only success." He wished to point out the sixteen years of fruitless hunting across Erador but decided otherwise. "When last we spoke, you were closing in on your prey."

The smoking visage grinned with wicked glee. "We strike this very night, Master."

That surprised The Eldan, lifting his spirits. "Truly?"

"Our quarry has grown comfortable. They have become lazy. Tonight, I will eliminate the Pendain threat."

A splinter of doubt crept into The Eldan's resolve. He couldn't help but think of the dozen boys and girls, abominations all, they had slain over the years. None had possessed the name Pendain and, to his knowledge, they had yet to learn of the boy's family name.

How many avenues had they exhausted searching the human genealogy that might bring the abomination into the light. Similarly, there had been no leads in Andara.

"You are certain, old friend, that this abomination *is* our quarry?"

"Yes, Master," he replied confidently. "This is Ilithranda's child. If any was to bring about the *Eikor*, it would be *her* spawn. The strength of the Vahlken flows through him."

The Eldan stopped himself from smiling. The *Eikor*! *The Dark Ones*! For all the advantages The Dawn Sword possessed over the common Andaren, he remained no more than a sheep like the rest of them. Still, he was right. If any were to take on the mantle seen through Ahnir's helm, it would be one of Vahlken blood.

"See it done, my friend," he said earnestly. "If we are to see the heavens restored there can be no margin of error. No threat you don't quash."

"It will be done, Master."

In the real world, The Eldan lifted his thumb from the needle. The realm of shadow and smoke evaporated to complete darkness until he opened his eyes. The warlock was watching him from afar as he wiped his thumb clean and returned the orb to its box.

"If you wish to *propel our efforts*," he remarked, raising his hand, "you'll find a way to refine *this*." After the warlock had noted the enclosed orb, The Eldan clipped it back on his belt. "Continue your studies," he added, gesturing at Govhul's bones. With that, he turned on his heel and made for the stone door.

"Where are you going?" the warlock asked after him. "You have only just arrived."

The Eldan paused and looked back. "You require a third *page*," he said, using the warlock's own terminology. "I know where to find it." A sharp smile cut across his face. "I think it's time we *took* it."

Walking away, his helm returned, The Eldan gave the warlocks no more thought. From there to Aran'saur he would formulate the words he would impart directly into the emperor's ear.

I will be the last, he swore.

25
MILD DREAMS

64 Years Ago...

Daijen craned his neck to take in the sheer wall above. There he saw the turrets of Ka'vairn protruding from the Hellion stone, though they seemed so far away. As far away as they were, the ground below seemed significantly further. The trees of The Dain'duil blew gently in the autumn breeze, a carpet of swaying green that would swallow him whole should he fall.

Deciding he wasn't for the Black Abyss that day, Daijen Saeth searched for the next handhold and pushed on. Unfortunately, he wasn't the only one. Below, Kastiek was in pursuit, a dagger gripped between his teeth.

"I really don't like this game," Daijen seethed.

Ilithranda looked down at him, her own position about twenty feet up and to the north. "You don't like it because you always lose," she replied.

"I don't like it because he's going to cut me!" Daijen fumed, his powerful muscles propelling him up at speed.

"You've suffered worse sparring with me," Ilithranda pointed out, her cat-like movements keeping her constantly ahead. "Besides, I thought you'd be accustomed to the feel of Kastiek's blade by now."

"I'm not going to taste that blade today," he vowed.

"We shall see," Ilithranda replied knowingly.

Foolishly, Daijen looked down again and caught sight of Kastiek. The Vahlken had given them a head start that was quickly beginning to mean very little.

"Just climb, Daijen!" Ilithranda called down.

And so he did, with all haste. He had climbed the cliff face many times, over the last three years, but it was a completely different exercise to be hunted up the wall. His fingers hooked into every crevice they could and his hips swayed and pivoted to get his feet higher and secured in the next hold. Still, Kastiek advanced. So smooth and swift was his ascent that it seemed he might have been able to make the climb with his eyes closed.

With a hundred feet left before they reached the ropes hanging over the side of Ka'vairn's solid stone, Daijen was finally closing on Ilithranda. He had only to get above her, be it by an inch or a foot, and Kastiek would divert his attention, his blade meant for the slowest. Yet it did not seem possible, the knotted end of the rope almost within Ilithranda's grasp.

Looking down again, Daijen ignored the dizzying height and focused solely on Kastiek. The Vahlken was almost within striking distance. The conclusion was obvious at this point—he was going to lose and he was going to bleed for it.

Or perhaps he wasn't...

Not far from his position was a rogue tree that had defied its surroundings and managed to grow out of the rock face. It wasn't particularly big and it didn't appear particularly strong, but it protruded about ten feet from the stone, its roots gripped between the cracks. It was foolish, bordering on sheer stupidity, to even consider it, but—as always—Daijen felt the urge to prove himself worthy of the body he had been blessed with.

As Kastiek came for him, his dagger in hand now, Daijen

pressed himself close to the cliff face and braced for the foolhardy leap.

He heard the swipe of cleaving steel as he left the safety of the wall.

For a brief moment there was naught but air beneath him. His right hand scraped gently down the cliff as he lined his feet up with the horizontal trunk. An uncanny sense of balance combined with decades of coming to grips with his new strength and agility prevented the young warrior from falling after landing quite precariously.

Regardless of the feat, he remained firmly in danger, for Kastiek was already preparing to make the same leap. Daijen, therefore, wasted no time enacting the rest of his plan. With his eyes up, searching for the hand and footholds he would need, the initiate ran along the trunk and used three of the largest protruding rocks as he might a set of steps. It was then, with the strength of Handuin flowing through his veins, that he made a jump no Andaren could hope to make. Straight up he went, covering precious feet of the cliff face in a single move.

Below, the roots protested against his every step. The trunk itself snapped a little over halfway along its length, compromising the entire structure. It left Kastiek with but one option—keep climbing. But he did not. As Daijen wrapped his hands around the rope and began his final and far easier ascent, the Vahlken pushed off from the cliff face and plummeted towards The Dain'duil. So powerful was his leap that he was taken far from the rock, where he was able to twist effortlessly in the air.

Frozen mid-climb, Daijen's jaw had fallen open and his heart was quickly making its way up into his throat. For all their enhancements, they possessed nothing that could save them from such a fall, and so Kastiek was now hurtling to his doom.

Daijen gasped when that fate was interrupted by Strix. The Aegre cut through the sky like an arrow, and perfectly in line with its falling rider. Kastiek simply reached out with one hand and caught his saddle before his descent was taken sideways and, ultimately, up. Had he been an ordinary Andaren or a human he would have suffered greatly, his arm ripped from its socket. But Kastiek was far from ordinary.

He was a Vahlken.

Daijen watched the Aegre soar, taking its companion up and over Ka'vairn until it was lost behind the top of the walls. The two initiates could only continue their climb until they reached the lip of the ramparts. Ilithranda was the first to step up onto the hewn stone—the winner. Daijen didn't mind. He was content to have survived the climb and complete it without the touch of Kastiek's blade.

It was that same blade that greeted him before he could get his chest over the top of the battlements. Kastiek was already there, one hand on the rope while the other pressed the biting edge of his dagger into the initiate's left cheek.

"You lose, Daijen Saeth."

Daijen grimaced, and not because of the blood he could feel trickling down his face. "You cheated," he fumed.

Kastiek's golden eyes twitched, narrowing for a second. "You cannot cheat in war. Always assume your enemy has the advantage." The Vahlken stepped back and took his dagger with him, leaving the initiate with a thin red line to sully his angelic features.

His breath hardly laboured, Daijen finished his climb feeling somewhat bitter about the whole exercise. He might not have been the victor, but it was the first time he had completed the climb to the fortress without being caught by Kastiek.

"Vahlkens don't sulk," Kastiek chastised, his soft voice contrasting with his harsh words. "Sometimes we fail and *always* we bleed. But we do not dwell on it. We rise again and *again* and *again*. There is no force that can keep us down. No will that can bind us. We are the line that cannot be crossed. Nothing more. So you keep your chin up, Daijen Saeth, and you try again."

"Such is the advantage you now have," The Valtorak interjected, approaching from behind the initiates. "Your greatest opponent will ever be the Dragon Riders, but their stamina cannot compare to yours. Where they will eventually falter, you will come at them again and again. You will wear them down as the tide does the shore."

"Slowly then," Daijen quipped, to which he suffered the master's intense gaze.

"*Inevitably,*" The Valtorak corrected.

"What of their magic?" Ilithranda questioned, diverting attention and reducing The Valtorak's ire.

"Don't get ahead of yourself," Kastiek told her.

"Quite," the master agreed. "You have other lessons to learn first. And accolades to acquire." The Valtorak looked to Kastiek, who simply nodded cryptically in response. "It seems you are both ready for the next step in your training."

Daijen's elation was enough to quash the injustice he felt, and he naturally thought of Laif and the other initiates. They had departed Ka'vairn a little over a year ago and weren't expected to return for another month or two. "We're going to The Weavers?" he asked, desperate to get out of the fortress and stretch his legs in the world.

Kastiek actually chuckled—a rare thing.

"No," The Valtorak said definitively. "Your fellow initiates have a decade on you," he reminded. "Your time with The Weavers is beyond the horizon. No. Your departure is to be staggered, but your destination is no further than The Dain'duil."

That was enough to spark some joy in Daijen. The Dain'duil was so vast as to be a world unto itself and, best of all, it wasn't surrounded by stone. No, he corrected himself. The best part was no Kastiek and no Valtorak. It was revelation not joy he saw in Ilithranda's eyes, who knew then exactly what they were to do.

"We're to retrieve our cloaks," she said.

Daijen heard the word cloaks and knew she meant pelts. He also knew what animal those pelts belonged to. It wasn't enough, however, to dampen his spirits. He was going into The Dain'duil!

The Valtorak wandered towards the edge of the rampart, where the valley and the forest below could be seen in all its glory. "Your bodies can take the cold, as you well know. But heed my words," the master warned, violet eyes cast high to the blue sky. "Up there, beyond even the limits of the dragons, where only our Aegres can soar, the air is so cold as to be the jaws of a beast. There are brews —potions—that can keep it at bay, but every Vahlken must be cloaked in victory."

Kastiek reached around his waist with both hands and produced a dagger in each. Daijen and Ilithranda accepted the weapons, having seen the other initiates do just the same years earlier.

"'Tis a badge of skill," Ka'vairn's master went on. "But it will also keep you warm in the coldest heights."

Daijen looked from his dagger to the white bear pelt Kastiek wore as a cloak, the lined fur reaching down to his ankles. It dawned on him then in a way that it hadn't when watching the other initiates make for The Dain'duil.

It was Ilithranda, though, who voiced his thoughts. "With this alone," she began, indicating the blade, "we have to kill a bear?"

"With that alone," The Valtorak replied, "you could slay a dragon."

There was something in the master's eyes that informed Daijen he wasn't exaggerating.

"You have two weeks," Kastiek said. "If you cannot claim a worthy pelt in that time you are to return here without it. Is that understood?"

Both initiates nodded without a word, as if tackling a fully grown bear with a small dagger was just another exercise.

"Daijen," Kastiek continued. "You will go first. Ilithranda, you will leave at dawn."

"I'm to leave right now?" Daijen checked, careful to keep any displeasure out of his voice.

"You have your weapon," The Valtorak replied. "You need no more. Take your horse and begone."

The master and Kastiek left them without another word on the matter, the pair falling into quiet conversation as they navigated the ramparts.

Daijen nudged Ilithranda with his elbow as they made for the interior lip of the battlements. "How great is this?"

She looked at him as if he had said something bewilderingly stupid, though her expression was only brief before they both stepped off the rampart and dropped into the courtyard.

"Are you not excited?" he pressed. "Normally, we only get to go out so we can climb back up again."

"It's only the forest," she replied soberingly. "And we go out to hunt and collect water all the time," she reminded.

"It's two weeks in the forest!" he pointed out, as they made for the stables.

"You have two weeks to claim a pelt, Daijen. That doesn't mean you have to spend all that time in The Dain'duil." Stoical was her expression, her features set like marble. "Hunt well—fight well—and you could be back here in a few days."

After so many years together, Daijen had learned to see her true feelings, hidden as they were. She was just as unsure as he was, only his excitement for adventure was drowning out his fear. Though, when he thought about it, tackling a bear with naught but a knife hadn't been what initially bothered him. In truth, he was more concerned about being so alone out there. Not a day had gone by without Ilithranda by his side. They had fought together, eaten all their meals together, and navigated Slait's thirst for violence together.

Despite holding on firmly to her colder side, he had seen episodes of the woman who lived under the shroud of the *warrior*. Though he called her friend, he never said the word aloud. She was a survivor through and through and survivors didn't collect friends lest they held them back. And, after so many years, he still knew nothing of her past, of the events that had led her from the palace in Aran'saur to the gates of Ka'vairn.

How many times had he broached the subject and been rebuked? After the first few years he had simply stopped asking her. Like him, perhaps, Ilithranda had severed herself from her previous life, before the pits of Handuin had forever changed them. Daijen could live with that, though he couldn't get away from one undeniable truth.

She was all he had.

Ilithranda was, in her own way, Daijen's tether to life. Had she been lost to the pit as Elivar was, Ka'vairn and its *traditions* would have broken him by now. He was sure of it.

"When did you last sleep?" she asked, a question that, in itself, was proof of her concern for him—that is, proof that he meant something to her.

"I slept last night," he reported, donning the light blue cloak he had left on a hook outside the stable.

"Good," she replied curtly. "You should have three days in you, perhaps four."

Daijen thought of the journey ahead and it brought a smile to his face. "I wish I didn't have to sleep at all. Though I will enjoy camping under a tree."

Ilithranda was shaking her head, a look of exasperation about her.

"What?" he enquired.

"Nothing. I sometimes forget you are little more than a boy," she answered patronisingly.

Thought his age had become hard to track over the long decades, Daijen didn't consider himself a child, but the years between them remained significant. How many of his lifetimes had Ilithranda already lived through? And he would have been lying if he said her remark hadn't stung.

That sting melted away when her hand came up to cup his right cheek. "Enjoy your adventure," she said warmly, showing a glimpse of that other self, the real her that Daijen craved more than anything. "But make sure you come back with a pelt," she finished in her usual hard tone. Added to that, she flicked him in the head, drawing a wince from the younger Andaren.

"Daijen." Kastiek's voice came from the main doors. "Why are you still here?"

Daijen bowed and slipped past Ilithranda to saddle one of the war horses they had arrived with years earlier. After filling his bags with some supplies and—per Kastiek's advice—a good helping of salt from the stores, he met Ilithranda's eyes one last time before the mount took him from the fortress. There was concern behind her eyes, and he liked to imagine her saying something to wish him well if not force a promise from him that he would be safe. But she said nothing. She didn't need to: Daijen knew. In some ways, he understood her silence better than he did her words.

It was the quiet concern that irked him. She doubted his abilities. All three of them did. Would Kastiek have even bothered saying they were to return in two weeks if it was Ilithranda and Elivar alone on that rampart?

He would prove their concern to be needless. Like every Vahlken before him, he would claim his victory cloak.

For three days, Daijen and his horse had journeyed north along the edge of The Dain'duil before seeking sleep. In truth, Daijen could have kept going for another day, but the horse had entered his twilight years and couldn't travel so far without rest. They had cut into the forest and found shelter that third night under the full branches of a White Oak that had enjoyed its summer months.

"Sleep well, my friend," Daijen bade, squeezing one of the antlers sloping over the horse's head. "Come the dawn," he said, looking further north, where branches of The Nheremyn weaved through the forest, "we will find ourselves a bear."

Having removed his saddle to use as a makeshift pillow, the initiate lay down and rested his head. Sleep didn't come as easily as it used to. These days his head was filled to bursting with knowledge. He had listened to Kastiek for what amounted to days on no more than human biology. So too had the Vahlken spoken at length on nature and ways in which the world could be used to their advantage.

When he wasn't thinking about any of that he was reliving the many many sparring matches with Ilithranda and the other initiates. Already his body was scarred and he had yet to don the mantle of Vahlken. Had he not been promised as much?

Then there were all the run-ins with Slait, of which there were too many to count. How quickly he would reveal his wicked side. And how quickly their encounters would turn violent.

Those wounds had always been the slowest to heal.

His years in Ka'vairn, it seemed, had been more eventful than those spent outside of it. They had certainly been more brutal. When, at last, sleep came to him, however, it was always the same. He closed his eyes and saw that infinite well, that void of streaking lights and stars. Though perfectly still beneath the White Oak, behind his eyes he was moving faster than thought. His life lay at his fingertips as it had in the pit. He had but to touch the memory and his mind returned to that moment, bringing the past into the clarity of the present day.

So while Daijen Saeth's body slept beneath that tree, his mind wandered the halls of time. Like many nights before, he chose the same memory to relive, and, for a time, it felt as if he wasn't alone anymore.

As it would, however, the autumn dawn broke and was upon the Andaren. He awoke as if he had never been asleep, his senses seamlessly adapting to the waking world. He also awoke with determination. He would find himself a bear that very day if not the next. Then, with his new pelt, he would spend what days he had left searching for Ilithranda. Hadn't they earned a little freedom? Some time in The Dain'duil would do them good after so many years of living through Kastiek's trials.

Daijen held on to that thought—that mild dream—as he saddled the horse and set off in search of the branching river. Attired in little more than his training leathers and a simple cloth shirt, the initiate adjusted his blue cloak to examine the dagger Kastiek had given him. The blade was an inch longer than his hand—so not that much longer than a bear claw.

He wouldn't get that close, he decided. The bear would be no more than a target board, like the ones that littered Ka'vairn's central courtyard. How many axes, spears, and knives had he thrown over the last three years, since being allowed to move beyond hand-to-hand combat? He would launch the dagger and strike the bear in the head. Now he had only to *find* a bear.

The morning stretched on, but not for long, before Daijen heard the rushing water, the sound reaching him before the sight of it. He guided the horse through the trees and onto the pebbled shore. It was a wide patch of land that had long ago been carved out of The Dain'duil, and the stream itself was divided here and there by small stony islands. A little further to the east there lay a large hollowed log, its top end intruding on the stream but not damming it.

It was beautiful.

Save for the sound of the stream there was naught but chirping birds in the trees behind him. The Morthil Mountains—gods made of stone—rested beyond the serene landscape, dominating the east. Daijen reconsidered his plan, wondering now if he shouldn't make camp by the stream for a few days. There was plenty of water and he could already see fish navigating upstream. It was also the most likely place to encounter a bear.

With the latter in mind, Daijen was sure to tether his mount to the strongest tree he could find. Were a bear to come along, the war horse wouldn't hesitate to charge and steal the kill. "Good boy," he praised, patting the mount as it lay down to rest.

He had considered naming the creature some time ago, but it was well known, if not tradition, to withhold names from the mutated war horses. Names bred emotional bonds and such tethers were considered pointless when considering the average lifespan of an animal bred to charge into battle.

"This isn't so bad," he said, moving to the edge of the stream. He crouched down and bathed his face in a handful of icy water before drinking some of it.

There he remained, poised in his crouch. What sense it was he couldn't say, but some part of him knew he wasn't alone on that shore anymore. Slowly, Daijen looked up, his cobalt eyes crossing the stream and the small island that sat in the middle.

A bear looked back at him.

The Andaren suddenly came to regret his plan of confronting the animal that very day. The peaceful environment had altered his mood, taking his thoughts far from violence. But the bear, it seemed, had taken umbrage with his presence. The animal padded out into the shallows and let loose a warning growl. Daijen stood up a little too quickly and the bear instantly mimicked him, rising on its back legs to display its superior height.

Not far away, the war horse sprang to his hooves and put his restraining reins to the test. The leather of those reins, however, had been made with war horses in mind, and Daijen had had the good sense to secure the mount to a thick and solid branch. And so, the beast could but protest and dig its powerful hooves into the earth.

Daijen had risen with the dagger in hand, the naked blade freed from its place on his belt. It seemed even smaller than before in the face of a real and present bear.

The offended animal bolted forward, splashing through the stream until it skidded onto the small island. If Daijen had to guess, he would say the bear didn't want to fight him as much as he didn't want to fight it.

"I have no quarrel with you," Daijen said softly, and uselessly. "But my path goes only forwards. Today," he lamented, "that will take me through you."

The bear roared in response, its imposingly long claws sinking into the pebbled island. It didn't care for his words, only his intentions.

"I will wear you proudly and with honour," Daijen went on, his right boot stepping into the stream. "And I promise you will touch the sky one day." The initiate's left foot followed, taking him one step closer. It was all the bear could take.

Six hundred pounds of predator charged at the Andaren.

But the two were not yet to meet.

An almighty blast interrupted their fated clash, the impossible explosion expanding from nowhere in the space between them. The sound of splitting stone, falling rubble, and the tumultuous eruption of water drowned out all else, while the flash of the brilliant light blinded even Daijen's mutated eyes.

Andaren and bear were cast back from whence they came, each ejected from the area at speed.

Handuin's magic was quick to aid Daijen's recovery, and he discovered he was face down beyond the shore. As he picked himself up, the initiate swept his mane of white hair from his marble-like face so he might see the calamity that had occurred.

He blinked.

In the place of an empty island, there now stood a lone *dwarf*.

26

NEW FRIENDS AND OLD FRIENDS

Joran saw it coming. How could he not? The man balling his fist was so drunk he might as well have told Gallien that he was about to take a swing at him.

"Don't," Drakalis warned, and wearily so.

The drunkard's expression scrunched into a grimace and his entire body moved to deliver the punch. Watching through the hatch in the kitchen, Joran did his best not to mimic Gallien, who side-stepped and let the man's momentum spell his downfall. He crashed through a chair, sending splinters of wood and three broken legs across the tavern floor.

"Oi!"

Joran's violet eyes shifted to the barrel of a man, his full cheeks sweaty and red from hours of drinking in the hot and cloistered tavern. So drunk was he that the rage he voiced could hardly be seen in his slack expression.

Gallien sighed and closed his eyes, a man resigned to a day that would never end. He turned around to see the drunkard's friend who had objected to the treatment of his companion. He was, however, a notch faster.

Joran winced as the man's fist glanced off Drakalis's chin, the attack aggravating the smuggler more than anything. The second swing was a back-hand, but Gallien saw it coming this time. He blocked it with his forearm and delivered a firm fist of knuckles to the man's ribs before landing the next across his cheek. He staggered into the doorframe, making it all the easier to grab him by his coat and shove him outside, into the early winter's evening.

The first was barely on his feet again before Drakalis grabbed him by the ear and towed him outside. A swift kick to the behind sent him stumbling into the hard-baked mud beside his friend.

"You can come back when you've sobered up, boys!" he called after them.

The patrons of The Brass Giant had already forgotten the incident as Gallien made his way back to the kitchen. Old Hux, however, the establishment's owner, was not one for forgetting.

"You broke a chair," he remarked gruffly, one hand plastered to the smooth surface of his round stomach. "I'll take it out of your wage," he added, his tone suggesting he was being perfectly reasonable.

Gallien frowned at the injustice. "You asked me to kick them out," he reminded him.

"I didn't tell you to break the place at the same time," Old Hux countered, as he dabbed the sweat from his balding brow. "Now back to the kitchen with you. Fresh orders are in." He didn't wait for Gallien to argue before turning his mouth over one shoulder. "Boy!" he yelled. "Bring the mop!" One of Hux's bulbous fingers was wagging at the puddle of ale that had sparked the initial incident.

Drakalis was quick to respond. "No," he said sharply, stepping forward. "I'll do it."

Old Hux was waving the notion away. "I need you in the kitchen. You've already wasted too much time with this chair business."

Gallien was already moving, likely anticipating Joran's response. Still, Joran did as commanded, chin to his chest, eyes down, and mop in hand. Drakalis intercepted the boy before he could clear the threshold. His way suddenly barred, those violet eyes flashed up at the smuggler. Upon seeing Gallien—who took the mop from him—he immediately understood that he was to turn back and make for the kitchen.

"I said, *I'll* do it." There was no argument or confusion in the smuggler's words now as he levelled his hard gaze on Old Hux.

The grizzled tavern owner hooked his thumbs into the straps of his breeches, and with a look about him that suggested he would rise to the challenge in Gallien's voice. He did not, however. Perhaps he saw the savage animal behind Drakalis's eyes, the one Joran glimpsed from time to time, when his secret was in jeopardy. Or, perhaps, he just didn't care enough to argue.

"Just be quick about it," he said instead, gesturing at the spill.

"Yes, Boss."

Upon his return to the kitchen, Gallien paused in the threshold. Joran recognised that look. The realisation that he was no longer a smuggler, free to roam the world but, in fact, a cook, condemned to four walls and the appetites of others. That same fact also explained why he could never get the smell of potatoes out of his hands or the scent of fish out of his nose, as he often complained.

Joran made no comment, returning to his own culinary duties: peeling carrots in the corner while keeping an eye on the stew bubbling in the pot beside him. Given their privacy—and the heat—Joran removed the strip of dark blue cloth from around his head, the material conveniently hiding his pointed ears. It did nothing to conceal his white hair, of course, but his work in the kitchen was the only time he didn't live under a hood.

"Put it back on," Gallien instructed.

"I'm hot," Joran protested, irritated by the cloth.

"If Old Hux walks in here—"

"Hux can't even fit in here," Joran was quick to point out.

"Just..." Gallien sounded exasperated. "Just put it back on."

"Fine," Joran said flatly, returning the fabric to his head.

He continued to prepare food in silence, dwelling as he did, on the injustice of his entire life. He had grown to loathe their nomadic lifestyle, though not because he hated the travelling—the only thing he did enjoy—but because it showed him that everyone else, wherever they went, was living their life as they were meant to. He saw boys and girls, teenagers of his age, interacting with each other, and without a parent breathing down their neck. How many times had Gallien stopped him from making connections?

Joran fell into his daydreams again. He thought of nothing but walking in the sun, passing through the streets like any other, his life of nocturnal activities at an end. In the dream, he didn't have to wear the cloth about his head or keep his hood drawn tight and eyes down. He was free.

"You can't be doing that," Drakalis told him, shattering the dream with no more than words.

"He called me out," Joran complained. "What was I supposed to do?"

"Leave *me* to handle it. We let Old Hux pay us next to nothing to turn a blind eye, but that won't stop everyone else from noticing you."

Joran ceased his relentless peeling, his shoulders heaving with deep breaths.

"It's for your own safety," Drakalis pointed out.

How many times had Joran heard those words? "No one is going to notice my eyes," he fumed—words Gallien had heard more than anything else. "They're too dark in low light."

"I'm not getting into this again," Gallien told him firmly.

Without another word, Joran went back to his preparation, cutting the carrots now, and vigorously so. After spending some time resenting his life-long jailer, he began to recall the times when he hadn't taken Gallien's instructions seriously. Times when they had been discovered at the wrong moment and his heritage exposed. Gallien hadn't been a jailer then.

He looked over his shoulder at the man. He was a friend, a brother, and a father all rolled into one. Ultimately, that meant the smuggler was irritating on not one, but three different fronts. It also meant Gallien was his *protector* on every front.

Gallien cleared his throat while preparing the next couple of dishes. "Maybe we can stay here a little longer," he posed, his words extending as a bridge between them. "It wouldn't be the worst place to spend winter."

Joran sighed. Gallien just didn't get it. His lack of response, however, only increased the smuggler's exasperation, leaving him to get on with his cooking. Simultaneously, Joran felt angry and guilty at Gallien's inability to navigate his emotions.

The evening inevitably rolled into the night and the demand for food was replaced by the need for drinks. It gave Gallien the time he needed to sort through the stores and make lists of supplies Old Hux would need to procure. It was simple work that Joran knew he had once found refreshing, years earlier, but it seemed all too apparent that the joy he had discovered in the ordinary was long gone. More and more he would talk wistfully of his days raiding ancient sites and lost tombs. Once or twice he had even spoken fondly of his time in the army, a hard but rewarding time he had assured. In his early forties now, that time was decades behind him.

Seeing that there were frothing tankards waiting to be delivered to patrons, Joran decided he would leave Gallien to the storeroom and stretch his legs. He knew he shouldn't. He knew it would infuriate Gallien.

He did it anyway.

His ears concealed and hair swept back by the strip of cloth, Joran picked up a tankard and, curiously, a cup of honey tea. The barmaid told him where to take them, leading the young man to a gloomy booth in the far corner. He thought nothing of the two patrons until he was standing before them. A sense of unease crept into his gut, a feeling that Gallien had long fostered in him. The smuggler had also taught him how to hide such feelings.

"Evening, sirs," he greeted happily enough.

They gave no response but to accept the tea and tankard, the latter being taken by a man who captured Joran's attention. He was handsome enough, his dark skin and chiselled features framed by a beard nearly as thick as Gallien's. There was similarity too in his hair with its long cords of black dreadlocks, curled neatly around one side of his neck and down over his chest.

His looks aside, the man wore a cuirass of steel and patterned bronze to match his vambraces and singular pauldron that guarded his right shoulder. Besides his mustard sleeves, an expensive colour, he wore a shoulder cloak of blue and cream to match the heavy battle skirt.

Protruding just over the table top were three exotic feathers of red, blue, and purple, each attached to the pommel of a dagger. That soon led Joran to the weapons piled on the seat beside the man. There stood a bow of dark wood with an ornate quiver full of arrows. Next to them was a curved sword of what appeared to be bone, the tip reminding Joran of a crab's claw. Lastly and, perhaps, the meanest looking of them all, was a short-sword, its jaunty-angled blade made predominantly out of some creature's large fangs.

"Thank you, young sir," an ancient voice croaked, turning his attention towards the other man in the booth.

Joran feigned a smile, taking in the man's terribly long white beard. His hair remained concealed within a voluminous green hood, where his weathered face sat in candle light. Curiously, the man had hesitated to accept his cup of tea, waiting to grip the handle until Joran's hand was well away. It was also impossible not to notice his penchant for the colour green, his robes dyed from hood to ankle in varying shades of it. Standing beside him was a tall staff, its end an arching hand of branches, and a sword housed in its scabbard.

"Have a good evening, sirs," Joran remarked on his departure, eager to be away from the unusual pair and their weaponry.

The moment he entered the kitchen, Drakalis grabbed him by the arm and pulled him in with a short sharp yank. "Who were those men?" he demanded.

Joran was flustered by the brash greeting and looked to the serving hatch, where he had been observed. "I don't know," he replied, shrugging himself free of Gallien's grasp. "Travellers by the looks of them."

"The hooded one. What did he say to you?"

"I'm sorry," Joran began. "I shouldn't have gone out there."

"What did he say?" Gallien asked again.

"He was just thanking me for the drinks," Joran told him, watching the man return to the serving hatch where he might watch them from afar. He knew that look in the smuggler, and damned if he wasn't always right. The man just knew trouble when he saw it.

"And the one with the blue cloak," he pressed. "Did he say anything?"

Taking Gallien's sixth sense seriously, Joran replied, "He didn't say anything. What's wrong?"

"You tell me, boy. What did you see?"

Joran was in no mood to be educated in the art of survival. "Why does this feel like another lesson? Can't I just go back to peeling potatoes?"

"If you want to live off your instincts you have to hone them first. Now tell me what's wrong with that picture," he commanded, nodding his chin at the distant booth.

Joran reluctantly joined him by the serving window and searched for the men through the patrons and barmaids. "They're an odd pair," he admitted. "More so the older one."

"And the other one?" Gallien probed.

"His clothes are expensive I'd say," Joran replied, thinking of the intricate gold pattern that lined the edges of his shoulder cloak and battle skirt. "Besides the fact that he can likely afford a better tavern, it seems outlandish that he would wear a cuirass and bracers with such finery."

"Their weapons?" Drakalis asked.

"The old man has a sword," Joran remarked. "The other man had the most *remarkable* swords. If I had to guess I'd say the blades were all made from—"

"Bone," Gallien finished, the word escaping his lips like the fall of a guillotine.

"Yes," Joran agreed, his attention returning to his protector.

Drakalis moved away from the serving window and stared hard at the back wall. "He's a *Kedradi.*"

A spark of wonder was ignited in Joran. "Truly? A real

Kedradi?" he asked, searching for the stranger again. He couldn't believe he was sharing a tavern with one, let alone having served him his drink.

Gallien grabbed him again and pulled him back. "That's *not* a good thing," he warned impatiently.

"But they're so *rare*."

"They're so *dangerous*," Drakalis corrected. "The only Kedradi you ever see outside of Qalanqath are rangers."

Joran's eyes went wide. "A monster hunter!" he exclaimed, wishing to hear the man's many tales.

"I've known them hunt *men*," Gallien uttered gravely.

Joran looked at his would-be father. He had that far-away look about him, the one he adopted when memories of his life under the Padoshi's thumb began to surface, memories he could hardly stomach anymore. Keeping Joran to one side, Drakalis alone moved to peer out of the serving window.

"He's gone," he reported sharply.

"What?"

"The Kedradi's gone," Gallien said again. "Gather your things," he instructed immediately, his apron coming off at the same time. "We're leaving Warth, *now*."

Joran looked out on the tavern, his violet eyes narrowing on the booth. Indeed, the suspected Kedradi was gone, leaving the old man to light his pipe.

When he turned back to the kitchen, Gallien had already retrieved his satchel—the other constant in Joran's life. He knew only two things about the satchel: it was enchanted, possessing infinite space inside, and it had belonged to a woman named Androma, who had died saving him as an infant. Drakalis had been sure to keep it with him at all times; often using it as a pillow.

Then there was the other *thing*. From nowhere, the axe appeared in Gallien's hand, leading Joran's gaze down to the sleek curves of its blade. Where it had come from was as much a mystery to Joran as it was to Gallien. They knew only that it came to him when threatened.

A Kedradi would do that, Joran thought.

"We're not fighting," Gallien said definitively. "We're getting out of here." As they reached the tavern's back door, the smuggler opened the satchel and dropped the axe inside. "Go get the horse," he added, as they walked out into the cool night air.

Both made it no further than a handful of steps before coming to a dead stop, their sudden departure halted by the group of rogues slinking out of the adjacent alley.

"Evening, Gallien." The greeting was issued pleasantly enough, but coming from such a shady-looking individual it might as well have been a threat.

"Craegor Stone," Gallien replied, his usual roguish charm replaced with something closer to disgust.

"You're one slippery little fish," Craegor went on, wagging a finger in the smuggler's direction.

"Stay behind me," Drakalis commanded quietly of Joran.

Craegor was shaking his head in disbelief. "So it *is* true. You *do* have a son. Kalem told us as much. You shouldn't have let him get away," he said with a wicked grin. "That gave us a fresh trail."

Joran recalled the man in question—one of three assassins sent by the Padoshi a couple of years earlier. Gallien had killed two but only maimed the third, who fled before the smuggler could bring the axe to bear again. Their last known location wasn't the only thing the Padoshi had learned from Kalem, for he had sent six this time, including Craegor. It seemed Thedaria's premier crime boss wasn't underestimating Gallien Drakalis anymore.

"Still barking for the Padoshi I see," the smuggler quipped.

The thug gave his best imitation of a barking dog, eliciting a chorus of harsh laughter from his crew of killers. "Do you have any idea how much trouble you're in? Every day you go on breathing is an insult to the master. He's mad like a demon now, Gallien. *Furious*. He doesn't even want you killed. No, no, no. He wants you *alive*. You're to be made an example of. Do you remember Rogan Norst?" Craegor made a sour expression. "The Padoshi wore his face for a whole week."

And just like that, the axe was in Gallien's grip again.

Craegor blinked. "Were you holding that a second ago?"

Drakalis's knuckles were paling around the haft. Joran knew what was coming—he had witnessed scenes such as this play out before. Gallien would likely lunge at Craegor first, the axe let fly. At such close range, the thug could do nothing to cheat his fate. As it always did, the axe would then return to the smuggler's hand, ready to tear through the others.

Craegor Stone, however, was dead before Gallien moved a muscle.

The arrow, lodged in his left eye socket, had flown free from the corner of The Bronze Giant. From that same location came the Kedradi. Vivid was the blue of his shoulder cloak and the battle skirt that flowed in the wake of his charge. In fact, compared to the others, his attire was vibrant. It was as if he wanted to stand out.

He came down in their midst with a kick that took one from his feet while his bow whipped around to catch another across the jaw. The remaining three attacked in unison with swords.

How exactly the Kedradi managed to block, parry, and evade all three blows at the same time was beyond Joran, who had pressed himself even closer to Gallien now. Together, they watched the hunter dispatch one thug after the other, his bow dropped in favour of a curved dagger, the weapon's hack and slash easily tracked as the blade was trailed by those exotic feathers. And so, with fist and blade, he broke bones, split flesh, and opened arteries.

Joran didn't know that death and grace could be wielded hand in hand.

With four corpses at his feet, the last two rose to meet him—though only one found their courage to face the Kedradi. The bolder of the two came at the hunter with a wild swing of his sword. It might have been enough to put a weaker man off balance, but a Kedradi could never be described as such. The hunter stepped forward, intercepted the swing at the wrist, and punched the air beside the thug's head. His blade, of course, was being held tip down at the time.

Joran blinked as he made sense of the dagger having passed directly through most of the man's throat. He dropped to his knees with blood pouring down over his chest before slamming into the street, face down.

Five of the six dead, that left but one, and he was running for his life. The Kedradi sheathed his dagger and used the toe of his right boot to flick his bow up into his waiting hand. In the same fluid motion, he retrieved and nocked an arrow. Joran intended to track it, but the Kedradi lowered his aim, the arrow retained.

The thug had skidded to a halt, his path blocked by the hooded man from the booth. He cut a tall lithe figure in the moonlight that streamed from the starlit heavens. His eyes alone were revealed in the shadow of his hood, illuminated briefly by the fiery ashes in the bowl of his pipe. While that remained gripped between his teeth, the old man held on to his staff with both hands, its end planted at his feet.

He said nothing to the Padoshi's man, cowering before him. Instead, he stamped his staff into the hard mud, and only once. That was all that was required to give life to the spell that exploded forth with the impact. The mud broke, creating a spiderweb of cracks that grew out from the end of the staff. Had that been all the magic achieved the thug might have turned and escaped. But the wave of energy that rippled out from the staff carried the man from his feet and flung him back towards his dead companions.

When he landed, it was clear that he was rolling limb over broken limb, as if he had been reduced to no more than a rag doll. At his final destination, next to Craegor Stone, he lay with a body of shattered and twisted bones, including his neck.

An uncomfortable silence fell over the street.

Gallien was pushing Joran back with one hand while raising the axe with the other. Joran had to wonder how the smuggler was going to fight a Kedradi and a wizard. He only knew that he would. Until his last breath, in fact.

"Stay back!" Gallien warned them.

The Kedradi gave Drakalis no more than a glance before turning to the approaching wizard. Joran didn't understand a word he said to the old man, the words spoken in the hunter's native tongue of Ked.

The wizard took the pipe from his mouth and exhaled a cloud of smoke. "Curious," he uttered, his eyes running down Gallien's arm to the axe he wielded.

"Who in the hells are you supposed to be?" Drakalis demanded.

The old man took a breath. "I assure you, Gallien Drakalis, we have come from no realm of hell."

"How do you know me?" the smuggler asked, his eyes darting between the wizard and the Kedradi. "The Padoshi of Thedaria doesn't send assassins to kill his own assassins."

The Kedradi was slinging his bow over one shoulder when he said something else in Ked to the wizard.

The wizard absorbed his companion's words while staring beyond Gallien. "You must be Joran," he assumed. "It is good to meet you at last."

Gallien side-stepped to block the wizard's view. "You talk to me," he stated firmly.

The old man looked to the darkened streets that surrounded them. "The Padoshi's men are not all that hunt you. We must take our leave at once if we are to stay ahead of our foe."

Gallien lowered the axe, though only a notch. "What are you talking about? Who *are* you?"

The wizard paused in his attempt to turn and lead the way. "My name is Aphrandhor, but most call me... *The Green Leaf.*"

27
CLOAKED IN VICTORY

64 Years Ago...

Where the explosion had erupted, there was now a scattered debris of large dark rocks and black dust covering the sandy pebbles and littering the clear stream. Where the rocks had come from, however, was a fleeting question, Daijen's attention entirely stolen by the lone dwarf standing in the centre of it all.

With a full beard and black dreadlocks that ran down to the waist, the Andaren would have assumed he looked upon a male of their species, but there was something in the face—the eyes especially—that told him he faced a female dwarf. Her skin was the antithesis of his own, being that of a smooth, rich oil that made the white of her eyes stand out like stars in the night's sky.

Her clothing was entirely forgettable, though her short sleeves revealed arms bulging with muscles and overlapping veins. It was the weapon she wielded that, ultimately, drew Daijen's focus. The hammer was unlike anything he had ever seen; a haft of silver coiled in bronze and elements of gold. The head was elegant—too elegant for the likes of a hammer. The haft snaked back before curving into a rectangular block of gold-coated steel encased in a trim of more bronze.

There within that trim, lining the hammer head, were runes he guessed to be dwarven. There was something about the weapon that lured the Andaren in with haphazard steps, as if he could sense its power. He might have approached the dwarf there and then had the bear not recovered.

With a deafening roar, the animal barrelled in. It navigated the new boulders and partially leapt up onto its back legs to swipe at the hammer-wielding dwarf. It would have taken her head in that moment, its front leg considerably stronger than either dwarf or Andaren. Fortunately for the dwarf, Daijen's new body wasn't so new anymore.

With enviable speed, the initiate dashed to her aid and managed to hook one arm around her waist as he took them both sideways. The bear's claws cut through air alone, its momentum taking it into the nearest rock. This, it appeared, only served to aggravate the bear all the more.

"*Gun'dov mai!*" the dwarf barked, her native tongue as baffling as her inexplicable appearance.

Her body language, though, informed Daijen that she had said something to the effect of, "Get off me!" The initiate gladly rolled aside, the two separating before the bear could pounce on their position.

The dwarf bellowed more of her harsh language and slammed her hammer into its side. The bear absorbed the blow and delivered one of its own, swatting her away. It naturally pursued the dwarf as she scrambled on her back to put as much distance between them as possible.

Daijen acted without thought, as he foolishly would when trying to protect another. Kastiek wouldn't have approved. Still, the Andaren was mid-air and incapable of changing his actions before coming down on the bear's muscled back. His dagger bit down and deep into the animal, just behind the joint of the front left leg. It moaned and instantly forgot about the dwarf.

Holding on with all his might, the initiate only dared to free his blade twice more to stab the bear, lest he be thrown down and brought within reach of its jaws. There seemed little he could do, however, when the animal reared up. Daijen tucked his knees in and pressed both boots into its back, from where he then sprang backwards, executing a deft flip. By the time the bear turned on him he had already landed and braced himself into a ready crouch.

So wide were its jaws then, a terrible roar unleashed from deep inside its chest. It had no effect on Daijen now. The mind of the warrior was upon him, changing his thoughts and feelings. He perceived his surroundings differently. Gone was the serenity and beauty of the stream. Now it was a battlefield.

Kastiek's words came back to him, spoken over him while he trained for a decade and more. "*In the blink of an eye, the world about you can become a storm. It will try to move you to its will. When your time inside these walls is at an end, you will see the truth of it. That* you *are the storm.*"

The bear was his enemy. Nothing more.

It came at the Andaren as the dagger flew from his hand. So too did the hammer fly from the dwarf's grip. It struck the bear before the dagger, turning the animal just enough that the blade sank into its shoulder in place of its skull. Still, it felt the sting of that blow and staggered.

Daijen cursed and moved to retrieve his only weapon. He planned on leaping and twisting over the animal while simultaneously grasping the hilt of the dagger, but that plan, like his previous one, did not come to pass.

Though staggered, the bear had enough strength to lash out and rake its claws across the initiate's chest. It tore through his leathers, shirt, and three of the claws succeeded in drawing a trio of thin red lines across his chalk-white skin. Added to that, the blow itself was powerful enough to throw him into the stream.

Sure that the bear would be advancing on him, Daijen ignored the pain in his chest and looked up from the stream bed. Struck by a rock, the bear turned away from the downed Andaren and once again faced the dwarf who had thrown it. It seemed the air rumbled as the animal let loose a prolonged growl.

Again, the protective instincts that lay in wait, just under the surface, rose up to challenge the stone-cold warrior that Kastiek had spent years forging in him. Those instincts put him to action and muscle memory took care of the rest.

Flipping onto his feet in a splash of water, Daijen dashed towards the bear, hardly pausing to scoop up the exquisite hammer. Legs that had finally become accustomed to their mutated strength propelled the initiate into a powerful jump. The hammer, firmly gripped in two hands, came down on the back of the bear's neck. The blow was absolute. To the bear, the world would have snapped painlessly to black and forever so.

In the wake of its sudden death, Daijen was left standing hunched over it with the hammer still in hand.

The dwarf stared at him. "*Aer gelvin dow Devonan*?" she asked.

Daijen resumed his full height and could only shrug at the question.

The dwarf rolled her eyes. "O' course ye don'," she said dryly, her words slipping into Andarneese. "Why learn me language when I can learn yers, eh? Typical Andaren." Her eyes slid down to the hammer in his hand. "I'll be takin' that back now," she said, her voice low.

Daijen glanced at the weapon, its gold and bronze elements glistening as the sun peeked over The Morthil Mountains. For just a moment, he considered withholding it, keeping it for himself. It was a prize of a weapon and with some kind of enchantment he guessed. But it wasn't his to claim. There was no honour in wielding a weapon he had simply picked from the ground.

The dwarf nodded with satisfaction as she accepted the hammer. Her fingers, thick and callused, wrapped around the haft and she carried it easily in one hand.

Daijen pushed his wet hair back. "Who are you?" he asked. "And where did you come from?" His second question reflected the depth of his curiosity and he even glanced at the site from which the dwarf had simply appeared.

The dwarf ran a hand down and through her black beard until

her finger and thumb were able to trace her jaw line. "Ye tell me yer name, bear-slayer, an' I'll tell ye mine."

Daijen didn't appreciate her suspicious tone. It had been her, after all, who had exploded into *his* life. Still, he saw nothing to lose from offering his name; two words that meant very little to anyone. And damned if he wasn't a little excited to have met his first dwarf, the first *anyone* outside of Ka'vairn's inhabitants in sixteen years.

"Daijen Saeth," he announced.

The dwarf frowned. "Is that a name or a herb?"

The unexpected response gave Daijen pause. "It's my name," he clarified.

"If ye say so," the dwarf replied, adjusting the hammer so she was now holding the haft near the engraved head.

"And your name?" the initiate prompted.

"Oh." She looked somewhat surprised, as if she had already forgotten the negotiation she herself had struck. "The name's Mordrith. Mordrith Underborn. Be seein' ye!" The dwarf turned back to the mountains. "An' thanks for killin' the bear!" she called back.

"Wait!" Daijen bounded after her, his long legs putting him in front of Mordrith with no more than two steps. "Where did you come from?" he asked again, his fingers pressed against the leathers around the claw marks. He was lucky the bear hadn't carved his heart out.

Mordrith gestured lazily at the rubble and shattered boulders. "Over there," she said, the answer obvious to her. Then she tried to leave again.

Daijen side-stepped to meet her. "But you weren't there. And then you were. Where were you before that?"

The dwarf looked a little put out by having her path blocked. "Not there," she answered unhelpfully. "Now, I suggest ye get out o' me way before I introduce ye to the business end o' me hammer..." Mordrith's attention began to immediately wander and her shoulders sagged. "Wrath an' ruin," she cursed, staggering away from the Andaren. "I thought I were past all this." The last word barely made it out of her mouth before she vomited into the stream.

"Are you alright?" Daijen pressed, his hands coming out as he sensed the dwarf's deteriorating balance.

"I jus' need... I jus' need a second to catch me..." The hammer slipped from her grasp and quickly sank to the bottom of the shallow stream.

Daijen then caught Mordrith before she joined it, his increased strength put to the test. He heaved her from the water and dragged her across the shore to his horse. By the time he had laid her on her back, the dwarf's eyes had closed and a deep slumber had overcome her.

The Andaren was left crouched beside her, utterly perplexed at how his morning had unravelled so quickly.

When the dwarf next awoke, a full and glorious moon cut through the valley, a sun in its own right that sat between the Hellion and Morthil Mountains. Daijen watched her eyes flutter before focusing on the fire he had started, its flames crackling into the quiet night.

From the fire she found him, and with her hammer cradled in his lap no less. He had been examining it for some time as, like Mordrith, the weapon was new to him, and anything new was of great interest to the Vahlken initiate.

"How are you feeling?" he asked.

Mordrith sat up and soon regretted it by the look of pain on her face. One hand came up to press against her forehead, though it appeared to offer her little balm. "I feel like me head's been split in two," she eventually replied, her words a touch slurred. "An' I feel like ye shouldn' be touchin' what ain' yers," she added pointedly, her eyes opening to focus on the weapon.

"You would have drowned had I not pulled you out," he told her, hoping his previous action would be enough to convince the dwarf he wasn't her foe.

"An' ye 'ave me thanks. But, ye also 'ave me hammer." Her free hand came up so her fingers might beckon its return.

Again, he willingly handed the hammer over, though Mordrith lacked the strength to hold it as she had before, and quickly placed it on the ground beside her.

"It doesn't burn," Daijen remarked, catching the dwarf off guard.

"Eh?"

The Andaren gestured at the fire. "I placed the head inside the flames. It didn't tarnish the craftsmanship. It didn't even get hot. I've never seen anything like it."

"Well now ye 'ave," Mordrith said, sniffing the waterskin he had deliberately left by her sleeping form. She gulped the water, draining the skin in seconds.

Though determined to get some answers, Daijen tried to keep his tone casual. "Is it made from silvyr?" he questioned, his knowledge on the subject limited to its durability.

"Good ol' fashioned steel," Mordrith reported, her voice less ragged now.

"Magic then," Daijen concluded. "I heard dwarves don't approve of magic."

"We don'."

The initiate waited for something more but the dwarf was content to sit and focus on her breathing. Indeed, she still appeared a touch sickly to Daijen's eyes.

Even though she wasn't looking at him, the Andaren still pointed lazily at the hammer. "Is that how you got here? I've never heard of magic that can take you from one place to another."

"Ye ask a lot o' questions," Mordrith observed, irritated.

Daijen wanted to inform the dwarf that it was a Vahlken's duty to be investigative, that asking questions was expected of him, but he wasn't ready to reveal so much about himself. "The first dwarf I've ever met appeared from thin air with a magic hammer," he stated instead. "Wouldn't you have a lot of questions?"

"That's another question," the dwarf said with an extended finger.

"Don't you have questions for me?" he countered.

Mordrith opened one eye to spy him across the fire. "No."

Daijen raised an eyebrow. "You're not the least bit curious as to why I'm out here?"

The dwarf shrugged. "I'm not even sure where *'ere* is," she confessed.

The Andaren glanced at the darkness that surrounded their little camp. "We're in The Dain'duil," he told her.

"The Dain'duil?" she echoed with a short sharp laugh. "I haven' been out 'ere since I were a little lass. I wonder why I thought o' this place..."

Daijen caught her words like a fish finding bait on a hook. "Is that how it works? The hammer. You just think about where you want to go and then..." He didn't know how to finish his theory, so he turned to the boulder-ridden site in the middle of the stream.

Something about Mordrith's expression softened and she sighed. "Ye 'ave me thanks, *truly*, for the bear an' keepin' me from drownin' an' all, but ye really don' want to get into this, laddy. Ye'd be better off pretendin' this never happened an' we never met." The dwarf made to stand but never managed to straighten up before her legs buckled and she returned to the ground in a heap.

Daijen moved to aid her before she shot out a hand to stop him.

"I'm alrigh'," she assured on her way back into a sitting position. "Maybe I'll jus' stay 'ere a while longer, eh?"

"Is this normal after..." Again, it felt ridiculous to voice words that spoke of magic that ported a person from one place to another, and so the initiate gestured at the hammer to speak for him.

Mordrith looked at him, scrutinised him even, before she picked up the weapon and placed it neatly over her crossed legs. "Aye," she admitted. "Though it's not been this bad in a while. Must 'ave been fightin' the bear straight after," she theorised.

Daijen slowly nodded along, glad to have made some progress. At least now he knew for sure that the hammer was the source of the magic that had conjured the dwarf so violently. He also knew its magic came with a price, and that price lessened over time. He hungered for more information, and not just about the unusual hammer but of the dwarf herself.

"So, you've come from within The Morthil Mountains," Daijen assumed, probing all the more. "From the realm of your people."

"Well, I didn' fall out o' the sky," she quipped. Her frown increased dramatically. "Alrigh'," the dwarf said, her patience having evaporated. "Why haven' ye tried to take it? Hmm? Most would try an' take it jus' for the craftsmanship. To know there's magic abou' it only adds to its value! Yet ye sit there with yer questions an' naught else."

Bemused, the Andaren couldn't help but smile. "I have no right to that weapon," he told her, as if that should be enough. "And I know *nothing* of magic."

Mordrith chewed that over. "That makes two o' us, I suppose," she muttered. "But it still ain' right. *Ye* ain' right, laddy. I don' like it."

"You would prefer I try and steal it from you?" he enquired, his amusement obvious.

"I've met yer folk before," the dwarf stated. "Me husband's traded with yer likes. Ye come for weaponry. Nothing else. Ye ain' interested in our gems or gold. Ye don' even ask us to build for ye. Jus' *weapons*." Mordrith patted the hammer. "This has to be the finest weapon ye've ever seen. I should be dead twice over an' ye the owner o' an enchanted hammer."

"But you're not," Daijen responded pleasantly, "and I can make no such boast."

Mordrith eyed him across the flames a while longer. "Alrigh', bear-slayer, I'll admit, ye've piqued me curiosity. What's a lonely Andaren such as yerself doin' out in the middle o' The Dain'duil? Ye've the look o' a soldier I'd say. Shouldn' ye be off killin' humans somewhere?"

"I *was* a soldier," the initiate answered, recalling his days guarding The Saible's messengers. He also recalled the many who had told him repeatedly that he was no such thing. Nevertheless, a soldier in the emperor's army he had been. "I suppose I'm not anymore," he continued, letting the flames distract him for a moment.

"So what then? Ye jus' like walkin' through forests an' pickin' fights with bears?"

Daijen laughed, stalling his answer. He didn't want to detail too much about himself, but he wondered if the dwarf would begin to feel comfortable speaking freely if she knew more about him. "I live in these parts," he began. "There's a... Well, I live in the mountains." He thumbed over his shoulder, to the west.

Mordrith became very still. Her eyes flashed beyond him and into the darkness, as if she could see the mountains that rose in the west. "Ye hail from the Hellions?" It was subtle, but Daijen didn't miss her hand tighten around the hammer.

"I do."

"There's only one kind o' Andaren I know that comes from such a place."

The initiate was careful to maintain his relaxed demeanour. "I suppose there is," he agreed, though, in truth, he had never expected a dwarf to know of Ka'vairn and those who dwelled within.

"Ye're a Vahlken then?" Her knuckles had paled around the haft now.

"Not yet," he answered honestly. "I'm told there's many years between now and then."

Mordrith must have drawn on her reserves, for the dwarf managed to rise to one knee and wield the hammer enough to point at him. "Ye stay right where ye are," she warned, a hint of fear behind her bravado. "I'll be takin' me leave now. Should ye feet touch the ground, I promise to bury this hammer in yer head. Ye hear?"

Daijen was shaking his head, his hands coming up to show his palms. "I mean you no harm, Mordrith Underborn. I came for the bear pelt," he added, with an innocent shrug.

"Ye're a killin' machine," the dwarf told him forcefully. "We've heard the stories. Ye're bred to slay dragons, they say. An' I've seen yer damned *slaiken blades* so I'll be believin' the stories. Hells, me

Thronghir's forged one for yer ilk! I'm not for tarryin' words with the likes o' some mutant berserker!"

Her last insult gave Daijen pause. "I assure you, Mordrith, I am none of those things." *Yet,* he thought. For now, though, he was content to follow his excitement and curiosity and enjoy the company of any who hadn't come from the dark halls of Ka'vairn.

"Says the bear-slayer!" the dwarf argued.

"Have I not proved my intent?" Daijen shot back, his voice still light and harmless. "I have two weeks to myself," he went on. "Two weeks outside of those walls and its traditions. I never imagined crossing paths with a dwarf. Until today I had only heard stories of your people. I just want..." The Andaren didn't know how to verbalise his emotions, something he had been forced to suppress in Ka'vairn. "Please," he insisted instead, gesturing to her spot beside the fire. "I would enjoy your company. Nothing more."

Mordrith remained where she was for the moment, sceptical perhaps. "Ye're a damned strange Andaren," she commented. "An' a stranger Vahlken," she added, before slowly returning to the ground.

"Would you like some food?" Daijen asked, his eyes flashing to the leathery canvas spread out not far from the dwarf. Upon it, and in pieces now, was the remains of a rabbit he had caught earlier in the day and cooked before the dwarf had risen from her stupor.

Mordrith had the look of a hungry wolf about her. Her paranoia wavered, though it did not fade from her expression entirely. She licked her lips. "Do ye 'ave any salt?"

"I do as it happens."

The dwarf accepted the salt and dragged the canvas towards her between finger and thumb. Daijen then watched, quite astonished, as Mordrith consumed bite after bite before moving on to pick the bones clean. He couldn't say if she ever paused to breathe but he had never seen another creature eat anything so quickly. The last piece of meat down her gullet, she sucked her fingers clean and belched into the night.

"Oh," she said with elation, her fingers having found a strip of meat hiding in her bushy beard. Like all else before it, the last of the rabbit was unceremoniously swallowed. Dark brown eyes landed on Daijen. "Ye didn' want any o' that, did ye?"

The initiate tried to keep any amusement from his face. "I had already eaten my fill," he replied politely.

Mordrith nodded along, her shoulders carrying less tension than before the meal. Words from Daijen's past surfaced for the first time in decades—spoken by his uncle before their falling out. *"The quickest way to make friends is to eat with them. Share your food, boy, and everything else will follow."*

That advice had rung hollow during his years training at The Saible. Perhaps, he thought, his uncle should have said something about choosing the right people to make one's friends. Of course, Daijen would never have guessed such a thing would apply to one of the stone bones.

"You say your husband—Thronghir?—has forged a slaiken blade. He must be a mighty smith."

Mordrith took a moment to get more comfortable and edged a little closer to the fire, her hammer now placed on the ground beside her. "That he is," she confirmed proudly. "Our guild hasn' known a better one. Though," she added with a quiet laugh, "I'd say he's matched by our son now."

Daijen found himself smiling. He hadn't known family for so long. His own had become a distant memory he could only view in his dreams, and the bond he had subsequently formed with his uncle had been fractured in many ways. The Saible might have provided him with a new kind of family, but even they had rejected him. What a travesty it was to consider Ka'vairn his home now and those inside his family.

Hearing of a normal, loving, family was simply a pleasure he had left west of The Gap, where the war had yet to touch. "Your son?" he probed. "He is still a boy?"

Mordrith chortled. "Grarfath wasn' a boy when he *was* a boy. Might as well 'ave been born with a hammer in his hand. Still, his dedication's paid off. He can work silvyr as well as the best, if not better."

Daijen smiled all the more. How long had it been since he had heard someone speak highly and fondly of another? "Silvyr," the initiate echoed wistfully. "I have heard of its splendour."

"Ye've heard o' its *strength*," Mordrith corrected. "Too few 'ave truly beheld its splendour. They're too busy usin' it to kill folk. Or *dragons*," she added dryly. "I suppose ye'll be knockin' at our door soon, hagglin' for yer own slaiken blade."

"Perhaps one day," he entertained, considering how much he had to survive in the meantime.

Mordrith, appearing more settled now, glanced at the dark lump that was the bear. "What did the bear do to deserve the wrath o' a Vahlken then? Were ye worried it were goin' to sprout wings an' start spittin' fire?"

Daijen laughed at the notion, enjoying himself all the more. "I had no quarrel with the bear," he said, a note of sadness tainting his response. "But it was demanded of me. Every Vahlken wears a... *a cloak of victory*. It's a symbol of our strength, I suppose."

"Ye're to be wearin' the bear then," the dwarf concluded.

"Yes."

Mordrith regarded the animal again. "Do ye even know how to skin a bear?"

Daijen opened his mouth to respond in the positive when it dawned on him that he had no idea. "Not really," he confessed.

"Ye're not the only ones who are partial to such a cloak. Though me kin prefer the tundra bears from Isendorn." The dwarf contorted her lips in thought for a moment. "Come the mornin', I'll help ye with it."

The Andaren was taken aback by the generous offer. "Thank you," he said. "That is most kind."

Mordrith shrugged with a tilt of her head. "It's the least I can do. Ye saved me life twice today." She waved away any further talk. "I'm thinkin' I need sleep now. No more questions for today, eh?"

"I will keep watch," Daijen vowed.

Mordrith gave a slow nod, perhaps questioning her choices as she rested her head against the nearest roots. "Wake me when it's me turn."

Daijen smiled and nodded in return. Sleep, he knew, would elude him. There had been too much excitement for that.

As promised, Mordrith spent all of the next morning helping Daijen to acquire the pelt. The initiate had watched her closely, absorbing her every technique. He wasn't entirely useless to the dwarf, his enhanced strength added to her own considerable muscle power in moving the bear.

By the time the sun had passed its apex, the pelt was stretched out and hanging between two trees, its excess fat removed and salt from the saddlebags applied to keep the skin fresh. It was to spend the rest of the day basking in the shade, a process that would eventually dry it out and make transporting the pelt so much easier.

Claiming to be tired from the morning's activities, Mordrith declared that she would camp with the Andaren one more night before finding her way back to The Morthil Mountains. It pleased Daijen all the more, for he had held all of his questions in reserve during their work with the bear.

"How did you come by a hammer such as that?" he asked later that evening, after the sun had set. "Or did your husband forge it?"

Mordrith regarded the hammer, its silver and bronze bathing in the light of their fire. "Thronghir's a master smith, but I feel this is beyond his craftsmanship. No, he didn' make it. I found it." The dwarf laughed. "That makes it sound like it was easy, don' it? It were years o' minin'. Years an' years o' diggin' through hard stone an' crawlin' through mud." She caught herself. "I shouldn' be tellin' ye any o' this, lad."

"For my own good?" Daijen queried, recalling her words from the previous night.

Mordrith eyed him across the flames, uncertainty about her. "Ye an' I are supposed to be enemies."

Daijen raised an eyebrow. "Last I heard we weren't at war with Morthil."

The dwarf narrowed her eyes at him. “Ye really don’ know, do ye?” she reasoned incredulously. “I thought as much when ye didn’ try an’ kill me for this.” Her hand landed on the hammer beside her. “Ye ’ave no idea what this is, do ye? Yer masters would. They’d guess who *I* am too.”

“My master would know who *you* are?” Daijen found that hard to believe. “What don’t I know? Who *are* you?”

Mordrith’s air of uncertainty increased tenfold. “We really shouldn’ be talkin’ abou’ it. Ask ye masters up there. Ask ’em who yer *real* enemy is.”

Somewhat rattled by the dark turn in their conversation, Daijen felt deeply uncomfortable. “I would hear it from you,” he said.

“It’s not me place,” she replied with a shake of her head.

“You just told me we’re *enemies*.”

“I know.”

“I would not call *you* foe,” Daijen told her earnestly.

Mordrith made to speak but sighed instead. “I shouldn’ ’ave said anythin’,” she finally voiced. “Ask me anythin’ else, lad. Anythin’. We’re not to be speakin’ o’ this.”

“If you knew we were enemies, why would you camp with me?”

Mordrith gave something of a disheartened shrug. “Maybe I don’ want ye for an enemy,” she posed before letting loose a frustrated groan. “I’ve broken so many damned rules. I shouldn’ even ’ave that,” she added, gesturing at the hammer.

Daijen tilted his head. “Mordrith,” he pleaded.

The dwarf waved her hand before he could go on. “No. I’m not even permitted to talk to me beloved abou’ it. Ye don’ know what I’m a part o’. They’d kill me for jus’ sharin’ a camp with ye.”

Daijen frowned at the notion. “Who are *they*?”

Mordrith’s dark eyes cut across the flames to find him. “Death.”

The word, and the gravity which the dwarf lent it, sat with Daijen for a moment. He had many questions to follow up with but Mordrith shook her head.

"No more," she said definitively. "Come the morn, I'm to find me way home." With that, the dwarf lay down to sleep, the hammer snug between her arms.

Daijen would have been distressed to know that this was how their time together came to an end had they not enjoyed some time together in the morning. The dwarf was quite content to eat breakfast in his company and even share some knowledge about the guilds and their high king. It was a hierarchy that reminded him of the Andaren system, whose numerous kings bowed to the radiant emperor.

"I would escort you to the mountains," he offered, desperate to learn more, to know more of Mordrith.

"That's very kind o' ye, laddy, but—Vahlken or not—ye'd better not be caught on the eastern banks o' The Nheremyn."

"So you do have patrols—the stories are true!"

Mordrith laughed. "I'm not givin' away all o' our secrets. Jus' be sure to stick to yer side o' the river."

"To the western banks then," he suggested, making his way towards the war horse.

"No need," the dwarf called back, walking into an open space beyond the trees.

Daijen looked back in time to see her casually raising the hammer by way of explanation. "Wait," he said, turning from his horse. "Will I ever see you again?"

Mordrith had stopped not far from the site where she had initially arrived. The smile she gave him was genuine. "I'll likely be back from time to time. This very spot," she added, her gaze taking in the streams of shallow water.

"We're sent out every two weeks," Daijen informed her. "We're to hunt food and collect water."

The dwarf was nodding happily enough. "Then perhaps we will meet again. Until then, Daijen Saeth..." She hesitated, weighing up her next words. "Ask yer masters abou'... Ask 'em abou' the *Skaramangians*."

Daijen narrowed his eyes, the most unusual name a cleansing fire that robbed him of thought.

"Though, I warn ye," she added, "ye might not want to see me again."

There was no time for further words before Mordrith swung the hammer over her head and struck the ground at her feet. There came a brief flash of light and the air rippled out from the impact, offering a glimpse of the dwarven realm. Mordrith was gone in that same instant, her presence replaced by fragments of Morthil stone.

Alone again, Daijen didn't feel like going off in search of Ilithranda anymore.

He would have his answers.

28
NEW FRIENDS

THE LIGHT WAS BLINDING. IT WAS TOO MUCH FOR THE EYES OF A NIMEAN. Kitrana staggered, disorientated, and quickly lost her footing as her left foot sank into cold water up to her knee. She splashed wholly into the bog, tasting the thick build-up of algae on its surface, before finding purchase on solid ground again.

Slowly, painfully, she opened her eyes enough to take in the world.

It was, indeed, a swamp. Gnarled trees, coated in moss, dotted the land between patches of bog water, and all in the shadow of the mountains. Still, the sky above was a bright white, the clouds illuminated by the sun beyond.

Feeling somewhat trapped inside her own head, Kit stretched her jaw and forced her ears to pop. Whatever had just happened, the Nimean knew she must have been taken far from the dwarven realm. From the Leviathan's prison.

Its gargantuan form flashed across her mind, a nightmare made flesh. Reason and logic told her she need not fear the demon now but, for the first time in her life, she wished to get out of the water.

Land, however, was no guarantee of safe harbour.

Still crouched from her climb out of the swampy waters, she felt the touch of cool steel against her throat.

It took no time at all to register the steel as the large curved head of an axe. Kit's eyes ran along the blade and up the long haft. Were her life not in danger, the Nimean would have been impressed to find the considerable weapon being wielded, if not balanced, by a single hand. Of course, that hand belonged to a dwarf.

What grit there was in her expression, a promise of death were the Nimean to make one bad move. Kitrana blinked, and hard, as she tried to focus on the dwarf's face, whose head was between her and the bright sky.

"Ye speak man's tongue," the dwarf stated in her gruff voice.

Kit tried to angle her head to better see the dwarf, but the axe blade moved with her, its edge biting slightly into her throat. "I do," she replied, her voice hoarse from years of disuse.

The sound of horrendous vomiting momentarily distracted the axe-wielding dwarf, turning her gaze over one shoulder. Kitrana took the opportunity and dived away from the sharp steel. The dwarf was quick to react, her axe going high into a potential throw. The Nimean turned her momentum into a roll that saw her returned to swampy waters that no dwarven eyes could pierce.

Her body seamlessly transitioned from one style of breathing to the next, and the skin between her fingers and toes secreted the natural oil that congealed to grant her webbing. All she had to do then was wait, for though the two worlds existed side by side, Kit was now residing beyond the surface dweller's reach.

Until she wasn't...

The slow but steady realisation inevitably dawned on the Nimean. There wasn't enough oxygen in the boggy water. Her chest began to spasm as she fought against her instincts to rise to the surface. When she could take it no longer, Kit pushed up from the bottom and broke the surface of the swamp at enviable speed. It was enough to clear her feet from the water and land in a crouch, ready to fight.

The dwarf was waiting for her. She came at the Nimean

swinging, her axe going high. Kit was agile enough to evade the attack, her body twisting and cartwheeling as she navigated the swamp, leaving the axe to sink deep into the mossy earth.

"Stay still!" the dwarf barked.

The axe whistled as it cut through the air, the blade intended to strike Kitrana across the hip. Again, the Nimean demonstrated her flexible skeleton and bowed backwards under the swing. When she snapped back, Kit had only to jump up on one foot and kick back with the other to score a blow across the dwarf's jaw.

Though staggered, the foot to the face wasn't nearly enough to put the dwarf down. If anything, it brought a wicked grin to her face. "Oh, ye're goin' to get it now, lassy," she vowed.

"Stop," the second dwarf managed, still on his hands and knees by the water's edge.

Kit tore her eyes from the red-head and looked upon the other, the one who had wielded the *hammer*. His cloak of white fur looked heavy with water, though not so heavy as the pack strapped to his broad back, its many compartments overflowing with supplies and tools.

Contrasting against the bright cloak, his skin was a smooth canvas of dark marble beneath a thick sable beard. His skin was beautiful, the colouring never to be seen amongst the underwater races, who dwelled so far from the sun. He bore other contrasts, such as the small bands of copper and bronze threaded amidst the long dreadlocks that flowed over his shoulders and chest.

He was also splattered with his own vomit.

"Stop," he said again, one hand coming up to point at the distant swamp. "What's that?"

His question was enough to grab the attention of the axe-wielder, who finally lowered her weapon and turned to follow his direction. "Grarfath," she intoned. "Get away from the water."

Kitrana shielded her eyes from the general light and looked out over the still waters. It was all too easy to spot the three distinct ripples that moved towards them. It reminded the Nimean of whales, who often swam so close to the water's surface that they pushed it up without actually breaking it. These were definitely not whales.

The one named Grarfath picked himself up and wiped his beard to clear the vomit before hefting the inexplicable hammer. The red-head was already grabbing him by the arm and dragging him back towards the giant pig.

"What is that?" he asked.

Kit knew she should be running for the answer to that question was undoubtedly bad, but she couldn't move for curiosity. That curiosity melted away when the three bulges dropped away. In its place there was only fear.

The Nimean turned and bolted.

A step behind her, the dwarves and their pig made all haste.

The quiet of the swamp was disturbed all at once, the water thrown high into the air and a chorus of roars unleashed upon the world. Kitrana had to look over her shoulder, to know that it wasn't the Leviathan. Of course it wasn't, but it was a monster all the same. Three heads with snaking necks lurched in the air above them, all joined to the same beastly body that was crawling out of the swamp.

Spit and bog water rained down on the trio, who were trailing the significantly faster pig. When the first of the three heads coiled round to attack from the side, Grarfath was pulled down by the red-head, where the two narrowly avoided the closing jaws. That same dragon-like head got in the way of its two companions, allowing the dwarves enough time to get up and run.

Too busy watching the event unfold, Kit failed to navigate the hard ground and splashed back into the swamp. The sound of distress was enough to redirect the monster, its three heads swivelling on the Nimean.

"Run!" she cried, at the dwarves before diving into the murky water.

Whether she could breathe or not, her body was still adept at moving through water. When the beast's body ploughed into the next segment of swamp, its heads snaking after her, Kitrana was already further ahead than it could have anticipated. Like the dolphins that enjoyed the waters of The Dawning Isles, Kit speared out of the bog and cleared the water altogether. The moment her feet touched down on mossy earth, they propelled her on, away from the pursuing creature.

Again, the swamp erupted as the monster burst out. Its high-pitched roar was multiplied by three, combining into an all-out assault on the battle maiden's ears. All the while, her vision was assailed by the light. Still, she could see enough to know that the red-headed dwarf was barrelling towards her astride the enormous hog.

"Yamnomora!" Grarfath shouted after her.

The Nimean leapt aside only a second before the charging pig rushed past. With a battle cry on her lips, the dwarf raised one of the two large axes she wielded and jumped into a crouch atop her saddle. It seemed too delicate a manoeuvre for one so squat and obviously heavy, yet the red-head did it all the same.

Despite every instinct screaming at her to keep running, Kitrana had to stop and watch the suicidal attack.

Naturally, the middle head dipped down, its jaw extending in the manner of a snake to scoop up its approaching meal. Yamnomora, however, vaulted from her precarious perch before the two could collide. While in the air, the dwarf twisted her body around and launched one of the axes at the left head while simultaneously avoiding the maw of the middle head. As she came down, her remaining axe chopped deep into the middle neck, severing all but a few strands of sinew.

While the left head reeled from the axe buried in one of its reptilian eyes, the right head curled in and down to take vengeance upon the vicious dwarf. It might have succeeded had the pig not slammed into the base of its neck, driving its steel-tipped tusks through scaly grey flesh. The right head reared up and screeched with pain, offering Yamnomora the perfect opportunity to heft her axe and let fly. Spinning horizontally, the weapon found its end in the right neck, just beneath the jaw. Dark blood spurted from the gaps in the wound and the head swayed high in the air.

Yamnomora groaned. "Give it up," she said wearily. "Ye were dead the second ye caught me scent."

Indeed, a moment later, it fell to the earth and joined the middle head in death.

Kitrana saw the calamity that was about to ensue, but it was Grarfath who called out the dwarf's name first, turning her to the remaining head. The beast was marred by the axe still lodged in its face, but it seemed that wouldn't be enough to prevent it from coming down on the red-head.

Still, the dwarf faced certain death with a grimace and balled fists, determined to meet her end fighting.

So fast did the hammer fly that Kitrana barely heard it before impact. It struck the side of the creature's head with a flash of light and a thunderous *clap*. It was enough to blind the Nimean, robbing her of the next few seconds.

What a sight awaited her when the world came back to her pained eyes.

The head—what was left of it—was already on the ground and steaming. Its mangled brain could be seen inside the remains of its skull, along with half of its tongue and a few fangs.

Both Kit and Yamnomora turned to lay eyes on Grarfath.

For all his exhaustion, the dwarf managed a shrug.

Yamnomora walked around the central head and marched across the swamp. "Where did ye send it?" she questioned urgently.

Only then did Kit realise that the hammer was not amidst the debris. Looking back at the dwarves, Grarfath was slowly lifting his head to the sky, his eyes moving beyond them.

Though it pained her to look, the battle maiden caught sight of the dark rain falling to the earth. The hammer landed first, its head sinking into the boggy ground so that its haft was left standing at a jaunty angle.

In its wake came the rest of the monster's head.

It was a pattering of wet *splats* and light *thuds*, but the creature was brought back together in a rain of gore and jagged flesh. The stench was quick to reach beyond the corpse and offend Kit's sense of smell, though even that could not distract her from the hammer of bronze and gold. Without thinking, she began walking towards it, the dwarves forgotten.

Though she had never seen the weapon before Grarfath used it under the mountain, the Nimean recognised so much about it: the bronze that coiled around the haft, its sleek curves and rearing head. Standing before it now, she could even see the glyphs carved into the back of the head, where it protruded from the ground. She knew those runes. Were it not a hammer, it could easily have been the axe she and Gallien had found in old Harendun.

Or the sword of Skara...

Kitrana thought of the hilt's design, the image burned into the mind of every battle maiden. The sword hadn't been seen in its whole form for eons, but the hilt was accented with bronze elements and what was left of the blade possessed a vertical line of glyphs running up the fuller.

It wasn't conscious thought that drew her hand towards the hammer, for surely it was the guiding hand of the Water Maiden. Who else could have entwined her path with a weapon of power, a weapon that must be linked to the blade?

A stubby dwarven hand appeared from nowhere to swat her away. "Get out o' it," Yamnomora warned, eyeing the Nimean with scorn. "Ye've no idea what me an' mine 'ave gone through to wield this. I'll not 'ave it taken by some fish lady."

Kit raised an eyebrow. "Fish lady?"

Yamnomora glanced at the Nimean's hands. "Do ye prefer *duck lady*?"

The battle maiden didn't need to look at her hands to know they were still webbed. She clenched her fists before wiggling every finger. The friction was enough to hasten the process and the webbing quickly dried and flaked away.

The hammer was yanked from the earth by Yamnomora, who went on to brush off the dirt clinging to the gold and bronze head. Using the weapon, the dwarf gestured for Kitrana to move out of her way. "Quack," she voiced mockingly.

Deciding she was in no fit state to pick a fight with the person who had just killed a three-headed monster the size of a house, Kit moved aside. Yamnomora's smug expression fell away upon spotting Grarfath. She dashed to his side and caught him before he collapsed to his knees.

"Take it easy," she bade.

Kitrana moved around them to better assess the situation. "What's wrong with him?"

Grarfath put one hand on Yamnomora's shoulder—a chunky and layered pauldron. "I don' feel right," he complained.

"Easy," she told him. "Sit down. We'll camp 'ere for the night to let you recover."

All thought of the sickly dwarf fled from Kitrana's concerns. "You can't be serious? Camp here? We'll never see morning."

"Bah!" Yamnomora spat. "There's no safer place than right 'ere. Do ye know what that thing is?" she asked, nodding at the monster.

Kit licked her lips, hating to admit any gap in her knowledge. "That thing is the reason we shouldn't stay here," she said instead. "What if another one comes along?"

Yamnomora removed the pack from Grarfath's back and deliberately laid him down so his head could rest against it. "*That*," she replied, jabbing one stubby finger at the corpse, "is a Three-Headed Dread Serpent. If there's one thing that's guaranteed to keep 'em away, it's the smell o' their own dead. As for everythin' else..." The dwarf shrugged her massive shoulders. "The Dread Serpent will already 'ave seen to 'em when it carved out its territory. Even Hell Hags fear these beasties."

Kitrana wanted to protest further but it was abundantly clear that Yamnomora's knowledge on such things was vastly superior to her own.

"Do feel free to camp elsewhere," the red-head added with far too much encouragement.

It dawned on the battle maiden that she had been thrown into the lives of others, and that they clearly had their own troubles to be dealing with. It seemed inescapable, however, that their troubles aligned, in some way, with her own quandary. For now, it would have to bind them together. There was, of course, one other, significant, problem that Kit couldn't escape.

"Elsewhere?" she echoed. "I don't even know where *here* is."

"The Swamps o' Morthil," Yamnomora stated as she removed several items from her saddlebags. The dwarf looked up, acquiring her bearings from the mountains in the distance. "That way," she directed, pointing in the opposite direction to the mountains, "ye'll find The Ice Plains o' Isendorn. If ye've keen eyes, ye'll notice The Dorth Road before ye wander all the way out there. Turn right an' go south for... a month or two, an' ye might reach the sea before the Andarens slit yer throat." The red-head didn't even look up from her preparations when she added, "Best o' luck to ye."

Considering the stink in her nose, Kit wondered if it wasn't the worst idea. Then the truth of things caught up with her and any thought of leaving came to a dead end.

"I'm in Andara," she muttered to herself.

How long had it been since she considered where she was in relation to the surface world? After so many years of mindlessly digging through stone it had become an inconsequential fact. For just a moment, the Nimean glimpsed a sliver of hope. If she was already on Andaren soil, she could more easily return to Harendun and retrieve the broken blade from its ancient foundations. After all, there was every chance that Gallien had fallen to the Vorge and the weapon still lay beside his corpse.

Dredging her memories of the man, however, informed her that such a chance was slim indeed. She had left him wielding not only the sword of Skara but an axe capable of returning to his grip from afar. Added to that, both the broken blade and the axe had reacted to each other, bringing to life the legend that surrounded the sword of Skara. It seemed more likely that the Vorge was ash and Gallien in the wind. Gallien and the sword.

Sixteen years is long enough for any trail to go cold, but all the more when the quarry was a smuggler by profession. Though he was undoubtedly in Erador by now, he could be anywhere in a realm that spanned thousands of miles.

The battle maiden's hope might have been crushed there and

then had her sight not landed on the hammer. She didn't know how, but she had to believe it would bring her and the sword back together. Kitrana thought of her people, scattered and alone or suffering under the oppression of the Merdians.

She needed that sword. More so, she needed it made whole again. Perhaps then, with the axe too, she would wield enough power to free every Nimean and rebuild her home.

"What are ye doin'?" The abrupt question cut right through Kit's thoughts. "Are ye jus' goin' to stand there? That way," she reminded, pointing into the distance.

The battle maiden reconsidered her strategy in the light of new... *beliefs*. She turned on her heel and walked away from the makeshift camp Yamnomora was beginning to put together. Upon her return, she presented the fiery dwarf with both of her axes, the weapons unceremoniously yanked from the tough flesh of the Dread Serpent.

All the while, Kitrana had been doing her best to recall a particular phrase she had heard among the surface-dwellers. "I think we got off on the wrong foot," she said, offering a sheepish smile. "My name is—"

"No," the dwarf interjected. "Don' need to know yer name."

Kit stood awkwardly for a moment, her body hardly aware of the icy temperature. "Can I at least sit with you?" she asked politely enough.

Time seemed to stretch on and on while Yamnomora scrutinised her. Finally, the dwarf thrust her chin at a patch of earth opposite her and Grarfath, who was already asleep.

Kit nodded appreciatively and crossed her legs as she lowered herself to the allocated spot. It was with disbelief that she took in her surroundings—a few feet from a dead monster and in the company of two dwarves in The Swamps of Morthil. Seemingly only minutes ago she had been inside the lair of the Leviathan and before that a lowly prisoner who had known naught but toil and torment for over a decade. It reminded her how quickly her life had changed the first time, when the Merdians had violated the laws of The Sanctum and killed her sister maidens.

Life, it seemed, was little more than a flipping coin.

Deciding that she would make certain the coin landed in her favour, Kitrana opened her mouth to start a fresh dialogue with Yamnomora.

"No." The word left the dwarf with all the subtlety of a brick. "I'm not for talkin' to ye."

"Why not?"

Yamnomora sighed. "Because ye've got naught but questions where *that's* concerned," she replied, gesturing to the hammer, "an' I'm not tellin' ye a damned thing."

Kit hesitated. "Maybe I wasn't going to ask *any* questions about it."

The dwarf responded with a sceptical look. "Oh aye, ye *weren'* goin' to ask any questions abou' the hammer that ported ye from one place to another," she said with dripping sarcasm.

The battle maiden opened her mouth to speak again.

"No," Yamnomora intervened again. "We're goin' to sit here quietly. Come night, ye're goin' to sleep an' I'm goin' to *watch* ye sleep—"

"You're going to watch me sleep?" Kitrana cut in, somewhat disturbed by the notion.

"The mountains," Yamnomora pointed out, "*literally* trembled before *ye* landed at our feet. So aye, I'm goin' to watch ye. I'm goin' to watch everythin' ye do, fish lady. Until dawn that is. Then," she promised, "we go our separate ways. Understood?"

Kitrana Voden had no intention of parting ways with that hammer. But she nodded all the same.

29
A SIMPLE QUESTION

64 YEARS AGO...

Though he was not cloaked in the bear yet, Daijen Saeth returned to Ka'vairn victorious. The pelt would need further treatment and considerable tailoring before it could be worn as the other initiates had before setting off to seek out the Weavers. Still, he returned with his head held high as he passed over the threshold with his horse's reins in hand.

Not that there was anyone to greet him and see as much.

The fortress looked abandoned. The ramparts were barren. The training areas stood idle. Even one of the main doors remained partially ajar, as if the occupants had left in a hurry. Yet the gates were open and the portcullis raised to allow him entry, so Kastiek must have seen him coming.

Perhaps proving that to be true, Strix launched into the sky, its eagle-like body previously concealed by one of the broken towers. The Aegre's call pierced the distant sky as its wings saw it rise effortlessly into the heavens.

As always, Daijen was enraptured by the sight of the creature.

He watched it soar until the ramparts blocked his view. "Where does he go?" he wondered aloud, though the war horse had little to say on the subject. If anything, the animal had become unsettled after sighting the winged predator. "Easy," he bade, patting his side. "No one's having you for lunch," he reassured.

It was then that the initiate spied Aramis nestled in the corner of the courtyard. The Aegre had been so still as to blend in with its environment, its dark feathers hard to distinguish against the fortress stone. It was well known among Ka'vairn's inhabitants that The Valtorak's Aegre *was* a predator worth keeping in your eyeline. How quickly it could rip the war horse to pieces.

Daijen was sure to never take his eyes from the Aegre as he led his mount into the stables. While he wasn't surprised to find that Ilithranda's horse was missing, the young Andaren was filled with mixed feelings to discover the other six horses in their stalls and the rack lined with saddles. The other initiates had returned earlier than expected.

Taking the heavy pelt with him, Daijen left the stables and made for the main doors. Voices echoed throughout the foyer, leading the initiate towards the Hall of Handuin. Indeed, Laif and the others occupied the heart of the great hall, lazing about the round table that sat before the ancient throne.

"Well, well, well..."

Daijen sighed at the sound of Slait's voice. What a wonderful year it had been without his manic presence, if wonderful was ever a word that could be applied to a year of Kastiek's rigorous training routines. The bald initiate stood up from his perch on the edge of the table and stalked towards Daijen, his gaze cutting across the gap to eye the pelt being carried in.

"I don't believe it," Slait said in his rough voice. "I would have bet my new armour you wouldn't return from the forest." He glanced over Daijen's shoulder. "Where's the princess? I'm assuming she's the one who put your bear down."

Daijen spared a moment to look over Slait's *new armour*. The extraordinary work of the Weavers was concealed beneath the tanned leather that coated his cuirass, but it was still a beautiful piece of craftsmanship that extended to the pauldrons and vambraces. Draped over his shoulders was his own cloak of victory, the fur an almost identical brown to Daijen's.

"I think that new armour is cutting off the blood supply to your brain," the younger Andaren quipped.

The other initiates shared a laugh at that, a fact that brought a snide smile to Slait's wide face. He even managed a snigger of his own. Then he shoved Daijen with both hands, launching him across the dusty floor.

In truth, it hardly hurt, but the shock of it was enough to see Daijen's anger boil over. He flipped deftly onto his feet and levelled a look on Slait that promised vengeance. Slait truly laughed now.

Daijen sneered and moved with such speed he appeared to skip across the hall. His first attack was a leaping knee to his opponent's chest. Slait was pushed back no more than a foot, however, and Daijen was consequently staggered upon landing. He was sure his knee had just slammed into Hellion stone.

Slait pounded a closed fist into his chest. "It seems to fit quite well," he remarked.

The pain was just enough to slow Daijen's reactions down, leaving him vulnerable to the humiliating backhand Slait delivered. Blood was flung from his mouth as his body angled for the cold floor once more.

"Slait." It was Laif who had spoken his name, and with a note of caution.

The bald initiate shrugged. "I'm just making sure he knows his place. He's had the run of the fortress for over a year. He's probably pissed on the walls—marking his territory." Again, his wicked laughter filled the hall, the sound a desecration of the hallowed stone in Daijen's mind.

The initiate's spine cracked in several places as he rose to his full height. His rage was peaking, reminding him of The Valtorak's callous nature upon Elivar's demise.

"*Hold on to it,*" Ilithranda had told him in that moment. "*Let it go at the right time.*"

Though he wished it to be, Daijen knew in his heart that it

wasn't the right time to unleash his wrath. For all his years in Ka'vairn, he was still in the early stages of his training. His skills needed honing from raw to refined. Until then, he was little better than a hammer.

He found Slait's golden eyes and saw how eager he was to spill more blood. Daijen worked to loosen his jaw and unclench his fists. "Welcome home," he managed bitterly, after taking a much-needed breath.

It was then that he caught sight of The Valtorak, his red robes standing out between the throne and the door that led down to the pits. How long had he been watching them? And to what end? Everything was a test inside those walls, a fact that bit into Daijen's already mounting frustration.

"You have your cloaks," The Valtorak announced, turning all eyes on him. "Now you have your armour. Your atori blades?" he questioned, to which the six initiates drew the short-sword from their belt. The curved steel of every blade was now bronze flecked with copper where the Weavers had worked their arcane magic.

"Very good," The Valtorak complimented. "You will now learn to move in your armour. To fight effectively. You will learn its limits before you hold the title of Vahlken. Wield your atori blades with skill and you will soon receive your sabres."

"What of our Slaiken blades?" Kovun enquired eagerly.

The Valtorak's hard stare was enough to let them all know that the master of Ka'vairn didn't enjoy being questioned so brashly. "Your time away has robbed you of decorum, Kovun. Perhaps *all* of you need reminding of your place."

Kovun swallowed and bowed his head apologetically.

"Your journey has been long," the master continued, his tone a touch softer now. "I'm sure that finding some rest in these familiar halls will remind you that your training still has a long way to go. But rest will have to wait," he was quick to add, his voice dropping. "Kastiek awaits you all in the courtyard. *He* will test the limits of your armour."

Disappointment flashed across the face of every initiate, though it was fleeting as they ensured they displayed nothing to suggest their real feelings. Daijen stepped aside and watched his peers trail one after the other. Of them all, only Soyra took note of the bear pelt on the floor. Her expression suggested she was impressed and she made no attempt to hide it from Daijen. The young Andaren had no idea what to make of the exchange after so many years of passive regard for his feats.

As she left the Hall of Handuin, only Daijen and The Valtorak remained. Ka'vairn's master, however, had closed the gap between them without a sound, and now stood mere feet away. "You return earlier than anticipated," he commented without inflection. "I was sure you would take all of the allotted time."

"*Ask 'em who yer* real *enemy is.*" Mordrith's words pressed upon the initiate.

"I must speak with you," he said.

The Valtorak's brow pinched in response. "You would speak to me as if I am some petulant child beckoned by his father?"

Daijen bowed his head and thought of a better way to begin. "Forgive me, Master. I only—"

"You will wait until *I* wish to speak to *you*," The Valtorak interjected, already walking away. "Kastiek will instruct you where your cloak is concerned," he added on his way to the nearest stairwell.

"Skaramangians." The name rang out to find every echoing wall inside the ancient hall.

The Valtorak stopped, his hand resting on the banister.

Daijen, his anticipation rising uncontrollably, watched his master's back intently. The Valtorak held his pose for several seconds, one foot raised to the first step. It was as if Daijen had voiced a spell and frozen the old Andaren to the spot. Quite deliberately, his head began to slowly swivel until his violet eyes consumed the initiate.

The master's jaw twitched before tensing. He glanced at the doors through which the other initiates had departed. "Not another word," he commanded, his voice under strain. "You will follow me."

Daijen did exactly that, and without another word as

instructed. It was in silence that he trailed The Valtorak up and across to the office that occupied the highest spot in the domed tower. As before, the master unlocked the door with his key and granted the initiate entry.

Continuing his vow of silence, Daijen watched The Valtorak move to one of the windows and peer down at the other initiates. The master observed them for an uncomfortable amount of time before addressing the room's only other occupant.

"Where did you hear that word?"

Daijen discovered his throat was dry, forcing him to clear his throat. "In The Dain'duil," he answered.

The Valtorak's eyes snapped from the window to the initiate. "Do not be clever with me, *boy*. From *whom* did you hear that word? I know for a fact that it cannot be found on any parchment you have access to."

Daijen did his best to appear unfazed by the rebuke. "I heard it from a dwarf," he answered again.

For the first time in sixteen years, there was a look of genuine surprise on The Valtorak's face. "You heard it from a *dwarf*?" he echoed in disbelief.

"Her name is Mordrith. Mordrith Underborn." He didn't know why, but her whole name felt like an important detail.

Apparently the name meant nothing to The Valtorak. "And why was this dwarf in The Dain'duil?"

Daijen opened his mouth to explain the hammer Mordrith had used to port in and out of the forest. But he said no such thing. He closed his mouth and considered the most important fact: he didn't have *all* the facts.

"She was lost," he said instead, not so far from the truth.

"Curious that a dwarf should wander west of The Nheremyn. All the more curious that you would engage her in conversation. Do you speak their tongue?"

"No," Daijen confirmed.

The Valtorak moved to the other side of his desk. "In what context did she use the word *Skaramangian*?"

"She told me to ask you about our *real* enemies."

The master of Ka'vairn gave nothing away, his expression chiselled from stone. "She had no right to burden you so. That word was not meant for you. Not *yet*."

"What does it mean?"

The Valtorak crossed to the other side of the room, where his finger was able to roam across the spines of his book collection. "Answer me this, Daijen: why is Erador at war with Andara?" Upon asking his question, the master retrieved a tome from one of the shelves and proceeded to open it across the only available space on his desk.

Daijen hesitated, his attention caught by the map spread over a double-page. "Erador invaded our lands," he finally said. "They sacked Tor Valan. Then their dragons scorched the stone black and all inside."

Seated behind his desk now, The Valtorak nodded along. "And what was our response?"

The details might have once been blurry, but Daijen had read numerous volumes inside Ka'vairn's library that recorded the early days of the war. "We assembled our forces and met the humans on The Plains Of Pelun."

"Where a monument now stands for all the dead," the master added dryly. "Go on," he insisted.

Daijen recalled, as he so easily could these days, a particular volume titled *The Spark of War*. "The Plains of Pelun was a disaster for both sides, our combined losses in the tens of thousands. The humans were forced to retreat, as they had foolishly entered into battle without their dragons."

The Valtorak was staring down at the map. "They believed we were weak after having taken Tor Valan so easily," he commented. "But slaughtering innocent Andarens is not the same as facing our warriors. They should have waited for their dragons. If they had, this war would look very different now." The master caught himself and gestured for Daijen to continue.

The initiate glanced at the map and used it to anchor the facts in his mind. "Emperor Qeledred officially declared war and assembled the Warmasters under the Archjusticiar." Daijen took a breath before recalling the next, and most bloody of battles. “Andara’s first act of aggression was to invade Erador. The emperor personally requested aid from the Vahlken and...” The initiate glanced at his master. “And it was given.”

Those violet eyes were consumed by the image of Daijen. “Go on.”

“Andara invaded Erador in the north, unaware that as they turned south into Dunmar, they turned their backs on Drakanan.” Daijen could imagine it. The newly swollen armies of Andara oblivious to the fact that the Dragon Riders’ home was now behind them. He envisioned those reptilian eyes spying them as they passed by, the beasts just waiting for the right moment.

“As battle commenced,” he continued, “the Dragon Riders attacked from the rear. For the first time, Aegres and dragons met in combat. Vahlken and Riders spilled blood in the air. Armies spilled blood on the ground. It became The Plains of Pelun all over again, only worse.”

“The carnage was such that the humans renamed it The Red Fields of Dunmar,” The Valtorak remarked. “I was there,” he breathed. “’Twas little more than a bog by the end. A swamp of blood and bodies. To this day I have not been able to get the smell out of my nose. So much death burns itself into the back of your eyes.”

A protracted silence reigned over the office, as if they were giving the long dead their moment of silence.

“Since then,” Daijen said in conclusion, “the war has gone on as it will. Invasions. Skirmishes. We built The Tower of Argunsuun and they built White Tower.”

“Very good,” the master replied, though he looked to be in deep contemplation.

Daijen wondered if his memories had taken a hold of him, dragging him down through time to relive so many battles. Those would be halls he never walked in *his* dreams. Just reading about the earlier battles was enough for Daijen.

“You still haven’t answered my question,” The Valtorak informed him.

The younger Andaren blinked. Though there was considerably more detail he could have produced, he knew he hadn't missed out the key events.

"Why is Erador at war with Andara? That was my question. You have told me of the events that transpired and in the correct order no less, but you have failed to answer my question."

The lecture irked Daijen, prompting a response he knew he shouldn't voice. "And you never answered mine," he said all the same.

"The answer to your question lies in the truth of mine," the master replied cryptically. "And if you speak to me again in such a manner, you will bleed for it."

Daijen felt himself shrink somewhat. "Apologies, Master," he said with a curt bow of the head. In all his years at Ka'vairn, he had never seen The Valtorak demonstrate his combat skills. Proof, he decided, wasn't required to know that he was out-matched in every way.

"Since you failed to grasp the nature of my question, I will rephrase it for you. Why did Erador amass its army, march hundreds of miles into foreign land, and proceed to besiege and destroy Tor Valan?"

Daijen's mind sifted through pages of manuscripts, tomes, and volumes searching for that specific answer. He found naught but lines from scripture, words taken from the Arkalon to explain the savage nature of humanity. As Slait had quoted years earlier, *Their Leviathans defeated, the Dark Ones unleashed new hell on earth, releasing the human scourge from their demonic flesh.* Knowing The Valtorak as he did, quoting the Arkalon would not be the answer he was looking for.

"I don't know," he was forced to admit.

"Don't look so concerned. I could ask that very question of every Andaren on Verda's green earth and they would answer with those same words. That's why the Arkalon is so convenient. Should anyone question Erador's motives, they have only to open its pages and read about monsters made flesh, demons born of the Dark

Ones themselves." The Valtorak locked his eyes on the initiate. "Are you sure you're prepared for the truth, boy?"

The question, and the gravity which the master's tone implied, made Daijen pause. "Yes," he uttered.

The Valtorak rested back in his chair. "Erador invaded because we told them to."

30
DEMONS IN THE NIGHT

THREE HORSES SET OUT FROM WARTH, AND AT A GALLOP THEY PUT THE town behind them. But it was with all haste that seven more departed in their wake. Seven pale demons on horseback, their white hair flowing out of equally white hoods.

Gallien's mind was taken back to his time with Androma. She had stood up to the Andarens and the giant who had led them into Erador, her final stand to give them time to escape. It chilled the smuggler's bones to know that the foreign assassins had been hunting them all this time.

"Ride!" the wizard called back, his black steed leading the way.

Gallien didn't need any encouragement. One glance over his shoulder was enough to tell him that Death and its riders were coming for them. For Joran. Drakalis could feel the boy behind him on the saddle, his hands clasped around his waist. He felt all too exposed to Gallien, who envisioned an arrow finding Joran's back.

Aphrandhor maintained their heading, his staff held high where it could illuminate the fields north of the town, his magic bathing the terrain in white light. Those fields would roll on for hundreds of miles, Gallien knew. Hundreds of miles of *nothing*. The worst hunters in the world could track them across those plains.

"We need to lose them!" he shouted over the thundering hooves.

Coming to the same conclusion, perhaps, the wizard waved his staff to the right, revealing the land that stretched between them and a wall of trees in the distance. His horse soon followed the light and the Kedradi guided his mount to follow. Gallien did the same, desperate to make Joran a harder target.

The trio of horses leapt over a fallen log and pierced the trees of The Morn Wood at speed. So too did their seven pursuers. The Andaren assassins moved with precision, weaving between the trees until they were spread out. Gallien realised all too late that it gave them more angles of attack.

The first salvo of arrows were clearly aimed at the Kedradi, with all but one of the missiles finding naught but the trees. That one, however, found its mark in the horse's side. The mount neighed in complaint and darted away from its companions, taking the hunter further out. The Kedradi could be seen struggling to control the animal until he finally gave in to the horse's direction and let it take him into the darkness.

Gallien would have cursed the man for abandoning them had two of the seven not peeled away in pursuit. The next wave of arrows came close to Drakalis and the boy, but it was clearly the wizard who had been targeted. Of the four arrows, two vanished in the shadows, missing the old man by no more than a foot. The other two collided with an unseen shield, their impacts creating ripples of light that revealed the faint shape of a sphere around Aphrandhor.

Deciding that the wizard was only good for attracting arrows, Gallien diverted to a path alongside him. The wizard, however, soon proved himself more valuable. In one hand, he began to wave his staff over his hooded head, the light creating a circle in the air. His spell complete, Aphrandhor slammed the head of his staff into the ground, just behind and to the side of his charging horse.

Besides the blinding light that shattered the night, the solid earth of The Morn Wood was violently churned. The ground rumbled and the dirt piled in on itself as the earth swallowed rocks and trees alike. The cacophony of splintering wood and cracking stone was interspersed with the cries of Andarens and their neighing horses.

The spectacle of it was a terror unto itself, reminding Gallien that he was in the company of a man who could kill with words and thoughts. The smuggler would have challenged any man not to be frightened by the display of raw magic, but it seemed the event had not had the same effect on Joran. The boy was twisted in the saddle, his violet eyes fixed on the nightmarish event. His expression was that of pure wonderment. He craved so much more of the world.

Fool.

"Eyes front!" Gallien barked.

For a time they continued through the wood unmolested, though the smuggler had lost any sense of direction. All he could do was follow Aphrandhor and the light of his staff. It was only when that sense of danger—a sense he had learned never to ignore—pricked the hairs on the back of his neck that Gallien turned his head over one shoulder.

There on the very edge of Aphrandhor's light, were three riders in white and red. Gallien swore. The spell had claimed only the two lives and succeeded in little more than slowing the other three.

"Wizard!" Drakalis cried.

Aphrandhor gave a double take upon seeing the truth of their situation. He proceeded to flick his staff across his shoulder, an action that played merry hell with the shadows, as well as sending a flash of light towards their quarry. The spell exploded on impact, kicking up dirt and debris right in front of the riders. Of the trio, the leader ploughed on, his horse leaping through the rain of dirt, while the other two skidded to a stop.

The wizard let loose another spell and struck a tree this time. Splinters of bark and a wild scattering of leaves blew across the lead assassin, forcing his horse to divert from the pursuit. He was delayed only a few seconds, though, and was even joined by the other two again, their hunt renewed.

"Look!" Joran yelled, daring Gallien to glance back.

The rider on the leader's left was slipping from his saddle, an arrow in the back of his neck. When he finally fell from his perch, his arm caught in the reins and his weight dragged the horse around with it. That would have left two assassins, but the rider on the leader's right spasmed and lurched forwards, an arrow in his back. His displaced weight similarly took the horse from its path and the mount veered away.

From the darkness, the Kedradi emerged.

The hunter leaned out of his saddle, his body stretching close to the ground, as he reclaimed the arrow from his victim's back. He fired it again from his bow, his aim just as accurate as his previous shots. It seemed impossible to Gallien, though he witnessed the leader bob his head and evade the arrow by an inch—without seeing it coming. The arrow went on, of course, and sank into the tree only feet away from the smuggler, who recoiled from the *thud*.

"This way!" the wizard called, his horse turning more to the left.

The slight change in direction gave the last of the Andarens the opportunity he needed to close the gap. Where before he had remained at their back, his robes of white and red could now be seen in the smuggler's peripheral vision. While his face was concealed behind the wall of his hood, his robes did nothing to conceal his size. It was *him*.

The Dancing Sword of the Dawn.

The Andaren turned his head towards them; enough to reveal the devilish smile in Aphrandhor's light. Gallien steered the horse to the right, putting a series of trees between them and the pale demon. It didn't last. The Andaren was soon coming up on their side again, only now he was wielding a curved dagger, its blade flashing in the light.

As his great mount began to close the gap, the Kedradi once again showed his quality. The hunter cut through the middle of them, his bow now replaced by a scimitar of bone—a scimitar already streaked with blood. He brought it down from on high and gave The Dawn Sword something else to think about.

And so the pair rode side by side, exchanging glances and

parried blows of steel and bone. More than once, it appeared The Dawn Sword attempted to draw his own scimitar, but the Kedradi never relented in his sweeping attacks. Locked in battle, the combatants were only separated sporadically by trees that got in their path. Their duel, however, was enough to slow their mounts down and allow Gallien and Joran to get ahead.

"Be done with him!" the wizard exclaimed over his shoulder.

The Kedradi adjusted his strategy immediately. His scimitar twisted in his grip, bringing the crab-like curve of its end into play. One decisive hammer blow to the skull killed the horse under The Dawn Sword. The animal went down head first, its body following its descent and over itself. It should have been the end of any rider, their life brought to a crushing end, but the pale assassin sprang from his saddle before he could be brought down and dragged beneath the horse's bulk.

Adding to the miraculous feat, he turned his flying momentum into a roll upon hitting the ground, and from his roll he sprang again, landing in a dead run.

He was damned fast. So fast, in fact, that Gallien had to question why he had even bothered with a horse to begin with. He skipped and jumped over every obstacle while, somehow, keeping pace with the Kedradi's mount.

The hunter cursed in his native tongue and sheathed the broad scimitar in favour of his bow again. One after the other, he launched arrows at The Dawn Sword. Every one was on target, the Kedradi's mastery of speed, distance, and wind second to none. Yet, through no more than micro-movements, the Andaren avoided them all.

"Ride!" Aphrandhor commanded.

The Kedradi returned the bow to his back and nestled down into his saddle. The shadows danced about the trio as they rode and rode hard, desperately putting The Dawn Sword's stamina to the test. Thus they moved, a light rushing through the darkness of The Morn Wood, edging further and further away from their pursuer.

When, at last, there was some space between them and the

fabled Andaren, The Green Leaf threw the end of his staff once more over his left shoulder. The spell was almost faster than Gallien could track, but there was no missing its impact or the concussive wave that took the Andaren from his feet. The blast was shortly followed by the sound of thick wood splitting and snapping.

The ground shook when the tree came down.

Drakalis looked back but could no longer see the pale demon in the fading light and rain of leaves and branches. Still, it would be some time yet before the smuggler dared to hope.

While the moon and stars reached for the western horizon, the companions rode ever onwards. They didn't stop until close to midday, when The Morn Wood was a dark smudge on the lower plains behind them. Fields of tough grass and rolling hills stretched out before them in every direction. Gallien recognised its beauty, but where he had once seen a land of opportunity, he now saw a world closing in on them.

A sudden movement caught his eye, turning the smuggler to the lone and pointed boulder that reigned over their hilly rise. Joran cast a heroic stance, his right foot raised to the highest point of the rock while he surveyed the realm. In the calamity of their escape, the cloth about his head had come loose, lost to The Morn Wood. His pointed ears were now clear to see amidst the mop of snow-white hair.

How often did he get to stand so tall without a hood to conceal him? He looked so alive in that moment, vibrantly so. No one could have looked at him and discerned his near-death experience only hours earlier. How quickly he adapted to a life of danger.

Gallien kept his horse's reins in one hand as he moved towards the boulder. "Where are we, Joran?" he asked, as he regularly had on their journeys across Erador.

Having bathed in the light for a while, Joran brought his smile under control. "A day's ride east, perhaps two, would take us to the coast. To The Dawning Isles!"

Mention of the coast brought the sea to Gallien's mind. Though they were far from The Hox, he liked to imagine he could feel the sea air on his face. The smuggler hadn't seen the ocean in a long time, a place he had once considered a realm of freedom. He knew better now. Before his thoughts could darken to the monsters that lurked beneath the waves—before he recalled all too much of Kitrana Voden—Drakalis considered that the boy was right and nodded his head in agreement, if not satisfaction.

"Where would you go from here?" he pressed.

Joran looked out on those rolling hills, but Drakalis knew it was a map of Verda he saw before him. "Hemon is the next port of civilisation," he replied confidently. "But we will not reach it before nightfall," he added, his vision cast back the way they had come. By the look in his eyes it was as if the boy could see The Dawn Sword watching them from the very edge of The Morn Wood.

"You know your way around the world, Master Joran."

The wizard's voice turned Gallien to his left, where the old man approached astride his black horse. "He knows his way around a *map*," the smuggler corrected. "Maps are nothing like the world."

His words deflated Joran, who quietly stepped down from the elevated boulder. His violet eyes flashed over Drakalis just once, enough to inform him that his response had been biting. The smuggler recognised then that it was *his* emotions that drove him to always blanket the boy, to keep him safe, even if it meant keeping him down. Seeing The Dawn Sword again had left him feeling exposed, vulnerable to an enemy he didn't dare to count as dead. There was nothing he could do with that feeling. There was no balm to quiet it nor words to settle those rattled nerves. For all his efforts over the last sixteen years, they were in the middle of it again.

Gallien watched Joran skulk to the other side of their horse. The smuggler desired nothing more than to make amends but he simply couldn't. *Wouldn't*. His statement was damned true and he didn't want the boy getting confused where his knowledge was concerned. He would, however, take the scornful looks if it meant Joran was still alive to give them.

The Kedradi approached from behind, one hand towing his mount by the reins. He looked up at Aphrandhor and voiced some opinion in Ked, his rich baritone seeming appropriate to the hunter's noble appearance.

"Agreed," the wizard said in response. "We should rest."

"What about The Dawn Sword?" Gallien asked. "Shouldn't we keep going?"

It was with great scrutiny that the wizard eyed him from his lofty vantage. "That's right—you've met him before. The Dancing Sword of the Dawn won't trouble us for now. He has lost the element of surprise and his numbers with it."

"He didn't look like he needed the numbers," Drakalis countered. "Wait. How do you know we've crossed paths before?"

"Nor will he risk moving against me so openly in daylight," Aphrandhor added confidently, his staff stealing his attention for a moment.

"You didn't answer my question," Gallien pointed out.

"I know a great many things, Mr Drakalis," the wizard replied cryptically. "Just as I know he will seek allies before moving against us again. Fodder for my magic and a shield to him."

Uncomfortable as it made him feel, Gallien knew when he wasn't going to get a straight answer and so moved on. "Where's he going to find allies? He's more than a thousand miles away from Andara."

The Green Leaf adjusted his hood. "He will find allies aplenty in these dark times, Mr Drakalis. The lines on the map don't mean what they used to."

The Kedradi spoke in his mysterious tongue once more.

"Yes," Aphrandhor agreed again. "The horses will need rest if we are to see the gates of Hemon before the next morn. I should like to be inside its walls sooner rather than later," he intoned.

Gallien turned on the hunter, his frayed nerves needling his attitude and wearing his patience thin. "If he's only going to speak in Ked, I'm only going to speak in Andarneese."

The Kedradi tilted his head, his expression serene as ever. "*If that would please you, northman,*" he said in perfect Andarneese.

Drakalis was taken off guard by the man's quick wit and, perhaps, more so by the word *northman.* He had spent years watering down his accent, chipping away at its edges until he sounded like he could have come from anywhere across Erador's central belt. It was the hair. It *had* to be the hair. The smuggler knew he shouldn't have adopted the style from his youth, shaving round from sideburn to sideburn so he might sweep it back and up into a knot on his crown.

The wizard was grinning with amusement above them both. "Perhaps a proper introduction is required," he suggested. "Gallien Drakalis meet Cob. Oh, and Joran of course," he added. "Cob here is a native of Qalanqath. His blood is that of the *Kedradi*. Though, I believe you have already come to that conclusion."

"Cob?" Gallien echoed, his scepticism obvious. "Just *Cob*? Am I supposed to believe that's your real name?"

"You are free to believe whatever you like," the Kedradi told him peacefully enough. "And it is an honour," Cob continued, his attention having shifted, "to finally meet you, Master Joran. We have been searching for you for some time."

The boy, who had moved away from the horse at the mention of rest, was clearly intrigued by the mention of any *honour*. "Why?" he asked earnestly.

Gallien deliberately side-stepped to put himself between Cob and Joran, his gaze fixed on the hunter from Qalanqath. "No," he intoned, shaking his head. "Not *here*, not *now*." He said no more than that, though his stance suggested the threat of violence.

Cob took the measure of him before looking up to consult the wizard by expression alone. Aphrandhor nodded his agreement with Gallien, at which the Kedradi backed off. Whatever the bond between wizard and hunter, it was becoming clear that one served at the will of the other. The smuggler found it most curious, if not disturbing, that any Kedradi—the proudest and most secretive of people—would ever be beholden to one outside of their culture.

"We can rest there," Joran called out, cutting through the tension.

Gallien followed Joran's arm to an outcropping of rocks that had long ago pushed their way up through the earth and curled over in the manner of a wave.

"Very good, Master Joran," Aphrandhor praised. "I for one could do with a cup of tea."

31
THE SKARAMANGIANS

64 Years Ago…

“Erador invaded because we told them to.”

Those seven words crashed into Daijen like a wall of water, robbing him of thought and reason. His natural reaction was to dismiss the master’s response—he was mistaken or simply lying. This was just another test, he told himself. It was preposterous. Nonsensical. Heresy even. More so it tainted the deaths of every Andaren who had fallen in the war, his parents included.

“I asked if you were prepared,” The Valtorak reminded.

“That’s not the truth,” Daijen managed. “It can’t be. You’re… You’re wrong. You’re *lying*.”

The master of Ka’vairn remained seated, his posture as rigid as his resolve. He wasn’t lying.

Daijen was shaking his head. “You’re saying that Emperor Qeledred—*our* emperor—had the humans invade on purpose. That he sacrificed every soul in Tor Valan to start a *war*.”

“That is not what I said,” The Valtorak corrected evenly. “I said *we*, meaning our fellow Andarens. The emperor had nothing to do with it. Nevertheless, the war was started by the machinations of Andarens, not humans."

"Why?" Disorientated by the revelation, it was the only question Daijen could ask.

"Because of the dragons," the master replied.

It was a second blow that rocked Daijen back. "The war... the war was started because of *dragons*?" He thought of the centuries of bloodshed and death, unable to reconcile it with such a simple and short answer. "Did we even know the dragons existed before the war?"

"Sit down," The Valtorak ordered, his eyes roaming over the chair beside Daijen.

The initiate did so, his muscles moving without conscious thought. Seated now, he looked expectantly at his master, waiting for the next audible blow to erase the foundations he had been standing on all his life.

The Valtorak took a breath, his attention wandering over the open map before settling on Daijen again. "Our enemy knew of dragons long before the war."

Daijen narrowed his eyes. "Our enemy?"

"The dragons are the greatest weapon of the human world," The Valtorak began. "A weapon they have turned against our lands. But it need not be so. The dragons and the humans themselves are not the problem, but a *symptom* of the problem."

Ka'vairn's master paused and lightly tapped the edge of his desk. It seemed clear for the first time that this was a conversation they weren't supposed to be having.

"Our *true* enemy is not so obvious," he continued. "They do not fly banners and their numbers, though legion, are spread thin, where they cannot be seen but their influence is reaching. They, Daijen, are the *real* reason Handuin formed this order. There came no whisper from a god, no *divine* inspiration. He simply saw the face of our enemy and knew they were the true evil we are meant to combat, and the reason *you* and the others must stand above your kin."

It was all too much to make sense of. "I don't understand."

"And you were never supposed to," The Valtorak imparted. "You and thousands of our people were intended to be no more than grunts, fodder in a war that would keep the masses occupied and our attention fixed mindlessly on the east. For centuries, before Erador invaded, ours was a *shadow war* not even the emperor knew about. But for all his efforts, Handuin's attempts to raise an army to combat them was not enough. That is not to say we haven't been a thorn in their side. Unfortunately, their ill intent towards the dragons provided them an opportunity to take out two birds with one stone."

Daijen's mind slotted the next piece of the puzzle into place. "The war."

"Yes," The Valtorak confirmed. "But our enemy held no sway over the Riders. Their reach is unimaginable, but Drakanan, it seems, is further still. They found the king's ear considerably easier to bend. And so they did what they have always done. They turned the wheels of war. With words alone, those few, but powerful, Andarens, had the humans invade our country. It worked tenfold for it not only thinned our numbers and that of the dragons but also kept us so occupied they were able to operate unchecked. Is there a better distraction than war?"

Daijen's hands tightened around the armrests, his enhanced strength threatening the wood. "An entire war. Thousands upon thousands dead. All to... what? Kill off dragons that weren't even threatening us? Distract us?" He could hardly believe it, the thought of it gripping his heart with icy fingers.

"That and more. War is useful to those who know how to wield it, and they have been bringing war to Andara for eons, be it with others or civil wars within our own borders. It masks their intentions. It moves coin from coffer to coffer without notice. It opens doors that might have remained closed to them. This war was their boldest move yet."

"But the dragons posed no threat before the war," Daijen insisted.

"Indeed. *Why* they fear the dragons is unknown. It is equally mystifying as to why they have chosen *now* to go to war with them.

For thousands of years they have been content to let Erador and their dragons exist. Yet, two hundred years ago they sparked a war to eradicate them."

"Who *are* they?" More than anything, Daijen needed the answer to that question and right now.

"As I said, they do not fly banners and they rarely gather in number. But we do know their name."

It was as if The Valtorak's eyes invaded Daijen's mind and drew the answer from his lips. "The Skaramangians."

The master didn't need to affirm Daijen's response, for there could be no other resolution. "We do not know the meaning behind the word," The Valtorak said instead, "only that it is the singular thing that binds them."

"What do they want?"

Again, The Valtorak paused, perhaps working through the barriers he himself had put up around this *true enemy*. "They have tried very hard to conceal the truth of their purpose, portraying a desire for wealth, power, control. But Handuin was taken into the heart of their order, if only for a time. They care little for those things; they are but a means to an end."

That made no sense to Daijen, who failed to see how there could be anything more to fight for. "What end?" he pressed.

"We've never had *all* the answers, Daijen. They're better at keeping secrets than *we* are. What we do know, is that they aren't evil for evil's sake. Nor are they moved by madness alone. They have a *purpose*. Beyond the wholesale slaughter of their own people they are driven by the beliefs of an ancient religion—a cult — that predates most of our recorded history."

Daijen swallowed. "What beliefs?"

The Valtorak held nothing back, his voice clear and his words concise. "The Skaramangians worship the Dark Ones. They have done since before the First Epoch. Since before the Arkalon would have us believe the heavens fell. From their own lips I have heard them confess their secret history; that they fought for the Dark Ones against the very gods."

Somehow, Daijen's ability to form coherent thoughts was

again numbed by the blistering wave of revelation. How could he —or any Andaren—have lived their whole life without knowing there were those among them who worshipped such wretched creatures? Further still, what could draw anyone to worship the evil that was once incarnate.

"You do not believe the words of the Arkalon?"

That sculpted facade seemed to crack, revealing something of an exhausted man beneath the burden of his heavy title. "I give no weight to it," he admitted. "The Dark Ones... the gods... Stories of war that have been exaggerated to make a better tale no doubt."

Daijen had to stop himself from looking around, for they were completely alone in the tower. Instinct, however, was hard to fight. Had The Valtorak voiced such heresy outside of Ka'vairn he would have been arrested and handed over to the clerics for trial.

"What about God Fall?" he had to probe. "Ahnir's body resides there. His bones have given us magic, the same magic that transformed us."

"I have no idea what lies in God Fall," The Valtorak admitted. "Handuin believed it was a god, yes. And so many more after him. But their belief is not my own."

"Then what do you believe?"

The master of Ka'vairn said nothing for a time, his thoughts coalescing. "I believe we don't know everything. I believe there were things walking the earth of Verda before us. If this war keeps up, there will likely be something that replaces us. Perhaps it will be *your* bones, Daijen Saeth, that gift magic to the next people."

It seemed a rather bleak belief, but Daijen had never been one for spreading the Arkalon's words. His own faith had mostly been born out of fear and what genuine belief he had dangled by a thread.

"What I believe doesn't matter," The Valtorak went on. "The Skaramangians believe it. They hold on to one verse in particular." He glanced aside as he recalled the exact words. "*Upon the hour of Reclamation, the darkness will rise to meet the light, to quash it, to conquer it, to consume it. The world will shake again, cast in the shadows of the Dark Ones. Should they find victory in that hour, those loyal to the black seed will know life eternal and hold sway over those fated to the Abyss.*"

He paused to take a breath. "It is that blind faith that drives them, that sees them commit the worst of crimes against our people. Whether or not there is any truth to their dark beliefs, the Vahlken cannot permit them to spill so much blood."

Daijen looked away as his mind latched onto a thread that he felt compelled to pull. "The Skaramangians told Erador to invade," he began, returning to The Valtorak's first revelation. "How could they do that?"

"Since the war started, we have learned that their order has grown beyond the confines of Andara. For generations now, there have been humans who call themselves Skaramangians, their lives and beliefs turned to the Dark Ones. *How* they have influenced the humans to begin with is beyond me, though the lives of men are fleeting. It makes them easily corrupted." The Valtorak paused again to make certain Daijen was looking at him before he continued. "The same can be said of *dwarves*."

Daijen thought of Mordrith and her parting words. "*I warn ye, ye might not want to see me again.*"

She was a Skaramangian.

For their brief time together, however, he would have said she was a goodly person. He had seen nothing of her that matched with The Valtorak's description of a Skaramangian— a worshipper of the Dark Ones.

"Why?" he asked, the question burning in him. "Why worship the creatures that ended the gods?"

The Valtorak closed the leather-bound book, its wodge of pages coming together with a resounding *clap*. "Because they hold to the Arkalon's words," he said, sounding exasperated, "to its promise of life eternal and power over others."

"But it also talks of Reclamation. Of the Dark Ones' defeat and the return of the heavens."

"The Arkalon talks of the future as if it is set upon scales, the weight of each outcome yet to be determined," The Valtorak explained. "It records as much because it was seen through the Helm of Ahnir. *But*," he emphasised, "the helm reveals *a* future, not *the* future. It can be changed, guided, if one knows the many possibilities."

That fact alone cleared Daijen's mind of clear thought. *A future?* How much of their peoples' faith was based on the Helm of Ahnir? On the words it had inspired in the Arkalon? It was all no more than a *possibility*.

"It's madness," he uttered, feeling so lost in his own culture.

"Madness is hard to reason with. Should you succeed, you will find only madness yourself. Focus on the facts. Follow them to reasonable ends and expose the truth. Such is the duty of any Vahlken."

"Who's under their influence?" he had to ask, eager to get away from the Arkalon.

"The highest levels of our clerics for certain. The warlocks too I would imagine."

"And the emperor knows nothing of this?" It seemed inconceivable to Daijen that the most powerful being in all of Andara could not be privy to this infection.

"I cannot say," the master lamented. "If not, then his closest advisors, perhaps a few of the warmasters. The archjusticiar even. Beyond them, they will have hidden their believers amongst our own, appearing as no more than common soldiers, imperators or castellans... a *messenger guard* even."

The latter caught Daijen off guard and his muscles tensed.

"Fear not, I do not suspect you," The Valtorak reported. "Anymore," he added, his tone a notch lower. "The Skaramangians wouldn't send such a naive pup into our midst. A discarded princess perhaps..."

Both statements were hard to swallow, though the added detail concerning Ilithranda begged more questions. Rather than ask direct questions about her past, Daijen focused on the matter at hand. "You suspect Ilithranda was planted here?"

"The Skaramangians have attempted to send *worthy* soldiers to join our ranks in the past. It is why Ka'vairn must adhere so closely to its traditions, to its secrets. They must be weeded out through trial and pain."

Daijen thought of his first time in The Valtorak's office, when the master had told him why the Vahlken are needed and why Handuin started their order in the first place. "Is that why you lied to me all those years ago? To all of us."

"I told you the truth, *mostly*. We *are* to protect the people, not those who govern them or even the land on which they live. The *people*. The Skaramangians pose the biggest threat to that mandate. At the very least their ancient beliefs will tear Andara apart."

"How could something so old and evil have been allowed to thrive?" The question left his lips without thought.

"No one wants to look in the shadows," the master stated. "We alone must tread where others dare not. We alone must bring the light." Something about his tone suggested they weren't his words, leading Daijen to wonder if they were, perhaps, passed down from Handuin himself.

Daijen looked back at The Valtorak, their eyes connecting again. "When were you going to tell me any of this? Do the others know?"

"Besides you, Kastiek, and the Vahlken who patrol our eastern borders, the only others who know that name are the Skaramangians themselves. Like everything else, the truth is earned, Daijen Saeth. Initiates are brought into the real war when they are capable of fighting in it. That is to say: when they are *Vahlken*. I suppose that brings us round to the dilemma of *you*," he added pointedly. "You have not earned this knowledge, yet you are burdened by it all the same." The Valtorak stood up. "You have your dwarf friend to thank for that. I'm hoping you have come to the conclusion that *she* is a Skaramangian and, therefore, your enemy."

Daijen nodded in agreement, feeling as naive as The Valtorak had previously remarked.

"Did she know who you are?" the master enquired, his hands gesturing to Ka'vairn itself.

"She knew what I am to become."

"Yet she did not try to kill you," The Valtorak mused. "Curious."

Thinking back, it seemed to Daijen that Mordrith had been conflicted regarding her part in the Skaramangian order. He said as much to The Valtorak, who absorbed the information as he wandered over to the window.

"Most curious." His thoughts remained his own for a time. "And she was lost? You could not find her again?"

Daijen knew what he should say and more, but he desired some degree of control in the chaos unravelling about him. "She made for the mountains. She will be across the river by now."

"A pity," he whispered, as if he was in counsel with himself. "In all my years I have never known one of their order to be... *conflicted.* We might have learned something." After another moment of silence, The Valtorak turned to Daijen again. "What to do with you then."

Daijen got up from his chair and genuflected before The Valtorak. "I will do as commanded, Master."

"That you will," he replied without a doubt. "Your training will continue as it has. You are to say nothing to the others."

Daijen hesitated but still found the courage to meet his master's eyes. "Can I do nothing to help?"

"*No,*" The Valtorak declared firmly. "Hear me, Daijen Saeth, when I say you are *useless* to our cause. Our enemy is everywhere, and even a Vahlken can fall to a knife in the back," he went on. "You would be dead before you reached The Saible."

Daijen took the emotional blow and bowed his head again, sure that his master's words would stay with him long after he left the office.

The Valtorak took a breath and moved to stand a little closer to the initiate. "Part of your duty is to investigate, to ask questions. You've always been good at that," he specified, his tone softer now, if tainted by a hint of irritation. "Survive the trials and your time will come. Until then, train hard and train *smart*. Listen to Kastiek."

Daijen swallowed his pride. "I will, Master."

"Very good." The Valtorak returned to his side of the desk,

leaving Daijen on one knee. "Now leave. You have a cloak to prepare."

"Master." The initiate rose and made for the door without another word.

"Daijen," The Valtorak called, giving him pause on the threshold. "Trust no one. Suspect everyone."

32
THE SWAMPS OF MORTHIL

GRARFATH STOOD IN AWE, HORROR EVEN. HIS EYES GORGED ON THE monster. A Three-headed Dread Serpent Yamnomora had called it. He thanked the All-Fathers it was dead. The smith had never seen anything like it. Creatures of such ilk had long been purged from the halls of Morthil, making dwarves the only real threat to other dwarves.

Damned if it didn't stink.

Grarfath was sure the stench had woken him. Still, Yamnomora's words had been the greater revelation, yanking his attention from the beast.

"I did what?" he asked, his memory a blur.

Yamnomora gestured casually at the demolished serpent head. "Ye threw the hammer, an' *hard*."

The smith looked over his shoulder, to the spot where the rest of the monster's head had apparently fallen from the sky. He licked his lips, fighting all he knew of the world as he tried to put the scene together. "So, the hammer can... what did ye call it? Port! It can *port* without me holdin' it? I jus' 'ave to throw it at somethin'?"

Yamnomora crouched by the ruined head and began chiselling away at the gum with her knife. "How do ye think yer mother was able to send the hammer into the mines?" she asked by way of an answer. "It were the only way to make certain they didn' get hold o' it." The determined dwarf gave the fang one strong tug and the root came free. "That'll do," she said happily enough. "Bludgeon!"

The Warhog was quick to heed its master's call and even quicker to take the large fang from her hand. The animal immediately settled down and began gnawing on its prize, like a dog with a bone.

"When ye say *they*, ye're talkin' abou' 'em... Skara... Skaramangians!"

Yamnomora grabbed him and roughly so. "Keep such words to yerself," she instructed, her eyes shifting towards their third companion.

Grarfath turned to regard the woman seated by their pitiful fire, her legs crossed and arms wrapped around her knees. Raven hair fell to just below her shoulders, framing an angular and perfectly symmetrical face. Her skin, though awfully pale, could not be compared to the silvery chalk of the Andarens. Such features, however, conjured images of their kind.

Then there were her eyes. The smith in him—who saw the detail in all things—was sure they were slightly larger than the norm, though it certainly wasn't obvious. What jewels they were, like rings of sapphire. Though he could see aspects of beauty, to his dwarven eyes she was not beautiful. Too lean. Too smooth. And where was the beard?

"Ye've spoken to her?" he enquired.

"Not really. We're to be partin' ways soon anyway."

"Where's she goin' to go?" the smith was compelled to voice. "Where did she even come from?" He recalled her striking the roof of the mine, expelled from the jet of water with some force.

Yamnomora shot him a look that suggested he was being stupid. "She came from under the mountains, Grarfath. She ain' human."

Of course that made sense to the smith, given what he had witnessed and what he had heard of humans, but it didn't help to inform him who or *what* she actually was.

"If she ain' human then..." Grarfath shrugged helplessly. "Well, what is she?"

"She's one o' 'em fish people," Yamnomora answered plainly. "I've heard the legends but only ever seen the monsters."

Grarfath's jaw had dropped. "Fish people?" he repeated in a hushed tone. Quite suddenly, the smith wished to return to The Morthil Mountains.

"I'm a *Nimean*, actually." The announcement drew the attention of both dwarves. "And you're not whispering either."

"Ye keep yer pointed ears out o' our business," Yamnomora snapped.

Grarfath narrowed his eyes but failed to see any *pointed ears* through her black hair. "So... So, it's true then? Ye from the *sea*?"

There seemed some reservation about her, but the so-called *Nimean* eventually nodded her head.

"Why did ye burst through the mines? Is it an *invasion*?" he asked suddenly, fearing what they left behind.

"That wasn't... That was just an accident. Well..." She paused. "I was actually fleeing for my life."

Her answer brought the smith a step closer. "Fleeing what?"

The woman glanced at the Dread Serpent behind the dwarves. "A monster," she uttered.

Yamnomora cut in before Grarfath could follow up with more questions. "A'right, a'right. There's enough light in the sky to see the way now. Let's be off. *Separately*."

"Wait," Grarfath demanded, holding out a hand to stop his dwarven companion from forging ahead. "I want to see it."

"See what?"

"Where it happened," the smith replied. "Where me mother died. I *need* to see it."

The hard features of Yamnomora's face softened somewhat. "Oh. *That's* why we're 'ere."

"Ye had jus' told me she were murdered 'ere," Grarfath said by way of an explanation. "That's no easy thing to forget. Please. Take me there."

The dwarven warrior looked away, her gaze wandering over

the gloomy and cold horizon. "As ye wish. But we should leave now. We're not meant for these lands. Our destination lies in the east, in Erador."

Grarfath blinked. "Erador?" he questioned, trailing her back to the camp now. "We're goin' to Erador? Ye must be jokin'! There's a war on, ye know. A war! We can' jus' go walkin' into man's world! An' why are we goin' there anyway?"

"One thing at a time, Underborn."

"*I* need to reach Erador," the Nimean spoke up, rising to her feet.

"Oh no," Yamnomora responded, her hand waving. "I've told ye—head east an' find the road. Beyond that, I don' care."

"Easy now," Grarfath bade, taken in by the Nimean's obvious plight.

"No," Yamnomora voiced, quick to turn to the smith. "We don' need fish problems on top o' our own." The dwarf began to pack sundries from about the camp while reeling off some list in her head. "We need to reach Erador. Got to get word to The Green Leaf. Got to keep that damned hammer out o' dangerous hands..."

"I won't get in your way," the Nimean reassured, her words aimed at Grarfath more than Yamnomora. "I might even be able to help. This isn't my first time up here. I used to work with a smuggler in fact. I could help to find a way into Erador."

"*I* can get us into Erador," the stubborn dwarf responded. "Ye need to be hittin' the road. It's *that* way."

The Nimean became more animated, moving now to intercept Yamnomora. "I won't survive these lands. The Andarens won't stop to see what I am—they'll just see a *human*."

"Ye'll do no better with us. An' besides, ye're likely to get *us* killed. The Andarens might turn a blind eye to our presence 'ere an' there, but they won' take kindly to a pair o' dwarves escortin' the enemy."

"I'm nobody's enemy," the Nimean stated.

"Like ye said: that won' stop 'em. Now get out o' me way."

The woman's demeanour held for another second before her shoulders sagged in defeat and she stepped aside.

Grarfath could only shrug in her gaze. "I'm sorry, lass. Wait. I don' even know yer name. I'm Grarfath—"

"No," Yamnomora insisted. "No names."

"I already know your names," the Nimean pointed out.

"Well we don' need to know yers." The dwarf shot eyes at the smith. "Names breed attachments, an' I don' need ye gettin' attached to baggage that *will* get us killed."

"My name is Kitrana Voden," the lady from the sea boldly declared. "My friends call me Kit."

Quite deliberate was the smile Grarfath shot Yamnomora's way. "I'm Grarfath, son o' Thronghir, o' the guild Underborn. It's a pleasure to meet ye, Miss Voden." The smith closed his fist and presented the outside of his forearm to the Nimean, who looked wholly unsure what to do in response. "Oh, it's a dwarven greetin'," he explained. Kitrana mimicked his action and Grarfath was able to knock his forearm against her own. "Well met," he said.

Yamnomora was shaking her head. "Ye're a dolt," she told him.

Grarfath ignored the insult and glanced beyond his dwarven companion, to the saddlebags attached to Bludgeon. "Ye got a cloak in there?"

Yamnomora's jaw clenched and unclenched. "Not to fit her."

"Jus' give her whatever ye've got," the smith instructed, already exhausted by the argument to come.

"I don't need it," Kit said in an appeasing tone.

"Ye hear that?" Yamnomora asked. "She don' need it. I imagine this is a hot summer's day compared to where ye've come from."

"Give her the cloak, " Grarfath repeated. "It'll help to conceal her some."

Indeed, the Nimean's attire was just as extraordinary as her biology, the clothing itself consisting of tight wraps and bindings that clung to her like a second skin. In the dawn light, the material glistened as a fish might when the sun catches its scales.

Yamnomora soon produced a cloak from one of her bags. It was thin and frayed at the edges with dotted patches of hard mud. It was pitiful compared to Grarfath's cloak of white fur or

Yamnomora's of light brown fur. Furthermore, it draped no lower than Kitrana's knees. Still, it concealed her hands and would do the same for her face when she pulled the hood up.

"There lies the edge o' me generosity, *Kitrana Voden*. Be on yer way."

Kit maintained her stance while she took in both dwarves. "Thank you," she said quietly.

Grarfath watched her, bare-footed, as she navigated the hard patches of ground to depart their camp. Fish person or not, she had changed his mind, if not his heart, on the matter in a short space of time. His initial fear, disgust even, had been transformed to curiosity, fascination in fact. Kitrana Voden was, quite possibly, the best thing to have happened on what could otherwise have been called the worst day of his life.

"This doesn' feel right," he voiced.

Yamnomora frowned before realising what he was talking about. It seemed the dwarf had already forgotten about the Nimean. "Don' be taken in, Grarfath. We ain' meant to trespass in each other's worlds. How many humans an' Andarens taken from their precious *ships* can attest to that? She ain' like us. She ain' even *close* to bein' like us."

Grarfath failed to see why that should matter, but he kept his opinion to himself. After all, it seemed all of his opinions came from a place of naivety. It was the result of a sheltered life, he knew.

A far cry from his mother's life apparently.

Quite resigned, he turned away from Kit. "Jus' take me to where it happened."

Trudging through The Swamps of Morthil was a slow and arduous task made all the harder by the large pack Grarfath had slung over his back. While his strength was second to none, his stamina over long distances was wanting. Even Bludgeon, burdened by

Yamnomora's saddle, supplies, two axes, and draping chainmail made the trek look easy.

"Is it much further?" he asked, bewildered by the sheer size of the swamps.

"No," Yamnomora replied, her hand leading the Warhog by the reins.

Grarfath adjusted the pack on his back and spared a moment to look over his shoulder. Kitrana was still following them from a distance, her lithe form failing to be hidden entirely behind the scrawny trees of the swamp. Yamnomora had taken notice of the Nimean some hours earlier and—to the smith's surprise—had responded with no more than an exasperated sigh.

"Over 'ere," the dwarven warrior beckoned, taking a jagged path between two bodies of water.

Grarfath took in the area at a glance. They had reached the base of The Morthil Mountains' eastern face, where the ground finally reached for the ancient stone without a break. The smith was no warrior, but he recognised the signs of battle from the area's edge.

A sword—a dwarven sword—stood partially buried in the earth. A spattering of arrows littered the flat ground, suggesting the quarry had been on the move. The midday sun revealed the blade of a two-handed axe abandoned across the clearing. Then there was the blood.

Grarfath shrugged off his pack while his eyes shifted from blood stain to blood stain. It marked the small rocks and darkened the mossy ground. There were even splatters across the mountain stone on the far side of the clearing.

For all the bloodshed and obvious death, there was but a single corpse.

The smith approached it, his feet drawn to the site as if by some unseen force. From a distance it was impossible to identify the body as anything other than a dead dwarf. Upon reaching it, the smith knew immediately that it wasn't his mother. Though the body had been ravaged by animals in parts and decay had set in, what remained of the skin revealed a considerably lighter tone than that of Mordrith's.

"Where are the rest?" he asked, looking around.

"In the bellies o' monsters I suspect," Yamnomora was quick to reply. "I'm amazed this one is still 'ere."

Her words brought on a crushing weight that demanded Grarfath fall to his knees. The smith withstood the grief, however, and remained on his feet, left there with the horrifying image of his mother's body being dragged into the swamp by some thing. It made her final resting place all the worse.

"She should be in the stone," Grarfath muttered, his dark eyes flitting over The Morthil Mountains that rose up in front of them.

"Oh, she is," Yamnomora said reassuringly, almost surprised by his assumption that Mordrith wasn't in the stone.

"She is?"

"O' course she is, ye dolt! Do ye think I watched Mordrith Underborn take her last breath an' then jus' walked away?"

There seemed a few reasons why that might have been the more likely case, but Grarfath only voiced the one. "Ye jus' don', ye know... Ye're not one for traditions is all."

Yamnomora gave a mirthless laugh. "Deduced that after a day in me company did ye?"

"Well, ye know..." The smith gestured at his own beard while observing her lack of one.

"I shave me beard jus' as Mordrith did," she retorted.

Grarfath was visibly stunned by the claim. "Me mother would never 'ave shaved her beard."

"On all the profit in Morthil she did," Yamnomora countered. "We spent a lot o' time in Erador ye know. Women folk there don' 'ave beards. They can' even grow 'em!"

Grarfath was nodding along if for no other reason than to hurry the dwarf along. "Where is she then?"

Yamnomora directed him with her eyes alone, turning the smith to a collection of rocks piled upon each other. They had been so piled on the rise, where The Morthil Mountains extended to meet the swamp like the roots of a great tree.

Seeing his mother made one with the mountains again brought about a sense of calm that Grarfath hadn't expected to feel. Without voicing that emotion, the dwarf began the short ascent so he might actually touch the stones that covered her.

"How did it happen?" he asked quietly, one hand resting atop the nearest rock.

Yamnomora rounded the site. "I was waylaid," she said, with an almost tangible heaviness about her. "We were to meet on the road. I found her camp—abandoned. *Their* tracks were easy enough to see," she elaborated with venom. "By the time I got 'ere, Mordrith had already killed most o' 'em. She was damned savage with that hammer."

Grarfath was shaking his head. He had known his mother for centuries and known her well—she was not a fighter. Not once had he seen her raise a violent hand to another. Not once had she wielded a weapon in the workshop and shown even an ounce of proficiency.

Savage?

It made no sense to the smith. "Ye were with her at the end," he stated, his true question threaded between the words.

"Aye. She told me to find ye. That only *ye* could retrieve the hammer."

"How did she die?" he asked, deciding that Yamnomora only recognised blunt language.

The dwarven warrior took a breath; the memory a sting perhaps. "She took a blade to the lungs. I came across her not long after. Like I said: I don' know which o' the kuds it were that delivered the blow, only that the order came from Tharg."

Grarfath could see the wretch standing in front of him, right there in his workshop. How could he have been so close to the dwarf that had ordered his mother's death and known nothing?

"Ye said Tharg were a Skaramangian," the smith began. "Like me mother. Why would he want her dead if they were from the same... guild?"

"It ain' a guild," Yamnomora specified. "It's more o' a cult. Mordrith were the one that..." The dwarf trailed off, her attention drawn back to the clearing and the exposed corpse. "For the love o' the All-Fathers," she cursed.

Grarfath turned around to spy the Nimean crouched beside the dead dwarf, her form mostly concealed within the cloak. It seemed she was looking at the corpse's left arm, her fingers holding back the sleeve.

"If ye're lookin' for an axe to the head ye've come to the right place, fish lady!" Yamnomora was already bounding down the rise and heading for Bludgeon.

Kitrana stood up, her fair features contorted with confusion. "Why does this dwarf bear that mark?" she demanded, her finger pointing down at the arm.

"I'll give ye a mark," the stout warrior vowed, her hand yanking one of the axes from the saddle.

Grarfath was quick to leave his mother's resting place and put himself between the two women. "Easy!" he cried, his arm strong enough to keep Yamnomora back.

"Why does this dwarf bear that mark?" the Nimean asked again, though her tone had adopted a sense of urgency now.

"What mark?" The smith approached her while keeping one eye on Yamnomora over his shoulder.

Kitrana crouched again and roughly tugged the corpse's sleeve back. Grarfath gave it his full attention and lowered himself to one knee to better inspect what he could now see was a tattoo on the dwarf's inside arm. It was a vertical line that almost connected elbow to wrist. In the centre of the line sat two four-sided diamonds, their tips touching in the middle of the tattoo. It looked to be a rune of some kind to Grarfath's eyes, though it was no rune he recognised.

"What's it to ye?" Yamnomora challenged, her axe hefted in two hands.

"I know this mark," Kitrana answered.

Something about Yamnomora changed in that moment, as if the dwarf fell away, a facade dropped by the killing machine that merely wore Yamnomora like a skin. "Grarfath. Move."

The smith knew that axe would swing the very second he was

clear of it. “Why don’ ye jus’ put the axe down an’ we can talk abou’ this first.”

“She knows their mark,” Yamnomora replied, her knuckles paling around the axe’s iron haft. “There’s only two kinds o’ people, Grarfath, an’ since I don’ know her, that makes her one o’ *’em.*”

“A Skaramangian?” the smith questioned incredulously. “She ain’ even a dwarf!”

Yamnomora groaned. “Yer like a babe!” she spat. “The Skaramangians ain’ bound by any race. They’re *everywhere*!”

“What’s a Skaramangian?” Kitrana Voden enquired, and on her feet since Yamnomora was becoming all the more threatening.

“*Stop speakin’ in man’s tongue!*” Yamnomora instructed in dwarven. “*Step aside, Grarfath, an’ I’ll chop their ranks down by one more kud.*”

“Would ye jus’ take a breath,” Grarfath barked, his language still that of the humans. “She don’ even know what ye’re talkin’ abou’! Hells, *I* don’ even know what ye’re talkin’ abou’!”

Yamnomora took a step towards the Nimean, her axe dangerously high. “There’s nothin to talk abou’! She jus’ admitted to knowin’ the mark!”

“If she really were a Skaramangian,” the smith posed, “why would she admit as much?”

That stumped the dwarven warrior, who looked from Grarfath to Kitrana. “It’s a trick,” she decided. “They’re damned crafty buggers!”

“That still don’ make no sense!” Grarfath argued, his wide frame firmly planted between them. “Jus’ put the axe down,” he ordered.

Yamnomora’s chest was heaving, her eyes large and wild. Her jaw clenched and unclenched as her thoughts tumbled over themselves. Finally, she threw the axe into the ground beside her, where the haft remained upright and within easy grasp.

“Speak then,” she pressed, her gaze fixed on Kitrana.

Her hood still shading her face, the Nimean glanced once at the tattoo beside her bare foot. "This mark is from *my* world," she explained. "How has it come to be on the skin of a dwarf?"

"Ye're askin' *me* questions!" Yamnomora growled. "Ye should assume ye're testifyin' to save yer life."

"I am a *battle maiden*," Kitrana declared boldly. "And I will not be threatened by the likes of you."

Yamnomora didn't appear phased in the slightest. "Ye're a *what*?"

"What's a battle maiden?" Grarfath asked for them both.

The Nimean's discomfort was obvious, though not so obvious as the threat that Yamnomora posed. "It's a... I'm a..." Kitrana seemed to deflate right there on her feet. "It's a guardian of sorts," she tried again.

"What are ye to guard?" the smith asked.

The Nimean looked at him with those vivid blue eyes. "It has no significance in your world," she said, before her gaze dropped to the tattoo again. "At least I didn't think it did," she added absently.

"Speak plainly or speak to me axe."

It was with resolve that Kitrana looked upon the dwarven warrior. "I was to protect a sword—an ancient sword. Others like me have done so for millennia. My entire order was built around it. *That*," she stated, her finger pointing to the tattoo, "is the mark of our order. We adopted it from the sword itself—that rune is on its hilt."

Yamnomora remained perfectly still, though only for a second. When she started forward, the heavy axe was returned to her grip, along with her expression of grim determination.

Grarfath cried out and thrust himself between, his hands raised to keep both of them at bay. "Stop!" he yelled.

"She protects Skaramangian artefacts!" Yamnomora pointed out. "Ye heard it from her own lips! Their mark is her *banner*! Get out o' me way!"

"I have no idea what you're talking about!" Kitrana asserted.

Grarfath reclaimed the hand keeping the Nimean at bay and used both to keep Yamnomora back. "See! She don' know anythin' abou' 'em!"

"Not all o' 'em do!" the dwarf shot back. "Some pledge their allegiance for coin or power! An' some are jus' plain ignorant! Whatever her reasons, she serves the Skaramangians, Grarfath. That means she serves evil, evil that I am sworn to destroy!"

"My order was brought about to keep the world *safe*," Kitrana voiced. "The sword I protect holds unimaginable power. Much like that," she added, looking to the hammer Grarfath had left beside his pack.

Yamnomora eyed the hammer before a flash of fierce curiosity crossed her face. "Where is this sword ye speak o'? I would see it."

The Nimean looked pained. "I lost it," she confessed.

"Ye lost it?" the dwarf echoed. "Some guardian ye are."

Anger creased Kitrana's features. "You know nothing of what I speak, of what I've truly lost."

"Pff! I probably know more abou' it than ye do, *battle maiden*. Ye don' even know who ye really serve."

"Battle maidens serve no one," the Nimean told her. "Like me, my sisters pledge their allegiance to each other alone. Our mandate is to safeguard the sword of..." If it was revelation that settled over her it was not easy to bear. "We are to protect the sword of *Skara*," she eventually finished.

Yamnomora shrugged, the revelation not shared. "Well, I ain' ever heard o' that, but I'd bet both me axes its connected to the *Skara*mangians," she said, emphasising part of the name.

Kitrana moved away, her world knocked perhaps.

"A'right, a'right," Grarfath intervened. "I'm abou' done with all this. It's time to lay it all out." His words were directed at Yamnomora. "I'm not leavin' this damned swamp until ye've told me everythin'. An' I mean *everythin'*. That goes for ye too," he added, looking to Kitrana.

Once again, Yamnomora slammed her axe into the ground. "Fine," she grumbled. "Where would ye like me to start?"

Grarfath considered the question before looking to his mother's grave. Though he was certain there were better places to begin, he could think only of Mordrith Underborn's tale, for hers had now become his.

33
DEFEAT

60 Years Ago...

To the sound of the running stream, Daijen Saeth moved through the ritual of his fighting routine. His shogue, a hooked blade on the end of a fine rope, whipped through the air, completing loops and sweeping arcs. Upon his shoulders he wore a cloak of light brown fur, though its considerable weight did nothing to slow him down.

And so, with his breath spilling into the winter air, he leapt from rock to rock, committed to a dance that would deliver death to any and all within range. As it was, the steel of his hook cut through naught but air and dirt as his mane of white hair flicked wildly about him.

Even after four years of being allowed to train with weapons, the feel of it in his hands was exhilarating. The shogue especially was an exciting weapon for it extended his reach which, when combined with his uncanny sense of balance and strength, made him all the more deadly.

How he longed to use his decades of skills on the *enemy*.

For the last four years, since The Valtorak had informed him of their true foe, that word had stumped the initiate. Their enemy, though clearly the humans from any Andaren's point of view, was not so clear. In fact, there was only one person in all the realm he knew for sure was his enemy.

Daijen sent a ripple through the rope, releasing the hook from its place in the hard earth, and tugged the blade back to his hand where he could coil the weapon about his arm. All the while, his gaze was fixed on the narrow strip of land that divided the stream. It was still strewn with foreign boulders and broken rocks from four years earlier.

How many times had he returned to this site? How many hunting trips had been extended so he might wait and watch? In four years Mordrith Underborn had yet to materialise. Such a length of time meant little to an Andaren, who could live at least a hundred times that, but it had felt an eternity to Daijen. He had learned a grave truth from the master of Ka'vairn before being instructed to never speak of it, their conversation meant for Vahlken alone.

Such an instruction had lent more weight to the isolation Daijen lived with. Enemy or not, he craved the opportunity to speak with the dwarf on the matter.

But it seemed he was out of time again. The island remained dormant and he was expected back at the fortress and with food and water no less. The initiate sighed and turned to his war horse, who had sat quietly for days and watched him practise Kastiek's routines.

"Perhaps next time," he said to the old war horse, his words steaming the air.

In the same moment he kicked snow and dirt over the fire, the air cracked behind him, as if thunder had been summoned so far from the sky. Daijen spun on his heel, his hope sparking into flame. There she was. Mordrith Underborn and with hammer in hand.

She was not alone.

Another dwarf had ported with her, his intentions undoubtedly violent. It was with a grimace that he barrelled into

Mordrith, taking them both to the ground amidst fresh rocks brought with them from the depths of Morthil.

Daijen dashed to intervene, his arm dropping to allow the shogue to unravel and the hook to hang free. Swift as he was, however, the matter was finished by the time he had splashed through the stream and reached the island.

Mordrith had come out of their tussle on top and brought her hammer to bear, the haft placed against her enemy's throat. One strong shove crushed the dwarf's windpipe, ending his fight. It was, ultimately, the hammer head that ended the brutal affair. When Mordrith finally rose to her feet, she unceremoniously yanked the weapon from the dwarf's skull and wiped the blood from her chin.

"Daijen Saeth," she said through laboured breath. "Forgive me intrusion into yer woods."

The Andaren might have replied had he not spotted a third dwarf on the ground—at least, it was half of a third dwarf. He was missing everything below the ribcage, though what should have been a gory wound was, in fact, scorched by an intense heat. At a glance, Daijen discerned the circular edge of the hammer's perimeter, a perimeter one poor dwarf had only partially crossed before Mordrith ported.

"Put the hammer down," he insisted, his voice calm but commanding.

Mordrith hesitated, her eyes shifting to scrutinise the landscape in the setting sun. "Ah, so ye did speak to yer masters after all."

"I did. And I would appreciate it if you put the hammer to one side."

Mordrith adjusted her grip on the weapon, considering. "I'll put it down, lad, but it stays close."

Daijen found that acceptable and nodded his agreement.

"Perhaps ye could discard whatever that is," the dwarf posed, her dark eyes landing on the shogue.

The Andaren began coiling the weapon. "I have a camp," he offered.

"Ye got any food?"

Daijen paused in his departure, fighting a smile. "I do," he confirmed.

"Well this day might end well after all," Mordrith remarked, stepping over the dead dwarf.

Settled around the smoking remains of the fire, their weapons put aside, Daijen made a point to look back at the body and a half they had left in the twilight. "Friends of yours?"

Mordrith was already seeing to a new fire, as if they had never left their original camp four years ago. "Maybe once, aye. It's amazing how quickly friends can turn into enemies though, eh?"

Daijen discovered her already looking at him as she made her comment. "Were we ever friends?" he asked lightly.

"Are we enemies, Daijen Saeth?" Mordrith countered.

"It was you who declared us so," he reminded.

"An' did yer master confirm as much?" The dwarf created a spark and blew new life into the fire.

"If you are a Skaramangian then yes, we are enemies."

Mordrith moved her dreadlocks to one side and tilted her head so the initiate could see the patch of skin behind her right ear. There he saw a small tattoo—a vertical line with a pair of four-sided diamonds in the middle. It wasn't a glyph or a sigil he recognised.

"All Skaramangians are so marked," the dwarf informed him. "Ye'll find identical tattoos on those kuds," she added, flicking her head towards the corpses.

Daijen had become quite adept at controlling his expressions during his years in Ka'vairn, a skill that allowed him to conceal his confusion. "They were Skaramangians as well?"

"Aye. That's two ye can cross off yer list, eh?" Without asking, the dwarf began rummaging through the Andaren's bag of supplies. "Ye've not got much," she complained.

"I've been here a while," he explained dryly.

"I've been back a couple o' times since our first meet," she said offhandedly. "We must 'ave missed each other."

"Apparently," Daijen replied, working hard to keep his stream of questions from bursting forth. "Why would you kill your own?" he had to ask, that particular question having risen to the top of his very long list.

Mordrith regarded the bodies that were steeped in long shadow now. "Ye weren' the only one that's learned a few truths in the passin' years."

Daijen's eyes narrowed on the dwarf. "And what truths did *you* learn?"

"I learned the truth o' what it *really* means to be a Skaramangian," Mordrith replied grimly.

The initiate's stony expression slipped for just a second, revealing his confusion. "You didn't know what it meant?"

Mordrith shrugged. "There are many layers to the order—rank upon rank. The higher up ye are, the more ye know. At my level, it's all grunt work. It were the same for me father—he brought me into the fold as it were."

Daijen couldn't believe what he was hearing. There were Skaramangians who didn't know what they were a part of. "What did you think you were doing then?"

"That's a complicated question," she told him. "What do ye actually know o' me kin?"

The question surprised Daijen, who could only call upon general knowledge. "You're legendary weapon makers. You can do anything with steel or stone. You have the only supply of silvyr in the realm..." The Andaren could have reeled off more from the list but he sensed the extent of his knowledge was miles away from what Mordrith was asking.

"Me father told me we were fightin' for what we once were," she said seriously. "Our work within the order would eventually restore Morthil to its grandeur, to a time o' the All-Fathers, before everythin' was done in the name o' *profit* an' *success*. There's stories o' such times, o' course. Me pa used to read 'em to me. He used to say that faith bred heroes." Mordrith gave a mirthless laugh. "Now such a title is only bestowed upon the most successful o' dwarves, those who bring in the most profit to their guild. Instead o' strivin' for immortality in the heavens, we look to the stone an' those that can afford the biggest statues. It's a soulless existence."

Daijen let the crackling fire have its moment between them. "What *was* that work?" he pressed. "What could you possibly do to restore such an era?"

"The commands that filtered down to me an' mine were simple, if unbelievable." The dwarf looked to the hammer. "We were to find *that*."

"Find it? You mean it was already forged."

"Forged and lost to time," Mordrith confirmed. "A *lot* o' time," she emphasised. "In our legends, it's known as The Anther, a weapon once wielded by the greatest o' heroes—a hero most believe is jus' a myth." The dwarf looked wistfully at the flames. "Duun, son o' Darl," she declared. "O' course, I thought the higher-ups were mad, but still we committed ourselves to the work. I led the minin' operation that, ultimately, put The Anther in me hands."

Daijen absorbed her every word as patiently as he could, but he needed more, his hunger for knowledge gnawing away at his bones. "What was the purpose in finding The Anther?"

"I asked that meself," Mordrith said. "Askin' questions ain' exactly encouraged though. Still, they deigned to answer: we were to make a new hero, one that could pave the way back to the beginnin'. Such a hero, o' course, would need a weapon to match."

"It was a lie," Daijen surmised, knowing roughly where her story ended.

"Oh aye. A damned big one." Mordrith paused to drink from the initiate's waterskin. "The Anther weren' the only thing we found down there," she added gravely.

"Down where?"

The dwarf snorted. "There ain' no more down, lad. Flat bottom o' the world we were. The Anther were jus' sittin' there beside it."

Daijen leaned forward. "Beside what?"

"Even to ye it would 'ave been a Giant," she described. "So old its bones were black. It had four arms an' a head like no other. I can tell ye, I were glad it were naught but bones."

"A monster?"

"Maybe. Though I've never known a monster's bones to be engraved with runes."

Everything stopped for Daijen Saeth. If the dwarf continued speaking he was no longer aware of her voice nor the flames of their fire or the running water of the stream.

Bones engraved with *runes.*

Old bones.

A weapon of *power.*

Like any Andaren, Daijen put the pieces together and arrived at one conclusion. Mordrith Underborn had unearthed a *god.* Her description matched the words of the Arkalon and that of Ahnir, whose bones lay under protection at God Fall in the far west. How many millennia had his people been searching for another of the fallen gods? How many millennia had his people been searching for another tool such as the Helm of Ahnir, found beside His bones?

"That's when I learned the truth," Mordrith was saying.

Daijen blinked, his mind snapping back to the present. "What?" he asked, his confusion there to see now. "What did you say?"

"I said they came for the bones," the dwarf reiterated for him. "The hammer too, but they were damned excited abou' the bones. Took everythin', the hammer included. I was curious, so I followed 'em. One thing led to another an' I started me own investigation o' sorts. It took time, but I found answers. I found *truth.*"

Daijen tried to put aside any thoughts concerning the gods for the moment and shot the dwarf an expression to suggest he was waiting for more.

"A little higher up the chain," she continued, "an' they were mostly excited abou' sellin' the bones an' makin' a huge profit. That alone shocked me, but like I said: that were only a little higher up the chain. Above 'em I discovered echelons o' Skaramangians who knew the bones were to be given to *yer* people—for *free,*" she emphasised, as if she had never heard anything so absurd. "That's when I learned that the order goes beyond Morthil. We're... *They're* everywhere. From Erador to Andara, their reach cannot be held back."

"But that's not all you learned," the initiate said cajolingly.

"No," she uttered in agreement. "I learnt what motivates those at the top. The *things* they worship."

"The Dark Ones," Daijen voiced.

"We call 'em the *Talakin*—the shadows born. It turns out our cultures 'ave somethin' o' a shared history. Our legends describe them as *the* monsters, the ones that birthed all the others."

That wasn't exactly in alignment with the Andaren belief, but it was close enough that Daijen couldn't disagree. "How does the hammer—The Anther—or the bones play into their machinations?"

"I didn' get that far before they were on to me," she replied while nodding her head at the dead dwarves in the distance. "Only that they're collectin' other relics like The Anther."

"They're amassing power," Daijen muttered, his gaze having settled on the magnificent hammer.

"*A means to an end,*" The Valtorak had said years earlier, his words returning like the sharp edge of a blade.

"But what end?" Daijen questioned aloud, his thoughts spiralling to think of what evil the Skaramangians intended for such powers as The Anther and others like it.

"Ain' that the question," Mordrith went on, her voice cutting through his thoughts. "Whatever their intentions, those at the top are all lookin' to the Talakin—to the *Dark Ones*. Jus' today I discovered 'em worshippin' the fiends, prayin' to monstrous statues an' idols. That's where I was before I came 'ere. That one ye saw me kill," she said, gesturing to the dwarf whose throat and skull she had crushed, "they called 'im The Bear. I guess that's why I thought o' this place."

"All this time," Daijen said, "you've been fighting them?"

"When I've had to, aye. I can' risk 'em usin' me family against me. After today though..." The dwarf gave it some thought. "It might be safer for them if I'm not around anymore. At least until I can be sure we're not under threat." Mordrith didn't look too optimistic about the latter.

"What of the bones?" the Andaren enquired, sure to keep his tone under control. "Where are they now?"

Mordrith shrugged. "I lost track o' 'em the moment they left the mountains. They'll be in Andaren hands by now I'm sure. No idea what they'll do with 'em though," she added as an afterthought.

Daijen made to reply when a distinct and all too-familiar sound caught his sensitive ears. He moved immediately but, swift as he was, the initiate was no match for Kastiek. The Vahlken fell like Death from the sky, his Aegre no more than a blur crossing over the trees.

Kastiek's drop and roll brought him to Mordrith in one smooth motion, his sabre drawn somewhere in the manoeuvre. The scarred Vahlken would have killed the dwarf in that moment had she raised the hammer in both hands. As it was, Kastiek stood over her, his blade pressing down against The Anther's steel haft, their battle reduced to raw strength.

Still a slave to his instincts, Daijen threw himself at Kastiek with abandon and grappled him by the waist. The two Andarens were then cast away from the fire and into the dancing shadows of early evening. Rolling and tumbling over each other, their wrestling displaced the snow and, ultimately, saw Kastiek's sabre left along the trail.

A twist of hips made the Vahlken the victor, placing him atop Daijen where he could press one knee into his chest. "What are you doing?" he hissed, his pale face contrasted by the blood trickling from a fresh wound above his left eye.

Daijen grabbed the knee resting on his chest but failed to budge it. "She's not the enemy," he managed.

Kastiek scowled at the response. "What madness have you let in?"

"Get off 'im!" Mordrith yelled, charging in with the hammer raised.

"No!" Daijen shouted back, one hand shooting up to warn her.

Kastiek sprang and collided with Mordrith's waist, taking her clear from her feet while taking the air from her lungs. The two hit the snow a second before the hammer did, the weapon parted from her grip. Credit to the dwarf, she landed a fist of dwarven bone across the Vahlken's jaw, whipping his head to the side. For all her strength, which was considerable, Mordrith lacked the skill to follow through and overcome her opponent.

With a single arm, Kastiek heaved the dwarf from the ground and with the other delivered a backhand to knock her down again. "Two options remain to you," the Vahlken declared as he moved to stand over her. "Answer all of my questions and die quickly or resist and die slowly. Either way," he vowed, "you will tell me everything I want to know."

There was a sleek and curved blade in his hand now, the weapon produced from within his heavy cloak. Light from the flames touched that blade and revealed its rough and coppery surface: an atori short-sword. Absent the sabre for a companion, the smaller sword was still an exquisite killing tool in the hands of a Vahlken.

Having identified it as such, Daijen made sure his next grapple immobilised Kastiek's sword arm. The Vahlken, however, was more attuned to the initiate's way of thinking now and moved at the last second. Daijen's grip wasn't where he intended and, subsequently, received an elbow to the nose and a knotted fist to the gut, lifting him to his toes.

"Stay out of this, Daijen," Kastiek instructed, his voice far from the familiar hush he used about the fortress. "I'll deal with you later."

Dropped to his hands and knees, the initiate fought against the urge to vomit while also tasting blood from his nose. "Run," he groaned, his eyes searching for Mordrith through strands of white hair. "Run!"

On her feet again, her beard wet with blood, the dwarf spat on the ground and faced Kastiek with balled fists. "I ain' leavin' ye," she replied.

"*Hold on to it.*" Ilithranda's voice sounded in his ear, her words having lingered there for years. "*Let it go at the right time.*"

Having stamped it down again and again, Daijen released just a portion of his unbridled rage. A lifetime of being underestimated, overlooked, and beaten into submission forced its way through that narrow gap and quashed the Andaren's pain.

With a roar, Daijen Saeth bolted from his hands and knees and charged into the back of Kastiek's legs. The Vahlken was flipped and tossed aside to land on his shoulder. Of course, he would be quick to recover and swift to exact vengeance, an inevitability that saw Daijen throw himself once again at his better.

Scrambling through the snow, with Kastiek's sword arm locked in a vice-like grip, the initiate over-extended the limb until the pain forced the Vahlken to release the atori blade.

"RUN!" Daijen screamed.

Mordrith hesitated before seeing sense. She picked up The Anther and gave the initiate one last look. With her expression alone, she conveyed but a single message. *Gratitude*. Down came the hammer, and with the thunder of its impact Mordrith Underborn was gone from The Dain'duil.

"Fool!" Kastiek barked.

Daijen released the Vahlken's arm and rolled away, though not to safety, for nowhere was safe while sharing space with Kastiek. Indeed, the older and more experienced Vahlken was on his feet first and advancing at speed.

Before Daijen could find his feet he was leaving the ground again, thrown back by a powerful knee to the chest. "You would side with the enemy," he spat, lifting the initiate with a swift kick to the gut. "You aren't fit to be a Vahlken!"

The boot to his back put the taste of dirt in his mouth, but it did nothing to hamper his hearing.

"I will be the judge of that," The Valtorak's ancient voice croaked from the shadows.

His curved staff preceded him, his robes of deep green revealed in the firelight. He looked older in that moment, the lines of his face exaggerated by the flames. "On your feet, Daijen Saeth."

"You were spying on me?" he asked on his way up.

"*We* will ask the questions," Kastiek snapped.

The Valtorak leaned into his staff with both hands. "We have been aware of your extended hunting trips. Kastiek has even kept a close eye on the site in between. It seems we arrived too late to intervene," he added, eyeing the Vahlken.

"Mordrith is not our enemy," Daijen blurted.

"Don't be so naive," Kastiek chastised.

"When was the last time you killed a Skaramangian?" the initiate countered venomously. "Mordrith killed two of them this very day!" He pointed to the bodies not far from where they argued.

Kastiek started forwards, his usually controlled composure abandoned in the face of the insult.

The Valtorak stamped his staff once into the ground, bringing the Vahlken's feet to a sudden stop. "You will not question Kastiek's deeds, *Initiate*. What you will do is return with me to Ka'vairn *and* without a word. There you will rest for the night. At dawn, I will find you outside my door where you will report every detail of this evening's activities. Fail to adhere to any one of my instructions and I will let Kastiek *break* you." With that, the master stood aside and gestured at the spot where Aramis made his timely landing.

Daijen looked to his horse, still bound to the tree beside the camp.

"Kastiek will free the horse," The Valtorak interpreted. "I'm sure he knows the way home by now."

Though it felt wrong to leave the animal to journey alone, to defy the will of The Valtorak felt so wrong as to open a pit in Daijen's stomach. He could but obey.

As if the evening hadn't been dramatic enough, flying back to Ka'vairn astride Aramis was exhilarating enough to rob Daijen of his much-needed sleep. He had kept himself awake for three days while waiting by the stream and now, standing outside the master's door at first light, his fatigue was catching up with him.

Granted entry, The Valtorak and Kastiek awaited him, each a statue of marble that had been chipped and worn down by time and violence. Continuing their statue-like existence, both Andarens remained silent while Daijen recounted his conversation with Mordrith. Unlike the first time he had detailed his meeting with the dwarf, the initiate included The Anther in his story.

When he was finished, master and Vahlken shared only a look.

"Did you hear what I said? The Skaramangians found a *god* under the mountains."

Kastiek regarded his master. "They have a weapon of power," he said gravely.

Daijen frowned. "No," he argued. "*Mordrith* has the hammer. She stole it back. She's been keeping it safe for years. Did you not hear what—"

"It's a trick," Kastiek insisted. "They're using you to get to us."

"She killed two of them," the initiate pointed out.

"An easy sacrifice to compromise this fortress," Kastiek countered.

"Mordrith could be our first ally outside of this order," Daijen shot back.

"*Our* first ally?" the Vahlken questioned with disbelief. "You only know the truth of our order because a *Skaramangian* told you. This isn't your war. Not yet. Maybe never," he threatened.

"Enough," The Valtorak said, ending it with a quiet word. "You are both right. Though to what degree is yet to be seen." The master consulted a map on his desk. "I will send word to Asled," he said to Kastiek. "He can investigate the movement of these *bones*."

"That will require him to leave his post," Kastiek replied gravely. "He guards the northern coast. He is the closest to The Tower of Argunsuun."

"He is also the closest to The Bronze Doors of Orgunthain," The Valtorak counteracted. "If these bones are, indeed, the same as those in God Fall they will be large and, therefore, ferried through those doors. They might still be on The Dorth Road."

"Asled?" Daijen questioned lightly. "He is a Vahlken?"

"He is not your concern," Kastiek told him sharply.

"Gaps in our defence are everyone's concern," the initiate interjected.

"You forget your place," the Vahlken glowered.

Daijen knew he should have shut his mouth there and then, but something drove him to double down. "Acquiring allies outside of these walls will eliminate the need to move Vahlkens around. It only furthers our reach, an advantage the Skaramangians have had over us since this shadow war began."

"You speak like you know what you're talking about," Kastiek seethed, "but you might as well have read everything you know in a book. You know nothing of *real* war."

"Easy, Kastiek," the master bade. "It is not incompetence that keeps Daijen from the war but *time*. And on that matter," he continued, looking at the initiate, "your time has almost run down."

Daijen frowned, fearing an ultimatum regarding his training. "Master?"

"Ilithranda awaits you in the courtyard. She has been preparing for your journey."

The Andaren glanced at Kastiek, who looked to be holding in a sigh. "A journey, Master?"

"The two of you are to make for The Weavers. You depart this very morn."

It was a turn in events Daijen could not have predicted, churning his emotions against the revelations of the past day. He wanted to stay and make plans with The Valtorak, to be a part of the effort against the Dark Ones and their worshippers. He wanted to discuss, at length, the meaning behind the runes on bones if not the discovery of the bones themselves. Mordrith's was a world-altering find that would affect every Andaren in the realm.

Yet he had longed not only to leave the valley and claim his armour but enjoy a long journey with Ilithranda. It was a big step in their training and would be a momentous accolade to return in the garb of a Vahlken.

"You can leave this matter to us," The Valtorak assured. "Continue your training, Daijen. Earn your place in this fight."

The initiate had so much more to say, to protest, to add... but he said nothing, sensing that to do so would ignite the master's ire. Instead, he bowed his head and left quietly, his feet taking him quickly to the courtyard.

Ilithranda wasn't alone out there, the other initiates taking advantage of the daylight and moving through various routines. Draped in the black fur of her own cloak, Ilithranda finished securing the straps on her saddle and turned to greet Daijen.

"What did you do wrong now?" she asked with some amusement. "The day has barely started."

How he wished to tell her everything. "Just the usual threats concerning my need to improve," he quipped, mustering half a smile.

Ilithranda glanced at the master's tower. "That seems... *inconsistent,* on the day you are to make for the lair of The Weavers."

"Hold!" Kastiek's voice didn't just stop Daijen and Ilithranda but all of the initiates.

"Now what?" Daijen uttered under his breath before presenting himself beside Ilithranda.

"It would be foolish to travel all the way to The Weavers," the Vahlken announced on his approach, "and not have your atori blades to be cast."

Daijen and Ilithranda stared at the short-swords Kastiek held out.

Ilithranda was the first to take hers in hand, a rare smile on her face.

Daijen accepted his, scrutinising the atori blade, its naked steel absent the coppery work of the mysterious Weavers. Even without their input it was a magnificent weapon, the guard forged into the shape of an eagle's claw, the talons pointing down towards the angled pommel.

"And your sabre," Kastiek continued, displaying the scimitar in his other hand.

Daijen blinked, rattled by disbelief, for the sabre was clearly being presented to him and him alone.

"It is tradition," Kastiek pointed out, "that only the atori blade is to be given to The Weavers."

Slait generated no more than a gust of air as he dropped down from the ramparts. "What's this?" he demanded. "Why does the *runt* get such honours?"

Kastiek maintained eye-contact with Daijen as he answered. "Because the *runt* defeated me in combat."

There was a prolonged moment where it seemed the fortress had been deprived of all air.

"Impossible!" Kovun stated, abandoning his axe.

"He disarmed me without a weapon," Kastiek explained, his tone leaving no room for argument. "He has... *earned* his sabre."

"When?" Ilithranda asked, though her question was aimed at Daijen.

"It doesn't matter," the Vahlken informed her. "Follow the map I gave you and see yourselves returned here as soon as possible. Your training does not end with The Weavers." Kastiek was quick to walk away and instruct the others to return to their routines.

Ilithranda's violet eyes bore into Daijen. "Concerns regarding your improvement..." she mused with suspicion.

Daijen could say nothing, though not because he was sworn to silence by the master. His mind was occupied by the weight of a sabre and short-sword that he had spent years longing for. At the same time, his respect for Kastiek grew tenfold, that the Vahlken would honour his word and publicly declare his defeat.

At last, a sense of pride swelled within the young Andaren.

He was one step closer to the war. The *real* war.

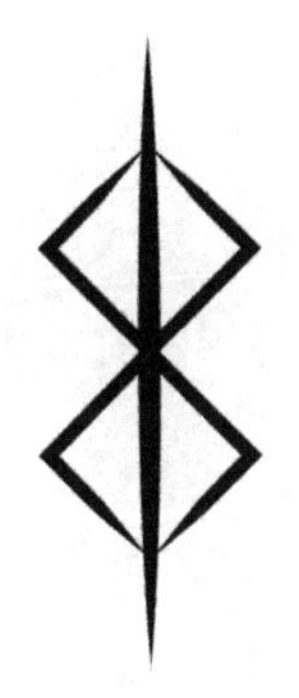

PART THREE

34
CHOOSING LIFE

It was black skies and heavy rain that greeted the four companions at the gates of Hemon. Thunder rolled in from the distance, as if the Almighty Kaliban Himself was riding His steed across the night. Gallien gave the coast no more than a glance, spying the flashes of lightning that illuminated the choppy waves of The Hox.

His attention was arrested by the wizard, as it had been since meeting the man in Warth. Leaving them astride their horses, Aphrandhor had made his way to the ordinary sized door inside the left-hand gate. He knocked with his staff and waited for a guard to slide open the rectangular hatch built into the door at eye level. There he had stood for several minutes, conversing with the man, their words lost to the rain until the guard closed the hatch again.

Gallien looked to Cob as, perhaps, some indicator as to whether events were going their way, but the Kedradi was ever unreadable. When, at last, the hatch in the door was slid aside again, the wizard exchanged words with a different guard. Theirs was a much shorter conversation and followed by some activity on the other side of the gates.

"If there's one thing I've learned in this life," Aphrandhor was saying on his way back to his horse, "it's to always make friends with the gatekeepers." He beamed at the smuggler, quite satisfied it seemed.

The great gates creaked and groaned as they were parted for the companions, the gap just big enough to accommodate a horse. Entering Hemon did nothing to get them out of the rain, its streets exposed to the raging skies. But they weren't alone for there were those who stumbled and staggered about, caring little for the rain as they sought the next tavern.

Indeed, so much of the city was still alive at the late hour. Torch and candlelight created a warm glow down many a street, where the gambling houses, brothels, and taverns were a hub of activity. Here and there, the homeguard patrolled in twos and fours, their red cloaks emblazoned with the plunging sword of dragon scale, the black sigil of blood Etragon—of the *king*.

While they certainly noticed the companions on their three horses, the homeguard gave them no reason for concern, leaving them to wander through the wet streets.

Joran moved in the saddle, drawing Gallien's attention. "Keep your hood up," he told the boy, who was craning his neck to take in the enormous arches that cut through the city.

"I've never seen anything so big," he said, his face plastered with rain.

Drakalis gave the arches a moment of his time. It had been more than two decades since he had entered Hemon. As high as the city's tallest spire, the stone walkways that crossed the city did so on a series of arches, all of which led into the central Parthadrel, blending into the palace's architecture. It was, in essence, a wheel of stone, its spokes the towering walkways.

Though the mighty walkways gave the city an extra sense of grandeur, the soldier that still lingered in Gallien suspected they would make for an advantage in an invasion. Soldiers could pour out from the Parthadrel and rain down hell upon the enemy. The lightning, however, revealed naught but banners hanging from the walkways, curtains of red and black.

"It's incredible," Joran observed.

Gallien couldn't help but smile—the boy was able to maintain his wonderment even at the worst of times.

"Does someone live in there?" he asked, looking to the central palace that rose in tiers to a single spire.

Gallien only raised his head until the intruding rain bothered him. "Some Blood Lord," he grumbled. "I forget which. Focus," he said, leaning in to Joran's ear. "Big cities have big problems."

The boy turned his head, though his features were still hidden by the fabric of his hood. "We have a Kedradi and a wizard for company," he reminded. "This might be the safest we've been in years."

Though his time with Androma had been short, the Dragon Rider had left a lasting impression on Gallien, her words seared into his memory. "*Trust me, smuggler,*" she had intoned, "*that boy will never be safe.*"

"Do not be fooled," he warned Joran. "Just because they haven't tried to kill us like everyone else doesn't mean they are of good intent. We each have one ally in this world and they're both sat in this saddle."

Joran might have been nodding inside his hood, but Drakalis wasn't convinced the boy was in actual agreement. He longed for more than their small life on the run.

"Where are we going?" Gallien asked their new companions, his mind eager to get away from thoughts of Joran being in danger.

"Somewhere safe," Aphrandhor told him. "Somewhere *dry*."

Somewhere safe was questionable and, upon seeing the building which they arrived at, so too was the possibility of it being dry. The house, if it had ever been such a thing, had suffered from fire damage, its roof and framework blackened by flames. The rain looked to be pouring in through a patchwork of jagged holes and gaps in the brickwork. For all the ruin, however, it seemed the door was still securely in place.

The wizard rifled through his saddle bag and produced a ring of keys—more than Gallien could count. After mumbling to himself and picking through the numerous keys, the old man finally unlocked the door, though he only opened it a crack.

"What's he doing?" Joran enquired.

Gallien watched the wizard run two fingers over the door's interior frame. It might have been a trick of the light, but the smuggler was sure he glimpsed faint runes come momentarily to life, as if reacting to the wizard's touch.

"He is making it safe," Cob answered on his dismount. "Follow him in. I will see to the horses."

Gallien felt at once quite concerned about being inside a confined area with the wizard, whose intentions were yet to come to light. Joran had no such concerns, his younger body seeing him nimbly from the saddle.

"Won't you come inside," Aphrandhor welcomed politely enough, a warm smile beneath his white beard. "No one has been here since my last visit," he assured.

"And where is *here*?" Drakalis questioned on his dismount, one hand subconsciously gripping the sword on his hip. Though the weapon gave him some peace of mind, his thoughts went to the satchel slung over his shoulders. He couldn't feel it, but he knew Kitrana's broken sword was inside, the jagged blade folded into some kind of intangible dimension. Then there was the axe, a weapon that had never failed to find him when threatened.

Recalling all too easily how Aphrandhor and Cob had dealt with the Padoshi's men, the smuggler had to wonder what good any of his weapons would do him if it came to a fight.

"A sanctuary to us," the wizard answered, navigating the old debris as he moved from room to room.

"And who, exactly, is *us*?"

"Oh," Aphrandhor answered lazily, "we're something of a... *council*."

Still feeling the rain find his hood in what had once been a kitchen, Gallien looked up to see compromised beams and deep cracks that threatened the integrity of every wall. "Last I checked, Hemon had plenty of taverns and inns."

"Indeed," Aphrandhor agreed. "And all with eyes and ears that report to our enemy—we are too close to The Red Hold to trust our surroundings."

"The Red Hold?" Joran glanced back at Gallien before aiming his next question at the wizard's back. "Where The Gilded come from?"

The Green Leaf paused in the final doorway and looked back at the boy. "I couldn't say if that's where the priests came from, but The Red Hold is undoubtedly where their strength comes from. 'Tis a fortress disguised as a church. People flock to its red walls every day, and every day it churns out new priestlings and sages. Spies all."

"Not a man of faith, Green Leaf?" Gallien quipped.

The wizard did not waver from his gaze. "That, Mr Drakalis, was the wrong question." At that, Aphrandhor entered the final room and began shifting debris about with the end of his staff.

The smuggler frowned. "And what was the right question?"

"Spies for *who*?" Joran enquired of the wizard.

The Green Leaf stopped his work to offer the boy a proud smile. "You have your mother's investigative mind—very good."

Though the comment had been delivered lightly and without a care, the wizard's response struck Joran, his surprise there to see. "My *mother*? You knew her?"

Gallien wished to immediately intervene, sensing more and more strands connecting Joran to a fate that lay beyond either of their control. He had already stopped Cob from speaking to the boy and prevented any meaningful talk on their journey to Hemon. It seemed cruel now to do the same when his mother had been mentioned, a topic he had deliberately feigned ignorance of, in response to all of Joran's questions.

Aphrandhor crouched and removed the remains of a tattered and heavily stained rug, under which there sat a trap door. "Oh yes," he replied offhandedly. "Though not so well as others. Still, hers was a *trained* mind." The wizard went on to, again, rifle through the many keys before seeing to the padlock that kept the trap door secured.

Once raised out of place, a spiralling staircase was revealed—or, at least, the top step, for all else was steeped in darkness.

"Where does *that* go?" Gallien had to ask, any thoughts of Joran's mother gone for the moment.

Aphrandhor took to the first step. "As I said: somewhere safe and dry."

Drakalis watched the wizard descend, a series of torches springing to life, their flames illuminating the steps behind him. Joran obviously made for the staircase without question, hungry to follow the man with, seemingly, all the answers he had ever wanted. Gallien reached out to grab the boy if for no other reason than to warn him, to remind him of their most recent conversation. But the smuggler retracted his hand at the last second.

He knew from experience that smothering him only served as a wedge between them. Now, more than ever, Gallien needed Joran to be receptive to his counsel.

The third to enter the stairwell, Drakalis was sure to keep Joran in view at all times. Though, admittedly, his gaze wandered round and high when they arrived in the chamber beneath the house. Walls overly stuffed with books and scrolls framed a long table that led the smuggler's attention to a cosy seating area atop several rugs. The more Aphrandhor advanced the more torches and candles came to life, revealing two-storeys worth of space and ladders that provided access to books at the very top.

"What is this place?" Gallien asked.

"The house was once owned by a wealthy merchant," the wizard explained as he approached the distant seating area. "He had this built in case of a siege—somewhere he and his family could wait it out."

Drakalis ran one finger along the table top and wiped away a layer of dust. "And he doesn't mind you using the place?"

"Alas, the owner has long passed and his wife too. The deed belongs to his son now." The wizard pointed his staff into the large fireplace that sat in the middle of the seating area, his magic enough to set it alight.

"And the son doesn't mind?" Gallien probed, a man who always liked to know where he was.

The Green Leaf chuckled to himself as the flames crackled behind him. "*I* don't mind at all," he commented.

Gallien said nothing. He absorbed the fact and hoped to build upon it. If nothing else, though, he had to assume the wizard had access to funds.

"Won't the smoke give us away?" Joran pointed out.

"Very astute, Master Joran, but no. The chimney system is a tad more complex than most you'll be happy to hear." Aphrandhor wandered over to bring their attention to a door just off from the seating area. "You'll also be happy to hear that there are sleeping quarters available. We will, at least, be comfortable while we wait."

"Wait for what?" Gallien was quick to follow up.

"We might not have taken the intended route," The Green Leaf replied happily enough, "but Hemon was always to be our destination. We are to meet a friend here. Like our enemy, we must seek allies."

The creak of a door turned Joran and Gallien around, where they watched the Kedradi enter the chamber, his large bow in hand. "All secure up top," he reported. "We were not followed."

"Very good. Thank you, Cob." Aphrandhor gestured at their surroundings. "Make yourselves at home. I will venture out tomorrow for fresh supplies."

"Wait," Joran called, his hand lightly reaching out to physically halt the wizard.

Gallien's eyes pinched in curiosity when Aphrandhor recoiled, the man not to be touched apparently.

Joran noticed it too and hesitated before speaking again. "You never said who The Gilded spy for."

The Green Leaf offered a disarming smile. "All in good time, my boy. Your world just got a lot bigger. Get some rest."

Joran's disappointment was there to see. How the boy hungered for information. For *more*. For the first time in his young life he was able to see the storm that had surrounded him. The truth, in Gallien's opinion, was unavoidable: the longer they remained in such company, the more likely it was that Joran would be swept up in that storm.

It was a path that led them right back to The Dancing Sword of the Dawn. A path to death.

He would not have it.

Without any windows it was impossible to know the hour but, judging by Joran's quiet and shallow breathing, Gallien presumed it was nearing dawn. Since they were sharing a room, it troubled no one to wake the boy, though the smuggler made certain his hand was covering Joran's mouth when he did.

With his eyes alone he asked Drakalis what was wrong.

"We're leaving," he whispered. "*Now.*"

"Why?" the teenager demanded, his pointed ears just protruding from a mess of ashen hair.

"They got us away from the Andarens—we don't need them anymore. Get your boots on, and *quietly.*" The smuggler moved to the door and checked the small hallway beyond.

"I don't want to go," Joran protested. "Gallien, he knew my *mother*. He knows why the Andarens have always been after me. We can't... I have to know."

"These people," Drakalis stressed, "have also been after you all your life. Just because they haven't tried to kill you like the Andarens doesn't mean they don't want to use you. We have to get out of here while we can. Hemon is a big enough city to get lost in. We can lie low, build up supplies, and then move on to—"

"Move on to where?" Joran interrupted. "Where are we going, Gallien? Where are we *ever* going? When does this end? The running. The hiding. Living on scraps. This can't be all there is."

"This is *life*," the smuggler told him. "*Living*. That's what this is, Joran. I don't know why they all want you, but I know being a child of both worlds puts you in danger *everywhere*. So the running, the hiding... It will never end so long as it means you're alive."

"I want more than just being alive," Joran declared quietly, if powerfully. "I can't believe that I am what I am for no other reason than to be hunted and killed."

Gallien turned on the boy, his patience evaporated. "That's because you're young and you know absolutely nothing about the world," he hissed.

"If I know nothing it's because you haven't given me a chance to learn anything," Joran countered, rising from his cot. "We're always on the move. You're always talking *for* me. You make us live in fear."

Drakalis closed the gap between them and grabbed the boy by his shirt. He had no idea of the things Gallien had done to keep them both safe. He said nothing for a time, allowing his rage to bubble over and dissipate, lest he say as much and divulge the blood he had spilled.

"It's fear that has kept you alive all these years," he eventually began. "I could have delivered you into the wizard's hands as a babe and got on with my life. But I didn't. I chose *life* for you. I know it's not the life you want but at least it's yours to live. Because, mark my words, The Green Leaf and his friends haven't been looking for you all these years just so they could give you everything you've ever wanted."

Joran appeared unfocused for a moment, his thoughts his own. "But we won't know what they want if we run," he argued. "Can't we at least stay until we find out?"

"It'll be too late by then," Gallien warned. "Listen," he said, his mind working furiously to find the right words. "We'll go to Valgala. Hmm? You've always wanted to see the capital. We can stay there for a while. It's the biggest city in the world," he added with wonder in his voice.

A spark of intrigue flared and died behind the boy's violet eyes. "How long is a while?" he asked.

Drakalis licked his lips, the hook taken—now he just needed to reel him in. "You know what? You're sixteen years old." Gallien let go of his shirt and gripped him by the shoulders. "We can decide things like that together from now on. But let's just get there first, eh?"

His answer didn't come immediately, but when it did there still seemed some reluctance. "All right. Let's go."

The smuggler gave the boy his broadest grin. "Good, lad. Get your boots on."

Together, they crept out of their room and entered the seating area beside the fire, its flames inexplicably strong even hours later. Using hand gestures alone, the smuggler directed Joran to follow him, past the long table and chairs. He saw the door in torchlight—it wasn't even locked.

Then again, it didn't need to be with a Kedradi standing in front of it.

"You cannot leave," Cob said evenly enough.

Gallien's jaw tensed. "The hells we can't. Stand aside."

The hunter didn't budge an inch, his arms folded to bring his vambraces of silver and gold together.

Drakalis kept his eyes on the Kedradi while one hand retrieved the dagger on his hip. It was a pitiful weapon when compared to the arsenal Cob possessed.

"We're going through that door," the smuggler vowed.

Cob eyed the knife from the head of the table. "No axe today?"

He must have seen it in Warth, Gallien reasoned. But did he see it appear from nowhere? Drakalis dismissed his concerns and focused on the immediate and, seemingly, unmovable problem.

"This'll do," he assured, adjusting his grip on the hilt so the blade tip pointed down.

Cob said nothing to that. Instead, he went about removing his every weapon, from the curved scimitar of solid bone on his hip to the short-sword of fangs on the back of his belt. With his bow put to one side and his feathered dagger left on the table, he moved to stand directly in front of the smuggler.

"I am under instruction not to kill you," he reported.

Gallien considered the unarmed man before him. More so, he considered the man's confidence to have relinquished his weapons. In most, he would believe it no more than arrogance but, in a Kedradi, it was likely his confidence was well earned. Still, they needed to get through that door.

Drakalis lunged, the knife slicing through the air to take Cob across the neck. The Kedradi's upper body curved like grass bending in the wind and he evaded the edge of steel with seeming ease. His counterattack was swift and definitive, leaving Gallien to wonder what exactly had transpired, for his right shoulder, arm, and ribs were all shooting with pain and the blade was now in Cob's hand.

"A good swing," he praised, his dark eyes roaming over the weapon in his hand. "A pity it was an *obvious* one." With some care, the Kedradi placed the weapon on the table, just beyond the smuggler's reach.

Gallien quit rubbing his shoulder and balled his fists. Every instinct told him that fighting a ranger—a man who hunted monsters for a living—was folly, but he gave his own life little concern when Joran's hung in the balance.

Like his first attack, lunging at the Kedradi with a closed fist invited a counterattack that left various parts of his torso stinging. Cob's arms moved like a pair of cobras, each darting out to find pinch points in Drakalis's form. It was all too easy for him to move Gallien's blows aside and deliver his own, always knocking the smuggler back. His last attack was an elbow to the chest that put Gallien on the floor.

Joran yelled out and leapt at the Kedradi. Gallien wanted to warn him away but he failed to summon enough air to voice the words. Instead, he watched Cob unravel the boy's attack and flip him over, bringing him down on the table top. The smuggler was quite surprised, and happily so, to see that Joran still possessed enough fight in him to hold the ranger over him and thrust a knee into his face.

The blow knocked Cob back, giving the boy time to grab the dagger and roll off the table. Advancing on his opponent, Joran managed two swipes of the weapon before the Kedradi snatched his wrist and claimed the blade as his own again. In the same fluid movement, the ranger dropped it and kicked out Joran's legs.

Seeing the boy thrown about and injured quashed Gallien's pains and put him on his feet. Facing the Kedradi again, the smuggler did so with the axe in hand. Again, Cob eyed the weapon in Drakalis's hands with naught but curiosity. Deciding to give him something else to think about, Gallien waded into their fight with a two-handed swing.

His form was clumsy, forfeiting skill for brute strength. His third swing missed so wildly that he reduced one of the chairs to splinters. By the time he had recovered his wits Cob was upon him, the edge of his hand chopping down on his clavicle. The blow ran down his arm and took the axe from his grip before the ranger's boot landed in his chest.

Thrown back against the wall, his blood boiling, Gallien felt his fingers coil around a haft of steel. The axe had returned to him no sooner than it hit the floor. He flashed the Kedradi a wicked grin and pushed off from the wall, the axe coming up to be launched.

It was then that a staff of maple wood cut across the smuggler and halted the axe.

Gallien followed the length of wood back to its owner, who had entered the chamber unheard amidst the violence. "You!" he exclaimed, holding back none of his shock.

"Gallien Drakalis. You're *late*."

The smuggler blinked. "You're *dead*."

The blind Dragon Rider brought the staff back into line with her body. "You're half right," Androma corrected.

35
THE WEAVERS

60 Years Ago...

The time beyond Ka'vairn and the boundaries of The Dain'duil passed all too quickly. In Daijen's eyes, the six weeks he and Ilithranda had been on their journey might as well have been six days. The first leg of their journey saw the pair return to The Saible for the first time since departing for the Path of Handuin.

The black fortress hadn't changed over the decades, though a new generation of humans had likely been born into servitude, never to know their homeland. Their arrival, however, had been a different affair, their status as initiates affording them a meeting with the justiciar himself. An Andaren of ancient stock and military breeding, he had accommodated their every need, giving them supplies for the journey, stabling their horses until their return, and even providing a row boat for the next leg of their journey.

How tempted Daijen had been to seek out Lornak, his direct commander while serving the emperor as messenger guard. Indeed, he might have had the justiciar not seen to their needs so promptly. And so his pride had nowhere to go as they set out on the cold waters of The Nheremyn. Of course, by the time they had taken its winding route through The Orsindil Mountains and reached Lake Iva, the feeling had long passed, his thoughts cast to what lay ahead.

After all, had those feelings not sprung from a long dead Daijen Saeth, from a young man who had yet to plunge into the pits of Handuin? Now there was only forward.

Now, after trekking on foot from the shores of Lake Iva, south through a narrow mountain pass, Daijen continued through the trees of The Sin'duil and looked upon The Ruins of Kharis Vhay. The ancient stone had been swallowed up in the heart of the forest, a two day expedition from any of its borders. Old as it was, the fortress was new to the initiate. How long had it been since he had encountered something new that wasn't accompanied by pain?

He was far from Ka'vairn's brutal traditions and Kastiek's trials, the world unfolding around him since taking to The Nheremyn. He had loved every minute of it.

Though every stone was exactly where it had been originally laid, there was evidence of fire damage on every wall and turret, the stone blackened and scorched. It was not dragon fire, Daijen knew, for the flames that had brought Kharis Vhay to ruin had merely marred the stone, not melted it.

"It looks abandoned," he observed, letting his pack drop to the ground. "Are you sure this is where Kastiek told us to go?"

Ilithranda dropped her own pack and craned her neck to take in the spires that reached for winter's bleak midday sky. "This is where we've always come." She looked at him. "You don't know the history? I thought you had read everything in the library."

Daijen smiled at her playful, if judgmental, comment. "Not *everything*," he replied. "Just more than you."

"I read everything before you were even *born*," Ilithranda quipped as she advanced on the ruins.

"Ah yes," Daijen called after her, "I forgot you're an old lady."

Ilithranda gave a soundless laugh. "Six weeks you've had that sabre and blade. Look how *bold* it's made you."

Daijen regarded the sabre sheathed on his left hip and the atori blade on his right. He had spent many an evening admiring each while Ilithranda practised her stoical nature. A part of him had to agree with her though. He *had* felt different since Kastiek had presented them to him. Though he could not boast of his skills, in appearance he was closer to that of a Vahlken than his quiet companion.

"Enlighten me then," he requested. "How does coming here help us find The Weavers?"

"You don't find The Weavers," Ilithranda corrected. "They find you."

Daijen made a show of looking around, where he spotted no more than a few out-buildings and the encircling line of trees. "And they'll find us *here*?"

"Kharis Vhay was once home to The Weavers. It was from here that they crafted their legendary works."

Daijen looked at the ruins with new eyes, imagining now a time when it was inhabited by the craftsmen.

And their *creatures*.

"What happened?" he asked.

"Hubris," she answered in a word, turning back to look at him.

And there she froze, her violet gaze cast beyond Daijen. For the first time in many years, he saw fear in Ilithranda's eyes. Gripping the hilt of his sabre, Daijen pivoted on his heel, his fur cloak sweeping out beside him. As steel rang free, the Andaren was faced with a spider so big it would have dwarfed his war horse. Worse still, the enormous spider reared up, baring a pair of oily fangs that dripped with venom. Its two front legs cast a shadow over the initiate, ready to come down and box him in.

Honed instincts moved Daijen from harm, seeing him dart, roll, and rise before the beast could spring. Like a hammer to the back, one of those front legs slammed into the initiate and threw him from his feet. It was, again, those instincts that Kastiek had drilled into him that prevented the Andaren from sprawling across the ground.

Instead, Daijen's body flexed, his fingers reaching out for the cold dirt, before flipping feet over head. Turning his momentum into a run, the initiate used speed and strength to dash across a wall of the ruins, his atori blade drawn and held aloft so he might wield it alongside his sabre. He came down in time to see a lunging attack from the spider, its entire body flying through the air.

"No!" Ilithranda's cry preceded her interference, barrelling into Daijen at the waist.

The spider skirted over their fall, a single hairy leg clipping Daijen's head before he hit the ground beneath Ilithranda.

"I had it!" he protested, sure that his blades would have sliced the creature's underside from end to end.

"I know!" Ilithranda snapped, rising beside him. "I wasn't saving *you*. I was saving *it*."

Daijen let his immediate question die on his lips. There was another one. The second spider leapt from high up the ruins and landed between them and the first hideous beast. Only then did the Andaren see the truth of things, that both spiders bore *riders*.

A tune of sharp *clicks* resounded from the new rider, and both creatures instantly ceased stamping their feet and settled down.

Still, Daijen was yet to lower his weapons. How could he in the face of such living nightmares? Their hairy bodies were the black of deep night and their eyes—all eight of them—were an inky abyss that could only be found when touched by the light.

Then there were the *riders* to consider. Silvery pale hands and flowing chalk-white hair revealed them to be Andarens certainly, but their faces remained a mystery behind a mask of silver, the surface of both intricately decorated with overlapping swirls. Indeed, the masks ran over the tops of their heads and appeared to be secured via a strap around the neck, connecting to the mask at the chin. Daijen had never seen anything like it, the eye holes narrow slits that must have inhibited vision.

Their dark robes were not so black when contrasted against the spiders, and fastened by belts laden with tools and what appeared to be a coiled whip. Daijen made a quick assessment and decided that the whip was the riders' only weapon; if it was even intended as such. Either way, the initiate came to one conclusion.

He was standing before a pair of Weavers.

"They are not our enemy," the second said to the first, turning in his saddle.

Compounding that statement, an arrow whistled between the trees, skimmed the corner of the ruins and struck the first Weaver in the neck. The Andaren couldn't even gasp with shock, his airway constricted. Instead, he gargled and sputtered before sliding from his saddle and over his spider's legs.

So much happened at once then that Daijen's warrior mind was forced to put certain things aside so he might focus on the most immediate danger. Therefore, he ignored the fact that the first spider sank its fangs into the dying rider and promptly scurried away with its meal. So too did he overlook the second spider and its rider crawling at speed up the side of the ruins and the uncoiling of a whip.

More so, he simply acknowledged the two humans charging towards him, their grey cloaks spreading out behind them as their swords flashed high.

The real danger came from afar, where Daijen spotted a pair of archers. They were partially hidden beside a knobbly tree and with fresh arrows nocked in their bows. Their aims, however, went high, searching for the spider that hurried around the spires.

Sure of the time he had, Daijen twisted his atori blade, raising it high. His command of strength and balance was enough to see the blade from his hand, across the gap, and into the heart of an archer.

How simple it had been. How easy to take a life.

For all his years of training: the years, decades, learning how to overcome the advantages of any opponent, wield any weapon, and kill any with proficiency, one thing had passed him by.

He had become a warrior without realising it.

Now, twenty years later, he had killed another human, bringing his tally of deaths to two. How different it felt in that instant. The archer had been a fly to him, unlike the man he had fought and beaten in the streets of Harendun. Compounding that, he knew the *truth* now, that for all their malice, the humans were little more than pawns, their actions commanded by the Skaramangians.

That is not to say that Daijen felt the sting of guilt or remorse in that definitive moment. Be he human, Andaren, or anything else for that matter, the archer posed a threat not only to the initiates but also the surviving Weaver and his extraordinary mount.

And, of course, there remained that incomparable feeling beneath all his conscious rationale. How glorious it felt to be the victor, to have utilised years of training and achieved the desired outcome. It was a rush that Daijen had to fight to keep contained, a battle he could only win with discipline and the stark reminder that humans as a people were not his enemy.

These men, however, were most certainly his present enemy.

The dying archer's limbs flailed, disturbing the man beside him, his arrow going wild. By the time he realised his companion was dead at his feet, a short-sword protruding from his chest, a would-be Vahlken was upon him.

Daijen leapt at the last second, his sabre pointed forward and arm coiled back. The archer's yell of surprise was cut short after Daijen came down with a thrusting blow, the curved steel piercing through flesh and bone to sever the top half of his head.

The Andaren was left standing there, his weapon embedded in the tree that had been behind the second archer. As blood pooled along the flat of the steel and dripped from its edge, Daijen finally saw the truth of his strength, which was magnitudes beyond what he had possessed the last time he had faced the men of Erador. Years of only fighting others who had survived the pits of Handuin had fogged his memory where human limits were concerned.

Still, he stood the victor, the seemingly eternal agony he had suffered in the pits bearing fruit. Added to that, he was unnervingly calm, his heart rate slow and regular, his breathing under control, and his hands steady. Fleeting though the thought was, Daijen was disgusted at how untroubled he was.

Ka'vairn had truly transformed him.

Moving forwards, as only he could, Daijen pulled his sabre free, retrieved his atori blade, and turned to challenge the two swordsmen.

He did so in time to see Ilithranda dispatch both with brutal efficiency. The first to meet her wrath suffered a pommel to the back of the head, cracking his skull before she plunged her atori blade into the charging second. The blow was a gutting one, a slow kill she turned into a swift kill as she jerked the blade up into his chest.

There she left her weapon, allowing it to fall with her victim. Instead, Ilithranda pivoted on her heel and approached the first, who staggering to his knees with blood dripping down the back of his head. The initiate loomed over him from behind, her hands locking his head in place.

Snap!

The man fell face down, there to join his kin in death.

Daijen navigated the forest trees to reach his companion, who was reclaiming her short-sword on his arrival. Ilithranda was crouched, where she could use one of the dead men's cloaks to wipe her blade clean.

"They were not soldiers," she stated, rising to meet him.

Upon a second glance, Daijen had to agree. None of them were attired in the black and red of Erador nor the plunging scaled sword of the human king. "Privateers?" he queried.

"Mercenaries," came the answer, though not from Ilithranda.

Daijen couldn't help but grip his sabre a little tighter at the sight of the giant spider, its rider sitting relaxed in its saddle.

The Weaver jutted his head into the air and made a series of clicks and hisses with his mouth. Again, the spider responded and dipped to one side, allowing him to dismount. His average height brought him to Daijen's chin as he moved to see the bodies between the initiates.

"They attacked us for the first time a week ago," the Weaver began. "We believe they have made anchor by the coast," he added, nodding his head to the east. "Chet, chet!" he called, and the spider scurried through the trees until it found one large enough to accommodate its bulk. The creature disappeared entirely up there, its dark body hidden by foliage and branches.

"Impossible," Daijen stated. "There are Vahlken who patrol the eastern border." The initiate called to mind the map he had seen on The Valtorak's desk and, specifically, the placement of names upon it. "Farengir patrols everything between here and Agandavael," he remarked, his words more for Ilithranda than the Weaver.

"That's a lot of terrain to cover," Ilithranda pointed out. "Farengir can't be everywhere all at once. These mercenaries must have slipped through. That would be far easier for a single craft," she noted.

"Why would mercenaries come here?" Daijen asked, his question aimed at the Weaver now.

"Why else?" the Weaver countered, his gaze glancing high as if he could see the spider.

"The silk," Ilithranda voiced.

There seemed a pinch of dramatic flair to the Weaver as he spun on his heel. "Forgive me. I have forgotten introductions. I am Abel Set-Sedaas. *You* are initiates of Ka'vairn," he stated, making a point to raise his gaze to both.

"We are," Ilithranda confirmed. "I am Ilithranda," she greeted, her family name notably absent.

"I am Daijen Saeth," he said, bowing his head.

"Our two orders have a pact," Ilithranda went on. "We have come to see you honour it."

Abel placed one hand over his heart. "And we will see it honoured, Ilithranda of Ka'vairn. You will follow me."

The Weaver walked away from the ruins and the bodies and called his spider mount with a short sharp *tick*. The creature hurried down the tree, barely disturbing the branches and leaves, and made its way over. Abel hopped on one of its legs, as if it were a stepping stone to the saddle.

"You may walk beside him," the Weaver instructed. "But never in front," he warned. "Do not show them your back. Not once. Not even for a second."

Daijen wasn't even that keen on walking by its side, but he made a mental note of Abel's warning all the same. And so, with one hand on the hilt of his sabre, the initiate mirrored the spider as it navigated the trees of The Sin'duil.

"Have you been troubled by mercenaries before?" Daijen asked, quickly disturbed by the sound of the spider's legs on the forest floor.

"Yes," Abel confirmed, his voice slightly muffled by the silver mask. "Though it was before my time. As you say, our borders are protected by Vahlken. I fear this... *gap in the net* is a result of war."

"What of your companion back there?" Ilithranda pressed. "Was he the first casualty of these mercenaries?"

"Halikon," the Weaver said, naming his companion with sorrow. "Sadly not. Though they did not take us by surprise, they succeeded in killing another of my order. His spider too, though I do not believe they intended to kill the creature but capture it."

Daijen tore his eyes from the spider to look solely at Abel. "And you haven't been to the forest's edge, to the coast?"

"We are not fighters, Daijen Saeth. We are tailors, smiths, armourers, tanners even. Violence is not our way. It is our mounts that have kept them mostly at bay."

Daijen thought of the three men he had killed—two this very day—and knew he and Ilithranda could not say the same. What were they if not fighters?

"And you were quite right, Ilithranda of Ka'vairn," the masked Andaren said. "I heard your conversation before Halikon confronted you. It *was* hubris that saw to the end of Kharis Vhay. Its carcass stands now to remind us of the past. Of our failings."

"What happened?" Daijen asked.

"We bent the spiders to our will here," the Weaver continued. "Forced them to live in cages, only to feed and breed as we allowed. We *took* their silk as if we were deserving of it. For generations they lived like this. It only took one spider to bring it all down."

"*One* spider?"

Abel glanced at the initiate and allowed his mount to continue for several steps before answering. "A female was mishandled. It broke free of containment and killed the keepers. Its actions resulted in more spiders being freed. It was chaos after that. Many died. They made Kharis Vhay their nest. Any who tried to flee never made it through The Sin'duil. Fear drove my predecessors to use fire. It killed some of the spiders but, in the end, it was a death blow to Kharis Vhay itself."

"But it was not the end of your order," Daijen commented, an evident observation.

Abel again glanced at the accompanying initiate. "You do not know your own history?"

Daijen didn't need to look at Ilithranda to know she was smiling with amusement. "I have read of your accomplishments and seen for myself the labour of your work," he replied. "I confess, I did not read so far as to know of your past."

"Our two orders overlapped centuries past," Abel explained. "It was the Vahlken who came to our aid. And it was the Vahlken who helped us rebuild. Thus, the price for our works has already been paid."

Fascinated, Daijen pictured Aegres descending from the sky to push back the vengeful spiders. What a sight that must have been, especially for the desperate Weavers. He imagined that scene as they trekked through The Sin'duil for several hours. Of course, it was inevitable, given their westerly heading, that they would meet the southern tips of The Orsindil Mountains.

There sat the mouth of a cave, a giant maw that reached high into the rock face. In the setting sun, the jagged entrance was cast in stark shadows, shadows that hid long and hairy legs. Daijen paused as he noted the distant spider move, its presence previously unseen amidst the uneven stone. Then it was gone altogether, swallowed up by the cave.

"Where are we?" he asked.

"Home," Abel simply replied.

As he answered as much, bright torches came to life from deeper inside the cavern, their light bouncing off a pair of silver faces. The new Weavers approached on foot, one behind the other and back to back. Their footsteps were perfectly timed, allowing them to walk through the cave at a regular speed and without tripping, as if they were a single animal on four legs.

"Where is Halikon?" a female voice asked, the Weaver who led the pair.

"The mercenaries," Abel answered, his two words enough to convey Halikon's fate.

If grieved, the female Weaver's expression was her own behind the mask of patterned silver, though there was a visible dip in her demeanour. "Initiates?"

"Yes," Abel replied with some passion. "Meet Ilithranda and Daijen."

"Greetings. I am Soveana. This is Melios," she added, shifting her shoulders to indicate the Weaver at her back. "You have come for your armour and atori blades," Soveana assumed, her gaze drifting over the initiates. "And you already possess a sabre," the Weaver observed with curiosity.

"Daijen's a quick learner," Ilithranda quipped, though Daijen was sure that he alone heard the humour in her voice.

"Very good," Soveana surmised evenly. "You will accompany us." The Weavers moved off as one and without any notable sign to the other, until Soveana paused and Melios mimicked her with immaculate precision. "You must walk as we do," she advised.

Daijen and Ilithranda shared a look, of trepidation perhaps. They had sparred together and against each other, their styles seamlessly flowing into one, but walking back to back in perfect harmony was a skill Kastiek had left out of their training. Worse still, they faced the wrath of giant spiders if they got it wrong.

Since the only alternative was to return to Ka'vairn without their armour—another badge of their station—the two initiates positioned themselves heel to heel and with Ilithranda leading. That left Daijen walking backwards, there to face Abel's trailing spider.

It was impossible to say where those eyes were looking, each an orb of glistening black. By the quivering of its fangs, however, Daijen guessed it to be watching his every step, just waiting for him to trip and take on the appearance of prey. Indeed, he caught Ilithranda's heel more than once and the pair had to pause while they repositioned themselves.

Once inside the cave, Abel's spider became one of many, though the majority were significantly smaller. It seemed thousands covered the walls, their sizes ranging from a fingernail to that of a dog, all of them crawling over each other. Those that dwelled in the jagged formations above were equal in size to Abel's. They sat perfectly still. Watching.

"In the forest," Daijen recalled, his words aimed at Abel, "you said your predecessors bent the spiders to your will and that Kharis Vhay stood to remind you of your failings. Yet," he said at length, "you saddle the spiders."

"Only the males," the Weaver informed. "And it is a mutually beneficial relationship. They offer themselves as able mounts in return for our protection."

"Protection from what?" Daijen enquired, having seen what little the Weavers could do in a fight.

"From the females," Abel answered simply, if ominously so.

Soveana and Melios soon led them into a tunnel that could not accommodate any of the abnormally large spiders. It was there that Abel dismounted and dismissed his spider while walking backwards after Daijen. Along the way, he collected his own torch, adding more light to the increasingly narrow tunnel.

Proportionately, the spiders that adorned the walls and ceiling became smaller and smaller, their webs forming an arch throughout the tunnel. When, at last, they passed through a door, Abel Set-Sedaas closed it behind him and dropped the locking bar into place.

"We are safe in here," Soveana declared, peeling away from Melios.

Daijen parted from Ilithranda and craned his neck to take in the new chamber. It was obviously a place for people with all the familiar trappings of a humble home. Rugs lay haphazardly on the cold floor as well as those others that hung from the walls. Though they were partially hidden behind drapes and personal decoration, the initiate made out individual beds on the far side.

Aside from a small kitchen and eating area, it was the workstation occupying the heart of the chamber that grabbed

Daijen's attention. Three large vats, cauldrons of iron, sat atop fires, their bubbling contents producing a purple light that spilled into the cave. They were surrounded by tables of ingredients, unusual tools, and alchemical devices—some of which Daijen recognised from Ka'vairn.

Inquisitive as he was, the initiate was drawn towards them. "What *is* this?"

Melios walked around the other side of the vats. "'Tis the beginning of our work," he said, tracking a small spider as it crawled over his fingers.

Ilithranda came up on Daijen's side, her violet gaze lost to the bubbling potions. "The magic of The Weavers," she uttered. "This is how you transform the spiders."

"A gift from Ahnir," Soveana interpreted. "The spells we enact are from His very bones."

"Much like yourselves," Abel pointed out, wandering around the workstation. "Is it not the will of Ahnir that you have come to be... something else?"

Daijen was about to agree, seeing the similarity between the two transformations, when Ilithranda cut him off.

"We follow the path of Handuin," she stated, and no more.

"Indeed," Soveana agreed knowingly.

Abel picked up a sieve on a long stick and stirred one of the vats before raising it above the cauldron. Daijen's sharp eyes couldn't miss the writhing spiders collected inside the sieve, some bigger than others. Some appeared dead.

"The females," Abel said, his eyes finding Daijen through the narrow slits of his mask. "So few survive the process," he explained, compounding all the more how similar the magic was.

"Those that do, however," Soveana interjected, "produce a silk unlike any other."

Daijen and Ilithranda both followed the Weaver's gaze to the far wall behind them. There, fitted about a crude mannequin, was a cuirass of battered and scarred leather. It was through the battle damage that they saw the delicate bronze weave—the silk of the

Weavers—that formed the underlay of every piece of Vahlken armour.

Soveana slowly walked towards the armour. "Though it cannot boast the durability of dwarven silvyr, it is stronger than steel and certainly more flexible than both. It can be applied to armour and weapon alike. As I said, it is the females that produce the desired silk and they do not part with it easily, nor are there many who can weave it."

Daijen held his question while Ilithranda walked in front of him to approach the mannequin. "How many are you?" he asked.

Soveana glanced at Melios and Abel. "We are three now," she reported, her grief audible.

Daijen adjusted his tone, softening his response. "I'm sorry for your loss."

"This..." The wonder in Ilithranda's voice turned all towards her. She stood with one hand hovering over the chest of the cuirass. "This was *his*," she whispered.

Melios rounded the cauldrons, his hands clasped at the waist. "You have a good eye," he praised.

Daijen looked from one to the other, his confusion evident. "It was whose?"

Ilithranda stepped back so he could see the cuirass and vambraces strapped to the wooden arms. "Handuin's," she answered in a word.

The initiate's lips parted in awe as he looked upon it with new eyes. "The armour of Handuin," he murmured.

"'Twas gifted us upon his death," Melios informed. "It, perhaps, deserves more grandeur than we can afford it here, but a gift such as that is not to be undervalued."

Daijen wholly agreed. Handuin's personal armour belonged in Ka'vairn, mounted beside his throne if not on display in the imperial palace in Aran'saur. And yet, somehow, it seemed to belong where it stood, in this, the most unpretentious of places. After all, were Handuin's true deeds and motivations not a secret, kept away from the world?

Again, Ilithranda made to touch the cuirass and retracted her fingers at the last second, daring not to touch so revered an item.

"Come," Abel bade, his body half turning to face another door in the corner. "I will show you to your quarters. Being only two of you, your stay with us shall not be so long as your predecessors."

"We won't be staying here," Ilithranda announced, strength returned to her voice. "You have a mercenary problem. Daijen and I will see to it. We will make camp at Kharis Vhay in the meantime."

"Your assistance is most welcome," Soveana replied. "Though you need not put yourselves in harm's way. They are not the first to come for our spells, nor the spiders. They will be deterred in time."

"You need not fear for our safety," Ilithranda told her. "Killing humans is what we were made for."

Daijen felt the grip of a cold hand in his gut. Ilithranda's perspective was skewed by centuries of Skaramangian propaganda, the truth yet to be earned. While that remained the case, she would slaughter humans like animals, unaware they were little more than puppets.

If he was to fight beside her—as Ilithranda would expect—then he would have to bring his blade to bear as she did. As much as he couldn't stomach the idea, there was another part of him that craved the battle to come.

That craved the *hunt*.

36
AN IRON BEAST

Day and night rolled over the realm of Verda again and again as Kitrana Voden put The Swamps of Morthil behind her. So too did the dwarves she trailed, their progress marked by the hoof prints of Bludgeon the Warhog.

Like the repetition of day and night, Kit relived the tale Yamnomora had brought to life, and only feet away from the resting place of Mordrith Underborn, the protagonist of her story.

While she was able to absorb so much of it, the broader picture was significantly harder to piece together. Her order, one that had stood beneath the waves for millennia, was connected to a cult of what she could only surmise to be demon-worshippers.

The Dark Ones...

Those words especially had plagued her in the days since setting off from the swamps. It conjured images of the Leviathan imprisoned beneath the mountains. A creature born of nightmares.

What's more, they were tethered to the engraved skeleton, a *god* to the Andarens. The battle maiden hadn't seen a skeleton of that description for sixteen years, not since she had stood beside Gallien Drakalis beneath Harendun. Including the one the Andarens called Ahnir, entombed in God Fall, and the one the dwarves had excavated, Kit knew there were, at least, three of them out there.

Three gods.

The Nimean didn't hold to that belief, especially since Yamnomora had told of their relevance to these *Skaramangians*.

"*They're everywhere,*" the dwarf had warned.

Kit thought of the Merdians and their Dread Queen. Were they connected to this cult? Or, as Yamnomora had insisted, were the battle maidens a branch, and a blind one at that? She couldn't believe the latter to be true, for she knew her order had been built out of a need to protect the world, not harm it.

Still, whatever the truth, Kitrana was left with a singular problem: she had no idea what she was in the middle of. That wasn't to say she didn't have a clear path. Her people, the proud citizens of Nimala, needed her. That was a war she could only wage with the sword of Skara in hand, and wholly forged at that.

By night, her dreams were filled with fantasies of freeing the Nimeans forced to excavate The Black Vault. With the sword in hand, she would reduce the Merdians to ash and emerge with an army at her back. Then the Dread Queen would suffer the wrath of a battle maiden.

Looking ahead now, at the bleak and cold landscape of Isendorth's southern plains, that future seemed a lifetime away. She didn't even have the hilt, let alone the rest of the blade. And the sea... How far away it seemed.

It was with such dwindling hope that she journeyed for more days still, The Morthil Mountains always on her right. Only when a great forest took shape on her left did the smith, Grarfath, slow his pace so they might walk together.

"Ye don' 'ave to hang back ye know. Ye can walk *with* us."

Kit spared Yamnomora a glance. "I would not have her go to the trouble of conjuring more threats," she quipped miserably.

Grarfath replied with an expression that was somewhere between amusement and apology. "I get the feelin' that trust is hard-earned with that one," he said.

"What's her story?" Kit asked.

Grarfath opened and closed his mouth while he thought about it. "Ye know, I 'ave no idea," he answered with a quiet laugh.

"But *you* trust her?"

The smith shrugged. "She knows things abou' me mother, things ye could only know if ye were friends. That'll 'ave to be enough for now."

"Even though your mother was a... Skaramangian?"

The dwarf looked uncomfortable, if not ashamed.

"I'm sorry," Kitrana was quick to add. "Who am I to comment on such things? I don't understand this... *secret war,* and I certainly don't understand how my people are connected to it. For all I know... For all I know, I'm one of these *demon worshippers*."

"Ye're not the only one tryin' to wrap yer head around it all. Giant skeletons. Weapons o' power. Secret cults. Three-Headed Dread Serpents! I'm a long way from home, I can tell ye that."

"That makes two of us," the Nimean remarked. "Where exactly are we?" she enquired, taking in the fogged horizon.

Grarfath sighed. "Damned if I know, lass. I've not been out o' the mountains in decades. Hells, I haven' seen the swamps since I were a pup. All I know is: I can' go back."

Though such a thought appeared to burden the dwarf, he shouldered it well. Either that, Kit considered, or some part of him was glad to be free of the place.

"Ye're still on The Dorth Road, ye dolts," Yamnomora called back from Bludgeon's saddle, her ears apparently tuned in to their conversation. "That there's The Morn'duil," she identified, her chin thrusting at the forest to the east. "Another day an' we'll reach The Yemmel Path. From there we can head towards the ruins."

"What ruins?" Kitrana demanded.

Yamnomora tutted. "The Ruins o' Tor Valan, ye useless fish. Ye both need to look at a map every once in a while. There's more to the world than mountains an' water."

Grarfath looked up at Kitrana. "Are ye to follow us there? Ye spoke o' Harendun, where ye lost yer sword."

How strange it was to hear a surface-dweller speak of the sword. In all her years searching the dry lands of Verda, she had never revealed the truth or significance of the blade. Until he saw its power, even Gallien Drakalis had been in the dark. Still, Kitrana had been sure to keep the whole truth to herself. The dwarves knew that the sword of Skara was important to her people, pivotal even to the war beneath the seas, but she had kept its similarities to the hammer to herself.

Picking up Grarfath's question, she looked to the southern horizon that concealed the distant city. "Harendun was under siege when last I was there. It will be in the hands of the Andarens again by now. My friend will be long gone and the sword with him."

"Harendun belongs to Erador," Yamnomora yelled over one shoulder.

Kit was struck by the statement. "Truly?"

"Aye. The humans 'ave held it for... it's got to be goin' on sixteen years now."

Knowing what she did of the war between Erador and Andara, that made no sense to the Nimean. "The Andarens haven't retaliated? They've always fought back. They've *always* taken ground back."

"Not this time," the dwarf reported with half a care. "Though, the dragon might have somethin' to do with it."

Yamnomora's words sparked a memory in the battle maiden, taking her back to The Raven's port side. There she had seen the silhouette of a creature so great that its wings seemed to encompass the city itself. It was with that dragon that Erador had taken Harendun and, apparently, kept it.

"The Vahlken haven't attacked?" she probed, her disbelief quite evident.

"How am I to know?" Yamnomora snapped. "I've been busy fightin' me own war. A fight, I'll add, that's takin' us to Erador. I suggest *ye* find yer way to Harendun," she strongly advised. "At least ye'll blend in there. Might even find yer friend an' that fancy sword, eh?"

"Ye've still got to get there," Grarfath pointed out. "That's a lot o' Andara to cross ain' it? An' I imagine the Andarens are watchin' the roads in an' out o' Harendun damned closely. Ye might be better off stickin' with us."

"*We*," Yamnomora emphasised, "would be better off if she didn'."

"Gallien was expecting the Andarens to attack," Kit recalled, ignoring the dwarf's remark altogether. "He will have put Andara's shores behind him." He may well have done so in chains, she thought.

Grarfath appeared to brighten up. "So ye're to accompany us then?"

Kitrana's crystal blue eyes roamed over the hammer in the smith's hand. She was sure it was a companion to the sword of Skara, just as Gallien's axe had been. How it might lead her back to the sword she couldn't rightly say, but being close to it gave her hope. Damned if she didn't crave it; like searching for a light in the dark.

"I suppose I am," the Nimean said. "If you would have me."

Grarfath gave a soft chuckle. "It's not every day the ocean spits out one o' its own, an' at me feet no less. I'd be glad o' yer company, lass."

Yamnomora's groan drifted back to find the pair.

The smith waved her response away and kept his dark eyes on the battle maiden. Kitrana could feel that gaze settle over her, inquisitive as it was. Though the dwarf obviously craved the comfort of his home and people, he was certainly curious about her, if not her world.

Kit dipped her head so she might see the dwarf past the edge of her hood. She said nothing, her question asked by expression alone.

It was enough to fluster Grarfath. "Apologies, Miss Voden," he said, acknowledging his stare. "I've never even seen the ocean is all, an' now I'm walkin' beside a fish... beside a Nomoan."

"Nimean," Kitrana corrected with a warm smile.

"Aye, that's it. A *Nimean*. What I'm tryin' to say is... Well, ye're like nothin' I've ever seen. Back at the swamp, ye said yer people had been attacked by another. There's a lot more o' ye down there then?"

Kit was nodding along. "The seas are as populated as the land," she divulged, seeing no harm in sharing with the inquisitive dwarf. "In fact," the Nimean added, eyeing the red-headed dwarf, "there might be more intelligent life beneath the waves than above it."

Grarfath appeared a touch bewildered. "An' to think that world were jus' beneath me own, a sheet o' rock between us."

The battle maiden thought of the Leviathan again, the monster far closer to the dwarven kingdom than any of the ocean's races. She had, like the power of the sword, left the creature out of her tale when it came to her turn in the swamp. There was something about the ancient beast, an obscene malevolence that kept her from voicing it, as if she might deny its existence by remaining silent.

"There are seven races," she told the smith, keen to have her mind move on from The Black Vault.

"*Seven*?"

The Nimean gave herself a moment, focusing solely on one foot after another as she trekked The Dorth Road. Peeling back the layers of the ocean world was to reveal something sacred, something pure and untouched by the grubby hands of the surface dwellers. Yet, Kitrana found the dwarf's curiosity, if not outright naivety, quite disarming. Speaking to him was akin to unburdening herself.

"You have humans, Andarens, and, of course, the magnificent dwarves," she beamed. "The folds of the ocean conceal many more. There are my people," she said proudly, "the Nimeans. The Merdians are enemy to us all it seems." Kitrana swallowed and collected her thoughts. "Then there's the Jinn, the Adakii, the Kells, the Fangoras... and the *Vorge*," she reluctantly added, almost offended by their inclusion, but demanded by their intelligence.

Grarfath blew his cheeks out, his eyes lost to the distance. "An' they're all like yerself?"

"No," the battle maiden replied, a laugh edging on her lips. "Some of us bear physical similarities, much like the humans and

Andarens. I suppose it's our cultures that separate us more than anything."

"Ye've war though," Grarfath replied, taking from her brief story, days earlier.

"There was peace for a long time," Kit lamented. "But it wasn't enough for the Merdians. Then they came for the sword."

The dwarf gave a solemn laugh. "Ye know, me people did away with the gods years ago, decided they weren' as important as industry an' profit an' the like. Yet 'ere we are, ye an' me. Two people from worlds that should never meet, an' with these Skaramangians in common. It seems to me the gods 'ave got their eye on us, eh?" he opined.

They weren't her gods, but Kitrana Voden had to agree. If nothing else, their fates appeared to have been bound together in some way.

"Ye said this sword o' yers is broken," Grarfath went on. "The blade is it?"

"Yes. Just under halfway. The hilt is an exquisite piece," she added, aware of who she was speaking to. "I would love to hear the thoughts of a dwarven smith on the matter."

"How does such a revered blade come to be shattered in two?" he enquired while adjusting the cumbersome pack over the white of his fur cloak.

The battle maiden hesitated, though not because she was reluctant to share her people's history. "It's a long story," she told him.

The dwarf eyed the path ahead. "It's a *long* road."

"That it is," Kitrana had to agree. "The sword," she began after a time, "traces back to an era my people now refer to as the Age of Skara, when all the races lived under one banner. A great warrior by our earliest records, Skara defeated a foe unlike any other and with a sword unlike any other. It was later decided that the weapon was too... *important* to be wielded by any but Skara.

"And so the sword was broken, its significance diminished. My order—the battle maidens—were formed to safeguard the hilt, while the blade itself was taken to the surface world and hidden."

Kitrana gestured to the dwarf's hammer. "Even whole, it would pale compared to a weapon that can port you from one place to another."

"Oh aye," Grarfath agreed, marvelling at the weapon. "It's more than a pretty trinket. It didn' half take it out o' me though. Felt like I could sleep for a week."

"I would say," the Nimean offered tentatively, "that you have strength enough to wield it."

Grarfath managed a smile at that, the first Kitrana had seen since his mother's tale had departed Yamnomora's lips.

The Dorth Road stretched on, consuming their journey for another two days before they reached the crossroads and an expanse of land Yamnomora called The Plains of Pelun. The time, however, gave Kitrana more opportunities to solidify a friendship with the smith, securing her place by their side. The dwarven warrior remained another matter altogether.

"That's *yer* road," Yamnomora informed, one stubby finger pointing to the path that continued south. "Follow The Annar Road until ye reach The Sael Road. Then follow that until ye reach Harendun. Best o' luck." The dwarf steered her Warhog to the easterly road. "Grarfath," she beckoned.

But the smith was distracted, her words failing to tether him.

"What's wrong?" Kit asked him, noting the concern on his face.

The dwarf didn't respond but lowered himself to one knee, where he could place a single hand to the ground. There he remained in a state of focus, his brow furrowed.

"What are ye doin'?" Yamnomora demanded, turning Bludgeon around.

"Somethin's comin'," he warned. "Somethin' *big*."

Kit looked to the flat vista in front of them and even that which lay behind them. Nothing. To their left, The Yemmel Path followed the southern wall of The Morn'duil, a route that could be seen for miles from the crossroads. Still nothing. The Annar Road to their right curled out of sight, behind a gravelled rise that hid much of the south. It was there that Grarfath's attention was drawn.

"It's nearly upon us," he snapped.

Indeed, Kit could feel the vibrations through her bare feet now. It was a constant rumble, as if the land was being struck by ten thousand hammers.

Perturbed by the unseen threat, Yamnomora directed Bludgeon towards The Annar Road, where she might see past the hills of stone. There she remained, still as the rocks themselves, her gaze taken by the south.

"What do ye see?" Grarfath asked.

The answer seemed obvious to Kitrana, who could hear the iron beast approaching now. "We need to hide," she said with no lack of urgency.

Indeed, Yamnomora was already riding Bludgeon back towards them, and at speed. "Over there!" she urged, pointing her weapon at a collection of boulders protruding from the base of the rise.

Together they raced for cover, reaching it only a second before the rumbling was given life. The battle maiden peered over the top of the boulder while the dwarves dared to stick their necks out to the side. What they saw was enough to see the trio retreat a step.

Kitrana felt like sinking into the stone, where she might not be seen.

"What in the hells?" Grarfath muttered.

Yamnomora coiled Bludgeon's reins about her fist, holding the animal fast. "Nobody move," she whispered.

The Nimean couldn't move, her feet rooted to the spot as she watched legion upon legion of Andaren soldiers march over the crossroads. The dozens quickly turned to hundreds which, in time, proved to be thousands. They moved across the land like a bronze snake, their armour gleaming in the midday sun, their obsidian cloaks contrasted by flowing white hair. It was with spears and shields that they advanced into the east, and with sabres resting on hips.

Dotted throughout were great caravans, carts filled with supplies and tools. Travelling alongside the main bulk were battalions mounted on their mutated war horses. Here and there, rising above the masses, were towering banners of the broken black circle against a yellow sunburst.

After watching the first few thousand pass by, Kitrana sank into a crouch, where she remained for some time. Indeed, the sun had moved through the sky when, at last, the cacophony of armour and thundering boots passed beyond the crossroads. In their wake there trailed a cloud of dust, as if the land was cleaning itself after suffering the walking Death.

The trio emerged, and cautiously so.

Yamnomora led them back to the crossroads, an axe in each hand. They seemed a cumbersome combination of weapons in Kitrana's eyes, each ideally requiring two hands to wield. Yet, somehow, she just knew the dwarven warrior wouldn't be troubled by that fact.

"It's not every day ye see the Andaren army out for a walk," Grarfath remarked, the hammer resting over one shoulder.

Yamnomora said nothing. She stood at the crossroads, watching the army churn up the land.

"What are the chances, eh?" the smith went on, his words aimed at Kit. "Ye askin' questions abou' 'em takin' Harendun back after so long an' 'ere they are."

Yamnomora was shaking her head, her gaze still fixed on the east. "That ain' the way to Harendun, ye dolt."

Grarfath frowned, looking from one road to the next. "Then where're they goin'?"

The battle maiden knew the answer to that, though she could hardly voice it with all the dust in the air. "That is to be our road," she managed.

Grarfath licked his lips. "They're goin' to the Ruins o' Tor Valan?" By his tone, the dwarf could make little sense of it.

"The emperor hasn' sent ten thousand Andarens to march on a *ruin*," Yamnomora told him. "They're followin' the road all the way to the towers. To Erador."

To *war*, the Nimean thought.

37
BLOOD IN THE WATER

60 Years Ago...

Among men and Andarens alike, Daijen knew he would be the predator, his skills and mutations placing him above their natural abilities. In the lair of a giant spider—a *female* spider—he felt as if he had returned to the walls of a burning Harendun, when he looked out on the encroaching fleet of Eradoran war ships as no more than a pitiful *messenger guard*.

He was prey for the taking.

Just ahead of him, Soveana, Melios, and Abel moved with vigilance as they advanced. Tight in their grips were long torches, the ends blazing in the darkness. Fire, they had said, was the only thing the females feared. Even so, Daijen wielded his Vahlken sabre in one hand and a torch in the other, his nerves comforted by the weight of steel.

Ilithranda remained close to his side, armed with a sword taken from one of the fallen mercenaries. Her violet gaze was cast high, to the chamber's vaulted ceiling. The flames, however, failed to reach such heights, allowing spiders to move unseen above them.

Adding to the peril, they were surrounded by webs. While some belonged to adolescent females, whose silk had yet to mature, and subjugated males, whose natural webbing was little more than an irritation, there were entire walls and deadly strands of bronze silk.

Daijen probed it with the flat of his blade, curious as to how it might behave on contact. Indeed, the sword bonded instantly with the bronze web, his touch sending ripples across the whole network. The initiate was forced to apply a portion of his mutated strength to prize the weapon away.

When he came across a single strand of the extraordinary silk, he brought the edge of his sabre to bear, dragging the blade down in a sawing motion. Had it been a length of rope it would surely have succumbed to that biting edge, but the spider silk resisted, the silk vibrating in the air.

"Would you *stop* that," Ilithranda hissed. "Just move around it," she suggested, her stress visible.

Daijen apologised for his inquisitiveness with expression alone, silently pledging to duck and weave between the webs. More than once they all stopped along the narrow path, sure that they had seen something at the edge of the light. It always came to nothing though, the females keeping to the darkness.

"Over there," Abel directed, taking the lead.

The Weaver was naturally drawn towards the dull glow that flared beyond a corner. Rounding that corner, the light intensified beyond their need for the torches to see.

"Melios." Soveana's command saw the Weaver take up a position at their rear, where he might keep his torch between them and any flanking spiders.

Daijen, like the others, was occupied by the jagged hole in the side of the cave, the floor littered with debris. The morning sun poured in, bathing the cave in light. The bronze webbing glistened in that light, revealing the alcove to have been a nest.

"This wall was blown in," Ilithranda observed, the tip of her boot knocking aside a small rock.

"There is but one power that could do this," Soveana surmised.

"Magic," Daijen uttered.

"Our suspicions were correct," Ilithranda concluded, moving to place one boot on the lip of the broken wall. "They have a *wizard.*"

Daijen had to agree, though in four months of probing the mercenaries' defences and brief skirmishes in The Sin'duil, they had never been challenged by the magic-user. Yet, in the dead of night, they had observed strange lights from the deck of their great ship.

"They have taken a female," Abel reported, his words directing the group to the back of the cave. There, in the light of his torch, they saw a swarm of spiders on the far wall, their writhing mass lending the wall a liquid-like appearance. "The mother would not abandon them so young."

Ilithranda looked beyond the cave, to the forest that dominated the view. Her white hair shone in the sunshine as the wisps were caught in the intruding breeze of spring. "We will see it freed from their grasp," she vowed. "It's time these mercenaries left our shores or died upon them."

Tracking the men through The Sin'duil proved easy enough, their trail also providing more evidence that a wizard was in their company. Besides the footprints, numerous trees had been uprooted and cast aside as if they had been no more than sticks in the way.

Ilithranda ran her fingers over the displaced roots that stood as tall as she did. "The humans believe our use of magic is abhorrent, that the mutations we create are unnatural and therefore *wrong.* Yet they use their magic to upturn the world around them, destroying whatever gets in their way."

Daijen could hear the venom in her voice. His companion had spent significantly more years in the war and those years had been spent earning her place in Ka'vairn. Unlike Daijen, she would have countless memories of them killing her comrades and friends on the battlefield. He wondered if the truth would even be enough to salve her hatred.

Hearing the waves of The Drifting Sea, Daijen bade her follow him through the last of the trees and onto the beach. For two days they had pursued their quarry across the forest, and not once had they come across one of their traps or been set upon by an ambush.

"They've pulled everyone back," Daijen determined as he set eyes on the mercenary vessel, the ship sitting idly on the distant waves.

"Because they have what they came for," Ilithranda said. "We should have brought an end to this sooner," she added in frustration.

Daijen knew the clipped remark was aimed at him, for it had been he who enforced their caution while investigating the human presence, if only to keep the death toll down. Now, however, the initiate saw no way around the impending violence, their crimes too steep.

"There," Ilithranda directed, her gaze leading Daijen to the large row boat making for open water.

Daijen set his sharp eyes to the scene and was immediately disturbed by what he saw. While the mercenaries operated the boat, the wizard stood in the centre, his arms outstretched and neck craned.

Above them all, slowly spinning on its axis, was the female spider.

The creature's hideous hide and bulbous body was laid bare in the twilight of the setting sun. So too was its binding in ropes, making it incapable of lashing out from its lofty placement. It made sense to Daijen now why the wizard had felled so many trees, for the spider's considerable bulk could not be squeezed through every part of the forest while suspended.

Beside him, Ilithranda had already removed her fur cloak and was dumping it at the base of the nearest tree. "The very moment the sun drops below the mountains, we make for the ship."

Daijen nodded his agreement and unclipped his cloak to add to hers. "How exactly do we get the spider back to shore?" he asked. "Melios tells me they can't swim."

"You grew up in Taranathen," Ilithranda pointed out needlessly.

Daijen eyed his companion with some exasperation. "You're assuming I know how to sail."

"I thought everyone from Taranathen could sail," she replied irritably.

"My uncle was a simple fisherman," he reminded. "I have no *idea* how to sail a ship that size. What I do know is they require a large crew for a reason."

"Then we convince them to bring the spider ashore," Ilithranda responded.

Daijen set his gaze to the distant ship again. He didn't imagine it would be as easy as that.

As always, though, there was only one path at Daijen Saeth's feet: forwards. Within the hour they were swimming through black water and under a black sky. The ship was aglow with torchlight, its anchor still firmly in place. It was the anchor chain that allowed the two initiates to ascend to the deck, where they got their first glimpse of the crew.

While maintaining his grip on the outside of the rail, Daijen made his assessment of those who manned the ship and arrived at a single word: young. If any of them had more than twenty winters under their belt the Andaren would be surprised. Most weren't armed, suggesting the sailors he could see weren't the mercenaries they had encountered over the last four months but simply the ship's crew.

"Get on with it!" came a call from the command deck—a true mercenary. "I want us out of these godforsaken waters!"

Daijen narrowed his eyes on the command deck and noted more of his ilk. They bore scars of their violent trade and wore a variety of tarnished weapons about them.

The wizard stepped out from behind the main mast, his robes of black and gold draping him from shoulder to decking. He had a sharp face, though his features were too harsh to be considered handsome, and his jet-black hair was cut short at the shoulders and slicked back behind his ears.

He was notably looking down at the deck, and with some scrutiny.

"It'll hold, Sir," the mercenary called down from the command deck.

"It had better, Mr Gertwig," the wizard shot back. "For all our sakes."

"He's not just any wizard," Ilithranda whispered, her voice so low only the ears of a Vahlken could hear her. "He's one of The Jainus."

Having only ever heard of their order, Daijen looked again at the wizard, and with a new perspective. "He's not working with the mercenaries. They're working for *him*."

"This is a Jainus operation," Ilithranda articulated, a steely resolve creeping into her hushed words. "We will have to kill him first," she advised. "He cannot be allowed to cast a single spell."

While Daijen agreed, he was still thinking of how they might convince the crew to make for shore. "If we dispatch the wizard and the mercenaries, the crew should see sense and take our command."

Ilithranda was already looking at him. "Daijen." Despite all that she intoned in that one word, she still voiced her intentions. "Everything on this ship dies tonight. Even the spider."

She left no time for discussion before scrambling along the side of the ship, her strength and sense of balance enough to keep her from making a sound. Daijen hesitated, his eyes lingering on the young crew who had, most likely, never even seen an Andaren before. Yet, Ilithranda would make them suffer for the lives their kin had taken centuries past. And all because they were pawns of the...

None but those who had survived the pits of Handuin's magic would have seen it.

Drawn in by movement from The Jainus, Daijen saw the man's voluminous sleeve fall down his arm as he adjusted the hair behind his ear. There, on the inside of his wrist, was a tattoo the initiate had only ever seen behind the ear of a dwarf.

Daijen's thoughts and reality had collided in the same moment.

"Skaramangian," he uttered to himself.

The revelation begged certain questions. Chiefly: were The Jainus working for the Skaramangians? Was everyone onboard a Skaramangian or simply in their pocket? For all his questions, Daijen knew there must be answers inside the wizard's head. It was with that thought that Daijen's objective shifted from freeing the spider and saving the crew to questioning The Jainus. How long had it been since The Valtorak, or any Vahlken, had had the opportunity to interrogate a Skaramangian?

There was, of course, a singular problem—an obstacle—that sat between Daijen and any of his objectives and, at that moment, the problem was creeping over the rail with a dagger between her teeth.

The wizard had his back to her, his attention having returned to the large grating built into the deck. Furthermore, Ilithranda's timing had been perfect as she slipped onboard while none were looking in her direction. The Jainus would be dead in mere moments.

"No!" Daijen cried, as he hauled himself seamlessly onto the deck.

The wizard was startled, a catalyst, perhaps, for the protective shield he erected. Fortunately for The Jainus, the spell he enacted was that of a sphere, protecting him from the knife he would have received to the brain stem. The shield flared on contact and the dagger was flung from Ilithranda's grip. So too was she flung when the wizard whipped his hand through the air, his magic coalescing in a wave of condensed air.

While the crew instinctively backed off from Daijen, his sabre already in hand, the mercenaries leapt into action, taking the steps from the command deck two or three at a time. Their advance mattered little, however, for the Skaramangian Jainus had turned his sights on him.

Daijen pivoted like a dancer, putting the thick mast between him and the wizard only a moment before a staccato of lightning exploded across the deck. It tore through the panelling, scattering splinters and debris in every direction before leaving the ship scorched and alight with flames. Without a line of sight, the next attack never came, granting the initiate time to deal with the approaching mercenaries.

Kastiek's training kicked in as the lives before him became no more than *threats*. Threats needed to be eliminated. His sabre sliced neatly through the midriff of the first mercenary, igniting a flash of excitement in his heart. How good it felt to unleash so many years of mere training!

One after the other they fell upon him. Their blades only clashed if Daijen willed it, his skill more than capable of taking their lives without such back and forth. But he enjoyed the parrying, deflecting, and evading with swift grace before delivering the final execution. All the while, he was in command of his footwork, ensuring the mast remained between him and the wizard that moved to get a clear shot.

Only when more spells rang out did Daijen realise The Jainus was occupied elsewhere. Ilithranda was back on her feet. A quick glance over the port side of the deck revealed a streak of corpses in her wake and a bloody sword in her hand. The wizard was destroying the ship in his attempt to bring her down, his human reflexes no match against Ilithranda's enhancements. In no time at all, there were more fires springing up, littering the deck with hungry flames.

Daijen ducked under an incoming mercenary's sword and elbowed another in the face while watching his companion close the gap on The Jainus. It was this split in his attention that caused him to take his next life without a care. Too late did he notice the heart he had pierced belonged to one of the young crewmen who had likely attacked out of fear.

He coughed a spattering of blood, his dark eyes roaming over Daijen's face, questioning that fateful moment. Daijen opened his mouth, as if he might apologise, but no words came forth. Instead, the young man slid from his sabre and collapsed on the deck, his time in Verda at an end. How many more years might he have lived had the Skaramangians not altered the course of their two realms?

Gripped by guilt, his attention slipped all the more. The mercenary named Gertwig took advantage and sprang from halfway up the steps to the command deck. It was luck alone that saved Daijen from death, the mercenary having attacked him with a hammer and what smelled like a keg of ale in his bloodstream. The weapon glanced off the initiate's shoulder, staggering him with pain and shock while giving Gertwig the time to swing again.

The pain triggered Daijen's anger, seeing him deliver one more blow than was necessary. He flicked his wrist once then twice, the first severing the mercenary's hand at the wrist and the second opening the artery in his neck. Mr Gertwig was to be dead before the minute was out.

Daijen glanced once more at the young crewman, lifeless at his feet, before a gargled cry returned his attention to the wizard. "No!" Daijen yelled, dashing towards The Jainus.

It was too late, of course, for there was no overcoming the dagger Ilithranda had launched into his throat. He wavered on his feet, his fingers still licked by small bolts of lightning. Blood trickled down his neck and began to soak his robes. It poured out when Ilithranda yanked the blade from the wound.

The Jainus fell to his knees before meeting the deck face first.

Ilithranda stood over her kill, cuirass smouldering and with half a face of cuts. If only she looked satisfied. A single bound placed the initiate on the command deck, where she unleashed her sword and darted from man to man. Daijen raced up the steps on the other side, challenging himself to stop her before she slaughtered every last one.

It was fear that drove the survivors. If they didn't lash out at Ilithranda with whatever they could find they tried to jump overboard. Even they who tried to flee could not escape her wrath, falling from the rails with bloody gashes down their backs.

"Stop!" Daijen barked, placing himself between Ilithranda and the last crewman on the command deck.

Ilithranda looked at him like he was a different person. "What are you doing?" she demanded. "You protect our enemy?" The edge in her voice was nearly as sharp as the sword in her hand.

"You don't understand," he began, and would have said more had the crewman not tried to thrust a small knife into his back.

Daijen intercepted the man's wrist and broke the bones therein, his hand held out wide and almost fully back on itself. There were numerous techniques the initiate might then have used to subdue the man, ending any further threat, but the whistle of steel brought, instead, an end to his life.

Letting him fall to the deck, Daijen looked from the dagger buried in the man's chest to Ilithranda, whose arm was still posed in the form of a throw. "Speak plainly," she instructed, "and speak sense. Anything else and you will join this ship at the bottom of the ocean."

Though she sounded like she meant every word of her threat, Daijen knew her well enough to know that she would more than hesitate to actually kill him. They had been through too much together and, ultimately, been bonded by their harsh experiences. He didn't need to know her past to know her, a fact he had reminded himself of many times in the last two decades.

"There isn't time," Daijen told her, gesturing to the flames that continued to explore every inch of the ship. "There might still be crew in the lower decks. If we act fast enough we might be able—"

"To what, Daijen?" Ilithranda interrupted. "Get them to lift anchor and steer the ship to shore? Save them and the spider at the same time?"

"We have to try!" he argued.

"Don't be so naive!" Ilithranda snapped. "The second they see us they'll force our hand or throw themselves overboard! And the spider," she went on, pointing at the large square grid on the main deck. "It'll kill us all the first chance it gets." Ilithranda marched towards him, retrieved her bloody dagger, and grabbed Daijen by the collar of his leathers. "You and I are swimming ashore and leaving this ship to burn," she commanded fiercely.

"You told the Weavers we would free it," he reminded.

"I told them I would free it from their grasp!" Ilithranda growled in his face. "Trust me, Daijen, there is freedom in death," she added, eyes glazed. "Now get in the water."

Standing amidst the carnage, the damage done, Daijen watched Ilithranda walk to the railing and deftly leap over the side without looking back. Feeling the heat of the growing fire, he took in the rest of the ship as it succumbed to flames. One spindly leg protruded through a gap in the grill, the length of it suggesting the female was considerably larger than the males he had seen. It probed the air and what it could of the surrounding deck, but the heavy grate was firmly locked into place.

The ship was no better than a tomb now.

Reluctantly, his heart filled with guilt and grief, Daijen Saeth followed his companion over the side and into the embrace of a cold sea.

38
REUNION

"You're *dead*," the smuggler spat, as if she needed reminding.

Androma retracted her staff, freeing Gallien to lower his weapon. "You're half right," she corrected, her thoughts flooded with images of the most beautiful and exquisite dragon to have ever lived. He possessed infinitely more attributes than those that made him the dragon she had poured her heart into, but to dwell on any one of them right then would prove a distraction she couldn't move past.

The sound of a staff tapping in step with someone's approach turned her ear down the length of the room.

"Androma," came the greeting.

How his voice had changed since first they met. How old he sounded now. "Aphrandhor," the old Rider replied, glimpsing the wizard's youth in her memory.

"You made good time," The Green Leaf complimented.

Androma considered what little sleep she had managed and how terribly wet she had got in her haste from Valgala. "Your message from Warth suggested you were closing in." The Rider turned her face to Gallien. "I had only hoped that we would meet under better circumstances."

"A misunderstanding," the wizard said happily enough.

"Joran," the smuggler beckoned.

Androma listened intently to the scramble of limbs that moved up from the floor and darted to Gallien's side. He was big, hardly a boy anymore. His breathing informed Androma that he was actually a little taller than she was. Brave too, she decided, if he had challenged Cob, and the Kedradi was most certainly present, his musk always that of sweat and spices.

"Joran," the old Rider began, her tone uncharacteristically soft. "You won't remember me, but I'm—"

"We were just leaving," Gallien interjected, sure to keep himself between Joran and all others.

"That is not an option," Cob told them.

"It isn't safe," Aphrandhor articulated, his tender approach differing from the Kedradi's blunt statement.

"We haven't been safe for years," Gallien retorted. "We were managing pretty well until you two arrived."

"You would be dead behind that tavern if it was not for..." Cob trailed off in response to Androma, who had raised her hand to calm him, if not all of them.

"We must *all* leave," she insisted, intoning a sense of urgency now.

"What has happened?" Aphrandhor demanded, his green robes rustling as he approached.

Androma gripped the wizard's arm. "Galahart," she answered in a word.

The Green Leaf sighed. "He belongs to the enemy then? It was only a matter of time, I suppose."

"Well," Gallien cut in, "it sounds like you have your hands full. Good to see you again, Androma. Glad you're not dead. Joran, let's go."

"Wait," Joran pleaded.

His voice. It was that of a man's now, his maturity almost solidified. The Rider, however, was sure she heard something of his mother's voice in that one word. The tragedy of Ilithranda's death lingered on the edges of her mind after that. The greater tragedy, of course, was that mother and son would never meet again in this life. What a force they would have been.

"We're *leaving*," Gallien persisted.

There followed a brief scuffle, ended only when Androma spoke again. "Galahart is the king's spymaster," she reported for the smuggler's sake. "I'm afraid the list of people hunting you down has just grown by a very *powerful* one."

Gallien had stopped, not quite reaching the door.

"As I said," Androma continued, "we must all leave. Right now."

"How long do we have?" Cob asked, as he strode about collecting his weapons of bone.

"I was not the only one to make haste from the capital," Androma warned. "Galahart has tasked his most trusted men. Make no mistake, they are ruthless killers all. They are likely here already."

"Their objective?" Cob pressed.

"I do not know," Androma replied honestly. "Capture or kill, we must get the boy to safety."

The wizard grizzled. "By dawn, Galahart will have every soldier and guard sentry on the lookout for us."

"It sounds like we'll have a better chance slipping out of the city on our own," the smuggler opined, moving for the door again.

Aphrandhor moved, his staff scraping along the floor. "You survived the Padoshi's men thanks to Cob, Mr Drakalis. You survived The Dancing Sword of the Dawn thanks to my magic. Trust me, it will take all of us to outwit the spymaster of Erador."

The Dawn Sword. Androma's mind wandered dangerously at the name. She was momentarily taken back to that night in The Edda Highlands, when the Skaramangian's favourite attack dog had ambushed them. His arrival had changed everything, altering the course they had intended for Joran and, perhaps, the world. The latter remained to be seen.

Gallien sounded like he was seething, a man forced into a corner. "Goddamn it," he muttered furiously. "Why is it every time you show up in my life, things get worse?"

Androma assumed the question was aimed at her. "You chose to keep Joran safe once, against any and all. Perhaps I should have trusted you with more; then you might have gone to Riverwatch as I instructed. That fault lies with me. But here we are. You must, again, make that same choice. Which way will you go, Gallien Drakalis?"

To the old Dragon Rider, the world was made up almost entirely by sound alone. In the narrow tunnels beneath Hemon, it was made up of hurried feet splashing through shallow puddles, laboured breathing, and the crackle of flickering flames.

Aphrandhor led them, having revealed the secret passage: a route to be taken in case the underground chamber was ever compromised. That was a chance they weren't taking with Galahart on the hunt. Following the cool air, the wizard soon brought them out into the world, only now they were beyond Hemon's walls and, judging by the sound of rushing water, among the river folk who lived outside the city, along the embankment.

"Why didn't we just *enter* the city this way?" Gallien asked, his voice just heard over the River Kyber.

"Always better to be seen coming than going," The Green Leaf called back. "This way."

"Where are we going?"

Joran's voice sounded from Androma's left. She resisted the urge to reach out and touch him, the one she had spent so long searching for. Now he was real, and a man at that. The old Rider desperately wanted to speak to him, to tell him everything. But keeping him alive—as it had been sixteen years ago—was still the priority.

"Somewhere safe," the wizard answered.

"You said that about the last place," Gallien pointed out irritably.

Their feet were now splashing through mud and puddles and the sound of a new day among the river folk was growing by the second. Their small village would be coming alive as the sun peeked in the east. Androma could already hear children playing, dogs barking, and fishermen calling out to friends and fellow workers.

For all that, the old Rider still heard one of Cob's arrows as it slid from the quiver on his back.

"Where?" she asked immediately.

"Other side of the river," the Kedradi reported. "They're making for the bridge down river."

"How many?" Androma demanded.

"Three."

"They don't look like soldiers," Joran observed.

"They wouldn't," Gallien told him knowingly. "Look at their swords. Too expensive for what they're wearing. What's the plan here?" the smuggler asked.

"We forge ahead," Aphrandhor replied.

"Have they seen us?" Androma asked.

"Yes," Cob informed.

Gallien cursed.

"What is it?" The old Rider had heard nothing to suggest things had escalated.

"We lost one—he's disappeared."

"Disappeared?"

"He's doubling back," the Kedradi guessed, though his guesses were rarely wrong. "More will be coming."

"Aphrandhor?" Androma called out.

"We're nearly there," the wizard assured. "I can see the boats from here."

"Boats?" Drakalis questioned. "We're going on the river?"

"It's the fastest way out of the city," The Green Leaf said, before asking some of the villagers to excuse his haste.

"The river only goes to one place from here," Gallien cautioned, fear in his voice.

"They're on the bridge," Cob described.

"Are they between us and the boats?" Androma asked, choosing to ignore the smuggler's concerns for the time being.

"Yes."

"Then remove them," she commanded evenly.

The *twang* of the Kedradi's bow was always followed by the sudden *thud* of impact, and there came no exception. The spymaster's thug let out no more than an unintelligible grunt before Androma heard the splash up ahead. It was hard to hear anything after that.

Screams from women, shouted names from mothers looking to gather their children, and cries from the men who abandoned their tasks and rushed to their families joined the sounds of the flowing river: a cacophony that bombarded the old Rider's ears. She did not, however, miss the distant sound of a sword being freed of its scabbard.

Again, and swiftly so, the Kedradi nocked and let loose another arrow. Androma imagined it passing through the narrowest of gaps, missing people and objects alike by a hair's breadth, before finding its mark.

Thud.

Cob was never one to disappoint. "More in pursuit," the Kedradi voiced.

Androma didn't bother turning back, for there was as much darkness behind her as there was right in front of her nose. The sound of running feet, on the other hand, turned her attention to her left, where the village buildings were lined up along the river. Unlike everyone else's, those feet were getting closer.

Centuries of instinct was enough to move the old Rider. Her staff flicked up and caught the nearest in the jaw, the blow shocking enough to stagger the man to the ground. The second cried out in anger, his voice coming from on high. He was leaping. Androma evaded with smooth ease while naming the Kedradi.

Cob intercepted Galahart's man as he landed. There came no sound of clashing steel nor even steel and bone. The Kedradi used his hands alone to disarm his enemy, break one of his legs at the knee joint and, finally, crack his neck.

But there were more than two emerging from that alley.

They had been quieter in their approach but no less swift.

Androma heard the blade of one slicing through air, the angle surely in line with her head. No more than a pivot was required to avoid the incoming sword, but the man was sure to attack again. At least he would have. Steel whistled through the air, its origins further than Cob, and took the man in the chest.

Gallien then rushed past the old Rider and met the fourth and final man. Their fight was brief, though certainly longer than if it had been Cob their enemy faced. Galahart's man cried out in pain as the smuggler cut him down with a low blow. He would never speak again after Gallien's second blow.

"It's good to know you haven't lost your edge after all these years," she quipped.

The first of Galahart's men to attack from the alley, who had taken Androma's staff to the jaw, made himself known again, his rise clumsy and loud. Androma planted her staff firmly before her and blocked the anticipated swing. Aware now of exactly where he was, the old Rider kicked out, catching her foe at the wrist and relieving him of his sword.

Confident her enemy was disarmed, Androma braced her legs and brought her staff round into a sweeping arc. The maple wood took the man in the side of the neck, dropping him to one knee, where his face then fell into line with her second attack. He was no better than a sack of meat after that, seemingly lifeless at her feet.

"Quickly!" came Aphrandhor's beckoning call.

Androma turned her ear back the way they had come. "More?" she asked any who could hear her.

"More," Drakalis reported gravely.

"Run," the old Rider barked.

Together, the four of them dashed to meet the wizard by the river's edge. Androma could hear them now; killers closing in on their prey.

"I had hoped to haggle somewhat," The Green Leaf bemoaned. "But today we are thieves it seems."

Androma allowed Cob to guide her into what she quickly deduced to be a row boat. "Where's Joran?" she asked.

"I'm here," he answered, his voice close behind.

"There are two boats," Cob told her.

"Go with Aphrandhor," she instructed the Kedradi. "Can you row, Joran?"

"He can row," Gallien replied on the boy's behalf, his voice strained as he pushed the boat out into the river.

Twang.

Cob unleashed his deadly skills upon more of the spymaster's men. Androma couldn't say how many were coming for them now, but there was certainly one less.

Twang.

Two less.

Splashing in the shallows told the old Rider that some were dangerously close. Gallien stood, up, his motion rocking the boat, and made a sound of exertion as something was launched from his grip. Like before, he hit his mark and another man cried out in death, his body falling fully into the river.

Then came the most unusual sound, as if the air was folding in on itself. It had been subtle, heard only because Androma was so close to the smuggler. A second later and Gallien threw another weapon, and a large one by the sound of steel cutting through the air.

What on earth was he throwing?

"Row, Joran!" he encouraged before that same, peculiar, sound repeated itself.

There came no more fighting after that. Even Cob saved his arrows on the boat ahead. Androma placed her staff horizontally across her lap and listened to the sound of Joran's breathing and the oars sweeping through the water. What a mess they had left behind.

"Always better to be seen coming than going," Gallien grumbled, and loud enough so those in the boat ahead could hear him. "I'd say they saw us going! And," he added, furiously, "there's only one place we *can* go!"

"'Tis a race, Mr Drakalis!" Aphrandhor shouted back. "The river will be our ally in this."

"A race to where?" Joran enquired.

Gallien sighed in place of answering him.

"We're going to Valgala, Joran," Androma answered instead. "We're going to the capital of the world," she added dryly, having hoped to get some distance from the largest nest of vipers in the realm, a nest she had only recently escaped, and by the skin of her teeth.

"Isn't that where those men were sent from?" the young man pointed out.

"You're damn right," Gallien uttered.

"Have no fear, Master Joran," the wizard called back. "We have speed on our side. When we reach Valgala, we will simply have to stay a step ahead of our enemy."

A single step, Androma lamented. How long would they remain there, on the precipice of death? She considered Joran behind her. He would change everything—it had been seen. Until then, the precipice would be their home.

39
NO PRINCESSES HERE

60 Years Ago...

Ilithranda's dagger ploughed into the stony beach at Daijen's feet, halting his progress. Like him, she was dripping wet in the moonlight, her back to the edge of The Sin'duil. Rage lay ruin to her fair features. The animal that lived in all who had borne Kastiek's training was there to see in her eyes.

It was not, however, enough to temper Daijen's.

He cleared the buried dagger and threw himself at her, one foot rising before he switched at the last second. It wasn't anything Ilithranda hadn't seen before, her hands coming up to bat his leg aside.

Both on solid ground, they fell into hand-to-hand combat across the moonlit beach, their boots kicking up waves of pebbles as they exchanged glancing blows.

"They didn't need to die!" Daijen berated, dropping to one knee and ramming an elbow into her gut.

"What is *wrong* with you?" Ilithranda spat, recovering from the blow to land a fist across his face.

Daijen's body twisted to follow his face and raised a sweeping leg. He felt his heel connect with the side of Ilithranda's head before hearing her impact the beach.

"You call *me* naive!" he yelled, ceasing his pursuit of violence. "You're running around with no idea about what's really going on! This is never what we were supposed to be!" he scolded, pointing to the great fire that burned atop The Drifting Sea.

Ilithranda picked herself up. "Black Abyss, Daijen!" she cursed, spitting a mouthful of blood at his feet. "What madness have you let in? You sound like you've lost your mind. And you could have got us both killed on that ship!" For just a moment, it seemed she would renew their battle.

Daijen wondered if fighting her would be easier than finding the words to explain his behaviour. Words he had been forbidden to voice. Yet it would be words alone that forged the path ahead.

Exhausted by the mere thought of it all, Daijen turned to face the flaming ship and sat down on the stony beach, his wrists coming to rest over his knees. Ilithranda remained standing, ready, perhaps, to continue their contest.

"I met a dwarf in The Dain'duil," he began, his statement the very beginning of a rabbit hole he was still falling through. It was also enough to disarm Ilithranda and see her mimic him, her own eyes now reflecting the distant flames.

The crescent moon slid across the heavens as Daijen broke his vow to The Valtorak and divulged his tale. He described his first meeting with Mordrith Underborn and the conversations that followed in The Valtorak's office. Word for word he repeated the truth as voiced by their master and Kastiek.

Ilithranda listened. She asked no questions and gave no interruptions. She simply listened.

Daijen was sure to emphasise the role the Skaramangians had played in starting the war, that it had been for little more than a means to destroy the dragons. That the humans had been played as much as the Andarens.

"You see," he finally said. "Our true enemy cannot be defined as human, Andaren or dwarf. They have bled into us all. The

Skaramangians have pitted us against each other so we're too occupied to fight *them*. And whatever it is they're trying to achieve, we must prioritise that over the—"

"We don't know their motivations?" Ilithranda's voice croaked.

Daijen shook his head. "Only that they desire the return of the Dark Ones. Those in power believe they were once real. But, like I said, they started the war because they need to purge the world of dragons first. What that has to do with the Dark Ones I cannot say."

"*Upon the hour of Reclamation, the darkness will rise to meet the light*," Ilithranda uttered, her words taken directly from scripture. There seemed no firm belief in her voice, however, the line spoken from memory alone.

"True or not," Daijen continued, "their faith in such evil leads to deeds of evil. They will see Andara and Erador drowned in blood if it is the means to their end. That's why I tried to stop you on the ship," he explained. "The Jainus—he bore their mark, the same as Mordrith's. I would have questioned him if not taken him back to Ka'vairn."

Ilithranda absorbed all that he said, her feelings on the matter guarded by a passive expression. "Why would The Valtorak keep this from us?" she asked, a hint of hurt in the question.

"I believe it is a testament to our enemy. The Skaramangians have infiltrated every layer of the empire, of the human kingdom. Even the dwarves are plagued. There is every chance they would try and infiltrate Ka'vairn."

"So we have to pass the trials first," Ilithranda surmised, her gaze beyond the horizon.

Daijen wondered if the revelation had disturbed her desire for freedom and power, the two things she believed attainable as a Vahlken. In many ways, he hoped it had. While she had been worthy of the path and he had stumbled upon it, they were both soldiers in the only war that had ever mattered now.

"I'm sorry you're learning of all this from me," he began. "You should have the opportunity to ask The Valtorak questions." Daijen shrugged. "I have very few answers. I haven't been permitted to act on my knowledge."

Ilithranda said nothing. It seemed, in fact, that she had become oblivious to Daijen's presence. He watched her while she watched the ship burning in the distance. Her silence was unbearable.

"If you need—" he began, before Ilithranda's whisper cut him short.

"It was all meaningless."

Daijen blinked, trying to find the context behind her comment. "The war," he reasoned solemnly.

"Tor Valan," she said, a woman grasping at any tangible thread. "Erador attacked Tor Valan. They started the war—that's why we've been fighting all these years!"

Daijen let her anger have its moment before repeating his earlier words. "The Skaramangians had them attack. Every step of the war has been orchestrated by them. The war allows them to pick off the dragons and the Vahlken in one fell swoop while keeping them free to... search for the Dark Ones, I suppose."

Ilithranda's glassy eyes were equalled by her distant voice. "All that fighting. All that..." The words died on her lips as she likely considered all those who had died upon her sword.

Without warning or explanation, Ilithranda stood up and strode into The Sin'Duil. Good as Daijen's eyes were, he soon lost sight of her in the shadows of the forest. He did not pursue. After all, how many decades of her life, centuries even, had he just exposed as a lie?

Instead, he remained on the beach and watched the ship burn, a smoking ruin of their work.

A month of near solitude followed that night. While Daijen had a few interactions with Soveana and her fellow Weavers, his time at their makeshift camp in Kharis Vhay was a quiet one. Ilithranda had avoided him whenever possible, never parting with a word when they crossed paths. The times he spied her from afar she seemed lost, mindless even.

How he wished to approach her. How many conversations had he played out in his mind? But what could he say? He didn't have the answers and he certainly didn't have the words to undo the damage the truth had caused.

It was four weeks from that night when the Weavers summoned them, their armour and atori blades finally completed. Without a word to each other, they entered the cave back to back, a torch each. The trio of Weavers led them into their dwelling, where they would be safe from the mutated spiders.

Despite the tension that lingered between them, Daijen gave all of his attention to the unveiling of his armour. Melios stepped aside, revealing the cuirass and vambraces, all on display as Handuin's were.

So fine were they, the bronze silk hand-crafted to fit their measurements and then hidden beneath tanned leather. Even that external layer was of exquisite make. Daijen ran his fingers over the Andaren glyphs and intricate pattern laid around the edges of the chest pieces and down into the panels that would protect his abdomen. The attention to detail was testament to their legendary skill.

Melios and Abel assisted him in donning the cuirass, if only to show him the clips they had fitted into the ribs-section, allowing Daijen to secure the armour without aid in the future. It was a weighty thing, though nothing his enhancements couldn't handle.

He moved his arms in wide circles, testing the limits of his agility with the sloping pauldrons in place. It was all so flexible, moving with him rather than against him.

The vambraces slipped on like an old pair of gloves, offering protection from elbow to knuckles. Daijen looked for any sign of the spider silk, but every seam was tight in place, concealing the true strength of the armour.

It was magnificent.

Even Ilithranda had managed to put aside her burdens. Like Daijen, she moved around, drawing and sheathing her sword to check for flexibility. Fully attired, her satisfaction looked like it was just creeping over into delight.

"Daijen. Ilithranda." Soveana had beckoned them, her arm outstretched to indicate the weapons displayed horizontally on the table beside her.

The initiates turned around, armoured and cloaked as a Vahlken, and looked upon their atori blades. Out of its scabbard, each weapon was revealed in all its bronze glory. Silk of the spiders had been woven about the steel blade, each strand touching the next so that none of the original metal could be seen. And yet, the edge had been worked so that it retained its sharpness from curved tip to hilt.

His attention roamed momentarily over the eagle's claw that gripped the rounded pommel. Another badge of his station. With sabre, armour, and cloak, he was only missing the mount of a Vahlken and his slaiken blade.

The initiate took the short-sword in hand, impressed to feel no change in its weight or balance. "Thank you," he said genuinely.

"The Vahlken will never have to thank us again," Abel told him. "This last month you have shown us the quality of your order, Daijen Saeth. After centuries, we are reminded that the Vahlken are still the noble warriors our history records."

Daijen bowed his head. The Weavers three had accepted his tale of that night on the ship. They had lamented the loss of the female spider, but it was surpassed by their gratitude and relief that the spider wouldn't be tormented in the hands of the humans.

"*There is freedom in death,*" Ilithranda had decreed on the command deck.

Daijen wasn't so sure the spider would have agreed with that statement, nor the humans who had gone down to their watery grave. Still, what was done was done. There was nothing he could do to change what had happened. There was, as ever, only forwards.

And so, it was without ceremony that the pair departed the caves and said farewell to the Weavers of The Sin'duil. With supplies willingly given, the pair made their way back to Kharis

Vhay, intending to camp one last night before making their return journey to Ka'vairn.

Deciding he had given her enough time and space, and decidedly tired of the isolation, Daijen climbed to the highest tower Kharis Vhay boasted. There he found Ilithranda, perched on the edge of the open window overlooking the tops of The Sin'duil. The circular room showed signs that it had been used as her personal camp for the last few weeks.

Equally as immune to the cold as Ilithranda, Daijen moved to stand beside her, his elbows resting on the rough stone of the window sill. He said nothing for a time, content to share in the view of the moonlit sky and the drifting clouds. Nor did *she* say anything, her long hair dancing lightly in the night breeze.

"I'm sorry," he began tentatively. "I shouldn't have told you the way I did. It should have come from The Valtorak, at the right time."

Ilithranda continued to take in the vista, her lips forming a tight line.

Daijen took a breath and reassessed his opening gambit. "Perhaps we should—"

"It was all meaningless," she interjected, her voice hollow. "All that war. All those campaigns. All that... *rage*." She sighed into the night, her demeanour as dulled as her cuirass in the moonlight. "For centuries I let it lead me into battle. *Rage* against the humans and their arrogance. *Rage* against my father for..."

Daijen was watching her intently, waiting for a sliver of detail pertaining to her life before Ka'vairn, before the war even. But she stopped herself, as she had in the past. It was, however, the first time she had referred to her father, a man all others called *Emperor*.

It came as no surprise, however, that anger had been such a driving force in her life. It had always been there, a second skin that clung to Ilithranda. Now, it seemed, he was witnessing all that rage-fuelled emotion dissipating, leaving her as hollow as her voice.

"It was all for nothing," Ilithranda lamented, refusing to meet his eyes. "Worse, it was all for some... *cult*. I wasted so much of myself fighting on no more than a board, oblivious to the players that moved us about." How quickly her rage was to return, a flame in her chest that would never die out. "I've seen more people die on battlefields than I've seen alive," she whispered.

Time stretched out between them, neither to utter a word while her statement sank in.

"Skaramangian," Ilithranda eventually voiced, venom dripping from every syllable. "You cannot understand," she told him. "You're too young. The war has been in my life since *I* was young. It's a revelation to you, to learn the name of your enemy. It's *humiliation* for me. To know I've been so easily fooled. It makes *me* the fool and all those who died believing the same."

It was *shame* then. Daijen pulled the word from between Ilithranda's and knew then exactly why she had hidden herself away from him. She was ashamed of her part in the war and had no idea what to do with that emotion. She only knew that she didn't want to be seen while she tried to make sense of two centuries of needless bloodshed.

"The Skaramangians have been working behind every major event since before the Arkalon was scribed," Daijen said softly. "They even claim to have fought for the Dark Ones when they waged war against the gods. Ilithranda, they've been fooling entire civilisations for eons. Secrecy, deceit, manipulation. These are their greatest weapons. But the blow they've landed isn't mortal," he intoned, his hand gripping her new vambrace. "It's wounded you," he continued, finally having drawn her eyes to his. "Now it's time to get back up and *fight*."

Her violet eyes were dark orbs in the gloom of a single candle. "Careful," she muttered. "You're starting to sound like a real Vahlken."

Daijen responded with a laugh through his nose. No one was more surprised at that statement than he was.

"If I was to fight," she began again, a familiar cord of strength returned to her voice, "how am I to do so against an invisible foe?"

Daijen smiled. "By learning how to see them."

From a pouch on his belt, the initiate retrieved a folded piece of parchment he had taken from the Weavers' dwelling. He carefully unfolded it and laid the square out on the window sill. Ilithranda scrutinised the symbol he had drawn on it: a vertical line with two four-sided diamonds connected at the centre.

"Have you ever seen this before?" he enquired.

"No," she answered confidently.

"Never? Not even in the palace?" he probed.

Ilithranda's gaze flickered from the mark of the Skaramangians to Daijen. "You think me a princess."

Daijen was careful with his tone. "We both died in those pits," he replied. "We both left our old lives behind. Whatever you were... it doesn't really matter to me. But," he qualified at length, "you were a Lhoris. Your blood is that of the emperor's—*was* that of the emperor's. His true allegiance remains unknown. If you ever saw anything—"

"I was permitted into the palace only once," she revealed, the first of anything from her previous life that wasn't from her days serving in the legions.

"You weren't a... princess?" Daijen hated using the word, the title used against her so many times by Slait.

Ilithranda sat with the question for some time and Daijen didn't push her, this being what he had waited years to hear.

"It was not my birthright. Only those born to one of the emperor's three wives can be granted the title, and I cannot call any of them *mother*."

"You were... illegitimate," Daijen reasoned, and lightly so.

"I was born to a plaything, a nameless concubine that lived only to serve Emperor Qeledred. I never even met her," Ilithranda whispered, those words finding life for the first time in, perhaps, centuries—if ever.

"I'm sorry," he said reflexively.

"I do not require your pity," she said quickly enough. "Surviving Handuin's magic has already elevated me beyond any *imperial offspring*."

"I didn't speak to offend," Daijen assured.

Ilithranda spared him a glance, her mouth contorted while she silently deliberated. "I was offered a chance to prove myself," she finally said, her ire somewhat reduced. "That was the reason for my one and only visit to the imperial palace."

"Prove yourself?"

"To be worthy of my blood," she explained. "To earn a place in the emperor's court. I would never be princess or in line to the throne, but if I was found worthy I could live with a taste of their life—a dream compared to my life on the streets. Just walking through the palace halls was like walking through the heavens."

Her life on the streets. That statement begged so many more questions and he was desperate to ask them all and, perhaps, would have were the narrative not so poignant.

"How were you to prove yourself?" he asked instead, hungry for it all now.

"I was to join the war effort. Learn the warrior's path. Kill humans for the empire," she added with mocking dramatic effect. "If I could rise high enough through the ranks then I might earn that life in Aran'saur."

"I would say you have more than earned it now," Daijen commented. "Who of imperial blood could claim to be a Vahlken?"

"It matters as little now as it did then," Ilithranda told him. "It was to be an impossible task, my death assured. I wasn't the first and I definitely won't have been the last. The runts are never to return."

"Why not just execute you?" Daijen had to ask, seeing the simpler alternative.

"The Lhoris bloodline is sacred," Ilithranda explained. "A fact you can find in any Arkalon. Of course," she went on, "I would have done anything for that life at the time. I stopped yearning for it all a long time ago."

Daijen frowned. "Truly?" he asked in disbelief, for even he had dreamed of palace life in his youth.

Thanks to the mutations his mind had undergone, he recalled perfectly the time when the imperial entourage had paraded down the main road of Taranathen, there to remind the serfs who ruled them. It had been a day of gold and gems, their horses and carriages just as bejewelled as the imperial family themselves.

"I couldn't exist in their world anymore," Ilithranda shared. "I have fought in countless campaigns since the day of that offer. I couldn't resign myself to a life of... *observation*. The imperial family doesn't live as we do. They simply watch from afar and enjoy the safety of their gilded cage."

Daijen could only take her word, his own life and experiences so far removed from those who dwelled in the heart of Aran'saur. "You gave your life over to the war then," he remarked.

Again, Ilithranda held on to her reply, while Daijen liked to imagine the walls that had stood for so long inside her mind were finally being torn down.

"For a long time I suppose I did," she eventually said. "But then I saw *him*."

"Saw *who*?"

"My first Vahlken," she said wistfully, her tone of wonder so incongruent with the undercurrent of seething anger that lived so close to the surface. "It was early in the war. The humans had taken Harendun and we drew the line at Yalafar. Orders came from The Saible, words from Emperor Qeledred himself, that we were to charge out and meet the marching horde at our gates. The paragon relayed as much to the Vahlken, ordering him on behalf of the emperor to lead us into battle."

Ilithranda paused, leaving Daijen with bated breath. It had been a long time since a story had held him so tightly. He could have stood by that window for another century listening to every second of her life.

"What happened?" he had to ask.

Ilithranda cut a smile. "He said *no*. Can you imagine it? Standing before an army, before the most powerful person *in* that army, whose very words are to be taken as the emperor's, and saying... *no*? And there wasn't a thing the paragon could do about it. He issued no commands, levied no threats. He could only accept the Vahlken's response."

Daijen's memory couldn't help but conjure The Valtorak's

words, that they were to exist outside of the emperor's laws, not above them. Still, he was enraptured by the tale. "What happened after that?"

"The Vahlken flew out and camped between the humans and Yalafar's gates. His presence alone was enough to dissuade them from advancing on us. But it was in that moment of defiance that I saw real *freedom*. Real *power*. After that, there was only one path for me."

Daijen smiled at that. "Do you know who it was?" he asked. Even if that particular Vahlken was still alive, the initiates had never met those in active service, their existence little more than names on a map.

Ilithranda turned to look at him. "Kastiek."

Daijen's mind explored that, liking to imagine the Andaren before the war had ravaged his body with battle scars. "Thank you," he said at last. "You didn't have to tell me anything."

"Nor did you," she replied. "It must have been a burden to keep such a truth all these years." Ilithranda gestured at the Skaramangian mark that sat between them. "As I said," she reiterated, moving past any emotions that could be rising between them, "I never saw anything like it. Nor have I since."

Daijen nodded along, content to have been let in at all. "You can't say anything," he told her, the thought just coming to him. "Even I'm not supposed to know any of this."

"Fear not, Daijen Saeth. I will survive the trials and hear it from The Valtorak myself," she vowed, before swinging her legs back into the chamber. "Come. I would eat *and* sleep before we begin our journey."

It was a warm smile that moved Daijen's lips. It had been a long time coming.

40
THE HAMMERHOLD

Even in death, Tor Valan clung to the mountains at its back. The city was a towering ruin, a black husk of six tiers and broken spires, its bridges destroyed and its majesty wiped from the face of Verda. It was no more than a place of shadows now.

Shadows and *ghosts*.

"I'm not goin' in there," Grarfath declared, his neck craned to take it all in. There were things moving inside, he was sure of it.

Yamnomora squinted into the blasting wind to spy him. "It's only goin' to get worse out 'ere!" she yelled over the rushing air. "Sun'll be down in minutes! Then it's goin' to get *really* cold!"

"*Then*?" the smith echoed, the northern chill invading every gap in his attire.

"We need shelter!" the warrior told him, ploughing through the snow towards the ruins. "Pick yer feet up, Smith!"

We need to go home, he thought. How he missed his workshop. How he longed to work the forge. He thought of his comfy armchair by the fire and the stool for his feet. The dwarf could practically taste the butter biscuits he kept stacked on the table. He might have voiced any and all of his desires had Kitrana Voden not walked past him.

Her ill-fitting cloak flapped wildly in the wind, exposing much of her body and the bare skin revealed by her unusual clothing. Grarfath winced as he watched her feet, absent any boots, disappear beneath the snow with every step. The Nimean was entirely unfazed by the weather.

"Ye're both mad!" Grarfath observed. "That's no place for the livin'!"

Yamnomora spun around. "The entire Andaren army has been camped 'ere for days! There's nothin' in these walls but the *filth* they've left behind!" With that, the dwarf made for the wide gap in the city's demolished outer wall.

Grarfath looked to his right, where the road continued south to a place Yamnomora had called The Watchtower of Argunsuun. The army was far from sight now, the Andarens having moved on hours earlier.

The smith groaned. "One night!" he called out reluctantly. "I'll stay one night!"

Keeping to Tor Valan's ground level—where they might make a quick escape should they need to—the trio had gathered closely around a small fire. Bludgeon had spent the first hour with his snout in the mud, searching for anything and everything the Andarens might have left that he could eat.

To Grarfath's surprise, Kitrana had wandered off to explore some of the ruins and had yet to return. The city's ominous feel and shadowed alcoves bothered her about as much as the weather did apparently. Yamnomora was her usual pleasant self, spending her time sharpening both axes while saying nothing at all.

Grarfath was miserable.

He regarded the hammer—The Anther. It rested beside him, its bronze accents brought beautifully to life in the firelight. The smith considered using it then. He had only to strike the earth and think of his home in The Morthil Mountains. The nausea and exhaustion would be worth it to sit in his chair again or sleep in his bed for the night.

Dark fingers reached out for the haft, his temptation mounting beyond control.

"Don' even think abou' it," Yamnomora warned, her eyes never leaving the dagger she had moved on to sharpening.

"*How* could ye know what I'm thinkin'?"

"Because ye're *soft*," the warrior told him bluntly.

Grarfath took offence. "I ain' soft!" he protested. "I killed a Three-Headed Dread Serpent!"

"Bah! I could slay one o' 'em with me eyes closed."

"Then next time," Grarfath retorted, "I suggest ye shut yer eyes! Because ye were doin' a piss poor job o' it back there!"

Yamnomora twisted her dagger so the tip was pointing at the smith. "Ye're sat there thinkin' abou' yer bed."

Grarfath opened and closed his mouth, dumbfounded by her accurate insight.

"Ye've known nothin' but the comforts an' protection o' them stone halls," the warrior went on. "Now ye're out 'ere, where there's no halls or hearths or even walls to keep out the big bad weather. Have ye even seen rain?"

The smith licked his lips, insulted by the truth. "I'm not soft," he reiterated. "An' I've seen *rain*," he added as a point of pride.

Yamnomora ran the back of her hand down her bristly cheek. "Ye can' be usin' The Anther for little trips like that—not *yet*. It'd wipe ye out. Leave ye vulnerable. Ye can bet every kronum ye've ever made that Tharg an' his boys are watchin' yer shop."

Grarfath sighed, the dwarf envisioning a future that held no more than shadows, ruins, and bad weather. "When's this goin' to end?" he complained. "When can I go home?"

"Ye're not gettin' it, are ye? Ye're the *Hammerhold* now. The Anther has passed to ye an' all the responsibilities that come with it."

"I'm the Hammerhold now?" he echoed incredulously, if not outright bemused. "I'm to be movin' the mountains next I suppose. What else did old Duun get up to? Oh, that's right, he defeated the Stonemaw an' *moved* The Nheremyn River." The smith chuckled. "I'll jus' be gettin' on with that then."

"Like I said: ye 'ave no *idea* what world ye're livin' in."

Grarfath leaned forward, his dark eyes narrowed. "I'm livin' in a world with one less Dread Serpent in it."

Yamnomora groaned. "Once I've delivered ye to The Green Leaf, ye can take it up with 'im. Hells, if the council has any sense they'll 'ave ye give *me* The Anther."

"*Council*? What council?"

Yamnomora laughed to herself, her voice bouncing off the walls. "The same council ye became a part o' when ye picked up that there hammer!"

Grarfath was shaking his head. "There's nothin' between yer ears *but* hammers. An' who *is* this Green Leaf fella ye keep mentionin'? Why 'ave I got to go to 'im? Why can' *he* come *'ere*?"

"He's a wizard, an' a *human* one at that. He can' exactly walk into Andara, ye dolt."

The smith rocked back, his eyes wide. "A *wizard*? Magic an' all that?"

Yamnomora grinned with amusement. "Magic an' all that," she confirmed.

"I don' want to see no wizard!" he exclaimed. "I'm not one for magic."

"Ye're sittin' next to a magical hammer," the warrior told him dryly.

"An' I ain' happy abou' that either!" The smith continued to grumble under his breath, cursing his mother.

"I'll not hear ye speak so foul abou' Mordrith Underborn," Yamnomora scolded. "It's not her fault yer thick head can' grasp the honour she's bestowed on ye. Ye can change the world with that hammer."

Grarfath sat with her biting words for a handful of minutes while his mind churned up memories of his mother. "Did she talk abou' me much?" he eventually asked.

"More than I'd 'ave liked," Yamnomora replied.

The smith ignored her tone. "What did she say?"

The warrior held on to her words for the moment. When her green eyes finally found him again, there was an impassioned look behind them. "She missed ye every day. Yer father too. She was mostly burdened by the guilt o' leavin' ye both. She wished she could go back an' explain *why*. Then there was the worryin'. Every day she feared the Skaramangians would come for ye, even if it were jus' to punish her for betrayin' 'em."

It pained Grarfath to hear of his mother's anguish, even if it wasn't quite enough to wipe clean the resentment he still felt towards her memory. "They never came," he uttered.

"Killin' ye would risk unnecessary exposure," Yamnomora said. "Ye were better as bait. Tharg will 'ave had ye watched since Mordrith left. If she were goin' to come back for anythin' it'd be her boys."

Her boys...

Grarfath had to look away, his resolve tested then. His mother had always referred to him and his father as her boys. For decades they believed she had jus' taken off without a care for them, breaking their hearts at the same time. He realised now that *three* hearts had been broken.

"But she was the *Hammerhold*," Yamnomora proclaimed. "Mordrith knew the legacy that rested on her shoulders. She knew that hammer was a weapon o' power, a weapon the Skaramangians *feared*."

"Why would they fear it?"

"Because Duun, son o' Darl, did more than move mountains an' rivers," the warrior explained. "He were the scourge o' the Talakin, the *shadowed beasts*. That's right, ye heard me. Them that the Skaramangians worship. Duun brought The Anther to bear an' crushed 'em."

"He fought the *Talakin*?" Grarfath repeated, as much aware of their mythology as Duun's. "Ye're startin' to get yer legends mixed up," he warned.

"Didn' ye hear a word I told ye abou' yer mother? Abou' the things she discovered? The Skaramangians live an' breathe for the Talakin's return. They're real, Grarfath. The council can debate it all day long, but I *know*. An' yer mother knew! They're *real*. Jus' like Duun. The Skaramangians 'ave suppressed his legend, guidin' the narrative so fools like ye believe what they want ye to."

Grarfath held up a hand so he might respond. "A'right, a'right. Let's say ye right—abou' *everythin'*. I'm what? The new Hammerhold? Me—a *smith*. I'm supposed to take up the mantle an' fight these Skaramangian fellas an' slay ancient monsters?"

Yamnomora drew in on herself before replying. "I don' know what ye're supposed to do," she said sullenly. "I only know what *I'm* to do, an' that's get ye an' The Anther to the council. Beyond that, yer fate is yer own."

"Ye're handin' me over to humans an' wizards then," he surmised glumly, feeling very much like his fate was not his own.

"The Green Leaf is wise," Yamnomora reassured. "He knows things. He knows *people*. Trust me. He's only to touch ye an' he'll 'ave a better idea o' what ye're capable of."

"What does that even *mean*?" Grarfath retorted. "I don' want no wizard touchin' me! I'm not for bein' magicked!"

Yamnomora looked at him like he was an irrational child. "Ye sound as stupid as ye look. The Green Leaf won' *magic* ye. In fact, ye an' 'im 'ave somethin' in common."

Grarfath frowned and his brow of dark slate knotted about his bushy eyebrows. "What could I have in common with a wizard?"

The dwarven warrior gestured at The Anther. "Ye both possess a weapon o' power."

The smith let his hand rest on the hammer for a time. "There's more than one o' these?"

"Aye, though they aren' all hammers."

"What *are* they then?"

"That's council talk. I'm jus' a humble servant. So are they," she added menacingly, her chin having indicated the two large axes beside the fire.

"This council," Grarfath queried. "Who's on it exactly?"

Yamnomora eyed him from across the fire. "The only person on the council ye need to be concerned with is *ye*."

The smith sat forwards. “Me? *I’m* on this council? Now what are ye talkin’ abou’?”

“Ye wield a weapon o’ power,” the warrior told him. “Whether ye like it or not, that means somethin’.”

Grarfath shrugged. “It means nothin’ to me. I’m only ’ere because ye started a fight in me shop an’ now I can’ go back!”

“I saved yer life!”

“I’ve done nothin’ but nearly die since we met!”

“Bah!” Yamnomora spat, waving his words away. “Ye wield The Anther. That puts *ye* on the council, ye stupid kud. As I said, I’m jus’ to deliver ye.”

Grarfath sat with that for a while. It was all so much to take in and, at the same time, difficult to believe a word of it. It seemed as if the world was sinking beneath his very feet, dragging him deeper and deeper into an entirely different realm. Besides weapons o’ power, secret cults, and water people, there were now mythical figures who were real and wizards he was to meet.

Surely, the dwarf thought, things couldn’t get any worse.

41
THE EYRIES

55 YEARS AGO...

"Do you know what today is, Runt?"

Daijen blinked, and slowly given the exasperation he was already feeling. Without a word in response, he kept his attention on the book laid out in front of him, his ice-blue eyes never wandering from the words therein. They were far more interesting than the words spouting from Slait's mouth.

Axium, he read, is a form of alchemical magic consisting of two substances individually stable, but volatile when combined. He had seen them on Kastiek's belt—two vials of purple and gold. The chapter he was reading detailed how axium could be used as a weapon against dragons. Specifically, their near-impenetrable scales. It was fascinating, but it seemed his time reading was at an end.

Heavy boots closed in from behind, approaching his chair with menacing purpose. "Today's the day I fly away from this hellish stone and your pathetic excuse for an existence." Slait came into view as he leaned down, inserting his bald head into Daijen's personal space. "You think that armour makes you worthy? Or the cloak? Even the weapons look ridiculous on you. We both know you don't belong here. It was pure chance—*dumb luck*—that you survived the pits."

Daijen regarded the armour he had been wearing for five years now. In that time, he had learned how to fight in it, how to move unheard in it. He could detach the leather from the silk underlay so he might make repairs or simply clean the intricate pattern of grooves. It was a second skin that he was always reluctant to take off.

"I thought you believed we were chosen by the gods," Daijen quipped, lazily turning the page. "I suppose you have just as much luck as I do."

Slait's top lip began to twitch, his rage burning hot as ever. "When your day comes to claim an Aegre, I guarantee it will eat you where you stand. Even animals know what it is to be dishonoured, and sharing breath with you is dishonour enough for me."

"*Smelling* your breath is enough for me," Daijen retorted casually, flicking the book closed with one finger, before looking up at Slait in defiance.

How many times had the brute tried to intimidate him? How many fights, verbal and otherwise, had he caused? Just last week, Ilithranda had launched her knee into his crotch to shut him up. Subsequently, Daijen had seen to her stitches himself.

Slait grabbed his shoulder in a vice-like grip, though even his significant strength wasn't enough to hurt Daijen through his pauldron.

"Do you know the first thing I'm going to do with my Aegre?" he asked, his voice low and threatening.

"Shave its head," Daijen suggested, while doing his damned hardest to keep any smile from his face.

Slait had murder in his eyes. "I'm going to take your little princess for a *ride*," he declared. "And you're going to watch."

Daijen might have let the comment roll over him had he not been confident that Slait meant every word. That was why he was already visualising the physical response he intended to give, the first being a swift palm to the throat.

"Try it," Slait provoked, sensing his intentions.

"Slait."

Both initiates froze at the sound of Kastiek's low whisper. The Vahlken was standing in the doorway of Ka'vairn's library, his white hair knotted at the back of his head. In the torchlight, his scars appeared all the more dramatic, giving him the look of a man put together from other parts.

"It's time. Meet the others in the courtyard."

Slait let go of Daijen's pauldron, sparing his fellow initiate one last glare, a promise of sorts. "As you say, Kastiek," he said on his way out. "Ahnir be raised! Today we fly!"

Kastiek waited until he was confident Slait was out of ear-shot. "You're coming too," he instructed Daijen. "Ilithranda's already in the courtyard."

Daijen nearly fell out of his chair he turned around so fast. "I'm coming? To the eyries?" He had read volume after volume in that very library about the Aegres and their dwellings high in the mountains above. He knew everything he could about them, preparing, hoping, for this day to arrive.

"To observe," Kastiek specified, injecting his dream with crashing reality. "You should see how the others form the bond. When your day comes, you must make that climb and face the Aegres with confidence."

Daijen cleared his throat and composed himself. "I see," he replied, his disappointment seen in the muscles of his jaw.

"Come along," Kastiek bade.

Was that a smile in the corner of his mouth?

It took a day and a night's walking for the initiates to reach the beginning of the path, just as the new dawn brought definition to The Morthil Mountains in the east. Daijen gave them one last look before entering a narrow valley cut into The Hellion Mountains.

Following Kastiek, the initiates could only walk in single file for the next two days, at which point they were all instructed to get some sleep before the climb—whether they felt the need to or not.

When the next sun brought light to the mountains, they began their ascent of the sheer walls, where their enhancements would be truly put to the test. To begin with, it felt no different to scaling the rock face up to Ka'vairn while being pursued by Kastiek. After a few hours, it became an entirely different ordeal.

Following in the handholds of those above, Daijen came across smears of blood again and again, their fingers cut and sliced by the unrelenting rock. He never complained, however, for Kastiek led them without so much as a groan, he who could have flown astride his own Aegre, Strix.

It was a small shelf that housed them for the night, where they ate and drank and gave their limbs time to recover. All before another day of climbing. There were times when they had to leap from hold to hold or raise their feet above their waists in order to pass a featureless rock. It was at times like that when Daijen was reminded there were no guarantees any would reach the eyries.

When, at last, the climb was behind them, the group of nine began the next leg of their journey. They followed the gentle incline until they came across the snows as the temperature continued to fall. From there, most used their atori blades to dig in and aid their ascent up the steep slopes.

Despite their ability to hold off sleep for days at a time, all nine of them, Kastiek included, required time to rest and slumber on the mountain side. It was their ability to withstand intense cold, however, that allowed them to camp with minimal shelter beyond their large bear pelts.

It was, perhaps, a little over a week after they departed the fortress that Kastiek brought them to the mouth of a cave, the site resting just higher than the clouds. Daijen felt that it could also have been a month since they set out, each miserable day blending into the next.

He tried not to think about the fact that he would have to make the exact same climb in the years to come.

Crouched by the cave entrance, Kastiek waited, his ear cocked to the darkness within. Apparently satisfied, he motioned them to follow him inside, and cautiously so. Within seconds, Daijen's sight adjusted to the shadows and viewed the cave's interior in detail, a feat no ordinary man could.

The smell hit him almost immediately. A thick animal musk mixed with filth and a hint of rot. Indeed, the cave floor was littered with bones, all picked clean and chipped by powerful beaks and sharp talons.

The tunnel, as it turned out to be, weaved through a portion of the mountain and branched here and there. Kastiek never hesitated in his choice of direction, leading the group directly to the heart of the eyries, where he crouched by the wall.

It was there that the tunnel opened up again, the darkness replaced by glorious sunlight. The jagged mountains dominated the view, revealing their position on the western slopes of the Hellion landscape. Somewhere out there, hidden beneath the clouds, were the tall trees of The Faern'duil, Andara's largest forest.

Daijen might have looked for any sign of them had his attention not been utterly captured by those who dwelled on the mountain top.

Aegres.

Countless, it seemed, were the number of times Daijen had seen Aramis or Strix during his decades at Ka'vairn, but never had he seen so many of their kind together, flying wild in their own domain. Some swooped low, their talons slicing through a mere inch of snow as they followed the slopes. Others roamed the outcroppings and with young by their side!

Daijen moved to see the small Aeglets, having only ever read about them in the volumes Handuin had personally written. "It took him years, you know," he remarked quietly to Ilithranda, who was equally fascinated by the creatures. "Handuin," he specified. "He started with the great eagles who already called the mountains home. He transformed them as he did us."

"Not them," Ilithranda corrected. "Handuin has been dead for millennia—as have the Aegres of his time. These were all *born*."

Daijen looked out on the majestic animals again, and with a fresh perspective. She was right, of course. It seemed such a simple and obvious observation, yet it made all the difference. These Aegres were natural born and had been for generations. Handuin hadn't just changed a few individuals—he had created a whole new and thriving species.

"Should any of you make the bond," Kastiek said, his voice so low that even Daijen's remarkable hearing struggled to catch every word, "today will be the hardest flight of your lives. Without a saddle you will have to feel for the changes in their muscles. You're also going to have to hold on for your life," he added casually.

"We're just holding on to feathers?" Yendi complained.

"All the way down," Kastiek answered with a wry smile. "Be bold," he instructed, his serious tone quick to return. "Aegres are predators. If you show any hesitation it will be taken as weakness. After that, you're no better than prey and they will not bond."

"You're just food," Slait remarked, his golden eyes finding Daijen.

Kovun was shaking his head. "We're just to go out there and... take one?"

Daijen resisted the urge to roll his eyes. Kovun—the largest of them all—had regularly neglected the essential reading, preferring always the courtyard to the library, his hands more comfortable holding a weapon than a book. The same might actually be said of Slait given how often he could be found reading the Arkalon.

"Handuin's magic flows through them as much as it does us," Kastiek told him. "They're sensitive to it in a way we couldn't imagine. It's not enough to keep them from killing you, but it'll give you the edge you need to survive long enough to make the bond."

Soyra nodded her head at the Aegres who had glided to a stop on the nearest slope. "Do you think they know why we're here?"

"They know why we're here," Kastiek replied. "We've been doing this since their first generation. It's as much a part of their tradition as it is our own."

"What do we do if they attack instead?" Kovun asked, his hand having been attached to the hilt of his sabre since they entered the tunnel.

"You submit to death," Kastiek said bluntly. "You are not permitted to spill Aegre blood," he went on, reiterating a lesson they had all been taught years earlier. "You can do nothing that might jeopardise the bonding of future generations. We must always be perceived as partners. Never enemies."

Laif shared an uneasy glance with Naelin. "Shouldn't we have attempted this decades ago?" he posed, aware of the years they might have wasted training for naught but death on a cold mountainside.

"It's only because of the years behind you that any attempt is viable," Kastiek pointed out. "When they look into your eyes," he explained, "they will see all that you are. It's your years of training, the trials you've overcome, that will endear you to them."

Kovun took a long breath, his confidence steadily rising to overcome his unease. At least it was until Ilithranda asked her one and only question.

"What's the success rate?"

Kastiek glanced at her. "A group this size... I would say one of you isn't getting off this mountain."

A ripple of nervous energy ran through the group. Daijen's thoughts were cast to the future, when he and Ilithranda would return as no more than a pair. Would only one of *them* return?

A shadow swept over the slopes.

While the group looked up, trying to see the newcomer, the other Aegres became skittish, their numbers scattering somewhat across the mountain.

"What was that?" Yendi asked.

Kastiek edged closer to the cave entrance. "*That...* was the exile."

The Aegre in question flew into view and came to land on the rocky plateau a hundred feet out. Unlike its kin, who were coated in feathers of varying brown and black, the *exile* was entirely white. Even its beak was a pale, sickly, colour that had no trace of the yellow boasted by the majority.

Given the creature's proximity, a pair of brown Aegres flapped their wings threateningly and put themselves between the exile and the Aeglets. The exile let loose a deep squawk and scraped its talons across the rocks, refusing to budge. Only when another, larger, Aegre descended onto the plateau did the white creature flex its wings and return to the sky.

"Why is it exiled?" Soyra enquired. "Because of its colour?"

Kastiek shook his head. "Because when that one's hungry, it hunts other Aegres. I remember the first winter after he hatched. The exile's been wild all its days. I think it only stays up here because of the instinct to mate—not that the others permit it."

"Maybe it just has nowhere else to go," Slait uttered, turning a number of surprised eyes upon him.

"Perhaps," Kastiek allowed. "Nevertheless, his presence has unsettled the rest. We should return to the other side of the mountain and try again tomorrow."

"I didn't come all this way to sit on a cold rock," Slait made known as he rose to his full height. "I fly today."

"No," Kastiek hissed, unable to reach the initiate and drag him back. "Slait! Do not go out there," he commanded.

"You've said it yourself countless times, Kastiek," Slait asserted, his tall frame occupying the entrance now. "You're not my master."

"Slait!" the Vahlken urged.

There was nothing any of them could do. Slait had already taken the necessary steps to move him from shadow to light, where every Aegre could see him. They all stopped their activity and immediately assessed the trespasser.

Kastiek was in a similar state of high alert, his body tensed and back plastered to the cave wall. "Once you make eye contact," he called out reluctantly, "do not break it for anything."

Save the few who ushered the Aeglets off the mountain side, the rest flapped their wings, squawked a short sharp warning, and closed in on the bald initiate.

Without looking at what he was doing, Kastiek rummaged through the pouches on his belt and retrieved a small wooden object no bigger than his middle finger. He quickly put it to his lips and blew into the hollow object, his fingers dancing over the holes along its length. It made no sound that Daijen could hear but every Aegre's head twitched, their gaze homing in on the cave beyond the intruder.

"What was that?" Ilithranda questioned.

"That's a Cuthar," Daijen answered, wondering if he was the only one to have accessed Ka'vairn's library. "Only the Aegres can hear it," he explained, "but only Strix will understand the call."

Somewhere between bold and foolish, Slait advanced with confident steps while the other initiates watched intently. It seemed that no two Aegres reacted the same to his presence, with one even flying away.

"What are they doing?" Naelin asked.

"Deciding who has the stronger bond," Kastiek informed. "Some will know right away that they don't wish to bond with him. While others are still intrigued, though, the rejecting Aegres will back off. It will come down to just one."

As always, Kastiek was proven right. While Slait stood his ground, the surrounding Aegres fell away one by one. The last two still approaching knocked heads and squawked at each other until the smaller of them peeled off. That left just one, its yellow eyes locked with Slait's.

Daijen was leaning forward, his anticipation rising to new heights. He had consumed books on this exact experience but it didn't compare to seeing the event unfold before his very eyes. In mere moments he would witness a lifelong bond be formed between man and beast that would culminate in a flight through the heavens. Even if it was Slait, it was still exhilarating.

The Aegre's talons tapped on the rock as it drew nearer. Soon, its true size was frighteningly clear, its head towering over Slait by six feet. Predatory eyes looked down on the initiate, its expression unreadable.

So close was it now that Daijen could see the details in its feathers—the grey flecks that spread out from its beak and the black repeating pattern that peppered its wings. It was graceful and dangerous all at the same time.

Kastiek was unnervingly still, his jaw tensed to the point that surely his teeth would soon shatter under the pressure. What was he seeing that Daijen couldn't? His fears that the white exile had disturbed the peace seemed unfounded now.

By the shape of Slait's cheeks, he was grinning up at the Aegre. "You're *mine*," he declared.

The Aegre's head twitched an inch. It blinked.

Then it pinned him beneath one mighty talon.

42
TEN THOUSAND EYES

Though bright, the midday sun failed in its battle against winter's bitter cold. Androma was sure to keep her cloak about her shoulders and gathered over her legs. There had been a time when the old Rider could conjure warmth from nowhere, her magic a spring that knew no end.

That was no longer the case.

In the hours since they had put Hemon and the river folk behind them, Joran and Gallien had taken it in turns to row the boat, taking them further north, where winter's hold would only increase. They had done so in relative silence while the smuggler's temper settled down.

"We had planned to set sail from the port," the wizard had explained, not long after they had taken to the river. "From there we could have followed the coast up to Sunhold, and without a shadow at that."

"Sunhold. Is that our final destination?" Gallien had asked at the time.

"No," Aphrandhor had told him, and nothing else.

It had only infuriated the smuggler all the more. Androma thought of enlightening him, but there were more pieces to put into place before then. Pieces that would ensure Joran went willingly. That was key.

Still, the hours of silence, and feeling Drakalis's scrutinising gaze on the back of her head, left the old Rider feeling uncomfortable. She also felt for Joran, the young man whisked from place to place, hounded by killers all the while and with never an explanation.

A cold breeze swept over them, momentarily robbing her of thought. The wind, however, did bring a hint of information, a faint scent that made her sensitive nose twitch. It was an old instinct that turned her head to the sky. She knew that smell—that animal musk. It brought a tight smile to her thin lips. Their guardian angel, she thought.

Deciding it served nothing to inform the others and, perhaps, even complicated things where Joran was concerned, the old Rider kept the possible revelation to herself.

"For sixteen years," Androma began, "I have wanted to ask you why you never went to Riverwatch. I understand now." She tilted her head ever so slightly. "I could hear it in your voice, Gallien. At what point, I wonder, did you come to love the boy?" she pondered, as if Joran wasn't sitting between them. "He is like a son to you, yes? I am glad," the old Rider added genuinely, knowing full well that his love for Joran had been the very thing that had kept the boy safe all those years. She couldn't have asked for a better protector. "I fear it will make what has to happen next that much harder for you."

Androma didn't need her sight to know that the smuggler had just tensed every muscle in his body.

"Whatever that is," Gallien said slowly, deliberately, "you're not getting to him without going through me."

"Gallien," Joran intoned, displaying a notch of his impressive maturity.

"Joran, you don't—" Gallien's warning was cut short by the boy, who had no problem speaking over him.

"We've met before, yes?"

The question came for Androma. After sixteen years of

anticipation, she thought she would be ready for such a question, yet the old Rider still hesitated, wondering then where to begin.

"I was there when you came into this world," she began, wishing to see his expression upon learning that. She had trusted Gallien with next to nothing which, in turn, meant Joran knew nothing of himself: where he came from or why he was so sought after.

"You *all* knew my mother then," he reasoned.

Androma didn't know what had been divulged, but it seemed apparent that The Green Leaf had said something. The wizard had always enjoyed a flippant comment, especially if it added to his air of mystery.

"Would *you* like to know about her?" the Rider offered, somewhat ashamed that she was using his dead mother as a hook.

"That's not fair," Gallien interrupted. "You're dragging him into something that could get him killed."

"Says the man with a Padoshi on his back," Cob remarked from the boat beside theirs.

Androma flexed her fingers to soothe the Kedradi. "He has a right to know, Gallien. He has a right to *choose*."

"There isn't much of a choice, Androma. You're talking about life and death."

"It's more complicated than that," the wizard commented. "Though I would point out; neither path is without peril. And," he added, "leave or stay, you will still be hunted by the Andarens, Galahart, and Thedaria's Padoshi."

"Stop," Gallien pleaded. "Just... *stop*." The smuggler's voice turned to a hush as he spoke directly to Joran. "Everything I said still stands. We can make our decisions *together*. It doesn't matter who comes after us. We'll stay ahead of them. We'll find a way to live, to live *well*. We can shore up right here and go anywhere."

Nobody said anything for a moment, all waiting on Joran's response.

"I would hear them out," he said at last. "But," he caveated, his voice projecting across the river, "I make no promises. My path —*our* path—is still our own. It just wouldn't hurt," he added, throwing his mouth over his shoulder, "to know why so many people want me dead."

Though they had never met, the boy harboured much of his mother in him, a fact that brought a smile to Androma's face. "Most wise," she praised.

The old Rider waited a short while, making certain there came no further argument from the smuggler, though not so long that Joran became impatient.

"It is quite the tale leading up to your birth. A tale," Androma added, gesturing to Cob and Aphrandhor beside them, "that involves us all, I suppose. But I would start with your mother."

"Why don't you start with yourself," Gallien cut in. "Joran should know who he's talking to."

Hearing no objection from the young man, she reassessed her words. "My name is Androma," she began, though her name had already been voiced. "I am... I *was*... a Dragon Rider."

Rather than dwell on those glorious memories, memories that threatened to shatter her in an instant, Androma focused on the silence that followed. It wasn't hard to imagine Joran's expression, his utter surprise at hearing that. The common man had more chance of being struck by lightning than meeting a Dragon Rider in the flesh. And, in the years following the start of the war, they had become more myth than anything else.

To Gallien, however, it would have come as no surprise. He had been present when The Dancing Sword of the Dawn ambushed them in The Edda Highlands. The beast had referred to her by title and the smuggler's command of Andarneese was good enough to catch it.

"You failed to mention that when *we* met," Drakalis remarked, his words barbed.

"It proves to be something of a distraction," Androma replied, sensing the onslaught of questions Joran was preparing. "Perhaps," she continued, getting ahead of him, "we can revisit my past another time. Yes, I *was* a Dragon Rider and *yes*, my use of the past tense is quite deliberate. I met your mother, Joran, before I lost... *everything*. I met her when I still had eyes to see how remarkable she was."

"What was her name?" Joran asked, the question bursting from his lips.

"Ilithranda," she told him.

A moment passed before the boy repeated her name, a hint of wonder about him. "Who was she?"

"Who she was cannot be summed up in only a few words," Androma told him, recalling the many facets to the Andaren. "*What* she was, however, can be voiced in a *single* word. Your mother was a *Vahlken*."

As before, her proclamation was met with deafening silence, though she did hear the oars slow down.

"A... *Vahlken*?" Gallien echoed in disbelief.

"An eagle rider," the boy uttered with amazement.

"A common word for a complicated creature," Androma corrected. "But yes, your mother was a class of warrior matched only by Dragon Riders. Her *Aegre* was equally fierce," she added. "Had she survived your birth I have no doubt the two would have gone on to change the world. Perhaps such a fate was intended for her legacy," she pondered aloud, and deliberately so. Still, the latter was not what grabbed the boy's attention.

"She died giving birth to me," he said, his wonder now replaced with sorrow, if not a tinge of guilt.

"The fault lies with none," Androma was quick to reassure. "The Vahlken are not just warriors born but warriors made, their bodies forged in magic. They were never intended to bear children." Hearing her own words said aloud reflected what little solace they truly offered.

"You were there," he stated, his voice hardened now.

"I was. You were born on the sparrow day, in the year 3117 of the sixth epoch. In Harendun. The city was under siege—*again*. While the war ships of Erador emptied legion upon legion onto Andara's soil, your mother gave birth to you. She was a warrior to her end."

It was difficult to know what was going through the boy's head without seeing him, but his bouts of silence suggested he was trying his best to absorb answers he had likely sought for most of his life.

"Why were *you* there?" he asked. "Why were *you* at my birth? I thought Dragon Riders and Vahlken were sworn enemies."

"The way you're *told* the world works and the way it *actually* works are seldom the same thing," Androma explained. "There is room for enemies to become allies... just as there is room for allies to become enemies," she added gravely. "I was fortunate. Your mother and those of her order saw me as a potential ally long before I saw it in them. The Vahlken have always known more about our enemy though. Their advantage. Our weakness."

"You speak of a *common* enemy," Gallien pointed out, his statement a question in itself.

"There *is* only one enemy," Androma specified. "They call themselves *Skaramangians*," she declared boldly, unafraid to voice their name.

There came more silence from the two in her boat.

"What in the hells are you talking about now?" the smuggler finally demanded, audibly exasperated already.

"I would caution a lowly smuggler from learning more," Androma replied, "but Joran should know his enemy."

"This lowly smuggler got you from Andara to Erador with ne'er a scratch," he said pointedly.

"That was hardly a smooth journey," Androma complained, his attitude grating against what little patience she had left.

"Who *are* the Skaramangians?" Joran's voice rose above their bickering. "And why do they want me dead?"

His first question had so many beginnings, each answer capable of unravelling history as it had been recorded. But, as she had said, the boy had a right to know. And how could he choose his path without knowing it all?

Androma cleared her throat. "The Skaramangians are, perhaps, the oldest religion in all of Verda, though theirs is a faith placed in the dark rather than the light. They have spent untold millennia worshipping creatures known by the Andarens as, the *Dark Ones*.

Over time, they have amassed wealth and influence, tools they use to orchestrate wars, genocide, anything that achieves their aims."

"Which is?" Gallien asked sceptically.

"They intend to raise the Dark Ones—"

"If they can *find* them all," Aphrandhor remarked offhandedly.

Assuming the wizard had also chosen that moment to look her way, Androma shot him an expression that, not-so-politely, informed him to wait for her invitation. Not only was it a complicated subject, but it had to be told just right while also allowing her to form a bond with Joran—preferably one of *trust.*

"I don't understand," Joran confessed.

"You can't be serious, Androma," the smuggler interjected. "You're talking about fairytales."

"I'm talking about the Andaren religion," she corrected.

"It's the same thing," he replied ignorantly.

"It predates human civilisation, Gallien."

"It can predate the dawn of time for all I care. You're talking about a group of people who have read the Arkalon too many times. Dark Ones," he sniggered.

"Gallien," Joran voiced again, his tone walking the line between pleading and impatience.

The smuggler sighed. "Do go on," he said patronisingly.

"What, exactly, are the Dark Ones?" Joran pressed.

He was hooked, and easily so. It told Androma of his hunger, his need for more. His need for *meaning* even. Here was a young man who knew he was meant for so much more than moving from town to town, tavern to tavern, always running, always hiding. It was a good start.

"God killers," Androma said simply. "The Andarens believe there was a time when the gods walked the earth as we do; that they even lived among us, *with* us. There isn't much to say where the Dark Ones came from, only that they threatened all life in Verda. The gods went to war to protect the realm and died finding victory."

"They are *monsters* then?" Joran followed up.

Androma considered the question, rarely having given it much thought. For all of her fight in this secret war, she had been more concerned with the Skaramangians, the lengths they would go to and the turmoil they would create.

"The Arkalon—the Andarens' holy book," she answered, "would suggest they are such. But," the old Rider added, and reluctantly so given Gallien's obtuse opinions, "there is little proof of their existence so long after the fact."

"Fairytales," the smuggler mumbled from the back of the boat.

"The Skaramangians believe it," Androma snapped back, "and they are *very* real. Their belief has brought war upon us all. The death toll at their feet cannot be counted nor the years they have spent amassing it. The Vahlken—your mother's order—were the first to fight them, Joran. In many ways, it was their fight that hastened the war."

"If *only* that was it," the wizard uttered.

Androma considered his dour addition. "We know more now than we used to," she went on. "The answers to bringing back the Dark Ones lie in magic, and so a race of sorts has begun."

"A race?" Joran enquired.

"A race for magic," Androma explained. "Be you Andaren or human, our collective knowledge of magic has only ever come from one source."

She hesitated, struggling to part with knowledge that had long been a secret, a secret she had even kept as a Dragon Rider.

"There is a place in Andara," she eventually continued. "They call it God Fall."

"I've heard of that," Gallien replied, his tone implying that whatever she said next would come as no revelation. "It's just a pile of bones," he described. "*Big* bones," he conceded, "but bones all the same. Hardly a god," he scoffed.

"A god?" Joran echoed, his wonder still intact.

"The Andarens believe so," Androma said, taking back control. "True or not, those *bones* are inscribed with every known spell. Without them, the Andarens, their clerics and warlocks, would know nothing of their alchemy."

"Wait," Drakalis interrupted. "The bones have... *spells* written into them?"

"Yes," she confirmed. "A fact that further lends to the Andarens' belief that the remains do, indeed, belong to a god: their parting gift magic itself. Whether you share in their faith or not, Gallien, it cannot be disputed that those bones belonged to something with knowledge of magic, a knowledge that predates our own."

Joran moved through the motions of rowing before responding. "If that's where the Andarens discovered magic, how did humans—The Jainus—come to possess it as well?"

Aphrandhor was chuckling to himself. "He is quite astute, Androma."

"Indeed he is," she agreed. "Perhaps, Green Leaf, you would be better answering his question."

The row boat beside them creaked as the wizard turned in his seat. "'Tis the best kept secret in all of Erador, I'd say. Known only to The Jainus."

"And the Dragon Riders," Androma inserted needlessly.

"True enough," Aphrandhor agreed. "Like those in Andara, who came to call themselves warlocks, we humans discovered magic beneath the ground, where the earth had tried to swallow the truth."

"Wizards," Androma muttered to herself, wondering if her old friend would ever speak plainly.

"Bones," he said at length. "Identical to those found in God Fall. Each bone a hard parchment inscribed with the secrets of the magic world. Spells upon spells. *Morvoren* was the first—the greatest wizard to have ever lived, they say! He founded The Jainus, tamed the Giants in The Spine, and had them build The Tower of Jain."

"There's *another* skeleton?" Gallien asked, somewhat animated now, as if he was finally investing in the knowledge they were imparting.

"There's actually three," Aphrandhor replied.

"*Three?*" the smuggler echoed, his curiosity delving into depths Androma would not have expected given his general attitude.

"The Skaramangians found another one in The Morthil Mountains," the wizard revealed. "They moved it, of course. We have never discovered its location or what they're doing with it."

Androma couldn't help but think of Mordrith Underborn who had, decades earlier, unearthed the third skeleton. It had been too long since the old Rider had crossed the dwarf's path and that of her apprentice, the fiery Yamnomora. Androma hoped the pair were safe, wherever they were. Both were assets they couldn't afford to lose, and Mordrith had become something of a friend over the long years.

"To answer *your* question, Master Joran," The Green Leaf continued, "The Jainus learned of their magic deep in the heart of The Silver Trees of Akmar."

"That forest is forbidden," Joran said, voicing the entirety of anyone's knowledge on the place.

"That it is," the wizard said definitively. "A request granted by the king of Morvoren's time and upheld by all who ascended the throne thereafter. It belongs to The Jainus, and they will kill any who enter."

"That brings us back to the business of war," Androma said, picking up the thread before Aphrandhor could replace his next five words with five hundred. "When the Skaramangians learned of a second skeleton, they took steps to retrieve it. This was, in fact, the very first skirmish between our two people, not Tor Valan as history would have you believe."

"What happened?"

Joran's question snapped out of his mouth at exactly the same time it burst from Gallien's, reminding Androma that the smuggler had once claimed to be a treasure seeker, a man who delved into the past in search of fortune.

"Andaren alchemy met human magic," Aphrandhor spoke up. "A collision the Skaramangians did not walk away from."

Androma knew everything the wizard was saying, only she recalled the men and women—Skaramangians all—who had suffered in order for them to learn it. Some had suffered at her hands, but most had revealed the truth while being questioned by a far more terrifying figure.

The image she conjured of Daijen Saeth was not the same Vahlken she knew now, for he had been younger when she still had eyes to see him. There were few who could keep their secrets from him. How thankful she was that he remained an ally.

"It led to war," Androma announced from the front of her boat, her voice projecting across the river. "The Skaramangians pitted the two realms against each other. Through bloodshed and chaos, they believed they could gain access to the bones in Akmar."

Joran had stopped rowing. "Why would they want the bones if they had their own?"

Androma turned her head to the other boat, signalling Aphrandhor.

"What do you know of magic, Master Joran?" The Green Leaf asked.

"Not much," he admitted. "Nothing really."

"The important thing to know, is that there is only one magic. But," he forewarned, "there is more than one way to *practice* it. The Andarens use methods pertaining to *alchemy*, a form of magic that incorporates many ingredients to their spells. It means they must prepare their spells in advance and store them—often in liquid form."

"I've heard people say it's unnatural," Joran commented.

"Yes," Aphrandhor drawled. "That's what The Gilded have been spouting since the war began. Those words were put in their mouths by their masters, of course—*The Jainus*."

"That's who they spy for!" Joran blurted, clearly referring to some conversation Androma must have missed.

"What have you been saying, Green Leaf?" she asked, her suspicion tinged with bemusement.

"This and that," he replied flippantly. "And yes, Master Joran, The Gilded are an extension of The Jainus, though most of the priestlings have no idea, the truth known only to the Gildessa and her most trusted sages."

"So, it's not true then?" Joran probed. "Their magic isn't... *unnatural*?"

"*All* magic is natural," Aphrandhor told him, a note of affection for the subject matter in the wizard's voice. "But it suits The Jainus to have the Andarens' magic looked upon as abhorrent by the people of Erador. A fact that the Skaramangians use to their advantage."

"Fuel for the fires of war," Androma remarked dryly.

"What's the other kind of magic?" Joran had managed to get back into the rhythm of rowing, his efforts likely employed to keep up with Cob.

"The other way..." The Green Leaf paused before determining. "Humans—The Jainus—use a more... *ethereal* form of magic."

As he said as much, the sound of flickering flames reached Androma's ears, though she could not feel the heat of the fire brought to life in the wizard's palm.

"Our spells derive from the glyphs inscribed on the bones, glyphs we have translated into words. These words can be spoken aloud or merely thought of and the spell is born. Of course, not everyone can actually *use* magic. Those of us capable of channelling its power can only do so with Demetrium, a natural ore that focuses our—"

"Aphrandhor," Androma chastened. "Why are there two forms of magic and why would the Skaramangians go to war for the bones? Before we reach Valgala, preferably." The old Rider was beginning to wonder if she wouldn't have been better keeping the wizard out of it.

"You never could tell a good tale," The Green Leaf criticised, a smile in his voice. "The crux of it is the spells we have at our disposal," he went on. "The glyphs etched into the bones, both here and in Andara, are different in nature and—most importantly—incomplete. We have been able to formulate much from what we have, but there is so much more to be learned. If only the three skeletons could be examined side by side we might put them together and complete them. Longer spells. More intricate spells.

More *powerful* spells. As long as we possess but one, our magic will be forever fractured."

"And these Skaramangians want *more* magic," Joran concluded.

"A means to an end, like all things," Androma chipped in. "More magic means more power, more leverage. They would use it as a weapon to see the Dark Ones returned, a weapon that would decimate both realms in the process."

"How could they bring back these... *Dark Ones*?" Joran enquired.

"Isn't that the question," Aphrandhor replied unhelpfully.

"We don't know," Androma said more succinctly. "There are few even in their own order who know such things."

"This has to be some kind of joke." Gallien's tone spoke of his disgust. "You can't be serious. The war was started over a pile of *bones*? Jealous wizards and ancient cults who believe in resurrecting fairytales."

"The Skaramangians have started wars for less," Cob said, speaking for the first time in a while.

"*You* believe this?" the smuggler asked of the Kedradi. "Your people are supposed to be pragmatists. You must see this as nonsense."

Cob gave no reply, content to row.

Androma placed her mouth over one shoulder. "You don't have to believe it, Gallien. But twice you have crossed paths with The Dawn Sword, their most favoured weapon. *Believe* that he is coming. That monster will never stop hunting Joran."

"Why?" he damn near growled.

Androma couldn't fathom the effect her next words would have on the young boy, but they were the final piece. *Then* he could choose.

"Because Joran is a threat to them."

It seemed both were taken aback, and rightly so. Androma said nothing, letting those words sit with the pair for a time.

"I'm a... *threat*?"

"*How* could he be a threat?" Gallien spat. "They've been after him since he was a baby! How can a *baby* threaten some cult as old as time? How could he threaten them *now*?"

"Is it because I'm *half* human?" Joran's voice was quieter than before, his wonderment retreated.

Androma turned so she was facing the young man. "It's not *what* you are or even *who* you are, Joran. It's who you're *going* to be. It's what you're going to *do* that threatens them."

The old Rider could already tell that the smuggler was making a face at her response.

"Now you're making even less sense," he accused.

"It has been seen," Androma said. "By *ten thousand eyes*, it has been seen."

And *heard*, she thought, though she declined to mention the name *Pendain*. None had come to understand the name or why it had been heard in the vision. She had no doubt, however, that Joran was the crux of it, for he was half Vahlken, a fact that had been recorded by the Andarens' grand clerics.

For precious seconds, there was only the sound of the river.

"What has been seen?" Joran dared to ask.

Androma didn't need to weigh her words, there were only four of them and they had been spoken by ten thousand lips.

"A time of dragons."

43
THE FALL

55 Years Ago...

Daijen was gripped with shock and sent reeling away from the mouth of the tunnel. Slait, however, could go nowhere, his body pinned to the ground. His armour, reinforced with silk of the Weavers, proved its strength and prevented the sudden blow from breaking every bone in his chest.

Not done with him, the Aegre thrashed its talon left and right, shaking the initiate like a rag doll, before hurling him away.

Yendi was the first to rise to his defence. "Slait!"

"No!" Kastiek cried, failing to reach her in time.

Laif tackled her at the threshold, though he required aid from Soyra to keep Yendi from breaking loose.

Outside, the Aegre reared up on its hind legs, its front talons flexing in the air. Even wounded, Slait was a testament to his vigorous training. The initiate flipped onto his feet, avoiding the incoming talons while, simultaneously, freeing his sabre.

"Slait, no!"

Kastiek's warning fell on deaf ears—Slait was going on the

offensive. He pivoted on one heel and brought his sabre round in a wide arc. The steel sliced into the Aegre's front left leg, spilling blood onto the rocks and snow. It shrieked in pain and flapped its wings, battering Slait to the ground.

Again, he absorbed the blow and rolled away; only this time he did so between the Aegre's front and back legs. As he emerged on its other side, he flicked his weapon up and round in an attack that cut the creature from gut to ribs.

"NO!" Kastiek bellowed.

The Aegre staggered but it wasn't to be brought down. Instead, it turned swiftly and swivelled its head down and around, slamming into Slait's wounded chest. He was flung from his feet and parted from his sabre. He might have crawled after it had the Aegre not mercilessly pursued him.

Slait cried out in a fresh wave of agony as his chest disappeared inside the animal's beak. Though protected from death by his cuirass, he was tossed into a jagged outcropping of rock as if he were no more than a sack of sundries.

"We have to help him!" Yendi growled.

"Keep her back!" Kastiek ordered.

Bleeding, the Aegre prowled towards Slait, its head dipped low to unleash its threatening squawk. Slait used the rock at his side to pick himself up, though his fate seemed all but sealed.

"Yendi's right," Kovun stated. "We have to help him—he's one of us!"

Taking no heed of the squabbling at its back, the Aegre closed in on Slait, its beating wings whipping up the snow into a flurry. The initiate offered his superior opponent a grimace of unrelenting determination. If nothing else, Kastiek had trained them never to give up, even when defeat was inevitable.

He had also trained them to be proficient killers, whatever their foe. It was with such proficiency that Slait dropped to one knee and threw out his right hand. That was not all he threw.

The Aegre managed one more step before momentum alone carried it forwards. The ground shuddered under its crashing weight, its talons lost entirely beneath its crushing bulk. Its horned head slammed unceremoniously into the plateau and skidded to Slait's boots.

With a sneer, the bald initiate reached down and gripped the hilt of his atori short-sword, the weapon lodged where it had impacted inside the Aegre's beak. He yanked it out to reveal red steel.

Kastiek was speechless, his mouth ajar.

Yendi shrugged free of her captors. "Slait," she muttered, breaking into a run.

Yendi was dead before her body hit the ground.

By the time Daijen registered what had happened, he was looking down at Yendi's body, pinned beneath three hooked talons. Blood had exploded from the back of her head where she had struck the ground and one of the talons had pierced her throat. She was gone.

That same Aegre thrust its head into the tunnel and snatched Kovun clear by one of his arms. The arm was soon severed above the elbow when the Aegre clamped its beak and threw the initiate across the slopes.

Daijen gasped seeing so much blood spurt through the air and plaster the Aegre's beak. Kovun made no such noise, silenced, perhaps, by the shock. Indeed, he had uttered his last words, the initiate never to be heard again after being set upon by two more Aegres. Their beaks and talons ripped him to pieces in seconds, spreading his remains across the eyries.

Naelin screamed with rage and freed her sabre and atori blade. Kastiek cried out, warning her to stay inside the tunnel, but grief clouded good sense. She delivered a glancing blow across the beak of the Aegre who had snatched Kovun from the cave and even succeeded in stabbing the creature at the base of its long throat.

It wasn't enough.

As Soyra reached out to drag Naelin back, the enraged initiate was mauled by three raking talons. The Weaver's armour was extremely durable, but it couldn't boast the substantial strength of dragon scales, and even they were torn asunder by Aegres' talons. Soyra suffered for the truth of that, her cuirass ripped in three jagged lines, mirroring the wounds inflicted upon her chest. Before she could fall to her knees, the Aegre engulfed her head and thrashed from left to right until it parted from the rest of the body.

Momentarily blinded by Naelin's blood, Soyra failed to get out of the way and found herself being dragged by the leg. As the Aegre backed away, taking the initiate with it, a group of Aeglets dropped out of the sky and wasted no time making Soyra their next meal. Her screams were silenced almost immediately. Almost.

"YOU!" Laif roared, his sabre pointed at Slait. "You did this!"

Laif raced from the tunnel entrance, leaping only once to run the edge of his blade along the throat of the Aegre responsible for the deaths of his brother and three sisters. The Aegre fell silently, its hot blood pooling and steaming in the snow.

Kastiek looked pained by the action but made not a sound, his utter shock robbing him of his protest.

Continuing his run, Laif brought his wrath down upon Slait, and sabre clashed with atori blade in a flurry of steel. "You did this!" Laif spat. "You should have listened!"

Slait was forced to evade more than deflect, his injuries taking their toll. Still, he kept Laif at bay and responded with more than one successful counterattack, splashing his fellow initiate's blood across the rocks.

All the while, Kastiek looked on with glassy eyes, his attention wandering from corpse to corpse. It seemed undeniable that his quiet fury was building, his sabre inching further from its scabbard. "They're all gone," he could be heard muttering over and over.

Daijen gripped his own sabre, determined to accompany Kastiek should he join the fight. Ilithranda placed a firm hand against his cuirass and shook her head, as if she had foreseen his death.

Leaving the Aegres to snap at each other and fight over the easy pickings of the dead, Slait and Laif took their fight atop a sill that split the plateau. Their battle rang out until Slait feigned his next attack and used the subsequent opening to grab Laif by the collar of his cuirass. Swift was the elbow slammed into the side of Laif's head, dazing him.

Kastiek's training, his instruction to always execute one's opponent without hesitation or remorse, was all too obvious when Slait slipped his atori blade through the gap under Laif's arm, plunging the short-sword to its hilt.

Laif's expression dropped in surprise. It lasted only until he realised his fate was to be that of his brother and sisters. It was with recognition and betrayal that he looked upon Slait.

Kastiek let loose a blood-curdling roar of his own, his fury now demanding he take action. Daijen called out a warning, fearing that any one of the frenzied Aegres could attack him. There was no stopping the Vahlken, however, his dead sprint clearing him from the tunnel in the blink of an eye.

Again, Ilithranda held Daijen back. "No," she hissed.

"We have to help him!"

"They're all gone!" Ilithranda yelled in his face. "Look! They're all gone! You'll die if you go out there!"

"Kastiek will die if I don't!" Daijen countered.

Like some villain of the old tales, Slait stood atop the ridge victorious, his blade coated in the blood of his kin. He himself was dripping blood from various places, his face streaked with red gashes. He looked out on the ravaged bodies of his brothers and sisters, they who had accompanied him every step of his journey for decades.

He just didn't care.

Hurtling towards him was Kastiek—a Wraith of vengeance.

His intrusion into their territory didn't go unnoticed. An adult Aegre flapped its wings to land in the Vahlken's path. Kastiek didn't stop, or even slow down, as if he knew what was about to happen.

Strix collided with the other Aegre at such speed that its kin was buried in the mountainside. Pinned and clawing with damaged legs, it succumbed to Strix's talons and plunging beak.

Through the rain of snow and debris, Kastiek leapt, taking him to Slait's ridge. There was no preamble—only wrath. Kastiek stabbed and thrust and swung his weapons, always bringing them to bear in such a way that Slait was forced to evade rather than parry. Inevitably, he was worn down by Kastiek's superior skills, and finally a kick that collapsed Slait to one knee.

With a mad cry, Kastiek whipped his sabre down, slashing through the initiate's face, lips, and chin. The attack put Slait on his back and saw him release his atori blade.

"You killed them all!" Kastiek spat, his voice hoarse.

"They were weak," Slait muttered, as he rolled to one side and tried to pick himself up.

Kastiek put a boot into his ribs and sent him crashing down from the ridge. "Why didn't you listen?" he roared, following him down and kicking him across the plateau again.

Slait changed tack and began crawling away.

"You're not fit to wear that cloak!" Kastiek bellowed, harassing him again and again with more kicks. "You're not fit to wear that armour! You're unworthy of the name Vahlken!"

Slait pushed himself up to his knees with undeserved speed. His hand whipped out and back and splattered Kastiek's face with the blood from his wounded face. The Vahlken was momentarily blinded, giving Slait all the time he needed to turn and jump, barrelling into his enemy with abandon.

Coming down on top of Kastiek, Slait immediately rammed his head down onto the Vahlken's nose. Never one to relent, he then reached out and grabbed Kastiek's wrist. Even Daijen's powerful sense of hearing couldn't hear the bones break through the feasting of the Aegres, but he certainly saw Kastiek's hand relinquish the sabre as it bent in towards his arm.

The Vahlken cried out and swung wildly with his other hand, bringing the edge of his atori blade into the side of Slait's head. At least it would have if Slait hadn't raised his arm and blocked the weapon with his vambrace, the silk of the Weavers keeping its bite at bay.

Daijen started for the opening again, his heart thundering in his chest.

"No!" Ilithranda grappled him.

"We have to do something!"

"We have to *survive*!" Ilithranda yelled back.

Slait pinned Kastiek's other arm down and repeated the same manoeuvre, snapping his wrist with a severe inflection of the joint. Again, the Vahlken groaned in pain and lost his grip on the weapon. His cry was cut short when Slait began laying into him, hammering fist after fist into his face.

"You always held me back!" the initiate moaned. "You always treated me like I was less than the others! You treated me like *dirt*!"

Bloodied, bruised, and battered, Kastiek could do naught but take the beating and barbed words.

Strix, on the other hand, didn't have to do anything of the sort.

The Aegre's front talons took purchase on the ridge of their plateau, startling Slait into retreat. Once, twice, he hammered down, the sharp point of his armoured beak piercing the stone beneath the snow.

Slait let loose the cry of a wild berserker.

Proving his mind to be plagued by real madness, Slait moved through his pain and actually advanced on the enraged Aegre.

As Strix's head came down, the initiate evaded and pounced, using the animal's head to reach its back. Worse, he reached the saddle. Strix flapped his wings and moved erratically, but it wasn't enough to prevent Slait from unclipping the slaiken blade strapped to the side of the saddle.

The curved and serrated blade was a few inches longer than Slait was tall, and from hilt to sloping tip it was pure silvyr, the strongest and lightest metal known to Verda. Free of its fastenings, the blade shone brilliant silver in the sunlight. It was soon to be dulled red.

Daijen lost some of the fight in him, his eyes reporting a scene he couldn't—*didn't*—want to comprehend. Slait had leapt forwards, the slaiken blade gripped in both hands, and brought all of his considerable strength to bear. Combined with the silvyr edge, it was enough to slice through most of Strix's neck, severing all but a few strands.

For all his injuries, Kastiek was distraught. His broken wrists made his rise awkward and, undoubtedly, painful, but still he found his feet and looked upon Strix's lifeless body. His tears mixed with the blood smeared across his face and his mouth fell ajar with a howling cry.

Shocked by the devastating outcome, Ilithranda's hold on Daijen slackened just enough for him to shove her away and bolt for the mountainside. He ran as fast as he could and, after years of practising just that, he was damned fast. He was not, however, faster than an Aegre.

It caught up with him and rammed him aside with its head of horns. He didn't even register the impact until he was skidding and tumbling over himself through the snow.

Quick to pick himself up, Daijen had to face the facts: he couldn't outrun the Aegre and nor should he slay to such a creature, sacred as they were.

There were few times in Daijen's life when he had felt something change him—the breaking of an old chain—but he felt it now, in Kastiek's moment of dire need. The feeling allowed him to dampen his instincts and push aside his emotions. He had only to rise. Rise to the challenge he would have previously cowered from.

As the Aegre came upon him, its front talons aloft and wings flared, Daijen wielded his sabre. He brought the edge up in a swift arc and met the creature's falling throat. There he held it in defiance, the steel coming to rest against the Aegre's flesh beneath brown feathers. The animal knew, of course. It was highly intelligent and knew when its life was at risk.

It left both locked in a battle of wills, frozen still and eye to eye.

"*Once you make eye contact, do not break it for anything.*" Intense as that moment was, the irony wasn't lost on Daijen that Kastiek's words of warning were jeopardised by the Vahlken's own impending doom.

Daijen was desperate to turn and see what was happening, but there was nothing he could do but look into those yellow eyes. There was a speckle of green in there, either side of the black slit that cut from top to bottom. Those eyes belonged to monsters and gods. It was fitting, perhaps, that they belonged to a creature that sat somewhere between the two.

Without warning, the Aegre slowly raised its head, clearing the sabre. It did so quite deliberately and with regal grace. It lifted its beak and released a short sharp squawk before taking a step back.

Daijen swallowed, wishing he could spare the time to appreciate the extraordinary exchange—the truce as it was—but he heard a gut-wrenching sound.

The initiate's head swivelled towards the noise and found Kastiek skewered on the end of his own slaiken blade.

Slait twisted the great sword, jerking the Vahlken to his knees. The weapon produced a metallic sound when he pulled it free, scraping against the silk of the Weavers beneath Kastiek's leathers.

"No!" Daijen yelled, breaking into a sprint.

Slait was mid swing, the long blade angled to part Kastiek's head from his body, when Daijen threw himself in the way. It took both his sabre and atori short-sword to block the slaiken blade and the silvyr dented both. Kastiek seemed hardly aware that he had just been saved from decapitation, his watery eyes fixed on Strix.

"Runt!" Slait growled, a wicked smirk pulling at one side of his lips. "*You're* even weaker than them!" he spat, rolling his head towards the dead initiates.

Daijen could conjure no retort, his fury demanding action alone. Using both weapons, he pushed the slaiken blade away and came at Slait with a flurry of steel. He scored naught but a cut down the initiate's arm before receiving an elbow to the chest and a solid fist to the jaw.

Slait was laughing amidst the gruesome feasting that surrounded them. He jabbed his sword in Kastiek's direction. "He's not going to save you now, little runt!"

Daijen spat blood onto the snow and launched himself back at his enemy. The sabre went high before the atori blade came in low. Slait deflected and evaded, a beast not to be controlled by his pain. He countered with a sweeping arc of the six-foot length of silvyr, forcing Daijen to dive over the top and roll away. His landing, however, caught the attention of a stray Aeglet.

The initiate managed to part his legs before the animal lunged and drove its beak into the ground. Next came its talons, mauling the snow and dirt beneath while Daijen scrambled away. Flapping its wings, the Aeglet found some height to renew its attack. It pursued Daijen until it was distracted by Slait, who was limping back to Kastiek. The creature squawked threateningly, but its cry only served to warn Slait of the imminent attack.

Round came the slaiken blade, and with no more than a simple backhand. The Aeglet, absent half of its head, crumpled into the mountainside with a crashing *thud*.

Daijen gritted his teeth and forced himself to his feet. He was going to kill that monster.

Leaping over Strix's legs, he fell upon Slait with lashes of steel, his sabre flashing silver and the atori blade gleaming bronze. Only once did he spy Ilithranda by the cave entrance. She was trying to reach them, to add her deadly talents to the battle, but a fully grown Aegre hounded her, always keeping her on the retreat.

"Come on then!" Slait baited. "Let's see what a messenger guard's really made of!"

Daijen cried out with rage as he thrust, twisted, and swept his weapons through the air. Even with such an unwieldy sword as a slaiken blade, Slait was the superior fighter, a glaring observation that Daijen refused to accept. It was, nonetheless, becoming harder to ignore, especially after Slait batted the atori short-sword from Daijen's grip and hammered the silvyr blade so hard it shattered his sabre and sent a jarring pain down his arms.

Not one, not two, but three headbutts put Daijen on his back, his face streaked with blood. He blinked again and again trying to align his senses. He could hear Slait's limping walk crunch through the snow, but it took him longer to realise he was moving away.

Kastiek!

Fear, as ever, was a powerful tool. It gave Daijen the strength to sit up and push through the pain and to focus his eyes. He wished it had taken him a moment longer, for he made sense of his environment only in time to witness Kastiek's final seconds on Verda's earth.

It seemed only a heartbeat that there existed a tangible connection, their eyes coming together in grim resignation.

You're ready.

Though he didn't say the words, it was the last message Kastiek conveyed before Slait cut off his head.

Daijen cried out, his body working furiously to put him back on his feet. He stumbled almost immediately and had to use Strix's still form to steady himself. His mind felt like a bottomless well, his thoughts and feelings dropping away to leave him cold and hollow. Over the sound of squabbling and feasting Aegres, he could just about register Ilithranda's voice shouting his name. He might have looked back at her had he not been gripped by the bloody sight of Kastiek, dead beside his winged companion.

A shadow ran over the scene.

Again, the Aegres became unsettled. Some even abandoned their easy meals and flew away.

The exile had returned, its white feathers matching perfectly with the snow.

Somewhat detached, Daijen watched the Aegre approach Slait. Its head dipped so their eyes might meet. Daijen almost smiled, sure that he was about to watch his foe be torn in half as he deserved. As the seconds went by, however, and Slait continued to breathe, the gravity of what was actually happening struck Daijen as powerfully as any blow.

They were bonding.

The exile had chosen the exile.

"No," Daijen uttered, pushing himself off Strix.

His right hand was clumsy in its search for the shogue on his belt. It barely occurred to the initiate that coordinating the hook and rope in his current condition would be near impossible. It was too late anyway. By the time he had the coiled weapon in his hand, Slait was mounting the exile and with Kastiek's slaiken blade in hand.

"No!" Daijen bellowed.

The white Aegre turned away and set off for the edge of the plateau in the south. Daijen broke into a run, his first few steps a stumble before he managed a dead sprint. His speed caught the attention of other Aegres, though none but a few Aeglets strayed from the easy pickings they already had. The latter were too far away to catch the initiate, who was using every ounce of magic Handuin's spells had imparted to him.

"Daijen, no!"

They were the last intelligible words he heard from Ilithranda. He cared little for her warning. There was only his prey. Slait hunkered down, pressing his chest close to the exile's back while gripping tightly to the feathers at the base of the animal's neck. The Aegre's talons kicked up snow as it leapt for the very edge of a sheer cliff. Its wings fanned majestically as all four legs left the mountainside.

So too did Daijen Saeth.

As he jumped into thousands of feet of nothingness, the initiate threw out his shogue. How many times had he done just that while leaping from the ramparts of Ka'vairn into the courtyard? Kastiek would toss a sack of sand into the air and Daijen's hook would find it. Every time. Today would be no different.

The shogue curled round and stabbed into the exile's rear. The animal shrieked in protest and dived. The rope went taut. Daijen yelped as he was pulled down at tremendous speed.

His hands ached and burned as he slipped down the rope. Still, he would not let go. That was considerably harder to maintain when the white Aegre unfurled its wings and changed direction. Daijen was swung up before he flew like the waves of the ocean in the creature's wake.

He was holding on with a single hand now, his entire body weight dragging behind his grip.

Looking ahead, Slait was basking in the glory of his achievements. He howled and hooted, thrusting Kastiek's slaiken blade in the air, a trophy of his bloody victory. That was the last he saw of the wretch, his grip utterly lost when the exile flapped its wings and ascended higher into the heavens.

Daijen could but watch the pair shrink into the blue above, as he plummeted into the rolling hills of white clouds below.

The clouds accepted him without protest and he entered a world of mist. His fur cloak billowed out above him and a number of sundries came loose from his belt. There was nothing he could do. There was no training to call upon. No way to save himself. There was only the fall.

As he broke free of the cloud bank, and the rocky slopes of The Hellion Mountains dominated his view, Daijen could only dwell on his failure. He would die soon enough having achieved nothing. He would never join the fight against the Skaramangians. He would never be declared a Vahlken. He would never be able to tell Ilithranda that she was a true sister in his eyes; that he loved her as such. She had become family in a way the others never could.

Worse than all of that—he would never avenge Kastiek and the others. The world had been robbed of six Vahlken. How much good they could have done!

For all his training, he had failed to slay their murderer. Daijen, of course, was responsible for his own doom too. Twice the fool then. And there was to be no serenity in these, his final moments. It was impossible to accept his fate knowing how much he had left undone. And yet, he was hurtling towards his death.

He could see The Faern'duil in all its glory now. The forest stretched out to the west, covering Andara in green for as far as the eye could see. Would he be shattered on the rocks below, there to dwell until his bones were dust? Or would his broken body find its way down to join the forest? Such morbid questions were to be his final companions.

So strong was the wind in his ears that he failed to hear the third and very *real* companion. It seemed as if the Aegre materialised from nowhere, appearing behind and beneath him, its wings tucked in. Daijen didn't hesitate, his survival instincts guiding his hands out to find purchase. The moment he gripped the creature's feathers it began to slowly fan its wings, slowing it down just enough that their falling speed lined up.

Hugging the animal as tightly as he could, Daijen braced

himself for the inevitable change in direction. The force of it drew a grunt from the initiate and would have broken his hold had the Aegre not levelled out and taken him across the top of The Faern'duil. Daring to ease his grip, Daijen carefully manoeuvred himself into a sitting position.

It wasn't the heavens, but it was no less a wondrous dream come to life.

The world was stretched out around him, a staggering vista of beauty that suddenly felt so very close.

Though the miraculous experience tried to keep him captivated, Daijen spared the time to scrutinise the Aegre upon which was seated. There was no doubt in his mind that it was the same one he had encountered on the mountain. They had been braced in death together, each capable of taking the other's life—each capable of sparing it.

Years ahead of schedule, he had done the unimaginable—he had bonded with an Aegre. As breathtaking as that revelation was, Daijen could only think of one thing.

He was flying!

44
THE WHISTLING PIG

"Tell me again." Gallien said the words before he even dropped into the booth.

Androma would have been looking at the smuggler had she the eyes to see. Instead, she continued to face him, her tattered blindfold concealing whatever lay beneath.

"It won't sound any different," she warned him.

Drakalis sighed, taking the moment to let his gaze roam over the tavern, The Whistling Pig. It was packed, but so was every other tavern in the capital city. They had arrived in the early evening, entering the city via the river that flowed into the circular lake. In the moonlight it had looked like a plane of black glass surrounded by a halo of candlelight. They would have to wait until dawn to see the white walls, buildings, and towering spires of Valgala.

Gallien hadn't cared for the view. Beautiful though the city was, he was more interested in a padded seat and a hot meal. There were only so many days he could commit to a row boat and sporadic camping before his mind began to unravel. He had to consider that it was too late for the latter.

A couple of men brushed past their table, setting the smuggler on edge. They made no comment nor trouble, but Drakalis knew their type by look alone. A couple more pints and they would start actively looking for a fight.

He had no love for the Kedradi in their party, nor the talkative wizard, but he wouldn't have minded sharing the table with them. Instead, the pair were absent altogether, having peeled away after entering the city in search of fresh supplies for the remainder of their journey—wherever that was.

Every few seconds, the smuggler scrutinised the thick crowd around the bar, always searching for Joran. He was easily identified, the only one with his hood up. It would be some time before he made it to the front and paid for their food and drinks—time Gallien intended to use to better understand the mess they were in.

"No one can see the future," he argued, his awfully strong opinion aimed at the blind Rider. "No one," he emphasised.

"The Andarens can," Androma countered. "And it's not *the* future," she went on to specify, and not for the first time. "It's *a* future. Thousands of Andarens were subjected to the Helm of Ahnir. *Thousands*, Gallien. They saw all kinds of things before it *killed* them. Of all the futures they witnessed there emerged a common thread, a singular vision that recurred more than the rest."

Gallien sat back in the booth, preparing himself to hear it again.

Androma leaned forward, as if she was chasing him across the table. "They saw Joran standing victorious on a *hundred* battlefields. He was a *Dragon Rider*. More so, they saw a future that every one of them described as a *time of dragons*. An age brought about *by* Joran. Do you understand how important that makes him?"

"No," Gallien said bluntly. "We've already got dragons and Riders—they're out there right now fighting in the damned war," he hissed.

Androma's demeanour sank, as did her head into her chest.

"The truth of that has been suppressed for years. For a century in fact."

"What *truth*?" Gallien demanded.

"The only truth," Androma replied, her voice ringing hollow. She sighed, her clasped hands sliding from the table top to rest on her lap. She tried once, twice, to speak but said nothing. It seemed the old Rider didn't know where to begin.

"Once there were heroes," she said at last. "Brave men and women who showed their quality to be above the rest. Those whose deeds earned them the heart of a warrior—*the heart of a dragon*. Those whose courage and strength resonated with an unborn dragon. In their eggs, they can wait years, *thousands* of years, for a warrior worthy of them.

"These... *heroes*," she continued. "They rose up on young battlefields and defended the weak and oppressed across all of Erador. They did so because they were *inspired*. They had only to look up and see. Dragon Riders... the last noble warriors in the realm. Only heroes can embolden the ordinary. For centuries, *millennia*, the Dragon Riders galvanised generation after generation, adding Riders to our ranks, birthing dragons from their eggs."

Androma remained unnervingly still for a time. Her expression was almost non-existent, though Gallien could see the subtle movements about her jaw, where the tension had crept in.

"But there are no more heroes," she eventually declared. "This war with the Andarens is like nothing the Riders have ever faced. The Vahlken and their Aegres have proven to be a formidable foe. We dwindled each other's numbers until we could no longer afford to fly into battle with the armies.

"Year upon year... *century upon century*," she corrected, "the bloodshed has raged on. In the place of heroes there are only soldiers now. Fodder for the machine of war. Instead of being there to inspire, the Dragon Riders are spread thin across the coastlines, patrolling the borders. Even then, there are gaps where the likes of The Dawn Sword can enter our lands."

The smuggler absorbed it all, though the picture was fractured in his mind. "If the Vahlken and the Riders know about the Skaramangians, why are you still fighting each other? Surely an alliance would—"

"They *don't* know," Androma interjected, her voice hushed. "Not all of them," she specified. "I am one of only two Riders who know the Skaramangians pose the real threat. The others do not. They know only the war. Their enemy is Andara and all who call it home. The Vahlken are forced to fight the Riders because they must defend their people. This has divided their attention, allowing the Skaramangians more freedom."

Gallien heard it all, but his concern always returned to Joran and Joran alone. "So you think that boy is going to inspire... what? A new generation of Dragon Riders? How's he going to do that, Androma? He's not even a Dragon Rider. Hells, he's not even a soldier. The only thing he fights is *my* good sense. Don't get me wrong," he was quick to add. "He's a *good* lad stuck in a world that hates him for no more than the way he looks, but he ain't what you want him to be."

"It's not the way he looks but what he represents," Androma pointed out. "He is living proof that our two peoples are compatible, that there can be peace."

Momentarily sidetracked from his own point, Gallien frowned at the old Rider. "One boy proves nothing. And there's got to be more like him after all this time. That doesn't matter," he told her, waving the topic away. "Joran washes dishes and keeps his head down. Do they sound like deeds worthy of a dragon?"

Androma had no immediate answer. In fact, she had no kind of response at all. Even the tension had left her jaw. She simply sat with the question, her thoughts her own for a time. "I don't know how he is to bond with an egg," she finally confessed, and quietly so. "I only know how all this ends. And I will fight to *my* very end for that future."

"You and how many others?" Drakalis argued. "How many will die fighting for *a* future? Will *Joran* die trying to be something he's not? Or will his *death* be the inspiration your precious heroes are looking for?"

Androma faced him. “I don’t know,” she uttered.

“That’s not good enough,” he stated. “I don’t care how many Andarens put that helmet on or what it showed them before blowing their heads off. It isn’t worth Joran throwing his life away...” Gallien trailed off, his thought taking him to their intended destination.

“He’s not a boy anymore, Gallien. What were *you* doing at his age? Had you joined the army yet? Or were you—”

“Drakanan,” the smuggler interrupted, his voice grave. Guarded though Androma’s reactions were, Gallien saw the truth reflected in the old Rider then. “That’s where we’re going. Isn’t it?”

Androma sat back, her hands reappearing on the table top. “It’s the only place he will be safe.”

“You mean it’s the only place he can train to become a Dragon Rider,” Drakalis corrected, his words barbed.

“The Skaramangians have no influence in Drakanan--”

“I don’t care.”

“You should care,” Androma snapped back. “They want him *dead*, Gallien. If he brings about a time of dragons the war will be tipped in Erador’s favour. They cannot allow that to happen. The majority of their power and control resides in Andara. Until their mission is fulfilled, they need to maintain that. They need the war to continue. Joran threatens that.”

“Their mission,” Gallien mocked. “The Dark Ones. More horseshit. The world’s full of monsters and when they die, they stay dead.”

“You heard what The Green Leaf said,” Androma reminded. “Those skeletons are the very definition of power and the Skaramangians possess *two* of them now. When they make their next move they will do so with magic we’ve never seen before. Spells we can’t imagine. For all we know, they’ve already mastered death. And if the Dark Ones prove to be real they might only be one step away from locating them. From bringing them back.”

Gallien thought of the fourth skeleton, his *secret* beneath Harendun. A god... The axe did possess a divine quality to it. The smuggler saw no reason to reveal such a thing though. Not until it served *his* interests. "They really believe Joran has the potential to end the war?" he had to ask, quite exasperated.

Androma shifted in her seat. "Ahnir was the god who saw *The End*. Why the Skaramangians would be allied against the gods no one can say, but they *believe* in the power they once held. In the power of the helm. So yes, they are taking the threat of Joran's future very seriously. Enough to have dispatched The Dancing Sword of the Dawn, and behind enemy lines no less. But even that beast cannot touch him in Drakanan."

Mention of the Riders' stronghold brought a question to the forefront of Gallien's mind. "And what are your friends in the north going to think when *we* turn up? You said they don't know about the Skaramangians. How are you going to explain our presence to a group of people who are legendary for disliking visitors?"

"I *said* I'm one of *two*," Androma reminded. "The other has awaited Joran's arrival in Drakanan for *sixteen years*."

Gallien knew the remark was spear tipped and aimed at his past decisions but he didn't care. "And the others?" he questioned, decidedly sure he didn't want to face an angry dragon at the end of their journey.

Androma shook her head. "I told you, they're patrolling the western coast. We will find no opposition in Drakanan. We just have to get there," she intoned.

Gallien scoffed. "Aye. We *just* have to leave Valgala—*unseen*. We *just* have to follow The North Road until our toes freeze off and hope we make it as far as Freygard before the Skaramangians catch up with us. Then there's *just* the matter of slipping through Drayshon without attracting attention. Aye," he drawled, "survive all that and we can just skip down The Dragon Path hand in hand, eh?"

"The journey is not without its perils," Androma admitted. "But when was the last time you felt safe? Truly safe. Or Joran for that matter. This is the only way, Gallien."

The smuggler had his witty response ready to deliver when a complete stranger sidled into the booth and sat down beside him.

He needed no more than a glance to know the man was rich, his clothes and jewellery elevating him to Valgala's higher echelons.

His greying hair and goatee were both immaculately trimmed, the latter attached to a strong jaw that jutted out at a severe angle. The tips of a scar could just be seen protruding both above and below the black eyepatch on the left side. The inherent thief that lived in Gallien also noticed the coin purse dangling from the stranger's belt.

"You should take her advice, Mr Drakalis," the man said pleasantly enough. "She has more than a few years on you, you know."

Gallien blinked. "And you are?"

"Apologies," he offered cheerfully. "Would you prefer I use your *other* name?"

The question flustered Gallien—no easy thing to do.

"Galahart," the old Rider interposed, her tone venomous.

"Androma," the spymaster replied with a grin.

And just like that, the axe returned to Gallien's grip, weighing his arm down to the tabletop.

Galahart raised a flawless eyebrow. "Now where did *that* come from?" he enquired with wicked wonder.

Drakalis pressed the axe blade into the spymaster's pristine shirt. "You should be more concerned with where I'm going to stick it."

"Well, didn't you just get more interesting," Galahart remarked, his eyes enraptured by the weapon.

Whether she was aware of the axe Gallien now wielded or not, Androma produced a curved dagger. "How could you have known we were here?" she hissed. "We left your men days behind."

"So you left some alive?" Galahart deduced. "I shall have to correct that upon their return."

"Answer me," the older Rider demanded, her knuckles paling around the dagger's hilt.

"Three years ago you sat in this very booth with The Green Leaf. Two years prior to that, you enjoyed a honey tea at that table over there, and with a pair of dwarves no less. Six months before that you stayed here for the night and met the Kedradi at dawn. After your meeting with the wizard," he went on casually, "I simply bought the establishment."

At that, the entire Whistling Pig came to a standstill, the noise sucked into a void. All eyes turned on their booth. All but three, whose attention pivoted to Joran who had been absorbed by the crowd around the bar. As one, they brought knives to bear, each positioned where they could deliver an instant kill.

Galahart let loose a light shot of laughter. "Money well spent," he said, complimenting his own work. "You should know by now, Androma. News in this city moves like The Kyber itself: *one way*. Everything passes through *me*. And my patience has paid off!" he declared. "The whole gang is here! Plus guests," he added, glancing at Gallien and gesturing at Joran. "But what *fine* guests they are."

The spymaster's attention turned fully on Joran now. "Such a ruckus for so insignificant a thing," he uttered. "You are the subject of quite the hunt, young sir." Galahart paused, as if he had only just noticed the axe blade resting threateningly against his chest. "Excuse me," he said, moving the weapon aside with naught but his finger and departing the booth.

Gallien pursued him, driven by fear for the boy. He made little more than a step beyond the booth before his path was barred by swords, the blades emerging from within the cloaks of what he had previously believed to be ordinary patrons.

Galahart moved into the open space, where he could address Joran more directly. "Perhaps there is more to you than meets the eye," he mused, pulling back his hood to reveal his violet eyes and shockingly white hair, through which the very tips of his pointed ears could be seen. "You are a leaf in a storm," he muttered.

"What have you done with Aphrandhor and Cob?" Androma demanded, cutting through the spymaster's opinions.

Galahart pivoted to face the blind woman. "Much like Joran here, it's not what I've *done* with them but what I'm *going to do* with them." The spymaster turned to wink at the boy. "Never good to be the crux of a prophecy, lad."

"Galahart," Androma growled.

"Like you, they are surrounded by enemies, soon to be questioned within an inch of their lives. I am so looking forward to interrogating the Kedradi. Their pain threshold is notoriously high. And The Green Leaf," he added mockingly. "Oh, *The Green Leaf.* Without his magic I imagine his old body won't stand up to much. Still, I would learn all that he knows before the end."

"I should have killed you when I had the chance," Androma lamented.

"I imagine the list of things you *should* have done is as long as your arm, Dragon Rider. Alas, you have as much time left as you do chances."

Gallien was listening, but his eyes had locked with Joran's, the two in silent conversation. Thus far, he had indicated his intention to launch his axe at the man holding a knife to the boy's throat. The commotion would be Joran's opportunity to leap over the bar and run through the back. By then, of course, the axe would have returned to his grip and the men barring his way would taste its steel. He could only hope that Androma chose to join the fight somewhere in there.

Before he could put any such plan into motion, however, the tavern door creaked open. A towering image of pale death walked in from the rain. Gallien's blood ran cold.

"You were supposed to wait outside," Galahart admonished.

The spymaster's men parted like long grass, not a man daring to block The Dancing Sword of the Dawn. Hood drawn high and standing in the gloom, only his strong and scarred jaw could be seen. That and his sword, of course, the steel dripping like his robes of stark white and red.

Gallien couldn't believe his eyes. Given everything he had seen of the warrior, he suspected the Andaren would have survived Aphrandhor's magic, but to have reached Valgala so soon he had to have forgone any sleep if not all rest. A beast indeed.

"The abomination yet lives," The Dawn Sword observed with a bad taste in his Andaren mouth. "Why?"

Galahart positioned himself so the hulking Andaren couldn't see the hand that had located the blade hidden in the shadows of his cloak. Gallien couldn't blame the man—who wouldn't feel threatened in the presence of such a creature? But weren't they allies? Drakalis sensed an opportunity emerging.

"Wait outside," the spymaster instructed.

The Dawn Sword didn't move. "The boy is to be put to death," he said simply, his voice deep and unnerving.

"Retreat to the shadows where you belong," Galahart told him firmly. "You're in *my* city now, *Slait*."

The beast's head twitched at the name. Then he took one step forward. "I am The Dancing Sword of the Dawn," he said quite deliberately. "I am the light that will banish the darkness. You *will* address me as such."

Galahart held his ground. "Leave," he ordered again.

"Why have you not killed the boy and his allies?" came The Dawn Sword's blunt response.

Gallien *felt* The Dawn Sword's gaze fall upon him rather than actually seeing it. He likened it to a weight on his shoulders, as if some predator was bearing down on him.

Slait, his true name revealed, made for Joran. "I would do it myself."

Galahart narrowed his one eye on the Andaren and stepped to block his path. "You have no such authority here. You will—"

Galahart held his tongue when The Dawn Sword flicked his wrist, bringing an Andaren sabre to rest on the spymaster's shoulder. The naked weapon sent a ripple of unease throughout the tavern, though not a man moved to defend their employer. More usefully, Gallien couldn't help but notice everyone's attention shifting away from him and Joran. The man standing beside Androma wasn't even looking at her anymore, and the old Rider had slowly positioned herself on the edge of her seat, ready to pounce.

"Your... *authority* is an illusion," The Dawn Sword retorted. "I am an instrument of the gods. There is no greater authority than theirs."

Galahart shifted his good eye to the men beside the Andaren who, credit to their courage, raised their swords to point at the colossal figure. "You are outnumbered," the spymaster informed him needlessly.

Looking down at Galahart, The Dawn Sword tilted his hooded head. "Whom do you serve, spymaster?" His tone of suspicion felt just as threatening as the blade he held to the man's neck.

Boldly, Galahart lifted his eyepatch and revealed a tattoo etched into the scarring where his eye used to be. "I am Skaramangian," he declared.

The Dawn Sword straightened up. "You speak our name so openly," he observed before his shadowed face scanned the rest of the tavern. "How many of you maggots bear the mark?"

Of the two dozen men, a mere three pulled back their sleeve or pulled down their collar to display the same glyph-like tattoo as Galahart's.

"You have brought outsiders into our crusade, Spymaster."

"They are loyal to me," Galahart reassured.

"The loyalties of men can be bought and bartered like sheep. You have overreached."

"I may do as I please in my city," the spymaster reminded him, seemingly oblivious now to the sword on his shoulder. "And I can assure you, our masters value my intellect and network over your brutality and bloodlust. So remove your sword and put Valgala behind you. The boy is in my custody now. You missed your chance." Galahart edged closer to the goliath. "You *failed*."

Gallien braced himself, no doubt in his mind that the Andaren was about to run the man through. Surprisingly, The Dawn Sword remained perfectly still, content to scrutinise the spymaster from within his hood.

"You have no intentions to kill the abomination," he uttered, as if he had just finished conducting an investigation into Galahart's mind. "I ask you again: whom do you serve?"

Galahart raised his chin proudly, defiantly. "As I have ever, Dawn Sword. I serve the *king of Erador*."

"HERETIC!" The Andaren's response was more bestial roar than any intelligible word.

If it shocked or deafened the spymaster there was no time to tell before The Dawn Sword thrust his blade into the man's gut, lifted him bodily from the floor, and pinned him to the ceiling. There he left Galahart, a bloody fixture that could do naught but watch his insides slide down the sabre. He was also forced to bear witness to the Andaren's savagery, and what savagery it was.

With his hands alone, The Dancing Sword of the Dawn snapped necks, crushed skulls, gouged out eyes with his thumbs, and even severed limbs. The spray from one such severed limb dotted Gallien with blood. In an instant, his mind was transported back to the battlefield, where blood, gore, and mud were worn like a second skin.

He shoved one of the spymaster's men and buried his axe in the other, clearing the path to Joran. Without hesitation, the smuggler threw his axe at the one who threatened the boy's throat, taking him in the head. Joran reacted well, throwing up an elbow into another's nose before pushing the other aside. As the axe reappeared in Drakalis's hand, Joran was leaping to safety beyond the tavern bar.

Not one to sit idly, Androma had already relieved her guard of his weapon and plunged it into his heart. "Get Joran out of here!" she yelled over the death cries of so many.

Gallien dashed across the tavern and skidded on his knees to reach the bar, narrowly evading the body being tossed through the air. Launching himself back to his feet, the smuggler barrelled into another of Galahart's men and pinned him against the bar. Joran emerged from nowhere and swung a glass bottle into the back of the agent's head. Drakalis saw to the end of the man, taking the axe by the handle that sat high in the middle of the blade and punching his foe in the face.

"You!" The Dawn Sword barked.

Gallien felt a strong hand grip the back of his neck and drag him away from the bar. He swung the axe wildly, but the Andaren had already released him, sending the smuggler staggering into a wooden post. As The Dawn Sword crushed a man's windpipe and flung another from his shoulders, he raised a meaty fist to drive Gallien's head into the wood.

He might have connected the blow had Androma's staff not whipped around and slammed into his ear. The impact dragged out a growl from the Andaren and saw him collide with a group of Galahart's men, two of whom succeeded in stabbing the behemoth with their swords. Their attack elicited a roar from The Dawn Sword, forcing him to lash out with new levels of barbarism.

"Gallien?" Androma called, only feet from where he rested against the post.

"I'm here," he answered, reaching out to grab her arm.

"Where's Joran?"

Drakalis spotted the boy that very moment, his eyes peering over the bar in time to see The Dawn Sword reclaim his weapon from the guts of Erador's spymaster. So quickly was the blade retrieved that Galahart himself fell straight to the floor. If he was still alive it was only for a moment more, the Andaren's blade dragged through his neck as the sword was raised into a devastating arc that cut through two more men.

"This way!" the smuggler urged, guiding the old Rider towards the bar. "Joran!" he bade.

The boy cleared the bar in one pivoting leap and joined them in their escape. None got in their way, every man charging in to bring down the Andaren monster. One of the poor fools slipped on blood before he could even raise his weapon, a misstep that saw him receive a backhand that broke every bone in his face.

That was the last atrocity Gallien witnessed before ramming through The Whistling Pig's side door. A night of pouring rain and a shadowed alley greeted the trio, their collective and laboured breath steaming the air.

The screams from inside were muffled now, mixed with shattering glass, snapping wood, and thunderous impacts. It was all too clear that only one would be walking out of the tavern now.

"We need to go," Androma hissed.

"Wait," Drakalis warned, hearing fast-approaching steps.

Pressing both the old Rider and Joran against the nearest wall, they observed a group of Valgala's homeguard rushing towards

The Whistling Pig's front door, swords in hand. The death toll was yet to reach its apex then.

"Now," Gallien directed.

The trio ran, putting as much distance between them and the tavern as possible. Here and there they were forced to take cover and wait out the passing of another patrol racing towards The Whistling Pig.

"Where's Aphrandhor and Cob?" Joran asked.

"They will find us," Androma assured. "We need to get out of the city, *now*."

Gallien didn't need telling twice. He kept reliving that first blow, nailing Galahart to the ceiling. He guided them away from the interior lake and navigated the maze of streets to Valgala's northern district. There they could leave via the road or the river that continued into Erador's north. The main gates, however, were shut and secured by a baulk of timber the size of a tree. Upon the ramparts were red-cloaked homeguards, all of whom were looking down at the three companions.

"What's wrong?" Androma demanded. "Why have we stopped?"

"The gates are shut," the smuggler reported, his axe still in hand.

"They never close the gates," she commented, an unfamiliar note of fear in her voice.

A man cleared his throat, the sound of it cutting through the night. As one, the trio's attention was drawn to the stone boathouse that arched high over the river and met the city's outer wall. There, in the doorway, his face and black robes illuminated by little more than the moonlight, was a bald man—a stranger to Gallien's eyes.

The man beckoned them with a gesture and retreated into the darkness of the boathouse.

"Who is it?" Androma asked.

"I have no idea," Gallien admitted. "But he hasn't tried to kill us yet, so let's find out."

His axe led the way across the courtyard and into the building, a glance spared for the homeguard who silently watched them all the way. The boathouse was filled with the sound of running water and revealed, in torchlight, its interior walls abound with the river's dancing reflection. It was also occupied by several men armed with bows, their arrows nocked but not aimed.

"You're alive!" Aphrandhor exclaimed, making himself known almost immediately. The wizard approached without being accosted by the armed men, including those who had been standing behind him, swords drawn.

"Green Leaf?" Androma replied. "What friends have you been making?"

Gallien exchanged a simple nod with Cob, the Kedradi surprisingly still in possession of his various weaponry. His dark eyes spared the smuggler half a glance, his focus swiftly returning to the archers.

The stranger who had beckoned them turned to Androma. "You've always had a talent for escaping by the skin of your teeth."

"Who are you?" Androma demanded.

The man clasped his hands behind his back and slowly approached them. "An old friend, of course."

"I do not know your voice," she confessed.

"Androma," the wizard interjected. "This is *Galahart*."

45
ALWAYS FORWARDS

45 Years Ago…

As if he were no more than a gargoyle, Daijen Saeth sat crouched on the edge of Ka'vairn's ramparts. His cloak of victory blowing out behind him, his icy blue eyes surveyed The Dain'Duil below. The forest was calm, the trees swaying gently in the spring breeze being funnelled through the valley.

Beyond The Dain'duil, The Morthil Mountains stood defiantly, a twin to The Hellion Mountains. Though familiar after so many years, the vista was no less beautiful.

It was marred now, and would be in Daijen's mind for the rest of his days. He looked down the sheer walls and jagged stone of the cliff to the strip of dirt that sat between the mountains and the edge of the forest. There, he laid eyes on the six marked graves.

Being the oak day, in the year 3072 of the sixth epoch, and exactly ten years since that fateful day, he was always going to have been drawn to them.

Of those who died upon the mountainside, only one had been recovered and given the rites of death tradition demanded. And so,

Kastiek's bones and ashes alone occupied that particular patch of earth—not far from Elivar, in fact.

Daijen could feel the memory repeating on him, as it had every day since. His jaw tensed and his knuckles cracked as he gripped the fortress stone. He wished to be rid of it, but he knew the sting would be useful, that the pain of the memory would be a source of strength.

Closing his eyes, he recalled the days immediately after, stranded in the great Faern'duil with his Aegre. They had inevitably landed and suffered communication problems. The initiate had desperately wanted to get back up to the mountain top and save Ilithranda, but the Aegre had not understood. Instead, the creature had hunted for them both, always taking to the skies without him.

Only after a week was he able to mount the Aegre again. Their first flight had been a disaster, the two incapable of coordinating their intended direction. They ended up on The Cliffs of Wren, south of the forest and no closer to The Hellion Mountains. Daijen had also fallen off moments before landing and injured his right shoulder.

It was days again before they took to the sky. His frustration and fear for Ilithranda had nearly driven him mad.

Doing his best to feel for the Aegre's micro-movements, Daijen began to gather some nebulous understanding of the creature's intentions while in flight. Though he was incapable of changing the direction, he was able to hold on for the plummeting dives and jarring landings.

Atop Ka'vairn, Daijen forced his memories to push on, moving through the numerous flights that ended in injury or resentment. Nearing on a month since Slait had abandoned Kastiek's command and most astute advice, Daijen again graced the tops of The Hellion Mountains.

The site had been forsaken by the Aegres, their eyries left to nature. There remained naught but picked bones and three enormous Aegre corpses, all frozen and untouched by their kin.

There had been no sign of Ilithranda nor any sign of her death—his only comfort at the time.

Daijen could still feel the cold of the snow as he dug his way through to Kastiek's body. He had heaved the Vahlken free—head and all—and dragged him away. It felt wrong to part him from Strix, even in death, but he was determined to return to Ka'vairn with a body to burn. Daijen had even contemplated retrieving the bones of his brothers and sisters, but failed to find any way to transport them all astride an Aegre. He might have taken Strix's saddle were the creature not dead on its side.

With his reclaimed atori blade and Kastiek, he had flown back to Ka'vairn—a precarious flight that had nearly cost him his own life several times. He thanked the gods upon sighting Ilithranda in the courtyard. He later learned of her ordeal and the near two weeks it had taken to climb down and find her way home. She had already informed The Valtorak of dark events. Together, they built a pyre for Kastiek and torched his body on behalf of the others too.

The funeral had been a grim affair. The Valtorak had acknowledged the blow to their order, fearing a gap between generations of Vahlken. He had also spoken highly, if not tenderly, of Kastiek. From that day forth, they shared a need for vengeance. Slait and his exile would need dealing with, another foe to add to their list.

How bitterly cold and empty the fortress had been since. The Valtorak had taken over their direct training. He continued to test Ilithranda as vigorously as he did Daijen, though he spared more time for Daijen, who required a dedicated regime to see his bond with the Aegre solidified.

For ten years, they had held on to the pain of their loss. For ten years, they had been gripped by fear for the future. For ten years, those two facts had kept Daijen from flying any further than the reach of the valley.

He had a sense that was about to change.

"You have delayed long enough," came The Valtorak's voice. "It is time, Daijen Saeth."

"I would wait for your return," he replied.

"*My* return?" The Valtorak queried sceptically. "Or *hers?*"

Daijen looked back, his eyes guided by the master to the courtyard. There he saw Ilithranda preparing to depart just as she had done a decade earlier.

"It's too soon," Daijen remarked, his words having grown bolder over the last few years.

"We have waited long enough," The Valtorak said simply.

"They will remember," Daijen stated firmly.

"You think ten years with an Aegre makes you an expert?" the master countered. "You remain in your infancy, *Initiate*."

Daijen returned his gaze to The Dain'duil. It was a barbed response and quite deliberate. It had been years since The Valtorak had given him permission to fly north and have the dwarves craft him his slaiken blade—the final step in his elevation to Vahlken. Again and again, Daijen had rejected the notion, always making excuses where his training was lacking; that he needed more time.

Lies, of course.

He had stayed for her. For Ilithranda. They had given the Aegres time to move on from the bloody event, but they were descendants of those mutated by Handuin's magic, their memories quite impeccable. They would recall their intrusion ten years earlier and likely attack on sight, regardless of any kinship.

"The Hellion Mountains is home to more than one eyrie," The Valtorak went on. "Those you encountered will never return to the site, but others certainly will. Nests already made. A vantage that puts them above all others. It would be too much to pass up for any Aegres searching for a new home."

"I'll wait all the same," Daijen told him.

The master of Ka'vairn clasped his hands behind his back and paced the ramparts. "I see now that I have been too easy on you since losing your brothers and sisters. You forget simple protocol, such as addressing me with the vernacular of an *initiate*. As you *insist* on remaining as such, you will adhere to those protocols or suffer the consequences."

"Yes, Master," Daijen uttered flatly.

The Valtorak came to stand just behind and to the side of his perch. "This is her time, just as it is yours. Ilithranda will make the climb and me with her. I have no doubt she will make the bond and we will fly home in a matter of days."

"If she doesn't—" Daijen started gravely.

"If she doesn't," the master interjected, "then she will die. Your remaining here will not change that. Go to the doors. Knock thrice. Bargain for your sword." At that, The Valtorak tossed a purse on the stone between them. "The very moment it is in your grasp, you will thenceforth—until your dying breath—be a *Vahlken*." He stepped closer. "You are so close, Daijen," he hissed. "Let Ilithranda walk her path. She does not need you shadowing her. Nor will she thank you for it."

That was a truth Daijen couldn't deny. More than once, Ilithranda had suspected his stunted progression was because of her and she had given him a verbal thrashing for it. There had also been a rather heated sparring session that had nearly ended in his decapitation. Of course, there had even been times when she had resented him for bonding with an Aegre so early, if not for doing so in the midst of tragedy. He could empathise with that. There was also nothing he could do about it.

"Will you tell her the truth?" he asked.

"About the Skaramangians?" The Valtorak queried. "Do I need to? How long ago did *you* tell her?"

Daijen's head whipped around to find his master looking at him knowingly.

"You would deny it?" The Valtorak pressed.

Daijen considered doing just that, if only for a heartbeat. "No," he said, shaking his head. "How did you know?"

The master of Ka'vairn half turned to regard Ilithranda in the distance. "When she arrived here, she was a product of the war, and so marked by years of fighting the humans. Her desire to exact vengeance upon Erador for all her dead brothers and sisters seemed an unquenchable fire. Only through fury did she believe freedom and power might be attained. Freedom to stand apart from house Lhoris. Power to wreak destruction upon the humans."

The Valtorak took a breath, considering his words. "At first, I thought her contempt for Erador had cooled—a result of her years away from the war. But then I realised the truth was far simpler and staring me in the face."

Daijen felt incredibly small under the scrutiny of those ancient violet eyes. He swallowed. "Forgive me, Master. I broke my oath."

"You have grown close, the two of you. Close enough that you would consider your bond before my command."

Daijen wished to argue that point, but he knew it to be the truth in his heart.

"I will not punish you for this," The Valtorak declared, surprising the initiate. "Knowledge of your own naivety will be punishment enough."

"Naivety?" Daijen questioned, his brow furrowed in offence.

"Ka'vairn's traditions are in place for a reason," the master told him. "Initiates are to prove themselves before enlightenment. Knowledge must be earned. Just like power and freedom."

"I had to tell her because—"

"You love her," The Valtorak interjected. "Because you hoped it would bring you closer. I can see that it worked and your trust in Ilithranda would seem well placed, but I told you to trust no-one and suspect everyone. I fear that your feelings for others will see you misplace your trust and forego your suspicions. So yes —naivety."

Daijen had much to say in his defence and was on the verge of voicing them all when reason had its moment. He could not—should not—argue with The Valtorak. Who was he to challenge the wisdom of centuries?

"You are a weapon," The Valtorak continued, his words adopting a sense of urgency now. "Do not withhold your skills from the war any longer. The Skaramangians gain ground every day. It's time to become the warrior you were never intended to be."

That tripped up Daijen's thoughts, reminding him of the life he had left behind. How had an average messenger guard risen up to the rank of Vahlken? It seemed the most unlikely of events, for surely someone of his previous skill should have perished in

Harendun, long ago. Yet here he was, garbed and armed as a Vahlken.

More so, he was privy to Verda's darkest secret, to its war of good and evil. Responsibility had been thrust upon him and he had looked the other way so he might protect the only person he really loved. He had stopped moving forwards for ten years now. He could not fight sense any longer.

"Say your farewells."

Without another word to his master, the initiate made his way down to the courtyard. Ilithranda was ready, her pack filled with supplies and skins of water. She knew what to expect from the climb this time.

"When next you see me," she said on his approach, "you will be looking up."

It brought a smile to Daijen's face. "I have no doubt," he lied. "I imagine you will return upon the largest Aegre the world has ever seen."

He paused, enjoying her return smile. How different she was now. It had taken decades, a few near-death experiences, and more than a few quiet moments to break down the wall that had stood between them. Whatever their backgrounds, whatever their blood, they were the same now.

"I'm going... I'm going to see the dwarves," he managed.

He hated to see that smile fade but fade it did. "Finally," she replied.

"I'm... I'm sorry we aren't going together," he added. "And up there," he said, glancing at the mountains that towered over the fortress. "I would have liked to have been there when you bond."

"And I would have liked to see the moment a messenger guard became a Vahlken," Ilithranda responded wittily, drawing a soundless laugh from Daijen. "Though," she continued with heart in her tone, "I've witnessed that moment many times over."

Daijen found a smile, if an awkward one. "I know we're made brothers and sisters in these walls," he began tentatively, all too aware that The Valtorak was still on the ramparts above. "I know that any... feelings that stir in us must be from the warrior's perspective; that we are brothers and sisters in *war*. But that's—"

"You've read too many books in that library," Ilithranda cut in dryly.

Daijen held out his hands to delay further interruption. "I know how this sounds. I've heard it inside my own head enough times. I just need to say it before we..."

"Go our separate ways for the first time in decades?"

Daijen nodded, though he was unable to speak before she did.

"You love me as a battle sister, a fellow warrior who might die beside you in combat, but you also love me more than this place would encourage. You love me like blood. Like family."

Daijen didn't know what to say. He had nothing else to say—Ilithranda had put it perfectly, taking the emotions right out of his mind. It then dawned on him how she had been able to so perfectly voice his feelings.

Ilithranda reached out and embraced him, pulling him into a hug that would have winded the average Andaren. "Go and get your slaiken blade," she whispered in his ear. "And keep one eye on the sky," she added playfully.

From his previous position atop the walls, Daijen watched The Valtorak and Ilithranda as they made the trek along the narrow path, down to the forest floor. Though saddened to see her depart, her words would nourish his soul for the journey ahead.

His own departure would ease the parting in their path—flying eased everything.

With all the strength in his legs, Daijen leapt from the ramparts with the confidence of a bird. He easily cleared the fortress wall and dived towards The Dain'duil at speed, a grin on his pale face. He grinned so eagerly for it was not Death waiting to greet him but another.

And she was coming in *fast*.

46
GETTING AHEAD OF THINGS

THINGS WERE FAR WORSE THAN GRARFATH COULD EVER HAVE EXPECTED.

From a snowy ridge, nestled between tall pine trees, the smith and his two companions looked out on the land that stretched west, where the extending hand of Andara met that of Erador's—where The Watchtower of Argunsuun met White Tower.

The latter was a speck on the horizon, seen only in the light of the flaming projectiles sailing through the night to deliver fiery death upon the men stationed therein. With Argunsuun at their backs, the Andaren forces had advanced with their machines of war. They unleashed them all. Amidst the ballistas and catapults, rank upon rank of archers clouded the dark skies with arrows.

The men of Erador resisted, fighting back with catapults of their own and trading ballista bolts that tore through the Andaren battalions. It wasn't, however, enough to stop the Andarens from marching over the land and closing the gap.

"How many Eradorans guard the way?" Kitrana asked, her eyes wide as she absorbed the battle.

"A few thousand maybe," Yamnomora answered, equally absorbed. "Not enough," she added gravely.

Grarfath imagined the Andarens crashing over the humans like a rockfall and razing White Tower to the ground all before the new day. The battle would be bloody but brief, a brutal spark of violence to light up the night. In the aftermath, a mountain of corpses would usher in the dawn.

The smith's eyes were drawn high again when another catapult fired its flaming missile in the distance. He watched its flight and inevitable descent before it impacted the side of White Tower, exploding in a ball of fire and debris.

By comparison, The Watchtower of Argunsuun stood a silent guardian, a colossal god of black stone, thick struts, and scattered balconies that bristled with idle ballistas. It was apparent that its occupants had emptied out of the tower and joined their fellow warriors on the invasion march.

Whether it was abandoned or not, Grarfath remained unsettled so close to its base. He looked to his right, where the south dropped off into a black ocean. Yamnomora had informed him it was called The Deep, a vast body of water that sat inside the curling arm of Erador by the look of the map the dwarf carried with her.

"Why don' we hug the coast," he suggested. "Avoid all o'... *that.*"

The smith didn't fancy trekking in the wake of the Andarens and the scar of blood and corpses they would leave behind. Then there were the potential survivors they might have to deal with. He glanced back at Bludgeon, eyeing the two axes strapped to his saddle. He knew *exactly* how Yamnomora would deal with survivors.

Lying on her belly like the others, the dwarven warrior flashed him an impressed expression. "That actually ain' a bad idea, hammer boy."

"*Hammer boy*?" Grarfath was quick to fire back.

"We should move while we still have the cover of night," Kitrana voiced, ignoring his comment altogether.

Yamnomora nodded once. "Agreed."

Kit turned to see the dwarf. "You agree with *me*?"

"I'm not to be makin' a habit o' it," Yamnomora assured. "We can follow the coast all the way around The Deep. We've only to reach The Sterling River an' that'll take us to The Spine o' Erador," she continued with an easy tone, as if she wasn't detailing weeks of travel.

"What's The Spine o' Erador?" Grarfath had to ask.

Kitrana offered an answer while Yamnomora sighed and rolled her eyes. "A long stretch of mountains that connect Erador's north to its south."

"The Misted Road cuts a path from west to east," Yamnomora informed. "We can take it straight to Valgala, the capital."

"Is that where this Green Leaf fella is?"

"The wizard?" Kitrana enquired.

Yamnomora looked from dwarf to Nimean as she answered their questions. "I don' know if he's there, an' *ye* need to keep yer ears out o' me business. We're goin' to Valgala because I can get a message to 'im from there." The warrior turned her head left and right again. "Any more questions or can we be off? There's only an *invasion* goin' on over there," she added sarcastically.

The smith picked himself up, grumbling all the while about his new name. Besides the cumbersome pack on his back, he was always sure to be holding The Anther. He had become accustomed to its size and weight now and easily handled it so his grip was just short of the sloping head. So occupied by the sight of it, the dwarf failed to realise that those in front of him had stopped.

Jostled, Yamnomora shot him a scowl over one shoulder. Before he could ask why they had stopped in the midst of the trees, where only the top of Argunsuun could be seen, the warrior placed a finger to her lips.

Grarfath held on to his question and immediately began to search his surroundings for threats. What had they heard? While distracted by the magnificent weapon, the smith had only been aware of the crunching snow beneath their collective boots.

Yamnomora let go of Bludgeon's reins and slowly slid one of

her axes from its loop on the saddle. How she had heard anything over the sounds of the Warhog's breathing he didn't know. Grarfath turned to see if Kitrana had detected any such threat, only to realise she had vanished. Startled by her sudden disappearance, the smith pivoted on his heel and searched frantically for the Nimean.

"Where'd she go?"

"Shh!" Yamnomora hissed, her feet slowly crunching through the snow.

Grarfath trailed her, walking backwards for a time while he tried to glimpse the Nimean. She was simply gone, as if the night had swallowed her whole. There was no time, however, to consider what might have given her cause to abandon them.

The Andarens attacked as one, springing from concealment either side of the pine trees. They made no war cry nor even so much as a grunt as they brought their spears to bear. Protected behind plates of bronze armour and trailed by obsidian cloaks, they cut menacing figures as they closed their trap, weapons poised to plunge into the dwarves.

Yamnomora roared in defiance and darted forward, ducking beneath a jabbing spear before swinging her axe. The curved blade chopped through her enemy's knee, severing everything below it from the rest of the body. While he fell into the snow, bleeding heavily and wailing in pain, the dwarven warrior ploughed ahead and swung her axe in the opposite direction, bringing the rounded pommel of her weapon up into the ribs of another. The Andaren grunted in pain and staggered back, positioning him perfectly for the two-handed execution of an over-head blow.

Blood splattered across the snow and up Yamnomora's grinning face. Stunned by her brutality, Grarfath could only watch the violence unfold. It was quickly escalated when Bludgeon charged in behind his master, tusks first. Through the slits in his visor, the third Andaren looked bewildered to see the animal and panicked. He made it three steps before Bludgeon mowed him down and drove his tusks deep into flesh.

A fourth made himself known, leaping over the savage

Warhog and with his spear held high in a throwing position. Grarfath began to move backwards, his instincts informing him without delay that he couldn't overcome a flying spear. Concerned as he was, the smith missed the rock protruding from the snow and he lost his footing. While his large pack cushioned the fall, it could do nothing to prevent the spear that had now been released.

It whistled through the air, thrown with speed and precision by a warrior who had potentially been perfecting his spear throw for centuries. Yamnomora could but watch the projectile, her jaw stretched wide as she cried out.

The spear stopped dead mere inches from Grarfath's chest.

The smith blinked, his mind racing to make sense of the blur that had emerged from behind the nearest tree.

Kitrana Voden, the spear gripped firmly in one hand, pivoted on her heel, twisting the weapon round as she did so. Like one of the ballistas they had witnessed behind the ridge, the Nimean launched the spear in a swift finale to her fluid dance.

The Andaren's armour was no match for the spear at such close range and thrown by a being whose body had the strength to navigate the seas. Impaled, the soldier hit the ground and skidded through the snow towards the base of the tree at his back.

"We're being surrounded," Kit informed them sharply, her toes springing one of the fallen spears into her waiting hand.

"Get up!" Yamnomora yelled at Grarfath. "It's time to start swingin' that hammer!"

"I'm a *smith*!" he protested. "I don' know how to do... all o' *this*!"

"I don' think they give a damn!" Yamnomora snapped back.

He could hear them now, rushing boots pounding through the snow. Why the Andarens had left any force behind was beyond the smith's understanding and they weren't likely to explain before skewering him.

Yamnomora stepped over the Andaren who had either passed out or died from his severed leg. Reaching her Warhog, the warrior removed the other axe from its holster so she might wield both at once. With one resting over a shoulder and the other lowered to the ground, the dwarf waited with heaving breath.

Kitrana was unnervingly still, the spear braced in one hand so the haft lay horizontally across both of her shoulders. Her bare feet were planted into the snow, her knees bent just enough that she might spring with a moment's notice.

Grarfath simply stood there, utterly bewildered to find himself being surrounded by Andaren soldiers on the border of Erador.

He had been holding hammers since he was old enough to grasp anything, but never had he used one in a fight. He could bend iron and even manipulate silvyr with a hammer in hand but the smith knew that wielding one as a weapon was a death sentence for his opponent and, therefore, a sure way of getting himself locked up in the High King's dungeons.

But he wasn't inside those walls anymore, as Yamnomora had pointed out. There were no laws; none but the law of *survival* at least. And damned if he wasn't going to see home again. Holding The Anther in both hands, the dwarf steeled himself.

"I'm the Hammerhold," he whispered to himself, wishing he believed it.

From between the pines, the Andarens were birthed by the shadows on all sides. This secondary, and larger, group of soldiers attacked with swords and spears in a display of acrobatics that no dwarf could hope to achieve. Some skidded into the clearing, while others leapt and spun in the air. It was a tactic that had no doubt been devised to disorientate their enemy, offering too many angles of attack.

It was little use against the eclectic group.

Bludgeon was the first to score a kill, goring one of the soldiers who had foolishly skidded on his knees hoping to strike a low blow. The animal's steel-tipped tusks bored through flesh and bone before the Andaren's body was thrashed violently from side to side.

Yamnomora was a storm of axes. The dwarven warrior swung her weapons out wildly and spun continuously on her heels. The axes went high and low, hacking and slicing through two soldiers that failed to anticipate such manic aggression.

Matching the Andaren's agility, while outmatching their flexibility, Kitrana evaded, deflected, and counter-attacked with mesmerising fluidity. The spear moved like an extension of her body, lashing out in devastating arcs before turning into deadly thrusts that dropped one enemy after another.

Still, they weren't enough to keep Grarfath from harm. Two soldiers, encased in their armour of bronze, came at him with a scimitar each. The dwarf rushed forwards as the first blade raced down to meet his head. The steel edge missed the smith but cut through his pack, spilling pots and pans onto the ground.

The second, and slower of the two Andarens, had enough time to adjust his intended attack and take into account Grarfath's proximity. There was little the dwarf could do to stop the boot from slamming into his face, and damned if it didn't hurt.

With a mouthful of snow, Grarfath didn't have time to consider any injuries he might have gained hitting the ground—he had to move. Rolling to one side, his pack was again struck by a scimitar that had been intended for his heart. It was more on instinct that he backhanded The Anther and landed a blow across his opponent's head.

The Andaren's helm was immediately distorted, the steel edges cutting into his cheek and eye. That aside, the force of the smith's blow sent the soldier reeling away until he tripped over his own feet.

Grarfath made it as far as his knees before the second Andaren fell upon him. Again, it was more the need to survive that drove the dwarf's actions and saw him raise the hammer horizontally to block the incoming scimitar. It didn't so much as scratch the haft.

It was with a face knotted in exertion that the soldier tried to press down with his sword. Grarfath's arms, however, were those of a dwarven smith and refused to budge even an inch. Grarfath let out a hearty chuckle, relieved and amused at the same time. Trained to fight, the Andaren simply changed his tactics and launched a foot into the dwarf's chest, knocking him back to the ground.

He might have succumbed to a mortal blow then, had he been on his own in the wilds of the world. As it was, he travelled with a Warhog. Bludgeon appeared from nowhere and at a dead run. The soldier was taken bodily from the ground and flipped wildly into the air. Before he could recover, the Warhog turned about and bit his foot, shattering the ankle. The Andaren cried out in agony, though his pain was short-lived when a two-handed axe *thudded* through his head and into the ground beneath.

"Get up!" Yamnomora growled at him.

The smith did just that, and in time to see the Nimean throw her spear into a charging soldier before simply flicking another up to her hand. Movement in the corner of his eye turned the dwarf away from Kitrana. An Andaren, his scimitar poised to thrust from shoulder height, lunged at the smith. Grarfath moved to avoid the curved tip of the scimitar but failed to dodge it altogether, his shoulder feeling its bite.

It was pain then that brought The Anther to bear.

The first swing took out the soldier's legs, sweeping them up to his waist before his shoulder crashed into the ground. The second swing was decidedly more definitive. Death was instantaneous, the Andaren's head crushed inside his helm.

The dwarf was struck by the cold fact that he had just killed someone, but it could do little more than simply register with him, his adrenaline raging through his blood. Having stepped over that line—a line that could no longer be seen by the likes of Yamnomora or Kitrana—Grarfath was able to swing The Anther with a new kind of confidence.

Indeed, the next Andaren to rush him felt the power that had long been held back by the smith. Hammering his cuirass, metal on metal, the soldier flew in the opposite direction as a wave of distorted air expanded outwards from the impact. With it there came flashes of fire and smoke and even the faint sound of men yelling.

Giving in to his fury, Grarfath swung again, striking another soldier emerging from the trees. Again, the distorted wave washed over them all with a collection of foreign sights and sounds. Twice more, the smith swung with abandon, each blow delivering death while steadily influencing The Anther's magical properties.

Grarfath didn't care. He wanted to survive. He wanted to see home again. He wanted to be done with all the people trying to kill him.

His next and final hammer stroke came from overhead, his enemy lying at his feet with a broken leg. The Anther thundered down and claimed another life. It also claimed all the land and people around it.

What had appeared as no more than a mirage became their solid reality, placing the companions and a pair of startled Andarens in the middle of merciless battle. Amidst smoke and small fires, their ears assaulted by clashing steel and cries of the dying, Grarfath looked out from the very top of White Tower.

They had ported right onto the nose of the invading army.

A quartet of archers—humans all—were altogether rattled by their sudden appearance. The Andarens who had been ported with them were quicker to recover and turned their blades on the men of Erador. One of the pale skinned soldiers was brought down by an arrow and sent tumbling over the tower's battlements. The other succeeded in reaching the men and even killing two of them before a sword found the gap under his arm and above his cuirass.

Given the state of battle they were in, the surviving archers made no distinction between the travelling companions, their Warhog, and the Andarens. They were all enemies of Erador now. With impressive strength of her own, Yamnomora threw her axes one after the other, slaying both men before they could nock their next arrow.

"Gods be damned!" she cursed at the top of her lungs. "Even the swamps would 'ave been better than 'ere!"

"This is White Tower," Kitrana remarked absently, her gaze taken by the sea of death that was almost upon them.

"I don' know how to use this thing!" Grarfath argued, feeling his previous meal rising into his throat. It took everything he had not to lie down right there and then and pass out.

"Ye could 'ave thought o' anywhere between 'ere an' Tor Valan!" Yamnomora complained, throwing her arms up. The dwarf flinched when a stray arrow bounced off her left pauldron, forcing her away from the edge.

"I've no idea what I'm doin'!" the smith protested, tossing the hammer across the white stone floor. Besides the onslaught of nausea and fatigue, the wound he had received to his shoulder was making itself known. The bite of the Andaren's scimitar would scar, he was sure.

"We're ahead of them," Kit voiced from the tower's edge.

"What?" Yamnomora spat.

"We're *ahead* of them!" the Nimean repeated, shouting over the din below. "We're ahead of the Andarens! We need to get out of here while they're still fighting!"

Yamnomora's eyes went high, her face contorted with dreaded revelation. "Get down!"

Grarfath glimpsed the blinding fiery ball only a second before it pounded the side of the tower. The impact knocked them all from their feet and dragged a rumbling roar from Bludgeon.

"Gettin' out o' 'ere is easier said than done," Yamnomora groaned on her way back up.

"The Andarens will need to camp here when the battle is done," Kitrana countered, picking up the spear as she rose. "We either get out now or face their entire army come the dawn!"

Yamnomora let loose a frustrated animalistic cry. "Fine! Ye!" She was pointing at the smith. "Pick up The Anther! Ye!" Her axe cut through the air to point at Kitrana. "Watch our backs on the way down!" An' ye!" she declared finally, her attention having found Bludgeon. "*Hunt!*"

One behind the other, led by an enormous Warhog, they descended the stairs that cut into the floor and spiralled down through the tower's interior. Bludgeon was considerably faster, his hooves rapidly pounding the stone steps. The first floor they reached was empty save for a single table and stacks of crates and sundries. Judging by the sounds that came up from the next floor, where Bludgeon had already reached, there were men occupying it.

Yamnomora followed her mount, reaching the floor before Grarfath. She barrelled into the nearest man, her bulk enough to bring him down to his knees where she then delivered a headbutt that took the soldier out of the fight. The Warhog was on the other side of the room, a man's head lost inside the animal's mouth.

"Bludgeon!" the dwarf called. "Drop!" The animal did as commanded, releasing the mangled and unrecognisable head. "On with ye!" she yelled.

Grarfath dragged his gaze from the horrific corpse and fell into line, crossing the room so he might descend to the next floor. He never made it to the stairs. There had been another human, his courage renewed, perhaps, in the Warhog's absence. Grarfath only became aware of the man after being shoved hard into the wall and struck by the pommel of a sword.

The blow wasn't nearly strong enough to break the skull of a dwarf, but it was enough to daze the smith. It made his counterattack all too sluggish, allowing the human to grab the haft of the hammer mid-swing. He yanked it once, failing to snatch it from Grarfath's grasp. An armoured vambrace to the face pushed the dwarf back into the wall and slackened his grip on The Anther. Through the pain erupting across his cheek and nose, he felt the cool metal slip from his fingers as it was claimed by the man.

Lacking a warrior's instinct, Grarfath could think only to raise an arm to shield himself against the inevitable attack. When it came though, it was the human who suffered the blow. From between his fingers, the smith witnessed Yamnomora's axe sink deep into the side of the man's head, robbing him of life in an instant. She yanked her axe free and the human crumpled in death, The Anther clattering on the floor beside him.

Yamnomora's eyes held the blazing fury of the sun itself. "Ye die holdin' this," she fumed, her bloody axe pointing down at the hammer. "Ye will not lose it again," she stated threateningly.

The dwarven warrior was gone before Grarfath could respond. He should never have been entrusted with it in the first place.

Given his current location and dilemma, it was a moot point. Instead, he glanced sheepishly at Kitrana and retrieved The Anther before descending to the next floor.

They were soon, however, trying to find their way through choking smoke that rose up through the stairwell. Down again, they came across the jagged hole that wounded White Tower's ancient masonry.

Unable to speak, Yamnomora grabbed Grarfath by the shoulder and dragged him along, her axe outstretched to find the wall. When the metal began to scrape across stone, she guided them to the next set of steps, where they were able to breathe at least.

After continuing for five more floors, they were again confronted with another of the Andarens' projectiles. Older than the previous one, much of the smoke had found its way out through the hole in the wall and there was precious little in the room to burn.

"Keep going," Kit yelled from the rear.

Grarfath navigated the debris, always sure to keep Yamnomora's red hair in sight. They passed by another floor, avoiding the open balcony from which archers attempted to keep the enemy at bay.

"Oi! Who are you?"

Grarfath turned around to see one of the archers entering the chamber, his quiver emptied. Kitrana didn't hesitate. The spear whipped up and round, taking the archer across the jaw and into the wall. A swift kick put the man on his back, where he showed no interest in getting back up.

"Run!" the Nimean shouted.

The trio made it to the next floor where an arrow chased after them, striking the wall beside Kitrana's head. Without stopping to face their challengers, the companions pressed on with all haste, rushing to the next set of steps before hurling themselves down two or three at a time. Grarfath hadn't been counting, but he guessed there to have been at least twenty floors by the time they reached the tower's base.

The heavy doors were already open, revealing a night of smoke and flames beyond. Men were shouting and running left and right, their swords drawn and red cloaks billowing in the frigid air. The clash of steel was a constant companion to the cries of death and colliding shields.

Yamnomora crashed into the edge of the doorframe and stuck her head out, surveying the chaos. "We need to go east," she hissed, as the others lined up beside her.

Grarfath ventured closer to the open doorway and peered out, spying the collection of small buildings dotted about the landscape. Every door was ajar, the dwellings emptied of soldiers. They had all charged into the west to meet their inevitable end.

"The Blooded Road should be on the other side," Yamnomora said, nodding her chin at the buildings.

"There!" The brash call turned the group back to the stairs, where two of the archers now stood nocking arrows.

"Run!" Yamnomora bellowed, hurrying into the night.

Two arrows whistled after them, one finding its end in Bludgeon's thick saddle. The turmoil made them invisible to those running about and organising the defences. Grarfath shoulder barged one man, clearing him from his feet, but never stopped to see if the man realised he had been struck by a dwarf.

They raced between the buildings, never daring to look back. With all looking to the west, however, there were none to prevent them disappearing into the east, where the black of night concealed them.

Once they were embraced by that darkness, Grarfath alone stopped, pausing to lay eyes on the carnage they had so narrowly escaped. White Tower, illuminated by fires at its base, had been battered by another flaming projectile, its pale walls partially hidden in black smoke. The stone fell like a waterfall, a precursor to what felt like an inevitable and total collapse of the entire structure.

It seemed the men who had occupied it would share a similar fate to those on the battlefield. Between the buildings, the smith could see the human ranks bursting apart, their numbers unable to keep back the enemy.

It was with a greeting of death that the Andarens had made themselves known.

"Grarfath," Kitrana called, breaking his daze. "We cannot linger here."

Here, he thought.

Here was a foreign land.

Here was *Erador*.

47
THE FINAL STEP

45 Years Ago...

Verda had never known such a magnificent creature. She swept by the cliff, her timing impeccable as ever. Daijen reached out with his own uncanny sense of timing and caught the handle at the head of his saddle, his direction changed in an instant. Handuin's magic allowed him to not only keep his arm in its socket, but also bring his whole body down into the saddle, where his feet slipped into the pockets folded into the hard leather.

That same magic flowed through the Aegre, as it had her ancestors. It made her powerful, placing her at the top of any food chain in Andara. Only the dragons could challenge her might.

Though what dragon could muster the courage to challenge *her*?

Valyra!

Her name was like a song in his heart. She was the companion he had long yearned for, though only ever comprehended as an absence in his life. As such, their coming together was always a joyous moment. Even after ten years, the feeling had never dulled.

Gliding low over the tree tops, Daijen marvelled at her crown of horns, each twisted into a loose spiral that flowed back over her head. They weren't as golden as her beak or as brown as the majority of her feathers, but somewhere in between. They stood out though against her head and neck, those feathers as white as Daijen's hair.

Valyra tilted slightly to the left, angling them steadily back towards Ka'vairn. Ten years weren't enough to stop the initiate from gazing in awe at the Aegre's impressive wingspan. He had never seen a dragon but he couldn't imagine they were much bigger. From one wing tip to the other, he could have lined up six mutated war horses end to end and there still might have been some room to spare.

Enjoying the moment, Daijen opened his arms and let his head fall back. The rushing wind swept back his ashen hair and the glorious sun brought out the smallest specks of silver across his nose and cheeks.

For all the enhancements he had enjoyed—the acute senses that attuned him to the world—nothing had come close to making him feel so alive as he did when astride Valyra. With the Aegre, he was free in a way no Andaren could fathom. She made him feel powerful too, her presence providing the kind of fortitude a paragon might experience with an army at his back.

For ten years they had practised routine after routine, running through flight drills alongside The Valtorak. He knew the subtleties of her movements, the fine twitches of her muscles. Aware that she was about to flap her wings and take them up towards Ka'vairn, Daijen shifted his weight to the right, away from the fortress.

"Not today," he said, a hint of excitement in his voice.

According to his movement, Valyra tilted to the right, her flight corrected to take them north, along the winding waters of The Nheremyn.

"We've been in the valley too long," he called out to her. "It's time we made this world our own."

Valyra squawked and Daijen patted the base of her thick neck, laughing as he did so.

"We're going to see the dwarves!" he exclaimed, pulling pack on the handles.

The Aegre naturally aimed her head up, sighting the tops of The Morthil Mountains and the clouds that drifted there. They would fly over the snow-capped points and follow them until The Ice Plains of Isendorn dominated the eastern view.

While the pair had taken excursions in the past, trips that had consumed weeks, those flights had consisted solely of navigating north and south of the valley. It would take only a few days, however, to leave the valley behind and dip down on the eastern side of The Morthil Mountains.

In that time, their camps were brief affairs, both eager to be on with their journey. While Valyra couldn't communicate a word to Daijen, she could listen. It had become an old observation, in fact, that the Aegre enjoyed listening to him. How much she understood could be debated by scholars for eons, but Daijen would have bet his atori blade and cloak of victory that she understood him better than most.

They had developed their own language that was made up from gestures, hand signals or—in Valyra's case—head tilts, scraping her talons, and variations in squawks. They didn't always see eye to eye, however, be it a breakdown in communication or opposing desires.

In those instances, a display of courage was required for, like the first time they had met, Daijen had to stand up to Valyra and prove his mettle. It always came to steel in his hand and an unwavering sense of defiance in the face of her threatening wing flaps.

Fortunately, their journey beyond the valley was a harmonious one. Valyra sensed that they weren't simply flying up and down, confined by the mountains, but were pushing their limits.

And so she glided gracefully over the top of The Morthil Mountains, briefly pierced the clouds and submerged into the realm below. The Ice Plains of Isendorn stretched out as far east as east could go, a flatland of nothingness.

Daijen clenched every muscle in his body, a signal to dive.

Valyra obliged obediently and tucked her feathered wings in. Like a yellow-tipped spear she plunged towards the ground. Daijen would have laughed were he able to breathe.

The Aegre required no instruction to level out before impact. Daijen moved with her body, his muscles doing just as much work as hers. Using his weight, the initiate turned them around, bringing their flight path in line with the mountains again.

Valyra squawked, a short sharp protest.

"Don't worry," he reassured. "We're not going back. We're going *there*."

The morning sun struck The Bronze Doors of Orgunthain, providing a glistening spot to aim for at the base of the dull mountains. When, at last, they passed over the approaching portal, Valyra reared up, flapped her wings, and set her talons to the hard ground.

As she finished the rest of the journey on land, Daijen remained in his saddle, eyes cast high to the intimidating doors of the dwarf lords. A hundred foot high and twice as wide, the bronze doors were a testament to dwarven ingenuity. By look alone they were impregnable, and Daijen guessed they were thick enough to be just so.

Each hulking slab of bronze bore imagery of the dwarves at war. They wielded hammers and axes, swords and spears, their faces filled with rage and battle lust. These were not doors built to welcome.

Dismounting, Daijen made for the doors, one hand running along Valyra's shoulder before her body rose higher than he could reach. She let loose a double squawk and dragged her front left talon through the earth.

"I wouldn't worry," he replied, patting the purse on his belt. "We have the only thing dwarves are interested in."

Valyra's subsequent squawk suggested she was not convinced.

Coming to stand before the doors, the initiate was made to feel so small as to be insignificant in the face of the dwarven kingdom. Perhaps that was the point, he mused.

"Knock thrice," he muttered, his eyes roaming over the wall of bronze.

He rapped his knuckles once against the door, immediately dissatisfied with the dull *thud* it made. Still, he knocked twice more, just to be sure. Nothing. There came no movement from the dwarves, the doors as still as the mountain that surrounded them. He glanced back at Valyra, feeling somewhat the fool. The Aegre tilted her head inquisitively.

Three more times he knocked, eliciting the same inconsequential sound. With a sigh, Daijen drew his sabre, the replacement blade gifted to him by The Valtorak after returning for the first time with Valyra. Using the pommel, he knocked again, three times as instructed. Metal on metal, and hammered by a Vahlken fist, the sound and reverberation travelled well across the doors.

It seemed an eruption of thunder followed in the wake of the last knock. The ground shuddered and unseen machinery rumbled behind the mountain stone. At once, the doors began to slowly open, forcing Daijen into a retreat. Valyra reacted as she would, her wings unfurled and weight lifted to sit threateningly on her back legs.

"Easy," the initiate bade, one hand raised towards her.

The doors came to a stop after parting just enough to allow a single person to pass through. Between the bronze slabs there stood a pillar of darkness that kept the dwarven realm a mystery.

Deciding that it would be best not to greet the dwarves with a weapon in hand, Daijen sheathed his sabre and waited patiently. He wasn't waiting long. A lone dwarf emerged from the darkness and marched towards him, bold as brass. In one hand, he dragged a mace on the end of a barbed chain. In the other, he wielded a two-headed axe. There was nothing to see of the dwarf, his entire body, face and all, encased in armour.

"*Well met,*" Daijen began, using his limited knowledge of their language—there was shockingly little about the dwarves and their culture in any library collated by Andarens.

"Don' even bother," the dwarf spat in Andarneese. "Ye've not the muscles for our words. State yer business, as if I couldn't bloody guess."

Daijen cleared his voice and started again. "I'm to commission a weapon. One befitting the craft of your people."

"One o' yer dragon killers, eh? I've seen many o' yer kin at these doors over the centuries. Ye always ask for silvyr. I hope ye've come with the coin to afford such a treasure."

"Of course," Daijen replied, hooking his thumbs into his belt, where the coin purse rested.

"Looks to be a very meagre purse," the dwarf observed sourly.

"It's not the size of the purse, but the quality of the coin inside," Daijen countered.

"Very good. Ye may enter the kingdom o' Morthil." The dwarf paused in turning back to the doors so he might point his beastly axe at Valyra. "An' that thing can stay outside."

Daijen took offence but understood all the same. Turning to the Aegre, he beat his chest once and threw his hand up to the sky—a command to take flight and fall into a circling pattern. Valyra squawked and lowered her head so her beak was level with the distant dwarf.

The initiate walked back to her and placed a hand over the top of her beak while the other rubbed the side of her face. "It'll be alright. Look for my return."

With some force, he pushed one hand up under her beak, encouraging the Aegre to lift her head and fly off. Only when her talons had left the ground did he follow the dwarf inside.

The Bronze Doors of Orgunthain closed behind him with a resounding *boom*. He could see the levers, mighty cogs, and colossal chains that operated the heavy doors—each twenty feet thick. Daijen couldn't help but marvel at the engineering, wondering all the while how the war might have differed if every Andaren town, city, and fort were behind such doors.

Upon tearing his gaze away from the doors, the initiate was nearly rocked back on his heels at the sight. The dwarven realm was a splendour, a feast for the eyes that demanded his attention be in all places at once.

Gargantuan stalactites hung from a cavern ceiling so vast it could have fitted all of Taranathen beneath it. The stalactites themselves appeared to have been hollowed out to create chambers, their many windows illuminated by candlelight. A network of bridges connected them all and the hanging towers were connected to the lower realm by several lifts.

Branching out from the main entrance, a bridge wide enough to accommodate an army ran from one end of the cavern to the other. At its heart, more bridges intersected and led Daijen's eyes to massive tunnels that snaked further into the mountains. Zig-zagging stairwells lined most of the walls, though it seemed most of the foot traffic was drawn to the many lifts.

Throughout it all, dwarves were going about their daily lives, creating a cacophony of noise that bombarded Daijen's sensitive ears. The slight pain, however, wasn't enough to keep him from staring in wonderment. He couldn't believe this world existed inside his own. How he wished to explore every inch of their domain!

"Ye'll be waitin' 'ere," the iron dwarf informed him bluntly.

Daijen blinked, utterly distracted by the view. "What?" he asked.

"Ye're to wait 'ere until yer escort arrives. Ye're not permitted to jus' go wanderin'."

"Of course," the initiate agreed, seeing sense in the precaution despite his disappointment. "I suppose you'll be wanting my weapons too," he added, reaching for the buckle on his belt.

The dwarf chuckled inside his visor. "No. Ye can keep 'em, lad."

Daijen let his hands fall away from his belt trying, as he did, not to feel offended at being considered no threat at all.

"Yer escort'll take ye to the smith district. Ye'll 'ave to convince 'em yerself o' course to actually forge ye a sword."

Daijen was nodding along until a name came to him, pulled from distant memory. "I want to see Thronghir Underborn," he announced.

The dwarf looked up at him. "Never heard o' 'im. Tell yer escort." With that, he turned and walked away, his spiked mace dragging over the stone behind him, as if it wasn't making the most awful noise.

Though some patience was required while waiting for his escort, Daijen enjoyed standing on the threshold of the dwarven realm, a silent observer. Every now and then, he was tempted to move on and peer over the edge of his platform and see what business was being conducted in the lower cavern. He refrained, however, sure that he was still under scrutiny by unseen guards.

When, at last, his escort arrived—a young dwarf with a short auburn beard—Daijen gave him Thronghir's name, specifying that he was a renowned smith. It seemed Mordrith's claims had some merit, for the dwarf knew where to take the initiate.

The journey was not what Daijen had expected.

Despite his assurances that he did not need sleep, they stopped every twelve to fifteen hours to rest and—in the dwarf's case—sleep. They repeated this pattern for three days as they delved deeper into the mountains. Daijen inevitably lost any and all sense of direction and time in the skyless realm. Still, it wasn't enough to stop him basking in the glory of their strange world.

They passed statues of dwarves that looked big enough to hold up the sky and climbed stairs that might have even reached the sky. Many of their crossroads were, in fact, bridges held aloft on pillars so thick they could have encased Giants, and every one was illuminated by a roaring hearth in the centre.

There wasn't a single dwarf who didn't stare at him. Indeed, Daijen saw no other foreigners among the native stone bones. He knew they had much business with the outside world, trading with both the humans and the Andarens, but it seemed that business was held outside of Morthil.

"This is the smith ye're lookin' for," the young dwarf declared—the most words he had said consecutively since their initial meeting.

Surprised by the announcement, Daijen required a moment to focus his eyes and thoughts from the sights and sounds and locate the premises in question.

"Conduct yer business," the dwarf commanded. "I shall wait 'ere."

Daijen bowed respectfully and entered the indicated building, unsure of its name due to the dwarven runes on the sign. He understood the imagery, however; a hammer and anvil.

The workshop was cramped, if very well organised. Daijen was able to walk without hitting his head on the ceiling, though only just. On the far side sat the forge, his eyes naturally drawn to the flames and the air disturbed by the heat. For every tool there appeared to be three replacements, though all seemed well used, as if they were regularly rotated.

"By all the profit in Morthil," came a deep and husky voice, "there's an Andaren in me shop."

Daijen turned to locate the voice. Though they had never met before, he knew it to be Thronghir Underborn. His white hair and beard, a tone darker than Daijen's, was a mane about his head, a contrast to his dark skin. A black leather apron protected his shirt and breeches, but it was the cords of the dwarf's forearms that caught the initiate's attention. The muscles there were like coiled ropes that had known naught but the swing of a hammer for centuries.

"I've not seen one o' yer kind in two-hundred years," Thronghir remarked, before limping around one of his work tables.

"My name is Daijen Sacth," he said with a bow of the head.

"Thronghir, son o' Enghir, o' guild Underborn." The dwarf pointed a stubby finger at the Andaren. "I'm knowin' why ye're 'ere."

Daijen cleared his throat. "I have come to commission a slaiken blade," he said anyway.

Thronghir blew out his cheeks. "That's six foot o' silvyr."

The initiate looked around. "Do you not have it?"

The smith chuckled. "Not on me, no. It's easy enough to acquire though, if ye've the coin to afford it," he added at length.

Daijen removed the coin purse from his belt. "The coffers of Ka'vairn are deep, master smith." He placed it on the table between them.

Thronghir looked at the meagre purse with great scepticism. "I'm worried ye've come a long way for naught, me pale friend. Even if that purse is full o' kronums, it ain' goin' to afford the amount o' silvyr ye need, never mind me own services."

Daijen smiled knowingly. "The vaults of Ka'vairn do not horde coins, son of Enghir."

His interest piqued, the dwarf untied the string and tipped the purse upside down. Precious gems of every colour scattered across the surface. A handful amongst them shone like stars as they caught the firelight from the nearby forge.

Thronghir's eyes seemed equally bright. "Aye," he drawled. "That'll do it."

For a week thereafter, Daijen Saeth remained a guest of the dwarves. That is to say, he was confined to a pair of adjoining chambers in what appeared to be a barracks half a day's trek from the Underborn workshop. It was entirely too small for the exceptionally tall Andaren and, worse, all too boring.

Time and time again he asked permission to leave if only to walk up and down the barracks. The answer was always the same. His food and drink were provided—too much of each in his opinion. And damned if the dwarves didn't love their meat and beer. After the third day they started bringing him water before he requested it. The notion of a salad, however, was little more than a joke to the stone bones.

Though he never fought the rules pressed upon him, Daijen was all too aware that the Skaramangians had their hooks in the halls of Morthil. He was behind enemy lines and a rich target at that. He could only hope that they didn't have enough operatives to penetrate the barracks of soldiers. The initiate could only imagine his fate should he have to kill any dwarves in order to survive.

The only solace Daijen took from his temporary imprisonment was the knowledge that, upon his release, he would hold a slaiken blade. *His* slaiken blade. The final step. Given all that he knew of the world's secret history—and especially the fear Skaramangians held for the dragons—it seemed a pity that the final step on his path to becoming a Vahlken was to wield a weapon designed to slay dragons.

While he lay on his cot, dreaming of a day when their two orders might call the other an ally, his escort returned with fantastic news. Thronghir had requested his presence!

How tempting it had been to run ahead and leave the escorting dwarf behind. Daijen could have retraced his steps in less than half the time.

He practically burst through the workshop doors, nearly knocking his head on a pair of hanging tongs. He was also met by not one but two dwarves this time.

"This is me son, Grarfath," Thronghir said by way of greeting.

"Well met," Grarfath declared, his voice deep and gruff like his father's.

"Well met," Daijen replied politely, desperate to tell Grarfath how highly his mother spoke of him.

"Grarfath's helped me forge yer sword," the smith explained, patting his son on the back. "I don't tell ye this because I'm expectin' twice the pay. I tell ye this so ye know that yer blade's been forged by the two premier smiths o' Morthil," he said proudly. "Ye'll find none who could craft so well as us, lad."

"I am honoured," Daijen told them, his tone conveying how genuine he was being. "Might I see it?" he had to ask.

"O' course," Thronghir answered with a short laugh. "It's yers!"

Grarfath moved to the longest table in the workshop, though much of it was concealed beneath a black and dusty sheet. With one callused hand, the younger smith removed the fabric, dragging it over a single object that sat atop the table.

Daijen was humbled in the seconds that followed.

His blue eyes shifted left and right, taking in the blade over and over again. He guessed it to be a little shorter than himself, though he was taller than every Andaren he had ever met, save for those who had survived the pits of Handuin. Every ordinary warrior of his kin would call the sword unwieldy, its exceptional length entirely impractical. Not in his hands.

The blade itself—crafted from pure silvyr—was shaped much like his sabre, with a straight edge that curved ever so slightly toward the end. Indeed, the blade and hilt appeared to be one solid piece of silvyr, with no cross guard between the two.

Moving closer, drawn towards the sword without thought, Daijen paused by the hilt, his eyes following the curve as it reached for the flat pommel. There was poetry to its overall shape, the tip being curved in the opposing direction to the sloping hilt.

Taking in the detail, he examined the grip. The initiate marvelled at the black leather with just a hint of green about it. He refrained from taking it in hand for the time being, aware of the significance of such an action.

"It's exquisite," he uttered.

Thronghir beamed. "That it is," he agreed.

The moment was disturbed when the shop door opened and another dwarf walked in.

Thronghir frowned and nudged his son's arm. "I thought I told ye to put the sign out. We weren' to be disturbed."

Grarfath shrugged with half an apology. "It's a customer," he argued. "He's 'ere to pick up the cuirass an' *pay us*," he emphasised.

The older smith waved the response away. "Go deal with it then."

Grarfath hesitated, looking to Daijen and the slaiken blade. Despite his pointed comment regarding the customer, he clearly wished to be a part of their transaction. "Fine," he muttered, walking off to greet the other dwarf—who had yet to stop staring at Daijen.

"Sorry abou' that," Thronghir said. "I had hoped to keep this a private matter."

Daijen was barely paying any attention to the dwarves and their business. He was enraptured by the slaiken blade.

"You're truly as skilled as she said you were." The words just slipped out of Daijen's mouth.

Thronghir's eyes twitched and he glanced at Grarfath on the

other side of the shop. "As who said?" he questioned, and quietly so.

Daijen tore his attention away from the weapon and looked down at Thronghir, son of Enghir. He had no idea how things had been left between the smith and his wife, only that Mordrith was wanted by the Skaramangians and that she had kept her husband and son in the dark to ensure their safety.

"I am a friend of your wife, Mordrith," he began tentatively.

Thronghir's eyes widened in surprise before he shot a glance towards Grarfath. The dwarf shifted his position so that Daijen now stood directly between father and son. "I'm not for knowin'," he said gravely.

"What?" Daijen asked with a frown.

"I'm no fool, lad. I know she's mixed up in somethin' jus' as I know it was her blasted father who got her into it. Whatever it is, I'm not for knowin'. There's a reason Mordrith didn' tell us—she didn' even leave a damned note!" he hissed. "I've seen shifty lookin' fellas hangin' abou' ever since. If not knowin' is what's keepin' me boy safe then that's that." The smith straightened out his apron. "Now, if ye'd take yer blade an' yer gems I'd be glad to be gettin' on with me day."

Daijen's reflexes had no trouble catching the purse of gems as it flew from Thronghir's meaty fist. By weight alone, he knew immediately that only some of the gems had been kept by the dwarf. "You can keep them all," he offered, feeling somehow guilty that the smith had lost his wife to a war he knew nothing about.

"I don't keep what I don' earn," Thronghir replied firmly.

Daijen only nodded as he attached the purse to his belt, feeling foolish now for pitying the proud dwarf. Deciding that he had overstayed his welcome, Daijen moved for his sword. His hand hesitated, hovering over the hilt.

"What she's been doing," he said, looking back at the smith, "the war she's a part of... Mordrith fights for us all. She is a true warrior."

Thronghir blinked, his eyes glassy. "Is she..." He cleared his throat and spared Grarfath one last look. "Is she alive?"

Daijen opened his mouth, the lie resting on the edge of his lips. The smith deserved better though.

"I don't know," he replied truthfully.

Thronghir dropped his chin to his chest, shoulders heaving with a protracted sigh. When he met the Andaren's eyes again, there was a measure of resolve about the dwarf. "Yer slaiken blade," he said, picking up the sword in two hands, the hilt offered forwards. "It is tradition among me kin," the smith explained. "A newly-forged weapon is to be given, so it may know the difference between they that craft an' they that wield."

Daijen's hand slowly reached out, his fingers flexing to account for the grip.

Not to delay the inevitable moment a second longer, the initiate took the weapon in hand, freeing it from the smith's grasp. It was extraordinarily light for such a long sword, giving the illusion that he was wielding no more than his atori short-sword. Moving past its weight and balance, he was left with the manifestation of a destiny he could never have foreseen.

From this moment to his very last, he was a *Vahlken*.

"Now be gone," Thronghir instructed, crushing the moment. "An' take yer war with ye."

Daijen opened his mouth to explain everything, but to do so would destroy Mordrith's sacrifice and the great work she had committed to. Instead, he offered the dwarf a curt bow of the head and left the son of Enghir behind.

Along with his grief.

PART FOUR

48
THE TRUTH IS A WEB

For the first time, the old Rider looked just as confused as Gallien. "Galahart's *dead*," Drakalis informed bluntly. "Watched it happen myself."

"The Dawn Sword is a volatile creature," the bald man commented, the crow's feet about his eyes drawing together. "A pity nonetheless—Galahart was a fine spy."

"I thought *you* were Galahart," the smuggler replied.

"That I am," came the expected, if infuriating, answer.

"I have met Galahart before," Androma asserted. "It was *his* voice in the tavern."

"And yet, I *am* Galahart. Perhaps we can move past this and address the matter at hand."

"He was a decoy," Joran concluded. "The other one."

"A spymaster must have many faces," the new Galahart remarked.

"And is this your real face?" Gallien probed. "Are you the *real* Galahart?"

"Yes," the spymaster told him, his voice so flat there was no discerning truth from lie.

Gallien eyed the small fellow, his black robes and cloak

betraying nothing of his wealth or position. Was Erador's spymaster one man or many? The smuggler suspected both were true.

"Are you wearing *your* real face, Mr *Drakalis*?"

Gallien said nothing. Like the dead Galahart, this one insinuated a wealth of knowledge where the smuggler's secrets were concerned.

"Why aren't you trying to kill us?" Androma enquired. "The other... *you*, threatened us all."

"Galahart always did enjoy any opportunity for theatrics. A quirk all of his own, I assure you. He was intending to keep up appearances, given The Dawn Sword's proximity. With the Andaren's escape the truth will out. My part in the game will have to change."

"What truth?" Joran asked before Androma could even open her mouth.

Galahart regarded the boy for precious seconds before deigning to respond. "The truth is a web, young sir. We're all just trying to find our way through before the spider finds us."

"Speak plainly," Cob instructed.

"I am Erador's premier spymaster, my Kedradi friend. Speaking *plainly* isn't in the job description."

"Galahart," Aphrandhor intoned, his hand reaching out for the spymaster's arm. "Since you haven't attempted to take our lives, perhaps you might enrich them with an explanation."

Galahart recoiled, removing himself from The Green Leaf's reach. "I know of your... *touch*, Wizard. I should like to keep my secrets, thank you."

"I nearly died learning you're a Skaramangian," Androma inserted before Gallien could ask what they were talking about.

"You might have learned a lot more had you not fled when you did," Galahart said dryly. "Obviously I am *not* a Skaramangian," he revealed without preamble. "They are enemy to us both—to us *all*. Every turn of the war. Every battle instigated. Every alliance made. Every betrayal. They keep us busy on all fronts. The Andarens too. More blood has been spilled in the last three centuries than the last three millennia. Worse: they are gaining ground."

"How do you know this?" Androma demanded. "How do we know you're telling the truth?"

"If my allegiances lay with the Skaramangians, you would all be dead by now."

"That's hardly proof," Gallien said, inserting himself.

"We simply have differing styles of warfare," Galahart told them. "While you have been running around the country like your boots are on fire, I have spent years *infiltrating* their ranks. The king's spymaster is a valuable asset, after all. At the price of an atrocity here and there, I have learned much of their ways. Until tonight, I even had their *trust*."

The spymaster sighed, his small eyes shifting momentarily to the water.

"Alas," he continued, "I am still a servant of the king. His will is my command, and he has willed it that Joran is to be brought before him. Hence our parting ways with the Skaramangians and *their* will to see Joran separated from his head."

"Wait." Gallien blurted the word and instinctively side-stepped to partially conceal the boy. "The *king*? The king of Erador wants to see Joran?"

"Do you know of any *other* king, Mr Drakalis?"

"Why?" Joran asked, cutting through the exchange.

"That would be the *king's* business," Galahart specified. "Like I said: I am but a servant."

"He is *not* going before the king," Gallien stated as a matter of fact. "We need to get out of this city. You don't have nearly enough men to challenge that thing back there."

"Agreed," the spymaster replied. "On both fronts," he added, surprising them all.

Gallien blinked, his understanding turned on its head. "I thought you said—"

"I cannot be seen to ignore the king's orders," Galahart interrupted. "That doesn't mean I have to succeed at them. I have gone so far as to break my cover within the enemy camp and lost good men in the process. You five, however, escaped in the chaos and are to be pursued on The North Road. As for The Dancing Sword of the Dawn... His training is magnitudes beyond any man I command. We will do what we can to contain him but I can offer no more than delaying him."

He was letting them go. Gallien couldn't believe it—*didn't* believe it. This was just another kind of trap.

"Why are you doing this?" Aphrandhor asked on behalf of them all.

"You fight your way, wizard, and I'll fight my way." His dark eyes fell on Androma before shifting to Joran. "I know the future you're fighting for. It is a *shard* of hope. Nevertheless, I would do my part to see it kindled. The king will have to wait for his audience. For now," he added ominously.

"You know what they saw?" Androma questioned lightly. "The Andarens."

"I wouldn't be much of a spymaster if I didn't," he replied dryly. "*A time of dragons,*" he uttered, as if the words were divine. "A vision worthy of our toil. Even more so if the Skaramangians fear a rise in their numbers."

"Of course they do," Gallien said as if it was obvious. "Dragons can end wars as quickly as they can start them."

"The Skaramangians do not fear any side losing the war," Galahart disclosed. "The war is a smoke screen—a tool that allows them to move the pieces on both sides of the board. They fear a time of dragons because it will interfere with their endgame."

"How so?" Aphrandhor asked.

"What plans?" Androma queried at the same time.

"That's the question, isn't it?" Galahart moved for the first time in minutes, his steps soundless. "Whatever they're doing—whatever they've been working towards for so many millennia—it is threatened by dragons. I would also say they are close to finishing their *great* work, else they wouldn't have started the war when they did. Adding to our list of problems, I hear reports every day of more Jainus succumbing to the Skaramangians' offers, their allegiances switching in the shadows. It seems inevitable that they will attain the bones in Akmar. Then they will possess *three* skeletons. I cannot say if there are more, just as I cannot imagine what magic they might wield with the knowledge of all three."

Androma gripped her staff as if it supported her. "They intend to bring back the—"

"Dark Ones," Galahart interrupted. "Yes, I know. From what I can gather, they are yet to actually discover one. I believe they intend to use the magic of the *so-called* gods to locate them. Perhaps they will use that same magic to bring them back," he mused. "Or, perhaps, they will come to see that myth and legend are just that. Either way, I have no doubt the Skaramangians will turn their new-found power on the rest of us. I suppose that's where you come in," he said, looking to Joran.

Gallien moved, always sure to have himself positioned between Joran and anything he considered a threat. "Right now," he said, doing his best to keep the conversation in the present, "we're just trying to get him somewhere he'll be safe."

"Safe?" the spymaster echoed incredulously. "And you're taking him to *Drakanan*?" he added, looking to Androma now.

Gallien looked to Joran at the mention of the name. The smuggler had learned from Androma, and so recently, that Drakanan was their intended destination. Still, there wasn't a soul in all of Erador that didn't know the purpose of Drakanan. The boy met his gaze with a hint of trepidation about him.

"I understand why," Galahart continued, "given what the boy must become, but Drakanan is the last place I would consider to be safe."

Androma was shaking her head. "You don't know what you're—"

"Why not?" Gallien blurted at the spymaster. "I thought Drakanan was the only place the Skaramangians *couldn't* get to."

"I see," Galahart drawled. "You haven't told them *everything*, Androma. A little fool-hardy for one usually so pragmatic. I recall you being quite the meticulous planner. Hmm," he croaked. "That's the problem with hope, I suppose. It makes us shortsighted."

Gallien couldn't be sure, but it seemed the spymaster might have been including himself in that final remark. "What are you talking about?" the smuggler demanded. "Why isn't Drakanan safe?"

"Yes," Galahart said, picking up the thread. "*Why* isn't Drakanan safe, Androma?"

It seemed with great reluctance that the old Rider responded at all. "It *is* safe," she reassured. "I told you," she went on, turning to face Gallien, "an *ally* awaits us in Drakanan."

Galahart tilted his bald and veiny head. "You need to get your house in order, Androma. That's if it *is your* house," he said provokingly. "I would have assumed with the death of—"

"You do *not* get to say his name," the old Rider asserted, her voice harder and colder than normal.

The spymaster straightened up and smoothed out his dark robes. "You are aware, yes, that Harendun sits apart from both Andara and Erador now? A fiefdom all of its own."

"I am aware," Androma replied, her jaw tight.

"Then you are also aware that *Vander* sits as king of the undying city, his authority emboldened by Herragax."

"I am," the old Rider answered.

"Vander?" Gallien knew that name. "The Dragon Rider? The one who invaded Harendun when *we* were there?" He recalled the Rider fighting a Vahlken in the streets, only to have his foe defeated by a common soldier driving a sword in his back. That same Rider then murdered the soldier and claimed the kill as his own.

The smuggler knew it was coming but he couldn't stop the vivid memory from being dredged up. The sound of crunching bone. The red dragon, Herragax, and its jaws dripping with thick blood. Astride the Aegre's body, the dragon had gripped the animal's head in its jaws and ripped one from the other.

There was nothing in the world like a dragon. As far Gallien was concerned, they were the *real* gods. *Terrifying* gods.

"The very same," Galahart confirmed. "After taking the city, he claimed it as his own. Thousands swore their allegiance to him. And why wouldn't they?" the spymaster asked. "He was the reason they had succeeded where so many before had failed. He was the reason they survived the battle. And who wouldn't bow in the shadow of a dragon? Now, a Rider sits on a throne in an Andaren city, and with a small army at his disposal no less. It is unprecedented."

"Vander is no king," Androma told them confidently. "He's just a puppet."

"Of course he is," Galahart agreed. "But he's a puppet with a dragon. This schism of yours has made a mess of things and it's only going to get worse."

"It's not my war anymore," Androma told him.

"Yet you would take the boy to Drakanan," Galahart pointed out. "*If* he has what it takes to become a Rider, their war will become his. *Baelon* will make him choose a side, just as he did with the others."

"Baelon lost Drakanan a century ago. It belongs to our side."

"*Our* side?" the spymaster noted. "I thought it wasn't your war anymore."

"Drakanan is safe," Androma retorted, doubling down. "He holds no power there."

"For how much longer?" the spymaster quizzed. "For a hundred years, he's done naught but think of a world under *his* rule. Positioning Vander in Harendun was Baelon's first move"

"That was sixteen years ago."

"What's that to an immortal?" Galahart argued. "How long until his next move? There are none who can track Baelon nor any of his Riders. Perhaps he's already made it and we don't even know yet. What if that next move is reclaiming Drakanan? Think of the eggs, Androma. Baelon will come for them and when he does, he will discover Joran."

"I *am* thinking of the eggs," the old Rider stressed. "There's nowhere else *to* go."

The spymaster regarded the portcullis that blocked the river. "Go if you must. But do not linger there. This dragon war will spread."

"I'm fighting a different war."

"It's all the same war," the spymaster stated. "The web is just far more complex than you can imagine."

"Stop" Drakalis pleaded, exhausted by his own lack of knowledge. "Who in the hells is Baelon?"

"Not our problem," Androma said. "He's not in Drakanan. We need to get Joran there as soon as possible. Nothing else matters."

"Nothing else matters," Galahart echoed, his tone suggesting he was really thinking about those words. "Have you considered the consequences of your actions?"

"What consequences?" Aphrandhor asked gravely.

"The Helm of Ahnir is a window to many futures," the spymaster affirmed. "Acting on the knowledge of any one of those futures may be the very work that undoes it. You believe taking Joran to Drakanan is the best way to see his future fulfilled. It might be the very thing that shatters any hope for a new generation of Dragon Riders."

"It won't," Androma was quick to respond, her words hard and unbending.

Galahart eyed the old Rider with some intensity. "We shall see. As I said, I will do my part to see it through." He gestured to the river. "When you're done with all this running and wish to get back in the fight, return to Valgala. I will gladly put you to work."

Cob inserted himself into the conversation. "I do not work for spymasters nor any man who wears so many faces."

"Hmm. Cob," he pronounced, as if he was testing the blunt name on his thin lips. "A butchery of your true name. If only I had ten thousand more of you, Mr Cob. I could end this war once and for all." Galahart's words were enough to put the Kedradi off balance—his intention no doubt. "You have all proven yourselves worthy adversaries of the Skaramangians. I only wish to aim you as one might a bow. With some precision—via the intelligence I have gathered—your collective skillset could deliver quite the blow to our phantom enemy."

The spymaster moved through them, making his way to the stone edge and the steps that descended to the water. There they saw one large row boat, its interior stocked with sacks of supplies.

"Our foe has eyes and ears to rival my own, I'm afraid. You cannot take the road to Freygard and beyond, not if you are to reach Drakanan. Take the river north. Go left at the fork."

"Left?" The Green Leaf questioned with concern. "That will take us to The Spine of Erador."

"And you must cross The Spine," Galahart replied. "The Dawn Sword will not think to follow you there. Take the mountain pass and keep Mount Kaliban on your left. Follow the path to The Giant's Throat. From there you have only to turn north and cross The Red Fields of Dunmar."

"Is that all?" the wizard quipped.

"From here to Drakanan you will face naught but the elements," the spymaster detailed. "You've all survived worse."

"The Skaramangians are not the only threat in this world," Cob warned.

"Then it is a good thing a ranger travels with you," Galahart's rasping voice countered. "I would say you have survived *much* worse," he added, glancing at the Kedradi's arsenal of weaponised bones.

After the spymaster stepped aside, the five companions made their way down to the boat and, one by one, found their place inside. All the while, a team of Galahart's men worked to raise the portcullis that barred their way north.

As they were being cast off, Androma turned up towards Galahart. "Should we return," the old Rider suggested, "how are we to find you?"

The spymaster's surly demeanour cracked for the first time and he let loose a cackling laugh as he departed in shadow.

49
DRAGON VERSUS AEGRE

40 Years Ago...

A whole head above his pale kin, Daijen offered nods to the Andaren soldiers as he passed through the highest chamber and climbed the steps to the flat roof that topped The Watchtower of Argunsuun. Five years he had spent roaming the world beyond the confines of Ka'vairn, and still the Vahlken felt uncomfortable under the scrutiny of his own people.

Before the pits of Handuin had transformed him in so many ways, he had been different to the soldiers churned out by The Saible. He had been considered weak or incompetent or simply of low blood; just another pitiful creature unfit to fight for his land and people.

Now, he was different for other, more obvious, reasons.

His armour and cloak were badges of his station, but so too was his stature and frame. Even his skin appeared healthier, his freckles as bright as silver. He was hardly aware of it, but he carried himself differently. Unlike the ordinary Andaren, it took days not hours to feel the burden of physical fatigue, and so his posture was strong, his chin high, and his eyes ever sharp.

Some marvelled at him, seeing the Vahlken as a fabled warrior from the stories of old. They felt safe around him, as if he could protect them from anything and everything. Then there were others, who regarded him as dangerous—they who had seen a Vahlken on the battlefield no doubt.

Whatever their opinion of him, he was to protect them, even if he didn't feel like he was one of them. The latter, however, was not a new feeling.

Leaving them behind, he ascended to the roof with a goblet in each hand. The scent of the wine had been stuck in his nose since they had arrived at the tower, days ago. "I think this might be older than you," he remarked, crossing the roof.

Ilithranda sat comfortably on the very edge of the wall, her back resting against one of the tall spikes that crowned the monolithic sentinel of black stone. The dizzying height was enough to make anyone's hands and feet sweat, but Argunsuun was half the height of Ka'vairn's position in The Hellion Mountains.

"They had no ale?" she asked.

Daijen refrained from shaking his head. "You're such a dwarf," he commented, handing her the goblet.

Ilithranda's first mouthful was fiendish, though she did acknowledge the wine's fine taste with an expression. "It'll do."

Daijen leaned against the wall, where his gaze should have been drawn to the magnificent view—to the distant White Tower that marked Erador's border. But he couldn't take his eyes off Ilithranda.

"You're staring," she stated flatly.

"Sorry," he replied sheepishly. "It's just..."

"We part ways tomorrow," she said for him.

"I know there aren't enough of us to stay together," Daijen went on, "but you're being posted in The Fangs and I'm stuck here," he complained, gesturing to the vista of snow."

"The sun will be a nice change," Ilithranda replied teasingly.

Daijen gave a silent laugh and finally turned away from his sister—his closest companion. The distance between them wasn't the only thing writhing under his skin. "This is exactly what they wanted," he began. "The Skaramangians wanted us distracted, busy fighting a foe that could cut us down."

"I think it's the other way around," Ilithranda opined.

Daijen didn't disagree, though he hated to think how many dragons had been slain by his kin, each a victory for the Skaramangians. It was all so infuriating. Questions were piling atop questions and, all the while, their foe drew ever closer to their inexplicable goal.

"We should be out *there*," he argued, his icy blue eyes cast out to the world. "We should be investigating, pursuing leads, challenging our enemy. I've a good mind to fly to Aran'saur and demand an audience with the emperor," he fumed.

Ilithranda barked a laugh. "And say what? Your grand clerics and closest advisors are part of an ancient cult bent on slaying dragons and bringing back the Dark Ones." She was shaking her head. "Trust me, Daijen, the Empyreal Throne will rob even you of your courage. It's a different world back there."

"We have to do *something*," he said hopelessly. "We can't spend the next century just guarding a border."

"Daijen..."

"I know," he was quick to reply. "We have a duty to protect the people."

"Daijen!"

Ilithranda was standing on the wall now, her grave tone finally piercing the fog of concern that spread through his mind. Following her gaze, Daijen looked out across the strip of icy land, where White Tower held sway over the eastern horizon. There was no missing the cause of Ilithranda's apprehension.

Dragons.

Three of them.

Daijen tore his eyes from their fast approach and leaned over the side of the tower. He saw a handful soldiers huddled around a fire on the tower's highest balcony, oblivious to Death riding on the wind.

"Sound the alarm!" he bellowed.

They looked up and spotted the Vahlken before turning their attention to the dragons. The group hesitated, ensnared by fear no doubt. One of them managed to run inside, where he began ringing a bell that was soon echoed all the way down Argunsuun.

Ilithranda was already blowing into her Cuthar, a whistle that only their Aegres could hear. Daijen's attention naturally turned to the sky, where he saw two dark objects plunging towards them against thick grey clouds.

They were too far away.

It was their first time in this part of the world and, for all their intelligence, there was no way of communicating something as complex as the no-man's land between the two towers. Now they weren't going to get back to Argunsuun in time.

"Ilithranda," Daijen intoned, warning her without the words to retreat from the edge.

She did just that, drawing her sabre at the same time. The weapon, of course, would prove useless unless the Dragon Riders dismounted. And why would they? Their dragons could annihilate the tower from the sky and be done with every Andaren that stood between them and Andara.

Daijen looked up again. Still too far.

The dragons, on the other hand, were much closer now. Daijen could make out their individual features, be it the variation in claw size or the number of horns that crowned their sloping heads. They were magnificent to behold, even if that awe was tinted with foreboding alarm. They seemed to exist somewhere between hideous monster and beautiful creature. One half of Daijen's mind demanded that he run and hide while the other refused to see him move, so he might marvel at them.

The Vahlken gripped the hilt of his sabre, a ritual he had adopted some years ago. He could feel his fear draining out of him, as if he were squeezing water from a cloth. His focus sharpened to a point worthy of Valyra's beak.

Overcome with a sense of ease, he looked again at the dragons, noting their colours now. In the lead, flying erratically, was a blue dragon. It was damned big. In its wake flew a red dragon—a sleeker and lithe-looking dragon with a long neck. Not far behind the red, a dragon of deep green swept in and down before its jaws snapped at the blue.

Daijen blinked. Had he just seen that?

"Get ready," Ilithranda urged, her knees bent.

Daijen didn't bother drawing his sabre—what was he going to do with it? Instead, he looked up, hoping to see the gleaming armour that covered Valyra's beak. Alas, she remained some distance away. And so he braced himself. Would he face teeth, claw or fire, the Vahlken wondered; a trifecta of death. His only hope was that the Riders fancied themselves a fight.

Inevitably, the moment was upon them.

The air was batted as a storm of dragons raced past the watchtower. They curled round at great speed and shot out towards the sea in the south. Not a one made to attack Argunsuun.

"They're chasing it," he muttered to himself, his words lost to the ringing of bells.

Valyra was first to reach them, her brown wings, tipped with white, unfurling to bring her level with the top of the watchtower. Though she came in to land with grace and precision, her yellow eyes were far beyond Argunsuun, tracking the dragons.

Then came *Oaken*.

The male Aegre waited a moment longer, flying in half way down the tower. His black feathers, a shade darker than the fur of Ilithranda's cloak, was a stark contrast against the white snow. He was a touch larger than Valyra, though *she*, it had been noted, was a notch more aggressive. They had become quite the pair over the last five years, their bond growing as if they were from the same eyrie. More importantly, they had become quite the force to be reckoned with, each aware of the other's strategies.

They had never faced a dragon, however. Now they faced *three*.

As Daijen deftly climbed into his saddle, Valyra's talons perched on the edge of the roof, Ilithranda swan dived from the raised wall. By the time Valyra had turned and let gravity pull her down the length of Argunsuun, Ilithranda was in her saddle and climbing astride Oaken.

Again, Valyra spread her wings and flapped hard, clearing the tower and aiming for the sky. Daijen looked to his left, where his slaiken blade sat strapped to his saddle, the hilt within easy reach. The weapon had sat idle for years, an ornament more than anything. He had a sinking feeling that it would taste blood today.

Guiding Valyra to come in alongside Oaken, Daijen cried out to be heard over the rushing wind. "We can't kill them!"

Ilithranda whipped head around. "*They* will kill *us*!"

"They're the only thing the Skaramangians fear! They *want* us to slay them!"

"They're in our territory!" Ilithranda pointed out. "Let's just remind them and be done with it!"

Daijen didn't see that happening without bloodshed. "I think they're chasing the blue one!" he informed.

Ilithranda shot him a scowl from her saddle. "Why would they hunt one of their own?"

Daijen nodded ahead. "Let's find out!"

The Aegres pursued the dragons all the way to the southern cliffs, where the land plunged towards a rocky shoreline and crashing waves. Here, the blue dragon dived down and the pursuing two gave chase, disappearing beneath the ridge. In the lead, Ilithranda and Oaken plummeted down after their prey first. When Daijen was vertical in her wake, the three dragons had spread their wings and were gliding along the coast.

The red one was swift and agile, following the contours of the cliff to gain some height over the blue. A jet of blazing fire erupted from its jaws, momentarily masking the blue and its rider. It seemed such a risk while moving at neck-breaking speeds, but the blue tucked in its wings and corkscrewed, taking the brunt of the fire across its hardened stomach.

It was protecting the Rider.

Daijen braced himself as Valyra came out of her dive and came in behind Oaken. He angled the Aegre so he could see past Oaken and continue to watch the dragons zig-zagging along the shore. The green attacked from below this time, its hard stomach skimming the jagged rocks. More fire burst forth, finding life from within the jaws of the hulking beast. The blue dragon was forced to fly towards the cliffs, where it no longer had the space to extend its wings.

The Vahlken could hardly believe his eyes. The blue dragon collapsed its wings and ran up and to the side of the cliff face. It avoided the flames and leapt out towards the sea, where its wings could, again, fan out and take flight.

"They're climbing!" Ilithranda called back, directing Oaken towards the sky.

Daijen pulled back on his handles and pushed down with his hips, taking Valyra into a vertical ascent. Above the cliffs and out to sea, the red dragon collided with the blue in an impact of gnashing jaws, raking claws, and thrashing tails. It was soon raining blood.

Without warning, the green dragon peeled away from the fight.

It turned to spy the trailing Aegres.

"It's coming for us!" Daijen yelled.

At least it was. The dragon vanished in the cloud bank above. Daijen's eyes roamed over every inch of cloud, searching desperately for any sign of the creature. He saw a tail cut through the clouds up and to his right. Then he saw the tip of a wing dip below to his left. Valyra squawked, perhaps having seen something his Vahlken eyes had missed. Either way, they both missed the fight that had grown out of control.

A blur of red and blue hurtled past them, the tail of each swinging within a foot of Aegre and Vahlken. Daijen looked over his shoulder and watched Ilithranda drive Oaken down, narrowly avoiding the mid-air battle.

Valyra squawked again and Daijen detected the subtlest of movements beneath his saddle, informing him of the imminent barrel roll. The world spun in a tight circle and something green flashed through the cone of blurring colours. Valyra had evaded the dragon's open maw by a hair's breadth but not its tail. It was a glancing blow but enough all the same to send the pair tumbling through the air.

Daijen grunted as the spinning fall tried to part him from Valyra. He clung to a single handle with a mere four fingers. The Aegre was a product of magic, however, and soon found the strength to correct her flight, bringing them back together.

Dipping to the right, Valyra brought the dragons back into view. The blue and red were coiling around each other, their Riders exchanging blows wherever they could in a dance of claws and silvyr. The green dragon, it seemed, still had an appetite for Aegre, ignoring its kin so it might take up the hunt with Oaken in its sights.

Ilithranda flattened herself against the long saddle, making herself part of the Aegre's body as he picked up speed.

"Bring him to me!" Daijen bellowed, the mechanics of his mind shifting into that of a cold and proficient killer in the wake of Ilithranda's potential doom.

Valyra angled herself head to head with Oaken, the hulking green on their tail. Daijen's mind was clear of any doubt now. The dragon had to die so Ilithranda could live. Without looking, his left hand found the leather grip of the slaiken blade. He had only to twist it and the latches released the naked weapon.

Channelling the spirit of Handuin himself, Daijen Saeth rode into battle astride his Aegre, slaiken blade held high in one hand. Was he to be a hero though, or was he to feed the Black Abyss?

In little more than a second, the three came together, occupying the same patch of sky. Oaken flapped his wings hard and launched higher into the air while, simultaneously, Valyra dived down, creating a tunnel for the green dragon to pass through.

Daijen leapt.

His momentum saw him fly over the top of the dragon, his cloak skimming the horns protruding from above the creature's eyes. Clearing the beast's head in an instant, his mind had mere fractions of time to comprehend the Rider seated in the saddle. His sword was drawn but in the wrong hand to lash out at the

Vahlken. It was also in the wrong hand to defend himself *against* the Vahlken.

Daijen flew past the Rider in the blink of an eye and whipped his slaiken blade around. The silvyr sliced through the Rider's head, separating everything above his mouth from the rest of his body in a spray of blood.

In accordance with Kastiek's rigorous training, Daijen had delivered a swift death.

What he could not do, however, was fly. His momentum died as the green dragon let loose an almighty roar that could have rivalled the loudest thunderclap. It knew its companion was dead. How long had they been bonded? How many centuries? Those questions were as fleeting as Daijen's fall was rapid. He hurtled towards the sea, though the water might as well have been stone from his height.

It didn't matter. He would be dead before impact.

The dragon, enraged—fury incarnate—had already turned around and was diving for him, jaws open. He was to be eaten then. At least that answered one of the questions that had plagued him. The Vahlken gripped his slaiken blade all the tighter, wondering how it might best be used before he joined the Rider in the Black Abyss.

Looking up, he could still see the dead Rider situated in his saddle, the corpse somehow fixed in place. It made for all the more an unnerving sight—a headless Rider plummeting after him astride a bloodthirsty dragon.

Like a spear hurled by Ahnir, Oaken slammed into the dragon, taking the creature off course. A second later and Valyra returned, sweeping past her Vahlken companion with wings spread flat. Daijen grabbed one of the handles and pulled himself back into the saddle, his feet quick to find their pockets and the sword its fastenings. Wanting to get back into the fight and aid Ilithranda, he leaned hard right and turned the Aegre back to land.

Oaken's beak, plated in armour, was clamped to the side of the dragon's head, the top point deep inside the beast's left eye. His front claws had found purchase inside its neck having made light work of the plated scale and sunk into flesh. The Aegre's back talons were raking at the dragon's front claws, keeping them at bay while Ilithranda leapt from one animal to the next.

Though the dragon writhed in pain and fought against Oaken, Ilithranda was nimble enough to navigate the rise and fall of its limbs, the flap of its wings, and the sharp spines that lined its back. Only then did Daijen see the value in their decades of training. How else could anyone bring down a dragon?

With nearly a human's entire lifespan of instruction, discipline, and relentless exercises under her belt, Ilithranda did exactly that. Death was immediate, her slaiken blade plunged between the dragon's horns and through its skull. Oaken detached and pushed away from the now falling corpse.

Ilithranda remained braced atop the head, riding the dragon down while holding on to her slaiken blade. When the creature's wings and limbs began to throw its descent into tumbling chaos, the Vahlken removed her weapon and jumped free. Instinctively, Daijen started to guide Valyra towards her, but Oaken's reappearance proved their interference unnecessary.

Astride their Aegres, both Vahlken turned to see the other. They could say nothing from so far apart, but they held a solemn moment as they digested the incredible feat they had performed. They might have come together and exchanged words were it not for the warring dragons vying for their attention.

The blue and red had descended back to the cliffs in their battle. It wasn't going well for the blue dragon. The red ploughed into it, driving the creature into the rocky face. A raking claw batted the blue's head aside, drawing lines of blood down its face while exposing the neck. The red lunged forward as the two scraped down the cliffs to the jagged beach. As they landed, the blue's neck was firmly inside the jaws of its opponent.

It took Daijen's sharp eyes another second to realise that both dragons were absent their Riders. At some point during their battle, the two humans had found themselves on the rocky beach, where the waves crashed about them, always threatening to wash them away.

They fought with swords and *magic*.

Daijen had witnessed humans wielding magic before, though only once and the Jainus wizard had required the Demetrium sewn into his robes to manipulate those otherworldly forces. The Riders required no such tools, their magic flowing out from their dragon bond. It dawned on the Vahlken then that all he knew of the Dragon Riders was what he had read about them in books. That would have made it a more daunting prospect had he not just slain one.

The Aegres glided across the sea, their talons cutting through the water's surface as they raced towards the shore. Flashes of light and brilliant colours exploded across the rocks, the Riders locked in heated battle. When their magic failed to thwart the other, they collided in a flurry of silvyr and acrobatics, dancing across the rocks as if it were no more than flat land. They were a marvel to behold. A worthy opponent.

Their presence, however, disturbed the duel. Of the man and woman bound in combat, the man turned to regard the approaching Aegres and hesitated. Daijen narrowed his eyes, taking the measure of the distant figure. Like the woman, he was attired in black plate—the tight-fitting armour of a Rider. Even from such a distance, the Vahlken could make out the red of his vambraces and pauldrons; the same shade of red as the dragon. His dusty cloak was heavy with water and sticking to his back, much like his blond hair which remained tightly bound at the back of his head.

Before the Aegres could reach the shore, the man was peeling away, darting for the dragons. The woman gave chase, her sodden blonde hair masking half of her face. None could close the gap, however, before the red Rider and dragon were reunited. Leaving the blue to lie strewn across the rocks, they fled into the sky. But not before Ilithranda had the last word of course.

Having ascended from the water's surface, Oaken was on an intercept path. When the distance was just right, Ilithranda hurled her vials of axium, the two chemicals knotted together. The glass shattered against the side of the dragon's neck and Andaren magic had its day. In a flash of violet, the chemicals mixed and were transmuted into an acid that even dragon scales couldn't stand up to.

The red dragon roared in pain as the acid bit into the flesh beneath, ensuring new scales would never grow in their place. Still it climbed, flying higher and higher until the clouds concealed it and Oaken turned back.

Valyra landed at a run, her talons taking them across the rocks and towards the downed blue dragon and its Rider. Daijen dismounted, sure to keep his slaiken blade in hand, and approached the cliff face. Up close, he could see the deep blue of its scales were speckled with gold and bronze—a tapestry that spoke of nature's majesty.

He could also see the damage wrought by the red dragon, its every natural weapon brought to bear against the blue. So much of its body was stained with blood and so many scales were missing altogether. One of the wings twitched, spasming out of control, and set the Vahlken back a step. Worse still, its breathing was laboured, haggard even. It turned Daijen's attention to the severe bite it had suffered across its neck.

Without thought, he slowly closed the gap, one hand coming up to touch the dragon's ribcage. It was an impulse he should have curbed but here he was, within reach of a real, living dragon. For decades he had read about them, trained to face them. But he had never even touched one. His pale fingers came within inches of the blue scales before a length of straight silvyr barred his way.

"You will not touch him!" the Rider barked in perfect Andarneese.

Daijen backed off and raised his free hand to ward off Valyra, who had instantly taken a dislike to the woman pointing a sword at him. In the seconds it took Oaken and Ilithranda to arrive, the Vahlken scrutinised the Rider before him, looking at her with the eyes Kastiek had given him.

Her long blonde hair was soaked through and pushed back now, revealing an angular face. Her lips were naught but a thin line that sat beneath a dimpled nose and a pair of exquisite blue eyes.

Where his were icy and vibrant, hers were like deep wells of ocean blue that drew him in.

She was also bleeding.

Her armour was scored across the ribs on one side and across the hip on the other. The other Rider's blade had sliced through the dark plate and found skin, for even her under armour—a fine suit of delicate blue scales—had succumbed to the silvyr. Besides the bruise to her jaw and the smaller cuts that formed a patchwork over her hands, she looked generally exhausted, distressed even.

Daijen looked beyond her, to the dragon. He had to wonder how wounded the creature was.

With two Aegres and two Vahlken sharing the rocky beach with her, the Rider altered her stance, adopting a new battle form. She was brave.

"Who are you?" she demanded, her silvyr sword held horizontally in both hands.

"You're in *our* territory," Ilithranda pointed out. "We will ask the questions, Rider."

"I'd rather just kill you both and get on with my day," the Rider retorted, unafraid.

"My name is Daijen Saeth," the Vahlken interjected, driving his slaiken blade into the beach at his side, his introduction cutting through the tension. "What is *your* name?"

The Rider maintained her battle readiness for another heartbeat before it cracked, her curiosity winning out. "You're not going to fight?"

"I think there has been enough fighting for one day," Daijen remarked, glancing at the dragon.

The Rider slowly lowered her sword, pausing a moment to take in Ilithranda. "My name is Androma," she declared boldly.

"Androma," Daijen repeated with some warmth in his voice. "Well met."

"That remains to be seen," she replied, her gaze travelling as far as the Aegres, lingering on Oaken's bloody beak.

"You're hurt," Daijen observed, his tone suggesting he cared.

"I've had worse," Androma told him.

"Why don't we all rest a while," the Vahlken suggested. "Your dragon is wounded, too wounded to fly I'd say. You're on our side of the line. We can offer you protection while you recover."

"No you can't," the Rider insisted. "There's more where Vander came from," she added, nodding at the sky. "And the Rider you killed—Gregorn. He was the weakest of them all. You won't survive what comes next."

Ilithranda stepped forwards, inserting herself into the conversation. "They want you dead so badly that they would cross the border *again*?"

Exasperated, Androma shook her head. "You have no idea what you're getting into here. Do yourselves a favour and return to Argunsuun. Leave us to fight each other."

"Why?" The question boiled out of Daijen. "Why would Dragon Riders want to kill Dragon Riders?"

Androma sighed, her wounds biting into her reserves by the look of it. Keeping her sword in hand, she sat on the nearest rock and let her head fall to her chest. When she looked up again, her attention was briefly drawn to the dragon at her back, as if the creature had said something to her.

"If we aren't to kill each other then," she said at length, if somewhat surprised by the fact, "perhaps there is room for words."

A spark of hope was ignited in the Vahlken. Words always championed steel, he believed.

If only his belief would be enough.

50
OVER THE MOUNTAINS

Not for the first time, Joran noticed that he didn't feel the extreme cold like everyone else. Barring The Green Leaf, who cocooned himself in magic to keep warm on the snowy slopes, Gallien, Cob, and Androma trekked for days with their cloaks pulled close, scarves bundled into their hoods, and no lack of discomfort on their faces—all of which were speckled with ice and snow.

Joran wouldn't have called it pleasant, but it wasn't unpleasant either. His tolerances aside, he was overjoyed to be somewhere in the world—anywhere—that meant he didn't have to hide who he was. His pointed ears found their way through his shockingly white hair and his violet eyes went ever high to take in the mountain tops.

Of course, he wasn't entirely free. When they camped and he closed his eyes to rest, he saw all those men being pulled apart by the beast. The same beast who hunted him. Joran didn't need to see The Dawn Sword to know he was out there, somewhere, coming for him. What man could stand up to that?

"Why is he called The Dancing Sword of the Dawn?" he felt forced to ask, the first of their voices to be heard in some hours.

Androma turned to regard him, her legs buried up to her knees in snow. "It's taken from Andaren scripture—from The Arkalon." The old Rider paused, swallowing to clear her throat and soothe the hoarse tone. "The Dancing Sword of the Dawn was an Andaren warrior from their first epoch. He is widely considered to be the greatest warrior to have ever lived. He rallied armies behind the gods and even died fighting the Eikor beside the god, Ahnir. It is a title that should be reserved for a hero. Not a violent brute."

Seeing her plough on, Joran took up pursuit so he might ask more questions. "He named *himself* after this hero?"

"Possibly," Androma entertained. "It's more likely his masters bestowed the title upon him. He's a religious zealot. Gifting Slait such a title would be an easy way to buy his loyalty and take advantage of his beliefs."

Joran's mind, again, conjured images of the monster slaughtering so many men. "He was... He seemed unnatural." He felt foolish saying as much, ever aware of his own unnatural existence.

"How human of you," Aphrandhor remarked, his tone even and without judgement. If anything, the wizard looked a touch amused.

"To any Andaren," Androma explained, "Slait's natural state has simply been adjusted."

"*Mutated*," Aphrandhor interjected, his tone—this time—suggesting that he was trying to be helpful. "It's all about perspective."

"Yes," Androma said forcefully, suggesting the wizard should keep his opinions to himself. "To a human, Slait would be considered unnatural. As are all the Vahlken."

Joran almost paused in his step. "Slait was a Vahlken?"

"Only in body," the old Rider replied. "He survived Handuin's magic and completed much of his training at Ka'vairn. But he never earned the title," she informed.

"He knew my mother?" The question simply escaped Joran's lips.

"He did," Androma answered. "They were bound by the same

order once. From what she told me, they were never friends. Barely allies. After his disgrace, he was recruited by the Skaramangians. His belief in the words of The Arkalon made him ripe for the picking."

"He is no more than a tool then," Joran concluded, as if thinking of the beast that way would make him any less formidable.

"He is a weapon," Androma corrected. "But we have weapons of our own."

For just a moment, Joran wondered if she was referring to him.

"Look," Gallien called out, his voice not far behind.

Joran followed the smuggler's gaze up to the clouds that drifted across the mountains. The last of them were clearing to the west and, like a curtain being pulled aside, it revealed the top of a mountain in its wake. Joran's lips parted and his neck craned all the more as he took in the majesty and sheer magnitude of Mount Kaliban.

It was a familiar name, though predominantly spouted by The Gilded. How many times had Joran passed through the streets of any town or city and heard their sages shouting scripture over the masses, always speaking of Kaliban's awesome power, the power of the one true god? The boy had naturally adopted Gallien's disinterest and overall passive faith. Seeing the mountain named after the god, however, was something else entirely.

It stood defiant against even the hardiest of adventurers, its black rock, walls of ice, and sharp slopes ready to claim any and all. Nothing could move it and no one could conquer it. That sounded like a god to Joran.

"We have to go over that?" he asked, his wonderment mixed with uncertainty.

"We go *round* it," Aphrandhor replied from the front. "Once we make that ridge," he explained, his staff pointing up the slope, "the path will become clear again. It will also go *down*," he added with some relief in his tone.

"Once on the other side," Androma said, coming up on Joran's right, "we can continue our journey north."

"To Drakanan," he concluded, his voice just heard over the wind.

Androma paused, her staff as buried in the snow as her knees. "Yes," she confirmed.

"We must rest here," Cob informed them all, the Kedradi further out from their procession.

"What is it?" The Green Leaf enquired.

Cob crouched and further examined the disturbed snow that ran parallel to the group. "Ydrits," he reported gravely. "Two of them."

The wizard immediately set his eyes to the slopes about them. "They are ahead of us?" he asked.

"Yes," the Kedradi replied, standing with his bow in hand. "If we rest now we will likely avoid them. Continue and we risk them catching our scent."

"What's an Ydrit?" Joran had to ask.

"Bad news," Gallien opined, his boots ploughing through the snow to bring him closer to Joran.

"The White Bears," Cob answered.

"That's what I said," Gallien quipped.

"Ydrits *eat* bears," Androma added ominously, as if their colloquial name was absurd. "And they are notorious for hunting their prey across many miles. I am inclined to agree with the ranger."

"As am I," the wizard announced. "The ridge can wait until tomorrow."

On a barren plateau of scattered rocks and snow, the company gathered around the fire Aphrandhor had produced with a mere word. The flames crackled as the stars made their first appearance in the distant east. Considering it had been talk of monsters that had brought the group to a halt, they all seemed rather relaxed to Joran.

"Shouldn't I have a sword?" he declared to no one in particular.

"A sword is a burden," Gallien said, his knees up to his chest. "It weighs down the mind. Makes you stop and think about using it when you should be running. You just concentrate on keeping one foot in front of the other."

Responding with action over words, Cob stood up and drew his great scimitar of bone. "There is yet light in the sky," he observed. "I would see how much Vahlken there is in your blood."

Gallien's head snapped up. "He asked for a sword not a lesson."

"What use is a sword if he can't wield it?" the Kedradi countered.

"And he's to wield *that* is he?" the smuggler went on, nodding at the heavy weapon.

"A Dragon Rider fights with silvyr," Androma spoke up, her voice coarse from hours of disuse. "But they *train* with steel."

"I think we're getting ahead of ourselves," Gallien interjected.

"What does *Joran* think?" the wizard posed, his question bringing an end to Gallien's protests.

Joran saw defeat in his protector's eyes, the smuggler well aware of what he was thinking. "I want to learn," he uttered.

"Then you may use my sword," Aphrandhor offered pleasantly. The wizard gripped the black scabbard and cleaved the air as he freed the blade.

Joran stood up and accepted the weapon, momentarily hypnotised by the reflection of flames dancing across the steel.

"Yalaqin," The Green Leaf breathed, naming the sword. "It means fire breather in the old tongue," he interpreted with pride.

Joran admired the light green leather of its hilt and the disc-shaped pommel that shone a brilliant silver in the firelight. It was also rather heavy, heavier even than Gallien's, a standard soldier's sword.

Cob moved, rounding Androma so that nothing stood between him and Joran. His shoulder cloak blew in the mountain wind, flapping blue and cream in an endless rhythm. His heavy dreadlocks flowed over his chest, partially concealing the patterned cuirass. How poised he looked, even with his sword held low.

Joran eyed his opponent's weapon. "Will the bone not break?"

The Kedradi flashed a smile. "This was the rib bone of a Draven," he said, twisting the hilt to display the crab-like claw at the tip of the sword. "They are native to Qalanqath—my homeland. The sharpest steel in the hands of the strongest man could not hope to dent it."

Gallien rocked back, a smug grin on his face. "Then how did you craft it into a sword, I wonder."

Cob's gaze never strayed from Joran—his challenger. "With patience," he answered flatly. "And the fang of a dragon."

It was all too brief, but Joran caught sight of a faint smile brightening Androma's face.

Movement in the corner of his eye was all the warning he had that their fight had begun. Cob came at him, his scimitar curling round and up before cutting down. Speed had ever been on Joran's side but damn if the Kedradi didn't move like a flash of lightning.

Rather than dash away or roll deftly to the side, Joran could only fall back and spread his legs to avoid the blade of bone as it bit into the snow and rock. Gallien was unfolding his limbs almost immediately and would likely have intervened had Androma not held out her hand.

"As long as there is a weapon in Cob's hand, the boy will be safe," she assured.

Joran scrambled to his feet, wholly disagreeing with the old Rider's statement. As Cob advanced again, Joran thrust ahead with Yalaqin only to have his blade batted aside. The Kedradi's second blow came down swift and hard, knocking the wizard's sword from his hand altogether. Retrieving it was impossible given the sharp piece of bone resting under his jaw.

Cob walked forwards, the edge of his sword pushing Joran back with each step. "You strike without thought," he chastised. "What would that thrust have done?" he asked, his free hand slapping the steel of his cuirass. "You have not the strength to pierce my armour nor the precision to strike at the gaps."

Joran opened his mouth to offer an explanation, if not a protest, but held on to his words when the Kedradi retracted his weapon and flicked Yalaqin with the tip of his boot, offering Joran a chance to grab the hilt.

"Again."

Joran felt he was ready this time, his focus homed in on his opponent. Cob's feet made powerful strides, taking him one way then the next before he leapt into a twist. Joran hunched, Yalaqin held firmly in both hands while he tried desperately to decipher where the attack would come from. Deciding the scimitar was coming down on him again, he raised the wizard's blade to defend himself.

He was wrong.

Partially hidden by his heavy battle skirt, Cob's feet crossed over each other as his hips turned, leaving his weapon out of the fight altogether. Instead, his boot shot out and caught Joran in the chest, launching him from his feet.

He heard the sound of steel clattering on the ground before his back met earth in a hard collision, robbing him of more breath. He could only groan as the Kedradi slowly approached.

"You are not a tree," Cob informed him needlessly. "Yet you stand as if you are rooted to the ground. To fight is to dance!" he exclaimed, revealing some of his fervour for combat. "You must be light on your feet, always moving."

Joran clenched his jaw and forced himself back to his feet. The second Yalaqin was firmly in his grip, he pivoted and lashed out with a backhand that should have sliced through Cob's arm. The Kedradi wasn't there, of course, having darted back a step. He watched the steel swing past by no more than a couple of inches before dashing in to deliver his own attack.

A dive and roll gave Joran some space, though not much. He came up and raised his sword to block an incoming blow that never landed, the Kedradi's angle of attack altered at the last moment. Instead, the flat of the bone blade hammered into the Joran's thigh, staggering him.

"You must learn all that can be done with a blade if you are to anticipate all that can be brought against you," Cob instructed.

Joran shook his injured leg and braced himself for the next

attack. Cob began to prowl like an animal, his feet moving sporadically every now and then. Joran mimicked him, ready to face the Kedradi head on.

"Do not move to the rhythm of your enemy," Cob warned. "Find your own rhythm and use it to put your opponent off balance."

Demonstrating as much, the Kedradi darted forwards and low, skidding by Joran's side with his scimitar swinging out. For all his speed, Joran failed to anticipate the attack and evade it. Fortunately, Cob again brought the flat of his blade to bear and struck him across the right leg. For the second time, he felt the hard embrace of the cold earth.

Pain and humiliation opened a pit of anger and frustration inside Joran. Without a groan this time, he pushed himself up and charged at the Kedradi. Cob avoided the first two swings of Yalaqin with little more than footwork and a shift in his posture. The third he blocked with his scimitar, the steel loudly knocking against the adamantine bone.

There was no fourth attack, Joran forced to retreat now as he deflected and blocked Cob's retaliation. After successfully defending himself against an astonishing five blows, Joran leaned into his anger a little more and came back swinging the wizard's blade in two hands. The Kedradi slipped past every swing, pivoting one way then the next before slapping Joran around the back of the head.

"Your emotions give you strength," he said. "They can see you through pain and hardship. They can keep you on your feet when you should already be dead. Use them, but never let them guide the path of your sword."

Panting for breath, Joran could only shrug his shoulders. "How in the hells am I supposed to do *that*?"

"Training," the Kedradi stated simply enough. "Then swordplay is second nature and requires little of your mind."

Seeing Cob raise his scimitar in both hands, Joran resumed his battle stance, the tip of Yalaqin pointed at the Kedradi. Again, his opponent struck first, his style undoubtedly aggressive. By the third attack, Joran's defence was cast aside and his torso exposed.

"Enough!" Gallien barked, on his feet now, his cloak of brown leather flapping in the wind.

Cob tilted his head to lay dark eyes on the smuggler. "You believe he has had all the training he requires?" he asked sceptically.

"We never said anything about training," Drakalis pointed out. "We agreed to go to Drakanan because Joran would be safe there. That's all. He doesn't need training."

"Gallien," Joran intoned, embarrassed. It was only days ago since the smuggler had promised to stop speaking for him; that they would make sense of their path and future together. How quickly he returned to his overbearing self.

"Are we even safe there?" Drakalis questioned, his temper fuelling him now. "Should we be worried about this *Baelon*?"

"No," Androma answered.

Gallien looked far from convinced. "He had Galahart damned concerned. The king's spymaster! Maybe we should think about going somewhere else."

The latter was aimed at Joran, but he gave no response verbal or otherwise as he sensed the lines between them shifting, placing Gallien on the other side and alone at that.

Androma kept her face pointed at the fire, her staff resting over her lap. "One step at a time, Gallien. First, let us reach Drakanan and reassure you that we will be safe there. We will only talk of training should Joran bond with an egg—which he *will*," she vowed.

Like before, when hearing of his potential future—seen at the expense of thousands of lives—Androma's words were so overwhelming as to numb the boy. He didn't know what to think or feel about something as outlandish as *destiny*.

And yet...

Joran could feel a sense of excitement growing in him. Was there anything more extraordinary than a Dragon Rider? The

Kedradi came close, he suspected but they couldn't boast having a dragon for a companion.

Then there was the other thing that had been niggling at the edges of his thoughts. As he was, humans and Andarens alike would reject him—an abomination The Dawn Sword had called him. So hated was he, for naught but being born of two worlds, that both worlds would happily kill him. But who could challenge him with a dragon at his back? All of Verda would be forced to accept him, to see him as more than the sum of his parts.

Since Gallien looked to be on the verge of renewing his argument, Joran returned Yalaqin to Aphrandhor with a quiet thanks and a short nod of the head to Cob. His movement was enough to give Drakalis pause which, in turn, gave Joran the time he needed to sit beside Androma.

"Who *is* Baelon?" he asked, his voice a light balm compared to Gallien's northern delivery.

Androma tilted her head to regard him, her fingers faintly tapping against her leg. "He is the oldest of the Riders," she began. "He wasn't always, but he..." Her mouth twisted and contorted while she collected her thoughts. "He challenged the Dragonlord for the title and won. His challenge was folly, we knew. There were none among us who could hope to beat Rhaymion.

"By then, of course, Baelon had turned others to his beliefs. While they duelled for the right to rule, those loyal to Baelon ambushed Rhaymion's dragon, Aila. They slaughtered her. Rhaymion felt her death through their bond and it broke him. That was when Baelon struck, the coward. He crowned himself Dragonlord after that."

"That's terrible," Joran whispered, though he couldn't imagine what it felt like to be so connected to another being that he knew the moment they had died. "Why did Baelon challenge Rhaymion?"

Androma's knuckles paled around the staff. When her hands finally relaxed, her shoulders followed suit and sagged somewhat. "Long ago," she explained, "when the written word was young, the Dragon Riders swore their allegiance to the king of Erador. The

Dragonlord was to be our commander and they answered only to the king. We kept the peace. We fought in the wars. We upheld the king's law."

The old Rider sighed, her mind weighed down by memory it seemed. "Centuries later, and the war with Andara began to reduce our numbers," she continued. "It shocked us all to lose so many. For Baelon, though, it was the beginning of a fire he couldn't put out. He and others within our ranks believed our allegiance to the king was to blame. They thought we were being thrown into a mismanaged war, our strategies discarded in place of those who had the king's ear.

"It created a schism within the order. On one side, Baelon and his followers wished to forsake their oaths to the throne and stand independent. On the other, many, including Rhaymion and myself, wished to remain loyal and continue fighting as we had sworn to do."

"A civil war," Joran surmised, astonished to hear of such a thing. The Dragon Riders were the proclaimed heroes of the realm, praised almost as much as Kaliban Himself.

"Our numbers truly dwindled after that," Androma uttered. "Those of us who remained loyal to the king were forced to take up stations along the coast, so we could ward off invasion. Without dragons in the war, Erador suffered heavy losses again and again. It was fortunate that the Vahlken were in a similar position, their ranks reduced after so much war. At least," she added, "that's how the king saw it. No one knew back then that the Vahlken could have been our greatest allies."

"You know the *king*?" Joran queried, a thread he had wanted to pick up since meeting the second Galahart.

"I *knew* the king," Androma specified. "This was fifty years ago, Joran, and he was an old man then. I never met his successors before..." She licked her lips and started again. "It has always been tradition that a newly knighted Dragon Rider accept the king's invitation to dine with him in Valgala. It's likely been forgotten after all this time." Perhaps sensing the source of his question, the old Rider added, "Truthfully, I don't know why the king would meet you. Who can say how much he knows about the Skaramangians or what was seen through the Helm of Ahnir?"

He probably wants me dead like everyone else, Joran thought, his dark opinion kept to himself.

"What's Baelon been doing for the last fifty years?" Gallien interjected, his concerns ever present.

"I have no idea," Androma replied. "The last time I saw him was forty years ago." Her last few words had come out as a clipped statement, spoken from an emotionless place. "Whatever his plans, he is in no rush apparently. We have time."

"Time before he comes for the eggs?" Gallien pressed, reminding them all that even Drakanan had a shadow coming its way.

"Yes," Androma said forcefully, intending to put the issue to bed.

"It has always surprised me," Aphrandhor commented, his hands preparing a fresh pipe, "that he and his followers haven't flown to Aran'saur and burned the city to the ground. You said he would often speak of such swift and simple strategies to end the war."

Androma was nodding along. "Perhaps his attention has been diverted from the war. Who can say? He was blood drunk long before I met him."

Joran looked to Androma then, eager to ask her how old she was—how many centuries she had witnessed. Noting her appearance now, her wrinkles and short grey hair, it was painfully clear that she was no longer immortal. The obvious conclusion—though he couldn't say for certain—was the loss of her dragon. His questions would have to pile up.

"What if you're wrong?" the smuggler posed. "What if Baelon arrives at Drakanan the very next day?"

"He will have to go through my friend first," Androma told him confidently.

"From what I've heard he probably will," Drakalis remarked, his fear bubbling over.

"She will not be easily cast aside. Nor her dragon—the *largest* of his kind," she added ominously.

Gallien made a sound of dissatisfaction and shook his head.

Joran took the opportunity while his would-be father fumed. "Your dragon," he said softly. "You lost him in the... civil war?"

Androma sat eerily still. "I didn't *lose* him. He was *taken* from me."

Joran waited a beat before continuing. "What was his name?"

For just a moment, it appeared Androma was to rebuke him, perhaps harshly so. "His name..." she echoed softly, her rising ire seemingly extinguished. "His name was... *Maegar*." The dragon's name left her lips with a hint of affection.

Joran began to ask his next question when the old Rider cut him off.

"I'm sorry, Joran," she said coldly. "I just... I would leave it be."

Androma said nothing else, her gaze—had she one—fixed on the flames. Joran understood. Years on and her grief was yet to ease, it seemed. Joran couldn't relate, but he could empathise, and so he offered a brief apology and turned his own gaze on the fire.

With the last of the evening light quickly fading, he looked back and up at the ridge they were to cross. Destiny was fast approaching.

51
THE ENEMY OF MY ENEMY, IS MY FRIEND

40 Years Ago...

"The Dragonlord is dead?" Ilithranda asked, taking the question right out of Daijen's mouth.

Androma was standing in the curve of her dragon's neck, her hands probing the damage wrought by Vander's dragon, Herragax. "Yes," she confirmed, despite having only just told them of recent events and the Riders that had hounded her.

Ilithranda shared a look with Daijen. "You're at war with yourselves," she muttered with great revelation.

"If only it were just ourselves," Androma replied dryly, wincing in pain as she overstretched her right arm.

"We shall have no more war today," Daijen said, feeling the faintest of spray from the crashing waves.

"War requires two agree to those terms," Androma retorted, glancing over one shoulder.

Daijen regarded his slaiken blade, several feet away. "I'm content to keep talking if you are."

The Dragon Rider turned from her wounded companion to face

the Andaren. "Keep talking?" she echoed incredulously. "Who *are* you? You're like no Vahlken I have ever met."

"Have you ever met a Vahlken you didn't try and kill?" Ilithranda commented flippantly.

Androma looked her square in the eyes. "The fact that I am standing before you would suggest I never *tried* anything."

Ilithranda's jaw became a knot of tense muscle. "I just killed a dragon without getting a scratch," she said threateningly, "and yours looks to be half dead."

At that, the blue dragon raised its head, defying its injuries so it might place Ilithranda in its gaze. What strength there was behind those eyes, black slits crowned with gold. He exhaled a sharp jet of hot air through his nostrils and displayed just a hint of his deadly fangs.

"Maegar understands your every word, Vahlken. I would caution against letting them just fly out of your head like that."

Ilithranda took a step forwards. "You can shove your caution right up your dragon's—"

"Easy," Daijen interjected, his tone enough to prevent his sister from charging the Rider. "We need not be enemies," he continued, looking directly at Androma now, though he did spare Maegar a fleeting glance.

The Rider frowned. "That's all we've ever been," she pointed out.

"And what's left of us now?" he countered. "We've killed each other to near extinction. A dragon is alive today because of our... *alliance*," he dared to call it.

"I'm not sure it counts when it comes at the price of another," Androma argued.

Ilithranda saw her moment for another barbed comment. "We should have let them tear you apart, as they did your Dragonlord?"

"Rhaymion was a good man!" Androma insisted, her anger mirrored in Maegar, who let loose a thunderous rumble from deep in his chest.

The dragon's reaction alone would have been enough to rob

any of their courage, but not Ilithranda. "If he'd had us by his side and not you, he might still be alive," she spat.

Androma raised her hand, absent any sword. It was a clear threat, for not even the Vahlken knew what sorcery she could conjure from thin air. There came no such response, however, the Rider's hand bearing her palm alone.

Beneath the concealment of his cloak, Daijen let go of his atori blade. "Enough," he intoned, speaking to both.

Androma lowered her hand while Ilithranda allowed her sabre to drop fully into its scabbard.

"I'm sorry your order has fallen into disarray," Daijen began again. "I'm sorry you've lost people close to you. We too have suffered great losses at the hands of our own. Let it not be a wedge but a pain we *share*."

Androma looked up at Maegar and said nothing despite the inexplicable moment that passed between them. "We appreciate your aid," the Rider eventually announced. "And we appreciate your... *presence* while on your side of the line. But we must know: why have you not attacked us where so many of your order have before?"

Daijen couldn't answer for his kin, though he imagined they were all in situations much like theirs had been while facing Gregorn and his dragon. Either that or they had lost sight of the *real* war and had embraced war with Erador for too long. Daijen hadn't got into the war for the sake of war itself nor his opportunity to prove himself and flex his abilities.

He intended to *end* it.

"We were never supposed to be enemies," he told her.

"Daijen," Ilithranda warned, well aware of the truth he was about to divulge.

"We can't keep killing each other," he told her firmly. "In fact," he went on, turning back to Androma, "we share an enemy, one that would pit us against each other. They have done so quite successfully," he added.

Androma's pain seemed to melt away as she stood a little

straighter, her blue eyes fixed on the Vahlken. "You know about *them*," she uttered.

Daijen made to speak but his surprise got in the way. Instead, he looked to Ilithranda as if he needed reassurance that Androma had actually spoken the words.

"*You* know about *them*?" Ilithranda replied.

Androma paused, taking the measure of both Vahlken before sharing another moment with Maegar. "The Skaramangians," she said at last, almost testing the word on the air.

Daijen had never heard the name from any but a handful and never from a human. It seemed unimaginable that the human would be a Dragon Rider, they who had remained beyond the Skaramangians' corrupting reach and always on the sharp end of their king's commands. They were also the Skaramangians' main target, making them the last people they would want knowing about them.

"How do the Riders know of them?" Daijen asked, his investigative mind shifting into control.

"How do *you* know of them?" Androma countered suspiciously.

Before Ilithranda could argue again, Daijen spoke up. "The Vahlken stand against the Skaramangians. It's why we were made."

Confused, the Dragon Rider sat down on a rock beside Maegar. "We always thought you were..." Androma shrugged, perhaps unsure what exactly her order had long believed. "You've known about the Skaramangians for centuries?"

"Yes, since the days of Handuin, our founder."

"Daijen," Ilithranda warned again, ill at ease with sharing such information.

The Vahlken turned to lay eyes on her. "This only works if we trust each other."

Ilithranda absorbed his response and refrained from further interjection.

"Our war with the Skaramangians was interrupted by war with Erador," he continued.

"A war they manufactured," Androma replied, filling in the rest of the information.

Her depth of knowledge gave him pause. "That's right," he said at length. "They had you invade Andara and lay siege to Tor Valan."

Androma sighed, her gaze drifting out beyond the crashing waves. "I wasn't part of the invasion, but I'm sorry for our part in destroying Tor Valan." The Rider looked up at Maegar before nodding her head. "There is only myself and one other Rider who know of the Skaramangians. We have tried to warn the others but our civil war has made that near-impossible. I told Rhaymion the morning of his duel with Baelon," she lamented.

"How did you come to hear of the Skaramangians?" Daijen queried, keen to find the root.

Androma didn't answer right away, her belief in their sincerity reserved it seemed. "A wizard—one of the Jainus."

"The Jainus are in league with them," Ilithranda was quick to point out.

"Aphrandhor is a friend," the Rider insisted. "He is young, yes, but wise beyond his years. More importantly, he is a good man. There aren't many of those left."

"This Aphrandhor," Daijen questioned, "how did *he* come to know so much?"

"Most Skaramangians aren't told the truth," Ilithranda added.

"Not all of the Jainus are in their pocket," Androma answered. "In fact, he tells me their numbers are few amongst the wizards. Aphrandhor, however, was part of a group assigned to The Silver Trees of Akmar." Seeing two blank pale faces looking back at her, the Rider expressed some revelation. "You don't know about Akmar," she reasoned.

"I have heard the name," Daijen confirmed, his memory recalling the map of Erador he had meticulously studied.

"You really don't know," the Rider said in disbelief. "That's why the Skaramangians started the war between us," Androma stated, emptying Daijen's mind of clear thought. "We have one of your *gods*," she informed.

Daijen blinked. "You have a skeleton," he blurted, thinking of Ahnir in God Fall and the skeleton Mordrith had uncovered beneath the mountains.

"The Skaramangians have wanted it for centuries but the Jainus guard it. They had hoped the war would push the boundaries back and the Silver Trees would fall under Andara's rule. That obviously hasn't happened."

Ilithranda was shaking her head. "No," she muttered. "They started the war to eliminate the threat of dragons."

Androma's expression relayed how idiotic that sounded. "If they wished to eliminate the threat of us then they shouldn't have started a war with us."

Daijen recalled his master's words from years earlier, that war served many purposes if one knew how to wield it. "It's all connected," he announced, seeing how the enemy might use the war to accomplish all of their goals at once. "The bones of the gods imparted magic to us. They seek *more*. With more magic they would be that much closer to their ultimate goal of resurrecting the Eikor. Perhaps dragons are a threat to the Eikor," he posed, though every legend and religious scripture spoke of the gods being the only ones capable of destroying the Eikor, and powerful though they were, dragons couldn't claim to be gods.

"The Eikor?" Androma asked.

"The Dark Ones," Daijen replied, his mind racing ahead.

"From your Arkalon," the Rider realised, bringing out a raised eyebrow from Ilithranda. "I read it a long time ago," she reported.

"Wait," Daijen cut in. "The wizard, Aphrandhor. You said he was assigned to the god—to the *bones*," he quickly corrected. "How did this reveal the Skaramangians?"

Androma appeared somewhat uncomfortable then. "That's a little more complicated. He was part of a team assigned to examine a relic, an artefact found amongst the bones." The Rider paused, her attention flitting to her scaled companion.

Maegar was rising to his feet, his sharp eyes cast out to sea.

Along with the others, Daijen followed the dragon's gaze to the south. As Maegar let loose a growl, Valyra and Oaken began to squawk, their talons scraping against the rocks.

Two dragons were on approach.

"Friends?" Daijen asked, the pair too far away even for his eyes.

"It's Vander," Androma said with disdain. "He returns with..." The Rider trailed off and looked up at her dragon as if she had misheard something. "*Baelon*," she uttered.

Daijen quickstepped to ascend the highest rock, his knee braced at waist height while he set his eyes to the approaching dread. They were flying in fast, the sun just catching the side of Herragax to reveal his scales of blood red. The other eventually came into focus, and with the infamous Baelon astride.

"That's a big dragon," Daijen whispered to himself, thankful that none could hear his apprehension over the waves. "Baelon's dragon?" he called over one shoulder.

"Kalaghan," Androma named him. "He's as old as Baelon. That's nine hundred years of hunting and killing you can't match. Leave him to us."

Ilithranda was running for Oaken's side. "We work together!" she cried back to the Rider.

"Wait!" Daijen shouted, halting Oaken and Ilithranda from taking to the air.

The two dragons had changed course, dipping to the east so they could follow the high shore line and glide the rest of the way. It wasn't an attack run—too slow, too obvious. It didn't stop Maegar from moving off where his wings might find some space away from the cliff face. On all four legs, his injuries were quite apparent, including a tail so badly ravaged that it was no longer whole.

Kalaghan fanned his wings high, taking all the speed out of his approach. So large was the dragon that he eclipsed Herragax, dominating the rocky shore. Enormous and intimidating as Kalaghan was, the dragon remained a beauty among creation. His scales were a dark honey speckled with bronze and silver. Between bright viridian eyes he displayed a singular horn, as if the two he had been born with had amalgamated into one black mass that curved back and up to the top of his skull.

His landing was felt along the rocky beach, shortly followed by Herragax, her long neck arching through the air to bring her head into view. Kalaghan came no closer, standing defiantly and notably taller than Maegar. Instead, the two Riders dismounted, making the jump down to the rocks and puddles.

Vander danced effortlessly across the rise and fall of rocks to meet Baelon's side. The red scales of his vambraces and pauldrons clashed with the yellow of Baelon's, who advanced ahead of his billowing cloak. Like Vander's and Androma's, it was a dusky sand colour that projected a sense of peace and humility, the very opposite of what the two men actually represented.

Daijen tilted his head to try and see anything of Baelon's features, but his face remained hidden beneath the lip of his hood.

Deciding he would walk out and meet the pair, the Vahlken stepped off his rock and approached with his hand resting on the hilt of his sabre. By his side, Androma was already wielding her sword of brilliant silvyr, reminding Daijen that he had returned his slaiken blade to Valyra's saddle during the Rider's tale. Ilithranda chose an even more aggressive path, guiding Oaken from her saddle so she might look down upon the Riders from behind her Aegre's armoured beak, the plates smeared with dragon blood.

Meeting somewhere in the middle, the group came to a natural stop. Baelon was a tall man, though not so tall as the Vahlken, and his pauldrons lent him a wide and imposing frame that exhibited strength. The sword on his belt was identical to Vander's and Androma's, the pommel tipped with a silvyr dragon's claw.

Both of Baelon's hands came up to find the rim of his hood and draw it back. Revealed was an aged man with grey trimmed hair and a short beard to match. He bore a single scar that ran up from his collar to touch the right side of his jaw.

"*Switching sides, Androma?*" he questioned in man's tongue. "*What would your precious king say?*" His voice was commanding, full of rich life and experience.

"*Your blade is still stained with Rhaymion's blood and you've the nerve to stand before me?"* Androma retorted, her injuries and pain replaced by the urge to fight.

"*Nearly five hundred years and you still fail to grasp our ways,*" Baelon replied, taking no heed of Oaken's overbearing form. "*Dragonlords have been challenged for millennia and Dragonlords have died at the hands of their betters for millennia. Rhaymion had his time. Now it's mine.*"

"*You've broken our order!*" Androma spat. "*You've drawn a line right through the middle of us!*"

Baelon smirked. "*It's a little off centre actually. You'll find there's more on my side of the line.*"

"*You had Aila slaughtered!*" the Rider spat. "*That is* not *our way. If it had been a fair fight, Rhaymion would have parted you head from body.*"

"*Fair?*" Baelon echoed, the word ringing hollow on the air. "*Do you know how many Riders—how many dragons—have died because some king opened his mouth? How fair is it that we, the immortals, should lose that most coveted gift so the mortals can live, breed, and die in the blink of an eye? How fair is it that our wisdom should be swept aside in favour of fools younger than my boots? We should have the right to rule ourselves—if not Verda itself!*"

Androma looked beyond Baelon, to his dragon. "*How can you agree with this madness, Kalaghan? You have the wisdom of your mother flowing through your veins!*"

"*Would that be the same mother who died at the beginning of the war?*" Baelon countered, his attention slipping towards Ilithranda and her Aegre. "*The king declared war and like good little soldiers we obeyed. Kalaghan's mother and so many more have paid the price for that fatuity. Never again.*"

"*We are to keep order,*" Androma told him fiercely. "*The king's order.*"

"*We* are *order!*" Baelon snapped, his emotions rising to crash upon them like the waves that beat the shore. "*As Dragonlord, it is my responsibility to ensure our future,*" he continued, finding some measure of calm again. "*Your recklessness puts that in jeopardy. I cannot have rogue dragons and Riders flying around causing chaos.*"

"*You'll not put us down like dogs,*" Androma promised, her tone laced with fury.

"*I am not the killer you believe me to be,*" Baelon assured. "*I didn't come here seeking your death, or Maegar's.*"

"*And what were Vander and Gregorn sent to do? Talk to me with a sword in my gut? With Maegar's neck in Herragax's jaws?*" Androma scoffed. "*Perhaps you're right, Baelon. Maybe you aren't a killer after all. You just have others do it for you.*"

"*I came here to offer you one last chance,*" Baelon said through a tight jaw. "*Join me and build a golden age of peace. Or join Rhaymion and become little more than a footnote in history.*"

Daijen inserted himself into their heated conversation, his cool tone delivering a firm threat. "*I would make certain of the ground beneath your boots, Rider. You're on our land. You're in no position to present terms.*"

Oaken scraped his talons over the rocks. "*I would say you've overstayed your welcome,*" Ilithranda put to them.

"*I won't be told what to do by a mutant,*" Baelon said plainly, not even deigning to meet the Vahlken's eyes.

Ilithranda drew her slaiken blade and held it steady at her side.

Beyond the Riders, Kalaghan's top lip curled to reveal a sliver of fangs.

Baelon returned his attention to Androma. "*This is it then? You would ally with the enemy over your own kin?*"

"*I would form an alliance with an army of Trolls if they stood against you.*"

Baelon took a breath, his eyes roaming over Androma and Maegar, calculating. "*So be it.*"

Daijen braced, his sabre lifting ever so slightly from its scabbard. He was confident of his reflexes but not his foe—a nine-hundred year old Rider and dragon were an unknown quantity.

To the Vahlken's great surprise, Baelon raised his hood once more and turned on his heel. Vander followed his master with no more than a lasting look of venom aimed at Androma. Together, the Riders returned to their mounts and climbed up to their saddles.

"*I want you to know, Androma!*" Baelon called out. "*This could have gone very differently!*"

With that, the two dragons pushed off from the shore and took to the sky. Daijen watched them intently, making certain they flew ever eastward. Looking to his right, he caught sight of Valyra, her powerful legs still crouched and her wings still braced to launch her into action.

"Why are we not fighting?" Ilithranda had to ask.

Androma sheathed her sword. "Trust me," she said, switching back to Andarneese, "he craves the fight. He's been fighting longer than any of us. He lives for it."

"Then why aren't we fighting?" Ilithranda asked again.

"Baelon's a master strategist," the Rider explained. "He likes to play the long game." Androma glanced at Oaken and Valyra. "He likely didn't want to win at the expense of injury to Kalaghan."

"You should return to Ka'vairn with us," Daijen suggested, taking both Androma and Ilithranda by surprise.

"Daijen." Ilithranda's tone was low and full of caution.

"Is it not fate that we have been brought together?" he asked of his fellow Vahlken. "Two Riders know of the Skaramangians, Ilithranda. *Two.*" Daijen gestured to Androma. "One of them is standing right there and she knows things we don't. We've been their enemy since the beginning. We should know *everything*. The only way we're going to make a difference is with knowledge." He looked back at Androma. "That means working together and sharing what we know. Ka'vairn is safe, beyond Baelon's strategies. Come with us."

"Nowhere is beyond Baelon's reach," Androma corrected. "He cares nothing for the lines on the map. And with you at Ka'vairn there will be a gap in your defences here."

"They won't know that," Daijen replied. "Please, Androma. Come with us. We've been fighting the same foe. Why not fight them together."

"Because we *are* foes," the Rider pointed out.

"We don't have to be," the Vahlken argued. "If we can win the war with the Skaramangians we can end the war between our two peoples. *That's* the peace we're fighting for."

Androma said nothing to that. Instead, she held silent counsel with Maegar. Daijen could but watch and wait with anticipation, sure that he was pulling on a thread that would unravel the Skaramangian war machine.

"That," the Rider said at length, "is a peace *we* would fight for. We will fly with you to Ka'vairn."

Daijen offered her a warm smile. "To Ka'vairn."

Ilithranda guided Oaken to walk past her brother. "The Valtorak is going to kill you," she informed him, her tone light despite the gravity of her words.

Daijen nodded at the distant dragons, flying into the east. "He can get in line behind them."

52
ON THE HEELS OF FATE

FOR YEARS, KITRANA VODEN HAD LIVED ON THE SURFACE WORLD AND acclimatised to land and the dry air that surrounded it. Her years in captivity, however, had returned her body and mind to the way of water. Her skin craved it, needed it. Just the feel of swimming was freedom personified.

She thought of the freedom her fellow Nimeans were experiencing though. How many would trade their abhorrent existence for life on dry land? How many would even be alive by the time she had the sword of Skara in her grasp and reforged?

I'm alive, Kit reminded herself.

She had survived the Vorge, the Merdians, years of imprisonment, and since returning to the surface world she had faced Andarens, humans, and even a Three-Headed Dread Serpent. Then there was the Leviathan she had come face to face with, a monster so inherently wicked and dangerous that it had been locked behind an impenetrable set of doors.

If she could survive all that then there was *hope*. The odds she had already defied suggested the Water Maiden Herself was at work pulling the strings of fate. She just had to keep going.

That mentality had brought her to the most extraordinary place she had ever seen. "What is this?"

Yamnomora came up on her side with Bludgeon's reins in hand. "The Red Fields of Dunmar," the dwarf answered.

Kitrana could see why. The plains of grass stretching out around them were a reddish bronze. Scattered throughout were great mounds and hills of colourful flowers and exquisite trees that bent at seemingly impossible angles. It was more like a dreamscape than any real landscape. The Nimean had noticed that the further south they trekked the redder the grass became, with some patches a vibrant scarlet.

Climbing one of the hills, Kitrana set her gaze across the fields of long red grass blowing in the northerly breeze. Judging by how wrapped up the dwarves were, it was likely more than just a northern breeze to their skin. Kit couldn't feel the freezing bite, but it seemed the plants, trees, and grass couldn't either.

"Winter doesn't bother them," she observed, pausing to run her fingers around the golden petals of a flower she couldn't identify.

"I suppose it wouldn'," Yamnomora replied. "It weren' nature that did this."

Kit turned away from the flower to lay eyes on the dwarven warrior. "Magic?" The Nimean possessed a healthy fear of magic, a supernatural skill ocean dwellers had yet to unlock.

"Not the kind ye're thinkin' o'," the dwarf told her. "This here is... *dragon magic*," she said with a shrug.

Kit's brow pinched in confusion. "Dragons have magic?"

"I'm not for knowin'." Yamnomora gave a more exaggerated shrug this time. "I only know what Androma told me."

Kitrana shook her head. "Who's Androma?"

"None o' yer business, fish lady." The dwarf gave the Nimean a double take. "An' show some respect, eh? That's a dead dragon ye're standin' on."

Kit looked down at her feet, her bare toes partially buried in the red grass. "A dead..." She looked out across the vista, quickly losing count of the hills and mounds coated in flowers and trees. "They're all... They're all dragons?"

Yamnomora didn't even bother slowing down and Grarfath was only just reaching the base of the hill. "Aye! Dragons all," she confirmed.

"I knew this was the site of an old battle," Kit went on, "but I didn't realise there were so many..." She trailed off, her words taken by the number of flowered graves again.

"They called it Dunmar back then," Yamnomora called back. "They say it rained blood for three days." The dwarf made a show of looking around. "I'm inclined to believe it."

"There are Aegres too?" Kit queried, making short work of the descent.

"I'm sure there were, but this place were picked clean long before the first flowers started sproutin'. There'll be Aegre skulls in the halls o' every Blood Lord from 'ere to Qalanqath."

Grarfath paused to inspect one of the hills. "They buried the dragons?"

Yamnomora stopped to shoot her fellow dwarf a look of exasperation. "*No*, they didn't *bury* the dragons," she said with a tone to match her expression. "It's all part o' the magic that gets released or somethin' when they die." The dwarf threw her hands up. "I'm not an 'istorical archive," she complained. "An' the Rider I've travelled with weren' much o' a talker."

"You've travelled with a *Dragon Rider*?" Kitrana immediately asked.

"Aye, though ye'll be glad to know I've travelled with no-one stranger than yerself, fish lady. An' that's sayin' a lot."

"Did me mother travel with a Dragon Rider?" The smith jogged to catch up.

"Aye, we all travelled together." Yamnomora waved her hand through the air. "This is council business." Her copper hair flung to the left as her head swivelled towards Kitrana. "*Secret* business. It's not for the ears o' women who spring up out o' the ground. Ye handled yerself at the towers, so I'll tolerate ye followin' us around like a lost pup, but when we get to where we're goin', ye're to take those big eyes an' get lost."

The battle maiden had no such intention, but she wasn't going to make an argument of it. "I've never been this far north," she remarked, noting the block of mountains that capped The Spine of Erador. "How long will it take to reach Valgala?" The Nimean couldn't help but wonder if they had made a mistake leaving the road behind for, though it went west before going south, it most certainly found its way to the capital. They had veered off the beaten path and taken to wild country, making immediately south and on the wrong side of the mountains.

"As long as it takes," Yamnomora replied unhelpfully.

The dwarven warrior continued between the colourful hills for a few more steps before she began to slow down. When she came to a complete stop, she tugged on Bludgeon's reins, bringing the Warhog to a halt beside her. She looked down at her feet before looking over one shoulder to find Grarfath.

The smith had also come to a stop. "I feel it too," he said gravely.

Kitrana scoured the ground at her feet. "Feel what?"

Grarfath lowered himself to all fours, his expression pensive. It reminded the Nimean of the crossroads in Andara, when the dwarf had detected the...

Kit made a dash for the nearest hill, her powerful legs bounding to the very top. Unlike before, she turned her gaze north, back the way they had come.

"What do ye see?" Grarfath shouted up.

"Like ye need to ask!" Yamnomora spat. "Pick up yer feet! We're movin'!"

The battle maiden looked upon the army that had haunted them across two countries now. Andarens, fresh from their latest victory and ready for war, were marching across The Red Fields of Dunmar, a dark scourge on a bright canvas.

"You said we'd be safe leaving the road!" Kit barked, tearing her eyes from the advancing horde.

"An' we should've been!" Yamnomora countered, hurrying ever

southward. "How was I to predict they'd abandon the road? I thought they'd burn everythin' on their way down!"

Kitrana was running after the dwarves until her thoughts churned enough to stagger her steps. "They would. Any invading army would." She looked ahead, to the plains and snow-capped mountains. "Why would they come this way?"

"What?"

"Why would their army come this way? Why cut through empty country when you can find your enemy on the road? What's the advantage?"

Yamnomora finally stopped rushing off and stopped to face the Nimean. "There is no advantage," she claimed. "They'd be funnelled through The Giant's Throat an' then again along The Misted Road if they cut through to the capital. Unless they intend to attack Thedaria first, but there's no strategic advantage to that either. Unless..." The dwarf looked to have had a thought.

"What is it?" Kit pressed.

"Unless they were never sent to lay siege to Erador," Yamnomora posed.

Grarfath frowned. "Why else would an entire army invade?"

The dwarven warrior looked the smith dead in the eyes. "To steal somethin'."

The battle maiden shook her head. "You don't send an army to steal anything. Armies *conquer*."

"Unless ye're to steal somethin' that cannot be stolen," Yamnomora countered, her attention turning back to the south. "The Silver Trees of Akmar lie beyond The Giant's Throat. That's why they're 'ere. They've come for the bones," she muttered.

The last word caught Kitrana off guard. "Did you say *bones*?"

"The situation is far worse than I feared," the dwarf declared. "We need to move, *now*."

53
A RED DAWN

40 Years Ago...

It was a moment of historical significance that wasn't lost on Daijen Saeth. From astride Valyra, he looked out to the north and marvelled at the dragon flying beside him. Maegar's blue scales glistened thanks to the speckle of silver and gold, lending him an air of majesty as he rode the currents.

Seated in her saddle, secured by clips that fastened to her belt, Androma looked back at him. The Vahlken wondered if she too was dwelling on the importance of their companionship. Dragon and Aegre flying side by side, and over Andara at that. It was the first time their coming together hadn't resulted in blood rain.

Then there was Androma herself. Daijen enjoyed looking at her too, though not for any historical significance.

Maegar turned his mighty head to lay golden eyes on him. It was as if the dragon could read his mind, as if he could see the Vahlken's desires.

It was unnerving and more than enough to put any attraction far from his thoughts. Instead, he looked beyond Maegar, to

Ilithranda and Oaken. They were flying high, above the clouds so as to avoid being seen from the ground. The last thing they needed was word getting back to The Saible, or the emperor himself, that a dragon was being escorted into Andara by two Aegres.

They had flown through the day and night and now the dawn broke behind them, as if the light itself was chasing the trio. Before setting off from the shore, Daijen had shown concern for Maegar's injuries and his ability to fly. They had quickly proved unfounded. Indeed, Androma displayed her own resilience, requiring no rest or sleep on their journey.

In an effort to show off—or, at least, compound their strength in the face of Daijen's concerns—Maegar began to take the lead. His claws skimmed the clouds while his great wings buffeted them, creating wisps that curled about him. He was a sight to behold.

Daijen couldn't help but wonder how many Vahlken and Aegres had seen such a sight before their final moments. Nearly three hundred years of killing each other, he lamented. It had to end.

But it was not to be that day.

Kalaghan burst from the cloud bank like a shark from the depths of the ocean. His jaws snapped shut around Maegar's throat and his upward thrust sent both dragons into a dizzying spiral.

Daijen's reflexes kicked in with the beat of his heart.

The slaiken blade was in his grasp as Vander and Herragax exploded from the carpet of clouds. Valyra tucked in her wings and corkscrewed to evade the gnashing of Herragax's razored maw. They levelled out as Vander thrust his lance, a silvyr-tipped spear twice as long as a slaiken blade. The Vahlken was able to bat it aside and save himself, though the deflection caused the sharp tip to slice along Valyra's back leg.

The Aegre let loose a defiant squawk and immediately banked to the south to renew their battle.

With what little time he had, Daijen looked around to spy his companions. Ilithranda and Oaken were flying towards them, her slaiken blade flashing in the sunrise. Further west, Maegar and Kalaghan were wrestling for dominance, their fight taking them higher and higher. Both Androma and Baelon were wielding their dragon lances, scoring blows to the other's mount wherever they could.

It was like thunder in his ear when Oaken rushed past, reminding Daijen that Herragax was coming for him. Seeing Ilithranda, however, appeared to be some kind of distraction, for the red dragon angled away from Valyra and made for Oaken. It was likely revenge on Herragax's part, the dragon still feeling the sting of Ilithranda's axium attack.

"I'll distract him!" she bellowed. "Kill the other one!"

With that, Ilithranda pushed down on her handles, directing Oaken into an immediate dive. Herragax's head followed their descent and her long neck arched, taking the rest of her bulk and Vander beneath the clouds.

Having recently seen Ilithranda execute a dragon, Daijen was content to leave her to her work.

He guided Valyra into a tight arc and then had her climb to reach the warring dragons. They were clawing at each other's bodies and biting limbs and throats and jaws. It was a wonder they could do all that—delivering and receiving so much damage—and stay aloft. That was, perhaps, the reason for Androma's repeated attacks on Kalaghan's wing joints, her lance thrusting again and again.

With a moment to spare before entering their battle, Daijen looked down and saw fire erupting throughout the clouds. It tempted the Vahlken to descend and aid his sister. An ear-piercing roar returned his attention to the dragons. Kalaghan had Maegar's left wing in his jaws and his front claws were sinking into the dragon's already wounded ribs.

Daijen gritted his teeth and flattened himself to his saddle. With all her speed, Valyra launched them into battle.

A downward swing cut through Kalaghan's snout. The pain was enough to see the dragon detach his fangs from Maegar's flesh and even push off.

Now we're in it, Daijen thought, as they circled and began flying towards each other.

What he wasn't prepared for, however, was the dragon lance. It was almost imperceptible on its flight path and the distance it had been thrown seemed far beyond the capabilities of any human. Daijen bobbed his head at the last possible second. The lance struck the top of his right pauldron and sprang up, clipping his cheek and ear as it whistled past. The Vahlken's sudden movement sent Valyra into a banking left turn and directly into the path of Kalaghan's fire.

The super-heated jet of flames consumed Daijen's view and banished the cold air. It was up to Valyra to save them and she didn't disappoint. The Aegre tilted and flew down at an awkward angle that kept Daijen away from the flames. When they cleared the torrent of fire and surged past Kalaghan's tail, the Vahlken looked in horror to see that the end of her right wing was alight. Fortunately, Valyra's instincts were just as superior as her intellect and she knew to climb and flap her wings hard. Where the air was thinner, the flames lost their grasp on life and extinguished.

Daijen sighed with relief. Since bonding with Valyra, he had envisioned the fateful day they would be pitted against the dragons of men. Too many times he had imagined her being swallowed whole by fire. It was a harrowing nightmare, but one they had just survived. For now.

Kalaghan and Baelon were far from done. The dark yellow dragon came at them with blood-smeared fangs and a red tongue. Seeing that open maw flying up towards them gave Daijen an idea that saw him sheath his slaiken blade. As he envisioned the flight path they would need to take, his right hand brought the two vials of axium to bear. The vials were knotted together with a length of rope that the Vahlken could hold and swing over his head.

And swing it he did.

His aim was perfect, as Kastiek would have insisted. As the vials flew across the sky, Daijen pressed his limbs into Valyra's body, being careful to shift his weight into the required position to see them skirt between Kalaghan's head and inside wing. It was all for naught. The dragon's superior experience became evident when Kalaghan snaked his body, creating a ripple effect that allowed him to slip under the axium's descent.

Worse, the rope was snatched from the air by Baelon.

Aegre and dragon soared past each other in a flash of feathers and scales. Daijen had Valyra turn around as fast as she could, fearing what Baelon might do with axium at his disposal.

It was then that the Vahlken saw Maegar spearing towards Kalaghan. The blue dragon was all rage, his wounds and pain replaced with grit and raw fury.

Kalaghan twisted mid-flight, barrelling over Maegar's incoming head. It also brought Baelon round, inverting him in his saddle. As Maegar swept under them, the Dragonlord launched the axium as any Vahlken might.

The vials slammed into the blue dragon's head and shattered. The two liquids came together, exciting the magic therein. Given Maegar's speed, however, the liquids struck the crown of his head and splashed beyond.

Androma screamed.

Daijen watched in horror as she clawed at her eyes. It would do no good, he knew. All she would achieve was burnt fingers. But pain obliterated sense.

Androma wasn't the only one in agony. Maegar roared as the acid bit through his scales, exposing bloody flesh between his eyes and horns. There was nothing any of them could do to stop events from unfolding.

Yet to be satisfied, Kalaghan took advantage of the mayhem caused by the axium. The one-horned dragon had gone high after barrelling over Maegar's initial attack and was now swooping down. Daijen and Valyra were already on an intercepting flight path and would have collided with Kalaghan had Herragax not re-emerged from the cloud bank below.

Valyra squawked and manoeuvred to one side, narrowly avoiding the red dragon and the stream of fire that preceded it. Ilithranda and Oaken were only a second behind, giving chase it seemed, but their momentary interference was enough to prevent Valyra from reaching Kalaghan in time.

Daijen cried out as the yellow dragon clamped shut his powerful jaws around Maegar's neck. His fangs bit deep and Maegar's entire body spasmed under the brutal attack.

Then, all at once, the blue dragon went limp.

In a gruesome scene, Kalaghan adjusted the grip of his jaws and ripped the top half of Maegar's head away before pushing off from his dead body.

Clipped into her saddle and blind, Androma was suddenly attached to a falling corpse, her screams taken by the rushing wind.

Daijen didn't hesitate.

He jumped into nothingness, as he once had in pursuit of Slait.

Unlike then, he now moved to save instead of kill, a difference that changed everything.

Clearing Valyra, his shogue unfurled in his hand and the hook flew out as Maegar's body fell past them. The hook snagged around one of the dragon's claws and pulled Daijen into a much faster descent.

Leaving his Aegre behind, if not the heavens themselves, the Vahlken called upon every ounce of strength his hands could muster, though he certainly felt the strain in his shoulders.

With the need to progress along the length of rope, he dared to slide one hand after the other, bringing him closer to the dragon. His efforts were eased by Maegar's slow tumble, his body rotating out of control.

Daijen growled under his breath, the length shortening with every new rotation.

Androma came round again and again, her body being held by the two straps hooked to her belt.

Not yet.

Nearly there.

The clouds swallowed Maegar, robbing Daijen of sight. It was an agonising handful of seconds until they cleared them and were faced by the world again. They were hurtling towards the eastern edge of The Morthil Mountains, a dark line that snaked across the realm beneath them. It would happily greet them all.

Daijen cried out in frustration, desperate now.

If he didn't reach the saddle in time, Maegar would roll again and he would find the end of the rope on the wrong side of the dragon.

Tilted by his wings, Maegar was completing another tumble, stealing Androma from sight for a few seconds. The rope shortened again and Daijen pulled himself closer and closer.

Seeing her shock of blonde hair come back into view, the Vahlken loosened his grip and slipped back up the rope until she rolled into him.

With all the strain on one arm, Daijen reached out, his fingers searching desperately for Androma's saddle. He couldn't find purchase, the leather too smooth and rounded.

Time running out, he used Androma's belt to pull himself over. Every one of his limbs was then required to brace against the edge of the saddle in order to keep him secure.

Unconscious now, Androma floated above him, connected by two very taut straps. Without her help, the Vahlken had to make sense of the fastenings. It didn't help that Maegar was still rolling through the air and so much strength was required to keep himself from being flung free.

Unable to work the straps and clips that stopped him from freeing Androma, the Vahlken carefully reached around his belt to retrieve his dagger. He began sawing through one of the two straps, praying to every dead god that the ground was nowhere near them.

When the last thread succumbed to the dagger's edge, Androma's body tilted up on the right, her entire weight being held by the final strap.

Andara's unwelcoming earth was getting closer and closer—a fact he had to put to one side for now, lest the threat of it cripple his critical thinking.

Daijen roared in defiance, using every ounce of strength Handuin's magic had gifted him. He severed the strap in one clean swipe, freeing Androma from her saddle and Maegar's dead weight.

Still holding on to the Rider, Daijen held out one arm, his hand open and ready—a signal to Valyra. The Aegre had remained close, as he had predicted—if not expected—and made her swooping entrance, so he could grab his saddle. His arm ached from so much exertion, but it was do or die, a time when every Vahlken showed their quality. Valyra took the pressure off him almost immediately by gliding up, offering his body some much-needed support so he could pull Androma closer.

Looking over the edge of Valyra's flying form, Daijen could see that the mountains of Morthil were above them now. Then he heard Maegar thunder into the earth with an almighty impact.

"Down, Valyra!" he called.

The Aegre knew the command but was slow to respond, aware that she bore more than one rider. Daijen was thankful, feeling real fatigue for the first time in a while.

He let himself lie flat beside Androma for a time, his arm wrapped tightly around her waist. Only after Valyra touched down did he truly see her face, taking the time to examine the damage wrought by the splash of axium.

He carried her in his arms, his attention fixed on the burns across her nose, cheeks, and eyes. The latter were gone, the blue orbs and soft lids melted, scorched black. The ends of her fingers were similarly burnt, the nails and skin fused together.

But she was alive.

Daijen placed her on the ground and removed her cloak. He bundled it into a makeshift pillow before unclipping his fur cloak and draping it over her. A distant squawk turned the Vahlken's gaze skyward, where he spied Oaken flying down to meet them. Searching the sky beyond the Aegre, Daijen saw no sign of Herragax or Kalaghan.

Oaken landed at a run and came right up to where Daijen was standing. Blood was dripping from a wound somewhere on the Aegre's back half, near his left leg, though it didn't seem to be bothering the animal. One of the three talons from his front right leg was missing and the armour that plated his beak was scratched and dented. Ilithranda climbed down, jumping the last few feet to join Daijen—she was entirely unharmed.

"Is she alive?"

"Yes," he confirmed, sparing a glance at the rolling clouds. "Herragax?"

"They have fled east," Ilithranda reported with a scowl. "They got what they came for," she added, her attention now on the crater to the west.

"Maegar?"

The hoarse voice turned both Vahlken around. Androma was rising unsteadily, her left hand outstretched to feel for a world she could no longer see.

"Maegar?" she called out, her voice trembling now. "I can't feel him. I can't hear him..."

Daijen approached her. "Androma," he said softly.

The sound of his voice brought the Rider to him, her hands gripping the edges of his cuirass. "Daijen," she said with panic. "I can't feel him. Where's Maegar?"

"Androma—"

"WHERE IS HE?" she screamed in his face.

Daijen looked to Ilithranda for advice. She nodded, agreeing with his silent question.

"He's over here," the Vahlken told her, positioning her hand around his arm.

"Take me to him," Androma whispered.

Together, they walked the short distance to Maegar's resting place. There was a small rise in the earth where the dragon's impact had pushed the ground away, but Daijen was sure to keep Androma on flat ground.

"He's here," Daijen informed, forcing himself to look upon Maegar's ruin.

The fall had severed one of his wings and forced numerous bones through his scaled skin. The dragon's blood had exploded out of every wound and darkened the soil. What remained of his bottom jaw had shattered on impact, lending the appearance that Maegar had been decapitated.

Daijen was thankful Androma couldn't see him.

The Rider tilted her head. "He's so quiet," she observed, her voice breaking.

A surge of emotion overcame her then. Daijen was pushed aside as she scrambled and fell down the slope. Androma was soon smeared in Maegar's blood, a fact that only became worse when she tripped over everything. Using her hands, the Rider began to feel her way around him, a path that eventually brought her to his neck. Another wave of devastation washed over her upon feeling the bloody stump at the end. It broke her, bringing her knees to the wet ground.

Daijen barely knew the Rider, but Androma's unbearable anguish and utter despair brought tears to his eyes. He couldn't imagine spending five hundred years with anyone, but he could empathise all the more for having his bond with Valyra.

Wishing he could do something to alleviate her suffering, Daijen made to descend the crater.

Ilithranda stopped him, her hand pressed firmly into his left pauldron. "Let her grieve."

Daijen retracted his foot and remained on the edge of the crater, utterly helpless. They could do naught but listen to Androma's howling wail, to her heartbreak.

54
THE RUINS OF GELAKOR

Gallien kicked a stone over the edge and peered out to watch The Giant's Throat swallow it up. The rocky canyon was a snow-covered mouth that sat open at the base of the mountains, as if it were some monster always ready to devour the slim pickings discarded by Mount Kaliban.

It sent a shiver up his spine and saw him move away from the lip. He adjusted the scarf that filled out his hood and brushed some of the snow and ice from his thick beard. He would be a happy man if he never had to trek over The Spine again. Besides the bitter cold and lack of shelter, he couldn't get the Ydrits out of his mind, nor the reminder that they could track their prey for many miles and days.

If there was one thing a smuggler hated, it was the feeling of being watched.

"Please tell me we're not going down there," he said, nodding at the dizzying drop to his left.

"We will continue north up here," the wizard replied, his staff gesturing along the jagged edge.

Gallien looked ahead, envisioning their journey as if it were on a map. They would have to traverse the mountains and leave The

Giant's Throat behind before crossing The Red Fields of Dunmar if they were to see Drakanan in the far north. The smuggler adjusted his brown leather cloak. They still had quite the trek ahead of them.

He spied Joran in the lead of their group, walking shoulder to shoulder with Cob. Ever since their sparring session on the other side of the mountains, the pair had regularly fallen into private conversation.

"I thought Kedradi were bound by their traditions," Joran was saying, the first thing Gallien had heard of their talks. "Don't you have to use the bones of your enemies in battle?"

"We do," Cob confirmed. "My first kill was a rabbit—for food. I killed it with my hands and used its bones to hunt a fox. I used the fox's bones to kill a panther. I still bear the scars of that encounter," he added dryly.

"But your bow," Joran countered. "It's made from wood," he pointed out.

Cob smiled, flashing his white teeth. "I can assure you it is bone," he replied confidently. "I accepted a ranger's contract out of Allisander. There had been reports of a monster in The Greenfold."

"A monster?" Joran's voice was brimming with wonder, a fact which caused Gallien to roll his eyes.

"My hunt led me into the heart of the forest," Cob went on. "There I fought a Skalagat, a *forest knight*."

"A Skalagat," Joran repeated, testing the word in his mouth. "I've never heard of that."

"They are creatures of wood," the Kedradi explained. "They are trees given life that spread only death." The ranger gestured to the bow slung over his shoulder. "I carved this from its leg."

"Incredible," Joran stated, clearly hungry for more tales.

Gallien slowed down, allowing the pair to walk beyond his hearing. Though the potential subjects of their discussions troubled him, he wasn't blind to his own feelings. Jealousy could be corrosive if he didn't manage it well. For sixteen years, however, they had only had each other, and now Joran was surrounded by fascinating people who were all fascinated with him.

For miles they walked and for miles it sat heavily in Gallien's chest, like a weight he couldn't shift. The smuggler fantasised again and again about taking Joran away from all this. He chastised himself just as much when he considered how much better the boy's life could have been, had he found somewhere safe for them to put down roots when he was a child.

Seeing Joran step in beside Aphrandhor and begin a new conversation with the wizard, Gallien skipped across a couple of rocks to close the gap. He trusted magic users about as much as he trusted magic itself. The Green Leaf was a hooded figure of sage from behind, his belt laden with vials, inexplicable tools, and strange devices. For all that, Joran's opening question was apparently in regards to the staff Aphrandhor walked with.

"You recall my mention of Demetrium?" the wizard replied to the young man. "A most fantastical ore. There is only one mine in existence, just north of Sunhold. The Jainus guard it as they do The Silver Trees of Akmar—ardently. Without Demetrium we wizards would be a menace to society. Our magic would be dangerous—"

"Would be?" Gallien interjected, his mind conjuring the old memory of his brother's death. "Isn't it already dangerous?" he asked, despite Joran's protesting expression.

Aphrandhor merely glanced back at the smuggler, a bemused smile pulling at his long beard. "Undoubtedly," he answered ominously. "But without Demetrium our magic would simply burst out, as if we were tapping into a well we couldn't control."

"Is it in the staff?" Joran queried, his mind an all-consuming creature that hungered for knowledge above all else.

Gallien both loved and loathed that characteristic in him.

The Green Leaf gave a light chuckle. "Not in it. Around it."

The wizard pointed out three coils of dark bronze. The one at the bottom of his staff was thin and kept the wood bound to a point. The Demetrium placed around the neck of the staff, where the wood branched out to one side, was a mesh about the size of a sword hilt. The final piece he drew their attention to was coiled about one of the branches and secured with nails.

"It's a little... *homemade*, I'll admit. But after abandoning my position within the order, I was forced to discard my robes."

Joran frowned. "Your robes?"

"Yes. Deep within The Tower of Jain, where none can observe their skill, there dwells a group of tailors. They are able to weave the Demetrium into the very fabric of a Jainus's robes. Without their knowledge, I am forced to use other methods of control." The wizard stamped his staff cheerily into the snow at his feet.

"Incredible," Joran remarked, his violet eyes roaming The Green Leaf's staff.

Gallien opened his mouth, a sharp comment regarding wizards in general readied, when Androma called his name from behind. The smuggler held on to his words and turned back. The blind Rider was maintaining a good pace, her staff sweeping regularly to check the ground for hazards. In the rear, Cob had come to a halt. The Kedradi was looking back the way they had come, his face angled high to the slopes that rose up on the group's right. His bow was in hand.

"Gallien," Androma said again.

"I"m here," he replied, his voice bringing her to his side.

Somewhat slower than Aphrandhor and Joran, Androma's more cautious speed put some distance between them, allowing her to speak without being overheard. "Magic has hurt someone close to you," she began, her theory sound.

Gallien's jaw stiffened and required some focus to soothe the muscles. "My brother," he said simply.

Androma nodded along while casually slipping a hand under his arm. "You have my word, Aphrandhor's magic will never harm Joran."

"And yours?" he asked, recalling her display the first time they were greeted by The Dawn Sword.

"My magic is spent," she assured. "That night, when Slait came for the boy, I used up all that lingered."

It took some effort, but Gallien managed a quiet, "Thank you."

"We are all here to protect him, Gallien," the old Rider went on. "Just like you, we have chosen to do so."

Drakalis wasn't so easily swayed. "Our reasons couldn't be further apart," he told her bluntly. "You've all bought into this vision. Worse, you believe without a doubt that Joran was seen in it."

"He was seen," Androma insisted. "By ten thousand eyes."

"And they're all dead, yes? So how could anyone know the person they saw is actually Joran? They were coming after him when he was only a baby!" he hissed.

"He is the son of a Vahlken," the old Rider reiterated. "There has never been such a child, but also to be half human? These were all details seen through the helm. He isn't just an abomination to the Andarens. He's a *powerful* abomination. He has to be the one."

"He doesn't *have* to be anything," Gallien replied forcefully. "Unless they named him in this vision, he's as likely to be *the one* as any other half blood." The smuggler freed himself of her hand and sped up.

"Gallien," she called again, giving him pause.

He watched her intently, sure that she had something profound to impart. He waited with what little patience he had left.

Instead, Androma gave an exasperated sigh and nodded ahead. "When we reach Drakanan," she said, her tone suggesting she had chosen to say something else entirely, "you will not be permitted to accompany Joran inside."

"The hells I won't," he growled.

"None of us will be," Androma informed him, her staff back to scouting the uneven ground. "Myself included," she added sullenly. "Riders and deemed potentials only. We will camp nearby," she offered as a balm.

"You failed to mention this earlier," he fumed.

"Nevertheless," she replied, with little more than a shrug.

Gallien wanted to shout and rage—to think that anyone could part him from Joran! *Let them try*, he thought.

"We'll see," he grumbled before picking up the pace.

They walked beside the chasm until nightfall, when exhaustion demanded they rest. They were all too tired to converse that night, including Joran, whose youthful font of energy had finally reached its end.

They shared food and drink in silence, the wizard, as usual, avoiding any direct contact. Gallien thought to enquire as to why that was but, instead, the smuggler put his head down and got some sleep.

It wasn't long after the dawn broke the very next day that the realm opened up before the companions. Gallien could see the head of The Giant's Throat and the northern half of The Red Fields of Dunmar that stretched from The Spine of Erador to The Blooded Road, the only path to Andara. Light from the east cast the famous fields in a burnished gold, its many hills creating long shadows that leaned into the west.

Drakanan was still too far away to be seen, hidden within the northern haze. It wasn't far enough in Gallien's opinion. Then again, he would need the width of Verda itself to convince Joran of another path.

They spent most of the morning descending the tiers of rock that made up The Giant's Throat. Around midday, they reached the lowest tier at the very head of the rift, though it was still several hundred feet above the Red Fields of Dunmar, a forest dominating the land before it. Gallien only saw a sliver of the landscape, his attention quick to be engaged by the ancient ruins they were soon to reach.

"What *is* that?" he asked to anyone.

"The Ruins of Gelakor," Aphrandhor proclaimed. "Perhaps we might rest there before finishing the climb down?"

"I'm starving," Joran replied. "At least we'd have a view while we eat," he said with an enthusiastic grin.

It did nothing to shift Gallien's stony expression. "You're always starving," he quipped. "And who in the hells is Gelakor?"

"Who *was* Gelakor," the wizard corrected.

Drakalis rolled his eyes as he made his way towards the ruins. "Who *was* Gelakor?"

"No idea," The Green Leaf replied with a hint of amusement. "I met a scholar from the Great Archives once—a jolly fellow. Enjoyed too much honey mead if I recall. Anyway, deep into our conversation, these very ruins came up. He had been researching them for years apparently."

Gallien walked past Aphrandhor, who had slowed in his recounting. "If there's a point, Wizard, I'd love to hear it."

The Green Leaf apologised with a short bow of the head. "The scholar told me there is no reference to any Gelakor in Erador's military history. He was even granted limited access to The Tower of Jain and the chronicles kept therein. Nothing. Only the ruins themselves speak of Gelakor and, even then, there are no inscriptions—no evidence at all—that specify Gelakor was master here. His is simply the only name to be found in the stone."

The smuggler turned to face Aphrandhor while continuing to walk backwards. "So there is no point," he concluded with a mocking grin.

The wizard shifted Yalaqin on his belt. "Knowledge is a goal unto itself, my dear smuggler."

Gallien pivoted on his heel so he could walk into the ruins, beneath an arch that might have once been the main entrance. The site itself was a collection of pillars and broken walls. Here and there, tiles could be seen on the ground, though they were all destined to be swallowed up by the earth one day. Whatever the ruin had been, it had been built with grandeur in mind, the hewn stone rising up to watch over the mountainside and offering several levels to ascend.

Cob was the first to begin the climb, though not out of interest. The Kedradi ranger was searching for threats, checking the shadowed areas where the midday sun failed to pierce the few ceilings that remained. Upon his return, he didn't inform them that they were safe, only that they were alone.

He came to a stop upon one of the broken pillars, his dark eyes cast down on Gallien. There he stood, as if he were a part of the ruins. His cold stare was unnerving and, in the smuggler's opinion, entirely uncalled for.

"What's your problem?" he demanded.

Cob began talking in Ked, his native tongue and a language Drakalis didn't understand. The ranger was pointing back the way they had travelled, his words coming out faster and faster and with a hard edge as he directed them at Aphrandhor. It became all the more unnerving when he started gesturing at the smuggler. The wizard responded in Ked, a hand batting the air to calm the Kedradi, though it only seemed to inflame the situation.

Gallien threw his arms out. "What's he talking about?"

"Leave it to them," Androma replied.

The Green Leaf stepped back when Cob jumped down, landing too close to the wizard. Gallien had no idea what was transpiring or what had brought it on, but his hand felt more comfortable resting on the hilt of his sword. Not that it made a difference when the ranger lunged at him, his scimitar of bone coming down from on high to carve through his skull. The smuggler had only his instincts in that moment and he threw up a helpless hand to protect his head.

The loud knock of hard bone on tempered steel rang clear through the ruins.

All eyes and Androma's ears turned to the source of the noise and found an exquisite and fierce-looking axe in Gallien's hand, the sleek and curving blade keeping Cob's scimitar at bay. The Kedradi might have retreated a step had Joran not leapt in and shoved him back.

"Cob!" Androma admonished.

"*That*," the ranger declared quite deliberately, "is a weapon of power."

Conscious of the attention, Gallien backed off a step and lowered the axe. He also put a hand into Joran's chest and directed him away from the Kedradi.

"We have not said a word," Cob continued, looking to the wizard and Rider now. "Not *one*. I would know how he has come to wield such a weapon."

Androma leaned into her staff. "We agreed this could wait, Cob."

"It has waited long enough," he argued. "We know of only three relics with that kind of power. Each was found beside a skeleton—the fourth and last has never been found." His dark eyes fell on Drakalis. "How did you come by that axe, Smuggler? Did you find it? Steal it? Kill for it?"

Gallien gestured at the Kedradi's sword. "Swing at me again and you'll see how *you're* going to come by it."

"He is not fit to wield it," Cob proclaimed. "The advantage to this council would be tenfold. It should be ours."

The Green Leaf waded in, placing himself between the men as he held on to the neck of his staff. "Mr Drakalis," he began, as if he were no more than an old man making a simple enquiry. "Perhaps you could enlighten us? After all, you do possess a weapon that might feel more comfortable in the hands of say... a *god*."

Gallien took a breath, his heart still pounding in his chest. They had clearly withheld their questions thus far to keep the peace and, more importantly, keep Joran on a path to Drakanan. But they had him now. Joran wanted to see it through.

But was now the right time to reveal his find in Harendun? It was all nonsense to him, but the location of a fourth skeleton was valuable leverage. Truthfully, the smuggler was wondering how he might apply that leverage to get Joran away from them.

Would they take the axe from him? Could they? For sixteen years it had shown him favour.

A darker thought crept into Gallien's desperate mind then. He could refuse them everything, including answers as to where he found it. The discord could provoke them into action and show their true colours. Joran would see them for what they were and they could part ways. The smuggler would happily leave the axe with them if it meant getting Joran as far away as possible from all this madness.

A barbed remark was forming on the edge of Gallien's lips when he noticed something. It completely threw him, sidelining any and all current concerns and replacing them with new ones.

"What is it?" Joran asked, the first to recognise the smuggler's troubled look.

Gallien's head began to tilt as he scrutinised the vambrace on Aphrandhor's right arm, the bracer having been revealed when The Green Leaf gripped his staff so high. It was predominantly silver in colour, with subtle accents of bronze in the folded steel. An intricate patter of copper laced the band, surrounding a copper tear drop that sat directly on top of the forearm.

Noting the smuggler's shift in attention, the wizard dropped his arm so his green sleeve concealed the piece of armour. "Are you quite alright, Mr Drakalis?"

Gallien was now staring at The Green Leaf's right arm as if he could still see it. "Where did you get that?" he asked quietly.

Aphrandhor glanced at Cob and Androma. "It's Demetrium," he answered. "A precaution in case I lose my staff."

The smuggler's eyes drifted up to the old man's grey eyes. "I'm a *very* good liar, *Mr Wizard*. You're just a *good* one. Where did you get that bracer?" he demanded again.

As he took a step closer, The Green Leaf took a step back.

"I've had it a long time, longer than you've been *alive*. And I don't like being called a liar."

Joran came up on his left. "Gallien, what's wrong?"

It took everything Drakalis had to tear his eyes away from the wizard and look at Joran. "The last time I ever saw my father, he walked away from me and my brother wearing that *exact* vambrace."

Aphrandhor's eyes twitched and narrowed. "Impossible," he mumbled.

"You don't forget a bracer like that," Gallien told him. "He was even wearing it on the same goddamn arm!" He took another step towards The Green Leaf.

The wizard stepped back again. "You must be mistaken."

"Don't tell me I'm mistaken!" Drakalis barked. "Where did you get it? Did you take it from him? Did you *kill* him for it?" With every question, the smuggler advanced on the wizard.

Cob moved around Aphrandhor only to be shoved aside by Gallien. "Stay out of it!" he growled at the ranger.

"It seems we all have questions for each other," Androma

intervened. "I'd say they can all wait until Joran is safely within Drakanan."

"Take it off," Gallien commanded, ignoring the old Rider altogether.

"I will not," Aphrandhor replied calmly.

Drakalis used the axe to point at the man's arm. "Take it off or *I'll* take it off."

Cob sniffed and brought his scimitar up to rest over one shoulder.

"Stop this," Androma insisted, her voice falling on deaf ears.

"You want to see what this thing can do?" Gallien asked the Kedradi threateningly.

"A weapon is no better than the one who wields it," Cob retorted, "and I have seen all you are capable of, Smuggler."

"This is getting us nowhere," the old Rider told them firmly.

"You have no idea what I'm capable of," Drakalis assured him.

Cob didn't shy away, presenting the smuggler with a wall of monster-hunting muscle.

"This isn't the time," Androma pressed.

"He hasn't denied it!" Gallien spat, levelling his axe at The Green Leaf. "I would have him say it. I would hear him describe the man he *prised* that bracer from."

"I *prised* it from no-one," Aphrandhor said evenly.

Gallien sensed some truth in that, though he also detected more than a hint of omission. "Liar!" he accused.

"Enough!" Androma snapped, her staff stamping once into the ground. "I forget how young you all are," she muttered to herself. "And I'm sure we're all lying about something," she groaned. "Our secrets will have to wait. Joran is all that matters."

"He's not going anywhere with *him*," Gallien vowed, eyeing the wizard.

"Drakalis!" Androma hissed.

"No!" the smuggler protested. "My father was a damn good fighter. There's no way he just handed that bracer over. That man's a killer."

"Aren't we all?" Cob retorted.

Gallien got right in the Kedradi's face. "There's a difference between fighting for your life and murdering folk!"

The old Rider sighed, exhausted by the back and forth. "Aphrandhor, tell him about..." Androma's words trailed off and her head slowly tilted to one side.

A second later, Joran mimicked her movement. "I hear it too."

Gallien and the others looked around, seeing naught but ruins. "Hear what?" he asked, irritated by the interruption.

Joran moved with light haste to reach the northern edge of the ruins, where the cliff dropped down to the fields and forest below. There he remained, paralysed by something the others couldn't see. Together, the companions crossed the site to join the young man, though Cob was sure to keep himself between Gallien and Aphrandhor.

"What is it?" Drakalis demanded as he reached the lip beside Joran.

As one, they looked down on a black mass that had previously been concealed by their elevation. The legions were advancing from the north and being steadily absorbed by the forest. Trees were being felled, their branches and leaves shrugging off snow as they were brought to the forest floor. In their wake, hulking war machines were being hauled along the new path.

The truth of what they were looking at struck Gallien with such revelation that he momentarily forgot that his father's potential murderer was standing three feet away. "Those are Andarens," he said absently.

"*Thousands,*" Joran observed gravely.

A low rumble resonated inside The Green Leaf's chest. "War has come to Erador."

55
BREAKING WITH TRADITION

40 Years Ago…

Daijen walked cautiously through the cold halls of Ka'vairn, his footing chosen with care lest he trip over the debris. There wasn't a single door still on its hinges in the west wing, and the contents of every room had been destroyed by a variety of spells. Some of the walls had even been knocked through, including one of the outer walls that now provided the Vahlken with a view of the valley beyond.

Decorative drapes and curtains lay in burnt heaps while patches of stone and shattered furniture sat frozen solid, their surfaces glistening. The wind had found its way inside and swept torn pages and sundries about the corridor. For nearly an hour he had listened to the carnage from the floors below, not daring to investigate until the Dragon Rider was spent.

Indeed, her magic had wrought all it could before her rage burned out.

In the furthest chamber, what remained of the door creaked under Daijen's boots as he entered. So much of the room was charred black. The window, its framework, and a foot of surrounding stone was completely gone, leaving a gaping hole in its place. The Vahlken's cobalt eyes came to rest on Androma, who lay on her side in the corner, her head resting on Ilithranda's lap.

Ilithranda had chosen to stay close by, though not so close that she found herself in harm's way. Her decision had surprised Daijen, given the heated exchange that had passed between both women on the shore. Something about Androma's loss and overwhelming grief, however, had impacted Ilithranda in a way Daijen couldn't have anticipated. Curiously, it seemed the loss resonated with her.

With Androma resting on her legs, Ilithranda stroked the Rider's head and met Daijen's eyes. They held a silent conversation, agreeing that more time would be required before she emerged from the darkest depths of her despair. Daijen nodded his head before twitching his eyes, a silent question to ensure that Ilithranda was alright to be left alone with the volatile Rider. The Vahlken bowed her head and blinked slowly, assuring him that she was safe.

Leaving the husk of a chamber behind, Daijen retreated into the bowels of Ka'vairn. Ten days had passed since they returned to the fortress with an exhausted Androma. Before that, they had spent three days beside Maegar, utterly powerless to move the Rider. She had been, and still was, inconsolable. Androma had fought them physically and with magic whenever they tried to peel her off the dragon. Only when she was too tired to fight back, were they able to bring her to Ka'vairn.

Since then, Androma had awoken from bouts of unconsciousness with renewed fury. She had demanded they take her back to Maegar, hearing none of their warnings about a human being discovered in Andara. Only once had The Valtorak attempted to introduce himself to the Rider. He had left that evening with a singed robe and a scowl that sent Daijen's eyes to his boots.

Arriving in the Hall of Handuin, he heard the tall double doors beyond the foyer being opened. He knew it couldn't be The Valtorak for the master of Ka'vairn moved everywhere without making a sound, his ability to simply appear anywhere inside the fortress lending him an almost supernatural air.

Daijen reached the end of the hall as Tovun stepped inside. He had only met the initiate ten days ago, and what a meeting for Tovun that had been! Even now, the young Andaren couldn't get his head around the fact that Androma—the enemy—was a guest and not a prisoner.

Since meeting the initiate, Daijen had tried to extend his patience. After all, he had only The Valtorak to instruct him—a far harsher mentor than Kastiek.

Still, he had survived the pits of Handuin while Daijen and Ilithranda had been out in the world. Like them, Tovun now boasted a wider frame of muscle and a whole head's worth of extra height. The other two potential Vahlken he had arrived with could not say the same, their bodies burned and buried beyond Ka'vairn.

"Master Daijen!" he hailed eagerly.

"Just Daijen," the Vahlken insisted.

Tovun straightened up. "Apologies," he blurted. "There's someone at the gate! Dwarves!"

"Dwarves?" Daijen was already past the initiate and charging up the steps to the ramparts.

Coming to a stop above the gates, he looked down upon a pair of dwarves surrounded by Aegres. Valyra barred their way forward while Oaken blocked any retreat. Gliding lazily above it all was Aramis, The Valtorak's faithful companion. Together they were a trinity of death that none could escape.

That said, the two dwarves appeared entirely unfazed.

Daijen couldn't help but smile. "Mordrith Underborn!" he called out.

The dwarf raised a flat hand to her brow and looked up at the ramparts. "That ye, Daijen Saeth?"

Valyra and Oaken squawked threateningly at the sound of their prey.

"Easy," Daijen bade from above. "Give me a moment," he said to the dwarves.

A few minutes later and the Aegres had taken to the skies and the Vahlken had the gates open. Mordrith led the way, closely followed by her companion, a younger dwarf with a short beard and thick mane of hair swept back over her head, both a rich copper. With one hand, the younger dwarf pulled on the reins of a large hog—too large to be natural, in Daijen's opinion.

"Well met," Mordrith greeted, her eyes cautiously roaming the fortress. "This is Yamnomora," she introduced without actually looking at the dwarf.

"So ye're the Vahlken," Yamnomora surmised, looking Daijen up and down. "I thought ye'd be bigger."

Daijen's response turned into a bemused smile. "It is good to meet you, Yamnomora. And it is good to see you again, Mordrith."

"Aye, it's been a while," the swarthy dwarf replied absently.

"Twenty years," the Vahlken specified.

Mordrith grunted. "Maybe it's not so long after all," she remarked, a testament to the long lives of her kin.

When they said nothing more, Daijen looked from one to the other expectantly. "I have to admit, this is the last place I thought to see you."

His comment prompted Mordrith and she took her eyes from Ka'vairn and finally settled on Daijen. "An' I wouldn' be 'ere if it weren' me only choice," she told him gravely.

Daijen glanced over the dwarves. "You are hunted?"

Mordrith stifled her laugh. "We're always hunted, lad. That ain' ever goin' to change."

"We're 'ere because the Skaramangians need a good slap," Yamnomora interjected passionately. "An' we know jus' where to slap 'em," she added with a wicked grin.

Mordrith calmed her companion with a raised hand. "There is a blow to be dealt, no doubt," she said before her demeanour sank. "We alone can only do so much." This comment brought out a snort of derision from Yamnomora, but the older dwarf ignored her. "There's no-one else to turn to in this war. Everyone else is on *their* side."

"Then, perhaps, we should take this inside." The suggestion came from behind Daijen, where The Valtorak was standing on the threshold of the keep, his bent staff in one hand. Just behind him, a silent observer, was a very confused Tovun.

Daijen returned his attention to the dwarves, a slight smile on his pale face. "Welcome to Ka'vairn, Mordrith Underborn."

In need of a space that would accommodate them all, the group settled in the library on the second floor in the east wing. The Valtorak had Tovun see to the torches and candles, adding some support to the narrow beams of dusty light that shone through the slitted windows high in the walls. Then the initiate was dismissed without explanation.

Daijen disagreed with his exclusion, believing that he needed to be brought in sooner rather than so many years later, but he wasn't the master of Ka'vairn. Its traditions were beyond his control, much to his annoyance. The initiate, however, did leave the door to the library open, so there was every chance his enhanced hearing would pick up their conversation. Daijen had said nothing to correct this.

"It seems unlikely," The Valtorak said patronisingly.

Yamnomora scowled up at the Andaren. "It's right *there*," she insisted, pressing one stubby finger into the map of Verda.

"Nareene?" Daijen queried, agreeing with his master's scepticism.

Yamnomora glanced at Mordrith. "Are we speakin' a different language? Aye," she said forcefully, "it's in Nareene. Can we go now?"

Daijen looked to Mordrith, his expression pleading for a modicum of reason.

The dwarf calmed Yamnomora with a flex of her fingers before placing The Anther on the table beside the map. The hammer drew the attention of both Vahlken, as it would any who looked upon it, but neither made a comment.

"It's there," Mordrith said with quiet confidence.

"But you haven't been there," The Valtorak pointed out, his remark verging on a question.

"No," Mordrith, confirmed before Yamnomora could snap at him. "But the one we interrogated was tellin' the truth."

The Valtorak raised an immaculate eyebrow. "How can you be sure if you haven't seen it yourself?"

"Because there's only so many pieces one can lose before the truth will out," Mordrith said grimly.

"He were singin' before the end," Yamnomora added darkly.

Daijen felt his master's violet eyes on him, an expectation that he would point out the flaw in their reasoning. He said nothing of the sort, the Vahlken's gaze landing intently at the map. Nareene was a large island inside The Deep, a body of water nestled neatly inside the hooking embrace of Erador. On a clear day, he might even have seen it from Argunsuun as a faded line on the distant horizon.

"The Skaramangians are known to be scattered," he began. "It's how they've avoided detection for so long. It does seem unlikely that they would have a meeting place as grand as you describe. It seems even more unlikely that it would be in Nareene. The island belongs to Erador," he pointed out. "The Skaramangian leadership is predominantly Andaren—they wouldn't risk travelling into enemy waters."

"We never said it were a meetin' place," Yamnomora spat.

Again, Mordrith extended her arm to soothe her capricious friend. "The nature o' the place remains a mystery. We only know that it's important to 'em."

"An' it's ancient," Yamnomora blurted.

Daijen frowned. "What could possibly be on a deserted island that holds any import to them?"

Mordrith rested both hands on the edge of the table. "The one we captured. Before he was finished being... *interrogated* by us, the Skaramangian told us we would die before we laid eyes on it."

"That means they're guardin' it," Yamnomora said needlessly. "Ye don' protect somethin' ye don' care abou'."

Daijen absorbed the new information. "And he gave you no indication as to what you would find there?"

"Only its name," Mordrith answered. "Though it don' really help to understand a damned thing."

Daijen remained poised, staring at the dwarf fervently—it wasn't very often they heard names from Skaramangian lore.

"The Tomb," she declared.

"That would suggest someone is buried there," The Valtorak concluded.

"Or *something*," Yamnomora countered.

Mordrith leaned forward, her dark eyes fixed on Daijen. "A Talakin," she uttered.

Daijen recalled the name from one of their old conversations. "A Dark One," he translated.

"This is becoming more unlikely by the minute," The Valtorak cut in.

"Whether there is an ancient god-killing monster on that island or not," came a hoarse voice from the doorway, "Nareene begs investigation."

Daijen turned to see Androma stepping into the library, her hand gripped to Ilithranda's arm. He whispered her name and made to approach until the Rider spoke again.

"My friend, Aphrandhor, was setting sail for the island when last I saw him."

"The wizard?" Daijen asked, his eyes wandering over her dark armour, the plates stained with crusted blood.

"He too has uncovered leads that point to this... *tomb*. He will have reached the island by now." Androma pulled herself a little closer to Ilithranda. "I should have gone with him," she muttered.

"Who's this?" Yamnomora asked bluntly.

Daijen made the introductions, naming both Androma and Ilithranda before doing the same for the dwarves.

Mordrith blinked and looked to Daijen questioningly. "Why do ye 'ave a blind human in yer keep?"

"An' what's with all this talk o' wizards?" Yamnomora challenged.

Daijen flinched at Mordrith's description and let his gaze wander over the Rider. Her face, while partially masked by matted blonde hair, was still streaked with angry burns and what remained of her eyes was a mess of damaged skin, the finer features lost to the bite of the axium.

"Androma is a—"

"*Was*," she quickly interjected.

Daijen paused, sharing a glance with Ilithranda. "Androma is a Dragon Rider," he asserted, feeling the title was still very much deserved.

Mordrith's bushy eyebrows went up. "Ye'll let anyone in these days."

"How does a dwarf get into Ka'vairn?" Androma asked, her voice low. "Better yet, how does a Dragon Rider get out?"

Daijen chose to ignore the latter and answer her first question by way of a short tale that recounted his meeting with Mordrith twenty-four years previously.

"You have a weapon of power?" Androma questioned, her hand probing the tabletop.

"Aye," Yamnomora replied on Mordrith's behalf, and sharply at that. "An' it's for her alone."

Androma retracted her fingers. "A Skaramangian traitor," the Rider pondered aloud. "You must have quite the price on your head."

"I see it as a good thing," Mordrith said. "Brings 'em all out o' hidin'."

Androma's thoughts were her own for a moment, her expression as stony as The Valtorak's. "As I said, Nareene begs investigation," she eventually announced, if miserably. "Anything the Skaramangians protect is worth destroying."

"We thank you for bringing us this information," The Valtorak said, moving to the head of the table. "The Vahlken will see to it from here."

Yamnomora's face fell, a prelude to the tirade just perched on the end of her tongue.

Mordrith dropped a heavy hand onto Yamnomora's right

pauldron, a command to be silent. "We didn' come all this way," she said firmly enough, "jus' to hand the fight over to ye."

"I assure you," The Valtorak replied cooly, "the Vahlken have been in this fight before your people knew there was even life outside the mountains. We will see it through. Again, I thank you for bringing this information to us."

"Ye'll see it through in another few thousand years," Yamnomora jibed. "We're actually goin' to end 'em."

"You are not equipped to battle this foe," The Valtorak argued. "The Vahlken were *made* to fight the Skaramangians."

"They're right," Daijen stated, robbing his master of breath. "We have been trying to win this war for so long. How many brothers and sisters have we lost? How much ground has our enemy gained? Our traditions aren't working."

The master opened his mouth to dispute that, but it seemed the argument died on his lips. Instead, he closed his mouth and raised his chin, allowing Daijen to say more.

"We've all been fighting the same war on different fronts," the Vahlken continued. "The Skaramangians don't need to divide and conquer us—we're *already* fighting apart. Think of what we each know. Think of the skills we each offer. If we pool them... If we form an alliance that transcends our traditions," he began again, his words aimed directly at his master, "then we might just pose a real threat."

"I'm for more than threatenin'," Mordrith expressed vehemently. "I mean to pull out the root an' *burn* it."

"Burning sounds good," Androma intoned.

Daijen spared Ilithranda a moment, gauging her thoughts through those violet orbs. "I didn't pass through eternity and torment for nothing," she voiced for them all. "I would see this war to its end."

Having heard from all parties except The Valtorak, Daijen turned to his master and waited.

"Outside of these walls, your tactics are your own—it is not my place to interfere." The ancient Andaren took a breath, his gaze drawn down to the map where, at its heart, lay the island of

Nareene. Without another word, he rounded the table and made for the doors.

It wasn't the permission Daijen had been hoping for, but the master's response was a reminder that he stood on his own two feet now. He was a Vahlken after all.

"So how are we gettin' there?" Yamnomora asked them collectively. "Do ye lot have a ship or somethin'? Bludgeon can' stand the water."

Daijen offered the surly dwarf a knowing smile. "How is he with flying?"

56
ONWARDS AND UPWARDS

Grarfath's lungs were burning. The dwarf wasn't built for running, a fact that was made all the worse by the burden of things he carried in his heavy pack. Then there was the hammer he was never to lose. The Anther was extraordinarily light compared to other hammers of its size, but it was still a great piece of steel added to his load.

When an arrow whistled inches from his ear and ploughed into a tree, the smith found the reserves needed to keep his speed up. He navigated the web of roots and clambered over boulders with all the grace of an anvil, unlike the battle maiden he travelled with.

Kitrana Voden exploded from the trees ahead and leapt over the dwarf and the ridge he was climbing. Her spear flew from her hand before she landed on the forest floor and took an Andaren from his charge. The pale warriors, draped in black cloaks, were filtering through from the north—a scouting party that always kept themselves one step ahead of the army.

One brought his sabre round in a sweeping arc, a sure swing that would split the Nimean across the waist. With incredible flexibility, Kitrana skidded under the blade and sprang back to her feet in time to reclaim her spear. She yanked it out of the soldier's bloody chest and whipped it around to deflect an incoming attack. Grarfath watched from the small ridge as the battle maiden danced around her foes, only pausing to angle the spear and thrust.

Thundering hooves turned the smith on his heel, though he witnessed little more than a blur as Bludgeon sped past. The Warhog jumped as Kit had, only instead of a spear, the animal wielded an axe-swinging dwarf. Yamnomora guided Bludgeon round in an arc that put them between Kitrana and the advancing soldiers. Her great axe swung once, twice, and a third time to claim three Andaren lives.

"Keep runnin'!" she bellowed up at Grarfath.

The Nimean was already scaling the short rise to join the smith and Bludgeon was dashing towards the slope further along. Grarfath turned from the corpses and ran through the last of the trees that formed the southern border of the small forest. They had been fleeing the Andarens for two days, barely pausing in order to stay ahead. The forest had slowed them down, but not nearly as much as it had slowed the army and their war machines.

The smith hesitated to go any further. "What is this?" he asked.

Yamnomora came riding out of the forest, her stubbled face glistening with a sheen of sweat. "The Giant's Throat," she answered. "It leads to The Silver Trees o' Akmar."

"For us it can only mean death," Kitrana said, jogging to meet them. "There will be nowhere to go but forwards and nowhere to hide from the Andarens," she added urgently, her eyes shifting from the rocky ascent to the forest and back.

"Well we can' go back," Grarfath pointed out.

"No," Yamnomora agreed, her neck craning. "But we can go *up*."

The smith looked up, his eyes easily picking out the hewn stone and building work that protruded from the lip of the nearest rocky shelf. His experience told him the stone was weathered—ancient even. What shelter could a ruin provide? That's if he could get up there.

"I can' climb that," he was sure to mention.

"No need," Yamnomora replied, directing the Warhog forward.

Grarfath looked ahead of his dwarven companion and discovered a steep track that zig-zagged up the face of the eastern cliff. "I'm still not sure I can climb that," he muttered.

The sound of clamouring armour and sharp orders barked in the Andaren tongue put the smith into action. It mattered little when one of those that pursued him emerged on horseback. The horse's neigh was more akin to a growl, demanding of Grarfath that he turn back and set eyes on his foe. It was one of their mutated war horses, a wicked looking creature with horns, a whipping thin tail, and six powerful legs.

The rider had the beast charging towards the smith, oblivious to Kitrana, who had been off to one side. That singular oversight proved to be the Andaren's fatal mistake, for he never could have predicted the spear hurtling towards his mount. The war horse let loose a garbled moan as it received the spear in the base of its wide neck.

The ground shook upon the creature's impact. The rider was thrown from his saddle and saved only by his armour upon meeting the rocky ground, though he tumbled and rolled, his dark cloak becoming entangled about his left leg. Still, it wasn't enough to keep the warrior down. Unsteady though he was, the rider picked himself up while drawing his sabre.

The sound of The Anther striking a steel helm was a deafening blast. It was also enough to kill the Andaren and lay him flat.

Grarfath stared at the blood smeared across the bronze and gold head of the hammer, the sight of it distracting him from the war horse, which was defying the mortal blow Kitrana had delivered.

Yamnomora's, though, cut through muscle, bone, and Grarfath's train of thought. He looked down at the dead horse, an axe buried in its skull.

"Ye've a lot to learn, blacksmith," the dwarf grumbled as she pulled her weapon free.

"More are coming!" Kitrana called out, running to retrieve her spear and make for the rising path.

Yamnomora looked from Grarfath to the cliff face. "On with ye!" she urged, but it was too late.

A trio of riders astride their war horses burst from the forest and galloped towards them, hungry for vengeance against those who had slain their kin. Given their size and speed, the horses alone would have been enough to kill the dwarves and Bludgeon, saving their riders the effort. Seemingly oblivious to this fact, Yamnomora raised her axe in both hands.

Fearing not only for his life but also for hers, Grarfath did the only thing he could and brought The Anther down, smashing the hammer into the weathered rock. Fuelled by fear and anger at his enemy's relentless pursuit, the smith poured as much of his will as he did his strength into the weapon of power.

Unlike before, the reaction was instantaneous.

The ground cracked and was partially replaced by the dirt track that climbed the cliff face. In turn, half way up the cliff, the dirt track that should have been beneath their feet was now the stone found at the bottom.

Bludgeon snorted and staggered into the wall before his legs gave out. Yamnomora blinked hard, accustomed to the effects of The Anther, and shook her head. She regained her senses just in time to reach out and grab Grarfath before he stumbled over the side of the path.

"Ye couldn' 'ave ported us to the very top?" the warrior queried, her tone as dry as the stone transported with them.

"Kitrana," Grarfath mumbled, sighting the Nimean far below. "Kitrana!" he yelled, fighting the nausea.

Ascending the zig-zagging path below, Kit was trying to stay ahead of the Andarens on horseback. Movement in the north turned the smith's attention to the treeline, where dozens of soldiers were emerging.

Unless there was a human army waiting for them amongst the ruins above, climbing the path was merely delaying the inevitable.

57
PALE DEATH

"I thought there were dragons guarding the pass," Gallien remarked, his anger still bubbling at the surface.

Androma ignored the unsaid accusation that she was somehow responsible for an entire army invading Erador. "The war between Riders has complicated our border security," she replied, straining her senses to learn what she could of the Andarens below. "They're entering The Throat?" she asked, staying well away from the edge.

"Yes," Cob answered, moving along the lip of the ruins and towards the interior of the cleft.

"The Skaramangians have two skeletons," Aphrandhor muttered into her ear. "Now they've come for a third."

"They're marching on Akmar," she voiced, thinking of the silver trees and the secret they housed. "In time, they will pass through The Giant's Throat. We must keep to ourselves up here and hope they choose not to investigate the ruins."

"We need to warn someone." Joran's urgent voice turned the old Rider back to the northern edge of the plateau. "Erador must be warned."

"The Andarens will meet magic before steel," The Green Leaf

informed him, still close by. “The Giant’s Throat will take them straight to The Silver Trees of Akmar, where the Jainus will intercept them.”

“Can they hold off an entire army?” Joran queried, incredulous. “Shouldn’t we get word to Galahart?”

“No,” the wizard replied. “And no,” he added, answering both questions.

“We do nothing then?” Joran’s voice was laced with concern and frustration.

Androma reached out and found the boy’s shoulder. “We can do nothing to halt that army,” she explained calmly, trying not to think about the days when she had the power to bring them to a stop. “The Jainus will likely slow them down long enough for Galahart to scramble forces through The Misted Road, if not from Thedaria. That’s if the Jainus allow soldiers anywhere near the forest,” she added, her comment for Aphrandhor alone.

“But how will Galahart know to send anyone?” Joran was sounding more desperate by the minute.

Gallien’s musk washed over Androma as he passed them. “Because they took White Tower getting into Erador,” he told the young man. “The soldiers there will have dispatched ravens and runners as soon as they saw the army.”

“The best thing we can do,” the old Rider addressed, “is let them pass us by. Our priority is still Drakanan.”

“I thought the war was our priority?” Joran argued. “Isn’t this the Skaramangians’ doing?”

“What are you going to do?” Drakalis posed, his temper and fear for the boy coming together in a melting pot. “Can you fight ten thousand Andarens?”

Androma held out her hand in Gallien’s direction, a call for cooler heads. “Your time is coming Joran,” she said quietly, deliberately. “When it does you have to be ready, because you’re going to change everything.” She gripped his shoulder a little tighter. “Facing the enemy today will only get you killed. You must train.”

"And preferably have a dragon at your back," The Green Leaf imparted before walking away.

"Ignore him," Androma said flippantly. "You must be able to fight every battle on your own. Your time in Drakanan will see to that," she promised.

"They're coming up the path!" Cob called out, his words sending Androma's heart into a thunderous beat.

"What path?" she demanded, her stick angled to sweep the ground around her.

An arm extended across the old Rider's chest, barring her way. Androma knew immediately from the staff across her midriff that it was Aphrandhor who had stopped her from going any further, and she heard Joran halt on her other side.

"Androma," the wizard said gravely.

The old Rider tilted her head, listening. She heard Gallien dash to join them and draw his sword. Aphrandhor retracted his staff and freed Yalaqin from its scabbard before Cob returned to them, his bowstring pulling taut.

A gentle breeze blew in from the south, carrying with it the scent of death and blood. Then there was the gentle tapping of steel on stone. Not steel, Androma realised. *Silvyr.*

"Slait," she uttered with revelation.

"*Their Leviathans defeated,*" Slait began, his rough voice booming across the ruins and filling it with Andaren scripture, "*the Dark Ones unleashed new hell on earth, releasing the human scourge from their demonic flesh. This new enemy, whose image was made in mockery of all Andarens, was set to infect the world with malice and darkness.*" His boots could be heard descending a set of steps, not far ahead. "I am the light dawning to meet that darkness," he concluded in man's tongue.

"He wields a slaiken blade," Aphrandhor warned quietly.

It was not the weapon he had attacked them with before, begging the question as to where he had been keeping it. "How did you track us?" she had to ask.

"You cannot escape the Black Abyss," he replied, a smile in his voice. "And I have been appointed to ensure you reach it."

Androma knew there was no reasoning with the religious zealot, his mind broken long before the Skaramangians corrupted it. Instead of offering a retort, the old Rider found Joran with her free hand and shoved him back behind the line they had formed.

"You cannot protect him," The Dawn Sword stated. "Reclamation is coming."

"I think not," Aphrandhor retorted, his staff coming down to stomp on a piece of ancient flagstone.

The magic unleashed tore through stone and earth, hurtling a shockwave of debris at Slait. Androma heard the numerous impacts a second before Cob's bow *twanged* and released an arrow, suggesting The Dancing Sword of the Dawn had evaded the wizard's initial attack. Aphrandhor grunted as he cast another spell, igniting the air with flames and the smell of sulphur. Somewhere to the old Rider's left, the ancient stonework exploded and Cob fired another arrow.

Androma began moving Joran back and to her right, away from the direction of mayhem. "Stay behind me."

A staccato of lightning erupted from the end of Aphrandhor's staff and again the Kedradi let loose his arrows. It seemed their target was hard to pin down.

"What's happening?" she asked, her question thrown at Gallien.

"The bastard's fast, that's what's happening." The stress in the smuggler's voice was all too audible. "Wait..." His stress was momentarily drowned out by confusion. "What in the hells is that?" There was a sharp silence before he spoke again. "That's an Aegre!" he exclaimed.

A genuine smile was brought to Androma's face, their guardian angel arriving in their hour of need. "Daijen," she whispered. "Daijen is coming!" she called out to The Green Leaf.

The squawk of an enormous Aegre pierced the air, a promise of cavalry—if cavalry was a four thousand pound mutated eagle with talons that could cleave through dragon scale.

"That isn't Daijen!" the wizard shouted between spells, his voice strained with dread.

Androma's hope was extinguished like a candle in the wind. She had been sure it was Valyra that had been silently watching over their journey. If not Valyra nor her Vahlken companion then who? The truth dawned on the old Rider as the Aegre descended on the ruins.

The exile—*Uthain.*

All at once, Androma came to understand how Slait had been tracking them as well as how he had been moving across the country as swiftly as he did. The Skaramangian assassin had been wise to keep his winged companion airborne, away from prying eyes, while he hunted Joran on horseback, disguised as a human. He had no need for the arts of subtlety or deception now.

Uthain, a white Aegre by all descriptions, flapped his wings, sending a gust of air over Androma and those beside her. They, however, were not the creature's prey. The Green Leaf called out, his words lost to the clap of magic he discharged.

"This way," Gallien hissed, the smuggler's hand gripping Androma's arm to drag her away.

His directions regarding trip hazards were short and sharp, but adequate enough to allow the old Rider to navigate between the broken pillars and over the uneven ground. "What's happening?" she demanded, fearing for Aphrandhor and Cob.

"They're fighting the damned Aegre!" Drakalis replied, shouting over the animal's squawks and the wizard's magic.

Androma pictured it in her mind; wizard and Kedradi in a dance to the death with a savage and unnaturally cruel Aegre. "Wait," she said, her critical thinking catching up with her imagination. "Where's Slait?"

The Dancing Sword of the Dawn answered that question himself.

The old Rider had detected his approach only a second before his slaiken blade was thrust between the pillars. Using her staff, she managed to push both Joran and Gallien out of the way, her hidden armour taking little more than a glancing strike across the back.

Sensing the next attack—and it came without delay—the old

Rider ducked and rolled under the sweeping blade. The sound of silvyr striking stone rang in Androma's ears, informing her of Slait's position.

"Run!" she cried, leaping from her crouch to bombard The Dawn Sword with blows from her staff.

"Get back!" Gallien barked at Joran, though it seemed the smuggler had no intention of leaving Androma to fight Slait alone.

Of her four consecutive blows, two struck her foe's cuirass and two were delivered across his jaw and cheek. Her years without Maegar, however, had slowly robbed the old Rider of the enhancements gifted through their bond. She no longer possessed the strength, speed, and stamina of a true Dragon Rider, and so the Andaren blessed with Handuin's magic absorbed her attacks and advanced.

Using her ears and intuition, Androma evaded Slait's counter attack, his slaiken blade whipping up and across with swift efficiency. She lashed out with the end of her staff only to be blocked by his vambrace. Again, she was forced to sidestep and evade his next swing, though it seemed The Dawn Sword was merely lining her up for a boot to the chest.

The air shot from her lungs as her feet left the ground, her body folding before meeting the ground several feet away. She should have died then, there at the mercy of her enemy, but she did not fight alone.

Gallien Drakalis replaced her, bringing his sword to bear. Androma heard it clash with Slait's once, twice, then shatter. Steel and human strength were no match against dwarven silvyr and Vahlken muscle.

The smuggler grunted, receiving some kind of blow. What remained of his broken sword hit the ground, the metal pommel creating a distinct sound as it impacted the stone ruins.

"Joran?" Androma called out, concerned that the boy was too close to a fight with only one conclusion.

"I'm here," he responded, breath ragged but close by.

Gallien roared in defiance and the two clashed again, only this time the steel in his hand did not relent. It was all the harder to imagine a smuggler of all people engaged in battle with a Vahlken and wielding a weapon of power no less. Still, he would not last. Drakalis would tire long before Slait, and that's if The Dawn Sword didn't simply outmatch him with sheer skill.

Let him die, she thought. Hadn't she once planned on killing him herself? While he died distracting Slait, she could hasten Joran to safety, back the way they had come. It would be hard for Joran to lose the man, she knew, but he was destined for an immortal life, a path down which Gallien couldn't hope to follow.

Pulling herself to her feet, Androma reached out clumsily and grabbed Joran's cloak. The old Rider was on the verge of directing him back to the south when the guttural noises evoked from Gallien's battle lodged themselves in her mind.

It was love that fuelled him, that made him blind to pain and inevitable death.

He fought as a father would—with abandon. Defying the odds, as he often did, the smuggler was keeping The Dancing Sword of the Dawn at bay, his axe cutting and chopping relentlessly.

He was a good man.

Be who you were meant to be...

The words were naught but a memory, she knew, but Maegar's voice always put fire in her blood.

With grim determination, Androma pushed Joran away rather than drag him into line. "Stay back," she warned him.

It was time to fight like a Dragon Rider.

Or die like one.

58
CENTRE OF THE WORLD

40 Years Ago...

Climbing down from his saddle, Daijen's feet pressed into Eradoran soil for the first time in his life. As a messenger guard, he had thought he would live out all of his centuries without even seeing Erador, let alone actually walking in it. To a human, the Vahlken supposed, his presence in Nareene was actually an invasion.

He might have found that amusing had his thoughts not led him to the only human in their group. Astride Oaken, Androma had flown with Ilithranda, the two having become inseparable. Whatever had bonded them remained beyond Daijen's understanding, but he was glad of the pairing while the Rider was in such need of support.

As Yamnomora chased after Bludgeon, the animal having sprinted away as soon as Valyra released the animal on land, Daijen approached Androma to see how she faired.

Mordrith intercepted him, The Anther strapped to her back. "Is it so wise bringin' her 'ere?" the dwarf asked, her dark eyes shifting to Androma. "We're likely to face those who don' want us pokin' our noses in. How's she goin' to fight what she can' see?"

"Androma is still a Dragon Rider," he told her quietly, if confidently.

"That don' mean much when ye've no dragon an' no damned eyes, lad. She's goin' to slow us down if not get us killed keepin' her safe."

"You wanted us here," Daijen reminded her. "Well, she comes with us."

Mordrith sighed. "So be it. But she's *yer* burden, not ours."

Daijen made a point to seek out Yamnomora who, at that moment, was struggling to wrangle her traumatised Warhog.

"Yamnomora ain' no burden," Mordrith told him easily enough. "Jus' don' get in her way when her axes come out."

"What's her story?" Daijen enquired.

"Her story's her own," the dwarf replied bluntly. "It ain' for me to tell."

Trust no-one. Suspect everyone.

The Valtorak's warning was never far from Daijen's mind. "Very well," he said in response, content to move on. For now.

Valyra flapped her wings in a short sharp manner while unleashing a cautioning squawk. Daijen knew it to mean she had detected a threat and knew to follow her gaze. Searching across the flat ground of black dirt and mounds of barren rock, the Vahlken found himself staring at the distant treeline of snow-covered pines. He saw nothing but forest, though he knew it was folly to doubt Valyra's eyes.

Oaken added his own call to the apparent threat before both Aegres took to the sky. They were upon the forest in no time, descending with enough speed that they were forced to run before coming to a stop. Both animals formed an arrowhead, squawking incessantly and scraping their talons over the ground.

"What is it?" Androma asked, her voice dry.

Daijen's eyes were able to pierce the distance but not the Aegres' flapping wings. "They've found something."

"Or *someone*," Mordrith posed, retrieving The Anther from over one shoulder.

The group advanced as one, including Yamnomora, who had finally got Bludgeon under control. When they were a little under half way to the treeline, Mordrith's comment was given credence as a figure emerged from the shadows. He did so slowly, and with his hands held high while under the intense gaze of two Aegres. At a glance, the stranger was weaponless save for the staff he held above his head. Robed in shades of green, his attire was bound tightly about his waist by a thick belt laden with all manner of things.

Walking between the Aegres, he used his free hand to pull back his hood, revealing a human man still in his youth. Daijen had yet to spend enough time around humans to gauge their exact age, but the man before him could have been anywhere from twenty to forty. His chestnut hair flowed down to his shoulders, framing an asymmetrical face with a crooked and hooked nose somewhere close to its centre. Much of his jaw was hidden behind a thick goatee, though it seemed a rather nasty scar cut up and across his chin.

"He's a wizard," Daijen guessed.

Androma's head twitched. "*Aphrandhor?*" she called out. "*Aphrandhor, is that you?*"

The wizard faltered in his approach. "*Androma? Androma! Is that really you?*"

His excitement faded to naught the closer he got. While he spared the dwarves and Andarens a passing look, his attention was drawn to the Dragon Rider. The extent of her injuries were concealed by the strip of cloth she had tied about her eyes before leaving Ka'vairn, but the staff she now used to navigate the ground compounded the truth of her wounds.

Aphrandhor's emotions moved quickly through shock and disgust to righteous anger. "What did you do to her?" he growled in Andarneese.

Daijen took a step back when the wizard's staff began to

crackle with small bolts of lightning. "Androma," the Vahlken intoned.

The Rider stepped away from Ilithranda, her hand coming up to calm her friend. "Green Leaf," she called him, her tone relaying her state of safety.

Aphrandhor's shoulder dropped a notch and his staff appeared as no more than a piece of wood. "What happened to you?"

Androma used his voice to close the gap and place a hand on his shoulder. "Baelon," she answered in a word.

The wizard looked confused, his gaze roaming the thick clouds overhead. "Maegar?" he uttered.

The Rider was unable to answer—unable to speak at all. The ruination of her eyes even prevented her from crying. It was answer enough for Aphrandhor, who stepped in and wrapped his arms around her.

"I'm so sorry," he whispered, holding her for some time. When they separated, the wizard looked again at his friend's most unusual companions. "What happened?"

"Her dragon got killed by another dragon." Yamnomora deposited the information as if it were no more than a casual piece of news. "What?" she queried under the Vahlkens' combined scrutiny. "We've not time for hugs an' kisses. This land belongs to *them*. An' they ain' exactly subtle," the dwarf added, gesturing at the Aegres. "The enemy probably knows we're 'ere."

Daijen looked to Mordrith in the hope she might censor her fiery companion.

"She's right," came the unhelpful response. "We need to find this tomb while we've still got the light."

Aphrandhor held up a hand. "Would someone *please* explain who you all are and how you know about the Skaramangians?"

Androma reached out, her hand extended towards the wizard. "See for yourself."

There was more than a little hesitation on The Green Leaf's face. He scanned those who were strangers to him before narrowing his eyes on the Rider.

"Trust me," Androma whispered, her fingers flexing in invitation.

It seemed peculiar, but Daijen was content to merely observe as the wizard reached into the satchel hooked across his torso. He removed an object the Vahlken immediately recognised as a vambrace, though it was quite ornate in appearance. More so, its accents of bronze, gold, and copper were enough to lead Daijen's gaze to the hammer in Mordrith's grip.

After inserting his right hand and securing the bracer to his forearm, Aphrandhor reached for Androma's hand. He hesitated again. If it was courage he needed the wizard soon found it, his hand grasping hers. Contact forced his eyes closed and he drew in a breath.

"We've no time for hand holdin' either," Yamnomora interjected.

The Green Leaf released his grip on Androma, his eyes snapping open with revelation behind them. "I see," he said at length, looking at the group with a fresh perspective.

"What was that?" Ilithranda asked.

"There is more than one weapon of power in the world," Androma replied cryptically.

"The bracer?" Daijen stepped towards the wizard, who adjusted the staff in his hand. The Vahlken came to a halt, his hands coming up in a symbol of peace. "How does it work?" His mind, starving for information, demanded answers.

"Daijen Saeth," Aphrandhor announced confidently. "Ilithranda Lhoris. Mordrith Underborn. Yamnomora." The Green Leaf's eyes eventually fell on the Warhog. "Bludgeon," he finally named.

"How does he know our names?" Yamnomora questioned, the numerous muscles in her brow knotting together.

"Because I know them," Androma said.

"He can read minds?" Ilithranda was quick to ask.

"No," Aphrandhor told her. "Not exactly. The bracer allows me to see the history of whatever I touch. I know where it's been, where it came from, what it's come into contact with."

"That's incredible," Daijen voiced, suddenly eager to wear the vambrace.

"It isn't perfect," the wizard explained. "I see fragments, shards of the past. With Androma, I learned your names and her general feelings towards you all. I lived through your meeting with... The Valtorak," he said, his mouth testing the name. "I confess, I don't have control—*yet*," he added. "But like all novices, I shall train."

"That's how you learned of this place?" Ilithranda deduced. "What did you touch?"

"I can assure you, there has been a lot more to my investigation than simply *touching* things. That said," he went on, looking deliberately at the dwarves, "my methods are... *cleaner* than others."

Yamnomora shrugged. "Same results."

Ignoring her companion's comment, Mordrith asked, "What did ye learn o' this place, Wizard?"

Aphrandhor faced the dwarf, though his eyes lingered on The Anther. "You too wield a weapon of the old world," he remarked. "What power does it possess?"

"Ye'll see soon enough, Wizard," Yamnomora answered on her charge's behalf, a wicked grin pulling at her beard.

"What did ye learn?" Mordrith asked again, her chin jutting towards the treeline.

The Green Leaf cleared his throat. "Like you, I know they call this place *The Tomb*. It is sacred to the Skaramangians. Those I have come into contact with have never been inside, however, so the truth of the site remains a mystery."

"The site?" Daijen's sharp gaze moved past the wizard, though he could not pierce the trees.

"Yes," Aphrandhor divulged. "It's about five miles south of here. In nearly twenty days I have only set eyes on it once. They guard it well."

Mordrith slung The Anther over one shoulder. "Not well enough," she stated with dwarven conviction.

Yamnomora chuckled to herself as she mounted Bludgeon. "Ain' that the truth."

The dwarves didn't wait for an invitation as they set off for the south. Ilithranda offered Androma her arm but the Rider politely refused, informing the Vahlken that she would walk with Aphrandhor.

"You don't wear it all the time?" Daijen asked, observing the wizard remove the vambrace and replace it inside his satchel.

"No. It's too much," he reported, his tone hinting at the burden of the thing. "Everything I touch fills my mind with sounds and images. Even the bark of a tree has a story to tell."

Daijen accepted the information with a nod and watched the two humans turn and make for the trees. Ilithranda gave Oaken instructions to remain in the area, so he might hunt and rest without tracking them south and giving their advance away. Daijen repeated her commands for Valyra, pausing only to rest his forehead against the smooth and cold curve of her armoured beak. He ran one hand down the same patch and patted her affectionately under the jaw. She squawked once in protest, her head thrusting towards the trees.

"Easy," he bade. "I will return. Now go. Hunt some whales," he added with a smile.

Leaving the anxious Aegres, the Vahlken fell in side by side at the rear of the group. "Is this wise?" Ilithranda posed. "Now there are *two* weapons of power on this island."

Daijen had to agree with her unease—the weapons had clearly been separated for a reason. "I get the feeling this island has something *worse* for us to worry about."

For the most part, their trek through the forest was well-paced and the group progressed swiftly. It was easy to forget that the island was infested with Skaramangians.

Androma conversed quietly with Aphrandhor, though her words could not escape Daijen's ears. Her recounting of events was staggered, the tale broken into bits that she could handle. The wizard listened patiently to it all, and without a word. In truth, the

Vahlken was hardly paying attention to their conversation. His thoughts drifted again and again to The Green Leaf's satchel.

A weapon of the old world, he had called it. It was a weapon to be brought against the Skaramangians, Daijen decided. So much of their world was shrouded in secrecy, their order broken into segments that didn't even know others existed. The bracer could unlock it all, reveal the truth, and bring them into the light.

Combined with The Anther, he thought, they would wield the power of... well, the power of a god. For years he had lived under the scepticism of The Valtorak. Now, beyond the walls of Ka'vairn, where he had witnessed godly relics in action, his faith was slowly filtering through again, like a light piercing the fog brought on by decades of brutal training.

However briefly, he imagined that fateful day of Reclamation, when the bones of Ahnir, Meliax, Govhul, and Yohem were given new life. The heavens would flourish again and the Black Abyss would be home to naught but the Dark Ones.

Could it really be as simple as that? Bring back the gods, even *one* god, and any threat of the Dark Ones would be extinguished? Even if he could be instrumental in such a thing, the Vahlken had no idea where to begin. How did one resurrect a dead god? The practicality clashed with his faith, leaving his belief in the Arkalon and its holy scripture standing on unsteady ground.

For the last mile of their trek, it felt only natural to Ilithranda and Daijen to separate and peel away from the group. They fanned east and west while progressing south. Without a sound they navigated the forest floor, moving from tree to tree, always finding the shadows. They kept the group in sight at all times but were ever vigilant for those that might be watching them from afar.

As the southern treeline came into view, Daijen nestled himself into a position at the top of a rocky outcropping, where he could perch on its many edges and maintain a lofty vantage. He spied the group in the distance, creeping ever closer to the edge of the forest. Beyond them, he could not find Ilithranda amongst the trees, though he hadn't expected to.

Unable to see the site Aphrandhor had spoken of, the Vahlken waited.

Despite having lived through an eternity in the pits of Handuin, his time perched in waiting felt excruciatingly long. Only when the sun began to set, streaming the forest with burnt light, did both he and Ilithranda regroup with the others.

"I thought you said this place was guarded," Ilithranda put to the wizard.

"It was—it *is*," he insisted.

"You've seen them?" Daijen checked.

"Oh yes. I have avoided them too."

Daijen spared a moment to meet Ilithranda's eyes. They shared their concern, feeling more than anything else, that something was wrong. The Vahlken had to wonder if a deer felt something similar before the lion sprang its trap.

"Maybe they're afraid," Yamnomora posited, hefting one of her two enormous axes over one shoulder. "Not everyone can stand up to dwarven steel."

"We've waited long enough," Mordrith voiced. "Guards or no guards, I'm for seein' what lies beyond."

"And if it's a trap?" Androma posed, the only other among them who had been trained as a warrior.

"I'm hopin' it is," Yamnomora said with a hungry smile. "It's been too long since me girls 'ave tasted Skaramangian," she added, looking proudly at her axes.

"It is a sight to behold," Aphrandhor reported, his sense of wonder edging into his voice.

That was enough for the dwarves, who turned and pushed through the treeline, Bludgeon between them. Ilithranda nudged Androma with her elbow and the Rider accepted, allowing the Vahlken to guide her through the last of the forest.

Daijen departed last, his blue eyes scanning the foliage they were leaving behind. He saw nothing, the forest dappled in the setting sun, but a land of quiet serenity. It just didn't sit right with him.

Drawing his sabre, the Vahlken followed the group out of the forest where, indeed, there was a sight to behold.

"What is it?" Androma enquired irritably, her lack of sight a burning frustration.

Daijen let his eyes roam over it all before answering. "It's a pyramid," he informed her, a hint of surprise about him.

Black as any abyss, the pyramid's surface possessed a sleek sheen, as if it were constructed from crystal or glass. All this was seen between the web of vines that had grown over it, the forest eager to extend its reach and swallow it up.

The structure dominated the clearing that sat with jagged cliffs at its back, guarding it from prying eyes. It was not the only thing in the clearing. Daijen's attention was drawn to the large hole in the ground, a perfect circle that plunged into the earth about two hundred yards out from the structure. He didn't need to get any closer to recognise the workings of a lift platform.

"A pyramid?" Androma echoed incredulously. "In Nareene?"

"Actually," The Green Leaf felt compelled to point out, "that is merely the capstone."

Daijen looked at the pyramid with fresh eyes, seeing now that the base of the visible pyramid was matte black. In disbelief, he looked at the ground as if he could see the rest of it—the majority of the pyramid—beneath him.

Yamnomora looked back at the wizard. "They built it underground?"

"No," Aphrandhor said at length. "The earth has swallowed it up." He laid a single eye on the dwarf. "'Tis *ancient*."

Androma broke away from Ilithranda, her staff tapping the ground at her feet. "How ancient?"

The wizard raised an eyebrow and offered something of a shrug. "It could be the oldest thing in all of Verda," he theorised. "It should be noted," he went on excitedly, eager to tell of his findings, "this is the very centre of Nareene, and Nareene lies at the heart of the known world."

Mordrith frowned. "Truly?"

"Oh yes. We might be behind Eradoran lines, but this island

sits perfectly between Erador and Andara. To the Elderlings, Nareene could have been the seat of power in their civilisation."

Daijen blinked and looked at the wizard. "Elderlings?"

"A theory," Androma was quick to insert.

"It is more than a theory," Aphrandhor argued. "I have seen them," he explained, holding up the arm that had previously worn the vambrace.

"What are they?" Mordrith asked, certainly the more curious of the two dwarves.

"They are the people who built this," The Green Leaf replied, as if it was obvious. "The people from which the Skaramangians were born."

"You're talking about Andarens," Ilithranda said, her confusion no less than Daijen's. "The Skaramangians came from Andara."

The wizard pursed his lips. "As I said, the bracer shows me shards of what was. I cannot put all the pieces together, but I have touched objects—relics—that have shown me people from eons past. *Humans*," he specified. "From what I can gather, they predate Erador's history."

Daijen was about as open-minded as an Andaren could be, and he wasn't convinced. "Surely you have just witnessed events that predate *recorded* history. Both our people have lived through ages without the written word." He gestured at Ilithranda, the only other Andaren among them. "There is nothing recorded before the first epoch, but we have found evidence that our people still populated Andara."

"Those who walked with your gods," Aphrandhor replied, nodding his head. "I know your history, Daijen Saeth. The time of your first epoch records the war with the Eikor, just as ours records a great exodus from a land of monsters. I believe *your* history," he went on, looking to the dwarves, "says something about dark days fighting the Talakin, great monsters of the deep."

Mordrith raised an eyebrow. "Aye," she said suspiciously. "It does."

The wizard smiled knowingly. "I have not seen a clear picture of the past, but I have seen enough to know we all share in the *same* past. As for my theory regarding the Elderlings; perhaps we should investigate the site a little further."

Daijen's mind wanted to lay out all of their collective history and see the truth revealed. But he also hungered to know exactly what The Tomb was. More importantly, what it was hiding in its depths.

Putting the wizard's theories aside for the time being, the Vahlken advanced with his sabre still in hand. He soon reached the large hole and peered over the edge to spy a deep well illuminated by torches all the way to the bottom. The lift platform rested at the surface, accessible via a narrow walkway that protruded from the lip.

"That's a big hole," Ilithranda remarked dryly.

Mordrith sniffed loudly. "I've dug bigger holes before lunch."

"I should like to walk the perimeter," Aphrandhor announced, looking at the capstone, "but I believe its secrets lie within."

"Agreed," Androma said, her tone clipped. "There is a way down?"

One by one they crossed the walkway and stepped onto the platform. Daijen barred Yamnomora's way.

"What are ye abou'?" she snapped.

"The pig stays here," he told her commandingly.

The dwarf shot him a scowl that could crack stone. "He's a Warhog, a title well-earned. Ye should be honoured to 'ave Bludgeon by yer side."

"By my side is exactly where I *don't* want a Warhog," Daijen countered. "We have no idea what's down there, but there's likely to be a structure of tight spaces. I can't have an unpredictable animal charging around making a mess of things. Bludgeon stays here," he repeated.

Yamnomora was about to give the Vahlken a piece of her mind when Mordrith interjected. "Jus' leave 'im up 'ere," she barked, keen to be on with their descent.

Yamnomora offered Daijen a sneer before leading the Warhog away from the hole. Upon her return, the group stood shoulder to shoulder, ready to bid farewell to the dying light. The Green Leaf used a touch of magic to activate the lever from afar. Chains rattled and wood creaked after the initial jerk, but the platform was slowly lowered underground.

Daijen looked up at the orange sky. He saw two rebellious Aegres flying overhead. Valyra always liked to have an eye on him—preferably two. It was then that the truth of their situation dawned on the Vahlken. Were their roles reversed and he were to set a trap for his foe, he would ensure his enemy had no hope of retreat and absolutely no hope of being aided by their dreaded Aegres.

Quite naturally, he turned to convey the sinking feeling he had with Ilithranda, only to find she was already looking at him, the concern evidently shared.

But the bait had been too much to pass up, and the six companions descended into the gloom.

Though it felt and certainly sounded rickety, the lift transported them to the bottom without fault. To Daijen's surprise, they weren't faced with the northern slope of the pyramid as he had expected.

"We're *inside*," Aphrandhor voiced for them all.

The Vahlken stepped off the platform, examining the entrance through which they had arrived. From inside the pyramid, he could see that the original excavation team had dug straight through the northern face rather than seek out an actual entrance.

The chamber they now stood in was twice the height of an average room, with two rows of thin pillars where the excavation team hadn't cut through the ceiling. Like the shaft, the space was illuminated by torches fixed to the walls—more proof that the pyramid was occupied.

"I'm to take it we're still alone?" Androma queried, her voice filling the chamber.

"For now," Daijen muttered, advancing between the pillars.

The Green Leaf whispered something into his staff, as if the stick could hear him. Perhaps it did, the Vahlken reasoned, for the end of the staff birthed an orb of light that outshone the torches.

The spell floated lazily above the wizard but always stayed a few feet ahead of him.

"I will take the lead," he offered, making for the door on the other side of the room.

Ilithranda placed Androma's hand on her shoulder, where the edge of the leather pauldron offered something to grip. She gave Daijen a look that told him to go ahead of them, just behind the dwarves who had fallen into line behind The Green Leaf.

Leaving the first chamber behind, they were immediately brought to a set of steps that took them even deeper into the pyramid. The steps turned back on themselves again and again, the companions cast in stark shadows as the orb of light moved ever forwards and down. Always down.

When, at last, they reached the end, an antechamber awaited them, only it boasted taller and thicker pillars that led Daijen's gaze towards a set of forbidding double doors that reminded the Vahlken of Ka'vairn's entrance.

Aphrandhor's attention, however, had been drawn to the walls either side of the pillars. "Would you look at this," he said with great interest.

Daijen managed only a glance at the imagery depicted in the stone before the dwarves demanded his attention.

"We didn' come 'ere to look at walls, Wizard." Yamnomora's words were strained as she pushed into one of the double doors.

Beside her, Mordrith applied her own strength to the other door. "Let's see what all this is for," she said.

The doors gave way with an unnervingly loud *crack* that forced Daijen to scrutinise every dark corner that surrounded them. The dwarves continued to push them until they were wide enough to permit entry.

There was naught but shadow to greet them.

"Aphrandhor," Daijen encouraged.

The wizard walked between the dwarves, who stood ready with weapons in hand. The orb of light preceded him, banishing what it could of the thick darkness. Daijen's keen eyes tracked the edges of the light, confounded by the lack of detail it revealed.

Seeing only the stone floor, the group could do little but depart the antechamber and brave the oppressive shadows.

"You're all quiet," Androma observed, her voice echoing far and high.

The Green Leaf noted the fleeing sound and turned to look back at the Vahlken, who gestured to the floating orb and jutted his chin up. The wizard understood and sent a silent command to his bright spell. The small globe began to rise, leaving them in semi-darkness.

Edging forwards, it also revealed what lay before the companions, the sight of it leading Daijen's eyes ever higher. The Vahlken's mouth slowly fell agape.

What madness had they found?

59
STEEL, FANGS, AND TALONS

Death had a face. It looked at Gallien Drakalis through golden eyes and a complexion of chalk white.

The Andaren towered over the smuggler, his armoured collar high enough to reach his chin but not high enough to conceal his psychotic grin or the scars that marred his entire head.

Their battle had already begun to feel more like a chase, as the Skaramangian assassin pursued him through the ruins and over the uneven ground. His cumbersome blade, which The Dawn Sword wielded with unimaginable grace, sliced through the ancient stone again and again as it came for Gallien's head.

The smuggler turned every accidental trip into a deliberate roll, using what agility he had to evade the incoming blade. It had to be silvyr, he reasoned, though such reasoning didn't help him to stay alive.

Deciding that he needed to do more than give Slait a distracting target, Gallien brought his axe to bear—his weapon of power. He lunged forwards, bringing the axe round in a two-handed swing. The Vahlken-trained assassin side-stepped the attack and then again when Drakalis reversed his swing. The third was a chopping attack aimed to split the Andaren down the middle.

Silvyr and steel came together in a ringing clash.

Slait's wicked grin faded as he tilted his head and examined the point where both blades were touching. The Dawn Sword grunted and came at the smuggler with a swing of his own. Gallien parried twice before his third block brought them close together.

Again, the towering Andaren scrutinised the axe, disgruntled and surprised to see that the silvyr had failed to even dent the steel. Drakalis used his opponent's momentary distraction and grasped the handle behind the curved blade. With his adjusted grip, he forced the sword away before swinging back with the pointed haft.

The Dancing Sword of the Dawn yelled in pain as the shaft struck his cheek, the sharp point tearing through his skin and lips. Another scar to be added to the ruinous tapestry.

The Andaren spat blood across the sandy stone and returned to the fight with a swift backhand. Drakalis barely registered the impact before he was sprawled across the ground. The taste of blood spoiling his mouth, he heard the axe clatter somewhere out of sight.

Footsteps sharpened his senses.

The sound of steel scraping over stone directed his attention to Slait, who now stood with the axe in hand. He turned it left and right, investigating the weapon's many facets. Gallien could have stayed flat out on the ground and accepted whatever death was to be delivered, but he knew who would suffer after him.

The smuggler decided he had a lot more blood to lose before he would allow Joran to face the pale beast.

Fighting his exhaustion and pain, Gallien picked himself up and took a breath, his shoulders squared. "That's mine," he declared gruffly.

Slait's golden eyes shifted towards Drakalis, his smug grin returning. "Then I shall give it to you," he replied mockingly.

Gallien mirrored his smile and raised his hand to display the axe.

Utterly shocked, The Dawn Sword looked from the axe to his own hand, now absent the weapon.

"Want to see it again?" Drakalis asked devilishly.

He didn't wait for an answer. The axe left his grip at speed, their proximity requiring hardly a notch of accuracy. Still, the Andaren's mutations granted him the ability to intercept the flying axe and bat it aside with his blade. The weapon, however, couldn't be heard to impact the stone.

Gallien smiled all the more, the axe returned to his grip. Having got a feel for the mechanism by which the magic worked, he threw it again and again, always waiting to see if it penetrated his foe's defences before recalling it to his waiting hand. Only once did it hit The Dawn Sword, his weapon knocked back, only for it to careen off his white pauldron.

It was enough to stagger the behemoth, blinding him, if briefly, to Gallien's charge. The smuggler leapt, using a slab of broken stone to gain height. His hand stretched high, the axe already comfortably in his grasp, he came down with a hammer stroke that would cleave anyone's skull, regardless of their enhancements.

But the axe stopped within an inch of Slait's left eye, the haft of the axe firmly within the Andaren's grip. Without the follow through, Gallien crashed into The Dawn Sword, a man-shaped wall of muscle and armour. It was enough to buckle the smuggler's knees, dropping him to the ground.

"My years of training alone dwarf your lifespan, human," The Dawn Sword told him. "This weapon will not change your fate."

Gallien craned his neck to offer the Andaren a bloody smile. "You're a slow learner."

Crouched at Slait's feet, Drakalis flexed the fingers of his left hand. Why the axe heeded *his* call he couldn't say, but he welcomed the cold steel as it vanished from the Andaren's hand and materialised in his.

He slammed the pointed shaft into The Dawn Sword's foot. If he roared with pain it went unnoticed by the smuggler, who knew naught but pain when Slait threw a solid fist into his face and launched him across the ground.

A curtain of black dropped over Gallien's world before reality rushed back into his senses. He was face down, his brown leather cloak strewn over one arm. Blinking long and hard, the smuggler discovered the trail of blood that led him back to Slait.

The Andaren staggered sideways and leaned against the nearest wall, his injured foot stealing his attention. One meaty hand rummaged through the pouches on his belt and produced a slender vial of luminous blue liquid.

Gallien could only squint, his head pounding, as The Dawn Sword proceeded to pour the blue liquid over his bleeding foot. A pained growl escaped his pale lips and his fist clenched until he shattered the vial.

What exactly the liquid had done was beyond Gallien's understanding, but the demonic glee that stretched Slait's face informed the smuggler that the wound was no longer so bothersome. Oblivious to the blood oozing from his injured palm, The Dawn Sword assumed his towering posture.

This was to be the moment then. What could he do in the face of such fury—fury that was paired with strength and skills beyond his own? Nevertheless, Gallien Drakalis wasn't to see out his final seconds lying on the ground. Fighting off the dizziness that tormented him, the smuggler once again picked himself up, rising with the axe in his hand.

"Too stubborn to die, I see," Slait remarked. "You should know when you're beaten."

Gallien spat a mouthful of blood on the ground. "I've been on the losing end of things all my life. But today," he added with a care-free smile, "I've got a magic axe."

He threw the weapon with reckless abandon, sure that he would make this, his final stand, count for the ages. The Andaren batted it away only to be hounded by the axe again and again, the steel slicing through the air time after time. With every step Gallien pressed forwards The Dawn Sword was pressed into retreat, his reflexes put to the test.

By the ninth or tenth throw, Slait intercepted the wrong part of the axe and the haft flipped round to strike him atop the head. His footing lost, The Dawn Sword fell back over a partially broken wall.

Gallien recalled the weapon and made to advance before a firm hand knocked against his arm. Despite her lack of sight, Androma had found him amongst the ruins, where their duel had taken the pair up a level.

Her hand glided down Drakalis's ribs until she located the worn leather of a satchel that she had once called her own.

Gallien didn't stop her. He didn't dare take his eyes from The Dancing Sword of the Dawn, who was already returned to his feet and navigating his way around the broken wall.

"There you are," Androma muttered, her right arm buried up to her elbow in the bottomless satchel.

Gallien's gaze was drawn up with Androma's rising hand, his eyes wide with awe.

The old Rider had pulled free from the depths a sword unlike any even a king could commission. The grip came out first, a crouching dragon of pale gold. The straight-edged blade that followed was magnificent, shining bright as it caught the sun's rays cutting between the ruins. The exquisite cross-guard curled up either side of the blade, each quillon resembling a fang in the same pale gold as the pommel. The weapon—a Dragon Rider's weapon—was gripped by a hilt of dark blue leather, the colour similar to the small scales that plated her vambraces.

Androma twisted the blade left and right, getting a feel for its weight and balance. The sword cut through the air with a fine whistle and came to a sudden stop, the flat of the blade an inch from her right cheekbone.

"You won't run away this time," she said, her words igniting a fresh wave of fury in The Dawn Sword. "Get Joran out of here," she barked over one shoulder.

Gallien was reminded of the last time they parted ways, when he whisked a much younger Joran from the clutches of the Andarens. Not this time, he decided. He would fight with her now and be rid of the menace that had chased them across the realm.

He struggled to maintain that resolve when Androma and Slait collided in battle. With her sword in hand, the old Rider was a Banshee unleashed, her fighting style that of a dancer and a Wraith combined. Gone was the uncertainty that came with her blindness—though, seeing her now, Drakalis had to wonder if some of it was an act.

Dropping low, her leg swept the floor, forcing The Dawn Sword to raise his good foot and put all of his weight onto his wounded foot. The larger opponent was immediately put off balance, compromising his defence, and leaving him vulnerable to the Rider's rising attack.

There was a sudden and sharp *ring*, the sound of metal slicing through metal, before Slait fell back into a shattered archway. He was quick to recover, however, puffing out his chest to display no more than a damaged cuirass where Androma's sword had cut diagonally up to his left shoulder. His cock-sure grin fell away when he noticed the blood dripping from the bottom rim of the cuirass, slowly being absorbed by his white robes.

The Andaren snarled and lunged at Androma. Gallien wasn't even close to the duel and he still retreated a step, disturbed by the ferocity. And yet, Androma had been ready for the beast. She pivoted one way then the next, narrowly evading the lash of his blade each time. In a deft counterattack Gallien couldn't have achieved *with* sight, the old Rider bashed her pommel into the back of his bald head before ducking and swivelling on one knee to whip her sword across her enemy's thigh.

The Dancing Sword of the Dawn cried out and staggered right, where the ground had long given way and sloped down into another empty chamber. The Andaren toppled over his own weight and disappeared from sight.

"Get Joran out of here!" Androma snapped. "Now!" she added when the smuggler didn't move.

Deciding he would leave Androma do what she had been trained to do, Gallien dashed from that section of the ruins, searching for the elevated edge where he could look out over the rest of the site. Slait's Aegre caught his attention first, the giant creature rearing up on its hind legs and flapping its wings.

Aphrandhor's magic exploded across the ruins, keeping the Aegre from tearing him to pieces. Indeed, the animal appeared wounded, with smoking patches of feathers and numerous arrows protruding from its sides.

Cob skipped across a portion of the ruins and came down on the Aegre with his scimitar of Draven bone. The creature swivelled its head towards the Kedradi, its beak already open and ready to snap at its prey. Cob struck first, bringing the scimitar down across the Aegre's face, just behind its beak. The animal let loose an angry squawk but was prevented from retaliation by the wizard.

"Yala!" The Green Leaf cried, sweeping his staff along the length of his sword, Yalaqin. The blade was set alight with hungry flames and waved from left to right in the Aegre's face.

Scanning the sprawling ruins, Gallien spotted the white of Joran's hair. The smuggler didn't waste any time in descending the rugged terrain, his hands and feet skidding down portions of the slopes.

"Joran!" he hissed.

The boy turned on his heel, his hands coming up to defend himself. "Gallien!" he called in relief, embracing the man in a bear hug. "We have to help them," he insisted.

Gallien grabbed the boy's shirt, the smuggler on the verge of dragging him as far away as possible, when there came new commotion from round the corner.

"Now what?" Drakalis fumed. Joran was quick to move, heading for the source, until the smuggler physically held him back. "Wait," he urged, all-too aware that the boy was absent any weapon.

Androma and Slait caught his eye, the two warriors colliding in battle on the ruins above. The sight of the Rider and her sword jogged Gallien's memory, reminding him that the axe wasn't the only weapon he had access to.

"Wait," he said again, his hand rummaging inside Androma's satchel. He felt numerous objects therein, from bound scrolls and leather-bound books to the small red dragon scale he had picked up in Harendun sixteen years earlier.

There! His fingers coiled around the hilt.

"Take this."

Joran flinched, his eyes roaming up and down the broken sword in Gallien's hand.

"Take it," the smuggler urged.

"Why do you have a broken sword?" Joran asked, accepting the hilt.

Gallien had never told him about the giant skeleton or the sword he had taken after Kitrana lost it beneath Harendun. Before he had lost Kitrana. As they did then, in the presence of a dead god, the axe and sword came to life in their hands. The sword adopted an orange hue, the blade illuminated by tiny shards. Similarly, the axe blade glowed with violet light.

Joran marvelled at the sword. "What is this?"

In truth, Gallien had no idea, but since the axe only began to glow a moment ago, he had to assume the effect was created when both weapons came together. What he did know was what he had witnessed sixteen years ago. It was hard to forget a sea monster being disintegrated.

"It's how you're going to survive," the smuggler said simply. "You only have to cut your enemy and the sword will do the rest."

"What are you talking about?" the boy demanded as the commotion they had heard turned into a clashing of steel.

It dawned on Gallien then, as it should have sooner, that Joran had never taken a life. Drakalis had hoped to spare the boy from killing anyone, a deed that marked everyone's soul, and nightmares, for the rest of their days. That seemed impossible with all the harbingers of Death that had circled Joran since his birth.

"Don't think about it," he told him, his words spilling out as the new threat grew louder. "Move and swing. That's all you have to do. Move, look for the opening, and drive your sword through. Don't dwell on it. Just stay on my shoulder. Guard my right. I'll guard your left."

Joran nodded through every instruction, his expression bordering on bewilderment.

Hugging the ancient walls and broken pillars, Gallien kept

Joran behind him as he moved to investigate the newcomers. It had to be the Andarens, he knew. The sound of clashing steel and parrying shields was an unnerving, if familiar, sound.

Much to his surprise, Aphrandhor and Cob had no part in whatever battle was taking place, the pair still locked in battle with the Aegre. Rounding the final corner, the truth of the matter came into view.

The Dawn Sword had struck his head, but it seemed the blow had been more potent than the smuggler had given it credit.

"You can see the dwarves, aye?"

Joran practically crashed into his side to lay eyes on them. "Dwarves!" he exclaimed.

There were two of them—men by the black beard of one and thick copper stubble of the other. They were fighting Andarens and fiercely so. The dwarf of dark skin landed wild blow after wild blow, his hammer sending soldiers to the ground. The considerably paler dwarf hacked and slashed with a two-handed axe in each hand.

Andaren blood was soon staining The Ruins of Gelakor.

Thundering hooves turned Gallien and Joran around on their heels. Despite having seen the army advancing below, it seemed an extraordinary sight to see an Andaren war horse charging towards them along the cliff path. It was also terrifying.

Gallien managed to raise his axe to deflect the swinging sword. At the same time, Joran bounded aside, partially mounting the slope beside them. Dissatisfied, the rider turned his horse about and charged again. Gallien braced himself, wondering if he had survived The Dancing Sword of the Dawn only to die at the hands of a common soldier.

A cloaked figure emerged from the ruins above and leapt with abandon, taking the pale rider from his saddle. The horse continued on, galloping towards the smuggler, its head down and horns presented. Without the rider to worry about, Gallien flattened himself to the wall on his left and waited for the mutated beast to pass him by.

The unseated rider and cloaked stranger wrestled fiercely as they tumbled down the slope. They landed on the ancient path in a heap, the stranger's spear rolling away. They exchanged fists on the ground, kicking up snow and mud, until they rose to their knees. Seeing only the stranger's back, he had no idea who had jumped in to save him, though he did wonder why they weren't wearing any boots.

The rider landed an elbow, eliciting a sharp yelp from the apparent woman. Taking what advantage he could, the Andaren drew a dagger from his belt. Gallien wasn't the only one to have witnessed this. Joran skidded down the slope and lunged at the rider. The broken sword plunged through a gap in the Andaren's cuirass, under his arm.

The smuggler shielded his eyes against the sudden flare of sparks and ash.

Reduced to dust, the Andaren simply blew away in the breeze. Joran was left in his wake, utterly stunned by the event. Gallien felt for him in that moment, though he was thankful his first kill was considerably less bloody than his own had been.

It seemed fitting, also, that the first life Joran should ever take was in defence of another.

"Joran..." he began, before the stranger looked over her shoulder. Gallien had to shut his eyes and shake his head. "Kit?"

"Gallien?" the Nimean blurted. Her head, however, was quick to swivel on Joran. "That's my sword!" she asserted.

Kitrana Voden started for the boy, her hand reaching for the sword in Joran's grip, when a shadow overcame them.

"Get down!" Gallien yelled.

Joran and Kit were able to drop flat onto the path as The Dawn Sword's Aegre descended on them beak-first. It snapped twice, its scarred mouth attempting to ensnare each as they scrambled away, but the slope and adjacent wall made it all too difficult for the large animal to navigate.

Desperate to protect Joran, Gallien stepped forward and launched his axe. It struck the beast above the right eye, enraging it before bringing its attention down on the smuggler. Drakalis swore, unsure what to do next. As the axe reappeared in his hand, the Aegre advanced, awkwardly navigating the slope, its beak snapping incessantly.

A mighty roar preceded the falling Kedradi. Having leapt from the ruins above, Cob came down with his scimitar in both hands. The claw-like point buried deep into the creature's left wing, the flash of pain and shock sending the Aegre into the wall.

"Get Joran out of here!" the ranger cried, yanking his weapon free.

Indeed, that was made possible when the mutated beast turned its ire on the Kedradi and followed him up the stony slope, while Joran recovered and ran down the path to join Gallien again.

Kitrana was on his heels.

"That's mine!" she barked, catching up with them. "I need it," the Nimean asserted, her path to Joran blocked by Gallien.

"I thought you were dead," the smuggler breathed.

The comment, if not his heartfelt tone, took some of the urgency out of her. "I should be," she replied, though he could make no sense of it.

Nor was there time to.

A pair of Andarens rushed them from the snowy ruins, ending any potential conversation. Gallien was soon reminded of Kit's graceful fighting style. She weaved between the soldiers, her body curving and bending in ways that would cause damage to any surface-dweller. Before the Andarens could swing a second time, Kitrana was behind them, her spear twisting to bring the sharp head to bear.

As one felt the thrust of her weapon, his chest cavity rammed by a weapon of his kin's own making, Drakalis raised his axe and deflected two more lashes of the steel scimitar. Seeing an opening, Joran lunged in with the broken sword. For all his awareness, the boy lacked the skill to execute without the element of surprise. The soldier pivoted and parried his clumsy attack, ending their brief clash with an elbow to Joran's face.

Gallien swung once and hard, the axe gripped in two hands and eight pale knuckles. A boot to the soldier's chest was soon required to free the axe from his head. Kitrana was similarly retrieving her spear and looked to be on the verge of renewing her argument for the broken sword when a familiar shadow returned.

This time, the smuggler was close enough to shove Joran out of the way before the Aegre's splayed talons came in to land. Drakalis himself, however, was unable to avoid the wing that swept him aside as if he were no more than a pebble.

His body having taken a severe beating in only a handful of minutes, the smuggler was slow to find his hands and knees. His ribs were burning on both sides, his hands were numb, and his back and head felt like they had substituted for an anvil.

Gallien looked up in time to see Kitrana flung into the air, her head struck by a closed beak. That left Joran, who was on his back and stuck between the Aegre and the ruins behind him.

At a glance, there was no sign of Aphrandhor or Cob, though the sound of battle still permeated The Ruins of Gelakor. With Kit down and Androma locked in a duel to the death with The Dawn Sword, only Gallien remained to save the boy.

But he was too far away.

Joran was very much in the Aegre's sights, its yellow eyes leading its bowing head and sharp beak towards the boy. Gallien called out to him, vowing his rescue, as he forgot his pain and found his feet. His words were about as useful as his ability to fend off an Aegre, but it was all he had in those precious seconds.

The white beast squawked fiercely in Joran's face, its enormous head plunging towards him in a promise of death.

"NO!" Drakalis raged, his axe coming up.

A buffeting wind launched the smuggler back and off his feet, robbing him of Joran's final moments.

His heart pounding, Gallien forced himself up, forced himself to look at his dead son if only to believe that such a thing could be true.

Such a black and grim reality was yet to dawn.

Gallien could hardly believe what he was seeing, but his eyes were adamant he looked upon not one, but *two* Aegres. More so, they were savagely tearing into each other. The new mutated eagle was a stark contrast to its white counterpart, its feathers more black than brown, and its beak plated in armour. It brought powerful talons to bear and ripped into the flesh of the pale beast.

Before he could become a casualty of their battle, Joran scrambled to his feet and darted for Gallien. "Where's the rider?" he asked hoarsely.

Drakalis took another look at the new Aegre, noting now that it wore a saddle laden with bags and pockets but no rider. "I don't know," the smuggler muttered, busy now trying to discover a way out of the ruins.

"This way!" Aphrandhor cried.

The wizard appeared in an archway, a figure of green in the light of his fiery sword. They were not the only ones to hear his call, his booming voice having garnered the attention of the Andarens. Aphrandhor flicked his staff at one, his magic sending the soldier flying through a broken wall. Another came at him with steel and found burning steel in return, his face and helm torn asunder.

Gallien turned back to see Kitrana picking herself up, if slowly. "Kit!" he yelled. "Over here!"

The Nimean was able to avoid the erratic Aegres as they pushed through ancient stone and kicked up mud and snow. She was already looking at the sword in Joran's hand.

"Not now," Gallien asserted, his tone conveying their dire situation.

"What in the hells is going on here?" she demanded.

"Later," he growled.

The orange hue of the broken blade had already caught Aphrandhor's attention. "A weapon of power," he uttered, his old face creased with turmoil. He looked to Gallien expectantly.

"It seems we both have questions," the smuggler posed, letting the wizard see and hear some of the enmity that still bubbled under his skin.

The Green Leaf paused, considering any response he might give. "Indeed," he drawled, before his eyes flitted beyond Gallien. "At least we still have allies!" he declared with elation.

The trio turned away from the wizard and looked back at the warring Aegres. There was no place for any man in that battle.

"There's no rider," Joran pointed out.

Aphrandhor offered the boy a sad smile. "You look upon Oaken. Your *mother's* Aegre."

Gallien watched Joran's emotions flood across his angular face, revealing some of his desperation to know the woman who had carried him and brought him into the world. It also revealed some of his heartbreak at knowing he never could.

"I suspected he had been following Androma—and for some time." The wizard glanced at the mountains that rose about them. "I never imagined he would track us this far north."

"Why has he been tracking Androma?" Joran asked.

"Only the Vahlken know how their Aegres think," The Green Leaf replied. "But," he added, "I would say he's been trying to find you, the son of Ilithranda. He is not the Aegre I had hoped to see this day, but he is a welcome sight all the same."

The moment was shattered as the group was set upon by the roaming Andarens, who were just as lost amongst the ruins as everyone else. The fight, however, never came to the companions, though it did come to the Andarens.

The red-headed dwarf thundered into the soldiers from the west, and astride an excessively large pig. The dwarf leapt from the saddle, an axe swinging in each hand. The Andarens tried to form some kind of defence, but it seemed they had never been trained to repel such a foe. Their swings missed, the dwarf able to roll this way and that before popping up with a hungry axe.

When there was naught but corpses on the ground, the dwarf turned to face the companions. "Green Leaf?" She—as her voice revealed—sounded just as perplexed as Gallien and Kitrana had been to see each other.

"Yamnomora?" The wizard wasn't to be left out, sounding just as confused.

All eyes moved to the ruins behind Yamnomora, where the hammer-wielding dwarf could now be seen running towards them. "More!" he shouted. "There's more!"

He wasn't wrong. A group twice the size of the one Yamnomora had just dispatched was charging round the corner. Aphrandhor stepped in the moment the running dwarf was behind him, his staff pointed to the ground before being swiftly flicked upwards. Dirt and snow were hurled at the approaching soldiers, blinding them as well as taking the speed out of their charge.

As one, the companions sprang into action. Gallien was sure to keep Joran behind him, but he didn't keep the boy out of the fight—it was the only way he was going to learn, and if today had taught the smuggler anything, it was that, alone, he couldn't survive the skill and number of foes coming for Joran.

The battle was made all the shorter by Cob's contribution, who ran in from the side and exhibited the prowess of a warrior only a Kedradi could boast. His bone sword was wielded with precision and his enemies executed with terrifying proficiency.

The last of the Andarens to die was by Joran's hand, and obviously so. Like his predecessor, the soldier exploded in a flare of hot ash that darkened the patches of remaining snow.

Yamnomora pushed past Kitrana with some familiarity and gestured at Joran with one of her axes. "That's a... That's a weapon o' power," she stated with amazement. She then noted the axe in Gallien's hand, the blade alight with purple shards. "Ye an' all!" she gasped. "Green Leaf!" The dwarf had become rather animated. "We've another! I found it! The Anther!"

All eyes fell on the dark-skinned dwarf, who looked to be entirely out of his element. The group's attention was quick to drop to the hammer in his hand. The head of gold and bronze was glowing, the shards scattered across its surface adding a blue hue to the ruins.

Yamnomora frowned. "It's never done *that* before," she reported.

A smile was beginning to break out across the wizard's face when a pained cry managed to breach the sound of the enraged Aegres. Like the others, Gallien turned to look up at the ruins above them, where Androma was battling The Dancing Sword of the Dawn.

She was losing.

Slait strode towards her, an air of strength and vitality about him that couldn't be seen in the old Rider. Still, with her sword in hand, Androma managed to evade his next attack and come back at him with one of her own. While she possessed fighting skills beyond the average warrior, she was still burdened with human limitations. Chiefly: fatigue. Her exhaustion was all too obvious and new injuries only added to her problems.

"We have to help her!" Joran cried.

"There is only one who can bring down that monster," Aphrandhor told him gravely. "And he is not here."

Gallien had no idea who or what the wizard was talking about, but he wasn't going to let Joran insert himself in their fight. "We need to get out of here," he said to the boy.

"No," Joran protested.

"She's distracting him so we can do just that," Gallien countered.

It didn't matter. The fight was coming to them.

Slait planted a boot in Androma's chest and launched her from the edge. She rolled and tumbled down the slope until Cob intercepted her.

The Dawn Sword stood defiantly above them, his razored scimitar dripping with blood. He smiled at them, his teeth and lips just as bloody as his blade.

"You are but flakes of the demon's flesh," he snarled.

His descent seemed impossibly fast, leaving Gallien to wonder if the blue liquid Slait had poured over his foot had completely healed the wound.

The Dawn Sword was soon amongst them, leaping at the last second to land in the middle of the companions. His slaiken blade swung round in a whistling arc, ringing against Yamnomora's axes and Aphrandhor's flaming sword before Cob blocked it with his scimitar—the bone notably dented.

Gallien stepped back, seeing the wizard on the verge of unleashing his repertoire of spells. The towering Andaren was cunning. He used the Kedradi and all else who challenged him as living shields. Every time The Green Leaf levelled his staff, Slait would pivot and engage another, ensuring they were between him and the wizard.

Not to be counted out yet, Androma waded back in. Her magnificent sword thrust towards the assassin, forcing him to retreat a step, bringing him closer to Yamnomora. It was with a battle cry that the dwarf joined the fight, her axes chopping and hacking.

Her chaotic and violent style was to Slait's advantage, for it seemed to disorientate the old Rider, who looked to be struggling to detect The Dawn Sword's movements. Yamnomora scored a glancing blow across the Andaren's left pauldron, but he turned it into a pivot that allowed him to backhand Androma, knocking her into Cob.

Completing a full spin, Slait retaliated with a flurry of attacks that pushed Yamnomora into a retreat and, ultimately, onto her back. Seeing the dwarf's inevitable doom, Joran started forward, the broken sword coming up in his hand. Drakalis wasn't taking any chances and held the boy at bay, an effort that required every ounce of his strength.

The situation became overly complicated when more Andarens arrived, the pale men and women of the west flooding in through every gap in the ruins. It dispersed the companions, forcing them to fight their own battles to survive. Worse, it prevented the wizard from bringing his magic to bear on The Dancing Sword of the Dawn.

Leaving Androma on her knees, Cob dashed back into the fray, slaying two soldiers in quick succession before facing Slait again. The Andaren assassin was supernaturally fast to defend himself, deflecting the ranger's attacks with smooth ease. Having fought the Kedradi, it seemed to Gallien an impossible feat when The Dawn Sword not only disarmed Cob but gripped him by the throat and head butted him. In one hand, he then raised the Kedradi clear from the ground and tossed him aside.

The Green Leaf and his fiery sword vanished behind a set of pillars, the wizard pursued by a handful of Andarens. Kit was a survivor and fought only to keep her enemies away, though it didn't escape Gallien that she kept close to him and, more importantly, Joran. Androma was slow to rise but, when she did, the old Rider cut the air with silvyr, her injuries and lack of sight unable to prevent her from felling foes.

Gallien Drakalis was a soldier once more. In some ways, it had never really left him—he had just found his own war. On his side was Joran and no other, and so he fought for their freedom. He swung the axe with everything he had left to give. Where he could, the smuggler threw the weapon, dropping an opponent before they could rush him, only to use the axe again in close quarters.

Here and there, Drakalis witnessed the flare of death delivered by Joran's broken sword. He remained close to Gallien, striking only when his blow was assured.

Slait was death to them all. He slaughtered any Andaren who came between him and his enemy. Indeed, they attacked him as well, unsure of his allegiance but confident he was a threat all the same.

Barrelling her way through, Yamnomora laid eyes on The Dawn Sword and pointed one of her axes at him. "Ye!" she spat.

Slait shoved one of his kin aside and twisted his slaiken blade so it flicked through the air. The two came together in a brief but brutal collision that elicited a sharp yelp from the dwarf. The Dawn Sword hopped on one foot and kicked out behind him. Yamnomora took the boot in the middle of her back and fell face down.

It was the first time Gallien had seen Kitrana breaking away from them, her efforts closing the gap so she might reach the fallen dwarf. For all her skill and natural talents, she could not breach the Andarens.

Slait flipped his scimitar, ready to plunge it into Yamnomora.

"No!" the dwarf cried.

It took Gallien an extra second to realise she wasn't shouting at The Dawn Sword. The smuggler followed Yamnomora's gaze and outstretched hand to the other dwarf. With one foot resting on a dead soldier, the thick-set dwarf was raising the hammer over his head, the haft gripped in two hands and the head glowing a brilliant blue.

A blur of silver, bronze, and gold crossed the ruins at speed. Drakalis was barely able to track the hammer's flight it moved so fast.

A flash of light and clap of thunder exploded the moment it impacted against Slait's cuirass.

Gallien saw only splinters of what had transpired and, like so much else that day, his mind struggled to comprehend the truth of it.

Slait was gone, The Dawn Sword taken from reality in the blink of an eye.

One moment he had been standing over Yamnomora and the next, he had vanished, as if he had been obliterated by the hand of a god.

It had also dumbfounded the remaining Andarens, giving Cob and Androma, who were always the quickest to recover, an opportunity to spill blood. The soldiers were wholly too late in banding together, falling one by one to the most skilled killers in all of Gelakor's ruins.

"No!" Yamnomora screeched, her hand slapping the hard ground. "What did ye do?" She was on her feet in no time and slamming into her fellow dwarf. "Where did ye send it? Where?"

He looked dazed, exhausted even. "I... I don' know."

"Ye don' know?" she bellowed in his face. "Ye don' know! Ye jus' lost The Anther!" Yamnomora's rage was a terrible sight to behold. "I'm goin' to kill ye!"

"Yamnomora," Aphrandhor chastised, the wizard appearing between the pillars, his chest heaving and a trickle of blood running down his brow.

"He lost it!" she barked. "He jus' threw it away! An' with the enemy no less! Do ye 'ave any idea what ye jus' did?"

The Green Leaf stepped into her vision. "If we do not focus on the here and now, The Anther won't be the only thing we lose today." The wizard then turned his head to look the other dwarf up and down. "Should we live through the day," he added, "we will deal with it then."

Yamnomora huffed and released the dwarf's shirt.

"I were tryin' to save ye," he explained hopelessly.

Yamnomora said something in her native tongue, her words sounding as harsh as her expression.

A deafening squawk pierced the air and a great flap of mighty wings buffeted air through the ruins. Slait's Aegre, bloody and savaged, was flying over the ruins, heading south. *Retreating* south.

Cob's attention snapped to his left, where he alone had a clear view between the ruins. "More are coming up the path!" he warned.

"Oaken," Androma voiced suddenly. "Where is Oaken?"

With no cohesive sense of direction, the group followed Cob who led Androma by the arm. They moved through the ruins, making their way to the northern edge, where the land fell away and The Red Fields of Dunmar dominated the view. There they discovered Oaken, still standing proud in spite of the wounds he bore.

"Joran!" the old Rider called.

Gallien naturally accompanied the boy who—much to the smuggler's annoyance—simply obeyed Androma.

"Stand back," she instructed the Kedradi. "Joran come here," she beckoned, drawing him closer.

Drakalis was now very aware that he stood under the glare of an Aegre, an intimidating and frightening creature.

"Oaken," Androma called, her open palm waiting high in the air.

The Aegre reacted in its own time, bringing its colossal head down so the old Rider's hand could rest against the smooth curve of its plated beak.

Androma swallowed and took a breath. "You have your mother's eyes, Joran. Show them to him."

"What's happening here?" Gallien interrupted.

"Quiet," came her hissing response. "We haven't time."

Joran did as instructed, looking up at Oaken with his violet eyes. The Aegre blinked, its stare so cold it could have been looking through the boy.

Androma pressed her free hand into Joran's chest. "Ilithranda," she declared.

The Aegre's head tilted and it blinked again.

The old Rider grabbed Joran's right hand and replaced her own upon Oaken's beak. She seemed to give the animal some time to acclimatise to his hand before stepping back.

As Oaken bowed his head all the more, a fresh wave of Andarens arrived, challenging the companions who had remained at a distance.

"Ignore it," Androma commanded of the boy, confident that the enemy would never reach them.

Indeed, the eclectic group of fighters met the Andarens with steel, magic, and bone, their defiance and skill enough to keep the soldiers at bay. For now.

Gallien glimpsed Kitrana among them, eager, if not desperate, to break away from the battle and join them by the edge. She wanted the broken sword, he knew, but such a weapon might keep Joran alive, and so the smuggler made no attempt to part it from the boy.

The smuggler turned back to the Aegre, which had lowered its entire body to the ground now.

Androma sighed with relief. "Joran, climb onto the saddle."

"No, no, no, no," Gallien blurted, putting himself in the way. "He is *not* getting on that thing."

"We don't have time for this, Gallien," Androma snapped.

"I'm not letting him fly away on an Aegre!" he fumed.

"We're all going to die up here," Androma said bluntly, her statement loud enough to breach the din of battle. "This is the only way he lives."

Joran was shaking his head. "I'm not leaving you here to die!" he voiced.

Gallien said nothing. Could say nothing. Androma's reasoning had struck as any real blow might. The smuggler continued to stare at the old Rider, but inside his mind he was seeing Joran die at the hands of invading Andarens.

"Will he be safe?" he asked absently, his question almost lost to the sound of clashing steel.

"Gallien?" Joran started before Androma interjected.

"I told you long ago," she answered, "he will never be safe."

Joran stepped away from Oaken and confronted Drakalis. "If I am to die here or die later then I choose *here*, beside all of you."

Gallien was shaking his head, his eyes glazing with tears. He placed one hand against the side of Joran's face. "I'd rather you didn't die at all," he whispered into the cold breeze.

"I'm staying," Joran said adamantly.

Drakalis took a breath, appreciating for the first time in years how beautiful Joran's eyes were. "You're going, boy." Gallien stepped in and lightly gripped him by the shirt, preventing him from walking away. "Listen to me. Listen to me," he said again, more forcefully, fighting against Joran's will. "Unlike the rest of us, you actually have something to live for. You're meant for something greater than dying on some forgotten rock. *Go*. Become everything they say you will. Then you can end all this death once and for all."

Joran's face was streaked with tears. "I don't want to leave you."

Gallien tensed his jaw and pulled the boy into a tight embrace. He squeezed, holding him close so he could feel something of his love.

"More are coming!" Cob yelled.

Gallien kissed Joran on the head and held him fast. "Go," he urged. "Live now. Fight for us later." The smuggler released him and stood his ground, vowing not to move until he saw the boy ascend the Aegre and fly to safety.

Androma began to guide Joran, instructing him on the best way to climb up and where to put his feet and hands. Shocked and uncertain, the boy did as commanded, glancing at Gallien whenever he could. The smuggler offered him reassuring nods, refusing the temptation to turn around and look upon the Andarens.

"Don't let go!" Androma told him firmly. "Oaken," she called. "Take him to Drakanan." The Aegre squawked. "To Drakanan!" she ordered, her arm flinging out to the north.

Oaken assumed his full height and turned to face the edge of the ruins.

"Gallien?" His own name was the last thing the smuggler heard from Joran's lips before the Aegre launched from the ancient stone.

The smuggler's leather cloak was blown out by the gust of wind, his neck craned to watch the boy's dramatic ascent. So too was the lone tear redirected towards his ear.

"His fate is his own now," the old Rider observed.

"As long as he doesn't share mine," Drakalis remarked darkly.

"Gallien! Androma!" The Kedradi's call turned them back to their miserable situation.

While the group had dispatched the most recent wave of soldiers, more Andarens were pouring from the path and scattering across the ruins like ants. Not even The Green Leaf's magic could save them from so many.

Drakalis moved away from the edge and returned to his unusual companions—those he would die with. Damned if he wasn't going to take as many Andarens with him as he could.

"My sword," Kit blurted, her large eyes tracking the distant Aegre.

"We have bigger problems," Gallien practically growled.

"What is it?" Aphrandhor asked.

Gallien followed the wizard's question to Cob, who stood above them on a jagged boulder. His dreadlocks blew out in the wind that drove up from the south. Curiously, his nose was twitching.

"Get ready to run," he informed them, a hint of revelation on his face.

"Run?" Yamnomora queried.

It did seem implausible given the number of Andarens crowding in front of them, shields presented and weapons poised.

Before the smuggler could question the ranger himself, the truth of the matter exploded into the ruins.

Gallien stepped back and braced himself, the deepest parts of his instincts crying out for retreat.

The Andaren line was decimated by the two Ydrits. While smaller than an Aegre, the monsters were all muscle and fur, their claws as big as a man's hand. The soldiers turned to fight the unexpected foe—a foe that had travelled far hunting others. Blood soon stained the Ydrits' white fur, though it was likely a mix of theirs and the Andarens.

As growls and roars mingled with screams and cries for help, Cob darted for a narrow gap in the chaos. "This way!"

One behind the other, the group followed in the Kedradi's wake. Yamnomora paused so she could guide Androma through the mayhem while Gallien and Aphrandhor took up the rear, each lashing out here and there to put down those that tried to bar their way.

The smuggler was sure to keep an eye on the creatures as he ran. The Ydrits' brutality was unrestrained, their days of hunting rewarded with rich pickings. The Andarens forgot their real foe as a result, turning their weapons as one on the monsters.

Impossible as it had seemed, the group was now moving south, putting the majority of the ruins behind them. The cries of dying Andarens became faint, if not drowned out altogether by the Ydrits' roars.

A sharp grunt and the clatter of steel on stone halted Gallien in his tracks. Turning around, he discovered the wizard on the ground, one hand pressed into his left leg. The green of his robes was dark and ragged there, where the blood had soaked through from a recent wound.

Hearing Andaren boots nearby, Drakalis rushed back to The Green Leaf. Of them all, he would see the wizard live so he might learn the truth of his father's fate.

"Come on!" he urged, reaching down to pick the old man up.

"No," Aphrandhor growled, one arm coming up to ward the smuggler off.

But it was too late. Gallien had grabbed the wizard with both hands and hauled him to his feet. The Green Leaf gasped, his eyes momentarily absent any life. He returned within a heartbeat, only now he looked at the smuggler with grave concern.

Gallien frowned at the wizard, disturbed by the reaction, and let go of his robes.

Aphrandhor gathered his staff to him, his back pressed against the stone. "You're not *Gallien Drakalis*."

60
CITY OF BONES

40 Years Ago...

Daijen's eyes worked furiously to understand what he was looking at. Aphrandhor had his floating orb move gently up and around, revealing the structure to be a pillar. It took some time for the light to find its curved edges, exposing a width so vast the Vahlken believed it could have held up the heavens themselves.

Massive though it was, the colossal pillar was not nearly as interesting as the rectangular holes that ran around its circumference. The small alcoves presumably ran from top to bottom, though that was impossible to discern as so much of the pillar remained in shadow. Daijen craned his neck to look at row upon row. They each housed the same contents.

Skeletons.

Drawn to them, his curiosity rising, Daijen homed in on the nearest alcove that rested at chest level. Inside, amidst a tangle of spider webs, lay a single skeleton. It appeared entirely average to him, the bones having belonged to either a human or an Andaren.

Glancing at the alcoves around it, he could see that every

skeleton was the same—just the remains of an ordinary person. Above each alcove, etched into the smooth stone, was a number—an ancient numerical symbol he hadn't seen since his studies as a child. Daijen reached out and followed the contours of the number with his fingers.

Two-hundred and fourteen.

Scrutinising the numbers either side, he could see that they were in order, running from left to right. Those above were lower numbers, suggesting the sequence began at the very top, where even his Vahlken eyes could not pierce the darkness.

Beside him, Mordrith, Yamnomora, and Aphrandhor had approached the pillar of the dead. They inspected the contents, appearing just as bewildered as Daijen did.

"Will someone say something!" Androma fumed. "Where are we? What can you see?"

Standing next to her, Ilithranda regarded the pillar before replying, "A monument to death."

"What does that mean?"

Ilithranda brought the Rider closer while describing what stood before them. "They are numbered?" Androma queried. "Who are they?"

"Who *were* they?" Mordrith specified. "I'd say there's years between these bones," she continued, walking along the alcoves. "The lower the number, the older the bones."

Not to be delicate, Yamnomora reached inside one of the alcoves and yanked on a leg. "It don' look too special," she remarked. "Jus' a bone."

"Then why keep so many?" Aphrandhor questioned.

"Is this typical human behaviour?" Mordrith asked of them all. "Or Andaren?"

Both Daijen and the wizard shook their heads. "We burn the dead and bury the remains," the Vahlken explained, his eyes wandering over the skeletons.

"We just bury our dead," Aphrandhor told her, his attention equally consumed by the pillar.

"Then what significance does this hold for the

Skaramangians?" Mordrith voiced on everyone's behalf. "I've borne their mark all me life—heard the teachin's they wanted me to *an'* those they didn'. They never mentioned anythin' like this."

"I think this place is only for those at the very apex of their order," Ilithranda reasoned.

"Perhaps that's who they were," Androma speculated. "This is where they keep their leaders after death."

"A reasonable conclusion," came a rasping voice from the darkness, "but I'm afraid you are incorrect."

The companions reacted as one, turning their backs on the pillar and bringing their weapons to bear. Daijen narrowed his eyes, searching desperately for the source of the voice. Aphrandhor's orb moved as he did, coming to float directly above the group, yet it failed to shine any light on their new company.

"When The Eldan dies," the rattling voice continued, "so too does the master cleric. A public affair to say the least," the voice added irritably.

Daijen spared half a second to meet Ilithranda's eyes, their gaze brought together by the mention of *The Eldan*. It wasn't a title either of them were familiar with, but they certainly knew of the master cleric, an Andaren who wielded almost as much power as the emperor himself.

"You really have no idea where you are." The voice began to laugh, a sound not dissimilar to a hacking cough. "All these years you've been dogging us, gnawing at our edges. What time we have wasted fearing you knew *anything*. And now you're here. You have no idea what an honour it is. To die at *his* feet," the voice hissed excitedly.

"Show yourself!" the wizard commanded.

Daijen winced at the volume in his ear but, more than anything, he had hoped to let the voice continue, hoping it might spill more secrets to the doomed.

Daijen and Ilithranda saw it first—movement just beyond the light. The diminutive figure was slow to approach, but appear they did, breaching the light where it remained hazy. The group looked upon a woman with a weathered and haggard face to match her ancient voice.

What there was of any hair sat in clumps on her scalp, long absent the colour of youth. Her skin was nearly so pale as to be considered Andaren, but she was undoubtedly human with her rounded ears. Her clothes were little more than rags and she approached with bare and dirty feet.

She would have been all too disarming if it were not for the scar that marked her forehead: a vertical line with two diamonds at its heart: the sigil of the Skaramangians.

Aphrandhor relaxed his staff, planting the tip on the stone beside him. "Who are you?"

"The question is," she countered, "who are *you*? Only *he* would know to find this place." The old woman looked over them all with pale eyes. "Perhaps he is already here," she said eagerly, if cryptically. "No," she drawled, her tone resigned to disappointment. "I would know if the lost had finally been found."

The strange, if not insane, woman licked her lips with a dark tongue. "You have killed our brothers and sisters then," she concluded. "Taken our secrets from bloody lips." She tutted like a disgruntled grandmother. "Your crimes mount against you."

"Speak plainly," Androma commanded threateningly. "Who are you?"

The old crone appeared unfazed by the biting words and harsh tone. "We are the curators," she declared pleasantly.

At the same time, more figures emerged from the darkness, their eyes blinking rapidly in the light. Like the hag, they all bore the mark of the Skaramangians upon their foreheads, an overt sign of loyalty not seen outside of Nareene. Dressed in rags, their ages varied from that of the old woman to children of no more than ten years.

The presence of these figures put the companions even more on edge, bringing them closer together.

"Ye should o' let me bring Bludgeon," Yamnomora muttered.

Daijen thought it an overreaction. They were currently faced by nearly two dozen unarmed men, women, and children. They posed no real threat to a group of warriors that boasted a Dragon Rider, two Vahlken, a wizard, and a pair of dwarves. Yet, he couldn't shake the feeling that he was missing something, for why else would these *curators* reveal themselves so confidently. It was madness.

"Curators?" Androma questioned. "In a *tomb*?"

The hag gave a knowing smile that displayed her black teeth before a rasping chuckle reverberated from deep in her chest. "You have a lot of questions. You are just children wandering through the forest, mindlessly picking at leaves. It is your ultimate undoing."

"Is that a threat?" Yamnomora spat.

"You were all doomed the moment you set foot on this island," the crone replied evenly.

"If that is true," Aphrandhor posed, "could the doomed not be enlightened before their end?"

The ancient-looking curator licked her lips with speed. "The doomed are damned to take what light they hold into the abyss," she said with a note of excitement. One of the other curators—a middle-aged man—dipped his head to whisper in her ear. She hissed at him, bearing those black teeth again, and he recoiled. "It has been so long since I have conversed with outsiders. It is only right," she went on, her hard tone aimed at her fellow curators, "that they know something of the glory to come before the darkness claims them. A pittance to take into the black."

When there came no further challenge from the others, she stepped a little further into the light. "Those beyond these walls call it The Tomb, but they were not born here as we were. This stone is like our bones. We are part of it." She grinned with glee. "It is no tomb, for there are no dead here. Only memories." The old crone looked directly at Daijen. "This is where he will remember who he is."

The curator was on the verge of continuing, her lips parted, when she noticed the skeletal leg and foot lying at Yamnomora's feet. Her large eyes twitched at the sight. Daijen recognised the spark of rage ignited behind that look.

"Heathens!" she fumed, her gravelly voice finding new life. The curator retreated one step into the shadows, her fiery gaze darting from companion to companion. "Your footsteps are unwelcome, but your meddling has desecrated our great work," she screeched, her disquiet rippling through the rest of her people.

Daijen stepped forward, his scimitar presented. "You don't have to die," he warned her, though he couldn't help but glance at the children among them. "Just walk away and let us leave."

The hag narrowed her eyes on the Vahlken. "You're still wandering through the forest, blind to the beasts that surround you." As one, each curator retrieved a small, fluorescent green, object from within the folds of their rags. "A gift," she explained, "from your kin."

It was an oval glass vial Daijen realised, but he didn't have time to query it before every one of the curators pushed them into their mouths and bit through the glass. Some yelped in pain while others groaned, but they all had blood oozing down their chins.

"Daijen," Ilithranda intoned.

The Vahlken stepped back, his eyes flitting from man to woman to child. They each began to fit, losing control of their limbs and collapsing to the floor. It only lasted a few seconds, however, before they regained some control and began clawing at their own skin. The sight of it put the wizard back a step and so his orb retreated with him, allowing the darkness to consume many of the curators. It could not drown out their agony, their screams echoing throughout the vast chamber.

"What's happening?" Androma asked over the din.

"They're killin' themselves," Mordrith informed her.

"No," Daijen corrected, his gaze fixed on the old hag. "They're *mutating*."

Before his very eyes, the woman turned into a beast. The bones of her fingers grew well beyond the limits of her flesh and fused into a single pincer. The legs underwent a similar metamorphosis, though the knees bent backwards, lending her an animalistic stance. Her skull cracked and elongated while her eyes filled with ink and expanded and multiplied into bulbous domes. Blood splattered across the floor as her ribs and spine extended away from the confines of her body, the smooth bones now mottled with small spikes. There was a crack and a pop as the hag's jaw dislocated and found a new extended shape, and lined with razored fangs.

The transformation complete, the monster unleashed a nightmarish shriek and a spray of hot spit. From the pitch black about it, the other curators slowly entered the edge of the light. Like the hag, they were fiends of darkness, their new form taken from the depths of Andaren magic.

Daijen didn't wait to be attacked—*he* was the predator.

The Vahlken lunged forwards and whipped his scimitar around to slice a bloody line across the hag's horrifying face. The creature reeled, its pincered arms coming up wildly. Daijen turned his swing into a roll and sprang up to face another beast, his blade flashing in the light of the orb. He cut through ragged flesh and tough bone, beating his enemy back, until one of the sharp pincers lashed out and caught him in the chest. The leather was torn immediately, but the Weaver's tailoring prevented the bone from plunging into his body.

It still hurt. And the force of it knocked him down to one knee.

There was a dance of shadows as Aphrandhor and the others surged forwards to meet the wave of monsters. Ilithranda dashed to Daijen's side and drove her atori short-sword up into the neck of the beast that had put him down. Still it resisted death, its face upturned and its bony arms flailing. Ilithranda drove the monster back, giving Daijen space to find his feet and add his scimitar to the battle.

The sharp points of its new legs dug down to challenge Ilithranda's strength, but couldn't hold against Daijen's sweeping blade. The steel hacked through bone and brought the creature down. Ilithranda yanked her atori blade free and slashed it across her foe's neck, severing most of the head. Only then did it accept death.

The wizard's orb was momentarily outshone by the staccato of lightning birthed by Aphrandhor's staff. His spell engulfed one of the beasts, burning everything it touched and hurling the creature from its bony limbs.

Yamnomora was spinning death. The dwarf pivoted again and again, her two axes swinging to deadly effect. She caught one monster after the other, chopping pieces of them away. The dwarf also lent a shriek of her own, an unnerving battle cry of sorts.

Mordrith wielded The Anther like it was an extension of her arm and little more than a paperweight. The hammer came down with mighty force, crushing limbs and shattering bones. Still, the creatures they faced would not perish so easily, their forms demanding decapitation before giving up the fight. The dwarf rose to the challenge, pulping the skulls of those Yamnomora brought down.

Androma, however, was drowning in enemies.

Daijen ducked and weaved his way through lashing limbs of bone and gnashing fangs to reach her. His scimitar cut one down, giving him room to grip the shogue on his belt. Using one beast as a stepping stone, the Vahlken leapt through the stark light and thrust out his arm. The rope uncoiled at speed and the hook found its end with a wet *thud* in the head of the monster. He dragged it away from the Rider before its intended bite could find flesh.

Yanked towards him, Daijen landed while lifting his scimitar up and round in a swift back swing. The creature cried with pain, its meagre midriff cut in half. That didn't stop the top half, where its hideous mouth and forked tongue remained, from continuing the battle.

Androma cleaved its head in a decisive blow, while simultaneously ducking under a swiping arm of bone. Vahlken and Dragon Rider fought back to back, but it wasn't enough to keep them in the light. With every attack that befell them, the pair were pushed further into shadow.

"Duck!" Daijen cried.

Androma doubled over, allowing the Vahlken to roll over her back and deliver a diagonal strike across the advancing head of a monster. From eyes to jaw, the beast's head parted in two and its body collapsed under its own weight. That left them faced by only one—the hag. She approached them slowly, her ruined face marred all the more by Daijen's initial attack.

Beyond the creature, the rest of the companions fought under Aphrandhor's light and that of the bodies set aflame by the wizard. Determined to get back to them, the Vahlken raised his scimitar in both hands and prepared to slay the old crone and be done with her.

Daijen might have delivered such a blow were it not for The Green Leaf's magic. Though he only glanced the wizard levelling his staff in their direction, the Vahlken certainly felt the power of his spell. The mutated curator took the brunt of it in her back, but the force carried her forwards, crashing into both Daijen and Androma. The monster's hard limbs made for a painful collision, but not nearly as painful as the door they were rammed through.

Daijen was only able to make sense of his surroundings when Androma rolled off him. They had apparently been flung through a door hidden in the darkness of the chamber.

They were not the only ones.

The hag shrieked, recovering slightly faster than either of the warriors. In the cramped space, the monster used its sharp arms to drag itself towards them. So long were they that neither Daijen nor Androma had the reach to strike without first tackling the deadly limbs.

Androma stretched out her hand, the monster easily located, and released a torrent of fire and excruciating heat. The hag screamed and squealed as the flames licked every inch of her disfigured body.

Closing her fist, the magic ended as suddenly as it had begun. It should have left a husk in its wake, for none could survive such a harrowing spell.

But Andaren magic could be cruel.

The burning hag kept coming, only now she posed the threat of fire too.

"Daijen?"

"Just run!" he urged, forcing her further down the new corridor.

They didn't even make it fifty yards before the ancient site swallowed them up. It was impossible to say why the floor was broken, missing vital slabs of stone that would have seen them continue down the corridor, but Daijen felt the jagged lip clip his head as he plummeted through the gap.

In total darkness, Rider and Vahlken collided with each other before smashing into various hard objects. Between the pain and disorientation, Daijen realised they were falling down some kind of rough slope made predominantly from dirt. When, at last, they came to a sudden halt, it was upon the cold of hewn stone.

The air was pushed from the Vahlken's lungs as he impacted face down. He groaned, his limbs slow to move. He could hear Androma going through the same thing not far away. Reaching his hands and knees, Daijen spat a mouthful of blood on the floor and felt the cuirass where it protected his chest. Again, the Weaver's work had guarded him against the damage such a fall could have inflicted, but he still ached from the ordeal. Androma could say the same, her under armour that of fine dragon scales.

"Daijen?" the Rider croaked.

"I'm here," he managed, rising unsteadily to his feet. "I'm coming." The Vahlken followed the sound of Androma's recovering steps and reached out in the pitch black.

"Your sword," she said, offering him his fallen scimitar.

"You have yours?"

Androma answered his question by lifting the silvyr blade. "A *Rider* never drops their weapon."

Daijen was glad she couldn't see him blush. "Perhaps a little light," he suggested, moving on.

The Dragon Rider conjured an orb of light not dissimilar from Aphrandhor's, the globe finding life in the unfurling of her fingers. "I suppose I will have little use for such a spell," she remarked bitterly.

Daijen's eyes adapted to the light immediately and without pain. "It didn't follow us," he observed, searching the rugged slope they had unceremoniously descended.

"Where are we?" Androma enquired.

Turning around, the Vahlken examined the new chamber. It was considerably less grand than that above, the ceiling barely twice his height. "The catacombs maybe," he guessed. "It looks older down here."

Forgotten, he thought.

Masses of cobwebs were revealed in the light, though none so complex and immense as those in The Sin'duil, where the Weavers worked their magic. The chamber itself was rather small, the walls coming into view, including what appeared to be a dais on the far side.

It was all so crowded, the walls lined with objects, rotten crates, and rusted weapons. All the more disturbing was the single skeleton in the centre of the floor, where a path had been forged that led directly to the dais. Daijen crouched by the remains and scrutinised the ancient bones, finding no violent cause of death.

Androma's foot discovered the skeleton and she knelt beside him, her hand running over the bones. "More of the dead," she commented.

"It seems they just laid down and died here," Daijen reasoned, utterly perplexed by it.

"What else do you see?" the Rider asked, standing and turning to the wall on her left. "A door would be useful."

Daijen followed her movement. More specifically, he followed the orb that floated towards the wall. His icy blue eyes narrowed on the images he saw there. Without thought, he approached them, drawn in by one image in particular.

"What is it?"

Using his scimitar, the Vahlken cut through the cobwebs and used his free hand to wipe them from the wall. "There's something here," he muttered.

"A door?" Androma asked hopefully.

Daijen's eyes roamed over the wall, drinking it in. "A *story*," he answered.

"I would have preferred a door," she replied dryly.

The Vahlken ran his fingers over the images, feeling the slight relief in the stone. Remarkably, some of the colours still remained, lending a touch more life to the carving.

"There are dragons," he said softly.

Androma's head twitched. She reached out as he had and touched the wall, her fingers finding the edges of a bat-like wing. "What do you see?"

"Seven dragons," he told her, wiping eons of dirt from the wall. "Six of them have Riders."

"And the seventh?"

"A saddle, but no Rider. They're flying towards... towards this pyramid."

"What else?"

Moving across the wall, Daijen examined the next image. "A battle. A big one. There's a figure standing in opposition to the dragons, but the image has faded too much."

"Is that all?" Androma pressed.

"No," he muttered. "Behind the figure stand four Giants cloaked in black." From the rim of those cloaks, the artist had stretched the black so it appeared as if the dark army was no more than an extension of the Giants.

The Vahlken moved along again, to the final image. "The dragon without a Rider," he described. "It's being..." He hesitated, trying to understand the artist's meaning. "It's being swallowed by darkness, as if it's sinking into the ground." His attention shifted along the image. "The four Giants are lying down—dead," he guessed. "A figure stands at the base of the pyramid," he went on. "They're cloaked in gold," he guessed, though the image was more yellow. "They're..." He paused, scrutinising the image all the more.

"They're what?" Androma probed.

"They're holding up an egg."

Androma came closer, her hand outstretched expectantly. Daijen guided her to the image, where she felt the edges of the figure and the egg being held aloft.

"What is this?" he was compelled to ask.

Androma's hand moved across the relief to find the dragon being consumed by darkness. "I don't know," she confessed.

Confounded by what could be a significant find, Daijen moved away, leaving the Rider to feel out the rest of the image. His attention turned to the dais, where he now noticed a pedestal surrounded by sundries and dusty relics. There was something atop the pedestal, its surface just catching the light of Androma's orb.

Without thought, his feet navigated the debris and brought him to the short set of steps. Shrouded in shadow and stark light, he ascended the dais and slowly approached the pedestal. He could see how ornate it was now, the stone crafted with great precision and attention to detail.

The Vahlken glanced back over one shoulder, checking that Androma was still occupied by the wall and the mystery it posed. His eyes, returning to the pedestal, were naturally drawn up, to that which rested upon it. The revelation of what he was looking at immersed him in the moment.

Sheathing his sword, he brushed away the cobwebs and picked it up with both hands. Cold to the touch, it wasn't nearly as heavy as he thought it would be, though it was certainly rougher than he had imagined. Depending on the light, its scaled surface was either dark purple or entirely black. There could be no question as to what it was, however.

Daijen Saeth was holding a dragon egg.

EPILOGUE

It was no use. Every time Joran closed his eyes he saw Gallien and the others dying amidst The Ruins of Gelakor. They succumbed to the Andarens, their numbers too large to quell: their broken bodies left to rot atop the cliffs. The only way to force the nightmare from his vision was to open his eyes and fill his mind with what he could actually see.

He didn't want to do that either.

When, finally, he found the courage to look upon the world, it was surely a world no man was ever meant to see. Oaken soared above the clouds, where the shocking cold failed to grip Joran as it might any other. The sky above was the most glorious blue he had ever seen, and entirely unending in its reign over Verda.

Daring to sit up a bit, he looked beyond Oaken's horned head and took in the carpet of clouds rolled out beneath them. The wind rushed in his ears and his dark cloak blew out wildly behind him, yet it was all so peaceful. It would have been easy to forget the realm below and the troubles that plagued it.

But Joran couldn't do that.

He looked back, his hand squeezing the saddle's handles all the tighter. How far north had they travelled? How far behind them were Gallien and the others? Even if he wanted to turn back, he had no idea how to command his mother's Aegre. He was stuck in the heavens until Oaken decided otherwise.

And so he was for that day and night and much of the second day. Exhaustion was beginning to set in, but he didn't dare close his eyes. The moment he fell asleep he would slip from the saddle and plummet.

Fortunately, the Aegre ceased flapping his wings a few hours after midday and slowly glided down, taking them through a world of mist before breaching the clouds altogether.

It was an icy vista that met them, the cliffs coated with snow and the surrounding flat land dominated by the white powder. Further north, where the horizon blurred beyond detail, Joran was sure he looked upon an ocean—The Night Sea! It was a body of water he had long resigned to know only on a map, never dreaming to travel so close to it.

Without any warning, Oaken's wings folded in and his considerable weight became quite apparent. Tilting forwards, the Aegre dropped like a stone.

Joran tried to scream but the air being forced into his throat prevented him from making so much as a sound. So too were his feet picked from the saddle's pockets and left to flail in the air above him. Only his grip on the handles kept him attached to Oaken.

Through thought alone, he pleaded with the Aegre to level out before he lost all feeling in his fingers. His silent pleas went unheard, the Aegre levelling out in his own time. Joran crashed into the long saddle and gulped in a much-needed breath. His toes sought out the pockets, where his feet were able to hook inside and secure his position. By then, Oaken was banking to the east and angling to come at the northern cliffs from a different direction.

Despite the sinking hollow feeling that ruled his stomach, the view was enough to eclipse his unease. He could see now that the canyon they were flying towards was shaped like a horseshoe. Furthermore, he could just make out a narrow road that cut across the land and ran directly into the heart of its enormous mouth.

Oaken continued to descend, the cliffs rising higher and higher until they towered over them. Scattered either side of the road, Joran spotted great statues, their shapes discernible through the snow that covered them. Looking ahead, he could make out similar statues and hulking pieces of relief across the cliffs, all depicting heroic warriors and mighty dragons.

They had arrived at Drakanan.

Gliding the remainder of the flight, Oaken took them past the threshold and well within the canyon. Eventually, all four of his legs reached out for the ground and the Aegre completed the journey at a run. Without any command to do so, Oaken began to slow down, his wings folding into his body.

Coming to a complete stop, they both filled the frigid air with their hot breath. Joran craned his neck to take it all in. Almost everywhere there seemed to be large balconies and platforms or massive alcoves that disappeared into the grey stone.

Oaken squawked, his front talons tearing at the ground.

"Easy," Joran bade, his voice weak from disuse.

He patted the back of the Aegre's neck and climbed down. He winced as the jagged blade of the broken sword dug into his thigh. If he wasn't careful it would cut through his belt soon enough.

Moving away from Oaken, there was only one place at ground level that drew his attention.

The squat iron doors were guarded by two hooded statues, each wielding a sword that they pointed at the ground.

"Do you think I should knock?" he asked the Aegre, hoping a bit of levity would make him feel better.

Oaken squawked again, only this time it had an edge to it, as if the Aegre had brought the noise up from somewhere deep in his chest. Joran turned to see his mother's companion looking up at the surrounding cliffs. His dark wings flapped once and he reared up, making himself appear bigger and more formidable.

Following his yellow eyes, Joran's heart felt like it had been brought to a stop.

Dragons.

Lots of dragons.

They snaked out of the cliff face, appearing on every side. Their hot breath spoiled the air as sharp eyes fixed on the trespassers. Some crawled down the rock, their claws disturbing the stone here and there. Others unfurled their wings and swiftly descended to surround the pair.

Joran instinctively retreated towards Oaken, his senses telling him the dragons meant him harm. A dragon with burnt orange scales landed in front of them and let loose an ear-shattering roar. It was enough to make Joran grip the broken sword, though what he would do with it he didn't know.

A brown dragon skidded down the remainder of the cliff and leapt to bar them from the west. It exhaled a cloud of hot air through its nostrils and licked its fangs, to which Oaken brandished his front talons and fanned his wings.

A pair of dark blue dragons thundered into the ground on the other side and roared in unison. One of them whipped its tail and destroyed a statue with the hard and pointed end. The other snorted and took a threatening step towards the newcomers. Oaken was quick to put himself between Joran and this overt threat, his squawk bordering on a growl.

"Perhaps," Joran uttered. "Perhaps we should just leave."

The burnt orange dragon curled its head and spat a cloud of fire into the air. Joran felt the heat on his face and hands, the intensity enough to put him back another step.

Despair gripped the boy, a hand so cold it could only have been sent by Death itself. He had travelled so far and survived what others would not only to die in a frozen hell. There would be no destiny, no great future that saw him rise to that of a Dragon Rider. Instead, he was to find his end in the belly of the same beast. How cruel fate could be.

There came a great gust of wind from the canyon's entrance. Raising his hand against the spitting snow and mud, Joran turned to lay eyes on yet another dragon. Revelation dawned on the boy, if slowly. This was not just *another* dragon come to eat him. It was different.

With scales of bone white, it cracked the earth upon landing, where its true size revealed a dragon considerably bigger than the others. Rearing up on its hind legs, the hulking dragon fanned its wings and cast them all in shadow. Its underside on display, Joran saw the long straps of a saddle, if no sign of a Rider.

Joran clapped his hands to his ears when the indomitable dragon opened its thick jaws and blasted the air with an explosive roar. The ground shook when its front claws dropped back down, threatening the boy's footing. It looked at the other dragons with cool blue eyes that spoke of unwavering resolve. They spoke a promise of death.

To a chorus of roars, the dragons on the ground and those gripped to the cliff took flight, their numerous wings bombarding the air and kicking up snow. Joran turned on the spot, watching them all flee. Indeed, they did not return to the shadowed halls dug into the cliff, but flew over the top of the horseshoe and vanished into the world beyond.

That left Joran under the scrutinising gaze of the largest creature he had ever seen. It inspired fear and awe, the two emotions fermenting in turmoil. Still, Oaken did not shy away. The Aegre faced the dragon with a courage Joran simply couldn't fathom.

"Wild dragons," came a biting female voice from the direction of the iron doors.

Joran swivelled on the spot, quickly locating the lone figure walking towards him. She pulled back the hood of her sandy cloak to reveal a sharp face, bald scalp, and an expression that could have been chiselled from the stone. Her dark skin was silky smooth, if marred by scars that cut across her face and eyebrow. Coming to a stop, she gestured at the high cliffs around them, revealing a portion of the black tattoos that ran over her scalp in intricate patterns.

"They have taken a liking to our home," she continued. "That's not to say they don't serve a purpose." She looked him up and down, one hand resting on the hilt of the ornate sword on her hip. "You must be *him*—the one Androma's been searching for."

"You have me at a disadvantage," he replied, trying to appear more confident than he actually was.

"Get used to it," she retorted. "Awfully bold of you to have brought an Aegre," she remarked, before he could respond.

"They're good in a fight," Joran told her, doing his best to appear anything but exhausted and haunted by what he had left behind. "Will they come back?" he asked, looking to the cliff top.

The Rider glanced at the white dragon. "Not unless he says so," she said, a touch bemused. "What is your name, boy?"

"I thought you knew who I was," Joran countered.

"I know who you're supposed to be," the Rider quipped. "But I see nothing of that. I would hear *your* name from *your* lips."

He swallowed and took a breath. "Joran," he declared. "This is—"

"Oaken," the Rider interjected. "We've met."

Joran couldn't help but wonder if that meant the Rider had also met his mother. Feeling that he was being tested in some way, he decided not to ask.

"My name is Kassanda," she announced proudly. "I believe Garganafan has already introduced himself."

Joran looked over his shoulder, pairing the name with the dragon. "Well met," he uttered, to which Garganafan exhaled a jet of steam from his nostrils, bathing the boy in hot air.

"Come along," Kassanda called, the Rider already returning to the iron doors.

Joran nearly tripped up taking after her. "Where are we going?"

"To see if you're everything she believes you are," Kassanda answered darkly.

Leaving Oaken and Garganafan behind, Joran approached the entrance to Drakanan, the ancient stone towering over him.

Ten thousand eyes, Androma had said. Ten thousand eyes had seen him arrive at this point in time and ten thousand *lives* had perished glimpsing what came next. All at once he felt the immense pressure to make those sacrifices count, to embrace the destiny that was no longer over the ridge but all around him.

Only Gallien could have instilled the courage required to face the odds stacked against him, courage that Joran now called upon to enter the dark halls of Drakanan. He did so with a set of beliefs in his bones.

He would heed the call of Fate.

He would end the war.

He would bring about *a time of dragons*.

A TIME OF DRAGONS

BOOK 2

THE SAGA CONTINUES IN 2024

PHILIP C. QUAINTRELL

Hear more from Philip C. Quaintrell including book releases and exclusive content:

PHILIPCQUAINTRELL.COM

FACEBOOK.COM/PHILIPCQUAINTRELL

@PHILIPCQUAINTRELL.AUTHOR

@PCQUAINTRELL

ABOUT THE AUTHOR

Philip C. Quaintrell is the author of the epic fantasy series, The Echoes Saga, as well as the Terran Cycle sci-fi series. He was born in Cheshire in 1989 and started his career as an emergency nurse.

Having always been a fan of fantasy and sci-fi fiction, Philip started to find himself feeling frustrated as he read books, wanting to delve into the writing himself to tweak characters and storylines. He decided to write his first novel as a hobby to escape from nursing and found himself swept away into the world he'd created. Even now, he talks about how the characters tell him what they're going to do next, rather than the other way around.

With his first book written, and a good few rejected agency submissions under his belt, he decided to throw himself in at the deep end and self-publish. 2 months and £60 worth of sales in, he took his wife out to dinner to celebrate an achievement ticked off his bucket list - blissfully unaware this was just the beginning.

Fast forward 12 months and he was self-publishing book 1 of his fantasy series (The Echoes Saga; written purely as a means to combat his sci-fi writers' block). With no discernible marketing except the 'Amazon algorithm', the book was in the amazon bestsellers list in at least 4 countries within a month. The Echoes

Saga has now surpassed 700k copies sold worldwide, has an option agreement for a potential TV-series in the pipeline and Amazon now puts Philip's sales figures in the top 1.8% of self-published authors worldwide.

Philip lives in Cheshire, England with his wife and two children. He still finds time between naps and wiping snot off his clothes to remain a movie aficionado and comic book connoisseur, and is hoping this is still just the beginning.